THE MATHEMATICS OF MAGIC

THE ENCHANTER STORIES OF L. SPRAGUE DE CAMP AND FLETCHER PRATT

L. Sprague de Camp, Volume 2

edited by Mark L. Olson

The NESFA Press
Post Office Box 809
Framingham, MA 01701
2007

Copyright 2007 by The Estate of L. Sprague de Camp

Introduction
Copyright 2007 by Christopher Stasheff

Dust jacket illustration
Copyright 2007 by Marc Fishman

"Arming the Incomplete Enchanter"
Copyright 2007 by Jerry Pournelle

ALL RIGHTS RESERVED. NO PART OF THIS BOOK MAY BE REPRODUCED IN ANY FORM OR BY ANY ELECTRONIC, MAGICAL OR MECHANICAL MEANS INCLUDING INFORMATION STORAGE AND RETRIEVAL WITHOUT PERMISSION IN WRITING FROM THE PUBLISHER, EXCEPT BY A REVIEWER, WHO MAY QUOTE BRIEF PASSAGES IN A REVIEW.

FIRST EDITION, February 2007

ISBN 10: 1-886778-65-5
ISBN 13: 978-1-886778-65-8

Acknowledgments

The introduction by Christopher Stasheff is original to this volume.

"The Roaring Trumpet" was first published in *Unknown*, May 1940.

"The Mathematics of Magic" was first published in *Unknown*, October 1940.

"The Castle of Iron" was first published in *Unknown*, April 1941 and expanded Gnome Press, 1950.

"The Wall of Serpents" was first published in *Fantasy Fiction,* June 1953.

"The Green Magician" was first published in *Beyond Fiction*, Vol 2, #3, 1954.

"Fletcher and I" was first published in *The Compleat Enchanter*, SF Book Club, 1975.

"Sir Harold and the Gnome King" was first published in the *World Fantasy Convention Program Book* in 1990 and then revised and expanded in *The Enchanter Reborn*, Baen Books, 1992.

"Sir Harold of Zodanga" was first published in *The Exotic Enchanter*, ed. by L. Sprague de Camp and Christopher Stasheff, Baen Books, 1995.

"Arming the Incomplete Enchanter" by Jerry Pournelle was first published in *Amra*, Vol 2, No 43, March 1967. Additional notes are original to this volume.

"REarming the Incomplete Enchanter" by Jerry Pournelle was first published in *Amra* II:58, January 1973

All stories appear by permission of the author's Agent.

Contents

Introduction *by Chirstopher Stasheff* 11
The Roaring Trumpet 15
The Mathematics of Magic 95
The Castle of Iron 187
The Wall of Serpents 305
The Green Magician 359
Fletcher and I 407
Sir Harold and the Gnome King 413
Sir Harold of Zodanga 441
Arming the Incomplete Enchanter
                           by Jerry Pournelle 489
An Enchanter Bibliography 507

The Mathematics of Magic
The Enchanter Stories of L. Sprague de Camp and Fletcher Pratt

L. Sprague de Camp, Volume 2

Introduction
by Christopher Stasheff

I grew up in a household with well-filled bookcases and acquired the habit of taking down a volume whenever I grew bored. One rainy Saturday when I was eleven, I scanned the shelves and found a volume with the title, *The Incompleat Enchanter*. I took it down to try a page or two, and...

BAM! I was hooked. De Camp's explanation of the syllogismobile was so clear that I had no trouble understanding it, and it transported me, along with Harold Shea, to the world of Norse myths. I was transfixed. I was mesmerized. I kept on reading. I learned of the world of Spenser's *Faerie Queene* and finished the book in a day. I took it to my father to sing its praises and he said something to the effect of, "You liked it, huh?" and showed me the flyleaf, which I had overlooked. It was inscribed to my parents and signed by L. Sprague de Camp.

For the first time, an author became real to me. I later learned that my parents had known the de Camps personally, which is, I think, why the de Camps were so kind to me when I finally started attending science fiction conventions. I had several long talks with them, which I enjoyed very much. They were able to deal with my thirty-something enthusiasms with patience and were always able to put in a kind word to keep me grounded. On one occasion, I went with them talking their ears off because I was concerned about people changing the rules of life too drastically, always going too far, and finally de Camp reminded me that in America, social change works like a pendulum—it goes too far in one direction, then too far in the other direction, but every time, the swing grows smaller until it finally comes to rest in the middle. It seemed so obvious, once he said it...

One of my few regrets in moving from New Jersey to the Midwest was that I no longer had opportunities for such conversations. However, my kind agent, Eleanor Wood, gave me the opportunity to contribute a Harold Shea story to a shared-universe anthology, so I had an excuse to contact de Camp again, at least by mail.

Thus I began my foray into the field by reading a science fantasy story. One prominent critic later stated that science fantasy breaks a fundamental rule by mixing the separate genres of fantasy and science fiction. However, he said that I somehow made it work. That was because I had learned from a master—de Camp. (The same reviewer had himself written an excellent science fantasy piece, by the way—*Day of the Giants*. His name was Lester del Rey).

The Incompleat Enchanter is also responsible from turning me from an omnivorous reader into a science fiction fan. Before that time, I had been reading normal eleven-year-old fare—the *Castle of Adventure* series, Dickens's *Barnaby Rudge*, some Jules Verne, some Costain novels, the usual stuff. All of a sudden, Dickens and Costain took a back seat to De Camp and, if I couldn't find a book by de Camp, then Williamson, Asimov, Del Rey, Heinlein—any science fiction or fantasy would do. So, much as I learned from de Camp, I learned even more from the other authors to whom his books directed me.

The *Enchanter* series also showed me that science fiction could be humorous. As I grew older, I learned that the adventures of Harold Shea could be described as good action stories with some comic relief and some love interest. When I began to write in my own turn, I tried to write according to the same plan—and found myself labeled a humorist. I suppose it was because most science fiction was pretty serious, so a book with any humor at all attracted notice.

Later in my career, other reviewers classified me as a romance writer—thanks, I think, to Harold Shea and Belphebe, the love of his life.

The Incompleat Enchanter introduced me to worlds I had never known existed—the worlds of classical myth and medieval romance. I followed the path that de Camp laid down for me, studying myths and fables and fantasies and using them as the raw material for stories of my own.

Mind you, the Enchanter books weren't the only de Camp stories I read. I delighted in *Lest Darkness Fall*, *Divide and Rule*, and *The Carnelian Cube*. "A Gun for Dinosaur" was my first introduction to the way small events can have large consequences that build up amazingly, if they're given enough time. His non-fiction showed me how much knowledge can underlie an amusing story. *The Dragon of the Ishtar Gate* made the ancient Middle East come alive for me. But most of all, *Land of Unreason* showed me that not only was it possible to be funny—you could also use humor to criticize political figures and cultural attitudes. If any of my readers think my humor is commenting on politics in general or public figures in particular, they're right. De Camp got me started on the right foot (or maybe the Left). Later in my career, I was surprised to discover how many of the precursors of science fiction and fantasy were using the genre to present political commentary in such a way that the reigning regime wouldn't notice—or if it did, wouldn't mind, because nobody

Introduction

would take comedy seriously, right? The list included Jonathan Swift, Cyrano de Bergerac, and Thomas More. I was in pretty good company.

I learned even more from de Camp when I had the privilege of working with him on *The Enchanter Reborn* and *The Exotic Enchanter*, even if it was by mail. He was adamantly opposed to the stereotype of the bad woman driver, especially when applied to Belphoebe; he pointed out that a champion archer would certainly have the coordination to steer a car safely. He was concerned about possible intolerance in the image of the Polovtsi; a tribe of Russian barbarians (whom I had scarcely known existed). He even corrected my spelling in transliteration from Chinese to English—I was still using the Yale system, blithely unaware that the Chinese had developed their own system. De Camp did know about it, of course. The two books involved a great deal of work, but working with a master was well worth it.

My eleven-year-old self had only one regret—that there were no more Harold Shea stories. A few years later, I was delighted to find that I was mistaken—in fact, there were several more volumes! By your good fortune, you are holding them all in one collection. You have many happy hours ahead. I hope you enjoy them as much as I did—and still do.

— Christopher Stasheff, 2006

THE ROARING TRUMPET
by L. Sprague de Camp & Fletcher Pratt
Unknown, May 1940

There were three men and a woman in the room. The men were commonplace as to face, and two of them were commonplace as to clothes. The third wore riding breeches, semi-field boots, and a suede jacket with a tartan lining. The extra-fuzzy polo coat and the sporty tan felt with the green feather which lay on a chair belonged to him also.

The owner of this theatrical outfit was neither a movie actor nor a rich young idler. He was a psychologist, and his name was Harold Shea. Dark; a trifle taller, a little thinner than the average, he would have been handsome if his nose were shorter and his eyes farther apart.

The woman—girl—was a tawny blonde. She was the chief nurse at the Garaden Hospital. She possessed—but did not rejoice in—the name of Gertrude Mugler.

The other two men were psychologists like Shea and members of the same group. The oldest, the director of the others' activities, was bushy-haired, and named Reed Chalmers. He had just been asking Shea what the devil he meant by coming to work in such conspicuous garb.

Shea said, defensively: "I'm going to ride a horse when I leave this afternoon. Honest."

"Ever ridden a horse?" asked the remaining member of the group, a large, sleepy-looking young man named Walter Bayard.

"No," replied Shea, "but it's about time I learned."

Walter Bayard snorkled. "What you ought to say is that you're going to ride a horse so as to have an excuse for looking like something out of *Esquire*. First there was that phony English accent you put on for a while. Then you took up fencing. Then last winter you smeared the place with patent Norwegian ski-grease, and went skiing just twice."

"So what?" demanded Shea.

Gertrude Mugler spoke up: "Don't let them kid you about your clothes, Harold."

"Thanks, Gert."

"Personally I think you look sweet in them."

"Unh." Shea's expression was less grateful.

"But you're foolish to go horseback riding. It's a useless accomplishment anyway, with automobiles—"

Shea held up a hand. "I've got my own reasons, Gert."

Gertrude looked at her wrist watch. She rose. "I have to go on duty. Don't do anything foolish, Harold. Remember, you're taking me to dinner tonight."

"Uh-huh."

"Dutch."

Shea winced. "Gert!"

"So long, everybody," said Gertrude. She departed in a rustle of starched cotton.

Walter Bayard snickered. "Big he-man. Dutch!"

Shea tried to laugh it off. "I've tried to train her not to pull those in public. Anyway she makes more money than I do, and if she'd rather have four dates a week Dutch than two on my budget, why not? She's a good kid."

Bayard said: "She thinks you're the wistful type, Harold. She told the super—"

"She did? Goddamn it..."

Chalmers said: "I cannot see, Harold, why you continue to—uh—keep company with a young woman who irritates you so."

Shea shrugged. "I suppose it's because she's the one not impossible she on the staff with whom I'm sure I'll never do anything irrevocable."

"While waiting for the dream-girl?" grinned Bayard. Shea simply shrugged again.

"That's not it," said Bayard. "The real reason, Doctor, is that she got the psychological jump on him the first time he took her out. Now he's afraid to quit."

"It's not a matter of being afraid," snapped Shea. He stood up and his voice rose to a roar of surprising volume: "And furthermore, Walter, I don't see that it's any damn business of yours..."

"Now, now, Harold," said Chalmers. "There's nothing to be gained by these outbursts. Aren't you satisfied with your work here?" he asked, worriedly.

Shea relaxed. "Why shouldn't I be? We do about as we damn please, thanks to old man Garaden's putting that requirement for a psychology institute into his bequest to the hospital. I could use more money, but so could everybody."

"That's not the point," said Chalmers. "These poses of yours and these outbreaks of temper point to an inner conflict, a maladjustment with your environment."

Shea grinned. "Call it a little suppressed romanticism. I figured it out myself long ago. Look. Walt here spends his time trying to become midwestern tennis champ. What good'll it do him? And Gert spends hours at the beauty parlor trying to look like a fallen Russian countess, which she's not built for. Another fixation on the distant romantic. I like to dress up. So what?"

"That's all right," Chalmers admitted, "if you don't start taking your imaginings seriously."

Bayard put in: "Like thinking dream-girls exist." Shea gave him a quick glare.

Chalmers continued: "Oh, well, if you start suffering from—uh—depressions, let me know. Let's get down to business now."

Shea asked: "More tests on hopheads?"

"No," said Chalmers. "We will discuss the latest hypotheses in what we hope will be our new science of paraphysics, and see whether we have not reached the stage where more experimental corroboration is possible.

"I've told you how I checked my premise, that the world we live in is composed of impressions received through the senses. But there is an infinity of possible worlds, and if the senses can be attuned to receive a different series of impressions, we should infallibly find ourselves living in a different world. That's where I got my second check, here at the hospital, in the examination of—uh—dements, mainly paranoiacs. You" —he nodded at Bayard— "set me on the right track with that report on the patient with Korsakov's psychosis.

"The next step would be to translate this theoretical data into experiment: that is, to determine how to transfer persons and objects from one world into another. Among the dements, the shift is partial and involuntary, with disastrous results to the psyche. When—"

"Just a minute," interrupted Shea. "Do you mean that a complete shift would actually transfer a man's body into one of these other worlds?"

"Very likely," agreed Chalmers, "since the body records whatever sensations the mind permits. For complete demonstration it would be necessary to try it, and I don't know that the risk would be worth it. The other world might have such different laws that it would be impossible to return."

Shea asked: "You mean, if the world were that of classical mythology, for instance, the laws would be those of Greek magic instead of modern physics?"

"Precisely. But—"

"Hey!" said Shea. "Then this new science of paraphysics is going to include the natural laws of all these different worlds, and what we call physics is just a special case of paraphysics—"

"Not so fast, young man," said Chalmers. "For the present, I think it wise to restrict the meaning of our term 'paraphysics' to the branch of knowledge that concerns the relationship of these multiple universes to each other, assuming that they actually exist. You will recall that careless use of the analogous term 'metaphysics' has resulted in its becoming practically synonymous with 'philosophy.'"

"Which," said Shea, "is regarded by some as a kind of scientific knowledge; by others as a kind of knowledge outside of science; and by still others as unscientific and therefore not knowledge of any kind."

"My, my, very neatly put," said Chalmers, fishing out a little black notebook. "E. T. Bell could not have said it more trenchantly. I shall include that statement of the status of philosophy in my next book."

"Hey," said Shea, sitting up sharply, "don't I even get a commission?"

Chalmers smiled blandly. "My dear Harold, you're at perfect liberty to write a book of your own; in fact I encourage you."

Bayard grinned: "Harold would rather play cowboy. When I think of a verbal pearl, I don't go around casting it promiscuously. I wait till I can use it in print and get paid for it. But to get back to our subject, how would you go about working the shift?"

Chalmers frowned. "I'll get to that, if you give me time. As I see it, the method consists of filling your mind with the fundamental assumptions of the world in question. Now, what are the fundamental assumptions of our world? Obviously, those of scientific logic."

"Such as—" said Shea.

"Oh, the principle of dependence, for instance. 'Any circumstance in which alone a case of the presence of a given phenomenon differs from the case of its absence is causally relevant to that phenomenon.' "

"Ouch!" said Shea. "That's almost as bad as Frege's definition of number."

Bayard droned: " 'The number of things in a given class—' "

"Stop it, Walter! It drives me nuts!"

" '—is the class of all classes that are similar to the given class.' "

"Hrrm," remarked Chalmers. "If you gentlemen are through with your joke, I'll go on. If one of these infinite other worlds—which up to now may be said to exist in a logical but not in an empirical sense—is governed by magic, you might expect to find a principle like that of dependence invalid, but principles of magic, such as the Law of Similarity, valid."

"What's the Law of Similarity?" asked Bayard sharply.

"The Law of Similarity may be stated thus: Effects resemble causes. It's not valid for us, but primitive peoples firmly believe it. For instance, they think you can make it rain by pouring water on the ground with appropriate mumbo jumbo."

"I didn't know you could have fixed principles of magic," commented Shea.

"Certainly," replied Chalmers solemnly. "Medicine men don't merely go through hocus-pocus. They believe they are working through natural laws. In a world where everyone firmly believed in these laws, that is, in one where all minds were attuned to receive the proper impressions, the laws of magic would conceivably work, as one hears of witch-doctors' spells working in Africa today. Frazer and Seabrook have worked out some of these magical laws. Another is the Law of Contagion: Things once in contact continue to interact from a distance after separation. As you—"

Shea snapped his fingers for attention. "Just a second, Doctor. In a world such as you're conceiving, would the laws of magic work because people believed in them, or would people believe in them because they worked?"

Chalmers put on the smile that always accompanied his intellectual rabbit-punches. "That question, Harold, is, in Russell's immortal phrase, a meaningless noise."

"No, you don't," said Shea. "That's the favorite dodge of modern epistemologists: every time you ask them a question they can't answer, they smile and say you're making a meaningless noise. I still think it's a sensible question, and as such deserves a sensible answer."

"Oh, but it is meaningless," said Chalmers. "As I can very easily demonstrate, it arises from your attempt to build your—uh—conceptualistic structure on an absolutistic rather than a relativistic basis. But I'll come back to that later. Allow me to continue my exposition.

"As you know, you can build up a self-consistent logic on almost any set of assumptions—"

Bayard opened his half-closed eyes and injected another sharp observation: "Isn't there a flaw in the structure there, Doctor? Seems to me your hypothesis makes transference to the future possible. We should then become aware of natural laws not yet discovered and inventions not yet made. But the future naturally won't be ignorant of our method of transference. Therefore we could return to the present with a whole list of new inventions. These inventions, launched into the present, would anticipate the future, and, by anticipating, change it."

"Very ingenious, Walter," said Chalmers. "But I'm afraid you overlook something. You might indeed secure transference to *a* future, but it would not necessarily be *the* future, the actual future of our own empirico-positivist world. A mental frame of reference is required. That is, we need a complete set of concepts of the physical world, which concepts condition the impressions received by the mind. The concepts of the future will be the product of numerous factors not now known to us. That is—"

"I see," said Shea. "The frame of reference for the actual future is not yet formed, whereas the frames of reference for all past worlds are fixed."

"Precisely. I would go beyond that. Transference to any world exhibiting such a fixed pattern is possible, but to such worlds only. That is, one could secure admission to any of H. G. Wells' numerous futures. We merely choose a series of basic assumptions. In the case of the actual future we are ignorant of the assumptions.

"But speculative extrapolation from our scanty supply of facts has already carried us—uh—halfway to Cloud-Cuckoo land. So let us return to our own time and place and devote ourselves to the development of an experimental technique wherewith to attack the problems of paraphysics.

"To contrive a vehicle for transposition from one world to another, we face the arduous task of extracting from the picture of such a world as that of the *Iliad* its basic assumptions, and expressing these in logical form—"

Shea interrupted: "In other words, building us a syllogismobile?"

Chalmers looked vexed for an instant, then laughed. "A very pithy way of expressing it, Harold. You are wasting your talents, as I have repeatedly pointed out, by not publishing more. I suggest; however, that the term 'syllogismobile' be confined for the present to discussions among us members of the Garaden Institute. When the time comes to try to impress our psychological colleagues with the importance of paraphysics, a somewhat more dignified mode of expression will be desirable."

Harold Shea lay on his bed, smoked, and thought. He smoked expensive English cigarettes, not because he liked them especially, but because it was part of his pattern of affectation to smoke something unusual. He thought about Chalmers' lecture.

It would no doubt be dangerous, as Chalmers had warned. But Shea was getting unutterably bored with life. Chalmers was able but stuffy; if brilliance and dullness could be combined in one personality, Reed Chalmers combined them. While in theory all three members of the Institute were researchers, in practice the two subordinates merely collected facts and left to the erudite Doctor the fun of assembling them and generalizing from them.

Of course, thought Shea, he did get some fun out of his little poses, but they were a poor substitute for real excitements. He liked wearing his new breeches and boots, but riding a horse had been an excruciating experience. It also had none of the imaginary thrill of swinging along in a cavalry charge, which he had half unconsciously promised himself. All he got was the fact that his acquaintances thought him a nut. Let 'em; he didn't care.

But he was too good a psychologist to deceive himself long or completely. He did care. He wanted to make a big impression, but he was one of those unfortunates who adopt a method that produces the effect opposite to the one they want.

Hell, he thought, *no use introspecting myself into the dumps. Chalmers says it'll work. The old bore misses fire once in a while, like the time he tried to psychoanalyze the cleaning woman and she thought he was proposing marriage. But that was an error of technique, not of general theory. Chalmers is sound enough on theory, and he has already warned of dangers in the practical application in this case.*

Yes. If he said that one could transport oneself to a different place and time by formula, it could be done. The complete escape from—well, from insignificance, Shea confessed to himself. He would be the Columbus of a new kind of journey! Harold Shea got up and began to pace the floor, excited by the trend of his own thoughts. *To explore—say the world of the Iliad. Danger: one might not be able to get back. Especially no*t, Shea told himself grimly, *if one turned out to be one of those serf soldiers who died by thousands under the gleaming walls of Troy.*
Not the Iliad. *The Slavic twilight? No; too full of man-eating witches and werewolves. Ireland! That was it—the Ireland of Cuchulainn and Queen Maev. Blood there, too, but what the hell, you can't have adventure without some danger. At least, the dangers were reasonable open-eye stuff you could handle. And the girls of that world—they were something pretty slick by all description.*

It is doubtful whether Shea's colleagues noticed any change in his somewhat irregular methods of working. They would hardly have suspected him of dropping Havelock Ellis for the Ulster and Fenian legendary cycles with which he was conditioning his mind for the attempted "trip." If any of them, entering his room suddenly, had come on a list with many erasures, which included a flashlight, a gun, and mercurochrome, they would merely have supposed that Shea intended to make a rather queer sort of camping expedition.

And Shea was too secretive about his intentions to let anyone see the equipment he selected: A Colt .38 revolver with plenty of ammunition, a stainless steel hunting knife—they ought to be able to appreciate metal like that, he told himself—a flashlight, a box of matches to give him a reputation as a wonder worker, a notebook, a Gaelic dictionary, and, finally, the *Boy Scout Handbook,* edition of 1926, as the easiest source of ready reference for one who expected to live in the open air and in primitive society.

Shea went home after a weary day of asking questions of neurotics, and had a good dinner. He put on the almost-new riding clothes and strapped over his polo coat a shoulder pack to hold his kit. He put on the hat with the green feather, and sat down at his desk. There, on sheets of paper spread before him, were the logical equations, with their little horseshoes, upside-down T's, and identity signs.

His scalp prickled a trifle as he gazed at them. But what the hell! Stand by for adventure and romance! He bent over, giving his whole attention to the formulas, trying not to focus on one spot, but to apprehend the whole:

"If P equals not-Q, Q implies not-P, which is equivalent to saying either P or Q or neither, but not both. *But* if not-P is not implied by not-Q, the counter-implicative form of the proposition—"

There was nothing but six sheets of paper. Just that, lying in two neat rows of three sheets, with perhaps half an inch between them. There should be strips of table showing between them. But there was nothing—nothing.

"The full argument thus consists in an epicheirematic syllogism in Barbara, the major premise of which is not the conclusion of an enthymeme, though the minor premise of which may or may not be the conclusion of a non-Aristotelian sorites—"

The papers were still there, but overlaying the picture of those six white rectangles was a whirl of faint spots of color. All the colors of the spectrum were represented, he noted with the back of his mind, but there was a strong tendency toward violet. Round and round they went—round—and round

"If either P or Q is true or (Q or R) is true then either Q is true or (P or R) is false—"

Round and round— He could hear nothing at all. He had no sense of heat or cold, or of the pressure of the chair seat against him. There was nothing but millions of whirling spots of color.

Yes, he could feel temperature now. He was cold. There was sound, too, a distant whistling sound, like that of a wind in a chimney. The spots were fading into a general grayness. There was a sense of pressure, also, on the soles of his feet. He straightened his legs—yes, standing on something. But everything around him was gray—and bitter cold, with a wind whipping the skirts of his coat around him.

He looked down. His feet were there all right—hello, feet, pleased to meet you. But they were fixed in grayish-yellow mud which had squilched up in little ridges around them. The mud belonged to a track only two feet wide. On both sides of it the gray-green of dying grass began. On the grass large flakes of snow were scattered, dandruffwise. More were coming, visible as dots of darker gray against the background of whirling mist, swooping down long parallel inclines, growing and striking the path with the tiniest *ts*. Now and then one spattered against Shea's face.

He had done it. The formula worked!

2

"Welcome to Ireland!" Harold Shea murmured to himself. He thanked heaven that his syllogismobile had brought his clothes and equipment along with his person. It would never have done to have been dumped naked onto this freezing landscape. The snow was not alone responsible for the grayness. There was also a cold, clinging mist that cut off vision at a hundred yards or so. Ahead of him the track edged leftward around a little mammary of a hill, on whose flank a tree rocked under the melancholy wind. The tree's arms all reached one direction, as though the wind were habitual; its branches bore a few leaves as gray and discouraged as the landscape itself. The tree was the only object visible in that wilderness of mud, grass and fog. Shea stepped toward it. The serrated leaves bore the indentations of the Northern scrub oak.

But that grows only in the Arctic Circle, he thought. He was bending closer for another look when he heard the *clop-squash* of a horse's hoofs on the muddy track behind him.

He turned. The horse was very small, hardly more than a pony, and shaggy, with a luxuriant tail blowing round its withers. On its back sat a man who might have been tall had he been upright, for his feet nearly touched the ground. But he was hunched before the icy wind driving in behind. From saddle to eyes he was enveloped in a faded blue cloak. A formless slouch hat was pulled tight over his face, yet not so tight as to conceal the fact that he was full-bearded and gray.

Shea took half a dozen quick steps to the roadside. He addressed the man with the phrase he had composed in advance for his first human contact in the world of Irish myth:

"The top of the morning to you, my good man, and would it be far to the nearest hostel?"

He had meant to say more, but paused uncertainly as the man on the horse lifted his head to reveal a proud, unsmiling face in which the left eye socket was unpleasantly vacant. Shea smiled weakly, then gathered his courage and plunged on: "It's a rare bitter December you do be having in Ireland."

The stranger looked at him with much of the same clinical detachment he himself would have given to an interesting case of schizophrenia, and spoke in slow, deep tones: "I have no knowledge of hostels, nor of Ireland; but the month is not December. We are in May, and this is the Fimbulwinter."

A little prickle of horror filled Harold Shea, though the last word was meaningless to him. Faint and far, his ear caught a sound that might be the howling of a dog—or a wolf. As he sought for words there was a flutter of movement. Two big black birds, like oversize crows, slid down the wind past him and came to rest on the dry grass, looked at him for a second or two with bright, intelligent eyes, then took the air again.

"Well, where *am* I?"

"At the wings of the world, by Midgard's border."

"Where in hell is that?"

The deep voice took on an edge of annoyance. "For all things there is a time, a place, and a person. There is none of the three for ill-judged questions and empty jokes." He showed Shea a blue-clad shoulder, clucked to his pony and began to move wearily ahead.

"Hey!" cried Shea. He was feeling good and sore. The wind made his fingers and jaw muscles ache. He was lost in this arctic wasteland, and this old goat was about to trot off and leave him stranded. He leaned forward, planting himself squarely in front of the pony. "What kind of a runaround is this, anyway? When I ask someone a civil question—"

The pony had halted, its muzzle almost touching Shea's coat. The man on the animal's back straightened suddenly so that Shea could see he was very tall indeed, a perfect giant. But before he had time to note anything more he felt himself caught and held with an almost physical force by that single eye. A stab of intense, burning cold seemed to run through him, inside his head, as though his brain had been pierced by an icicle. He felt rather than heard a voice which demanded, "Are you trying to stop *me*, niggeling?"

For his life, Shea could not have moved anything but his lips. "N-no," he stammered. "That is, I just wondered if you could tell me how I could get somewhere where it's warm—"

The single eye held him unblinkingly for a few seconds. Shea felt that it was examining his inmost thoughts. Then the man slumped a trifle so that the brim of his hat shut out the glare and the deep voice was muffled. "I will be tonight at the house of the bonder Sverre, which is the Crossroads of the World. You may follow." The wind whipped a fold of his blue cloak, and as it did so there came, apparently from within the cloak itself, a little swirl of leaves. One clung for a moment to the front of Shea's coat. He caught it with numbed fingers, and saw it was an ash leaf, fresh and tender with the bright green of spring—in the midst of this howling wilderness, where only arctic scrub oak grew!

Shea let the pony pass and fell in behind, head down, collar up, hands deep in pockets, squinting against the snowflakes. He was too frozen to think clearly, but he tried. The logical formulas had certainly thrown him into another world. But he hardly needed the word of Old Whiskers that it was not Ireland. Something must have gone haywire in his calculations. Could he go back and recheck them? No—he had not the slightest idea at present what might have been on those six sheets of paper. He would have to make the best of his situation.

But what world had he tumbled into? A cold, bleak one, inhabited by small, shaggy ponies and grim old blue-clad men with remarkable eyes. It might be the world of Scandinavian mythology. Shea knew very little about such a world, except that its No. 1 guy was someone named Odinn, or Woden, or Wotan, and there was another god named Thor who threw a sledge hammer at people he disliked.

Shea's scientific training made him doubt whether he would actually find these gods operating as gods, with more-than-human powers; or, for that matter, whether he would see any fabulous monsters. Still, that stab of cold through his head and that handful of ash leaves needed explaining. Of course, the pain in his head might be an indication of incipient pneumonia, and Old Whis-

kers might make a habit of carrying ash leaves in his pockets. But still—
The big black birds were keeping up with them. They didn't seem afraid, nor did they seem to mind the ghastly weather.

It was getting darker, though in this landscape of damp blotting paper Shea could not tell whether the sun had set. The wind pushed at him violently, forcing him to lean into it; the mud on the path was freezing, but not quite gelid. It had collected in yellow gobs on his boots. He could have sworn the boots weighed thirty pounds apiece, and they had taken in water around the seams, adding clammy socks to his discomfort. A clicking sound, like a long roll of castanets, made him wonder until he realized it was caused by his own teeth.

He seemed to have been walking for days, though he knew it could hardly be a matter of hours. Reluctantly he took one hand from his pocket and gazed at his wrist watch. It read 9:56; certainly wrong. When he held the watch to a numbed ear he discovered it had stopped. Neither shaking nor winding could make it start.

He thought of asking his companion the time, but realized that the rider would have no more accurate idea than himself. He thought of asking how much farther they had to go. But he would have to make himself heard over the wind, and the old boy's manner did not encourage questions.

They plodded on. The snow was coming thickly through the murky twilight. Shea could barely make out the figure before him. The path had become the same neutral gray as everything else. The weather was turning colder. The snowflakes were dry and hard, stinging and bouncing where they struck. Now and then an extra puff of wind would snatch a cloud of them from the moor, whirling it into Shea's face. He would shut his eyes to the impact, and when he opened them find he had blundered off the path and have to scurry after his guide.

Light. He pulled the pack around in front of him and fumbled in it till he felt the icy touch of the flashlight's metal. He pulled it out from under the other articles and pressed the switch button. Nothing happened, nor would shaking, slapping, or repeated snappings of the switch produce any result.

In a few minutes it would be too dark for him to follow the man on the pony by sight alone. Whether the old boy liked it or not, Shea would have to ask the privilege of holding a corner of his cloak as a guide.

It was just as he reached this determination that something in the gait of the pony conveyed a sense of arrival. A moment more and the little animal was trotting, with Shea stumbling and skidding along the fresh snow behind as he strove to keep pace. The pack weighed tons, and he found himself gasping for breath as though he were running up a forty-five-degree angle instead of on an almost level path.

Then there was a darker patch in the dark-gray universe. Shea's companion halted the pony and slid off. A rough-hewn timber door loomed through the storm, and the old man banged against it with his fist. It opened, flinging a flood of yellow light out across the snow. The old man stepped into the gap, his cloak vividly blue in the fresh illumination.

Shea, left behind, croaked a feeble "Hey!" just managing to get his foot in the gap of the closing door. It opened full out and a man in a baggy homespun tunic peered out at him, his face rimmed with drooping whiskers. "Well?"

"May I c-c-come in?"

"Umph," said the man. "Come on, come on. Don't stand there letting the cold in!"

3

Shea stood in a kind of entry hall, soaking in the delicious warmth. The vestibule was perhaps six feet deep. At its far end a curtain of skins had been parted to permit the passage of the old man who preceded him. The bonder Sverre—Shea supposed this would be his host—pulled them still wider. "Lord, use this as your own house, now and forever," he murmured with the perfunctory hurry of a man repeating a formula like "Pleased to meet you."

The explorer of universes ducked under the skins and into a long hall paneled in dark wood. At one end a fire blazed, apparently in the center of the floor though bricked round to knee height. Around it were a number of benches and tables. Shea caught a glimpse of walls hung with weapons—a huge sword, nearly as tall as he was, half a dozen small spears or javelins, their delicate steel points catching ruddy highlights from the torches in brackets; a kite-shaped shield with metal overlay in an intricate pattern—

No more than a glimpse. Sverre had taken him by the arm and conducted him through another door, shouting: "Aud! Hallgerda! This stranger's half frozen. Get the steam room ready. Now, stranger, you come with me."

Down a passage to a smaller room, where the whiskered man ordered him: "Get off those wet clothes. Strange garments you have. I've never seen so many buttons and clasps in all my days. If you're one of the Sons of Muspellheim, I'll give you guesting for the night. But I warn you for tomorrow there be men not far from here who would liefer meet you with a sword than a handclasp." He eyed Shea narrowly a moment. "Be you of Muspellheim?"

Shea fenced: "What makes you think that?"

"Traveling in those light clothes this far north. Those that hunt the red bear"—he made a curious motion of his hand as though tracing the outline of an eyebolt in the air—"need warm hides as well as stout hearts." Again he gave Shea that curiously intent glance, as though trying to ravel some secret out of him.

Shea asked: "This is May, isn't it? I understand you're pretty far north, but you ought to get over this cold snap soon."

The man Sverre moved his shoulders in a gesture of bafflement. "Mought, and then mought not. Men say this would be the Fimbulwinter. If that's so, there'll be little enough of warm till the roaring trumpet blows and the Sons of the Wolf ride from the East, at the *Time*."

Shea would have put a question of his own, but Sverre had turned away grumpily. He got rid of his clammy shorts instead, turning to note that Sverre had picked up his wrist watch.

"That's a watch," he offered in a friendly voice.

"A thing of power?" Sverre looked at him again, and then a smile of comprehension distended the wide beard as he slapped his knee. "Of course. Mought have known. You came in with the Wanderer. You're all right. One of those southern warlocks."

From somewhere he produced a blanket and whisked it around Shea's nude form. "This way now," he ordered. Shea followed through a couple of doors to another small room, so full of wood smoke that it made him cough. He started to rub his eyes, then just in time caught at the edge of his blanket. There were two girls standing by the door, neither of them in the least like the Irish colleens he had expected to find. Both were blonde, apple-cheeked, and rather beamy. They reminded him disagreeably of Gertrude Mugler.

Sverre introduced them: "This here's my daughter Aud. She's a shield girl; can lick her weight in polar bears." Shea, observing the brawny miss, silently agreed. "And this is Hallgerda. All right, you go on in. The water's ready to pour."

In the center of the small room was a sunken hearth full of fire. On top of the fire had been laid a lot of stones about the size of potatoes. Two wooden buckets full of water sat by the hearth.

The girls went out, closing the door. Shea, with the odd sensation that he had experienced all this at some previous time— *It must be part of the automatic adjustment one's mind makes to the pattern of this world* he told himself— picked up one of the buckets. He threw it rapidly on the fire, then followed it with the other. With a hiss, the room filled with water vapor.

Shea stood it as long as he could, which was about a minute, then groped blindly for the door and gasped out. Instantly a bucketful of ice water hit him in the face. As he stood pawing the air and making strangled noises a second bucketful caught him in the chest. He yelped, managing to choke out, "Glup...stop...that's enough!"

Somewhere in the watery world a couple of girls were giggling. It was not till his eyes cleared that he realized it was they who had drenched him, and that he was standing between them without his protecting blanket.

His first impulse was to dash back into the steam room. But one of the pair was holding out a towel which it seemed only courtesy to accept. Sverre was approaching unconcernedly with a mug of something. *Well,* he thought, *if they can take it, I can.* He discovered that after the first horrible moment his embarrassment had vanished. He dried himself calmly while Sverre held out the mug. The girls' clinical indifference to the physical Shea was more than ever like Gertrude.

"Hot mead," Sverre explained. "Something you don't get down south. Aud, get the stranger's blanket. We don't want him catching cold."

Shea took a gulp of the mead, to discover that it tasted something like ale and something like honey. The sticky sweetness of the stuff caught him in the throat at first, but he was more afraid of losing face before these people than of being sick. Down it went, and after the first gulp it wasn't so bad. He began to feel almost human.

"What's your name, stranger?" inquired Sverre.

Shea thought a minute. These people probably didn't use family names. So he said simply, "Harold."

"Hungh?"

Shea repeated, more distinctly. "Oh," said Sverre. "Harald." He made it rhyme with "dolled."

Dressed, except for his boots, Shea took the place on the bench that Sverre indicated. As he waited for food he glanced round the hall. Nearest him was a huge middle-aged man with red hair and beard, whose appearance made Shea's mind leap to Sverre's phrase about "the red bear." His dark red cloak fell back to show a belt with carved gold work on it. Next to him sat another redhead, more on the sandy order, small-boned and foxy-faced, with quick, shifty eyes. Beyond Foxy-face was a blond young man of about Shea's size and build, with a little golden fuzz on his face.

At the middle of the bench two pillars of black wood rose, from floor to ceiling, heavily carved, and so near the table that they almost cut off one seat. It was now occupied by the gray-bearded, one-eyed man Shea had followed in from the road. His floppy hat was on the table before him, and he was half leaning around one of the pillars to talk to another big blond man—a stout chap whose face bore an expression of permanent good nature, overlaid with worry. Leaning against the table at his side was an empty scabbard that could have held a sword as large as the one Shea had noticed on the wall.

The explorer's eye, roving along the table, caught and was held by that of the slim young man. The latter nodded, then rose and came round the table, grinning bashfully.

"Would ye like a seat companion?" he asked. "You know how it is, as Havámal says:

> *Care eats the heart If you cannot speak*
> *To another all your thought.*

He half-chanted the lines, accenting the alliteration in a way that made the rhymeless verse curiously attractive. He went on: "It would help me a lot with the *Time* coming, to talk to a plain human being. I don't mind saying I'm scared. My name's Thjalfi."

"Mine's Harald," said Shea, pronouncing it as Sverre had done.

"You came with the Wanderer, didn't ye? Are ye one of those outland warlocks?"

It was the second time Shea had been accused of that. "I don't know what a warlock is, honest," said he, "and I didn't come with the Wanderer. I just got lost and followed him here, "and ever since I've been trying to find out where I am."

Thjalfi laughed, then took a long drink of mead. As Shea wondered what there was to laugh at, the young man said: "No offense, friend Harald. Only it does seem mighty funny for a man to say he's lost at Crossroads of the World. Ha, ha, I never did hear the like."

"The where did you say?"

"Sure, the Crossroads of the World! You must come from seven miles beyond the moon not to know that. Hai! You picked a queer time to come, with all of *Them* here"—he jerked his finger toward the four bearded men. "Well, I'd keep quiet about not having the power, if I was you. Ye know what the Havámal says:

> *To the silent and sage Does care seldom come*
> *When he goes to a house as guest.*

Ye're likely to be in a jam when the trouble starts if ye don't have protection from one of *Them*, but as long as *They* think ye're a warlock, Uncle Fox will help you out."

He jabbed a finger to indicate the small, sharp-featured man among the four, then went on quickly: "Or are ye a hero? If ye are, I can get Redbeard to take ye into his service when the *Time* comes."

"What time? Tell me what this is all—" began Shea, but at that moment Aud and another girl appeared with wooden platters loaded with food.

"Hai, sis!" called Thjalfi cheerfully, and tried to grab a chop from the platter carried by the second, a girl Shea had not previously seen. The girl kicked him neatly on the shin and set it before the late-comer.

The meal consisted of various meats, with beside them a big slab of bread, looking as though it had been cut from a quilt. There was no sign of knife, fork, or any vegetable element. Of course, they would not have table silver, Shea assured himself. He broke off a piece of the bread and bit into it. It was better than it looked. The meat that he picked up rather gingerly was apparently a boiled pork chop, well-cooked and well-seasoned. But as he was taking the second bite, he noted that the shield girl, Aud, was still standing beside him.

As he looked round Aud made a curtsy and said rapidly: "Lord, with this meal as with all things, your wishes are our law. Is there aught else that you desire?"

Shea hesitated for a moment, realizing it was a formula required by politeness and that he should make some remark praising the food. But he had had a long drink of potent mead on an empty stomach. The normal food habits of an American urged him to action.

"Would it be too much to ask whether you have any vegetables?" he said.

For one brief second both the girl and Thjalfi stared at him. Then both burst into shrieks of laughter, Aud staggering back toward the wall, Thjalfi rolling his head forward on his arms. Shea sat staring, red with embarrassment, the half-eaten chop in his hand. He hardly noticed that the four men at the other side of the table were looking at him till the big red-headed man boomed out:

"Good is the wit when men's children laugh before the Æsir! Now, Thjalfi, you shall tell us what brings this lightness of heart."

Thjalfi, making no effort to control himself, managed to gasp out: "The...the warlock Harald wants to eat a turnip!" His renewed burst of laughter was drowned in the roar from Redbeard, who leaned back, bellowing: "Oh, ho, ho, ho, ho! Turnip Harald, ha, ha ha!" His merriment was like a gale with the other three adding their part, even the blue-cloaked Wanderer.

When they had quieted down a little Shea turned to Thjalfi. "What did I do?" he asked. "After all—"

"Ye named yourself Turnip Harald! I'm afeared ye spoiled your chance of standing under Redbeard's banner at the *Time*. Who'd want a hero that ate turnips? In Asgard we use them to fatten hogs."

"But—"

"Ye didn't know better. Well, now your only chance is Uncle Fox. Ye can thank me for saying ye're a warlock. Besides, he loves a good joke; the only humorist in the lot of them, I always say. But eating turnips—ha, ha, that's the funniest thing I've heard since the giant tried to marry the Hammer Thrower!"

Shea, a trifle angry and now completely mystified, turned to ask explanations. Before he could frame the words there was a pounding at the door. Sverre admitted a tall man, pale, blond and beardless, with a proud, stately face and a huge golden horn slung over his back. "There's another of *Them*," whispered Thjalfi. "That's Heimdall. I wonder if all twelve of *Them* are meeting here."

"Who the devil are *They*?"

"*Sh!*"

The four bearded men nodded welcome to the newcomer. He took his place beside the Wanderer with lithe grace, and immediately began to say something to the older man, who nodded in rapt attention. Shea caught a few of the words: "—fire horses, but no use telling you with the Bearer of Bad Tidings present." He nodded contemptuously toward Uncle Fox.

"It is often seen," said the latter, raising his voice a trifle but addressing the red-bearded man as though continuing a conversation begun before, "that liars tell few lies when those are present who can see the truth."

"Or it may be that I have that to tell which I do not wish to have repeated to our enemies by the Evil Companion," said Heimdall, looking straight at Uncle Fox.

"There are even those," continued the latter evenly, still paying Heimdall no attention, "who, having no character of their own, wish to destroy all character by assassinating the reputations of others."

"Liar and thief!" cried Heimdall angrily, bringing his fist down on the table and almost snarling. Shea saw that his front teeth were, surprisingly, of gold.

"Here," rumbled the large redhead, judicially. "Let there be an allaying of the anger of the Æsir in the presence of mortals."

"Let there also," snapped the small man, "be an allaying of insults in the mouth of—"

"All insults are untrue," said Heimdall. "I state facts."

"Facts! Few are the facts that come from that long wagging chin. Facts like the tale of having nine mothers, or the boast of that horn and the great noise it will make— Beware lest mice nest in it and it fail to give a squeak."

"You shall hear my trumpet at the *Time*, Father of Lies. And you will not like the sound."

"Some would say that called for the sword."

"Try it. Here is the blade that will carve your stinking carcass."

"Why, you—" Foxy-face and Heimdall were on their feet and bellowing at each other. Their voices had a volume that made Shea wince. The other three bearded men rose and began shouting also. Above their heads the two black birds who had been the Wanderer's companions fled round and round with excited cries.

Just as it looked as though the two original disputants were certain to fling themselves at each other's throat, the bigger redhead grabbed the smaller one by the shoulders and forced him down. "Sit down!" he thundered. The Wanderer, his sonorous voice full of outraged dignity, shouted: "This is disgraceful! We shall have no respect left. I command you to be quiet, both of you!"

"But—" yelled Heimdall.

The Wanderer silenced him with a gesture. "Nothing you can say will be heard. If either of you speaks to the other before bedtime, he shall have nothing less than my gravest displeasure."

Heimdall subsided and went over to a far corner to sit and glare at Foxface, who returned the glare. Thjalfi whispered to the awed Shea: "It's like this every time three or four of *Them* get together. They're supposed to set us a good example, but the first thing ye know they're at it like a gang of drunken berserks."

"I'd still like to know who *They* are," said Shea.

"Do you mean ye really don't know?" Thjalfi stared at him with eyes full of honest rustic perplexity. "Don't that beat all, now? I wouldn't have believed it if ye hadn't asked for those turnips. Well, the one that was scrapping with Heimdall is Loki. The big red-bearded one next to him is Thor. The old man, the Wanderer, is Odinn, and the fat one is Frey. Have ye got them straight now?"

Shea looked hard at Thjalfi, but there was nothing in the latter's face but the most transparent seriousness. Either he had stepped through the formula into some downright dream, or he was being kidded, or the five were local Scandinavian chieftains who for some reason had named themselves after the gods of the old Norse pantheon. The remaining possibility—that these were actually gods—was too wildly improbable for consideration. Yet, those birds—the glance he had received from Odinn—and he knew that Odinn was always represented as one-eyed—

The big redhead called Thor got up and went over to the pair whom Thjalfi had identified as Odinn and Frey. For a few minutes they muttered, heads together. At the conclusion of the conference Odinn got up, clapped his floppy hat on his head, whirled his blue cloak around him, took a last gulp of mead and strode out the door.

As the door banged behind him, Loki and Heimdall half rose to their feet. Immediately Thor and Frey jumped up, with the former rumbling: "No more! Save your blows, sons of Asgard, for the *Time*. Or if you must deal buffets, exchange them with me." He lifted a fist the size of a small ham, and both subsided. "It is time for bed, in any case. Come along, Loki. You, too, Thjalfi."

Thjalfi rose reluctantly. "I'll speak a word for ye to Uncle Fox in the morning," he murmured in farewell. "Working for these Æsir is no fun. They're an ornery lot, but I suppose we're better off with 'em than without 'em, what with the *Time* coming. Ye know what Ulf, the poet says:

> Bare is the breast Without banner before it
> When heroes bear weapons To the wrack of the world.

Good night."

Shea was not at all sure he wanted to work for Loki as a warlock, whatever that was. There was something sly about the man, uncomfortable. The graceful and forthright Heimdall had impressed him more in spite of the latter's lack of a sense of humor, he mused.

A small noise at the door was Sverre, putting his head in for a look around and then vanishing again. Of the buxom young women nothing had been seen since they took up the wooden platters. Though the house was obviously going to bed, Shea found himself not in the least sleepy. It could hardly be much after nine o'clock. But in a world without artificial light other than that of torches, people would rise and set with the sun. Shea wondered whether he, too, would come around to that dismal habit. Probably, unless he succeeded in getting back to his own world. That was a rather upsetting thought. But, hell, he had taken the risk with his eyes open. Even if this was not the world he had expected to land in, it was still one in which his twentieth century appliances should give him certain advantages. It would be time enough to worry when—

"Hai, turnip, man," said Heimdall suddenly from his corner. "Fill a couple of mugs and bring them hither, will you?"

Shea felt his temper rise at this dictatorial manner. But whatever or whoever Heimdall was, he looked fully capable of enforcing authority. And though the words were peremptory, the tone of voice was evidently meant for kindness. He obeyed.

"Sit down," said Heimdall. "You have been called Harald. Is that correct?"

"Yes, I was told you are Heimdall."

"Nothing less than the truth. I am also known as the Watcher, the Son of Nine Mothers, the Child of Fury, and the Golden. I prefer the titles."

"Well, look here, Heimdall, what's all this—"

"Children of men use the titles or call me sir," said Heimdall severely and rather pompously.

"Sorry, sir."

Heimdall looked down his long nose and condescended a smile that showed the gold teeth. "To me this familiarity is not unpleasant, for I have also been called the Friend of Men. But the Lord of Asgard disapproves."

"You mean Odinn?"

"None other."

"The old guy—pardon me, I mean the elderly one-eyed gentleman?"

"You are a well of knowledge."

"I ran into him out on the moor yesterday and followed him here."

"That is not hidden. I saw you."

"You did? Where were you?"

"Many miles eastaway. I also heard your remarks to him. Lucky you were not to have been struck dead."

Shea almost said, "Aw, don't try to kid me." Just in time he remembered the piercing, icy glance Odinn had given him and held his tongue. It wouldn't do to take chances till he knew more about what chances he was taking, what system of natural laws governed this world into which he had fallen. Heimdall was watching him with a slightly amused smile.

"I also heard you tell Thjalfi that you are no warlock, but you know not what it means. You must be from far. However"—he smiled again at Shea's expression of consternation—"few are sorry for that. I'll keep your secret. A joke on the Master of Deception—ho, ho, ho!"

He drank. "And now, child of an ignorant mother," he went on, "it is yet to be seen that you have knowledge of strange things. I propose that we amuse ourselves with the game of questions. Each shall ask of the other seven questions, and he who answers best shall be adjudged the winner. Ask, mortal!"

Seven questions. Shea considered a moment how he could make them yield him the most information. "Where has Odinn gone?" he asked finally.

"One," said Heimdall. "He has gone to the gates of Hell to summon from her grave a woman centuries dead."

"Did you say Hell, honest?" asked Shea.

"It is not to be doubted."

"Well, well, you don't say so." Shea was covering his own incredulity and confusion. This man—god—individual was more difficult than any psychopathic he had ever questioned. He gathered his mental forces for the next try. "What is Odinn doing that for?"

"Two," replied Heimdall. "The *Time* is coming. Balder dies, and the Æsir need advice. The Wanderer believes that the spae-wife buried at the gates of Hell can tell us what we need to know."

The vaguely ominous statements about the *Time* were beginning to get on Shea's nerves. He asked, "What is meant by the statement, 'the *Time* is coming?' "

"Three. Ragnarök, as all men know. All men but you alone, dewy-eyed innocent."

"What's Ragnarök?"

"Four. The end of the world, babe in a man's body."

Shea's temper stirred. He didn't like this elaborate ridicule, and he didn't think it fair of Heimdall to count his last question, which had been merely a request to explain an unfamiliar word in the previous answer. But he had met irritatingly irrelevant replies at the Garaden Institute and managed to keep himself under control.

"When will all this happen?"

"Five. Not men, or gods, or Vanir, or even the dwarfs know, but it will be soon. Already the Fimbulwinter, the winter in summer that precedes Ragnarök, is upon us."

"They all say there's going to be a battle. Who will win?" Shea was proud of himself for that question. It covered both the participants and the result.

"Six. Gods and men were glad to have the answer to that, youngling, since we shall stand together against the giant folk. But for the present there is this to be said: our chances are far from good. There are four weapons of great power among us: Odinn's spear, Gungnir; the Hammer of Thor that is called Mjöllnir; Frey's sword, the magic blade Hundingsbana; and my own good sword which bears the name of Head." He slapped the hilt of the sword that hung by his side. "But some of the giants, we do not know how or who, have stolen both the great Hammer and Frey's sword. Unless they are recovered it may be that gods and men will drink of death together."

Shea realized with panic that the world whose destruction Heimdall was so calmly discussing was the one in which he, Harold Shea, was physically living. He was at the mercy of a system of events he could not escape.

"What can I do to keep from getting caught in the gears?" he demanded, and then, seeing Heimdall look puzzled, "I mean, if the world's going to bust up, how can I keep out of the smash?"

Heimdall's eyebrows went up. "Ragnarök is upon us, that not gods know how to avoid—and you, son of man, think of safety! The answer is nothing. And now this is your seventh question and it is my turn to ask of you."

"But—"

"Child of Earth, you weary me." He stared straight into Shea's eyes, and once more there was that sensation of an icicle piercing his brain. But Heimdall's voice was smooth. "From which of the nine worlds do you come, strangest of strangers, with garments like to none I have seen?"

Shea thought. The question was a little like, "Have you quit beating your wife?" He asked cautiously, "Which nine worlds?"

Heimdall laughed lightly. "Ho—I thought I was to be the questioner here. But there is the abode of the gods that is Asgard, and that is one world; and the homes of the giants, that are Jötunheim, Muspellheim, Niflheim, and Hell, or five worlds in all. There is Alfheim where live the dwarfs; and Svartalfheim and Vanaheim which we do not know well, though it is said the Vanir shall stand with us at the *Time*. Lastly there is Midgard, which is overrun with such worms as you."

Shea yawned. The mead and warmth were beginning to pull up on him. "To tell the truth, I don't come from any of them, but from outside your system of worlds entirely."

"A strange answer is that, yet not so strange, but it could be true," said Heimdall, thoughtfully. "For I can see the nine worlds from where I sit and nowhere such a person as yourself. Say nothing of this to the other Æsir, and above all to the Wanderer. He would take it ill to hear there was a world in which he held no power. Now I will ask my second question. What men or gods rule this world of yours?"

Shea found himself yawning again. He was too tired for explanations and flipped off his answer. "Well, some say one class and some say another, but the real rulers are called traffic cops. They pinch you—"

"Are they then some form of crab-fish?"

"No. They pinch you for moving too fast, whereas a crab pinches you for moving too slowly."

"Still they are sea gods, I perceive, like my brother Ægir. What is their power?"

Shea fought a losing battle against another yawn. "I'm sorry I seem to be sleepy," he said. "Aren't you going to bed soon, Golden?"

"Me? Ho, ho! Seldom has such ignorance been seen at the Crossroads of the World. I am the Watcher of the Gods, and never sleep. Sleepless One is, indeed, another of my titles. But it is to be seen that it is otherwise with you, youngling, and since I have won the game of questions you may go to bed."

An angry retort rose to Shea's lips at this calm assumption of victory, but he remembered that icy glare in time. Heimdall, however, seemed able to read his mind. "What! You would argue with me? Off to bed—and remember our little plot against the Bringer of Discord. Henceforth you are Turnip Harald, the bold and crafty warlock."

Shea risked just one more question. "What is a warlock, please, sir?"

"Ho, ho! Child from another world, your ignorance is higher than a mountain and deeper than a well. A warlock is a wizard, an enchanter, a weaver of spells, a raiser of spirits. Goodnight, Turnip Harald."

The bedroom proved to have a sliding door. Shea found it no bigger than a Pullman section and utterly without ventilation. The bed was straw-stuffed and jabbed him. He could not find comfort. After an hour or so of tossing, he had the experience, not uncommon on the heels of a day of excitements, of finding himself more wide-awake than in the beginning.

For a time his thoughts floated aimlessly; then he told himself that, since this was an experiment, he might as well spend the sleepless hours trying to assemble results. What were they?

Well, firstly, that there had been an error either in the equations or his use of them, and he had been pitched into a world of Scandinavian mythology— or else Scandinavian history. He was almost prepared to accept the former view.

These people talked with great conviction about their Ragnarök. He was enough of a psychologist to recognize their sincerity. And that icy stare he had felt from Odinn and then Heimdall was something, so far as he knew, outside ordinary human experience. It might be a form of hypnosis, but he doubted whether the technique, or even the idea of hypnotism, would be known to ancient Viking chiefs. No, there was something definitely more than human about them.

Yet they had human enough attributes as well. It ought not to be beyond the powers of an experimental psychologist to guide his conduct by analyzing them a little and making use of the results. Odinn? Well, he was off to the gates of Hell, whither Shea had no desire to follow him. Not much to be made of him, anyway, save a sense of authority.

What about Loki? A devastatingly sharp tongue that indicated a keen mind at work. Also a certain amount of malice. Uncle Fox, Thjalfi had called him, and said he was fond of jokes. Shea told himself he would not be surprised to find the jokes were often of a painful order. Working for him might be difficult, but Shea smiled to himself as he thought how he could surprise the god with so simple an object as a match.

Frey he had hardly noticed, Thor apparently was no more than a big, good-natured bruiser, and Thjalfi, the kind of rustic one would find in any country town, quoting Eddic lays instead of the Bible.

Heimdall, however, was a more complex character, certainly lacking in Loki's sense of humor, but also in the malice that was the basid of that humor. And he quite evidently felt he had a position of dignity to maintain with relation to the common herd—as witness his insistence on titles. But equally evidently, he was prepared to accept the responsibilities of that position, throw himself heart and soul and with quite a good mind into the right side of the scales—as Loki was not. Perhaps that was why he hated Loki. And Heimdall, underneath the shell of dignity, had a streak of genuine kindness. One felt one could count on him—and deciding he liked Heimdall the best of the lot, Shea turned over and went to sleep.

4

Shea awoke with a set of fur-bearing teeth and a headache that resembled the establishment of a drop-forging plant inside his brain—whether from the mead or the effect of those two piercing glances he had received from Heimdall and Odinn he could not tell. It was severe enough to stir him to a morning-after resolution to avoid all three in the future.

When the panel of his bedroom slid back he could hear voices from the hall. Thor, Loki, and Thjalfi were at breakfast as he came in, tearing away with knives and fingers at steaks the size of unabridged dictionaries. The foxy-faced Loki greeted him cheerfully: "Hail, hero of the turnip fields! Will your lordship do us the honor of breakfasting with us?"

He shoved a wooden platter with a hunk of meat on it toward Shea and passed along one of a collection of filled mugs. Shea's mouth was dry, but he almost gagged when a pull at the mug showed it contained beer and sour beer at that.

Loki laughed. "Ridiculous it is," he said, "to see the children of men, who have no fixed customs, grow uneasy when customs about them change. Harald of the Turnips, I am told you are a notable warlock."

Shea looked at his plate. "I know one or two tricks," he admitted.

"It was only to be expected that a hero of such unusual powers would be modest. Now there is this to be said: a man fares ill at Ragnarök unless he have his place. Would you be one of my band at the *Time?*"

Shea gulped. He was still unconvinced about this story of a battle and the end of the world, but he might as well ride with the current till he could master it. "Yes, sir, and thank you."

"The worm consents to ride on the eagle's wings. Thank you, most gracious worm. Then I will tell you what you must do; you must go with us to Jötunheim, and that will be a hard journey."

Shea remembered his conversation with Heimdall the night before. "Isn't that where some of the giants live?"

"The frost giants to be exact. That lying Sleepless One claims to have heard Thor's hammer humming somewhere in their castle; and for all of us it will be well to find that weapon. But we shall need whatever we possess of strength and magic in the task—unless, Lord Turnip Eater, you think you can recover it without our help."

Shea gulped again. Should he go with them? He had come looking for adventure, but enough was enough. "What is adventure?" he remembered reading somewhere, with the answer, "Somebody else having a hell of a tough time a thousand miles away." Only—

Thjalfi had come round the table, and said in a low voice: "Look. My sister Röskva is staying here at the Crossroads, because the Giant Killer don't think Jötunheim would be any place for a woman. That leaves me all alone with these Æsir and an awful lot of giants. I'd be mighty obliged if ye could see your way to keep me company."

"I'll do it," said Shea aloud. Then he realized that his impulsiveness had let him in for something: If Loki and Thor were not sure they could recover the hammer without help, it was likely to be an enterprise of some difficulty. Still, neither Æsir nor giants knew about matches—or the revolver. They would do for magic till something better came along.

"I've already spoken to the Lord of the Goat Chariot," Thjalfi was saying. "He'd be glad to have ye come, but he says ye mustn't disgrace him by asking to eat turnips. Ye'd best do something about those clothes. They're more than light for this climate. Sverre-bonder will lend you some others."

Sverre was glad to take the inadequate polo coat and riding breeches as security for the loan of some baggy Norse garments. Shea, newly dressed in accordance with his surroundings, went outside. A low, cheerless sun shone on the blinding white of new snow. As the biting cold nipped his nose Shea was thankful for the yards of coarse wool in which he was swathed.

The Roaring Trumpet

The goat chariot was waiting. It was as big as a Conestoga wagon, notwithstanding that there were only two wheels. A line of incised runic letters was etched in black around the gold rim; the body was boldly painted red and gold. But the goats constituted the most remarkable feature. One was black, the other white, and they were as big as horses.

"This here's Tooth Gnasher," said Thjalfi, indicating the nigh goat, "and that there's Tooth Gritter," waving at the off goat, the black one. "Say, friend Harald, I'd be mighty obliged if ye'd help me tote the stuff out."

Shea, ignorant of what the "stuff" was, followed Thjalfi into the bonder's house, where the latter pointed to a big oak chest. This, he explained, held the Æsir's belongings. Thjalfi hoisted one end by its bronze handle. Shea took hold of the other, expecting it to come up easily. The chest did not move. He looked at Thjalfi, but the latter merely stood, holding his end off the floor without apparent effort. So Shea took his handle in both hands and gave a mighty heave. He got his end up, but the thing seemed packed with ingots of lead. The pair went through the door, Thjalfi leading, Shea staggering and straining along in the rear. He almost yelled to Thjalfi to hurry and ease the horrible strain on his arms, but this would involve so much loss of face that he stuck it out. When they reached the chariot Shea dropped his end into the snow and almost collapsed across the chest. The icy air hurt his lungs as he drew great gasps of breath.

"All right," said Thjalfi calmly, "you catch hold here, and we'll shove her aboard." Shea forced his unwilling body to obey. They manhandled one end of the chest onto the tail of the chariot and somehow got the whole thing aboard. Shea was uncomfortably aware that Thjalfi had done three-quarters of the work, but the rustic seemed not to notice.

With the load in, Shea leaned against one of the shafts, waiting for his heart to slow down and for the aches in his arms and chest to subside. "Now it is to be seen," said a voice, "that Thjalfi has persuaded another mortal to share his labors. Convenient is this for Thjalfi."

It was the foxy-faced Loki, with the usual note of mockery in his voice. Once more Shea's temper began to rise. Thjalfi was all right but it *did* look as though he had talked Shea into coming along for the dirty work. If—Whoa! Shea suddenly remembered Loki's title—"Bringer of Discord," and Thjalfi's warning about his jokes. Uncle Fox would doubtless think it very funny to get the two mortals into a quarrel, and for the sake of his own credit he didn't dare let the god succeed.

Just then came a tug at his cloak. He whirled round; Tooth Gritter had seized the lower edge of the garment in his teeth and was trying to drag it off him. "Hey!" cried Shea, and dragged back. The giant goat shook its head and held on while Loki stood with hands on hips, laughing a deep, rich bellylaugh. He made not the slightest move to help Shea. Thjalfi came running round and added his strength to Shea's. The cloak came loose with a rip; the two mortals tumbled backward. Tooth Gritter calmly munched the fragment he had torn from the cloak and swallowed it.

Shea got up scowling and faced a Loki purple with amusement. "Say, you," he began belligerently, "what the hell's so damn funny—" At that instant Thjalfi seized him from behind and whirled him away as though he were a child. "Shut up, ye nitwit!" he flung into Shea's ear. "Don't ye know he could burn ye to a cinder just by looking at ye?"

"But—"

"But nothing! *Them's* gods! No matter what they do ye dassn't say boo, or they'll do something worse. That's how things be!"

"Okay," grumbled Shea, reflecting that rustics the world over were a little too ready to accept "that's how things be," and that when the opportunity came he would get back some of his own from Loki.

"Ye want to be careful around them goats," continued Thjalfi. "They're mean, and they eat most anything. I remember a funny thing as happened a fortnight back. We found five men that had frozen to death on the moor. I says we ought to take them in so their folks could give 'em burial. Thor says all right, take 'em in. When we got to the house we was going to stay at, the bonder didn't see as how there was any point in bringing 'em inside, 'cause when they got thawed out, they'd get kind of strong. So we stacked 'em in the yard, like firewood. Next morning, would ye believe it, those goats had gotten at 'em and et 'em up. Everything but their buckles!" Thjalfi chuckled to himself.

As Shea was digesting this example of Norse humor, there came a shout of "Come on, mortals!" from Thor, who had climbed into the chariot. He clucked to the goats, who leaned forward. The chariot wheels screeched and turned.

"Hurry!" cried Thjalfi and ran for the chariot. He had reached it and jumped aboard with a single huge bound before Shea even started. The latter ran behind the now rapidly moving vehicle and tried to hoist himself up. His fingers, again numbed with cold, slipped, and he went sprawling on his face in the snow. He heard Loki's infuriating laugh. As he pulled himself to his feet he remembered bitterly that he had made this "journey" to escape the feeling of insignificance and maladjustment that his former life had given him.

There was nothing to do but run after the chariot again. Thjalfi pulled him over the tail and slapped the snow from his clothes. "Next time," he advised, "ye better get a good grip before ye try to jump. Ye know what it says in Havámal:

> It is better to live   Than to lie a corpse;
> The quick man catches the cart.

Thor, at the front of the chariot, said something to the goats. They broke from a trot to a gallop. Shea, clutching the side of the vehicle, became aware that it had no springs. He found he could take the jolting best by flexing his legs and yielding to the jerks.

Loki leaned toward him, grinning. "Hai, Turnip Harald! Let us be merry!" Shea smiled uncertainly. Manner and voice were friendly, but might conceal some new malicious trick. Uncle Fox continued airily: "Be merry while you can. These hill giants are uncertain of humor where we go. He, he, I remember a warlock named Birger. He put a spell on one of the hill giants so he married a goat instead of a girl. The giant cut Birger open, tied one end of his entrails to a tree, and chased him around it. He, he!"

The anecdote was not appetizing and the chariot was bounding on at the same furious pace, throwing its passengers into the air every time it hit a bump. Up—down—bang—up—down—bang. Shea began to regret his breakfast.

Thjalfi said: "Ye look poorly, friend Harald; sort of goose-green. Shall I get something to eat?"

Shea had been fighting his stomach in desperate dread of losing further prestige. But the word "eat" ended the battle. He leaned far over the side of the chariot.

Loki laughed. Thor turned at the sound, and drowned Loki's laughter in a roar of his own. "Haw, haw, haw! If you foul up my chariot, Turnip Harald, I'll make you clean it." There was a kind of good-natured contempt in the tone, more galling than Uncle Fox's amusement.

Shea's stomach finally ceased its convulsions and he sat down on the chest, wishing he were dead. Perhaps it was the discomfort of the seat, but he soon stood up again, forcing himself to grin. "I'll be all right now. I'm just not used to such a pace."

Thor turned his head again and rumbled. "You think this fast, springling? You have in no wise any experience of speed. Watch." He whistled to the goats, who stretched their heads forward and really opened out. The chariot seemed to spend most of the time in the air; at intervals, it would hit a ridge in the road with a thunderous bang and then take off again. Shea clung for dear life to the side, estimating their speed at something between sixty and seventy miles an hour. This is not much in a modern automobile on a concrete road, but something quite different in a two-wheeled springless cart on a rutted track.

"Wow! Wow! Wow!" yelled Thor, carried away by his own enjoyment. "Hang on; here's a curve!" Instead of slackening speed the goats fairly leaped, banking inward on the turn. The chariot lurched in the opposite direction. Shea clung with eyes closed and one arm over the side. "Yoooeee!" bellowed Thor.

It went on for ten minutes more before Thjalfi suggested lunch. Shea found himself actually hungry again. But his appetite quailed at the sight of some slabs that looked like scorched leather.

"*Ulp*—what's that?"

"Smoked salmon," said Thjalfi. "Ye put one end in your mouth, like this. Then ye bite. Then ye swallow. Ye have sense enough to swallow, I suppose?"

Shea tried it. He was amazed that any fish could be so tough. But as he gnawed he became aware of a delicious flavor. *When I get back*, he thought, *I must look up some of this stuff. Rather,* if *I get back.*

The temperature rose during the afternoon, and toward evening the wheels were throwing out fans of slush. Thor roared "Whoa!" and the goats stopped. They were in a hollow between low hills, gray save where the snow had melted to show dark patches of grass. In the hollow itself a few discouraged-looking spruces showed black in the twilight.

"Here we camp," said Thor. "Goat steak would be our feasting had we but fire."

"What does he mean?" Shea whispered to Thjalfi.

"It's one of the Thunderer's magic tricks. He slaughters Tooth Gnasher or Tooth Gritter and we can eat all but the hide and bones. He magics them back to life."

Loki was saying to Thor: "Uncertain is it, Enemy of the Worm, whether my fire spell will be effective here. In this hill-giant land there are spells against spells. Your lightning flash?"

"It can shiver and slay but not kindle in this damp," growled Thor. "You have a new warlock there. Why not make him work?"

Shea had been feeling for his matches. They were there and dry. This was his chance. "That'll be easy," he said lightly. "I can make your fire as easy as snapping my fingers. Honest."

Thor glared at him with suspicion. "Few are the weaklings equal to any works," he said heavily. "For my part I always hold that strength and courage are the first requirements of a man. But I will not gainsay that occasionally my brothers feel otherwise, and it may be that you can do as you say."

"There is also cleverness, Wielder of Mjöllnir," said Loki. "Even your hammer blows would be worthless if you did not know where to strike; and it may be that this outlander can show us some new thing. Now I propose a contest, we two and the warlock. The first of us to make the fire light shall have a blow at either of the others."

"Hey!" said Shea. "If Thor takes a swat at me, you'll have to get a new warlock."

"That will not be difficult." Loki grinned and rubbed his hands together. Though Shea decided the sly god would find something funny about his mother's funeral, for once he was not caught. He grinned back, and thought he detected a flicker of approval in Uncle Fox's eyes.

Shea and Thjalfi tramped through the slush to the clump of spruces. As he pulled out his supposedly rust-proof knife, Shea was dismayed to observe that the blade had developed a number of dull red freckles.

He worked manfully hacking down a number of trees and branches. They were piled on a spot from which the snow had disappeared, although the ground was still sopping.

"Who's going to try first?" asked Shea.

"Don't be more foolish than ye have to," murmured Thjalfi. "Redbeard, of course."

Thor walked up to the pile of brush and extended his hands: There was a blue glow of corona discharge around them, and a piercing crack as bright electric sparks leaped from his fingertips to the wood. The brush stirred a little and a few puffs of water vapor rose from it. Thor frowned in concentration. Again the sparks crackled, but no fire resulted.

"Too damp is the wood," growled Thor. "Now you shall make the attempt, Sly One."

Loki extended his hands and muttered something too low for Shea to hear. A rosy-violet glow shone from his hands and danced among the brush. In the twilight the strange illumination lit up Loki's sandy red goatee, high cheekbones, and slanting brows with startling effect. His lips moved almost silently. The spruce steamed gently, but did not light.

Loki stepped back. The magenta glow died out. "A night's work," said he. "Let us see what our warlock can do."

Shea had been assembling a few small twigs, rubbing them to dryness on his clothes and arranging them like an Indian tepee. They were still dampish, but he supposed spruce would contain enough resin to light.

"Now," he said with a trace of swagger. "Let everybody watch. This is strong magic."

He felt around in the little container that held his matches until he found some of the nonsafety kitchen type. His three companions held their breaths as he took out a match and struck it against the box.

Nothing happened.

He tried again. Still no result. He threw the match away and essayed another, again without success. He tried another, and another, and another. He tried two at once. He put away the kitchen matches and got out a box of safety matches. The result was no better. There was no visible reason. The matches simply would not light.

He stood up. "I'm sorry," he said, "but something has gone wrong. If you'll just wait a minute, I'll look it up in my book of magic formulas."

There was just enough light left to read by. Shea got out his *Boy Scout Manual*. Surely it would tell him what to do—if not with failing matches, at least it would instruct him in the art of rubbing sticks.

He opened it at random and peered, blinked his eyes, shook his head, and peered again. The light was good enough. But the black marks on the page, which presumably were printed sentences, were utterly meaningless. A few letters looked vaguely familiar, but he could make nothing of the words. He leafed rapidly through the book; it was the same senseless jumble of hen tracks everywhere. Even the few diagrams meant nothing without the text.

Harold Shea stood with his mouth open and not the faintest idea of what to do next. "Well," rumbled Thor, "where is our warlock fire?"

In the background Loki tittered. "He perhaps prefers to eat his turnips uncooked."

"I...I'm sorry, sir," babbled Shea. "I'm afraid it won't work."

Thor lifted his massive fist. "It is time," he said, "to put an end to this lying and feeble child of man who raises our hopes and then condemns us to a dinner of cold salmon."

"No, Slayer of Giants," said Loki. "Hold your hand. He furnishes us something to laugh at, which is always good in this melancholy country. I may be able to use him where we are going."

Thor slowly lowered his arm. "Yours be the responsibility. I am not unfriendly to the children of men; but for liars I have no sympathy. What I say I can do, and that will I do."

Thjalfi spoke. "If ye please, sir, there's a dark something up yonder." He pointed toward the head of the valley. "Maybe we can find shelter."

Thor growled an assent; they got back into the chariot and drove up toward the dark mass. Shea was silent, with the blackest of thoughts. He would leave his position as researcher at the Garaden Institute to go after adventure with a capital A, would he? And as an escape from a position where he felt himself inferior and enclosed. Well, he told himself bitterly, he had landed in another still more enclosed and inferior. Yet why was it his preparations had so utterly failed? There was no reason for the matches' not lighting or the book's turning into gibberish—or for that matter the failure of the flashlight on the night before.

Thjalfi was whispering to him. "By the beard of Odinn, I'm ashamed of you, friend Harald. Why did ye promise a fire if you couldn't make it?"

"I thought I could, honest," said Shea morosely.

"Well, maybe so. Ye certainly rubbed the Thunderer the wrong way. Ye'd best be grateful to Uncle Fox. He saved your life for you. He ain't as bad as some people think, I always say. Usually helps you out in a real pinch."

The dark something grew into the form of an oddly shaped house. The top was rounded, the near end completely open. When they went in Shea found to his surprise that the floor was of some linoleum-like material, as were the curving walls and low-arched roof. There seemed only a single broad low room, without furniture or lights. At the far end they could dimly make out five hallways, circular in cross section, leading they knew not where. Nobody cared to explore.

Thjalfi and Shea dragged down the heavy chest and fished out blankets. For supper the four glumly chewed pieces of smoked salmon. Thor's eyebrows worked in a manner that showed he was trying to control justifiable anger.

Finally Loki said: "It is in my mind that our fireless warlock has not heard the story of your fishing, son of Jörd."

"Oh," said Thor, "that story is not unknown. But it is good that men should hear it and learn from it. Let me think—"

"Odinn preserve us!" murmured Thjalfi in Shea's ear. "I've only heard this a million times."

Thor rumbled: "I was guesting with the giant Hymir. We rowed far out in the blue sea. I baited my hook with a whole ox-head, for the fish I fish are worthy a man's strength. At the first strike I knew I had the greatest fish of all: to wit, the Midgard Serpent, for his strength was so great. Three whales could not have pulled so hard. For nine hours I played the serpent, thrashing to and fro, before I pulled him in. When his head came over the gunwale, he sprayed venom in futile wrath; it ate holes in my clothes. His eyes were as great as shields, and his teeth *that* long." Thor held up his hands in the gloom to show the length of the teeth. "I pulled and the serpent pulled again. I was braced with my belt of strength; my feet nearly went through the bottom of the boat.

"I had all but landed the monster, when—I speak no untruth—that fool Hymir got scared and cut the line! The biggest thing any fisherman ever caught, and it escaped!" He finished on a mournful note: "I gave Hymir a thumping he will not soon forget. But it did not give me the trophy I wanted to hang on the walls of Thrudvang!"

Thjalfi leaned toward Shea, singing in his ear:

> A man shall not boast   Of the fish that fled
>   Or the bear he failed to flay;
> Bigger they be   Than those borne back
>   To hang their heads in the hall.

At least that's what Atli's Drapar says."

Loki chuckled; he had caught the words. "True, youngling. Had any but our friend and great protector told such a tale, I would doubt it."

"Doubt me?" rumbled Thor. "How would you like one of my buffets?" He drew back his arm. Loki ducked. Thor uttered a huge good-natured laugh. "Two things gods and mortals alike doubt—tales of fishing and the virtue of women."

He lay back among the blankets, took two deep breaths and seemed to be snoring instantly. Loki and Thjalfi also lapsed into silence.

Shea, unable to sleep, let his mind go over the day's doings. He had shown up pretty badly. It annoyed him, for he was beginning to like these people, even the unapproachable and tempestuous Thor. The big fellow was all right: someone you could depend on right up to the hilt, especially in any crisis that required straightforward courage. He would see right and wrong divided by a line of absolute sharpness, chalk on one side, coal dust on the other. He became annoyed when others proved to lack his own simple strength.

About Loki, Shea was not quite so sure. Uncle Fox had saved his life, all right, but Shea suspected that there had been a touch of self-interest about the act. Loki expected to make some use of him, and not entirely as a butt of jokes, either. That keen mind had doubtless noted the unfamiliar gear Shea had brought from the twentieth century and was speculating on its use.

But why had those gadgets failed to work? Why had he been unable to read simple English print?

Was it English? Shea tried to visualize his name in written form. It was easy enough, and showed him that the transference had not made him illiterate. But wait a minute, what was he visualizing? He concentrated on the row of letters in his mind's eye. What he saw was:

ᚼᛏᚱᚠᛁᛏ   ᛒᚱᛀᛏᛏ   ᛋᚼᛏᛏ

These letters spelled Harold Bryan Shea to him. At the same time he realized they weren't the letters of the Latin alphabet. He tried some more visualizations. "Man" came out as:

ᛉᛏᚦᛀ

Something was wrong. "Man," he vaguely remembered, ought not to have four letters.

Then, gradually, he realized what had happened. Chalmers had been right and more than right. His mind had been filled with the fundamental assumptions of this new world. When he transferred from his safe, Midwestern institute to this howling wilderness, he had automatically changed languages. If it were otherwise, if the shift were partial, he would be a dement—insane. But the shift was complete. He was speaking and understanding old Norse, touching old Norse gods and eating old Norse food. No wonder he had had no difficulty making himself understood!

But as an inevitable corollary, his knowledge of English had vanished. When he thought of the written form of "man" he could form no concept but that of the four runic characters.

ᚢᛏᚦᚼ

He couldn't even imagine what the word would look like with the runes put into other characters. And he had failed to read his *Boy Scout Handbook*.

Naturally his gadgets had failed to work. He was in a world not governed by the laws of twentieth century physics or chemistry. It had a mental pattern which left no room for matches or flashlights, or non-rusting steel. These things were simply inconceivable to anyone around him. Therefore they did not exist save as curiously shaped objects of no value.

Well, anyway, he thought to himself drowsily, *at least I won't have to worry about the figure I cut in front of these guys again. I've fallen so low that nothing I could do would make me a bigger fool. Oh, what the hell—*

5

Shea awoke before dawn, shivering. The temperature was still above freezing, but a wind had come up, and the gray landscape was curtained with driving rain. He yawned and sat up with his blanket round him like an Indian. The others were still asleep and he stared out for a moment, trying to recover the thread of last night's thoughts.

This world he was in—perhaps permanently—was governed by laws of its own. What were those laws? There was one piece of equipment of which the transference had not robbed him; his modern mind, habituated to studying and analyzing the general rules guiding individual events. He ought to be able to reason out the rules governing. this existence and to use them—something which the rustic Thjalfi would never think of doing. So far the only rules he had noticed were that the gods had unusual powers. But there must be general laws underlying even these

Thor's snores died away into a gasping rattle. The red-bearded god rubbed his eyes, sat up, and spat.

"Up, all Æsir's men!" he said. "Ah, Harald of the Turnips, you are already awake. Cold salmon will be our breakfast again since your fire magic failed." Then, as he saw Shea stiffen: "Nay, take it not unkindly. We Æsir are not unkind to mortals, and I've seen more unpromising objects than you turn out all right. Make a man of you yet, youngling. Just watch me and imitate what I do." He yawned and the yawn spread into a bristling grin.

The others bestirred themselves. Thjalfi got out some smoked salmon. However good the stuff was, Shea found the third successive meal of it a little too much.

They were just beginning to gnaw when there was a heavy tramp outside. Through the rain loomed a gray shape whose outline made Shea's scalp tingle. It was mannish, but at least ten feet tall, with massive columnar legs. It was a giant. The giant stooped and looked into the travelers' refuge. Shea, his heart beating madly, backed up against the curving wall, his hand feeling for his hunting knife. The face that looked in was huge, with bloodshot gray eyes and a scraggly iron-gray beard, and its expression was not encouraging.

"Ungh," snarled the giant, showing yellow snags of teeth. His voice was a couple of octaves beneath the lowest human bass. " 'Scuse me, gents, but I been looking for my glove. How 'bout having a little breakfast together, huh?"

Shea, Thjalfi and Loki all looked at Thor. The Red God stood with feet wide apart, surveying the giant for some minutes. Then he said, "Good is guesting on a journey. We offer some smoked salmon. But what have you?"

"The name's Skrymir, buddy. I got some bread and dried dragon meat. Say, ain't you Thor Odinnsson, the hammer thrower?"

"That is not incorrect."

"Boy, oh, boy, ain't that something?" The giant made a horrible face that was probably intended for a friendly grin. He reached around for a bag that hung at his back and sitting down in front of the shelter, opened it. Shea got a better view of him, though not one that inspired a more favorable impression. The monster's long gray hair was done up in a topknot with bone skewers stuck through it. He was dressed entirely in furs, of which the cloak must have come from the grandfather of all the bears, though it was none too large for him.

Skrymir took from his bag a slab of Norse bread the size of a mattress, and several hunks of leathery gray meat. These he slapped down in front of the travelers. "All right, youse guys help yourselves," he rumbled. "Let's see some of that salmon, huh?"

Thjalfi mutely handed over a piece of the salmon on which the giant set noisily to work. He drooled, now and then wiping his face with the back of his huge paw, and getting himself well smeared with salmon grease.

Shea found he had to break up his portion of the bread with his knife-handle before he could manage it, so hard was the material. The dragon meat was a little easier, but still required some hard chewing, and his jaw muscles were sore from the beating they had taken in the last twenty-four hours. The dragon meat had a pungent, garlicky flavor that he didn't care for.

As Shea gnawed he saw a louse the size of a cockroach crawl out from the upper edge of one of Skrymir's black fur leggings, amble around a bit in the jungle of hair below the giant's knee, and stroll back into its sanctuary. Shea almost gagged. His appetite tapered off, though presently it returned. After what he had been through lately, it would take more than a single louse to spoil his interest in food for any length of time. What the hell?

Loki, grinning slyly, asked: "Are there turnips in your bag, Hairy One?"

Skrymir frowned. "Turnips? Naw. Whatcha want with 'em?"

"Our warlock"—Loki jerked his thumb at Shea—"eats them."

"What-a-at? No kiddin'!" roared the giant. "I heard of guys that eat bugs and drink cow's milk, but I ain't never heard of nobody what eats turnips."

Shea said: "That's how I get some of my magic powers," with a somewhat sickly smile, and felt he had come out of it fairly well.

Skrymir belched. It was not an ordinary run-of-the-mine belch, but something akin to a natural cataclysm. Shea tried to hold his breath until the air cleared. The giant settled himself and inquired: "Say, how come youse is traveling in Jötunheim?"

"The Wing Thor travels where he will," observed Loki loftily, but with a side glance.

"Aw right, aw right, butcha don't have to get snotty about it. I just was thinking there's some relations of Hrungnir and Geirröd that was laying for Thor. They'd just love to have a chance to get even witcha for bumping off those giants."

Thor rumbled: "Few will be more pleased than I to meet—"

But Loki interrupted: "Thank you for the warning, friend Skrymir. Good is the guesting when men are friendly. We will do as much for you one of these days. Will you have more salmon?"

"Naw, I had all I want."

Loki continued silkily, "Would it be impertinence to ask whither your giantship is bound?"

"Aw, I'm going up to Utgard. Utgardaloki's throwing a big feed for all the giants."

"Great and glorious will be that feasting."

"You're damn right it'll be great. All the hill giants and frost giants and fire giants together at once—say, that's something!"

"It would give us pleasure to see it. If we went as guests of so formidable a giant as yourself, none of Hrungnir's or Geirröd's friends would dare make trouble, would they?"

Skrymir showed his snags in a pleased grin. "Them punks? Haw, they wouldn't do nothing." He picked his teeth thoughtfully with thumb and forefinger. "Yeah, I guess you can come. The big boss, Utgardaloki, is a good guy and a friend of mine. So you won't have no trouble. If youse'll clear outta my glove, we can start right now."

"What?" All four spoke at once.

"Yeah. My glove, that's what you slept in."

The implications of this statement were so alarming that the four travelers picked up their belongings and scrambled out of the shelter with ludicrous haste—the mighty Thor included.

The rain had ceased. Ragged serpents of mist, pearly against the darker gray of the clouds, crawled over the hills. Outside, the travelers looked back at their shelter. There was no question that it was an enormous glove.

Skrymir grasped the upper edge of the opening with his left hand and thrust the right into the erstwhile dwelling. From where he stood, Shea couldn't see whether the big glove had shrunk to fit or whether it had faded out of sight and been replaced by a smaller one. At the same time he became suddenly conscious of the fact that he was wet to the skin.

Before he had a chance to think over the meaning of these facts, Thor was bellowing at him to help get the chariot loaded.

When he was sitting hunched up on the chest and swaying to the movement of the cart, Thjalfi murmured to him: "I knew Loki would get around the Hairy One. When it's something that calls for smartness, ye can depend on Uncle Fox, I always say."

Shea nodded silently and sneezed. He'd be lucky if he didn't come down with a first-class cold, riding in these wet garments. The landscape was wilder and bleaker around them than even on the previous day's journey. Ahead Skrymir tramped along, the bag on his back swaying with his strides, his sour sweat smell wafting back over the chariot.

Wet garments. Why? The rain had stopped when they emerged from that monstrous glove. There was something peculiar about the whole business of that glove. The others, including the two gods, had unhesitatingly accepted its huge size as an indication that Skrymir was even larger and more powerful than he seemed. He was undoubtedly a giant—but hardly that much of a giant. Shea supposed that although the world he was in did not respond to the natural laws of that from which he had come, there was no reason to conceive that the laws of illusion had changed. He had studied psychology enough to know something of the standard methods used by stage magicians. But others, unfamiliar both with such methods and the technique of modern thought, would not think of criticizing observation with pure logic. For that matter, they would not think of questioning the evidence of observation—

"You know," he whispered suddenly to Thjalfi, "I just wonder whether Loki is as clever as he thinks, and whether Skrymir isn't smarter than he pretends."

The servant of gods gave him a startled glance. "A mighty strange word is that. Why?"

"Well, didn't you say the giants would be fighting against the gods when this big smash comes?"

"Truly I did:

> *High blows Heimdall.   The horn is aloft;*
> *   The ash shall shake   And the rime-giants ride*
> *   On the roads of Hell—*

leastways that's what Voluspö says, the words of the prophetess."

"Then isn't Skrymir a shade too friendly with someone he's going to fight?"

Thjalfi gave a barking laugh. "Ye don't know much about Oku-Thor to say that. This Skrymir may be big, but Redbeard has his strength belt on. He could twist that there giant right up, snip-snap."

Shea sighed. But he tried once more. "Well, look here, did you notice that when Skrymir put his gloves on, your clothes got wet all of a sudden?"

"Why, yes now that I think of it."

"My idea is that there wasn't any giant glove there at all. It was an illusion, a magic, to scare us. We really slept in the open without knowing it, and got soaked. But whoever magicked us did a good job, so we didn't feel the wet till the spell was off and the big glove disappeared."

"Maybe so. But how does it signify?"

"It signified that Skrymir didn't blunder into us by accident. It was a put-up job."

The rustic scratched his head in puzzlement. "Seems to me ye're being a little mite fancy, friend Harald." He looked around. "I wish we had Heimdall along. He can see a hundred leagues in the dark and hear the wool growing on a sheep's back. But 'twouldn't do to have him and Uncle Fox together. Thor's the only one of the Æsir that can stand Uncle Fox."

Shea shivered. "Say, friend Harald," offered Thjalfi, "how would ye like to run a few steps to warm up?"

Shea soon learned that Thjalfi's idea of warming up did not consist merely of dogtrotting behind the chariot. "We'll race to yonder boulder and back to the chariot," he said. "Be ye ready? Get set; go!" Before Shea fairly got into his stride, his woolens flapping around him, Thjalfi was halfway to the boulder, gravel flying under his shoes, and clothes fluttering stiffly behind him like a flag in a gale. Shea had not covered half the distance when Thjalfi passed him, grinning, on the way back. He had always considered himself a good runner, but against this human antelope it was no contest. Wasn't there *anything* in which he could hold his own against these people?

Thjalfi helped pull him over the tail of the chariot. "Ye do a little better than most runners, friend Harald," he said with the cheerfulness of superiority. "But I thought I'd give ye a little surprise, seeing as how maybe ye hadn't heard about my running. But" —he lowered his voice—"don't let Uncle Fox get ye into any contests. He'll make a wager and collect it out of your hide. Ye got to watch him that way."

"What's Loki's game, anyway?" asked Shea. "I heard Heimdall suggesting he might be on the other side at the big fight."

Thjalfi shrugged. "That there Child of Fury gets a little mite hasty about Loki. Guess he'll turn up on the right side all right, but he's a queer one. Always up to something, sometimes good, sometimes bad, and he won't let anyone boss him. There's a lay about him, the Lokasenna, ye know:

> *I say to the gods   And the sons of gods*
> *The things that whet my thoughts;*
> *By the wells of the world   There is none with the might*
> *To make me do his will.*

That agreed fairly well with the opinion Shea had formed of the enigmatic Uncle Fox. He would have liked to discuss the matter with Thjalfi. But he found that while he could form such concepts as delayed adolescence, superego, and sadism readily enough, he could think of no words to express them. If he wanted to be a practicing psychologist in this world, he would have to invent a whole terminology for the science.

He sneezed some more. He was catching cold. His nose clogged, and his eyes ran. The temperature was going down, and an icy breeze had risen that did nothing to add to his happiness.

They lunched without stopping, as they had on the previous day. As the puddles of the thaw began to develop crystals and the chariot wheels began to crunch, Shea blew on his mittens and slapped himself. Thjalfi looked sympathetic. "Be ye really cold, friend Harald?" he said. "This is barely freezing. A few years back we had a winter so cold that when we made a fire in the open, flames froze solid. I broke off some pieces, and for the rest of the winter, whenever we wanted a fire, I used one of them pieces to light it with. Would 'a' come in mighty handy this morning. My uncle Einarr traded off some as amber."

It was told with so straight a countenance, that Shea was not quite certain he was being kidded. In this world it *might* happen.

The terrible afternoon finally waned. Skrymir was walking with head up now, looking around him. The giant waved toward a black spot on the side of a hill. "Hey, youse, there's a cave," he said. "Whatcha say we camp in there, huh?"

Thor looked around. "It is not too dark for more of progress."

Loki spoke up. "Not untrue, Powerful One. Yet I fear our warlock must soon freeze to an ice bone. We should have to pack him in boughs lest pieces chip off, ha-ha!"

"Oh, dote bide be," said Shea, "I cad stad it." Perhaps he could; at least if they went on he wouldn't have to manhandle that chest halfway up the hill.

He was overruled, but, after all, did not have to carry the chest. When the chariot had been parked at the edge of a snowdrift, Skrymir took that bulky object under one arm and led the way up the stony slope to the cave mouth.

"Could you get us fire?" Thor asked Skrymir.

"Sure thing, buddy." Skrymir strode down to a clump of small trees, pulled up a couple by the roots, and breaking them across his knee laid them for burning.

Shea put his head into the cave. At first he was conscious of nothing but the rocky gloom. Then he sniffed. He hadn't been able to smell anything—not even Skrymir—for some hours, but now an odor pricked through the veil of his cold. A familiar odor—chlorine gas! What—

"Hey, you," roared Skrymir behind him. Shea jumped a foot. "Get the hell outta my way."

Shea got. Skrymir put his head down and whistled. At least he did what would have been called a whistle in a human being. From his lips it sounded more like an air-raid warning.

A little man about three feet tall, with a beard that made him look like a miniature Santa Claus, appeared at the mouth of the cave. He had a pointed hood, and the tail of his beard was tucked into his belt.

"Hey, you," said Skrymir. "Let's have some fire. Make it snappy." He pointed to the pile of logs and brush in front of the cave mouth.

"Yes, sir," said the dwarf. He toddled over to the pile and produced a coppery-looking bar out of his jacket. Shea watched the process with interest, but just then Loki tucked an icicle down his back, and when Shea had extracted it the fire was already burning with a hiss of damp wood.

The dwarf spoke up in a little chirping voice. "You are not planning to camp here, are you?"

"Yeah," replied Skrymir. "Now beat it."

"Oh, but you must not—"

"*Shut up!*" bellowed the giant. "We camp where we damn please."

"Yessir. Thank you, sir. Anything else, sir?"

"Naw. Go on, beat it, before I step on you."

The dwarf vanished into the cave. They got their belongings out and disposed themselves around the fire, which took a long time to grow. The setting sun broke through the clouds for a minute and smeared them with streaks of lurid vermilion. To Shea's imagination, the clouds took on the form of apocalyptic monsters. Far in the distance he heard the cry of a wolf.

Thjalfi looked up suddenly, frowning. "What's that noise?"

"What noise?" said Thor. Then he jumped up—he had been sitting with his back to the cave mouth—and spun around. "Hai, Clever One, our cave is already not untenanted!" He backed away slowly. From the depths of the cave there came a hiss like that of a steam-pipe leak, followed by a harsh, metallic cry.

"A dragon!" cried Thjalfi. A puff of yellow gas from the cave set them all coughing. A scrape of scales, a rattle of loose stones, and in the dark a pair of yellow eyes the size of dinner plates caught the reflection of the fire.

Æsir, giant, and Thjalfi shouted incoherently, grabbing for whatever might serve as a weapon.

"Here, I cad take care of hib!" cried Shea, forgetting his previous reasoning. He pulled out the revolver. As the great snakelike head came into view in the firelight, he aimed at one of the eyes and pulled the trigger.

The hammer clicked harmlessly. He tried again and again, click, click. The jaws came open with a reek of chlorine.

Harold Shea stumbled back. There was a flash of movement past his head. The butt end of a young tree, wielded by Skrymir, swished down on the beast's head.

The eyes rolled. The head half turned toward the giant. Thor leaped in with a roaring yell, and let fly a right hook that would have demolished Joe Louis. There was a crunch of snapping bones; the fist sank right into the reptile's face. With a scream like that of a disemboweled horse the head vanished into the cave.

Thjalfi helped Shea up. "Now maybe ye can see," remarked the servant of gods, "why Skrymir would as lief not take chances with the Lord of the Goats." He chuckled. "That there dragon's going to have him a toothache next spring—if there is any spring before the *Time*."

The dwarf popped out again. "Hai, Skrymir!"

"Huh?"

"I tried to warn you that a fire would bring the dragon out of hibernation. But you wouldn't listen. Think you're smart, don't you? Yah! Yah! Yah!" The vest-pocket Santa Claus capered in the cave mouth for an instant, thumbing his nose with both hands. He vanished as Skrymir picked up a stone to throw.

The giant lumbered over to the cave and felt around inside. "Never catch the little totrug now. They have burrows all through these hills," he observed gloomily.

The evening meal was eaten in a silence made more pointed for Shea by the fact that he felt it was mostly directed at himself. He ought to have known better, he told himself bitterly.

In fact, he ought to have known better than to embark on such an expedition at all. Adventure! Romance! Bosh! As for the dream-girl whose fancied image he had once in a rash moment described to Walter Bayard, those he had seen in this miserable dump were like lady wrestlers. If he could have used the formulas to return instantly, he would.

But he could not. That was the point. The formulas didn't exist any more, as far as he was concerned. Nothing existed but the bleak, snowbound hillside, the nauseating giant, the two Æsir and their servant regarding him with aversion. There was nothing he could do—

Whoa, Shea, steady, he remarked to himself. *You're talking yourself into a state of melancholy, which is, as Chalmers once remarked, of no philosophical or practical value.* Too bad old Doc wasn't along, to furnish a mature intellect and civilized company. The intelligent thing to do, was not to bemoan the past but to live in the present. He lacked the physical equipment to imitate Thor's forthright approach to problems. But he could at least come somewhere near Loki's sardonic and intelligent humor.

And speaking of intelligence, had he not already decided to make use of it in discovering the laws of this world? Laws which these people were not fitted, by their mental habit, to deduce?

He turned suddenly and asked: "Didn't that dwarf say the fire fetched the dragon out of hibernation?"

Skrymir yawned, and spoke. "Yeah. What about it, snotty?"

"The fire's still here. What if he, or another one comes back during the night?"

"Prob'ly eat you, and serve you right." He cackled a laugh.

"The niggeling speaks sooth," said Loki. "It were best to move our camp."

The accent of contempt in the voice made Shea wince. But he went on: "We don't have to do that, do we, sir? It's freezing now and getting colder. If we take some of that snow and stuff it into the cave, it seems to me the dragon would hardly come out across it."

Loki slapped a knee. "Soundly and well said, turnip-man! Now you and Thjalfi shall do it. I perceive you are not altogether without your uses, since there has been a certain gain in wit since you joined our party. Who would have thought of stopping a dragon with snow?"

Thor grunted.

6

When Shea awoke he was still sniffling, but at least his head was of normal weight. He wondered whether the chlorine he had inhaled the previous evening might not have helped the cold. Or whether the improvement were a general one, based on his determination to accept his surroundings and make the most of them.

After breakfast they set out as before, Skrymir tramping on ahead. The sky was the color of old lead. The wind was keen, rattling the branches of the scrubby trees and whirling an occasional snowflake before it. The goats slipped on patches of frozen slush, plodding uphill most of the time. The hills were all about them now, rising steadily and with more vegetation, mostly pine and spruce.

It must have been around noon—Shea could only guess at the time—when Skrymir turned and waved at the biggest mountain they had yet seen. The wind carried away the giant's words, but Thor seemed to have understood. The goats quickened their pace toward the mountain, whose top hung in cloud.

After a good hour of climbing, Shea began to get glimpses of a shape looming from the bare crest, intermittently blotted out by the eddies of mist. When they were close enough to see it plainly, it became clearly a house, not unlike that of the bonder Sverre. But it was cruder, made of logs with the bark on, and vastly bigger—as big as a metropolitan railroad terminal.

Thjalfi said into his ear: "That will be Utgard Castle. Ye'll need whatever mite of courage ye have here, friend Harald." The young man's teeth were chattering from something other than cold.

Skrymir lurched up to the door and pounded on it with his fist. He stood there for a long minute, the wind flapping his furs. A rectangular hole opened in the door. The door swung open. The chariot riders climbed down, stretching their stiff muscles as they followed their guide.

The door banged shut behind them. They were in a dark vestibule, like that in Sverre's house but larger and foul with the odor of unwashed giant. A huge arm pushed the leather curtain aside, revealing through the triangular opening a view of roaring yellow flame and thronging, shouting giants.

Thjalfi murmured: "Keep your eyes open, Harald. As Thjodolf of Hvin says:

> *All the gateways   Ere one goes out*
> *Thoughtfully should a man scan;*
> *Uncertain it is   Where sits the unfriendly*
> *Upon the bench before thee.*

Within, the place was a disorderly parody of Sverre's. Of the same general form, with the same benches, its tables were all uneven, filthy, and littered with fragments of food. Above the fire in the center hung a pall of smoke under the rafters. The dirty straw on the floor was thick about the ankles.

The benches and the passageway behind them were filled with giants, drinking, eating, shouting at the tops of their voices. Before him a group of six, with iron-gray topknots and patchy beards like Skrymir's, were wrangling. One drew back his arm in anger. His elbow struck a mug of mead borne by a harassed-looking man who was evidently a thrall. The mead splashed onto another giant, who instantly snatched up a bowl of stew from the table and slammed it on the man's head.

Down went the man with a squeal. Skrymir calmly kicked him from the path of his guests. The six giants burst into bubbling laughter, rolling in their seats and clapping each other on the back, their argument forgotten.

"Hai, Skridbaldnir!" Skrymir was gripping another giant on the bench by the arm. "How's every little thing wit' you? Commere, I wantcha to meet a friend of mine. This here guy's Asa-Thor!"

Skridbaldnir turned. Shea noticed that he was slenderer than Skrymir, with ash-blond hair, the pink eyes of an albino, and a long, red ulcerated nose.

"He's a frost giant," whispered Thjalfi, "and that gang over there are fire giants." He waved a trembling hand toward the other side of the table, where a group of individuals like taller and straighter gorillas were howling at each other. They were shorter than the other giants, not much more than eight feet tall. They had prognathous jaws and coarse black hair where their bodies were exposed. They scratched ceaselessly.

Halfway down the hall, at one side, sat the biggest hill giant of all, in a huge chair with interwoven serpents carved on the legs and arms. His costume was distinguished from those of the other giants in that the bone skewers through his topknot had rough gold knobs on their ends. One of his lower snag teeth projected for several inches beyond his upper lip. He looked at Skrymir and said: "Hai, bud. I see you got some kids witcha. It ain't a good idea to bring kids to these feeds; they learns bad language."

"They ain't kids," said Skrymir. "They're a couple of men and a couple of Æsir. I told 'em they could come wit' me. That okay, boss?"

Utgardaloki picked his nose and wiped his fingers on his greasy leather jacket before replying: "I guess so. But ain't that one with the red whiskers Asa-Thor?"

"You are not mistaken," said Thor.

"Well, well, you don't say so. I always thought Thor was a big husky guy." Thor stuck out his chest, scowling. "It is ill to jest with the Æsir, giant."

"Ho, ho, ain't he the cutest little fella?" Utgardaloki paused to capture a small creeping thing that had crawled out of his left eyebrow and crack it between his teeth.

"A fair arrangement," murmured Loki in Shea's ear. "They live on him; he lives on them."

Utgardaloki continued ominously: "But whatcha doing here, you? This is a respectable party, see, and I don't want no trouble."

Thor said: "I have come for my hammer, Mjöllnir."

"Huh? What makes ya think we got it?"

"Ask not of the tree where it got its growth or of the gods their wisdom. Will you give it up, or do I have to fight you for it?"

"Aw, don't be like that, Öku-Thor. Sure, I'd give you your piddling nutcracker if I knew where it was."

"Nutcracker! Why you—"

"Easy!" Shea could hear Loki's whisper. "Son of Odinn, with the strong use strength; with the liar, lies." He turned to Utgardaloki and bowed mockingly: "Chief of giants, we thank you for your courtesy and will not trouble you long. Trusting your word, lord, are we to understand that Mjöllnir is not here?"

" 'Tain't here as far as I know," replied Utgardaloki, spitting on the floor and rubbing his bare foot over the spot, with just a hint of uneasiness.

"Might it not have been brought hither without your knowledge?"

Utgardaloki shrugged. "How in hell should I know? I said as far as I knew. This is a hell of a way to come at your host."

"Evidently there is no objection should the desire come upon us to search the place."

"Huh? You're damn right there's objections! This is my joint and I don't let no foreigners go sniffing around."

Loki smiled ingratiatingly. "Greatest of the Jötun, your objection is but natural with one who knows his own value. But the gods do not idly speak; we believe Mjöllnir is here, and have come in peace to ask it, rather than in arms with Odinn and his spear at our head, Heimdall and his great sword and Ullr's deadly bow. Now you shall let us search for the hammer, or we will go away and return with them to make you such a feasting as you will not soon forget. But if we fail to find it we will depart in all peace. This is my word."

"And mine!" cried Thor, his brows knitting. Beside him Shea noticed Thjalfi's face go to the color of skimmed milk and was slightly surprised to find himself unafraid. *But that may be because I don't understand the situation,* he told himself.

Utgardaloki scratched thoughtfully, his lips working. "Tell you what," he said at last. "You Æsir are sporting gents, ain't you?"

"It is not to be denied," said Loki guardedly, "that we enjoy sports."

"I'll make you a sporting proposition. You think you are great athaletes. Well, we got pretty tough babies here, too. We'll have some games, and if you beat us at even one of 'em, see, I'll let you go ahead and search. If you lose, out you get."

"What manner of games?"

"Hell, sonny, anything youse want."

Thor's face had gone thoughtful. "I am not unknown as a wrestler," he remarked.

"Awright," said Utgardaloki. "We'll find someone to rassle you down. Can you do anything else?"

Loki spoke up. "I will meet your best champion at eating and our man Thjalfi here will run a race with you. Asa-Thor also will undertake any trial of strength you care to hold."

"Swell. Me, I think these games are kid stuff, see? But it ought be fun for some of the gang to see you take your licking. HAI! Bring Elli up here; here's a punk that wants to rassle!"

With a good deal of shouting and confusion a space was cleared near the fire in the center of the hall. Thor stood with fists on hips, waiting the giant's champion. There came forward, not a giant, but a tall old woman. She was at least a hundred, a hunched bag of bones covered by thin, almost transparent skin, as wrinkled as the surface of a file.

Thor shouted: "What manner of jest is this, Utgardaloki? It is not to be said that Asa-Thor wrestles with women."

"Oh, don't worry none, kid. She *likes* it, don'tcha, Elli?"

The crone bared toothless gums. "Yep," she quavered. "And many's the good man I put down, heh, heh."

"But—" began Thor.

"Y'aint scared to work up a reputation, are you?"

"Ha! Thor afraid? Not of aught the giant kindred can do." Thor puffed out his chest.

"I gotta explain the rules." Utgardaloki put a hand on the shoulder of each contestant and muttered at them.

Shea felt his arm pinched and looked into the bright eyes of Loki. "Great and evil is the magic in this place," whispered Uncle Fox, "and I misdoubt me we are to be tricked, for never have I heard of such a wrestling. But it may be that the spells they use are spells against gods alone and not for the eyes of men. Now I have here a spell against spells, and while these contests go forward you shall take it." He handed Shea a piece of very thin parchment, covered with spidery runic writing. "Repeat it forward, then backward, then forward again, looking as you do at the object you suspect of being an illusion. It may be you will see on the wall the hammer we seek."

"Wouldn't the giants hide it away, sir?"

"Not with their boasting, and vainglorious habit. It—"

"Awright," said Utgardaloki in a huge voice, "go!"

Thor, roaring like a lion, seized Elli as though he intended to dash her brains out on the floor. But Elli might have been nailed where she was. Her rickety frame did not budge. Thor fell silent, wrenching at the crone's arms and body. He turned purple in the face from the effort: the giants around murmured appreciatively.

Shea glanced at the slip Loki had given him. The words were readable, though they seemed to consist of meaningless strings of syllables—"Nyi-Nidi-Nordri-Sudri-Austri-Vestri-Altjof-Dvalinn." He obediently repeated it according to the directions, looking at a giant's club that hung on the wall. It remained a giant's club. He turned back to the wrestling where Thor was puffing with effort, his forehead beaded with sweat.

"Witch!" Thor shouted at last, and seized her arm to twist it. Elli caught his neck with her free hand. There was a second's scuffle and Thor skidded away, falling to one knee.

"That's enough!" said Utgardaloki, stepping between them. "That counts as a fall; Elli wins. I guess it's a good job you didn't try to rassle with any of the *big* guys here, eh, Thor, old kid?" The other giants roared an approval that drowned Thor's growl.

Utgardaloki continued: "Awright, you, stand back! Get back, I say, or I'll cut the blood-eagle on a couple of you! Next event's an eating contest. Bring Logi up here. We got some eating for him to do."

A fire giant shuffled through the press. His black hair had a reddish tinge, and his movements were quick and animal-like. "Is it lunch time yet?" he rasped. "Them three elk I et for breakfast just kinda got my appetite going."

Utgardaloki explained and introduced him to his opponent. "Please to meetcha," said Logi. "I always like to see a guy what appreciates good food. Say, you oughta come down to Muspellheim sometime. We got a cook there what knows how to roast a whale right. He uses charcoal fire and bastes it with bear grease—"

"That'll do, Logi," said Utgardaloki. "You get that guy talking about the meals he's et and he'll talk till the *Time* comes."

Shea was pushed back by giants as they crowded in. An eddy of the crowd carried him still farther away from the scene of action as the giants made way for a little procession of harried-looking slaves. These bore two huge wooden platters, on each of which rested an entire roasted elk haunch. Shea stood on tiptoe and stretched. Between a pair of massive shoulders he glimpsed Utgardaloki taking his place at the middle of a long table, at each end of which sat one of the contestants.

A shoulder moved across Shea's field of vision, and he glanced up at the owner. It was a comparatively short giant, who bulged out in the middle to make up for his lack of stature. A disorderly mop of black-and-white hair covered his head. But the thing that struck Shea was that, as the giant turned profile to watch the eaters, the eye that looked from under the piebald thatch was bright *blue*.

That was wrong. Fire giants, as he had noted, had black eyes, hill giants gray or black eyes, frost giants pink. Of course, this giant might have a trace of some other blood—but there was a familiar angle to that long, high-bridged nose and something phony-looking about the mop of hair. Heimdall!

Shea whispered behind his hand: "How many mothers did you have, giant with the uncombed thatch?"

He heard a low chuckle and the answer came back: "Thrice three, man from an unknown world! But there is no need to shout; I can hear your lightest whisper, even your thoughts half formed."

"I think we're being tricked," continued Shea. He didn't say it even in a whisper this time, merely thought it, moving his lips.

The answer was pat: "That is what was to be expected, and for no other reason did I come hither. Yet I have not solved the nature of the spells."

Shea said: "I have been taught a spell"—and remembered Heimdall's enmity to Loki and all his works, just in time to keep from mentioning Uncle Fox—"which may be of use in such a case."

"Then use it," Heimdall answered, "while you watch the contest."

"Awright, ready, you two?" Utgardaloki shouted. "Go!"

The giants gave a shout. Shea, his eyes fixed on Loki, was repeating: "Nyi-Nidri-Nordri-Sudri." The sly god bounced in his oversize chair as he applied his teeth to the elk haunch. The meat was disappearing in hunks the size of a man's fist at the rate of two hunks per second. Shea had never seen anything like it, and wondered where Loki was putting it all. He heard Thjalfi's voice, thin in the basso-profundo clamor of the giants: "Besit yourself, Son of Laufey!!"

Then the bone, the size of a baseball bat, was clean. Loki dropped it clattering to the platter and sat back with a sigh. A whoop went up from the assembled giants. Shea saw Loki start forward again, the eyes popping from his head. Utgardaloki walked to the opposite end of the table. He bellowed: "Logi wins!"

Shea turned to look at the other contestant. But his head bumped a giant's elbow so violently that he saw stars. His eyes beaded with tears. For one fleeting second he saw no Logi there at all, only a great leaping flame at the opposite end of the table. A flicker—the teardrop was gone, and with it the picture.

Logi sat contentedly at the other end of the table, and Loki was crying; "He finished no sooner than myself!"

"Yeah, sonny boy, but he et the bone and the platter too. I said Logi wins!" boomed Utgardaloki.

"Heimdall!" Shea said it so loud that the god thrust a hand toward him. Fortunately the uproar around drowned his voice. "It is a trick, an illusion. Logi is a flame."

"Now, good luck go with your eyes, no-warlock and warlock. Warn Asa-Thor, and use your spell on whatever you can see, for it is more than ever important that the hammer be found. Surely, these tricks and sleights must mean the *Time* is even nearer than we think, and the giants are desirous not to see that weapon in the hands of Redbeard. Go!"

Utgardaloki, posted on the table where the eating contest had been held, was directing the clearing of a section of the hall. "The next event is a footrace," he was shouting. "You, shrimp!"—Utgardaloki pointed at Thjalfi. "You're going to run against my son Hugi. Where is that young halfwit? Hugi!"

"Here I am, pop." A gangling, adolescent giant wormed his way to the front. He had little forehead and less chin, and a crop of pimples the size of poker chips. "You want me to run against him? He, he, he!" Hugi drooled down his chin as he laughed.

Shea ducked and dodged, squeezing through toward Thor, who was frowning with concentration as he watched the preparations for the race. Thjalfi and the drooling Hugi placed themselves at one end of the hall. "Go!" cried Utgardaloki, and they raced for the far end of the hall, a good three hundred yards away. Thjalfi went like the wind, but Hugi went like a bullet. By the time Thjalfi had reached the far end his opponent was halfway back.

"Hugi wins first heat!" roared Utgardaloki above a tornado of sound. "It's two outta three."

The crowd loosened a little as the contestants caught their breath. Shea found himself beside Thor and Loki.

"Hai, Turnip Harald," rumbled the Redbeard, "where have you been?"

"It is more like anything else that he has been concealed under a table like a mouse," remarked Loki, but Shea was too full of his news to resent anything.

"They're trying to put over tricks on you—on us," he burst out. "All these contests are illusions."

He could see Thor's lips curl. "Your warlock can see deeper into a millstone than most," growled he angrily to Loki.

"No, but I mean it, really." Hugi had just passed them to take his place for the second heat, the hall's huge central fire on the other side. "Look," said Shea. "That runner of. theirs. He casts no shadow!"

Thor glanced and as comprehension spread across his features, turned purple. But just then Utgardaloki cried "Go!" again, and the second race was on. It was a repetition of the first. Utgardaloki announced over a delighted uproar that Hugi was the winner.

"I am to pick up their damned cat next," growled Thor. "If that be another trick of theirs, I'll—"

"Not so loudly," whispered Loki. "Soft and slow is the sly fox taken. Now Thor, you shall try this cat-lifting as though nothing were amiss. But Harald here, who is only half subject to their spells because he is a mortal and without fear, shall search for Mjöllnir. Youngling, you are our hope and stay. Use, use the spell I gave you."

A chorus of yells announced that Utgardaloki's cat had arrived. It was a huge beast, gray, and the size of a puma. But it did not look too big for the burly Thor to lift. It glared suspiciously at Thor and spat a little

Utgardaloki rumbled: "Quiet, you. Ain'tcha got no manners?" The cat subsided and allowed Thor to scratch it behind the ears, though with no appearance of pleasure.

How had he seen through the illusion of the eating contest? Shea asked himself. A teardrop in the eye. Would he have to bang his head again to get another one? He closed his eyes and then opened them again, looking at Thor as he put an arm around the big cat's belly and heaved. No teardrop. The cat's belly came up, but its four big paws remained firmly planted.

How to induce a teardrop? A mug of mead stood on the table. Shea dipped a finger into the liquid and shook a drop into his eye. The alcohol burned and stung, and he could hear Thor's grunt and the whooping of the giants. He shook his head and opened the eye again. Through a film of tears, as he repeated "Sudri-Nordri-Nidi-Nyi—" It was not a cat Thor was lifting, but the middle part of a snake as big around as a barrel. There was no sign of head or tail; the visible section was of uniform thickness, going in one door of the hall and out the other.

"Loki!" he said. "That's not a cat. It's a giant snake that Thor's trying to lift!"

"With a strange shimmering blackish cast over its scales?"

"Yes; and no head or tail in sight."

"Now, right good are your eyes, eater of turnips! That will be nothing less than the Midgard Serpent that curls round the earth! Surely we are surrounded by evil things. Hurry with the finding of the hammer, for this is now our only hope."

Shea turned from the contest, making a desperate effort to concentrate. He looked at the nearest object, an aurochs skull on a pillar, tried another drop of mead in his eye and repeated the spell, forward, backward, and forward., No result. The skull was a skull. Thor was still grunting and heaving. Shea tried once more on a knife hanging at a giant's belt. No result.

He looked at a quiver of arrows on the opposite wall and tried again. The sweet mead was sticking his eyelashes together and he felt sure he would have a headache after this. The quiver blurred as he pronounced the words. He found himself looking at a short-handled sledge hammer hanging by a rawhide loop.

Thor had given up the effort to lift the cat and came over to them, panting. Utgardaloki grinned down at him with the indulgence one might show a child. All around the giants were breaking up into little groups and calling for more drink.

"Want any more, sonny boy?" the giant chieftain sneered. "Guess you ain't so damn good as you thought you was, huh?"

Shea plucked at Thor's sleeve as the latter flushed and started to retort. "Can you call your hammer to you?" he whispered.

The giant's ears caught the words. "Beat it, thrall," he said belligerently. "We got business to settle and I won't have no snotty little mortals butting in. Now, Asa-Thor, do you want any more contests?"

"I—" began Thor again.

Shea clung to his arm. "*Can* you?" he demanded.

"Aye, if it be in view."

"I said get outta here, punk!" bellowed Utgardaloki, the rough good nature vanishing from his face. He raised an arm like a tree trunk.

"Point at that quiver of arrows and call!" shouted Shea. He dodged behind Thor as the giant's arm descended. The blow missed. He scuttled among the crowding monsters, hitting his head against the pommel of a giant's sword. Utgardaloki was roaring behind him. He ducked under a table and past some foul-smelling fire giants. He heard a clang of metal as Thor pulled on the iron gloves he carried at his belt. Then over all other sounds rose the voice of the red-bearded god, making even Utgardaloki's voice sound like a whisper:

"Mjöllnir the mighty, slayer of miscreants, come to your master, Thor Odinnsson!"

For a few breathless seconds the hall hung in suspended animation. Shea could see a giant just in front of him with mouth wide open, Adam's apple rising and falling. Then there was a rending snap. With a deep humming, the hammer that had seemed a quiver of arrows flew straight through the air into Thor's hands.

There was a deafening yell from the swarms of giants. They swayed back, then forward, squeezing Shea so tightly he could hardly breathe. High over the tumult rose the voice of Thor:

"I am Thor! I am the Thunderer! Ho, ho, hohoho, yoyoho!" The hammer was whirling round his head in a blur, sparks dancing round it. Level flashes of lightning cracked across the hall followed by deafening peals of thunder. There was a shriek from the giants and a rush towards the doors.

Shea shot one glimpse as the hammer flew at Utgardaloki and spattered his brains into pink oatmeal, rebounding back into Thor's gloves. Then he was caught completely in the panic rush and almost squeezed to death. Fortunately for him, the giants on either side wedged him so tightly he couldn't fall to be trampled.

The pressure suddenly gave way in front. Shea caught the giant ahead of him around the waist and hung on. Behind came Thor's battle howl, mingled with constant thunder and the sound of the hammer shattering giant skulls—a noise that in a calmer moment Shea might have compared to that made by dropping a watermelon ten stories. The Wielder of Mjöllnir was thoroughly enjoying himself; his shouts were like the noise of a happy express train.

Shea found himself outside and running across damp moss in the middle of hundreds of galloping giants and thralls. He dared not stop lest he be stepped on. An outcrop of rock made him swerve. As he did so he caught sight of Utgard. There was already a yawning gap at one end of the roof. The central beam split; a spear of blue-green lightning shot skyward, and the place began to burn brightly around the edges of the rent.

A clump of trees cut off the view. Shea ran downhill with giants still all around him. One of the group just ahead missed his footing and went rolling. Before Shea could stop, he had tripped across the fellow's legs, his face plowing up cold dirt and pine needles. A giant's voice shouted: "Hey, gang! Look at this!"

Now they've got me, he thought. He rolled over, his head swimming from the jar. But it was not he they were interested in. The giant over whose legs he had fallen was Heimdall, his wig knocked askew to reveal a patch of golden hair. The straw with which he had stuffed his jacket was dribbling out. He was struggling to get up; around him a group of fire giants were gripping his arms and legs, kicking and cuffing at him. There was a babble of rough voices:

"He's one of the Æsir, all right!" "Sock him!" "Let's get out of here!" "Which one is he?" "Get the horses!"

If he could get away, Shea thought, he could at least take news of Heimdall's plight to Thor. He started to crawl behind the projecting root of a tree, but the movement was fatal. One of the fire giants hallooed: "There's another one!"

Shea was caught, jerked upright, and inspected by half a dozen of the filthy gorillalike beings. They took particular delight in pulling his hair and ears.

"Aw," said one of them, "he's no As. Bump him off and let's get t' hell out of here."

One of them loosened a knife at his belt. Shea felt a deadly constriction of fear around the heart. But the largest of the lot—leadership seemed to go with size in giantland—roared: "Lay off! He was with that yellow-headed stümper. Maybe he's one of the Vanes and we can get something for him. Anyway, it's up to Lord Surt. Where the hell are those horses?"

At that moment more fire giants appeared, leading a group of horses. They were glossy black and bigger than the largest Percherons Shea had ever seen. Three hoofs were on each foot, as with the ancestral Miocene horse; their eyes glowed red like live coals and their breath made Shea cough. He remembered the phrase he had heard Heimdall whispering to Odinn in Sverre's house—"fire horses."

One of the giants produced leather cords from a pouch. Shea and Heimdall were bound with brutal efficiency and tossed on the back of one of the horses, one hanging down on either side. The giants clucked to their mounts, which started off at a trot through the gathering dusk among the trees.

Far behind them the thunders of Thor still rolled. From time to time his distant lightnings cast sudden shadows along their path. The redbeard was certainly having fun.

7

The agonizing hours that followed left little detailed impression on Harold Shea's mind. They would not, he told himself even while experiencing them. The impression was certainly painful while being undergone. There was nothing to see but misty darkness; nothing to feel but breakneck speed and the torment of his bonds. He could twist his head a little, but of their path could obtain no impression but now and then the ghost of a boulder or a clump of trees momentarily lit by the fiery eyes of the horses. Every time he thought of the speed they were making along the rough and winding route his stomach crawled and the muscles of his right leg tensed as he tried to apply an imaginary automobile brake.

When the sky finally turned to its wearisome blotting-paper gray the air was a little warmer, though still raw. A light drizzle was sifting down. They were in a countryside of a type totally unfamiliar to Shea. A boundless plain of tumbled black rock rose here and there to cones of varying size. Some of the cones smoked, and little pennons of steam wafted from cracks in the basalt. The vegetation consisted mostly of clumps of small palmlike tree ferns in the depressions.

They had slowed down to a fast trot, the horses picking their way over the ropy bands of old lava flows. Now and again one or more fire giants would detach themselves from the party and set off on a tangent to the main course.

Finally, a score of the giants clustered around the horse that bore the prisoners, making toward a particularly large cone from whose flanks a number of smoke plumes rose through the drizzle. To Shea the fire giants still looked pretty much alike, but he had no difficulty in picking out the big authoritative one who had directed his capture.

They halted in front of a gash in the rock. The giants dismounted, and one by one led their steeds through the opening. The animals' hoofs rang echoing on the rock floor of the passage, which sprang above their heads in a lofty vault till it suddenly ended with a right-angled turn. The cavalcade halted; Shea heard a banging of metal on metal, the creak of a rusty hinge, and a giant voice that cried: "Whatcha want?"

"It's the gang, back from Jötunheim. We got one of the Æsir and a Van. Tell Lord Surt."

"Howdja make out at Utgard?"

"Lousy. Thor showed up. He spotted the hammer somehow, the scum, and called it to him and busted things wide open. It was that smart-aleck Loki, I think."

"What was the matter with the Sons of the Wolf? They know what to do about old Red Whiskers."

"Didn't show. I suppose we gotta wait for the *Time* for them to come around."

The horses tramped on. As they passed the gatekeeper, Shea noticed that he held a sword along which flickered a yellow flame with thick, curling smoke rising from it, as though burning oil were running down the blade. Ahead and slanting downward, the place they had entered seemed an underground hall of vaguely huge proportions, full of great pillars. Flares of yellow light threw changing shadows as they moved. There was a stench of sulfur and a dull, machine-like banging. As the horses halted behind some pillars that grew together to

make another passage, a thin shriek ululated in the distance: "Eee-e-e."
"Bring the prisoners along," said a voice. "Lord Surt wants to judge 'em."
Shea felt himself removed and tucked under a giant's arm like a bundle. It was a method of progress that woke all the agonies in his body. The giant was carrying him face down, so that he could see nothing but the stone floor with its flickering shadows. The place stank.

A door opened and there was a babble of giant voices. Shea was flung upright. He would have fallen if the giant who had been carrying him had not propped him up. He was in a torchlit hall, very hot, with fire giants standing all around, grinning, pointing, and talking, some of them drinking.

But he had no more than a glance for them. Right in front, facing him, flanked by two guards who carried the curious burning swords, sat the biggest giant of all—a giant dwarf. That is, he was a full giant in size, at least eleven feet tall, but with the squat bandy legs, the short arms and huge neckless head of a dwarf. His hair hung lank around the nastiest grin Shea had ever seen. When he spoke, the voice had not the rumble of the other giants, but a reedy, mocking falsetto:

"Welcome, Lord Heimdall, to Muspellheim! We are delighted to have you here." He snickered. "I fear gods and men will be somewhat late in assembling for the battle without their horn blower. Hee, hee, hee. But, at least, we can give you the comforts of one of our best dungeons. If you must have music, we will provide a willow whistle. Hee, hee, hee. Surely so skilled a musician as yourself could make it heard throughout the nine worlds." He ended with another titter at his own humor.

Heimdall kept his air of dignity. "Bold are your words, Surt," he replied, "but it is yet to be seen whether your deeds match them when you stand on Vigrid Plain. It may be that I have small power against you of the Muspellheim blood. Yet I have a brother named Frey, and it is said that if you two come face to face, he will be your master."

Surt sucked two fingers to indicate his contempt. "Hee, hee, hee. It is also said, most stupid of godlings, that Frey is powerless without his sword. Would you like to know where the enchanted blade, Hundingsbana, is? Look behind you, Lord Heimdall!"

Shea followed the direction of Heimdall's eyes. Sure enough, on the wall there hung a great two-handed sword, its blade gleaming brightly in that place of glooms, its hilt all worked with gold up to the jeweled pommel.

"While it hangs up there, most stupid of Æsir, I am safe. Hee, hee, hee. Have you been wondering why that famous eyesight of yours did not light on it before? Now you know, most easily deceived. In Muspellheim, we have found the spells that make Heimdall powerless."

Heimdall was unimpressed. "Thor has his hammer back," he remarked easily. "Not a few of your fire giants' heads will bear witness—if you can find them."

Surt scowled and thrust his jaw forward, but his piping voice was as serene and mocking as before. "Now, that," he said, "really gives me an idea. I thank you, Lord Heimdall. Who would have thought it possible to learn anything from one of the Æsir? Hee, hee, hee. Skoa!"

A lop-eared fire giant shuffled forward. "Whatcha want, boss?"

"Ride to the gates of Asgard. Tell them I have their horn tooter here. I will gladly send the nuisance back to his relatives; but in exchange I want that sword of his, the one they call Head. Hee, hee, hee. I am collecting gods' swords, and we shall see, Lord Heimdall, how you fare against the frost giants without yours."

He grinned all around his face and the fire giants in the background slapped their knees and whooped. "Pretty hot stuff boss!" "Ain't he smart." "Two of the four great weapons!" "Boy, will we show 'em!"

Surt gazed at Shea and Heimdall for a moment, enjoying to the utmost the roar of appreciation and Heimdall's sudden pallor. Then he made a gesture of dismissal. "Take the animals away and put 'em in a dungeon before I die laughing."

Shea felt himself seized once more and carried off, face downward in the same ignominious position as before.

Down—down—down they went, stumbling through the lurid semidark. At last they came to a passage lined with cells between whose bars the hollow eyes of previous arrivals stared at them. The stench had become overpowering.

The commanding giant thundered: "Stegg!"

There was a stir in an alcove at the far end of the passage, and out came a scaly being about five feet tall, with an oversize head decorated by a snub nose and a pair of long pointed ears. Instead of hair and beard it had wormlike excrescences on its head. They moved. The being squeaked: "Yes, Lord."

The giant said: "Got a couple more prisoners for you. Say, what stinks?"

"Please, lord, mortal him die. Five days gone."

"You lug! And you left him in there?"

"No lord here. Snögg say 'no,' must have lord's orders to do—"

"You damn nitwit! Take him out and give him to the furnace detail! Hai, wait, take care of these prisoners first. Hai, bolt the door, somebody. We don't take no chances with the Æsir."

Stegg set about efficiently stripping Shea and Heimdall. Shea wasn't especially afraid. So many extraordinary things had happened to him lately that the whole proceeding possessed an air of unreality. Besides, even the difficulties of such a place might not be beyond the resources of a well-applied brain.

Stegg said: "Lord, must put in dead mortal's cell. No more. All full."

"Awright, get in there, youse." The giant gave Shea a cuff that almost knocked him flat and set him staggering toward the cell which Stegg had opened. Shea avoided the mass of corruption at one side and looked for a place to sit down. There was none. The only furnishings of any kind consisted of a bucket whose purpose was obvious.

Heimdall followed him in, still wearing his high, imperturbable air. Stegg gathered up the corpse; went out, and slammed the door. The giant took hold of the bars and heaved on them. There was no visible lock or bolt, but the door stayed tight.

"Oh, ho!" roared the giant. "Don't the Sleepless One look cute? When we get through with the other Æsir we'll come back and show you some fun. Have yourselves a time." With this farewell, the giants all tramped out.

Fortunately the air was warm enough so Shea didn't mind the loss of his garments from a thermal point of view. Around them the dungeon was silent, save for a drip of water somewhere and the occasional rustle of a prisoner in his cell. Across from Shea there was a clank of chains. An emaciated figure with a wildly disordered beard shuffled up to the bars and screamed, "Yngvi is a louse!" and shuffled back again.

"What means he?" Heimdall called out.

From the right came a muffled answer: "None knows. He says it every hour. He is mad, as you will be."

"Cheerful place," remarked Shea.

"Is it not?" agreed Heimdall readily. "Worse have I seen, but happily without being confined therein. I will say that for a mortal, you are not without spirit, Turnip Harald. Your demeanor likes me well."

"Thanks." Shea had not entirely forgotten his irritation over Heimdall's patronizing manner, but the Sleepless One held his interest more than the choleric and rather slow-witted Thor or the sneering Loki. "If you don't mind my asking, Golden One, why can't you just use your powers to get out?"

"To all things there is a limit," replied Heimdall, "of size, of power, and of duration. Wide is the lifetime of a god; wider than of a thousand of your feeble species one after the other. Yet even gods grow old and die. Likewise, as to these fire giants and their chief, Surt, that worst of beings, I have not much strength. If my brother Frey were here now, or if we were among the frost giants, I could overcome the magic of that door."

"How do you mean?"

"It has no lock. Yet it will not open save when an authorized person pulls it and with intent to open. Look, now"—Heimdall pushed against the bars without effect— "if you will be quiet for a while, I will try to see my way out of this place."

The Sleepless One leaned back against the wall, his eyes moving restlessly about. His body quivered with energy in spite of his relaxed position.

"Not too well can I see," he announced after a few minutes. "There is so much magic here—fire magic of a kind both evil and difficult—that it hurts my head. Yet this much I see clearly: around us all is rock, with no entrance but the way by which we came. Beyond that there lies a passage with trolls to watch it. *Ugh*, disgusting creatures." The golden-haired god gave a shudder of repugnance.

"Can you see beyond?" asked Shea.

"A little. Beyond the trolls, a ledge sits over a pile of molten slag at the entrance of the hall where the flaming swords are forged, and then—and then" —his forehead contracted, his lips moved a trifle—"a giant sits by the pool of slag. No more can I see."

Heimdall relapsed into gloomy silence. Shea felt considerable respect and some liking for him, but it is hard to be friendly with a god, even in a prison cell. Thjalfi's cheerful human warmth was missing.

Stegg reentered the cell hall. One of the prisoners called out: "Good Stegg, a little water, please; I die of thirst."

Stegg turned his head a trifle. "Dinner time soon, slave." The prisoner gave a yell of anger and shouted abuse at the troll, who continued down to his alcove in the most perfect indifference. Here he hoisted himself into a broken-down stool, dropped his chin on his chest, and apparently went to sleep.

"Nice guy," said Shea.

The prisoner across the way came to the front of his cell and shrieked, "Yngvi is a louse!" again.

"The troll is not asleep," said Heimdall. "I can hear his thoughts, for he is of a race that can hardly think at all without moving the lips. But I cannot make them out. Harald, you see a thing that is uncommon; namely, one of the Æsir confessing he is beaten. But there is this to be said: if we are held here it will be the worst of days for gods and men."

"Why would that be?"

"So near is the balance of strength, gods against giants, that the issue of what will happen at the *Time* hangs by a thread. If we come late to the field we shall surely lose; the giants will hold the issues against our mustering. And I am here—here in this cell—with my gift of eyesight that can see them in time to warn. I am here, and the Gjallarhorn, the roaring trumpet that would call gods and heroes to the field, is at Sverre's house."

Shea asked: "Why don't the Æsir *attack* the giants before the giants are ready, if they know there's going to be a war anyway?"

Heimdall stared at him. "You know not the Law of the Nine Worlds, Harald. We Æsir cannot attack the giants all together before the *Time*. Men and gods live by law; else they would be but giants."

He began to pace back and forth with rapid steps, his forehead set in a frown. Shea noted that even at this moment the Sleepless One was careful to place one foot before the other to best display the litheness of his walk,

"Surely they'll miss you," said Shea. "Can't they set other guards to watch the giants get together, or"—he finished lamely at the glint in Heimdall's eye— "something?"

"A mortal's thoughts! Aye!" Heimdall gave a short bark of bitter laughter. "Set other guards, here and there! Listen, Turnip Harald; Harald the fool. Of all us Æsir, Frey is the best, the only one who can stand before Surt with weapons in hand. Yet the worlds are so made, and we cannot change it, that one race Frey fears. Against the frost giants he has no power. Only I, I and my sword Head, can deal with them; and if I am not there to lead my band against the frost giants, we shall live to something less than a ripe old age thereafter."

"I'm sorry—sir," said Shea.

"Aye. No matter. Come, let us play the game of questions. Few and ill are the thoughts that rise from brooding."

For hours they plied each other with queries about their respective worlds. In that ominous place, time could be measured only by meals and the periodic shrieks of "Yngvi is a louse!" About the eighth of these cries, Stegg came out of his somnolent state, went out, and returned with a pile of bowls. These he set in front of the cells. Each bowl had a spoon; one was evidently expected to do one's eating through the bars. As the troll put the bowls in front of Shea's cell, he remarked loftily: "King see subjects eat."

The mess he put in them consisted of some kind of porridge with small lumps of fish in it, sour to the taste. Shea did not blame his fellow prisoners when they broke into loud complaints about the quality and quantity of the food. Stegg paid not the slightest attention, relapsing into his chair till they had finished, when he gathered up the bowls and carried them out.

The next time the door opened, it was not Stegg but another troll. In the flickering torchlight this one was, if possible, less handsome than his predecessor. His face was built around a nose of such astonishing proportions that it projected a good eighteen inches, and he moved with a quick, catlike stride. The prisoners, who had been fairly noisy while Stegg was in charge, now fell silent.

The new jailer stepped quickly to Shea's cell. "You new arrivals?" he snapped. "I am Snögg. You be good, nothing hurt you. You be bad, zzzp." He made a motion with his finger to indicate the cutting of a throat, and turning his back on them, paced down the row of cells, peering suspiciously into each.

Shea had never in his life slept on a stone floor. So he was surprised, an indefinite time later, to awaken and discover that he had done it for the first time, with the result of being stiff.

He got up, stretching. "How long have I been asleep?" he asked Heimdall.

"I do not know that. Our fellow prisoner, who dislikes someone called Yngvi, ceased his shouting some time since."

The long-nosed jailer was still pacing. Still muzzy with sleep Shea could not remember his name, and called out: "Hey, you with the nose! How long before breakf—"

The troll had turned on him, shrieking: "What you call me? You stinking worm! I—*zzzp!*" He ran down to the alcove, face distorted with fury, and returned with a bucket of water which he sloshed into Shea's surprised face. "You son of unwed parents!" he raged. "I roast you with slow fire! I am Snögg. I am master! You use right name."

Heimdall was laughing silently at the back of the cell.

Shea murmured: "That's one way of getting a bath at all events. I guess our friend Snögg is sensitive about his nose."

"That is not unevident," said Heimdall. "Hai! How many troubles the children of men would save themselves, could they but have the skill of the gods for reading the thought that lies behind the lips. Half of all they suffer, I would wager."

"Speaking of wagers, Sleepless One," said Shea, "I see how we can run a race to pass the time."

"This cage is somewhat less than spacious," objected Heimdall. "What are you' doing? It is to be trusted that you do not mean an eating race with those cockroaches."

"No. I'm going to race them. Here's yours. You can tell him by his broken feeler."

"The steed is not of the breed," observed Heimdall, taking the insect. "Still, I will name him Gold Top, after my horse. What will you call yours, and how shall we race them?"

Shea said: "I shall call mine Man o' War after a famous horse in our world." He smoothed down the dust on the floor, and drew a circle in it with his finger. "Now," he explained, "let us release our racers in the center of the circle, and the one whose roach crossed the rim first shall win."

"A good sport. What shall the wager be? A crown?"

"Seeing that neither of us has any money at all," said Shea, "why don't we shoot the works and make it fifty crowns?"

"Five hundred if you wish."

Man o' War won the first race. Snögg, hearing the activity in the cell, hustled over. "What you do?" he demanded. Shea explained. "Oh," sniffed the troll. "All right, you do. Not too noisy, though. I stop if you do." He stalked away, but was soon back again to watch the sport. Gold Top won the second race—Man o' War the third and fourth. Shea, glancing up, suppressed an impulse to tweak the sesquipedalian nose that the troll had thrust through the bars.

By and by Snögg went out and was replaced by Stegg, who did not even notice the cockroach racing. As he hoisted himself into his chair, Shea asked whether he could get them some sort of small box or basket.

"Why you want?" asked Stegg.

Shea explained he wanted it to keep the cockroaches in.

Stegg raised his eyebrows. "I too big for this things," he said loftily and refused to answer another word.

So they had to let the racers go rather than hold them in their hands all day. But Shea saved a little of his breakfast and later, by using it as bait, they captured two more cockroaches.

This time, after a few victories for Shea, Heimdall's roach began to win consistently. By the time the man across the passage had yelled "Yngvi is a louse!" four times Shea found himself Heimdall's debtor to the extent of something like thirty million crowns. It made him suspicious. He watched the golden god narrowly during the next race, then burst out: "Say, that's not fair! You're fixing my cockroach with your glittering eye and slowing him up!"

"What, mortal! Dare you accuse one of the Æsir?"

"You're damn right, I dare! If you're going to use your special powers, I won't play."

A smile slowly spread across Heimdall's face. "Young Harald, you do not lack for boldness, and I have said before that you show glimmerings of wit. In truth, I have slowed up your steed; it is not meet that one of the Æsir should be beaten at aught by a mortal. But come, let that one go, and we will begin again with new mounts, for I fear that animal of yours will never again be the same."

It was not difficult to catch more roaches. "Once more I shall name mine Gold Top, after my horse," said Heimdall. "It is a name of good luck. Did you have no favorite horse?"

"No, but I had a car, a four-wheeled chariot, it was called—" began Shea, and then stopped. What was the name of that car? He tried to reproduce the syllables—nyrose, no—neelose, no, not that either—neroses, nerosis—something clicked into place in his brain, a series of somethings, like the fragments of a jigsaw puzzle.

"Heimdall!" he cried suddenly, "I believe I know how we can get out of here!"

"That will be the best of news," said the Sleepless One, doubtfully, "if the deed be equal to the thought. But I have looked, now, deeply into this place, and I do not see how it may be done without outside aid. Nor shall we have help from any giant with the *Time* so near."

"Whose side will the trolls be on?"

"It is thought that the trolls will be neuter. Yet strange it would be if we could beguile one of these surly ones to help us."

"Nevertheless, something you said a little while back gives me an idea. You remember? Something about the skill of the gods at reading the thought that lies behind the lips?"

"Aye."

"I am—I was—of a profession whose business it is to learn people's thoughts by questioning them, and by studying what they think today, predict what they will think tomorrow in other circumstances. Even to provoke them to thinking certain things."

"It could be. It is an unusual art, mortal, and a great skill, but it could be. What then?"

"Well, then, this Stegg, I don't think we can get far with him, I've seen his. type before. He's a—a something I can't remember, but he lives in a world of his own imaginings, where he's a king and we're all his slaves. I remember, now—a paranoiac. You can't establish contact with a mind like that."

"Most justly and truly reasoned, Harald. From what I am able to catch of his thought this is no more than the truth."

"But Snögg is something else. We can do something with him."

"Much though I regret to say it, you do not drown me in an ocean of hope. Snögg is even more hostile than his unattractive brother."

Shea grinned. At last he was in a position to make use of his specialized knowledge. "That's what one would think. But I have studied many like him. The only thing that's wrong with Snögg is that he has a…a feeling of inferiority—a complex we call it—about that nose of his. If somebody could convince him he's handsome—"

"Snögg handsome! Ho, ho! That is a jest for Loki's tongue."

"*Sssh!* Please, Lord Heimdall. As I say, the thing he wants most is probably good looks. If we could…if we could pretend to work some sort of spell on his nose, tell him it has shrunk and get the other prisoners to corroborate—"

"A plan of wit! It is now to be seen that you have been associating with Uncle Fox. Yet do not sell your bearskin till you have caught the animal. If you can get Snögg sufficiently friendly to propose your plan, then will it be seen whether confinement has really sharpened your wits or only addled them. But, youngling, what is to prevent Snögg feeling his nose and discovering the beguilement for himself?"

"Oh, we don't have to guarantee to take it all off. He'd be grateful enough for a couple of inches."

8

When Snögg came on duty at nightfall, he found the dungeon as usual, except that Shea's and Heimdall's cell was noisy with shouts of encouragement to their entries in the great cockroach derby. He went over to the cell to make sure that nothing outside the rules of the prison was going on.

Shea met his suspicious glower with a grin. "Hi, there, friend Snögg! Yesterday I owed Heimdall thirty million crowns, but today my luck has turned and it's down to twenty-three million."

"What do you mean?" snapped the troll.

Shea explained, and went on: "Why don't you get in the game? We'll catch a roach for you. It must be pretty dull, with nothing to do all night but listen to the prisoners snore."

"Hm-m-m," said Snögg, then turned abruptly suspicious again. "You make trick to let other prisoner escape, I—*zzzzp!*" He motioned across his throat again. "Lord Surt, he say."

"No, nothing like that. You can make your inspection any time. *Sssh!* There's one now."

"One what?" asked Snögg, a little of the hostility leaving his voice. Shea was creeping toward the wall of his cell. He pounced like a cat and came up with another cockroach in his hand. "What'll his name be?" he asked Snögg.

Snögg thought, his little troll brain trying to grasp the paradox of a friendly prisoner, his eyes moving suspiciously. "I call him Fjörm, after river. That run fast," he said at last.

"That where you are from?"

"Aye."

Heimdall spoke up. "It is said, friend Snögg, that Fjörm has the finest fish in all the nine worlds, and I believe it, for I have seen them."

The troll looked almost pleased. "True word. Me fish there, early morning. Ho, ho! Me wade—snap! Up come trout. Bite him, flop, flop in face. Me remember big one, chase into shallow."

Shea said: "You and Öku-Thor ought to get together. Fjörm may have the best fish, but he has the biggest fish story in the nine worlds."

Snögg actually emitted a snicker. "Me know that story. Thor no fisher. He use hook and line. Only trolls know how to fish fair. We use hands, like this." He bent over the floor, his face fixed in intense concentration then made a sudden sweeping motion, quick as a rattlesnake's lunge. "Ah!" he cried. "Fish! I love him! Come, we race."

The three cockroaches were tossed into the center of the circle and scuttled away. Snögg's Fjörm was the first to cross the line to the troll's unconcealed delight.

They ran race after race, with halts when one of the roaches escaped and another had to be caught. Snögg's entry showed a tendency to win altogether at variance with the law of probability. The troll did not notice and would hardly have grasped the fact that Heimdall was using his piercing glance on his own and Shea's roaches and slowing them up, though Snögg was not allowed to win often enough to rouse his sleeping suspicions. By the time Stegg relieved him in the morning he was over twenty million crowns ahead. Shea stretched out on the floor to sleep with the consciousness of a job well done.

When he awoke, just before Snögg came on duty the next night, he found Heimdall impatient and uneasy, complaining of the delay while Surt's messenger was riding to demand the sword Head as ransom. Yet it speedily became obvious that the Snögg campaign could not be hurried.

"Don't you ever get homesick for your river Fjörm?" asked Shea, when the troll had joined them.

"Aye," replied Snögg. "Often. Like 'um fish."

"Think you'll be going back?"

"Will not be soon."

"Why not?"

Snögg squirmed a little. "Lord Surt him hard master."

"Oh, he'd let you go. Is that the only reason?"

"N-no. Me like troll girl Elvagevu. Haro! Here, what I do, talk privacy life with prisoner? Stop it. We race."

Shea recognized this as a good place to stop his questioning, but when Snögg was relieved, he remarked to Heimdall: "That's a rich bit of luck. I can't imagine being in love with a female troll, but he evidently is—"

"Man from another world, you observe well. His thoughts were near enough his lips for me to read. This troll-wife, Elvagevu, has refused him because of the size of his nose."

"Ah! Then we really have something. Now, tonight—"

When the cockroach races began that night, Heimdall reversed the usual process sufficiently to allow Snögg to lose several races in succession. The long winning streak he later developed was accordingly appreciated, and it was while Snögg was chuckling over his victories, snapping his finger joints and bouncing in delight that Shea insinuated softly: "Friend Snögg, you have been good to us. Now, if there's something we could do for you, we'd be glad to do it. For instance, we might be able to remove the obstacle that prevents your return to Elvagevu."

Snögg jumped and glared suspiciously. "Not possible," he said thickly.

Heimdall looked at the ceiling. "Great wonders have been accomplished by prisoners," he said, "when there is held out to them the hope of release."

"Lord Surt him very bad man when angry," Snögg countered, his eyes moving restlessly.

"Aye," nodded Heimdall. "Yet not even Lord Surt's arm is long enough to reach into the troll country—after one who has gone there to stay with his own troll-wife."

Snögg cocked his head on one side, so that he looked like some large-beaked bird. "Hard part is," he countered, "to get beyond Lord Surt's arm. Too much danger."

"But," said Shea, falling into the spirit of the discussion, "if one's face were altogether changed by the removal of a feature, it might be much easier and simpler. One would not be recognized."

Snögg caressed his enormous nose. "Too big—You make fun of me!" he snapped with sudden suspicion.

"Not at all," said Shea. "Back in my own country a girl once turned me down because my eyes were too close together. Women always have peculiar taste."

"That's true." Snögg lowered his voice till it was barely audible. "You fix nose, I be your man: I do all for you."

"I don't want to guarantee too much in advance," said Shea. "But I think I can do something for you. I landed here without all my magic apparatus, though."

"All you need I get," said Snögg, eager to go the whole way now that he had committed himself.

"I'll have to think about what I need," said Shea.

The next day, when Stegg had collected the breakfast bowls, Shea and Heimdall lifted their voices and asked the other prisoners whether they would cooperate in the proposed method of escape. They answered readily enough. "Sure, if 'twon't get us into no trouble." "Aye, but will ye try to do something for me, too?" "Mought, if ye can manage it quiet." *"Yngvi is a louse!"*

Shea turned his thoughts to the concoction of a spell that would sound sufficiently convincing, doing his best to recall Chalmers' description of the laws of magic to which he had given so little attention when the psychologist stated them. There was the law of contagion—no, there seemed no application for that. But the law of similarity? That would be it. The troll, himself familiar with spells and wizardry, would recognize an effort to apply that principle as in accordance with the general laws of magic. It remained, then, to surround some application of the law of similarity with sufficient hocus-pocus to make Snögg believe something extra-special in the way of spells was going on. By their exclamation over the diminishing size of Snögg's nose the other prisoners would do the rest.

"Whom should one invoke in working a spell of this kind?" Shea asked Heimdall.

"Small is my knowledge of this petty mortal magic," replied Heimdall. "The Evil Companion would be able to give you all manner of spells and gewgaws. But I would say that the names of the ancestors of wizardry would be not without power in such cases."

"And who are they?"

"There is the ancestor of all witches, by name Witolf; the ancestor of all warlocks, who was called Willharm. Svarthead was the first of the spell singers, and of the giant kindred Ymir. For good luck and the beguiling of Snögg you might add two who yet live—Andvari, king of the dwarfs, and the ruler of all trolls, who is the Old Woman of Ironwood. She is a fearsome creature, but I think not unpleasant to one of her subjects."

When Snögg showed up again Shea had worked out his method for the phony spell. "I shall need a piece of beeswax," he said, "and a charcoal brazier already lit and burning; a piece of driftwood sawn into pieces no bigger than your thumb; a pound of green grass, and a stand on which you can balance a board just over the brazier."

Snögg said: "*Time* comes very near. Giants muster—When you want things?"

Shea heard in the background Heimdall's gasp of dismay at the first sentence. But he said: "As soon as you can possibly get them."

"Maybe tomorrow night. We race?"

"No—yes," said Heimdall. His lean, sharp face looked strained in the dim light. Shea could guess the impatience that was gnawing him, with his exalted sense of personal duty and responsibility. And perhaps with reason, Shea assured himself. The fate of the world, of gods and men, in Heimdall's own words, hung on that trumpet blast. Shea's own fate, too, hung on it—an idea he could never contemplate without a sense of shock and unreality, no matter how frequently he repeated the process of reasoning it all out

Yet not even the shock of this repeated, thought could stir him from the fatalism into which he had fallen. The world he had come from, uninteresting though it was, had at least been something one could grasp, think over as a whole. Here he felt himself a chip on a tossing ocean of strange and terrible events. His early failures on the trip to Jötunheim had left him with a sense of helplessness which had not entirely disappeared even with his success in detecting the illusions in the giants' games and the discovery of Thor's hammer. Loki then, and Heimdall later had praised his fearlessness—*ha*, he said to himself, *if they only knew!* It was not true courage that animated him, but a feeling that he was involved in a kind of strange and desperate game, in which the only thing that mattered was to play it as skillfully as possible. He supposed soldiers had something of that feeling in battle. Otherwise, they would all run away and then wouldn't be any battle—

His thoughts strayed again to the episode in the hall of Utgard. Was it Loki's spell or the teardrop in his eye that accounted for his success there? Or merely the trained observation of a modern mind? Some of the last, certainly; the others had been too excited to note such discordant details as the fact that Hugi cast no shadow. At the same time, his modern mind balked over the idea that the spell had been effective. Yet there was something, a residue of phenomenon, not accounted for by physical fact.

That meant that, given the proper spell to work he could perform as good a bit of magic as the next *man*. Heimdall, Snögg, and Surt all had special powers—built in during construction as it were—but their methods would do him, Shea, no good at all. He was neither god, troll—thank Heaven!—nor giant

Well, if he couldn't be a genuine warlock, he could at least put on a good show. He thought of the little poses and affectations he had put on during his former life. Now life itself depended on how well he could assume a pose. How would a wizard act? His normal behavior should seem odd enough to Snögg for all practical purposes.

The inevitable night dragged out, and Stegg arrived to take over his duties. Snögg hurried out. Shea managed to choke down what was sardonically described as his breakfast and tried to sleep. The first yell of "Yngvi is a louse!" brought him up all standing. And his fleabites seemed to itch more than usual. He had just gotten himself composed when it was time for dinner again and Snögg.

The troll listened, twitching with impatience, till Stegg's footfall died away. Then he scurried out like a magnified rat and returned with his arms full of the articles Shea had ordered. He dumped them in the middle of the passage and with a few words opened the door of Shea's and Heimdall's cell.

"Put out all but one of the torches," said Shea. While Snögg was doing this the amateur magician went to work. Holding the beeswax over the brazier, he softened it enough to work and pressed it into conical shape, making two deep indentations on one side till it was a crude imitation of Snögg's proboscis.

"Now," he whispered to the popeyed troll, "get the water bucket. When I tell you, pour it into the brazier."

Shea knelt before the brazier and blew into it. The coals brightened. He picked up a fistful of the driftwood chips and began feeding them onto the glowing charcoal. They caught; little varicolored flames dancing across them. Shea, on his haunches and swaying to and fro, began his spell:

> *Witolf and Willharm,*
> *Stand, my friends!*
> *Andvari, Ymir,*
> *Help me to my ends!*
> *The Hag of the Ironwood*
> *Shall be my aid;*
> *By the spirit of Svarthead,*
> *Let this spell be made!*

The beeswax, on the board above the brazier, was softening. Slowly the cone lost its shape and slumped. Transparent drops trickled over the edge of the board, hung redly in the glow, and dropped with a hiss and spurt of yellow flame into the brazier.

Shea chanted:

> *Let wizards and warlocks*
> *Combine and conspire*
> *To make Snögg's nose melt*
> *Like the wax on this fire!*

The beeswax had become a mere fist-shaped lump. The trickle into the brazier was continuous: little flames rose yellowly and were reflected from the eyes of the breathlessly watching prisoners.

Shea stuffed handfuls of grass into the brazier. Thick rolls of smoke filled the dungeon. He moved his arms through the murk, wriggling the fingers and shouting:

"Hag of the Ironwood, I invoke you in the name of your subject!"

The waxen lump was tiny now. Shea leaned forward into the smoky half-light, his eyes smarting, and rapidly molded it into something resembling the shape of an ordinary nose. "Pour, now!" he cried. Swoosh! went the water into the brazier, and everything was blotted from vision by a cloud of vapor.

He struggled away and to an erect position. Sweat was making little furrows in the dirt along his skin, with the sensation of insects crawling. "All right," he said. "You can put the light back on now." The next few seconds would tell whether his deception was going to work. If the other prisoners did not fail him—

Snögg was going along the passage, lighting the extinguished torches from the one that remained. As the light increased and he turned to place one in its bracket on the opposite side of the wall, Shea joined involuntarily in the cry of astonishment that rose from every prisoner in the cells.

Snögg's nose was no bigger than that of a normal human being.

Harold Shea was a warlock.

"Head feel funny," remarked Snögg in a matter of fact tone.

9

The troll put the last torch in place and turned to Shea, caressing the new nose with a scaly hand. "Very good magic, Harald Warlock!" he said, chuckling and dancing a couple of steps. "Hai! Elvagevu, you like me now!"

Shea stood rooted, trying to absorb events that seemed to have rushed past him. The only sound he could utter was "Guk!"

He felt Heimdall's hand on his shoulder. "Well and truly was that spell

The Roaring Trumpet

cast," said the Sleepless One. "Much profit may we have from it. Yet I should warn you, warlock, that it is ill to lie to the gods. Why did you tell me, at the Crossroads of the World, that you had no skill in magic?"

"Oh," said Shea, unable to think of anything else, "I guess I'm just naturally modest. I didn't wish to presume before you, sir."

Snögg had gone off into a ludicrous hopping dance around the hall. "Beautiful me!" he squealed. "Beautiful me!"

Shea thought that Snögg, with or without nose, was about the ugliest thing he had ever seen. But there seemed little point in mentioning the fact. Instead, he asked, "How about getting us out of here now, friend Snögg?"

Snögg moderated his delight enough to say: "Will be do. Go your cage now. I come with clothes and weapon." Shea and Heimdall exchanged glances. It seemed hard to go back into that tiny cell, but they had to trust the troll now, so they went.

"Now it remains to be seen," said Heimdall, "whether that scaly fish-eater has betrayed us. If he has—" He let his voice trail off.

"We might consider what we could do to him if he has," grinned Shea. His astonishing achievement had boosted his morale to the skies.

"Little enough could I accomplish in this place of fire magic," said Heimdall, gloomily, "but such a warlock as yourself could make his legs sprout into serpents."

"Maybe," said Shea. He couldn't get used to the idea that he, of all people, could work magic. It was contrary to the laws of physics, chemistry, and biology. But then, where he was the laws of physics, chemistry and biology had been repealed. He was under the laws of magic. His spell had conformed exactly to those laws, as explained by Dr. Chalmers. This was a world in which those laws were basic. The trick was that he happened to know one of those laws, while the general run of mortals—and trolls and gods, too—didn't know them. Naturally, the spells would seem mysterious to them, just as the changing color of two combined chemicals was mysterious to anyone who didn't know chemistry. If he had only provided himself with a more elaborate knowledge of those laws instead of the useless flashlights, matches, and guns—

A tuneless whistle cut across his thoughts. It was Snögg, still beaming, carrying a great bundle of clothes and something long.

"Here clothes, lords," he grinned, the tendrils on his head writhing in a manner that no doubt indicated wellbeing, but which made Shea's skin crawl. "Here swords, too. I carry till we outside, yes?" He held up a length of light chain. "You put round wrists, I lead you. Anybody stop, I say going to Lord Surt."

"Hurry, Harald," said Heimdall as Shea struggled into the unfamiliar garments. "There is yet hope, though it grows dim, that we may reach the other Æsir before they give my sword away."

Shea was dressed. He and Heimdall took the middle and end of the chain, while Snögg tucked the other end in his belt and strode importantly before them, a huge sword in either hand. They were as big as Hundingsbana, but with plain hilts and rust-spotted blades. The troll carried them without visible effort.

Snögg opened the door at the end of the dungeon. "Now you keep quiet," he said. "I say I take you to Surt. Look down, you much abused."

One of the prisoner called softly. "Good luck go with you, friends, and do not forget us." Then they were outside, shambling along the gloom of the tunnel. Shea hunched his shoulders forward and assumed as discouraged an expression as he could manage.

They passed a recess in the tunnel wall, where sat four trolls. Their tridents leaned beside them, and they were playing the game of odds-and-evens with their fingers. One of the four got up and called out something in troll language. Snögg responded in the same tongue, adding: "Lord Surt want."

The troll looked dubious. "One guard not enough. Maybe they get away."

Snögg rattled the chain. "Not this. Spell on this chain. *Goinn almsorg thjalma.*"

The troll seemed satisfied with the explanation and returned to his sport. The three stumbled on through the dimness past a big room hewn out of the rock, full of murky light and motion. Shea jumped as someone—a man from the voice—screamed, a long, high scream that ended with gasps of "Don't...don't...don't." There was only a glimpse of what was going on, but enough to turn the stomach.

The passage ended in a ledge below which boiled a lake of molten lava. Beside the ledge sat a giant with one of the flaming swords. As he looked up, his eyes were pits beneath the eyebrow ridges.

Snögg said: "Prisoners go to Lord Surt. Orders."

"The giant peered at them. "Say," he said, "ain't you the troll Snögg? What happened to your nose?"

"'I pray Old Woman of Ironwood. She shrink him!" Snögg grinned.

"Okay, I guess it's all right." As they passed, the giant thrust a foot in front of Shea, who promptly stumbled over it, in sickening fear of going down into the lava. The giant thundered, "Haw, haw, haw!"

"You be careful," snapped Snögg. "You push prisoners in, Surt push you in, by Ymir."

"Haw, haw, haw! Gawan, Scalyface, before I push you in."

Shea picked himself up, giving the giant a look that should have melted lead at twenty paces. If he could remember that face and sometime—but, no, he was romancing. *Careful, Shea, don't let things go to your head.*

They turned from the ledge into another tunnel. This sloped up then leveled again where side tunnels branched in from several directions. Snögg picked his way unerringly through the maze. A tremendous banging grew on them, and they were passing the entrance of some kind of armory. The limits of the place were invisible in the flickering red glare, through which scuttled naked black things, like licorice dolls. Heimdall whispered: "These would be dark dwarfs from Svartalfheim, where no man nor As has ever been."

They went on, up, right, left. A sultry glow came down the tunnel ahead, as though a locomotive were approaching around the curve. There was a tramp of giant feet. Around the corner came a file of the monsters, each with a flaming sword, marching and looking straight ahead, like somnambulists. The three flattened themselves against the wall as the file tramped past, their stench filling the passage. The rearmost giant fell out and turned back.

"Prisoners to Lord Surt," said Snögg. The giant nodded, cleared his throat, and spat. Shea got it in the neck. He retched slightly and swabbed with the tail of his cloak as the giant grinned and hurried after the rest.

They were in the upper part of the stronghold now, moving through forests of pillars. Snögg abandoned his bold stride, put a finger to his lips and began to slide softly from pillar to pillar. The tread of a giant resounded somewhere near. All three squeezed themselves into a triangle of shadow behind a pillar. The footsteps waxed, stopping just on the opposite side, and all three held breath. They heard the giant hawk, then spit, and the little *splat!* on the floor. The footsteps moved off.

"Give me chain," whispered Snögg. He rolled it into a tight ball, and led the way, tiptoeing into another maze of passages. "This is way," he whispered, after a few minutes. "We wait till passage clear. Then I go make giant chase. Then you go, run fast. Then—ssst! Lie down on floor, quick!"

They fell flat at the word, next to the wall. Shea felt the floor vibrate beneath him to the tread of invisible giants. They were coming nearer, toward them, right over them, and the sound of their feet was almost drowned for Shea in the beating of his own heart. He shut his eyes. One of the giants rumbled heavily: "So I says to him, 'Whassa matter, ain'tcha got no guts?' And he says—" The rest of the remark was carried away.

The three rose and tiptoed. Snögg motioned them to stop, peering around a corner. Shea recognized the passage by which they had entered the place—how long before? Snögg took one more peek, turned and handed Shea one sword, giving the other to Heimdall. "When giant chase me," he whispered, "run; run fast. Dark outside. You hide."

"How will you find us?" asked Shea.

Snögg's grin was visible in the gloom. "Never mind. I find you all right. You bet." He was gone.

Shea and Heimdall waited. They heard a rumbling challenge from the sentry and Snögg's piping reply. A chain clanked, the sound suddenly drowned in a frightful roar. "Why, you snotty little—" Feet pounded into the night, and shoutings.

Shea and Heimdall raced for the entrance and out past the door, which swung ajar. It was blacker than the inside of a cow, except where dull-red glows lit the under sides of smoke plumes from vents in the cones. They headed straight out and away, Shea, at least, with no knowledge of where they were going. It would be time enough to think of direction later, anyway. They had to walk rather than run, even when their eyes had become accustomed to the gloom, and even so, narrowly missed a couple of bad falls on the fantastically contorted rock.

The huge cone of Surt's stronghold faded into the general blackness behind. Then there was a hiss in the dark and they were aware of Snögg's fishy body smell. The troll moved light and sure, like a cat. He was chuckling. "Hit giant in nose with chain. Should see face. He, he, he!"

"Whither do you lead us, troll?" asked Heimdall. "Where you want to go?"

Heimdall thought. "The best would be Sverre's house, the Crossroads of the World. Or failing that, the gates of Hell, where one may hope to find even yet the Wanderer at his task. He must know, soon as ever, what we have seen. That were a fortnight's journey afoot. But if I could get to some high cold place, where this fire magic is not, I could call my horse, Gold Top."

"Look out!" said Snögg suddenly. "Giants come!"

A flickering yellow light was showing across the lava beds. Snögg vanished into a patch of shadow, while Shea and Heimdall crouched under the edge of a dyke in the lava flow. They heard the crunch of giant feet on the basalt. The shadows swayed this way and that with the swinging of the fiery swords. A giant voice rumbled. "Hey, you, this is a rough section. There's enough pockets to hide fifty prisoners."

Another voice: "Okay, okay. I suppose we gotta poke around here all night. Me, I don't think they came this way, anyhow."

"You ain't supposed to think," retorted the first voice, nearer. "Hey, Raki!"

"Here," growled a third, more distant, giant.

"Don't get too far away," shouted the first.

"But the other guys are clear outta sight!" complained the distant Raki.

"That don't matter none. We gotta keep close together. Ouch!" The last was a yell, mixed with a thump and a scramble. "If I catch those scum, they'll pay for this."

The light from the nearest giant's sword grew stronger, creeping toward Shea and Heimdall inch by inch. The fugitives pressed themselves right through it. Inch by inch—

The giant was clearly visible around the end of the lava dyke, holding his sword high and moving slowly, peering into every hollow. Nearer came the light. Nearer. It washed over the toes of Shea's boots, then lit up Heimdall's yellow mane.

"Hey!" roared the giant in his foghorn bass. "Raki! Randver! I got 'em! Come, quick!" He rushed at a run. At the same time there was a thumping behind them and the nearest of the other two leaped up out of nowhere, swinging his sword in circles.

"Take that one, warlock!" barked Heimdall, pointing with his sword at the first of the two. He vaulted lightly to the top of the dyke and made for the second giant.

Shea hefted his huge blade with both hands. You simply couldn't fence with a crowbar like this. It was hopeless. But he wasn't afraid—hot dog, he wasn't afraid! What the hell, anyway? The giant gave a roar and a leap, whirling the fiery sword over his head in a figure eight to cut the little man down in one stroke.

Shea swung the ponderous weapon up in an effort to parry that downstroke. He never knew how, but in that instant the sword went as light as an amusement park cane. The blades met. With a tearing scream of metal Shea's sword sheared right through the flaming blade. The tip sailed over his head, landing with a crackle of flame in some brush behind. Almost without Shea's trying, his big blade swept around in a perfect stop-thrust in carte, and through the monster's throat. With a bubbling shriek the giant crashed to earth.

Shea spun around. Beyond the lip of the dyke Heimdall was hotly engaged with his big adversary, their blades flickering, but the third giant was coming up to take a part. Shea scrambled up on the dyke and ran toward him, surprised to discover he was shouting at the top of his voice.

The giant changed course and in no time was towering right over him. Shea easily caught the first slash, with a simple parry carte. The giant hesitated, irresolute; Shea saw his chance, whipped both blades around in a bind in octave, and lunged. The giant's flaming sword was pushed back against its owner, and Shea's point took him in the stomach with such a rush that Shea almost fell onto the collapsing monster's body.

"Ho, ho!" cried Heimdall. He was standing over his fallen opponent, terrible bloody slashes in the giant's body showing dim red in the light of the burning swords on the ground. "Through the guts! Never have I seen a man who used a sword as he would a spear, thrust and not strike. By Thor's hammer, Warlock Harald, I had not expected to find you so good a man of your hands! I have seen those do worse who were called berserks and champions." He laughed, and tossed his own sword up to catch it by the hilt. "Surely you shall be of my band at the *Time*. Though in the end it is nothing remarkable, seeing what blade you have there."

The big sword had become heavy again and weighted Shea's arm down. There was a trickle of blood up over the hilt onto his hand. "Looks like a plain sword to me," he said.

"By no means. That is the enchanted sword, Frey's invincible Hundingsbana, that shall one day be Surt's death. Hai! Gods and men will shout for this day; for the last of the war weapons of the Æsir is recovered! But we must hurry. Snögg!"

"Here," said the troll, emerging from a clump of tree ferns. "Forgot to say. I put troll spell on sword so light from blade don't show giants where we go. It wear off in a day or two."

"Can you tell us where there is a mountain tall and cold near here?" asked Heimdall.

"Is one—oh, many miles north. Called Steinnbjörg. Walk three days."

"That is something less than good news," said Heimdall. "Already we have reached the seventh night since Thor's play with the giants of Jötunheim. By the length of his journey the Wanderer should tomorrow be at the gates of Hell. We must seek him there; much depends on it."

Shea had been thinking furiously. If he knew enough to be a warlock, why not use the knowledge?

"Can I get hold of a few brooms?" he demanded.

"Brooms? Strange are your desires, warlock of another world," said Heimdall.

"What you want him for?" asked Snögg.

"I may be able to work a magic trick."

Snögg thought. "In thrall's house, two mile east, maybe brooms. Thrall he get sick, die."

"Lead on," said Shea.

They were off again through the darkness. Now and then they glimpsed a pinpoint of light in the distance, as some one of the other giant search parties moved about, but none approached them.

10

The thrall's hut proved a crazy pile of basalt blocks chinked with moss. The door sagged ajar. Inside it was too black to see anything.

"Snögg," asked Shea, "can you take a little of the spell off this sword so we can have some light?"

He held it out. Snögg ran his hands up and down the blade, muttering. A faint golden gleam came from it, revealing a pair of brooms in one corner of the single-room hut. One was fairly new, the other an ancient wreck with most of the willow twigs that had composed it broken or missing.

"Now," he said, "I need the feathers of a bird. Preferably a swift, as that's about the fastest flier. There ought to be some around."

"On roof, I think," said Snögg. "You wait; I get." He slid out, and they heard him grunting and scrambling up the hut. Presently he was back with a puff of feathers in his scaly hand.

Shea had been working out the proper spell in his head, applying both the Law of Contagion and the Law of Similarity. Now he laid the brooms on the floor and brushed them gently with the feathers, chanting:

> *Bird of the south, swift bird of the south,*
> *Lend us your wings for a night.*
> *Stir these brooms to movement, O bird of the south*
> *As swift as your own and as light.*

He tossed one of the feathers into the air and blew at it, so that it bobbed about without falling.

"Verdfölnir, greatest of hawks, I invoke you!" he cried. Catching the feather, he stooped, picking at the strings that held the broom till they were loosened, inserted the feathers in the broom, and made all tight again. Kneeling, he made what he hoped were mystic passes over the brooms, declaiming:

> *Up, up, arise!*
> *Bear us away;*
> *We must be in the mountains*
> *Before the new day.*

"Now," he said, "I think we can get to your Steinnbjörg soon enough."

Snögg pointed to the brooms, which in that pale light seemed to be stirring with a motion of their own. "You fly through air?" he inquired.

"With the greatest of ease. If you want to, I guess that new broom will carry two of us."

"Oh, no!" said Snögg, backing away. "No thank, by Ymir! I stay on ground, you bet. I go to Elvagevu on foot. Not break beautiful me. You not worry. I know way."

Snögg made a vague gesture of farewell and slipped out the door. Heimdall and Shea followed him, the latter with the brooms. The sky was beginning to show its first touch of dawn. "Now, let's see how these broomsticks of ours work," said Shea.

"What is the art of their use?" asked Heimdall.

Shea hadn't the least idea. But he answered boldly. "Just watch me and imitate me," he said, and squatting over his broom, with the stick between his legs and Hundingsbana stuck through his belt, said:

> *By oak, ash, and broom*
> *Before the night's gloom*
> *We soar to Steinnbjörgen*
> *To stay the world's doom.*

The broom leaped up under him with a jerk that almost left its rider behind. Shea gripped the stick till his knuckles were white. Up—up—up he went, till everything was blotted out in the damp opaqueness of cloud. The broom rushed on at a steeper and steeper angle, till Shea found to his horror that it was rearing over backward. He wound his legs around the stick and clung, while the broom hung for a second suspended at the top of its loop with Shea dangling beneath. It dived, then fell over sidewise, spun this way and that, with its passenger flopping like a bell clapper.

The dark earth popped out from beneath the clouds and rushed up at him. Just as he was sure he was about to crash, he managed to swing himself around the stick. The broom darted straight ahead at frightening speed, then started to nose up again. Shea inched forward to shift his weight. The broom slowed up, teetered to a forty-five degree angle and fell off into a spin. The black rock of Muspellheim whirled madly beneath. Shea leaned back, tugging up on the stick. The broom came out of it and promptly fell into another spin on the opposite side. Shea pulled it out of that, too, being careful not to give so much pressure this time. By now he was so dizzy he couldn't tell whether he was spinning or not.

For a few seconds the broom scudded along with a pitching motion like a porpoise with the itch. This was worse than Thor's chariot. Shea's stomach, always sensitive to such movements, failed him abruptly and he strewed Muspellheim with the remains of his last meal. Having accomplished this, he set himself grimly to the task of mastering his steed. He discovered that it had the characteristics of an airplane both longitudinally and laterally unstable. The moment it began to nose up, down, or sidewise the movement had to be corrected instantly and to just the right degree. But it could be managed.

A thin, drawn-out cry of "Haaar-aaald!" came to him. He had been so busy that he had had no time to look for Heimdall. A quarter mile to his right, the Sleepless One clung desperately to his broom, which was doing an endless series of loops, like an amusement park proprietor's dream of heaven.

Shea inched his own broom around a wide circuit. A hundred yards from Heimdall, the latter's mount suddenly stopped looping and veered straight at him. Heimdall seemed helpless to avoid the collision, but Shea managed to pull up at the last minute, and Heimdall, yellow hair streaming, shot past underneath. Shea brought his own broom around, to discover that Heimdall was in a flat spin.

As his face came toward Shea, the latter noted it looked paler than he had ever seen it. Then the As called: "How to control this thing, oh very fiend among warlocks?"

"Lean to your left!" shouted Shea. "When she dives, lean back far enough to level her out!" Heimdall obeyed, but overdid the lean-back and went into another series of loops. Shea yelled to shift his weight forward when the broom reached the bottom of the loop.

Heimdall overdid it again and took a wild downward plunge, but was grasping the principle of the thing and pulled out again. "Never shall we reach Odinn in time!" he shouted, pointing down. "Look, how already the hosts of Surt move toward Ragnarök!"

Shea glanced down at the tumbled plain. Sure enough, down there long files of giants were crawling over it, the flaming swords standing out like fiery particles against the black earth.

"Which way is this mountain?" he called back.

Heimdall pointed toward the left. "There is a high berg in that direction, I think; though still too strong is the fire magic for me to see clearly."

"Let's get above the clouds then. Ready?" Shea shifted back a little and they soared. Dark grayness gripped them, and he hoped he was keeping the correct angle. Then the gray paled to pearl, and they were out above an infinite sea of cloud, touched yellow by a rising sun.

Heimdall pointed. "Unquestionably the Steinnbjörg lies yonder. Let us speed!"

Shea looked. He could make out nothing but one more roll of cloud, perhaps a little more solid than the others. They streaked toward it.

"There must be an arresting!" cried Heimdall. "How do you stop this thing?" They had tried three times to land on the peak; each time the brooms had skimmed over the rocks at breathless speed.

"I'll have to use a spell," replied Shea. He swung back, chanting:

> *By oak, ash, and yew*
> *And heavenly dew,*
> *We've come to Steinnbjörgen;*
> *Land softly and true!*

The broomstick slowed down, and Shea fishtailed it into an easy landing. Heimdall followed, but plowed deep into a snowdrift. He struggled out with hair and eyebrows all white, but with a literally flashing smile on his face. "Warlocks there have been, Harald, but never like you. I find your methods somewhat drastic."

"If you don't want that broom any more," Shea retorted, "I'll take it and leave this old one. I can use it."

"Take it, if it pleases your fancy. But now you, too, shall see a thing." He put both hands to his mouth and shouted. "Yo hoooo! *Gulltop!* Yo hooooo, *Gulltop!* Your master, Heimdall Odinnsson, calls!"

For a while nothing happened. Then Shea became aware of a shimmering, polychromatic radiance in the air about him. A rainbow was forming and he in the center of it. But unlike most rainbows, this one was end-on. It extended slowly down to the very snow at their feet; the colors thickened and grew solid till they blotted out the snow and clouds and crags behind them. Down the rainbow came trotting a gigantic white horse with a mane of bright metallic yellow. The, animal stepped off the rainbow and nuzzled Heimdall's chest.

"Come," said Heimdall. "I grant you permission to ride with me, though you will have to sit behind. Mind you do not prick him with Hundingsbana."

Shea climbed aboard with his baggage of sword and broom. The horse whirled around and bounded onto the rainbow. It galloped fast, with a long reaching stride, but almost no sound, as though it were running across an endless feather bed. The wind whistled past Shea's ears with a speed he could only guess.

After an hour or two Heimdall turned his head. "Sverre's house lies below the clouds; I can see it."

The rainbow inclined downward, disappearing through the gray. For a moment they were wrapped in mist again, then out, and the rainbow, less vivid but still substantial enough to bear them, curved direct to the bonder's gate.

Goldtop stamped to a halt in the yard, slushy with melting snow. Heimdall leaped off and toward the door, where a couple of stalwart blonds stood on guard.

"Hey," called Shea after him. "Can't I get something to eat?"

"Time is wanting," shouted the Sleepless One over his shoulder, disappearing through the door, to return in a moment with horn and sword. He spoke a word or two to the men at the door, who ran around the house, and presently were visible leading out horses of their own.

"Heroes from Valhall," explained Heimdall, buckling on his baldric, "set to guard the Gjallarhorn while the negotiations for my release were going on." He snatched up the horn and vaulted to the saddle. The rainbow had changed direction, but lay straight away before them as Goldtop sprang into his stride again.

Shea asked: "Couldn't you just blow your horn now without waiting to see Odinn?"

"Not so, Warlock Harald. The Wanderer is lord of gods and men. None act without his permission. But I fear me it will come late—late." He turned his head. "Hark! Do you, hear—Nay, you cannot. But my ears catch a sound which tells me the dog Garm is loose, that great monster."

"Why does it take Odinn so long to get to Hell?" said Shea, puzzled "He goes in disguise, as you saw him on the moor, riding a common pony. The spae-wife Grua is of the giant brood. Be sure she would refuse to advise him, or give him ill advice, did she recognize him as one of the Æsir."

Gold Top was up out of the clouds, riding the rainbow that seemed to stretch endlessly before. Shea could think only how many steaks one could get from the huge animal. He had never eaten horseflesh, but in his present mood was willing to try.

The sun was already low when they pierced the cloud-banks again. This time they dropped straight into swirls of snow. Beneath and then around them Shea could make out a ragged, gloomy landscape of sharp black pinnacles, too steep to gather drifts.

The rainbow ended abruptly, and they were on a rough road that wound among the rock towers. Gold Top's hoofs clop-clopped sharply on frozen mud. The road wound tortuously, always downward into a great gorge, which reared up pillars and buttresses on either side. Snowflakes sank vertically through the still air around them, feathering the forlorn little patches of moss that constituted the only vegetation. Cold tore at them like a knife. Enormous icicles, like the trunks of elephants, were suspended all around. There was no sound but the tread of the horse and his quick breathing, which condensed in little vapor plumes around his nostrils.

Darker and darker it grew, colder and colder. Shea whispered—he did not know why, except that it seemed appropriate— "Is this Hell of yours a cold place?"

"The coldest in the nine worlds," said Heimdall. "Now you shall pass me up the great sword, that I may light our way with it."

Shea did so. Ahead, all he could see over Heimdall's shoulder now was blackness, as though the walls of the gorge had shut them in above. Shea put out one hand as they scraped one wall of the chasm, then jerked it back. The cold of the rock bit through his mitten into his fingers like fire.

Gold Top's ears pricked forward in the light from the sword. They rounded a corner, and came suddenly on a spark of life in that gloomy place, lit by an eerie blue-green phosphorescence. Shea could make out in that half-light the tall, slouch-hatted figure of the Wanderer, and his pony beside him. There was a third figure, cloaked and hooded in black, its face invisible.

Odinn looked toward them as they approached. "Hai, Muginn brought me tidings of your captivity and your escape. The second was the better news," said the sonorous voice.

Heimdall and Shea dismounted. The Wanderer looked sharply at Shea. "Are you not that lost one I met near the crossroads?" he asked.

"It is none other," put in Heimdall, "and a warlock of power is he, as well as the briskest man with sword that ever I saw. He is to be of my band. We have Hundingsbana and Head. Have you won that for which you came?"

"Enough, or near enough. Myself and Vidarr are to stand before the Sons of the Wolf, those dreadful monsters. Thor shall fight the Worm; Frey, Surt. Ullr and his men are to match the hill giants and you the frost giants, as already I knew."

"Allfather, you are needed. The dog Garm is loose and Surt is bearing the flaming sword from the south with the frost giants at his back. The *Time* is here."

"Aieeee!" screeched the black-shrouded figure. "I know ye now, Odinn! Woe the day that my tongue—"

"Silence, hag!" The deep voice seemed to fill that desolate place with thunder. "Blow, son of mine, then. Rouse our bands, for it is *Time*."

"Aieeee!" screeched the figure again. "Begone, accursed ones, to whatever place from whence ye came!" A hand shot out, and Shea noticed with a prickling of the scalp that it was fleshless. The hand seized a sprinkle of snow and threw it at Odinn. He laughed.

"Begone!" shrieked the spae-wife, throwing another handful of snow, this time at Heimdall. His only reply was to set the great horn to his lips and take a deep breath.

"Begone, I say!" she screamed again. Shea had a bloodcurdling glimpse of a skull under the hood as she scooped up the third handful of snow. "To whatever misbegotten place ye came from!" The first notes of the roaring trumpet sang and swelled and filled all space in a tremendous peal of martial, triumphant music. The rocks shook, and the icicles cracked, and Harold Shea saw the third handful of snow, a harmless little damp clot, flying at him from Grua's bony fingers...

"Well," said the detective, "I'm sorry you can't help me out no more than that, Dr. Chalmers. We gotta notify his folks in St. Louis. We get these missing-person cases now and then, but we usually find 'em. You'll get his things together, will you?"

"Certainly, certainly," said Reed Chalmers. "I thought I'd go over the papers now."

"Okay. Thanks. Miss Mugler, I'll send you a report with my bill."

"But," said Gertrude Mugler, "I don't want a report! I want Mr. Shea!"

The detective grinned. "You paid for a report, whether you want it or not. You can throw it away. So long. Bye, Dr. Chalmers. Bye, Mr. Bayard. Be seein' you." The door of the room closed.

Walter Bayard, lounging in Harold Shea's one good armchair, asked: "Why didn't you tell him what you think really happened?"

Chalmers replied: "Because it would be—shall I say—somewhat difficult to prove. I do not propose to make myself a subject of public ridicule."

Gertrude said: "That wasn't honest of you, Doctor. Even if you won't tell me, you might at least—"

Bayard wiggled an eyebrow at the worried girl. "Heh, heh. Who was indignantly denying that Harold might have run away from her maternal envelopment, when the detective asked her just now?"

Gertrude snapped: "In the first place it wasn't so, and in the second it was none of his damn business, and in the third I think you two might at least cooperate instead of obstructing, especially since I'm paying for Mr. Johnson's services!"

"My dear Gertrude," said Chalmers, "if I thought it had the slightest chance of doing any good, I should certainly acquaint your Mr. Johnson with my hypothesis. But I assure you that he would decline to credit it, and even if he did, the theory would present no—uh—point of application for his investigatory methods."

"Something in that, Gert," said Bayard. "You can prove the thing in one direction, but not the reverse. If Shea can't get back from where we think he's gone, it's a cinch that Johnson couldn't. So why send Johnson after him?" He sighed. "It'll be a little queer without Harold, for all his—"

Wham! The outward rush of displaced air bowled Chalmers over, whipped a picture from the wall with a crash of glass, and sent the pile of Shea's papers flying. There may have been minor damage as well.

If there was, neither Gertrude nor Chalmers nor Bayard noticed it. In the middle of the room stood the subject of their talk, swathed in countless yards of blanket-like woolen garments. His face was tanned and slightly chapped. In his left hand he held a clumsy broom of willow twigs.

"Hiya," said Shea, grinning at their expressions. "You three had dinner yet? Yeah? Well, you can come along and watch me eat." He tossed the broom in a corner. "Souvenir to go with my story. Useful while it lasted, but I'm afraid it won't work here."

"B-but," stammered Chalmers, "you aren't going out to a restaurant in those garments?"

"Hell, yes! I'm hungry."

"What will people think?"

"What do I care?"

"God bless my soul," exclaimed Chalmers, and followed Shea out.

The Mathematics of Magic
by L. Sprague de Camp & Fletcher Pratt
Unknown, October 1940

"Steak," said Harold Shea.

"Porterhouse, sirloin—?" asked the waitress.

"Both, so long as they're big and rare."

"Harold," said Gertrude Mugler, "whatever this is all about, please be careful of your diet. A large protein intake for a man who doesn't do physical labor—"

"Physical labor!" barked Shea. "The last meal I had was twenty-four hours ago, and it was a little dish of oatmeal mush. Sour, too. Since then I've fought a duel with a couple of giants, done acrobatics on a magic broomstick, had a ride on a god's enchanted brewery-horse— Well, anyway, I've been roasted and frozen and shaken and nearly scared to death, and by Thor's hammer I want food!"

"Harold, are you—are you feeling well?"

"Fine, toots. Or I will be when I surround some grub." He turned to the waitress again: "Steak!"

"Listen, Harold," persisted Gertrude. "Don't! You pop out of nowhere in that crazy costume; you talk wildly about things you couldn't expect anyone to believe—"

"You don't have to believe I popped out of nowhere, either," said Shea.

"Then can't you tell me what's wrong?"

"Nothing's wrong, and I'm not going to talk about it until I've consulted Dr. Chalmers."

"Well," said Gertrude, "if that's your attitude—come on, Walter, let's go to a movie."

"But," bleated Walter Bayard, "I want to listen—"

"Oh, be a gentleman for once in your life!"

"Oh, all right, Gert." He leered back at Shea as he went. "Anyway you didn't bring back any dream-girls."

Shea grinned after them. "There goes the guy who used to kid me about how Gert had gotten the psychological jump on me," he said to Chalmers. "I hope she rides herd on him."

Reed Chalmers smiled faintly. "You forget—uh—Walter's infallible defense mechanism."

"What's that?"

"When the pressure becomes too great, he can simply go to sleep on her."

Shea gave a suppressed snort. "You know not what you—ah, food!" He attacked his plate, working his mouth around a piece of steak big enough to choke a horse; with effort, like a snake engulfing a toad. An expression of pure bliss spread over his face as he chewed. Chalmers noted that his colleague ignored the fact that half the restaurant was staring at the tableaux of a long-faced young man in baggy Norse woolens.

"A—uh—somewhat less rapid rate of ingestion—" Chalmers began.

Shea shook a finger, gulped down his mouthful, and spoke: "Don't worry about me." Between mouthfuls he told his story.

Reed Chalmers' mild eyes bugged as he watched and listened to his young friend. "Good gracious! That's the third of those steaks, somewhat inadequately called small. You'll—uh—render yourself ill."

"This is the last one. Hey, waitress! May I please have an apple pie? Not just a segment; I want a whole pie." He turned back to Chalmers. "So the spook said, 'Go on back to where you came from,' and here I am!"

Chalmers mused: "While I have known you, Harold, to commit venial sins of rhetorical exaggeration incompatible with true scientific accuracy, I have never known you to engage in deliberate fabrication. So I believe you. The general alteration in your appearance and bearing furnishes persuasive corroboration."

"Have I changed?" asked Shea.

"You show the effects of physical hardship, as well as exposure to the sun and wind."

"That all?"

Chalmers pondered: "You would like me to say, would you not, that your air of self-conscious brashness has been replaced by one of legitimate self-confidence?"

"Well—uh..."

Chalmers continued: "Those conscious of shortcomings are always eager to be informed of radical improvement. Actually such improvements, when they occur at all in an adult, take place slowly. No miraculous change is to be expected in a couple of weeks." He twinkled at Shea's discomfort, and added: "I will admit that you seem to show some alteration of personality, and I think in the right direction."

The Mathematics of Magic

Shea laughed. "At least I learned to appreciate the value of theory. If you'd been along we'd really have gotten somewhere in applying the screwy laws of the world of Scandinavian myth."

"I—" Chalmers stopped.

"What?"

"Nothing."

"Of course," said Shea, "you'd never have stood the physical end of it."

Chalmers sighed. "I suppose not."

Shea went on: "It checked your theory of paraphysics all right. In that universe the laws of similarity and contagion held good—at least, the magic spells I figured out with their help worked."

Chalmers brushed his gray mop out of his eyes. "Amazing! I asserted that the transfer of the physical body, to another spacetime frame by symbolic logic—what did you call it? A syllogismobile!—was possible. But it is a shock to have so—uh—far-fetched a deduction confirmed by experimental proof."

Shea said: "Sure, we've got something all right. But what are we going to do with it?"

Chalmers frowned. "It is rather obscure. Presents a whole new world-picture, unlike anything but some of the Oriental religions. An infinity of universes, moving along parallel but distinct space-time vectors. But, as you put it, what can be done with it? If I publish the results of your experiment they'll simply say poor old Chalmers has...uh...a tile loose, and in any case an experimental psychologist has no business venturing into physics. Think of Oliver Lodge!" He shuddered. "The only satisfactory proof would be to send some of the doubters to another universe. Unfortunately, we could hardly count on their encountering Grua with a handful of enchanted snow. They would be unable to return, and the doubters left behind would be doubters still. You perceive the difficulty."

"Huh-uh. Wonder how the fight came out? It might be worth while going back to see."

"It would be inadvisable. The Ragnarök was only beginning when you left. You might return to find the giants had won and were in charge. If you wish adventure, there are plenty of other and less—" The voice trailed off.

"Other what?"

"Well, perhaps nothing of importance. I was about to say—systematic attainable universes. Since you left I have been engaged in the development of the structural theory of a multiple-universe cosmology, and—"

Shea interrupted. "Listen, Dr. Chalmers. We both know too much psychology to kid each other. Something's eating you besides paraphysical mathematics."

"Harold"—Chalmers gave a sigh—"I've always maintained that you'd make a better...uh...salesman or politician than psychologist. You're weak on theory, but in offhand, rule-of-thumb diagnosis of behavior patterns, you are incomparable."

"Don't evade, Doctor."

"Very well. Were you perhaps thinking of making another journey soon?"

"Why, I just got back and haven't had time to think. Say! You aren't suggesting you'd like to go along, are you?"

Reed Chalmers rolled a fragment of bread into a precise gray pill. "As a matter of fact that's what I was suggesting, Harold. Here I am, fifty-six years old, without family or intimate friends—except you young men of the Garaden Institute. I have made—or believe I have—the greatest cosmological discovery since Copernicus, yet its nature is such that it cannot be proved, and no one will credit it without the most exhaustive proof." He shrugged slightly. "My work is done, but to a result that will afford me no appreciation in this world. May I not...uh...be permitted the foible of seeking a fuller life elsewhere?"

Back in Shea's room and seated in the best arm chair, Chalmers stretched his legs and meditatively sipped a highball. "I'm afraid your suggestion of Cuchulainn's Ireland does not meet with my approval. An adventurous life, no doubt—but culturally a barbarism, with an elaborate system of taboos, violations of which are punished by the removal of heads."

"But the girls—" protested Shea. "Those piano-legged Scowegian blondes—they all reminded me of Gertrude—"

"For a person of my age amorous adventure has few attractions. And as my partner in this enterprise I must ask you to remember that while you have...uh...certain physical skills that would be useful anywhere, I am limited to fields where intellectual attainments would be of more value than in ancient Ireland. The only non-warriors who got anywhere in those days were minstrels—and I can neither compose lays nor play the harp."

Shea grinned maliciously. "All right, you leave the girls to me, then. But I guess you're right; we'll have to drop Queen Maev and Ossian." He peered around the bookshelves. "How about this?"

Chalmers examined the volume he handed down. "Spenser's *Faerie Queene*. Mm-m-m—'vision unrolled after vision to the sound of varying music,' as Dr. Johnson said. Certainly a brilliant and interesting world, and one in which I personally might have some place. But I am afraid we should find it uncomfortable if we landed in the latter half of the story, where Queen Gloriana's knights are having a harder time, as though Spenser were growing discouraged, or the narrative for some reason was escaping from his hands, taking on a life of its own. I'm not sure we could exercise the degree of selectivity needed to get into the story at the right point. After all, in your last experience, you attempted Ireland and arrived in Scandinavian myth."

"But," protested Shea, "if you're going adventuring you can't avoid—" and then stopped, his mouth open.

"You were about to say 'danger,' were you not?" said Chalmers, with a smile. "I confess—"

Shea got to his feet. "Doctor...Doc—" he burst out. "Listen: why shouldn't we jump right into that last part of the *Faerie Queene* and help Gloriana's knights straighten things out? You said you had worked out some new angles. We ought to be better than anyone else in the place. Look what I was able to do in the Ragnarök with the little I know!"

"You are immodest, Harold," replied Chalmers, but he was leaning forward. "Still, it is an...uh...attractive plan; to look in another world for the achievement denied in this. Suppose you fill my glass again while we consider details."

"Well, the first detail I'd like to know something about is what new wrinkles in theory you have in mind."

Chalmers settled himself and took on his lecture-room manner. "As I see it, our universes have a relation analogous to that of a pencil of parallel vectors," said he. "The vectors themselves represent time, of course. That gives us a six-dimensional cosmos—three in space, one in time, and two which define the relationships of one universe of the cosmos to another.

"You know enough mathematics to be aware that the 'fourth dimension,' so called, is only a dimension in the sense of a measurable quality, like color or density. The same applies for the interuniversal dimensions. I maintain—"

"Whoa!" said Shea. "Is there an infinite number of universes?"

"Ahem—I wish you would learn to avoid interruptions, Harold. I used to believe so. But now I consider the number finite, though very large.

"Let me continue. I maintain that what we call 'magic' is merely...the physics of some of these other universes. This physics is capable of operating along the interuniversal dimensions—"

"I see," Shea interrupted again. "Just as light can operate through interplanetary space, but sound requires some such conducting medium as air or water."

"The analogy is not perfect. Let me continue. You know how the theme of conjuring things up and making them disappear constantly recurs in fairy tales. These phenomena become plausible if we assume the enchanter is snatching things from another universe or banishing them to one."

Shea said: "I see an objection. If the laws of magic don't operate in the conducting medium of our universe, how's it possible to learn about them? I mean, how did they get into fairy stories?"

"The question is somewhat obvious. You remember my remarking that dements suffered hallucinations because their personalities were split between this universe and another? The same applies to the composers of fairy stories, though to a lesser degree. Naturally, it would apply to any writer of fantasy, such as Dunsany or Hubbard. When he describes some strange world, he is offering a somewhat garbled version of a real one, having its own set of dimensions quite independent of ours."

Shea sipped his highball in silence. Then he asked: "Why can't we conjure things into and out of this universe?"

"We can. You successfully conjured yourself out of this one. But it is probable that certain of these parallel universes are easier of access than others. Ours—"

"Would be one of the hard kind?"

"Ahem. Don't interrupt, please. Yes. Now as to the time dimension, I'm inclined to think we can travel among universes only at right angles to the pencil of space-time vectors, if you follow my use of a...a somewhat misleading analogy.

"However, it appears likely that our vectors are curved. A lapse of time, along the inner side of the curve would correspond to a greater lapse of time along the outer. You know the theme in certain fairy tales—the hero comes to fairyland, spends three days, and returns to find he has been gone three minutes or three years.

"The same feature would account for the possibility of landing in someone's imagined idea of the future. This is clearly a case where a mind has been running along one of the outer curved vectors at a speed which has outstripped the passage of time along our own inner side of the curve. The result—Harold, are you following me?"

Shea's highball glass had rolled onto the rug with a gentle *plunk*, and the suspicion of a snore came from his chair. Fatigue had caught up with him at last.

Next weekend, Harold Shea went up to Cleveland. He was approaching this second time-journey with some misgivings. Chalmers was an astute old bird—no doubt about that. A good theorist. But it was the pursuit of the theory rather than its result that interested the old boy. How would he work out as a companion in a life of arduous adventure—a man of fifty-six, who had always led a sedentary life, and for that matter, who always seemed to prefer discussion to experience—

Well, too late to pull out now, Shea told himself, as he entered the shop of the Montrose Costume Co. He asked to see medieval stuff. A clerk, who seemed to think that the word "medieval" had something to do with pirates, finally produced an assortment of doublets and hose, feathered hats, and floppy boots of thin yellow leather. Shea selected a costume that had once been worn by the leading man in De Koven's *Robin Hood*. It had no pockets, but a tailor could be found to remedy that. For Chalmers, he bought a similar but plainer outfit, with a monkish robe and attached hood. Chalmers was to go as a palmer, or pilgrim, a character which both felt would give him some standing.

The costume company's assortment of arms and armor proved not only phony but impractical. The chain mail was knitted woolens dipped in aluminum paint. The plate was sheets of tin-can thinness. The swords had neither edge, balance, nor temper. The antique shops had nothing better; their antique weapons were mostly Civil War cavalry sabers. Shea decided to use his own fencing epee. It had a rather stiff blade, and if he unscrewed the point d'arrêt, ground the end down to a sharp point, and contrived some kind of sheath, the weapon would do till he got something better.

The most serious question, as he explained to Chalmers on his return, was concern with the formulas of the magic they intended to use on their arrival. "How do you expect to read English in the land of Faerie when I couldn't in Scandinavia?" he demanded.

"I've allowed for that," Chalmers replied. "You forget that mathematics is a...a universal language, independent of words."

"All right. But will your mathematical symbols mean the same things?"

"Glance at this sheet, Harold. Knowing the principles of symbolic logic to begin with, I can look over this pictured equation with an apple at the left and a great many apples at the right, and thus realize it means that an apple belongs to the class of apples. From that I shall infer that the horseshoe-shaped symbol in the center means 'is a member of the class of.'"

"You think that'll work, honest? But, say, how do we know that you and I will land in the same part of the Faerie world?"

Chalmers shrugged. "For that matter, how do we know we shan't land in Greek mythology? There are still laws of this method of transference to be worked out. We can only hold on to each other, read the formulas in chorus, and hope for the best."

Shea grinned. "And if it doesn't work, what the hell! Well, I guess we're ready." He inhaled deeply. "If P equals not-Q, Q implies not-P, which is equivalent to saying either P or Q but not both. But if not-P is not implied by not-Q— Come in, Mrs. Ladd."

Shea's landlady opened the door, and opened her mouth to say something. But the something failed to come forth. She stared agape at a pair of respectable psychologists, standing side by side in medieval costumes, with rucksacks on their shoulders. They were holding hands and with their free hands holding sheets of paper. Chalmers purpled with embarrassment.

Shea bowed easily. "We're doing an experiment, Mrs. Ladd. We may be away for some time. If Mr. Bayard asks for us, let him in and tell him he can look at the papers in the top right-hand drawer. And you might mail this letter. Thanks." He explained to Chalmers: "It's to Gert; to tell her not to waste her money by setting Johnson after us."

"But, Mr. Shea—" said the landlady.

"Please, Mrs. Ladd. You can sit down and watch if you like. Let's go, Doctor—a conclusion can be drawn concerning the relation between two classes even if the evidence refers only to a part of some third class to which both are related. Whatever is predicated affirmatively or negatively of a class may be predicated in like manner of everything asserted to be contained in that class—"

Mrs. Ladd watched, ample bosom heaving. Her eyes bulged from her head; she'd have material for backfence conversation for months to come.

Pfimp! There was a movement of air, muttering the papers on the table and whirling ashes from the ash trays. Mrs. Ladd, pulling herself together, moved a trembling hand through the space where her strangely dressed lodgers had stood.

It met no resistance.

2

Chalmers spoke first. "Astounding! I should have thought the passage more difficult."

"Uh-huh." Shea looked around, sniffing the air with his head up. "Looks like a plain forest to me. Not as cold as the last one, thank God."

"I...I suppose so. Though I'm sure I don't know what type of tree that is."

"I'd say some kind of eucalyptus," replied Shea. "That would mean a warm, dry climate. But look where the sun is. That means late afternoon, so we better get started."

"Dear me, I suppose so. Which direction would you suggest?"

"Dunno, but I can find out." Shea dropped his rucksack and swarmed up the nearest tree. He called down: "Can't see much. No, wait, there's a slope off that direction." He waved an arm, almost lost his footing, and slid down again in a small torrent of bark and leaves.

They started toward the slope in the hope that it represented a river valley, where they could expect to find human habitations. After half a mile a scraping sound halted him wordlessly. They crept forward, peering. A tall, spotted buck was rubbing its horns against a tree. It flung up its head as it heard them, gave a sneeze-like snort, and leaped gracefully away.

Shea said: "If he's just getting rid of his velvet, it ought to be late summer or early fall."

"I wasn't aware you were so much of a woodsman, Harold."

"What the hell, Doc...Doctor, I've been having practice. What's that?"

Something far off had gone *"Ow-ooh,"* a sort of musical grunt, as though somebody had casually scraped the C string of a cello.

Chalmers fingered his chin. "It sounds remarkably like a lion. I trust we need not expect to encounter lions in this country."

The noise came again, louder. "Don't bet on it, Doctor," said Shea. "If you remember your Spenser, there were plenty of lions around; also camels, bears, wolves, leopards, and aurochs, as well as human fauna like giants and Saracens. Not to mention the Blatant Beast, which had the worst qualities of all and slandered people besides. What worries me is whether lions can climb trees."

"Merciful Heavens! I don't know about lions, but I'm afraid I shouldn't be equal to much climbing. Let's hurry."

They strode on through the wood, a wood of open glades with little underbrush and no recognizable paths. A little breeze came up to make the leaves whisper overhead. The coughing roar of the lion came again, and Shea and Chalmers, without realizing, stepped up their pace to a trot. They glanced at each other and slowed down again.

Chalmers puffed: "It's good for a man of my age to have a little...uh...exercise like this."

Shea grinned with one side of his mouth. They came out onto the edge of a meadow that stretched a couple of hundred yards downhill. At the bottom of the valley, more trees evidently concealed a stream. Shea scrambled up another tree for a look. Beyond the stream and its wide, shallow vale stood a castle, small in the distance and yellow in the low sun, with pennants writhing lazily from its turrets. He called down the news.

"Can you make out the devices on any of the pennants?" Chalmers answered. "I was...I am...not altogether inexpert in matters of heraldry. It might be wise to learn something of the character of the institution."

"Not a damn thing," said Shea, and swung himself down. "Air's too quiet and she's too far away. Anyhow, I'd rather take a chance on the castle than on being part of a lion's breakfast. Let's go."

In the tone of an announcer offering the express for East Chicago, Laporte, and South Bend on Track 18, a voice cried at them: "Who would enter Castle Caultrock?"

There was nobody in sight, but the travelers' eyes caught a flash of metal on one of the projecting balconies where the drawbridge chains entered the wall. Shea shouted hack the rehearsed answer: "Travelers, to wit, Harold Shea, gentleman and squire, and Reed Chalmers, palmer!" *Wonder what they'd say about the "gentleman," thought Shea, if they knew my father was head bookkeeper of a meat-packing concern?*

The answer floated back: "This is a castle of deeds and ladies. The holy palmer may enter in the name of God, but no gentleman unless he be accompanied by his fair dame, for such is the custom of this place."

Shea and Chalmers looked at each other. The latter was smiling happily. "Perfect selectivity!" he murmured. "This is exactly right; right at the beginning of Spenser's fourth book—" His voice trailed off and his face fell. "I don't quite know what to do about your being left out—"

"Go ahead in. I've slept in the open before."

"But—" Just then a movable section in the bars of the portcullis creaked outward, and a man in armor stumbled through, apparently pushed from behind. There was a shout of derisive laughter. A horse was squeezed through the opening behind. The man took the reins and came toward them. He was a small man with close-cropped hair. A scar intersected one corner of a mouth drawn into a doleful expression.

"Hi," said Shea. "Did they throw you out?"

"I hight Hardimour. Aye; it is even the hour of vespers, and being ladyless I am put forth from the fair entertainment within." He smiled wryly. "And what hight you? Nay, tell me not now; for I see my dinner and bed approach, mounted on the back of a jennet."

The travelers turned to follow Hardimour's eyes behind them. Across the even meadow came a pair of horses, bearing an armored knight and his lady. The latter rode sidesaddle, clad in rich garments of a trailing, impractical kind.

The little knight vaulted to his saddle with a lightness that was surprising, considering the weight of his hardware. He shouted, "Defend yourself, knight, or yield me your lady!" and snapped down his visor with a clang.

The smaller horse, with the woman, swung to one side. Shea gave a low whistle as he got a look at her: a slim, pale girl, with features as perfect as a cameo, and delicately rounded eyebrows. The other rider, without a word, whipped a cloth covering from his shield, revealing a black field on which broken spear points were picked out with silver. He swung a big black lance into position.

Heads appeared along the battlements of the castle. Shea felt Chalmers pluck at his sleeve. "That Sir Hardimour is in for trouble," said the older psychologist. "Sable, semé of broken spears is the bearing of Britomart."

Shea was watching the knights, who had spurred their horses to a heavy gallop. *Wham!* went lances against shields, and there were sparks in the fading light. The head of the little knight from the castle went back, his feet came up, and he turned a somersault through the air. He landed on his head with the sound of thirty feet of chain being dropped on a manhole cover.

The stranger knight reined in and brought his horse back at a walk. Shea, followed by Chalmers, ran to where Sir Hardimour sprawled. The little knight seemed to be out cold. As Shea fumbled with unfamiliar fingers at his helmet fastenings, he sat up groggily and helped get it off. He drew in a long breath.

"By'r Lady," he remarked with a rueful grin, "I have stood before Blandamour of the Iron Arm, but that was as rude a dint as ever I took." He looked up as the knight who had overthrown him approached. "It seems I was too ambitious. To whom do I owe the pleasure of a night with the crickets?"

The other pulled up his visor to reveal a fresh young face. "Certes," he said in a light, high-pitched voice, "you are a very gentle person, young sir, and shall not spend a night with the crickets and bug-bears if I can help it. Ho, warder!"

The castle guard's head came through the gate in the portcullis. "Your worship," he said.

"Have I fairly gained admittance to Castle Caultrock as the knight of this lady?"

"That is most true."

The knight of the shivered spears on their field of black put both hands up to his own helmet and lifted it off. A sunburst of golden hair burst forth and flowed down to his—her—waist. Behind him Shea heard Chalmers chuckle, "I told you it was Britomart." He remembered that Britomart was the warrior girl who could beat most of the men in the *Faerie Queene*.

She was speaking: "Then I declare I am the lady of this good knight who has been overthrown, and since he has a lady he may enter."

The warder looked worried and scratched his chin. "The point is certainly very delicate. If you are her knight—and yet his lady—how can she be your lady and he your knight? Marry I warrant me this is a case Sir Artegall himself could not unravel. Enter, all three!"

Shea spoke up: "Beg pardon, miss, but I wonder if I could arrange to go in as your friend's man?"

"That you may not, sir," she replied haughtily. "She shall be no man's lady till I restore her to her husband; for this is that Lady Amoret who was foully stolen from her spouse's arms by Busyrane, the enchanter. If you wish to be her knight, you must even try Sir Hardimour's fate against me."

"Hm-m-m," said Shea. "But you're going in as Sir Hardimour's lady?" They nodded. He turned to the latter. "If I had a horse and all the fixings, Sir Knight, I'd fight you for the privilege of being Miss Britomart's man. But as it is I'll challenge you to a round on foot with swords and without armor."

Hardimour's scarred face registered an astonishment that changed to something like pleasure. "Now, that is a strange sort of challenge—" he began.

"Yet not unheard of," interrupted the statuesque Britomart. "I mind me that Sir Artegall fought thus against three brothers at the Ford of Thrack."

Chalmers was plucking at Shea's sleeve again. "Harold, I consider it most unwise—"

"*Shh!* I know what I'm doing. Well, Sir Knight, how about it?"

"Done." Sir Hardimour unbuckled himself from his chrysalis of steel. He stepped forward, his feet feeling uncertainly on the smooth grass which he was used to crossing in metal shoes.

Hardimour stamped and swung his sword a couple of times in both hands. He shifted it to one and moved toward Shea. Shea waited quietly, balancing the epee. Hardimour made a couple of tentative cuts at Shea, who parried easily. Then, feeling surer of his footing, Hardimour stepped forward nimbly, swinging his sword up for a real clash. Shea straightened his arm and lunged, aiming for Hardimour's exposed forearm. He missed, and jumped back before the knight's sword came down, gleaming red in the setting sun.

As the blade descended, Shea flipped it aside with a parry in carte, being careful not to let the heavy blade meet his thin epee squarely. Hardimour tried again, a forehand cut at Shea's head. Shea ducked under it and pricked Hardimour's arm before he could recover. Shea heard Chalmers' quick intake of breath and an encouraging word from Britomart, "Bravely done, oh, bravely!"

Hardimour came on again, swinging. Shea parried, lunged, missed again, but held his lunge and drilled the knight's arm properly with a remise. The slim steel needle went through the muscles like butter. Britomart clapped her hands.

Shea withdrew his blade and recovered, keeping the epee flickering between them. "Had enough?" he asked.

"By God's wounds, no!" gritted Hardimour. The sleeve of his shirt was turning dark red, and he was sweating, but he looked thoroughly grim. He swung the sword up in both hands, wincing slightly. The epee flickered out and ripped his now-dripping shirtsleeve. He checked, and held his sword out in front of him, trying to imitate Shea's fencing position. Shea tapped it ringingly a couple of times, gathered it up in a bind in octave, and lunged. Hardimour saved himself by stumbling backward. Shea followed him. *Flick, flick, flick* went the thin blade, Hardimour's eyes following it in fearful fascination. He tried to parry the repeated thrust, but could no longer control his big blade. Shea forced him back zigzag, got him into the position he wanted, feinted, and lunged. He stopped his point just as it touched the smaller man's chest. Hardimour put a foot back, but found no support. His arms went up, his sword whirling over and over till it went *plunk* into the moat. Sir Hardimour followed it with a great splash.

When he came up with a green water plant plastered on his forehead, Shea was kneeling at the edge.

Hardimour cried: *"Gulp...pffth...ugh!...*help! I can't swim!"

Shea extended Chalmers' staff. Hardimour caught it and pulled himself up. As he scrambled to his feet, he found that villainous epee blade flickering in his face.

"Give up?" demanded Shea.

Hardimour blinked, coughed up some more water, and sank to his knees. "I cry craven," he said grudgingly. Then: "Curse it! In another bout I'll beat you, Master Harold!"

"But I won this one," said Shea. "After all, I didn't want to sleep with the crickets, either."

"Right glad am I that you shall not," said Hardimour honestly, feeling of his arm. "What galls me is that twice I've been put to shame before all these noble lords and ladies of Castle Caultrock. And after all, I must stay without."

Chalmers spoke up. "Hasn't the castle some rule about admitting persons in distress?"

"I bethink me this is even the case. Sick or wounded knights may enter till they are well."

"Well," said Shea, "that arm won't be well for a couple of months."

"Perhaps you caught a cold from your ducking," advised Chalmers.

"I thank you, reverend palmer. Perhaps I did." Hardimour sneezed experimentally.

"Put more feeling into it," said Shea.

Hardimour did so, adding a racking cough. "Ah me, I burn with ague!" he cried, winking. "Good people of the castle, throw me at least a cloak to wrap myself in, ere I perish! Oooo-ah!" He sank realistically to the ground. They got him up, and supported him, staggering, across the drawbridge. Britomart and Amoret followed, the former leading the three horses. This time the warder made no objection.

A trumpet blew three notes as they passed through the gate in the portcullis. The last note was sour. As the travelers entered a paved courtyard littered by heaps of dirty straw, they were surrounded by a swarm of little page boys in bright-colored costumes. All were chattering, but they seemed to know what to do. They attached themselves two by two to each of the new arrivals and led them toward the door of a tall, graystone building that rose from the opposite side of the court.

Shea was taken in tow by a pair of youths who gazed at him admiringly. Each wore medieval hose, with one leg red and the other white. As he mounted a winding stair under their guidance, one of them piped: "Are you only a squire, sir?"

"*Shh!*" said the other. "Have you no manners, Bevis? The lord hasn't spoken."

"Oh, that's all right," said Shea. "Yes, I'm only a squire. Why?"

"Because you're such a good swordsman, worshipful sir. Sir Hardimour is a right good knight." He looked wistful. "Will you show me that trick of catching an enemy's blade sometime, worshipful sir? I want to slay an enchanter."

They had arrived at the entrance of a long, high room, with a huge four-poster bed in one corner. One of the pages ran ahead and, kneeling before a cross-legged chair, brushed it off for Shea to sit on. As he did so, the other reached around him and unbuckled his sword belt, while the first ran out of the room. A moment later he was back, carrying a big copper basin of steaming water, a towel over his arm.

Shea gathered he was expected to wash his hands. They needed it.

"In the name of Castle Caultrock," said the little Bevis, "I crave your lordship's pardon for not offering him a bath. But the hour of dinner is now so near—"

He was interrupted by a terrific blowing of trumpets, mostly out of tune and all playing different things, that might have heralded the arrival of the new year.

"The trumpets for dinner!" said the page who was wiping Shea's hands for him, somewhat to his embarrassment. "Come."

It had fallen dusk outside. The winding stair up which they had come was black as a boot. Shea was glad of the page's guiding hand. The boy surefootedly led the way to the bottom, across a little entry hall where a single torch hung in a wall bracket. He threw open a door, announcing in his thin voice, "Master Harold de Shea!"

The room beyond was large—at least fifty feet long and nearly as wide, wretchedly lighted—according to American standards—by alternate torches and tapers along the wall. Shea, who had recently been in the even dimmer illumination of Bonder Sverre's house, found the light good enough to see that the place was filled with men and ladies, gabbing as they moved through an arch at the far end into the dining hall.

Chalmers was not to be seen. Britomart was visible a few feet away. She was the tallest person in the room with the exception of himself, and fully equal to his own five feet eleven.

He made his way toward her. "Well, Master Squire," she greeted him unsmilingly, "it seems that since I have become your lady you are to take me to dinner. You may give the kiss of grace, but no liberties, you understand?" She pushed her cheek toward him, and since he was apparently expected to do so, he kissed it. That was easy enough. With a little make-up she might have been drawn by George Petty.

Preceded by the little Bevis they entered into the tall dining hall. They were led to the raised central part of the U-shaped table. Shea was glad to see that Chalmers had already been seated, two places away from him. The intervening space was already occupied by the cameo-like Amoret. To the evident discomfort of Chalmers, she was pouring the tale of her woes into his ear with machine-gun speed.

"—and, oh, the tortures that foul fiend Busyrane put me to!" she was saying. "With foul shows and fantastic images on the walls of the cell where I was held. Now he'd declare how my own Scudamour was unfaithful to me; now offer me great price for my virtue—"

"How many times a day did he demand it?" inquired a knight beyond, leaning down the table.

"Never less than six," said Amoret, "and oft, as many as twenty. When I refused—as ever I must—the thing's past understanding—"

Shea heard Chalmers murmur: "What, never? No never. What, *never*—"

The knight said: "Sir Scudamour may well take pride in such a wife, gentle lady, who has borne so much for his sake."

"What else could she do?" asked Britomart coldly.

Shea spoke up: "I could think of one or two things."

The Petty girl turned on him, blue eyes flashing. "Master Squire, your insinuations are vile, and unworthy the honor of knighthood! Had you made them beyond that gate, I would prove them so on your body, with spear and sword."

She was, he observed with some astonishment, genuinely angry. "Sorry; I was joking," he offered.

"Chastity, sir, is no subject for jest!" she snapped.

Before the conversation could be carried further, Shea jumped at another tremendous blast of trumpets. A file of pages pranced in with silver plates. Shea noted, there was only one plate for him and Britomart together. Looking down the table, he saw that each pair, knight and lady, had been similarly served. This was apparently one of the implications of being a knight's "lady." Shea would have liked to inquire whether there were any others; but in view of Britomart's rebuff at his mild joke at Amoret, he didn't quite dare.

The trumpets blew again, this time to usher in a file of serving men bearing trays of food. That set before Shea and Britomart was a huge pastry, elaborately made in the form of a potbellied medieval ship, upon which the page Bevis fell with a carving knife. As he worked at it, Chalmers leaned around Amoret's back, and touching Shea's sleeve, remarked: "Everything's going according to plan."

"How do you mean?"

"The logical equations. I looked at them in my room. They puzzled me a bit at first, but I checked them against that key I made up, and everything fitted into place."

"Then you can really work magic?"

"I'm pretty sure. I tried a little enchantment on a cat that was strolling around. Worked a spell on some feathers and gave it wings." He chuckled. "I daresay there will be some astonishment among the birds in the forest tonight. It flew out the window."

Shea felt a nudge at his other side, and turned to face Britomart. "Will my lord, as is his right, help himself first?" she said. She indicated the plate. Her expression plainly said she hoped any man who helped himself before her would choke on what he got. Shea surveyed her for a second.

"Not at all," he answered. "You go first. After all, you're a better knight than I am. You pitched Hardimour down with a spear. If you hadn't softened him up, I couldn't have done a thing."

Her smile told him he had gauged her psychology correctly. "Grace," said she. She plunged her hand into the pile of meat that had come out of the pastry ship, put a good-sized lump into her mouth. Shea followed her example. He nearly jumped out of his chair, and snatched for the wine cup in front of him.

The meat tasted like nothing on earth. It was heavily salted, and sweet, and almost all other flavors were drowned in a terrific taste of cloves. Two big tears of agony came into Shea's eyes as he took a long pull at the wine cup.

The wine reeked of cinnamon. The tears ran down his cheek.

"Ah, good Squire Harold," came Amoret's voice, "I don't wonder that you weep at the tale of the agonies through which I have passed. Was ever faithful lady so foully put upon?"

"For my part," said the knight farther down the table, "I think this Busyrane is a vile, caitiff rogue, and willingly would I take the adventure of putting an end to him."

Britomart gave a hard little laugh. "You won't find that so easy, Sir Erivan. Firstly, you shall know that Busyrane dwells in the woods where the Losels breed, those most hideous creatures that are half-human in form, yet eat of human flesh. They are ill to overcome. Secondly, this Busyrane conceals his castle by arts magical, so it is hard to find. And thirdly, having found it and Busyrane himself, he is a very stout and powerful fighter, whom few can match. In all Faerie, I know of only two that might overthrow him."

"And who are they?" asked Erivan.

"This one is Sir Cambell, who is a knight of great prowess. Moreover, he has to wife Cambina, who is much skilled in the white magic that might pass both through the Losels and Busyrane's enchantments. The other is my own dear lord and affianced husband, Sir Artegall, justiciar to our queen."

"There you see!" cried Amoret. "That's the kind of person who was after me. Oh, what sufferings! Oh, how I ever—"

"*Ssst,* Amoret!" interrupted Chalmers. "Your food's getting cold, child,"

"How true, good palmer." A tear trickled down Amoret's lovely pale cheek as she rolled a huge ball of food between her fingers and thrust it into her mouth. As she chewed she managed to exclaim: "Oh, what would I do without the good friends who aid me!" There was certainly nothing weak about the frail-looking lady's appetite.

Trumpets sounded the end of the course, and as one set of serving men took away the plates, another emerged with more dishes. Pages came running to each couple with metal bowls of water and towels. Sir Erivan, beyond Chalmers, lifted his wine cup and then set it down again.

"Ho, varlet!" he cried. "My wine cup is empty. Is it the custom of Caultrock to let the guests perish of thirst?"

The servitor signaled another, and a small wizened man in a fur-lined jacket hurried up and bowed to Sir Erivan.

"My very gracious lord," he said, "I crave your pardon. But a most strange malady has befallen the wine, and it's turned sour. All the wine in Castle Caultrock. The good Fray Montelius has pronounced an exorcism over it, but to no purpose. There must be a powerful enchantment on it."

"What?" shouted Sir Erivan. "By the seven thousand demons of Gehenna, do you expect us to drink *water?*" And then, shrugging his shoulders, he turned toward Chalmers. "You see how it is, reverend sir. Daily we knights of Faerie are compassed closer about by these evil spells till we know not what to do. I misdoubt me they will make trouble at the tournament."

"What tournament?" asked Shea.

"The tournament of Satyrane, the woodland knight, at his forest castle, three days hence. It will be a most proud and joyous occasion. There's to be jousting, ending with a melee, for the prize among knights, and also a tourney of beauty for the ladies after. I've heard that the prize of beauty is to be that famous girdle of the Lady Florimel, which none but the most chaste may bind on."

"Oh, how you frighten me!" said Amoret. "I was kidnapped from a tournament, you know. Now I shall hardly dare attend this one, if there will be enchanters present. Just think, one might win the prize of valor and I be awarded to him of right!"

"*I* shall be in the lists for you," said Britomart, a trifle haughtily.

Shea asked: "Does the winner of the men's prize get the winner of the prize of beauty?"

Sir Erivan looked at him in some astonishment. "You are pleased to jest— No, I see you are really a foreigner and don't know. Well, then, such is the custom of Faerie. But I misdoubt me these enchanters and their spells." He shook his head gloomily.

Shea said: "Say, my friend Chalmers and I might be able to help you out a little."

"In what manner?'"

Chalmers was making frantic efforts to signal him to silence, but Shea ignored them. "We know a little magic of our own. Pure white magic, like that Lady Cambina you spoke of. For instance— Doc, think you could do something about the wine situation?"

"Why...ahem...that is...I suppose I might, Harold. But don't you think—"

Shea did not wait for the objection. "If you'll be patient," he said, "my friend the palmer will work some of his magic. What'll you need, Doc?"

Chalmers' brow furrowed. "A gallon or so of water, yes. Perhaps a few drops of good wine. Some grapes and bay leaves—"

Somebody interrupted: "As well ask for the moon in a basket as grapes at Caultrock. Last week came a swarm of birds and stripped the vines bare. Enchanter's work, by hap; they do not love us here."

"Dear me! Would there be a cask?"

"Aye, marry, a mort o' 'em. Rudiger, an empty cask!"

The cask was rolled down the center of the tables. The guests buzzed as they saw the preparations. Other articles were asked and refused till there was produced a stock of cubes of crystallized honey, crude and unstandardized in shape, "—but they'll do as sugar cubes, lacking anything better," Chalmers told Shea.

A piece of charcoal served Chalmers for a pencil. On each of the lumps of crystallized honey he marked a letter, O, C, or H. A little fire was got going on the stone floor in the center of the tables. Chalmers dissolved some of the honey in some of the water, put the water in the cask and some of straw in the water. The remaining lumps of honey he stirred about the table top with his fingers, as though playing some private game of anagrams, reciting meanwhile:

> *So oft as I with state of present time*
> *The image of our...uh...happiness compare,*
> *So oft I find how less we are than prime,*
> *How less our joy than that we once did share:*
> *Thus do I ask those things that once we had*
> *To make an evening run its wonted course,*
> *And banish from this company the sad*
> *Thoughts that in utter abstinence have their source:*
> *Change then! For, being water, you cannot be worse!*

As he spoke, he withdrew a few of the lumps, arranging them thus:

```
      H   H
   H  C   C  O  H
      H   H
```

"By the splendor of Heaven!" cried a knight with a short beard, who had risen and was peering into the cask. "The palmer's done it!"

Chalmers reached over and pulled the straw from the top of the cask, dipped some of the liquid into his goblet and sipped. "God bless my soul!" he murmured.

"What is it, Doc?" asked Shea.

"Try it," said Chalmers, passing him the goblet. Shea tried it and for the second time that evening almost upset the table.

The liquid was the best Scotch whiskey he had ever tasted.

The thirsty Sir Erivan spoke up: "Is aught amiss with your spell-wrought wine?"

"Nothing," said Chalmers, "except that it's rather...uh...potent."

"May one sample it, Sir Palmer?"

"Go easy on it," said Shea, passing down the goblet.

Sir Erivan went easy, but nevertheless exploded into a series of coughs. "*Whee!* A beverage for the gods on Olympus! None but they would have gullets of the proper temper. Yet methinks I should like more."

Shea diluted the next slug of whiskey with water before giving it to the serving man to pass down the table. The knight with the short beard made a face at the flavor. "This tastes like no wine I wot of," said he.

"Most true," said Erivan, "but 'tis proper nectar, and makes one feel wonnnnnnderful! More, I pray you!"

"May I have some, please?" asked Amoret, timidly.

Chalmers looked unhappy. Britomart intervened: "Before you sample strange waters I myself will try." She picked up the goblet she was sharing with Shea, took a long, quick drink.

Her eyes goggled and watered, but she held it well. "Too...strong for my little charge," said she when she got her breath back.

"But, Lady Britomart—"

"Nay. It would not—Nay, I say."

The servitors were busy handing out the Scotch, which left a trail of louder talk and funnier jokes in its wake. Down the table some of the people were dancing; the kind of dance wherein you spend your time holding up your partner's hand and bowing. Shea had just enough whiskey in him to uncork his natural recklessness. He bowed half-mockingly to Britomart. "Would my lady care to dance?"

"No," she said solemnly. "I do it not. So many responsibilities have I had that I've never learned. Another drink, please."

"Oh, come on! I don't, either, the way they do here. But we can try."

"No," she said. "Poor Britomart never indulges in the lighter pleasures. Always busy, righting wrongs and setting a good example of chastity. Not that anyone heeds it."

Shea saw Chalmers slip Amoret a shot of whiskey. The perfect beauty coughed it down. Then she began talking very fast about the sacrifices she had made to keep herself pure for her husband. Chalmers began looking around for help. *Serves the Doc right*, thought Shea. Britomart was pulling his sleeve.

"It's a shame," she sighed. "They all say Britomart needs no man's sympathy. She's the girl who can take care of herself."

"Is it as bad as all that?"

"Mush worst. I mean much worse. They all say Britomart has no sense of humor. That's because I do my duty. Conscientious. That's the trouble. *You* think I have a sense of humor, don't you, Master Harold de Shea?" She looked at him accusingly.

Shea privately thought that "they all" were right. But he answered: "Of course I do."

"That's splendid. It gladdens my heart to find someone who understands. I like you, Master Harold. You're tall, not like these little pigs of men around here. Tell me, *you* don't think I'm too tall, do you? You wouldn't say I was just a big blond horse?"

"Perish the thought!"

"Would you even say I was good-looking?"

"And how!" Shea wondered how this was going to end.

"Really, truly good-looking, even if I am tall?"

"Sure, you bet, honest." Shea saw that Britomart was on the verge of tears. Chalmers was busy trying to stanch Amoret's verbal hemorrhage, and couldn't help.

"Thass glorious. I'm so glad to find somebody who likes me as a woman. They all admire me, but nobody cares for me as a woman. Have to set a good example. Tell you a secret." She leaned toward him in such a marked manner that Shea glanced around to see whether they were attracting attention.

They were not. Sir Erivan, with a Harpo Marx expression, was chasing a plump, squeaking lady from pillar to pillar. The dancers were doing a snake dance. From one corner came a roar where knights were betting their shirts at knucklebones.

"Tell you shecret," she went on, raising her voice. "I get tired of being a good example. Like to be really human. Just once. Like this." She grabbed Shea out of his seat as if he had been a puppy dog, slammed him down on her lap, and kissed him with all the gentleness of an affectionate tornado.

Then she heaved him out of her lap with the same amazing strength and pushed him back into his place. "No," she said gloomily. "No. My responsibilities. Must think on them." A big tear rolled down her cheek. "Come, Amoret. We must to bed."

The early sun had not yet reached the floor of the courtyard when Shea came back, grinning. He told Chalmers: "Say, Doc, silver has all kinds of value here! The horse and ass together only cost $4.60."

"Capital! I feared some other metal would pass current, or that they might have no money at all. Is the...uh...donkey domesticated?"

"Tamest I ever saw. Hello, there, girls!" This was to Britomart and Amoret, who had just come out. Britomart had her armor on, and a stern, martial face glowered at Shea out of the helmet.

"How are you this morning?" asked that young man, unabashed.

"My head beats with the cruel beat of an anvil, as you must know." She turned her back. "Come, Amoret, there is no salve like air, and if we start now we shall be at Satyrane's castle as early as those who ride late and fast with more pain."

"We're going that way, too," said Shea. "Hadn't we better ride along with you?"

"For protection's sake, mean you? Hah! Little enough use that overgrown bodkin you bear would be if we came to real combat. Or is it that you wish to ride under the guard of my arm?" She shook it with a clang of metal.

Shea grinned. "After all, you *are* technically my ladylove—" He ducked as she swung at him, and hopped back out of reach.

Amoret spoke up: "Ah, Britomart, but do me the favor of letting them ride with us! The old magician is so sympathetic."

Shea saw Chalmers start in dismay. But it was too late to back out now. When the women had mounted they rode through the gate together. Shea took the lead with the grumpily silent Britomart. Behind him, he could hear Amoret prattling cheerfully at Chalmers, who answered in monosyllables.

The road, no more than a bridle path without marks of wheeled traffic, paralleled the stream. The occasional glades that had been visible near Castle Caultrock disappeared. The trees drew in on them and grew taller till they were riding through a perpetual twilight, only here and there touched with a bright fleck of sunlight.

After two hours Britomart drew rein. As Amoret came up, the warrior girl announced: "I'm for a bath. Join me, Amoret?"

The girl blushed and simpered. "These gentlemen—"

"Are gentlemen," said Britomart, with a glare at Shea that implied he had jolly well better be a gentleman, or else. "We will halloo." She led the way down the slope and between a pair of mossy trunks.

The two men strolled off a way and sat. Shea turned to Chalmers. "How's the magic going?"

"Ahem," said the professor. "We were right about the general worsening of conditions here. Everyone seems aware of it, but they don't quite know what causes it or what to do about it."

"Do you?"

Chalmers pinched his chin. "It would seem—uh—reasonable to suspect the operations of a kind of guild of evil, of which various enchanters, like this Busyrane mentioned last night, form a prominent part. I indicate the souring of the wine and the loss of the grapes as suggestive examples. It would not even surprise me to discover that a well-organized revolutionary conspiracy is afoot. The question of whether such a subversive enterprise is justified is of course a moral one, resting on that complex of sentiments which the German philosophers call by the characteristically formidable name of *Weltansicht*. It therefore cannot be settled by scientific—"

Shea said: "Yeah. But what can we do about it?"

"I'm not quite certain. The obvious step would be to observe some of these people in operation and learn something of their technique. This tournament—Good gracious, what's that?"

From the river came a shriek. Shea stared at Chalmers for three seconds. Then he jumped up and ran toward the sound.

As he burst through the screen of brush, he saw the two women up to their necks in a little pool out near the middle of the river. Wading toward them, their backs to Shea, were two wild-looking, half-naked men in tartan kilts. They were shouting with laughter.

Shea did a foolish thing. He drew his epee, slid down the six foot bank, and plowed into the water after the men, yelling. They whirled about, whipped out broadswords from rawhide slings, and splashed toward him. He realized his folly: knee-deep in water he would be unable to use his footwork. At best his chances were no more than even against one of these men. Two...

The bell guard of the epee gave a clear ringing note as he parried the first cut. His riposte missed, but the kilted man gave a little. Shea out of the tail of his eye saw the other working around to get behind him. He parried, thrust, parried.

"Wurroo!" yelled the wild man, and swung again. Shea backed a step to bring the other into his field of vision. Cold fear gripped him lest his foot slip on an unseen rock. The other man was upon him, swinging his sword up with both hands for the kill. "Wurroo!" he yelled like the other. Shea knew sickeningly that he couldn't get his guard around in time...

Thump! A rock bounced off the man's head. The man sat down. Shea turned back to the first and just parried a cut at his head. The first kiltie was really boring in now. Shea backed another step, slipped, recovered, parried, and backed. The water tugged at his legs. He couldn't meet the furious swings squarely for fear of snapping his light blade. Another step back, and another, and the water was only inches deep. Now! Disengage, double, one-two, *lunge*—and the needle-point slid through, skin and lungs and skin again. Shea recovered and watched the man's knees sag. Down he went.

The other was picking himself out of the water some distance down. When Shea took a few steps toward him, he scrambled up the bank and ran like a deer, his empty swordsling banging against his back.

Amoret's voice announced: "You may come now, gentlemen." Shea and Chalmers went back to the river to find the girls dressed and drying their hair by spreading it to the sun on their hands.

Shea asked Britomart: "You threw that rock, didn't you?"

"Aye. Thanks and more than thanks, Squire Harold. I cry your grace for having thought that slaughtering blade of yours a toy."

"Don't mention it. That second bird would have nailed me if you hadn't beaned him with a rock. But say, why did you just sit there in the pool? A couple of steps would have taken you to the deep water. Or can't you swim?"

"We can swim," she replied. "But it would not be meet to expose our modesty by leaving the pool, least of all to the wild Da Derga."

Shea forbore to argue about the folly of modesty that exposed one to death or to a fate that Britomart would undoubtedly consider worse. The blonde beauty was showing a much friendlier disposition toward him, and he did not wish to jeopardize it by argument over undebateable questions.

When they rode on, Britomart left Amoret to inflict her endless tale of woe on Chalmers, while she rode with Shea. Shea asked leading questions, trying not to reveal his own ignorance too much.

Britomart was, it transpired, one of Queen Gloriana's "Companions" or officers—a "count" in the old Frankish sense of the term. There were twelve of them, each charged with the righting of wrongs in some special field of the land of Faerie.

Ye olde tyme policewoman, thought Shea. He asked whether there were grades of authority among the Companions.

Britomart told him: "That hangs by what matter is under consideration. In questions involving the relations of man to man, I am less than those gallant knights, Sir Cambell and Sir Triamond. Again, should it be a point of justice, the last authority rests with Sir Artegall."

Her voice changed a trifle on the last word. Shea remembered how she had mentioned Artegall the evening before. "What's he like?"

"Oh, a most gallant princely rogue, I warrant you!" She touched her horse with the spurs so that he pranced, and she had to soothe him with: "Quiet, Beltran!"

"Yes?" Shea encouraged.

"Well, for the physical side of him, somewhat dark of hair and countenance; tall, and so strong with lance that not Redcross or Prince Arthur himself can bear the shock of his charge. That was how I came to know him. We fought; I was the better with the spear, but at swords he overthrew me and was like to have killed me before he found I was a woman. I fell in love with him forthwith," she finished simply.

Singular sort of courtship, thought Shea, *but even in the world I came from there are girls who fall for that kind of treatment.* Aloud he said: "I hope he fell for you, too."

Britomart surprised him by heaving a sigh. "Alas, fair squire, that I must confess I do not know. 'Tis true he plighted himself to marry me, but he's ever off to some tournament, or riding to some quest that I know not the end or hour of. We'll be married when he gets back, quotha, but when he does return, it's to praise my courage or strength, and never a word to show he thinks of me as a woman. He'll clap me on the back and say: 'Good old Britomart, I knew I could depend on you. And now I have another task for you; a dragon this time.'"

"Hm-m-m," said Shea. "Don't suppose you ever heard of psychology?"

"Nay, not I."

"Do you ever dress up? I mean, like some of those ladies at Castle Caultrock."

"Of what use to me such foibles? Could I pursue my tasks as Companion in such garb?"

"Do you ever roll your eyes up at Artegall and tell him how wonderful he is?"

"Nay, marry beshrew me! What would he think of so unmaidenly conduct?"

"That's just the point; just what he's waiting for! Look here, in my country the girls are pretty good at that sort of thing, and I've learned most of the tricks. I'll show you a few, and you can practice on me. I don't mind."

They dined rather thinly that night, on coarse brown bread and cheese which Britomart produced from a pack at the back of her saddle. They slept in cushiony beds of fern, three inches deep. The next day they rode in the same arrangement. Chalmers rather surprisingly consented. He explained: "The young lady is certainly very...uh...verbose, but she has a good deal of information to offer with regard to the methods of this Busyrane. I should prefer to continue the conversation."

As soon as they were on the road Britomart pulled up her visor and, leaning toward Shea, rolled her eyes. "You must be weary, my most dear lord," she said, "after your struggle with those giants. Come sit and talk. I love to hear—"

Shea grinned. "Overdoing it a little, old girl. Better start again."

"You must be weary—Hola, what have we here?"

The track had turned and mounted to a plateau-like meadow. As they emerged into the bright sun, a trumpet sounded two sharp notes. There was a gleam of metal from the other side. Shea saw a knight with a shield marked in wavy stripes of green drop his lance into place and start toward him.

"Sir Paridell, as I live!" snapped Britomart, in her policewoman's voice. "Oft an illdoer and always a lecher. Ha! Well met! Gloriana!" The last shouted word was muffled in her helmet as the visor snapped shut. Her big black horse bounded toward this sudden opponent, the ebony lance sticking out past his head. They met with a crash. Paridell held the saddle, but his horse's legs flew out from under. Man and animal came down together in a whirlwind of dust—

Shea and Chalmers reached him together and managed to pull the horse clear. When they got Paridell's helmet off he was breathing, but there was a thin trickle of blood at his lips. He was unconscious.

Shea gazed at him a moment, then had an inspiration. "Say, Britomart," he asked, "what are the rules about taking the arms of a guy like that?"

Britomart looked at her late opponent without pity. "Since the false knave attacked us, I suppose they belong to me."

"He must have heard I was traveling in your company," piped Amoret. "Oh, the perils I go through!"

Shea was not to be put off. "I was wondering if maybe I couldn't use that outfit."

Paridell's squire, a youth with a thin fuzz of beard on his chin and the trumpet over his shoulder, had joined them. He was bending over his master, trying to revive him by forcing the contents of a little flask between his lips. Now he looked up. "Nay, good sir," he said to Britomart, "punish him not so. He did but catch a glimpse of you as you rode up, and mistook this dame for the Lady Florimel."

A flush of anger went up Britomart's face. "In very truth!" she cried. "Now if I had no thought before of penalties, this would be more than I needed. Sir, I am Britomart of the Companions, and this Paridell of yours is a most foul scoundrel. Strip him of his arms!"

"What about me?" asked Shea insistently. "That tournament—"

"You could not ride in the tournament in a knight's arms without being yourself knight, fair squire."

"Ahem!" said Chalmers. "I think my young friend would make a very good addition to the knights of your Queen Gloriana's court."

"True, reverend sir," said Britomart, "but the obligation of knighthood is not lightly undertaken. He must either watch by his arms in a chapel all night, and have two proved knights to vouch him; or he must perform some great deed on the battlefield. Here we have neither the one nor the other."

"I remember how my Scudamour—" began Amoret. But Chalmers broke in, "Couldn't you, swear him in as a kind of deputy?"

"There is no—" began Britomart, and then checked herself. " 'Tis true, I have no squire at present. If you, Master Harold, will take the oaths and ride as my squire, that is, without a crest to your helmet, it might be managed."

The oath was simple enough, about allegiance to Queen Gloriana and Britomart in her name, a promise to suppress malefactors, protect the weak, and so on.

Shea and Chalmers pulled off Sir Paridell's armor together. His squire clucked distractedly through the process. Paridell came to in the middle of it, and Chalmers had to sit on his head until it was finished.

Shea learned that a suit of armor was heavier than it looked. It was also a trifle small in the breastplate. Fortunately Paridell—a plump young man with bags under his eyes—had a large head. So there was no trouble with the well-padded helmet, from which Britomart knocked off the crest with the handle of her sword.

She also lent Shea her own shield cover. She explained that Paridell's engrailed green bars would cause any of half a dozen knights to challenge him to a death duel on sight.

They had eaten the last of their provisions at lunch. Shea had remarked to Chalmers on the difficulty of getting a bellyful of adventure and one of food on the same day. So the sight of Satyrane's castle, all rough and craggy and set amid trees, held a welcome promise of food and entertainment. Unlike that of

Caultrock, it had portcullis and gate open onto the immense courtyard. Here workmen were hammering at temporary stands at one side.

The place was filled with knights and ladies, most of them familiar to Britomart and Amoret. Shea quite lost track of the number he was introduced to. In the hall before the dinner trumpet he met one he'd remember: Satyrane himself, a thick bear of a man, with a spade beard and huge voice.

"All Britomart's friends are mine!" he shouted. "Take a good place at the table, folks. Hungry, not so? We're all hungry here; like to starve." He chuckled. "Eat well, good squire; you'll need strength tomorrow. There will be champions. Blandamour of the Iron Arm has come, and so have Cambell and Triamond."

4

At ten the next morning, Shea came out of the vaultlike castle and blinked into the morning sun. Armor pressed his body in unfamiliar places. The big broadsword at his side was heavier than any he had ever handled.

The stands were finished and occupied by a vocal swarm of gentlemen and ladies in bright clothes. At their center was a raised booth under a canopy. In it sat an old man with frosty-white hair and beard. He held a bundle of little yellow sticks.

"Who's he?" asked Shea of Britomart, walking just a step ahead of him across the wide courtyard to a row of tents at the opposite side.

"*Sssh!* The honorable judge of the lists. Each time one of the knights scores a brave point he shall notch the stick of that knight, and thus the winner will be chosen."

They had reached the row of tents, behind which grooms held horses. A trumpet blew three clear notes and a mounted herald rode right past them. Behind him came Satyrane on a big white horse. He had his helmet off, and was grinning and bobbing his head like a clumsy, amiable bear. He held a richly carved gold casket. As he reached the front of the stands, he opened it up and took from it a long girdle, intricately worked and flashing with jewels. The trumpeter blew another series of notes, and shouted in a high voice:

"This is that girdle of Florimel which none but the chaste may wear. It shall be the prize of the lady judged most beautiful of all at this tourney; and she shall be lady to that knight who gains the prize of valor and skill. These are the rules."

"Some piece of rubbish, eh, folks?" shouted Satyrane and grinned. Shea heard Britomart, next to him, mutter something about "No manners." The woodland knight completed his circuit and came to a stand near them. A squire passed up his helmet. From the opposite end of the lists a knight came forward, carrying a long slim lance, with which he lightly tapped Satyrane's shield. Then he rode back to his place.

"Do you know him?" asked Shea to make conversation.

"Nay, I ken him not," replied Britomart. "Some Saracen: see how his helmet ends in a spike and crescent peak and his shoulder plates flare outward."

The trumpet sounded again, two warning notes.

The antagonists charged. There was a clang like a dozen dropped kettles. Bright splinters of wood flew as both spears broke. Neither man went down, but the Saracen's horse was staggering as he reached Shea's end of the lists and he himself reeling drunkenly in the saddle, clutching for support.

Satyrane was judged winner amid a patter of applause. Shea caught sight of Chalmers in the stands, shouting with the rest. Beside him was a heavily veiled woman, whose slender-bodiced figure in the tight gown implied good looks.

Another knight had taken his place at the opposite end of the lists. The crowd murmured.

"Blandamour of the Iron Arm," remarked Britomart, as the trumpet blew. Again came the rush and the *whang* of metal. This time Satyrane had aimed more shrewdly. Blandamour popped out of his saddle, lit on the horse's rump, and slid to the ground amid a shout of applause. Before he could be pulled aside another knight had taken his place. Satyrane rode him down, too, but came back from the encounter with his visor up, calling "Givors!" and shaking his head as though to clear it.

A squire hurried past with a cup of wine. Britomart called at him: "Am I needed yet?"

"No, my lady," he replied. "Ferramont is to ride the next run." Shea saw a little dark man with a black triangle on gold across his shield climb aboard his horse and take Satyrane's place. The pace of the jousting began to quicken. After Ferramont's second trip down the lists, two knights appeared at the opposite end. A page pushed past Shea calling for someone whose name sounded like "Sir Partybore" to join Ferramont for the defenders.

This time there was a double crash from the lists, which were getting dusty. Sir Partybore, or whatever his name was, went down. But he got up, clanked over to his horse, and pulled a big broadsword from the saddle bow. He waved it at the knight who had overthrown him, shouting something muffled in his helmet. The other turned back and dropped his broken lance. He drew a sword of his own, and aimed from the stirrups a blow that would have decapitated an elephant. The defender turned it easily with upraised shield. The man on foot and man on horseback circled each other, banging away with a frightful racket. Ferramont had downed another opponent in a cloud of dust, and new knights from either side were preparing to ride.

Shea turned to Britomart. "Aren't you going to get in?"

She smiled and shook her head. "Those are the lesser knights of either side," she said. "You must know, good squire, that it is the custom of these tourneys for one or two knights of good report to ride at the beginning, as Satyrane has done for us and Blandamour for them. After that, those younger men have their opportunity to gain reputation, while such as we of the Companions remain aside until needed."

Shea was about to ask who chose the sides. But Britomart gripped his arm. "Ha! Look! With the gyronny of black and silver."

At the other end of the lists Shea saw a big blond man ducking into a helmet. His shield bore a design of alternating black and silver triangles all running to the same point, which must be "gyronny." "That is Sir Cambell and none other," continued Britomart impressively.

As Britomart spoke, the big man came storming into the press. One of the lesser knights on foot, attempting to stop him, was knocked down like a ninepin, rolling over and over under the horse's hoofs. Shea hoped his skull had not been cracked.

Ferramont, who had secured another lance, was charging to meet Cambell. Just before black-and-gold and black-and-silver came together, Cambell dropped his own lance. With a single clean, flowing motion he ducked under the point of Ferramont's lance, snatched a mace from his side and dealt Ferramont's a terrific backhand blow on the back of the head. Ferramont clanged heavily from his saddle, out cold. The stands were in a bedlam, Britomart shouting, "Well struck! Oh, well!" and shifting from foot to foot.

Near by Shea saw Satyrane's face go grim and heard his visor clang shut as Cambell turned back into the melee, laying furiously about him with his mace and upsetting a knight at every stroke. Shouts warned him of Satyrane's approach. He turned to meet the chief defender and swerved his horse quickly, striking with his mace at the lance head. But Satyrane knew the answer to that. As the arm went up, he changed aim from Cambell's shield to his right shoulder. The long spear took him right at the joint and burst in a hundred shivering fragments. Down went Cambell with the point sticking in his shoulder.

With a yell of delight the defenders threw themselves on Cambell to make him prisoner. The challengers, more numerous, ringed the fallen knight round and began to get him back. Those still mounted tilted against each other around the edges of the melee.

A trumpet blew sharply over the uproar. Shea saw a new contestant entering the arena on the side of the challengers. He was a big, burly man who had fantastically decked every joint in his armor with brass oak leaves and had a curled metal oak leaf for a crest. Without any other notice, he dropped a big lance into position and charged at Satyrane, who had just received a fresh weapon on his side of the lists. *Whang!* Satyrane's spear shivered, but the stranger's held. The chief defender was carried six feet beyond his horse's tail.

He landed completely out. The stranger withdrew and then charged again. Down went another defender.

Britomart turned to Shea. "This is surely a man of much worship," she said, "and now I may enter. Do you watch me, good squire, and if I am unhorsed, you are to draw me from the press."

She was gone. The wounded Cambell, forgotten amid the tumult around this new champion, had been dragged to the security of the tents at the challengers' end of the lists. The press was now around Satyrane, who was trying groggily to get up.

A trumpet sounded behind Shea. He turned to see Britomart ready. Oakleaves heard it, too. He wheeled to meet her.

His lance shattered, but Britomart's held. Though he slipped part of its force by twisting so it skidded over his shoulder, his horse staggered. Oakleaves swayed in the saddle. Unable to regain his coordination, he came down with a clatter.

The warrior girl turned at the end of the lists and came back, lifting a hand to acknowledge the hurricane of cheers. Another of the challengers had taken the place of the oakleaf knight. Britomart laid her lance in rest to meet him.

Then a knight—Shea recognized Blandamour by the three crossed arrows on his shield and surcoat—detached himself from the mob around Satyrane. In two bounds his horse carried him to Britomart's side, partly behind her. Too late she heard the warning shout from the stands as he swung his sword in a quick arc. The blow caught her at the base of the helmet. Down she went. Blandamour leaped down after her, sword in hand. Somebody shrieked: "Foully done!" Shea found himself running toward the spot, dragging at the big sword.

Blandamour had swung up his sword for another blow at Britomart. He turned at Shea's approach and swung at his new adversary. Shea parried awkwardly with the big, clumsy blade, noticing out the corner of his eye that Britomart had reached a knee and was yanking a mace from her belt.

Blandamour started another swing. *Can't do much with this crowbar,* thought Shea. He was trying to get it round, when he got a violent blow on the side of the head. He reeled, eyes watering with pain. More to gain balance than to hit anything, he swung his sword round like a hammer thrower about to let go.

It caught Blandamour on the shoulder.

Shea felt the armor give before the impact. The man toppled with a red spurt of blood. The world was filled with a terrific blast of trumpets. Men-at-arms with halberds were separating the contestants. Britomart snapped up her visor and pointed to the man in armor at her feet, jerking like a headless chicken.

"A favor for a favor," she remarked. "This faitour knave struck you from behind and was about to repeat the blow when my mace caught him." She noticed that the groveling man's surcoat bore the green bars of Sir Paridell.

"Yet still I owe you thanks, good squire. Without your aid I might have been sped by that foul cowardly blow that Blandamour struck."

"Don't mention it," said Shea. "Are we taking time out for lunch?"

"Nay, the tournament is ended."

Shea looked up and was dumfounded to see how much of the day had gone. The herald who had opened the proceedings had ridden across to the booth where the judge of the tournament sat. Now he blew a couple of toots, and cried in his high voice:

"It is judged that the most honor of this tournament has been gained by that noble and puissant lady, the Princess Britomart." There was a shout of approval. "But it is also judged that the knight of the oak leaves has shown himself a very worthy lord and he also shall receive a chaplet of laurel."

But when Britomart stepped up to the judge's stand, the knight of the oak leaves was nowhere to be found.

The stands emptied slowly, like those at a football game. Some spectators hooted after Blandamour and Paridell as they were helped out. Shea caught a glimpse of Chalmers, hurrying after the veiled girl who had been his neighbor in the stands.

She moved slowly, with long, graceful strides, and he caught up to her at the entrance to the castle. Someone, hurrying past, bumped them into each other. A pair of intense eyes regarded Chalmers over the low face veil.

"It is the good palmer. Hail, reverend sir," she said in a toneless voice.

"Ahem," said Chalmers, struggling to find something to say. "Isn't it...uh...unusual for a woman to...uh...win a tournament?"

"Ywis, that it is." The voice was toneless still. Chalmers feared he had managed things badly. But she walked by his side down the great hall till a blast of warmth came from a fireplace where a serving man had just started a blaze.

"The heat!" she gasped. "Bear it I cannot! Get me to air, holy sir!"

She reeled against the psychologist's arm. He supported her to a casemented window, where she leaned back among the cushions, drawing in deep breaths. The features outlined against the thin veil were regular and fine; the eyes almost closed.

Twice Chalmers opened his mouth to speak to this singularly abstracted girl. Twice he closed it again. He could think of nothing to say but: "Nice weather, isn't it?" or "What's your name?" Both remarks struck him as not only inadequate, but absurd. He looked at his knobby knuckles with the feeling of being attached to a set of hands and feet seven times too big for him. He felt an utter fool in his drab gown and phony air of piety.

Dr. Reed Chalmers, though he did not recognize the sensations, was falling in love.

The girl's eyelids fluttered. She turned her head and gave him a long, slow look. He squirmed again. Then his professional sense awoke under that intent gaze. *Something* was the matter with her.

Certainly she was not feebleminded. She must be acting under some sort of compulsion—posthypnotic suggestion, perhaps—Magic!

He leaned forward, and was nearly knocked from his seat by a violent clap on the back.

"Good fortune, palmer!" cried a raucous voice. The dark Blandamour stepped past him, one arm bound tightly to his side. "Gramercy for your care of my little rosebud!" With the undamaged arm, he swung the girl expertly from her place in the casement and kissed her with a vigor that left a damp spot on her veil.

Chalmers shuddered internally. The girl submitted with the same air of preoccupation. She sank back into the casement. Chalmers meditated on a suitably horrible end for this jolly roughneck. Something humorous and lingering, with either boiling oil or melted lead.

"Hi, Doc, how are we doing?" It was Shea. "Hi, Sir Blandamour. No hard feelings, I hope?"

The knight's black eyebrows came down like awnings. "Against you, you kern?" he roared. "Nay, I'll give you a meeting beyond the castle gate and spank you with the flat o' my blade."

Shea looked down his long nose and pointed toward Blandamour's bandaged shoulder. "Be careful that iron arm of yours doesn't get rusty before you go that far," he remarked. He turned to Chalmers. "Come on, Doc, we got some reserved seats for the beauty parade. They're starting now."

As they left, Chalmers said: "Harold, I wish I could talk to that girl...uh...in private. I believe she's the...uh...key to what we're looking for."

Shea said: "Honest? She's Blandamour's lady, isn't she? I suppose if I fought him for her and beat him, she'd be mine."

"No, no, Harold, I implore you not to start any more fights. Our superiority over these people should be based on...uh...intellectual considerations."

"Okay. It's funny, though, the way they pass women around like bottles of liquor. And the women don't seem to mind."

"Custom," remarked Chalmers. "Beyond that, deep-rooted psychology. The rules are different from those we're accustomed to, but they're strict enough. A knight's lady is evidently expected to be faithful to him until he loses her."

"Still," Shea persisted, "if I had a lady, I'm not sure I'd want to enter her in this beauty contest, knowing she'd be turned over to the winner of the tournament."

"Custom again. It's not considered sporting to hold out on the other knights by refusing to risk an attractive lady."

They had been bowed into a kind of throne room with a raised dais at one end. At one side of the dais the bearish Satyrane sprawled in a comfortable chair. Six musicians with tootle-pipes and things like long-stemmed ukeleles were setting up a racket unlike any music Shea and Chalmers had ever heard. The knights and ladies appeared to find it charming, however. They listened with expressions of ecstasy till it squeaked and plunked to a close.

Satyrane stood up, the famous girdle dangling from his hand. "All ye folks know," he said, "that this is a tournament of love and beauty as well as a garboil. This here girdle goes to the winning lady. It used to be Florimel's, but she lost it and nobody knows where she is, so it's finders keepers."

He paused and looked around. "Now, what I want to say is that this here is a very useful little collop of jewelry, both for the lady and her knight. It has a double enchantment on it. For the lady, it makes her ten times fairer the minute she puts it on, and it hides her from anyone who would do her wrong. But, also, it won't stay around the waist of any wench who's not perfectly chaste and pure. That's for the benefit of the knight. The minute this lady can't keep her belt on he knows she's been up to tricks." He ended with a bellowing laugh. A few echoed it. Others murmured at his uncouthness.

Satyrane waved for quiet and went on. "Now, as to who wins, the honorable judges have eliminated the contestants down to four, but among the claims of these four they say they can't decide nohow. So they ask, lords and ladies, that you yourselves choose." Satyrane turned to the opposite side of the dais where four women sat, with veils over their heads, and called: "Duessa! Lady to Sir Paridell."

One of the girls rose and advanced to the front of the dais. Satyrane removed her veil. Her hair was red almost as bright as her heavily rouged lips. Eyebrows slanted low at the center. She looked a queenly, disdainful scorn at the audience. The company murmured its appreciation. Satyrane stepped back a pace and called: "Cambina! Lady and wife to Sir Cambell."

She came forward slowly—blond, almost as tall as Cambell himself, and of the mature, Junoesque beauty she dwarfed without outshining the fiery little redhead.

Shea whispered to Chalmers: "A little bit too well upholstered for me."

Just then there was a clang as an iron glove was thrown on the floor. Cambell's deep voice boomed, "My challenge to any one who tries to take her from me!"

There was no acceptance. Satyrane never turned a hair. He whipped off the next veil crying: "The Lady Amoret!" She stepped forward bravely, turning her head to show the perfect profile, but as Satyrane announced, "Lady and wife of Sir Scudamour," the delicate nostrils twitched. They gave an audible sniffle. Then, abandoning all efforts at self-control, she burst into a torrent of tears for the absent Scudamour. The Lady Duessa looked angry contempt. Cambina tried to comfort her as the sobs became louder and louder, mixed with words about, "—when I think of all I've been through for him—" Satyrane threw up his hands despairingly and stepped back to the fourth contestant. Shea saw one of the judges whisper to Satyrane. "What?" said the woodland knight in an incredulous stage-whisper. He shrugged and turned to the company.

"Sir Blandamour's lady, Florimel!" he announced, and drew the veil from the woman with whom Chalmers had been talking. Shea heard Chalmers gasp. The girl who advanced to the front of the dais with a sleepwalker's step and wide eyes was the most beautiful thing Shea had ever seen. Clapping and murmurs foretold who would win.

But there was a buzz of talk as well. Shea's ear caught Britomart's remark to Chalmers: "Good palmer! You who are skilled in magic and supersticerie, mark her well!"

"Why...why, Miss Britomart?"

"Because there's something here very strange. She's as like that Florimel of the Sea to whom the girdle really belongs as one pea to another. Yet I will swear it is not the same woman, and see!—all here are of the same mind."

In truth the hall was shouting for Florimel as the winner, but they were shouting for "Blandamour's Florimel," as though to distinguish her from the true owner of the girdle. Satyrane bowed and extended the jeweled trinket toward her.

With a word of thanks she took the belt. She clasped it around her middle. There seemed to be some difficulty about buckling it. She fumbled, worked at it a second, snapped it tight, lifted her hands—and the enchanted belt, still buckled, slid down her hips and thumped on the floor.

A low murmur of laughter ran around the room. Everyone looked at Blandamour who turned beet-color. Florimel stepped out of the circle of the belt and picked it up, a frown of puzzlement on her perfect features.

"Here, let *me* put it on," said the red-haired Duessa, and snatching it, suited the action to the word. As soon as she clasped it, the girdle popped open and slid down. She caught it and tried again. Same result. Shea noticed her lips were moving as though pronouncing a charm.

"At least, I can do it," said Cambina, and Duessa threw the belt at her angrily. But Cambina could not make the belt stay either. No more could the others, as they tried one after another. With each effort the knights' jokes grew louder and more barbed. Satyrane looked worried. Shea sympathized with him. This backwoods knight had tried so hard to give a polite tournament and party. Blandamour had ruined one with his back blow at Britomart, while the girdle was ruining the other.

But Satyrane was not done yet. "Ladies!" he shouted. "Cease, I pray you! The rules of the contest only provide that this girdle should go to the winner with nothing about her trying it on. That's Florimel, and she is now the lady of the winner of the tournament, who is—by the seven thousand virgins of Cologne, it's the Princess Britomart!"

The tall blonde stepped forward and said something to Satyrane, then turned to the company. "I do refuse this gift," she said, "since I am sworn to accompany Amoret till she finds her Scudamour."

Chalmers whispered: "Harold, I've simply got to talk to that girl. For...uh...scientific reasons. Couldn't you persuade Britomart to accept her for—"

"I say to me!" Blandamour's shout drowned every other sound. "If the winner won't have her, the she's mine again by right of reversion!" Satyrane scratching his head, was the middle of a knot of knights.

"Assotishness!" shouted Sir Cambell. "If the winner won't have her, then she reverts to the champion of the other side and, marry, that am I!"

"I overthrew more knights than you today," cried Sir Ferramont. "If it comes to a question of the second best—"

Britomart cut in icily: "Good knights and gentles, I have changed my mind and will accept the charge. of this lady."

"By my halidome, no!" bellowed Blandamour. "You refused her once, and she's mine!"

"Hey," Shea put in. "Didn't I knock you for a loo this morning? Then doesn't that—"

Blandamour spat. "That for you, springald! Pox on these legal points! I'm on my way!" He strode across the room, grabbed Florimel's wrist, and dragged her after him, snarling something inaudible through his mustache. Florimel whimpered with pain.

Shea bounded after them, spun Blandamour round and slapped his face. He jumped back and got the epee out just in time.

"Stop, fair sirs!" wailed Satyrane. The clash of steel answered him. His guests scattered, pushing furniture back. To them, stopping a good fight would be wicked waste of entertainment.

Shea remembered that in dealing with these broadsword men, you had to rely on footwork. If they got close enough for a good swing, you might get your blade snapped on a parry. He felt rather than saw the approach of a corner, and drove in a stop-thrust to keep from being backed into it. He heard a voice: "Nay, bid them cease. Blandamour uses but one arm."

"So does the other," came the answer, "and he has the lighter blade. Let them go."

Back and forth they went, *Swish, clang, tzing!* Shea caught a ferocious backhand cut with a parry sixte, but his light blade was borne back by the force of the blow. The edge chopped through the sleeve of his jacket and barely nicked the skin. Blandamour laughed. Shea, thinking fast, grunted as if with pain, jumped back and dropped his epee. But he caught it with his left hand, and as Blandamour came hurling in, nailed him just above the knee. The knight's blade whistled round and clipped the tip off Shea's hat feather before

Blandamour crashed to the floor on the stabbed leg.

"Enough!" shouted Satyrane, jumping between them. "Let there be an end of manslaying! Now I rule that Sir Blandamour has his just deserts for unknightly behavior, both here and at the tourney. Let any who challenge this prove it on me! Squire Harold, ye have won Florimel for your lawful paramour— Why, pest take it, where is she?"

Florimel, the fair bone of this knightly contention, had disappeared.

5

Shea said: "I get sick of the flatness of this country. And doesn't it ever rain?" He sat on the white gelding he had purchased at Castle Caultrock, the armor that had been Sir Paridell's bundled up behind him. He had tried wearing it, but the heat made it unbearable.

Chalmers was just taking his bearings with a crude jackstave he and Shea had managed to patch together. He remarked: "Harold, you're an incorrigible varietist. If we had cliffs and a downpour you'd doubtless complain about that."

Shea grinned. "Touché, Doc. Only I get bored. I'd even welcome a lion for the sake of excitement."

Chalmers climbed back onto the ass. "Giddap, Gustavus," he said, and then: "I daresay you'll have plenty of excitement if this wood harbors as many enchanters as they say. I rather wish you wouldn't challenge all the...uh...hard characters we encounter on the strength of your ability to fence."

"Well, what the hell, I've gotten away with it so far."

"Undoubtedly. At the same time it is just as well not to carry matters too far. I should hate to be left alone."

"A nasty, selfish point of view. Say, Doc, it's too bad the girls wouldn't come with us. That ebony spear of Britomart's gave me a feeling of solid comfort."

"You're not acquiring a...uh...sentimental fondness for that brawny lady?"

"Good Lord, no! She reminds me of Gert. I was just giving her practice in the theory and practice of feminine charm, for snaring her own boyfriend. But, say, if anybody's loopy over a girl it's you! I saw the look on your face when Satyrane suggested Florimel had been carried off by enchantment."

"Why...ahem...nothing of the sort...that is, very well." Chalmers looked worried. "The trouble with traveling with a fellow psychologist is that concealments are impossible. However, I will say that Florimel's manner gave me to pause. When the girdle refused to stay on anyone, I became certain of the operation of magic. The laws of probability should have produced at least one faithful lady among so many." Chalmers gave a sigh. "I suppose Florimel was just an illusion. It was fortunate in a way. It gave us a good excuse to ask how to find an enchanter. Otherwise they might have suspected us of trying...uh...to make common cause with their enemies. The Faerie knights seem convinced that all enchanters are working against them. Perhaps they are right."

They rode in silence for a while. Then Shea said: "Looks like the woods begin about here." A little stream crossed the track in front of them, and beyond it the sparse timber gave place to dense forest. They dismounted, tying up Gustavus and the horse, which had been christened Adolphus, and produced their lunch.

Both munched in silence for a moment. Then Chalmers said: "Harold, I wish you'd promise not to get into any more fights if—"

"Hey!" said Shea, and leaped to his feet.

Out from among the trees loped a pair of naked, hairy, seven-foot ape men. They had huge ears with tufts of hair sprouting from them, and throat pouches like orangutans. In their hands were clubs. For a moment they stood at gaze, then came splashing through the stream at a gallop.

Chalmers ran to untie the animals, but they were leaping about, crazy with fear. In a glance Shea decided he could never reach Sir Paridell's sword. He would have to use the epee, feeble as that toothpick was against those huge clubs.

The first of the ape men ran at him, bellowing. Shea never knew whether he had gained his senses or lost his nerve, but the next instant he and Chalmers were running round and round the tethered animals, with the ape-men foaming through their tusks behind.

One of the creatures boomed something to the other. On the next circuit the fugitives were surprised to run head-on into one ape-man who had stopped and waited for them. Shea was in front. He saw the club swing up in two hairy hands and did the only thing possible—extend the epee and fling himself forward in a terrific flèche.

His face was buried in fur and he was clutching at it for support. The hilt was wrenched from his hand, and the animal-man went screaming off, with the weapon sticking through him.

Shea himself was running; over his shoulder, he saw Chalmers was running, with the other ape-man gaining, twirling up his club for the blow. Shea had an instant of horror and revulsion—the poor old Doc, to pass out this way, when he couldn't help—

Twunk!

The feathered butt of an arrow appeared in the thing's side, as though it had just sprouted there. The club missed Chalmers as the creature staggered and turned. *Twunk!* The second arrow took it in the throat, and it collapsed in a clump of bracken, screeching and thrashing. Shea tried to stop; Chalmers careened into him and they went down together.

Shea sat up and wiped leaf mold from his face. Footsteps preceded a tall-ish, slim girl in a short-skirted tunic and soft leather boots. She had a bow in one hand and a light boar spear in the other, and she moved toward them at a springy trot as though it were her normal gait. A feathered hat like Shea's sat on her red-gold hair, which was trimmed in a long bob.

Shea got up. "Thanks, young lady. We owe you a life or two. I think the thing's about dead."

"I'll make certain. Those Losels are hard to kill," said the girl. She stepped to the bracken and jabbed. She seemed satisfied as she pulled the spear out, wiping its point on some moss. "Is the old man hurt?"

Chalmers gained breath enough to sit up. "Just...*puff*...winded. I am...uh...merely middle-aged. To whom do we owe our rescue?"

The girl's eyebrows went up, Shea noticing they were a delightful color. "You know me not? I hight Belphebe."

"Well," said Shea, "I...ah...hight Harold Shea, esquire, and my friend hight Reed Chalmers, the palmer, if that's how you say it."

"That would be your blade sticking in the other Losel?"

"Yes. What happened to it."

"I will even show you. The creature died when erst I saw it."

Losels. Shea recalled the table at Castle Caultrock, with Britomart telling Sir Erivan he would not find it easy to come to grips with Busyrane the enchanter, because Busyrane's castle was in "the wood where the Losels breed."

"We're on the right track, Doc," he said to Chalmers as he helped the latter up and followed Belphebe.

Chalmers merely gave him a sidelong glance and sang softly:

> *But when away his regiment ran,*
> *His place was at the fore, oh,*
> *That celebrated, cultivated, underrated nobleman,*
> *The Duke of Plaza-Toro!*

Shea grinned. "Meaning me, I suppose? I was just setting a good pace for you. Here's our other Losel." He pulled the epee from the repellent corpse.

Belphebe gazed at the instrument with interest. "Marry, a strange weapon. May I try its balance?"

Shea showed her how to hold the epee and made a few lunges, enjoying to the full his first recent chance to show off before an attractive girl.

Belphebe tried. "*Ouch!* These poses of yours are as awkward as a Mussulman at Mass, Squire Harold." She laughed and tossed the epee back to him. "Will you show me more another day?"

"Glad to," replied Shea. He turned to Chalmers. "Say, Doc, it seems to me we were eating lunch when the fracas started. Maybe the young lady would like to help us finish it."

Chalmers gulped. "I had—this harrowing experience had quite driven the thought of food out of my mind, Harold. But if Miss Belphebe would like to—by all means—"

"If I may give that I may get," she said. "Hola, attend!" She pulled out an arrow and tiptoed slowly away from them, peering intently into the greenery. Shea tried to follow her gaze, but could see nothing but foliage.

Then Belphebe brought up the bow; aimed, drew, and released all in one movement. To Shea it looked as though she had loosed at random. He heard the arrow strike. Down from the trees fell a large green macaw-like bird. It struck the leaf mold with a thump, and a couple of green feathers gyrated down after.

Gustavus and Adolphus still trembled and tugged at their reins when the three approached them. Shea soothed them and took them down to the stream to drink while Chalmers started a fire and Belphebe stripped the feathers from the parrot. Presently she was toasting the bird on the end of a stick. She was so deft in rustling a meal in the open that Shea felt no desire to compete with her in scoutcraft.

Chalmers, he was surprised to observe, was holding his right forefinger against his left wrist. He asked: "What are you doing, Doc? Taking your pulse?"

"Yes," said Chalmers gloomily. "My heart seems to be—uh—holding up all right. But I'm afraid I wasn't cut out for this type of life, Harold. If it were not for pure scientific interest in the problems—"

"Aw, cheer up. Say, how's your magic coming along? A few good spells would help more than all the hardware put together."

Chalmers brightened. "Well, now—ahem—I think I may claim some progress. There was that business of the cat that flew away. I find I can levitate small objects without difficulty, and have had much success in conjuring up mice. In fact, I fear I left quite a plague of them at Satyrane's castle. But I took care to conjure up a similar number of cats, so perhaps conditions will not be too bad."

"Yeah, but what about the general principles?"

"Well, the laws of similarity and contagion hold. They appear to be the fundamental Newtonian principles in the field of magic. Obviously the next step is to discover a system of mathematics arising from these fundamentals. I was afraid I should have to invent my own, as Einstein was forced to adapt tensor analysis to handle his relativity equations. But I think I have discovered such a system ready made, in the calculus of classes, which is a branch of symbolic logic. Here, I'll show you."

Chalmers fished through his garments for writing materials. "As you know, one of the fundamental equations of class calculus—which a naive academic acquaintance of mine once thought had something to do with Marxism—is this:

$$\forall \alpha, \alpha \in I : \alpha + \sim\alpha = I$$

"That is, the class *alpha* plus the class *non-alpha* equals the universe. But in magic the analogous equation appears to be:

$$\forall \alpha, \alpha \in I : I \in \alpha + \sim\alpha$$

"The class alpha plus the class non-alpha *includes* the universe. But it may or may not be limited thereto. The reason seems to be that in magic one deals with a plurality of universes. Magic thus does not violate the law of conservation of energy. It operates along the interuniversal vectors, perpendicular, in a sense, to the spatial and temporal dimensions. It can draw on the energy of another universe for its effects.

"Evidently, one may readily have the case of two magicians, each summoning energy from some universe external to the given one, for diametrically opposite purposes. Thus it must have been obvious to you that the charming Lady Duessa—somewhat of a vixen, I fear—was attempting to operate an enchantment of her own to overcome that of the girdle. That she was unable to do so—"

"The fowl is ready, gentlemen," said Belphebe.

"Want me to carve?" asked Shea.

"Certes, if you will, Master Harold."

Shea pulled some big leaves off a catalpa-like tree, spread them out, laid the parrot on them, and attacked the bird with his knife. As he hacked at the carcass he became more and more dubious of the wisdom of psittacophagy. He gave Belphebe most of the breast. Chalmers and he each took a leg.

Belphebe said: "What's this I hear anent the subject of magic? Are you practitioners of the art?"

Chalmers replied: "Well—uh—I would not go so far as to say—"

"We know a couple of little tricks," put in Shea.

"White or black?" said Belphebe sharply.

"White as the driven snow," said Shea.

Belphebe looked hard at them. She took a bite of parrot, and seemed to have no difficulty with it. Shea had found his piece of the consistency of a mouthful of bedsprings.

Belphebe said: "Few are the white magicians of Faerie, and all are entered. Had there been additions to the roster, my lord Artegall had so acquainted me when last I saw him."

"Good lord," said Shea with sinking heart, "are you a policewoman too?"

"A—what?"

"One of the Companions."

"Nay, not a jot I. I rove where I will. But virtue is a good master. I am—but stay, you meet not my query by half."

"Which query?" asked Chalmers.

"How it is that you be unknown to me, though you claim to be sorcerers white?"

"Oh," said Shea modestly, "I guess we aren't good enough yet to be worth noticing."

"That may be," said Belphebe. "I, too, have what you call 'a couple of tricks,' yet 'twere immodesty in me to place myself beside Cambina."

Chalmers said: "Anyhow, my dear young lady, I—uh—am convinced, from my own studies of the subject, that the distinction between 'black' and 'white' magic is purely verbal; a spurious distinction that does not reflect any actual division in the fundamental laws that govern magic."

"Good palmer!" cried Belphebe. "What say you, no difference between 'black' and 'white'? 'Tis plainly heresy..."

"Not at all," persisted Chalmers, unaware that Shea was trying to shush him. "The people of the country have agreed to call magic 'white' when practiced for lawful ends by duly authorized agents of the governing authority, and 'black' when practiced by unauthorized persons for criminal ends. That is not to say that the principles of the science—or art—are not the same in either event. You should confine such terms as 'black' and 'white' to the objects for which the magic is performed, and not apply it to the science itself, which like all branches of knowledge is morally neutral—"

"But," protested Belphebe, "is't not that the spell used to, let us say, kidnap a worthy citizen be different from that used to trap a malefactor?"

"Verbally but not structurally," Chalmers went on. After some minutes of wrangling, Chalmers held up the bone of his drumstick. "I think I can, for instance, conjure the parrot back on this bone—or at least fetch another parrot in place of the one we ate. Will you concede, young lady, that that is a harmless manifestation of the art?"

"Aye, for the now," said the girl. "Though I know you schoolmen; say 'I admit this; I concede that,' are ere long one finds oneself conceded into a noose."

"Therefore it would be 'white' magic. But suppose I desired the parrot for some—uh—illegal purpose—"

"What manner of crime for ensample, good sir?" asked Belphebe.

"I—uh—can't think just now. Assume that I did. The spell would be the same in either case—"

"Ah, but would it?" cried Belphebe. "Let me see you conjure a brace of parrots, one fair, one foul; then truly I'll concede."

Chalmers frowned. "Harold, what would be a legal purpose for which to conjure a parrot?"

Shea shrugged. "If you really want an answer, no purpose would be as legal as any, unless there's something in the game-laws. Personally I think it's the silliest damned argument—"

"No purpose it shall be," said Chalmers. He got together a few props—the parrot's remains, some ferns, a pair of scissors from his kit, one of Belphebe's arrows. He stoked the fire, put grass on it to make it smoke, and began to walk back and forth pigeon-toed, holding his arms out and chanting:

> *Oh bird that speaks*
> *With the words of men*
> *Mocking their wisdom*
> *Of tongue and pen—*

Crash! A monster burst out of the forest and was upon them before they could get to their feet. With a frightful roar it knocked Chalmers down with one scaly forepaw. Shea got to his knees and pulled his epee halfway out of the scabbard before a paw knocked him down too...

The pressure on Shea's back let up. He rolled over and sat up. Chalmers and Belphebe were doing the same. They were close to the monster's chest. Around them the thing's forelegs ran like a wall. It was sitting down with its prey between its paws like a cat. Shea stared up into a pair of huge slit-pupiled eyes. The creature arched its neck like a swan to get a better look at them.

"The Blatant Beast!" cried Belphebe. "Now surely are we lost!"

"What mean you?" roared the monster. "You called me, did you not? Then wherefore such surprise when I do you miserable mortals the boon of answering?"

Chalmers gibbered: "Really—I had no idea—I thought I asked for a *bird*—"

"Well?" bellowed the monster.

"B-but you're a reptile—"

"What is a bird but a reptile with feathers? Nay, you scaleless tadpole, reach not for your sorry sword!" it shouted at Shea. "Else I'll mortify you thus!" The monster spat, whock, *ptoo!* The green saliva sprayed over a weed, which turned black and shriveled rapidly. "Now then, an you ransom yourselves not, I'll do you die ere you can say 'William of Occam'!"

"What sort of ransom, fair monster?" asked Belphebe, her face white.

"Why, words! The only valuable thing your vile kind produces."

Belphebe turned to her companions. "Know, good sirs, that this monster, proud of his gift of speech, does collect all manner of literary expression, both prose and verse. I fear me unless we can satisfy his craving, he will truly slay us."

Shea said hesitantly: "I know a couple of jokes about Hitler—"

"Nay!" snarled the monster. "All jests are stale. I would an epic poem."

"An—epic poem?" quavered Chalmers.

"Aye," roared the Blatant Beast. "Ye know, like

> *Herkeneth to me, gode men*
> *Wives, maydnes, and alle men,*

Of a tale ich you wil telle,
Hwo-so-it wile here, and there-to dwelle.
The tale of Havelok is i-maked;
Hwil he was litel, he yede ful naked.

Shea asked Chalmers: "Can you do it, Doc? How about *Beowulf?*"
"Dear me," replied Chalmers. "I'm sure I couldn't repeat it from memory..."
The monster sneered: "And 'twould do you no good; I know that one:

Hwet! we Gar-Thena   *in gear-dagum*
    theod cyninga   *thrym gefrunon,*
   hu tha æthelingas   *ellen fremedon.*

" 'Twill have to be something else. Come now; an epic or shrive yourselves!"
Shea said: "Give him some of your Gilbert and Sullivan, Doc."
"I—uh—I hardly think he—"
"Give it to him!"
Chalmers cleared his throat, and readily quavered:

Oh! My name is John Wellington Wells,
I'm a dealer in magic and spells,
In blessings and curses
And ever-filled purses,
And ever-filled purses,
And ever-filled—

"I can't! I can't remember a thing! Can't *you* recite something, Harold?"
"I don't know anything either."
"You must! How about *Barbara Frietchie?*"
"Don't know it."
"Or Chesterton's *Lepanto?*"
"I don't—hey, I do know one long poem. But—"
"Then say it!" cried Chalmers.
Shea looked at Belphebe. "Well, it's hardly suitable for mixed company. Monster, if you'll let the young lady go—"
"Nay!" roared the Blatant Beast. "To your verses, tadpole!"
Shea turned a stricken face to Chalmers. "It's *The Ballad of Eskimo Nell.* What'll I do?"
"Recite it, by all means."
"Oh, Lord!" Chalmers was right, of course. But Shea had begun to feel an affinity for the red-haired huntress. He drew a deep breath and began:

> *When Deadeye Dick and Mexican Pete*
> *Set forth in search of fun,*
> *'Twas Deadeye Dick who...*

He wished he knew a bowdlerized version; he didn't dare try to change the wording extempore.

> *They hit the strand of the Rio Grande*
> *At the top of a burning moon,*
> *And to slake their thirst and do their worst*
> *They sought Black Mike's saloon.*

On he went, getting redder and redder.

> *Soon Deadeye Dick was breathing quick*
> *With lecherous snorts and grunts...*

Out of the corner of his eye he saw Belphebe's face. It registered puzzlement.

> *Then entered into that hall of sin,*
> *Into that Harlot's Hell,*
> *A lusty maid who was never afraid:*
> *Her name was Eskimo Nell...*

Shea went faster and faster to get to the end of the awful epos. He finished with a sigh of relief, and looked up to see how the Blatant Beast was taking it.

The monster got slowly to its feet. Without a word to its late captives, it lumbered off into the woods, shaking its reptilian head.

Shea next looked at Belphebe. She said: "A life for a life. Truly we should be friends henceforth, and fain would I be such, did I but understand your craft of magic. That magic is white that draws such a monster nigh, you'll hardly assert. That poem—half the words I understood not, though meseems 'twas about a battle betwixt a warrior maid and a recreant knight."

"You might put it that way," said Shea.

"Riddle me those words, Squire Harold. For ensample—"

Shea interrupted hastily: "Some other time, Miss Belphebe, if you don't mind. Right now we want to get our bearings. Is this what they call 'the wood where the Losels breed?' "

"Aye. Some say the enchanters created that gruesome race of monsters to be their cattle."

Shea asked innocently: "Why, is the place infested with enchanters too?"

"Marry, a mort of 'em. Take care lest you fall into their snares."

Chalmers broke in: "Ahem...could you tell us where there are any—uh—magicians to be found?"

Shea scowled at his partner. Belphebe's face changed. "Now wherefore would you know such things?"

"We're trying to rescue somebody we think they have, and we thought if we could—uh—gain the confidence of one—"

"Meseems that is a strange and not well-thought-on plan," said the girl coolly. "Yet, since you wish, straight on, and I warrant me you'll find enough of the naughty rogues." She waved her hand. "And now, good gentles, if you will even pardon me, I must trim the ears from the Losel I slew—"

"You must *what?*" demanded Shea.

"Trim the ears from the Losel. For trophies. Already I have pairs an hundred and twenty and two. Good morrow, gentles."

"That," said Shea when they were on their way, "is my idea of a real girl. And you had to put her off us by that crack about magicians!"

"Very fine girl, provided she doesn't put an arrow through you and cut off your ears for trophies. I confess my taste runs to a somewhat more sedentary type of female. I doubt whether I can stand much more excitement of this sort."

Shea said: "I know how you feel. Traveling through Faerie is just one damned encounter after another." His two narrow escapes in one day had left Shea feeling like a damp washcloth.

Chalmers mused: "It is logical that it should be so. The *Faerie Queene* indicates that this is a world wherein an endless and largely planless concatenation of encounters are a part of the normal pattern of events—Merciful Heavens, another one! What's that?"

"That" was a big black leopard which leaped out suddenly into their path. It snarled with the sound of tearing sheet iron. The mounts bucked and started to whirl against the bits.

"Stop, Doc!" yelled Shea, manhandling Adolphus around and reaching behind him for the broadsword. "If you run, it'll jump you sure!"

He tumbled off, snubbed his reins around a convenient stump, and faced the leopard with the broad-sword in one hand and the epee in the other. This was getting to be a worse bore than the Garaden Institute. *If I stand my ground,* he thought, *it probably won't attack, but if it does—* There was a book he had read once—what was its name?—about a Lithuanian who hunted jaguars with a spear. If it springs, impale it with the epee; if it stands off and claws, chop with the broadsword—

The leopard snarled again. It seemed uncertain. Then, to Shea's astonishment, it swelled and changed into a huge lion. He felt a prick of fear. A man might handle a 150-pound leopard, but a 600-pound lion—not even a mortal stab would keep it from ripping him up, once it got to close quarters. He was in for it—

"Harold!" Chalmers' voice was not too near. "It's all right."

The hell it's all right! thought Shea, holding his ground for want of anything better to do.

The lion did not spring. Instead it grimaced. The fanged mouth became a beak, wings sprouted from its shoulders, and it was a griffin. That, Shea realized, was not kosher; griffins did not—

Chalmers called, closer. "It's the man we're looking for."

Shea relaxed. "Take off the false whiskers, Mr. Magician; we know you," he said. The griffin began to dwindle and dissolve. Shea turned to Chalmers, who was struggling with a patently balky Gustavus. "Didn't you say something about when away his regiment ran, his place was in the fore, oh—"

"I couldn't control this confounded beast. And it's '*at* the fore, oh,' not *in*. How do you do, sir?" This was to the ex-griffin, which had become a stout, dark, bald man, who stood glowering at them, fists on hips.

"I do right well," said the man. "What do you two here? Eh? Seek trouble? You've come to the right market."

Shea grinned. "In a way, I suppose we are, if you call yourself trouble."

"Ho, you seek my professional service! I warn you I handle no minor matters, like turning cows sour or the manufacture of love philters. That's witch-wife work. I'm a master magician."

"Then we're delighted—"

"Ahem," said Chalmers. "Excuse me, Harold. I should like to explain to the gentleman that our interest is professional, looking to an exchange of information that might be mutually profitable."

"Ho!" cried the enchanter. "You two claim to be magicians? How do I know you speak sooth? Tell me that, eh?"

"Well...uh—"

"Work a spell for him, Doc," said Shea.

"Oh, dear me. I don't suppose he'd be satisfied with more mice—or cats. All I can think of now is one I prepared for conjuring up a dragon."

"What the hell, that's fine! Go ahead with your dragon!"

The magician's ears caught the last word. "Dragon? D'you think you can really produce a dragon? Let's see you do it!"

"But won't it be...uh...dangerous?" This was Chalmers.

"Have no fear. I'll get a counterspell ready. Dolon protects you. *The* Dolon." He strutted.

"Show him, Doc."

Chalmers, with a look of baffled and apprehensive resignation, began to make a list of the properties needed. A small red salamander was discovered under a stone. Most of the other things they had already, but a snapdragon plant was called for, and there was none in sight. "Conjure one up," said Shea, coolly. The harassed psychologist looked annoyed. But, with the aid of a roadside weed, he produced a snapdragon plant the size of a tree. *The* Dolon snorted.

Chalmers laid out his properties, lit a fire with flint and steel, and began an incantation:

> *By Fafnir and Hydra,*
> *Apophis and Yang:*
> *With the length of Nidhöggr,*
> *Tiámat's sharp fang,*
> *The shape of the lizard;*
> *The strength of the bear,*
> *Thou, scaled like the serpent,*
> *Emerge from your lair!*
> *Steed of Triptolemus.*
> *Beowulf's bane.*
> *Symbol of Uther.*
> *And bringer of rain—*

Shea prudently hitched the animals' reins around a tree. If the dragon turned out to be winged and hungry— He wished that his damned reckless impulsiveness had not made him force Chalmers' hand. If *the* Dolon's counterspell didn't work—

The oyster-colored smoke of the fire thickened and darkened. Chalmers bit off his chant in mid-stanza and scrambled back. A reptilian head a yard long was poking toward them out of the smoke.

The head had a scaly neck behind it. Then came a foreleg and another. The dragon seemed to be crawling from nothingness through an orifice somewhere in the smoke, ballooning out as it came. There it was, complete to stinger-tipped tail, gazing at them with yellow cat's eyes.

Shea breathed, not daring to attract its attention by a movement: "If it starts for us, Doc, you get on Gustavus and I'll let go the reins."

Dolon's face was twisting as though he had swallowed too big a mouthful. The dragon lurched a few steps, not toward them but off at right angles, opened its terrible mouth, gave a whistling *"beeep!"* and began to crop the grass contentedly.

"God bless my soul!" said Chalmers.

"He'd better," replied Shea. "Look!"

A second draconian head was pushed through the smoke. This one was squirted out in a few seconds. It looked at the three men, then wandered over to a clump of bright-colored flowers, sniffed, and began to eat them. Now a third and a fourth head were already in sight. As fast as the dragons were extruded, more followed them. The field down to the very confines of the trees was crowded with them, new arrivals butting the others to make room or scratching their sides on trees. Shea was counting: "Thirty-three, thirty-four— We better untie the animals and move or we'll get stepped on. Thirty-six, thirty-seven—"

"Dear me," remarked Chalmers, fingering his chin, as they backed among the trees. "I rather feared this. The same thing happened with the mice."

"Fifty-two, fifty-three—" Shea continued. "My God, the country will be overrun with them!"

Dragons had overflowed the field and were lurching through the trees with their ungainly gait, munching everything green in sight, and mooing at each other with the same plaintive beeping sound. "Ninety-eight, ninety-nine, one hundred. Oh, boy!"

The fire suddenly died, and the cascade of vegetarian dragons ceased. "My God!" said Shea in an awe-struck voice. "One hundred reptilian Ferdinands!"

Dolon's voice was that of a man shaken to the core. "Forsooth, you do things not by halves. Though I mind me I once succeeded with a bushel measure full of pearls." Dolon snapped his fingers. "By Ahriman's toenails, are you not those who even now bested the Blatant Beast?"

"That's us," said Shea. "How did you hear about it?"

"The Beast passed me a few hours ago, and warned me of a prow company. He said he demanded a trifle of poesy, as is his custom, and you gave him a lay full of such—ah—spice that even he durst not repeat it for shame. The like had never before happened to him, and he seemed much downcast thereby. But was there not another of you? The Beast mentioned three."

Chalmers cleared his throat, but Shea quickly answered: "No; he's got us mixed up with another bunch."

" 'Tis a thing conceivable; the Beast is in sooth of the lower orders, and cannot count beyond two." Dolon shook a finger and said with a slight leer: "Now about these dragons: Tell me, fellow magicians, was't not by error you got eaters of grass? Eh? No secrets in the trade!"

"Ahem. No use taking unnecessary risks," said Chalmers, still looking a trifle wall-eyed.

"Doubtless," remarked Dolon with a glance that Shea just barely saw, "you can exorcise them as rapidly."

"We could," said Shea, before his companion had a chance to answer. "For the dragon-disappearing spell, though, we need an aneroid comptometer, and we lost ours. Do you have one with you?"

"An...ah, certes, an ameroid combompeter. Nay, I fear me not so. Last spring came a black frost that killed all the plants on which ameroid combompeters grow." He spread his hands regretfully. "However, meseems these dragons will in the long run be a benefit, making rare good sport and food for our friends and servants, the Losels. And now, Sir Magicians whom I have not seen, explain your purpose in Loselwood."

Chalmers spoke. "Uh...we're looking for a lady named Florimel, and were advised we might find her here. Do you know the young person?"

Dolon chuckled. "The real Florimel or the false?"

"The real or— The one who was at Satyrane's tournament recently."

"That would be the false one, made by the Witch of Riphœa. A fair piece of work—though I will say I care not much for these witches. Duessa is the only one who has any standing in the Chapter— And that brings me to remark, magical sirs, are you members of one of the outland Chapters? My memory is practically infallible, and I do not recall having seen you at our meetings."

Chalmers stammered: "We...uh...that is...can you tell me a little more about this Florimel? The...uh...false one."

Dolon waved his hand. "A mere witch's thing—a creature made of snow, of no special value. You must let me show you the really fine chess player I made sometime, or the imps I conjured up to handle my torture work. Really an achievement. Busyrane, our archmagician, doubtless called this false Florimel in for inspection." He accented the last word and snickered. "But you haven't answered my question, magical sirs."

Shea spoke up boldly. "The point is, we'd like to join up with you."

"You mean you have been working independently and we know it not?" Dolon narrowed his eyes suspiciously. "Aye; Busyrane opened the Chapter but a twelvemonth ago and you may well have slipped his attention. I trust you have not refused his invitation. Our archimage is not soft or slow with unlicensed magicians. He has a spell that turns 'em into spiders. Witty, is he not, eh?"

"Good gracious!" said Chalmers. "But how does one acquire a license?"

"That falls somewhat upon the applicant. Our charter calls for a round twenty-one master magicians, the magic number... Naturally, you behold in me one of the leading masters, whether by ability or seniority. There is also a class of journeymen, who handle the ordinary work, and one of apprentices. Perhaps you have talent enough to be elected to mastership. There are three or four places unfilled, I believe. The next meeting comes in five days, and with my backing your election would be certain."

6

Dolon, in the form of a handsome stallion, trotted in front. Shea leaned back in his saddle and, watching the stallion's ears carefully, murmured: "Doing all right, aren't we, Doc?"

"I suppose so, but I admit to being somewhat apprehensive as to what will happen if both the Companions and the Chapter of Magicians learn we've been cooperating with the other party. This...ah...playing both ends against the middle may get us in trouble."

"Maybe," said Shea. They rode on in silence. Once a tiger glided out from between the trunks ahead. Gustavus and Adolphus, both rapidly approaching nervous breakdowns, tried to bolt from the trail. Dolon turned himself from a stallion into an immense buffalo. The tiger slunk off, snarling.

The sun was already low when the trail made a right-angled bend and dipped under a bank. A huge oak door was set into the earth. Dolon, again in his natural form, waved a hand, and the door flew open. "Fear not for the safety of your mounts," he said. "An invisible wall, which none may penetrate without my warrant, surrounds this place."

Shea, dismounting, said: "That ought to be nice for keeping the mosquitoes out."

Dolon laughed dutifully, then shook his head. "Ah, good 'prentice, how true! Is it not sad that a man of genius must concern himself with petty moils and worries?"

The air was stuffy inside. The first thing Shea saw was a huge pile of dirty dishes. Dolon was evidently not the neat type of bachelor. Beyond was an object that made his scalp prickle. It was the life-sized nude statue of a young man, stiff, at one side of the room, emitting a faint bluish glow. It held aloft a torch, which Dolon set alight.

The enchanter noticed Shea's glance of inquiry. "A former 'prentice of mine," he remarked. "I found he was a spy from Queen Gloriana's court, where a few of those high-born grandees practice a kind of magic they call 'white.' So there he stands, with all his sensations alive and the rest of him dead. Eh, Roger?" He pinched the statue playfully and laughed. "I'm really the best humorist in the Chapter when I'm in the mood. Let me show you my collection of Mallamies."

"What's a Mallamy?" inquired Chalmers.

Dolon looked at him hard, then decided it was a kind of joke and laughed. He began taking bottles off a shelf and holding them up to the light. Each contained a human figure about an inch tall. "Homunculi from the hand of great master, Mallamy himself," he explained. "He specialized in this art, and none other has been able to shrink folk to so small size. Even I, Dolon, cannot equal his art. This is the finest collection of his figures in existence.

"It wants only a blond Saracen. Busyrane has one, but he will not yield it, though I have offered him a water fay, which his own collection lacks. He insists that water fays are not permanent, since any accident will bring water in contact with the bottle and they can work a spell of their own and so escape."

He sighed. "You see how things fall short of perfection even for the greatest of us. But come in, good sirs, and seat yourselves in my cabinet. Only 'ware the cockatrice as you go down this passage."

"A cockatrice?" said Shea.

"Aye. A rare, priceless idea of Busyrane's. All masters of the Chapter are supplied with them. They are just outside our inner cabinets and under an enchantment, so they may not look on any member of the Chapter—or his friends. But should any of Gloriana's people essay to enter, the cockatrice looks on them and they turn to stone."

Dolon threw open a door and led the way down a dimly lighted passage. Behind bars at one side the beast stalked to and fro with a clatter of its scaly tail. It turned its head this way and that. The stench made Shea want to vomit. Over his shoulder he saw Chalmers' lips moving. He hoped it was with a protective counterspell, not prayer. Dolon's voice floated back: "—had to get them after Cambina, one of those 'white magic' practitioners, got into Mallamy's cabinet and drowned him in a pool of alkahest. Thank Lucifer, she married that oaf, Sir Cambell, and marriage cost her some of her powers—"

The door banged behind them. Shea gasped for air as though he had swum up from the bottom of the ocean.

The table was ready and the food—*thank Heaven*, thought Shea—not too highly spiced. Whittling at a steak, he asked: "What's this meat? It's good!"

"Fried Losel," said the magician calmly.

Shea saw Chalmers halt a mouthful in midair. He felt himself gag momentarily; it was, after all, on the borderline of cannibalism, and after the cockatrice— He forced himself to go on eating. Squeamishness right now was a luxury.

Dolon poured out some wine, sat back and, rather to the travelers' astonishment, produced and lit a clay pipe.

"Aye," he pronounced, "competition is the curse of our business. One playing against another, and those curst companions of Gloriana making sad work of us all—that's how matters stood till Busyrane organized our Chapter. Why, I mind me, I had a very good thing once, very good. Found a man of property who wanted a love philter. I made it for him, and he refused to pay. As he was more ass than human, I promised him his ears should grow an inch a day, with the price doubled for each inch they grew till he got me to take the spell off." Dolon laughed and puffed. "I told you I was a good deal of a humorist.

"Well, what does he do but go to Malingo, who gives him a counterspell at half price! No more of that now."

Shea had a question: "Look here! If you magicians all cooperate so well, what went wrong at Satyrane's tournament? That girdle wouldn't stay on the false Florimel, or on Duessa either for that matter. I should've thought Busyrane would see to that."

Dolon chuckled. "Briskly questioned, springald! The trick with the girdle was doubtless Duessa's doing. It's in her style. She tried to remove the enchantment already on it, but when she found she couldn't do that, clapped another atop, so 'twould fit nobody. But Florimel's case was an error, I fear me much." He shook his head. "Especially if in good sooth Busyrane has sent for her. Nothing would gall those high knights and ladies of the court half so much as having one of their queens of beauty, approved chaste by the test of the girdle, to live with an enchanter. But now, alack, there's a doubt."

Shea saw Chalmers start and run his tongue around his lips at the mention of the connection between Busyrane and Florimel. He pressed questions about the Chapter to give Chalmers a chance to recover. But now Dolon shut up like a clam, with suspicious glances. Shea had uneasy memories of the cockatrice and the spy in the outer room.

The magician finally rose. " 'Tis time we retired, eh, magical sirs? 'Twere wise to set out for Busyrane's tomorrow. If we arrive ere the meeting be called, I'm sure that my connections and the skill in intrigue for which I'm known will enable me to secure your election."

A whisper: "Hey, Doc, you asleep?"

Another: "Merciful Heavens, no. Not in this place. Is *he?*"

"If he isn't, that's a damned good magical snore. Say, can't we do something about that poor guy he made into a statue?"

"It would be injudicious to attempt it, Harold. Moreover, I'm not certain I know how. It would jeopardize our whole plan of campaign."

"Didn't know we had one. Are we stringing along with him?"

"I suppose we must if we really intend to help Queen Gloriana and the Companions. I may also mention Florimel. Dolon remarked that she was made of snow—created. I find it difficult to credit and rather awful. I fear we must join this Chapter and...uh...bore from within, as if it were."

"I suppose," said Shea thoughtfully, "that the Chapter explains why the Land of Faerie is sort of running down."

"Yes. The enchanters had just discovered the—"

"Say, Doc!" Shea's whisper was almost loud. "If the Chapter was formed a year ago, *Faerie Queene* time, and it had already been started when Spenser wrote, which was four centuries ago, Earth time—Faerie time must be much slower than ours. If we go back, we'll land somewhere in the twenty-fifth century—along with Buck Rogers."

"*If* we go back. And also if the curvature of the spacetime vectors is uniform. There might be sine curves in the vectors, you know."

"Never thought of it. Say, how come your dragon spell was so extremely successful?"

Chalmers permitted himself an under-the-breath chuckle. "A property of the mathematics of magic. Since it's based on the calculus of classes, it is primarily qualitative, not quantitative. Hence the quantitative effects are indeterminate. You can't—at least, with my present skill I can't—locate the decimal point. Here the decimal point was too far rightward, and I got a hundred dragons instead of one. It might have been a thousand."

Shea lay still a moment digesting that thought. Then: "Can't you do something about that?"

"I don't know. Apparently the professionals learn by experience just how much force to put into their incantations. It's an art rather than a science. If I could solve the quantitative problem, I could put magic on a scientific basis. I wish, Harold, that tomorrow you could...uh...manage to distract Dolon for long enough to allow me to possess myself of one of his textbooks. His place is such a hurrah's nest that he's certain not to miss it."

The three riders—Dolon had conjured up a horse because, he said, taking the form of one for a long journey would be fatiguing—had been going for miles through Loselwood. They saw deer, but no other living creatures. Conversation was scarce till they came out on a road, once wide and well graded, now much overgrown. Shea reasoned that this was one more sign of how the enchanters were getting the best of the Faerie knights.

He pushed his mount alongside the magician. "With your superlative powers, Dolon, I wonder they didn't elect you head of the Chapter instead of Busyrane."

Dolon shrugged. "I could have had the post at good cheap, ho-ho! But I would not strive and moil for it. I'm really a very good judge of human nature, so I arranged Busyrane's election, knowing he would do it well."

"You must be just about perfect," said Shea.

" 'Just about,' my 'prentice friend, is a weak phrase. I *am* perfect. I've no doubt that people in ages to come will date the history of true wizardry from my entry into the field."

"Modest, too," remarked Shea, drawing a quick glare from Chalmers.

Dolon dropped his eyes. "Too modest, I sometimes think. Yet do I guard against such affectation—hola! Here's an encounter!" An armored horseman had appeared at the far end of the defile through which they were riding. His lance came down and he trotted toward them.

Dolon cried: "Ten thousand devils, 'tis Artegall himself! Flee, or we are undone!" Looking a bit undone himself, the magician whirled his horse sharp round on its hind legs.

A woman's voice behind them called, "Stand, all of you!" Belphebe was perched on a rock at the side of the defile, covering them with bow bent full.

"To the air!" screeched Dolon, the last word going beyond human pitch as he changed to hawk and flapped slanting upward. There was the flat snap of the bow, the whistle of the arrow, and there was a puff of feathers. Down hurtled the hawk, changing to Dolon with an arrow through his arm as he fell. He landed, *plop,* in a soft spot. Shea observed that these people really knew something about swearing in the minute or two before Artegall's lance jabbed him.

"Dismount, runagates!" roared the knight. It seemed the best thing to do. The man was as big as Cambell, cased in steel, yet moved quickly. Besides, Belphebe had another arrow already nocked.

Artegall pushed up his visor to show a stern, swarthy face with a broken nose. He produced a couple of looped chains, which he slipped over the victims' heads, tightened, and locked. "You're in arrest," quoth he.

"What for?" asked Shea.

"For judgment by the high justice of the court of her majesty, Queen Gloriana."

Chalmers groaned. "The high justice," he explained in a low voice, "means the death penalty if we're found guilty."

"Then I'll take low," said Shea.

"You had better not ask it. He probably has the privilege of low justice himself, which means he can sentence you to about five years in prison right here. He probably would."

Belphebe had come down from her rock. "Dolon, by the splendor of Heaven!" she cried. "I bear witness, Sir Artegall, that when I met this pair in Loselwood but yesterday, they were asking after magicians. Guard the young one well; he bears a blade of much power, which I doubt not has some enchantment on it."

"Say you so!" observed Artegall, with an unpleasant expression. "By my halidome, we are well met, then. A pretty gift for the queen's justice! Let's see that little sword." He yanked Shea's baldric up over his head, nearly taking off an ear.

He climbed back on his horse, holding the end of the chains. The prisoners had no choice but to trot along behind him.

Chalmers managed to whisper: "Don't try to tell them we're on the right side. Britomart will clear us if necessary. We must...uh retain Dolon's confidence."

They plodded on. The more Chalmers thought about it the less he liked the idea of being dragged off to the Faerie court for judgment. If they were released with Britomart's help, any enchanters they met afterward might reasonably ask them how they came to escape when Dolon was condemned. Of the master magician's condemnation there could be little doubt. Artegall looked at him with pure detestation. Belphebe, trotting along beside them, was amusing herself by catching the enchanter's eye, putting one hand around her neck, and making strangling sounds. The great Dolon did not seem to be enjoying it.

Shea? Shea was admiring Belphebe's springy stride. Anything Chalmers did would have to be on his own. Fortunately, Chalmers had succeeded in purloining and sneaking a look into one of Dolon's textbooks that morning. There was a simple weakness spell in it; not much of a spell, lasting only a few hours and easily guarded against if one knew it were coming. But it required no apparatus beyond twelve blades of grass, a small piece of paper, and some water.

Chalmers stooped and pulled up the grass blades as he stumbled along, holding them in his mouth as though he merely wanted something to chew on. He slipped a hand inside his robe, ostensibly to scratch, really to tear a page corner from Dolon's book. This also went into his mouth; saliva ought to be a fairish substitute for water. He mumbled the incantation. If it worked, Artegall and Belphebe ought to be weakened enough to let the prisoners escape.

Shea decided that he liked the little spray of freckles across Belphebe's nose, but that it was difficult to admire a girl who had a bead drawn on one's right kidney with a longbow. He would like to see more of Belphebe. She had about everything, including an adventurous spirit not unlike his own

Why the devil was he so tired? He could barely drag one foot after the other. He should be hardened to strenuous living by now. Belphebe was drooping, too; the spring had left her walk. Even the horse's head hung.

Artegall swayed in his saddle. He made one monstrous effort to balance himself, overcompensated, and slowly fell into the road with the dignity of a toppling factory chimney. The crash halted the procession. The horse sat down jerkily and sprawled beside its rider, its tongue lolling out. Chalmers and Dolon followed suit, their chains jangling.

Artegall heaved himself up on one elbow. "Sorcery!" he drawled languidly. "The rascals have tricked us! Skewer them, Belphebe!"

The girl fumbled with her bow. Chalmers rolled over and reached hands and knees. "Come on, Harold! Rouse Dolon!" he said. He smothered a yawn and started to crawl. "Dear me, I wish I could learn to keep these spells within bounds!"

Shea tried to leap over Dolon; lost his balance and fell across the magician. Dolon grunted as Shea's knees dug into him, but he, also, made his hands and knees. The three prisoners set off down the road in that fashion.

Shea looked back. Belphebe was still on her feet, trying to draw the bow, but lacking strength to pull it more than a few inches. She aimed up and let fly at random. The recoil knocked her over backward. The arrow soared in a whispering parabola and thwunked into the seat of Dolon's pants with just enough force to stick. The magician yelped and increased his speed to almost a mile an hour.

"Hurry," said Shea. "They're coming after us." Belphebe was crawling along at a fair rate, regardless of the abrasion of her bare knees. Behind her, Artegall brought up the rear of the bizarre parade like some monstrous tailless lizard. In his armor he could barely move.

"Belphebe's gaining," remarked Shea, after a minute.

"That sorrows me not," said Dolon, with a nasty expression. He fished a knife from his boot.

"Hey," said Shea, "not that!"

"And wherefore not?"

While Shea was trying to think of a reasonable answer, a man in a kilt appeared at the side of the road. For a moment he stared in astonishment at the singular procession, then put a willow whistle in his mouth and blew.

"The Da Derga!" gasped Dolon. "Ah, woe are we, to be caught thus!"

A swarm of the wild men came trotting through the trunks. All wore tartan kilts. With them were a number of lean, rough-coated dogs. The five crawlers were efficiently bowled over and frisked for weapons. Shea found himself looking into the ugly, bearded face of a gigantic redhead, who moved a rusty broadsword back and forth an inch from the prisoner's throat as though he were sawing. The redhead seemed to think it very funny.

"Sure and is it not a strange thing to find them so?" remarked a benign-looking graybeard. "The folk would be taking poison to make them so weak."

"Do we be takin' them back entire," asked another, "or just their heads to put in the hall, now?"

"Shame on you, Shawn! 'Tis a month now since the gods have had a proper sacrifice. 'Tis a lack of proper reverence you show, I'm thinking."

Shea could have thought of one or two terms more appropriate than lack of reverence. But he was not consulted. He was tied up and suspended from a pole. For the next hour or so, as the carriers of the pole jounced along, the pain in his wrists and ankles was too exquisite for him to think coherently.

They followed deer trails, ultimately emerging into a clearing with tents around it. The Da Derga were evidently on a raiding expedition; there were no women or children to be seen. The captives were dumped in a row near a rough-hewn wooden altar with ominously dark stains down its sides.

Shea whispered: "Can't you work a spell, Dolon?"

"Aye, as soon as I recover from this curst weakness. Malediction on the bungling knave who clipped us in it!"

"I'm afraid I was...uh...responsible," said Chalmers humbly.

"May Beelzebub fly away with you then! After this, stick to your dragon-juggling tricks, and leave true magic to the great Dolon. Was it not the grass-and-paper spell?"

"Yes."

"I trow I recognized the symptoms. Haro! 'Twill not wear off for hours, and by that time we shall be dead as Judas Iscariot. Ah, 'tis foul that the greatest master of magic the world has seen should come to an end thus, like a netted herring! The tragedy of it makes me weep."

He lapsed into gloomy silence. Shea thought desperately—what could they do? If neither the wily Dolon nor the powerful Artegall could help, the case appeared hopeless. Another last-minute rescue from outside would be too much of a coincidence to hope for.

Three men in long white robes, absurdly garlanded with leaves, came out of a tent. One of them thoughtfully whetted a long knife. The sound it made on the stone was hard to bear.

The one with the knife came over and looked down at the captives. The amiable-looking chieftain remarked: "Sure, 'tis a likely lot they are, isn't it?"

"They'll do," replied the Druid. "For a chance-met lot, they'll do. The two younger are the handsomest. We take them first. But if it's so weak they are, how shall we ever get them to walk to the altar?"

"A couple of the lads will support them. Oh, Murrahu! Would you be getting your pipes?"

The Da Derga had formed a circle around the clearing. One of the Druids stood with his arms out and face to the sky, chanting, while another gestured symbolically over the altar. A third marched round the clearing, followed by the bagpiper. The piper cut loose with a sound like a thousand angry beehives. It seemed to Shea that a procession of ghostly figures was following the two marchers, floating in some medium of faint iridescence that made their forms and even their existence uncertain. The Da Derga bowed low as priest and piper passed, and stayed bent over till that trail of misty things had gone by.

It was extremely interesting. Shea wished he were in a position to appreciate it without being dominated by the thought that these were probably his last sense impressions. He wondered if the gods of the Da Derga had something in common with the ancient Celtic deities—By the great horn spoon, he had an idea!

A barbarian was cutting his bonds. Two others heaved him and Belphebe to their feet and supported them by the arms. Their expressions were of rapt ecstasy. Shea muttered out of the side of his mouth: "Hey, Belphebe, if I get you out of this, will you call a truce till we can explain?"

The girl nodded. The Druid with the knife took his place at the altar. Another came over to the captives, faced about, and started to lead them. Summoning all his strength, Shea barked: "Hey, Mr. Priest!"

The Druid turned. He had a kindly expression. "Now, laddie," he said, "it's no good shouting! Sure, 'tis an honor to be the first to go to the gods."

"I know it. But you don't think the gods will be satisfied with a bunch of weak fish like us, do you?"

"True enough for you. But the gods do be giving credit when a man offers the best he has, and faith, you are that."

"You could make us better, though. We're under a spell. You're a pretty good magician; why not take this weakness off us?"

The Druid's expression showed cunning. "I'm thinking you're saying that for your own benefit and not for ours, but 'tis rare good sense you speak, my boy." He looked at Shea, then at Belphebe and waved his hands toward them, mumbling. Shea felt the force flow back into his body. The old priest addressed the two with him: "Hold them tight, now, lads. It wouldn't do at all, at all, if they used their strength to get away."

The rough hands of the Da Derga clamped down on Shea's arms till he winced. He saw that Belphebe wasn't enjoying their grip either. He held himself relaxed, as though putty in their hands.

The procession approached the altar. The piper was red-faced, but seemed to be maintaining himself by that unique power all pipers have of keeping going long after ordinary people would collapse for lack of breath. Shea's feet dragged. The Druid with the knife awaited him with the supremely peaceful expression of a man who is rendering his own happiness sure by a great and noble act. The altar was only four paces away. He glanced toward Belphebe. Three. She was looking anxiously at him as though awaiting a signal. Two. He felt what he was waiting for—the relaxation of the tired, sweaty hands of the huskies. One. It was now or never.

Shea snapped his left heel up and back. It hit a hairy kneecap, and the barbarian went down with a yell of pain. He let go. Shea spun around on the other heel, driving his left knee into the other guard and at the same time punching him in the Adam's apple. The second guard, not expecting this demoniac burst of energy, let go and dropped, strangling in the agony of the throat punch.

What followed took seconds. The other two guards got their signals crossed, and instead of one of them holding Belphebe, both let her go to run at Shea. The woods girl pounced on the Druid with the knife and sank her teeth into his hand.

The guards were good rough-and-tumble fighters, but under the handicap of having to take their captives unharmed. Shea was under no such inhibition. He jabbed one in the eyes with his fingers and kicked the other in the belly. Somebody screeched. Belphebe ran past with a bloody knife in her hand, yanking Shea after her.

The other Da Derga were too dumfounded by the sacrilege to interfere. She and Belphebe raced through a hole in their circle just as the barbarians began reaching for their broadswords.

Then they were among trees, running madly. Belphebe glided ahead of Shea without even breathing hard. He guessed she could leave him behind if she wished. She seemed to know the woods by instinct. She swerved right, squeezed between a pair of trunks, down to a brook, splashed along its bed for fifty yards, then off into the woods again.

"Up!" cried Belphebe suddenly, and climbed a trunk with the agility of a small boy, lending a hand to help Shea. They crouched together in a crotch and listened.

Scattered sounds of pursuit came, now here, now there. The Da Derga had spread and were beating the woods. Shea and Belphebe held themselves still, almost breathless. There was a rustle of snapped twigs and a pair of the barbarians walked past a few yards from their tree, leading one of the huge dogs. "Sure, 'tis a terrible thing," said one of them. "Three men cut up, and one of them a holy man."

"A wicked, cruel thing. And poor Fion, with his lovely neck all broke in. It's inhuman monsters they are, those two."

The sounds died. They waited, and Shea explained his and Chalmers' plan to her in a whisper.

Belphebe gave Shea a level glance. Apparently satisfied with his sincerity, she asked: "Why said you not so sooner, good squire?"

"I couldn't in front of Dolon without giving the whole show away. If you don't believe me, Britomart will give us good characters. Honest."

"You mean you plan still to go on with this witless scheme?"

"Of course, if we can rescue our people."

"You think Artegall would let Dolon go?"

Shea hesitated. "I don't know Artegall. But you're right; he's the kind that, once he gets an idea, he won't change it for hell or high water."

Belphebe gave a gurgling little laugh. "You should be a court jester, Squire Harold. But your wit is well taken; that describes Artegall exactly."

"Well, we'll have to see to it that Artegall can't interfere till we've left."

"Nay. In honor I cannot take the side of that foul enchanter—"

"Look, Belphebe. Use your head. The knights of Faerie have been trying for years to catch up with these enchanters, haven't they?"

"That is good sooth."

"And they haven't made out very well, have they?"

"Gentle Squire, you argue like a doctor. But I fear me you are right."

"All right. This riding around in an iron shirt and knocking off an occasional enchanter isn't going to get you anywhere, either. Now, my boss and I have a plan for getting into their organization and rounding up the whole batch at once. Why not let us try?"

"But how shall I—"

"Oh, tell Artegall we made a private truce to escape the Da Derga, and one of the conditions was that we get a head start before—" He stopped, listening.

Faintly, the drone of bagpipes wafted to them.

Belphebe cried: "The ceremony has begun again. Haste, or our friends are sped!" She began to climb down, but as they went Shea asked: "What can we do?"

"I'm not without some knowledge of things in the woods and their secret ways." She dropped to the ground and started to whistle a strange little tune. When the whistle reached an ear-piercing pitch, a unicorn came trotting forward. It nuzzled up to her, pawing the ground, and she vaulted onto its back. "How about me?" asked Shea.

Belphebe frowned. "Right glad would I be to have *you* ride with me, but I misdoubt this steed will bear the weight. And they are ever jealous beasts, not liking to go two and two. You could hold the tail."

That seemed unsatisfactory. But Shea thought, *after all, I know some magic and ought to be able to conjure one up, and a conjured unicorn probably won't object to this one.* "If you'll show me that brook, I'll see what I can do," he said.

He composed his incantation on the way to the stream. At its bank he made a model, as well as he could, of the animal's head in wet sand, and stuck a stick in it for a horn. Then he recited:

*Oh, steed that feeds on the lightning
And drinks of the whirlwind's surge,
In the name of the horse of Heimdall,
I conjure you now, emerge!*

*Strong and docile and valiant,
Decked with the single horn,
In the name of the horse of Mohammed,
I conjure you to be born!*

The brook exploded outward with a *whoosh of* spray. Shea jumped up and rubbed the water from his eyes—then rubbed them again to make sure. Once more, the travelers' magic had been almost successful.

Standing in the creek was a fine big bull Indian rhinoceros.

7

Shea had a moment of panic. Then he remembered that the bad reputation of the rhinoceros tribe is based on the cantankerousness of the two-horned black rhino of Africa. Anyway, he couldn't fool around conjuring up more animals. As he had asked for a docile one, this was presumably it. He landed astride the rhino's back.

The rhinoceros might be docile, but it was unaccustomed to riders. When it recovered from the shock of its arrival in an unfamiliar section of spacetime, it scrambled out of the creek and galloped off through the trees in the wrong direction. Shea dug his fingers into the folds of its armor and hung on, yelling at Belphebe: "Hey! See if...ugh...you can...ugh...herd this thing!"

The rhino, seeing the unicorn on its right, charged snorting and baring its incisor tusks. The unicorn whirled aside and poked the rhinoceros in the ribs as it lumbered past. The rhinoceros, now thoroughly upset, tried to flee. Belphebe skillfully herded it toward the camp of the Da Derga.

The bagpipes were louder. The rhinoceros, now more afraid of the unicorn than of this noise, headed straight for the sound. Shea clung to its back, hoping it wouldn't ram a tree. The trees sprang apart in front, and there was the camp of the Da Derga. A couple of guards held Chalmers across the altar. The Druids had found another knife.

Shea yelled: *"Yeeeeeow!"*

Heads turned toward him. The upraised knife hung suspended. Shea had a blurred picture of the camp streaming past, and everywhere the backs of the Da Derga departing in a swirl of tartan. They screamed most gratifyingly.

Beyond the altar Shea tumbled off his mount and walked back. Belphebe had already cut the bonds from the others; but, stiff and weak as they were, they could not move.

"I trust," said Chalmers feebly, "that you are...uh...convinced of the inadvisability of visiting the world of Irish myth, Harold."

Shea grinned, "Well, yes, since you mention it." He turned to Dolon. "I can take this weakness off you. But I'm sure a master like you would have a much better method than anything I could use. If you'll give the spell to me, I'll use it instead of my own."

"Marry, that will I. Few youngsters are so polite as to appreciate the powers of the masters these days. Bend down—"

Artegall raised a feeble hand to Belphebe. "What ails you, girl? Fall on these caitiffs! Slay them."

"The squire and I have a truce."

"A truce!" he growled. "Make a truce with the devil, or the Da Derga, but not with these enemies of human kind. The queen's majesty shall hear of this."

Shea was working the spell on Chalmers. As he got up he grunted: "Thank you, Harold. Really, do we have to go on—"

"Shut up, Doc," snapped Shea. He didn't intend to have his delicate bit of finagling gummed up at this stage. Then he turned to Dolon and worked the spell again.

The magician seemed annoyed that Chalmers should have preceded him, but it turned out to be a good idea. The moment Dolon was on his feet, he snatched up one of the discarded sacrificial knives and flung himself toward the helpless Artegall. Belphebe tripped him as he tried to go past. Before he could get up, Shea was on his back with one hand on his neck and the other on his wrist. "Drop that!" he yelled.

The magician's bulbous body heaved convulsively. Shea found himself gripping the neck of an enormous snake of the python type. With horror he felt the immense rubbery strength of the thing as it writhed a section from under him and tried to throw a coil around his body.

But, as the snakes have no hands, Dolon had perforce dropped the knife. Shea put the edge of it against the scaly throat. "Change back," he gritted, "or I'll saw your head right off!"

Dolon changed back. "Are you clean daft?" he sputtered. "There's a stinking fool 'prentice for you—ruining our chance to get rid of our greatest enemy."

"Not at all, master," said Shea, relaxing his grip a trifle. "You forget there's a truce on. Belphebe and I agreed not to have any scrapping until we've separated."

"You mean to keep your word with *them?* 'Tis against nature and therefore void."

Shea clamped down his grip again and turned to Artegall. "If I release you from the weakness spell, will you give me your word of honor to let us have a two-hour start?"

"Fool! Doltard!" shouted Dolon. But Artegall settled the question. "Covenant with an enchanter? Not I! Slay me if you will; you shall not rid yourselves of all Gloriana's knights so easily!"

Shea sighed at the unreasonableness of men. "Doc, watch Dolon for a minute, will you?" He got up and said to Belphebe: "Take care of him after we go." Then, more softly: "Say, how can I get in touch with you again?"

She thought. "If you go not beyond the confines of this great wood and know but how to call my unicorn of the forest—not that ungainly great beast of yours—"

"Can you whistle the tune for me—softly?" She did so, and he followed till he could do it. But she finished with a smile. "I misdoubt you could entice her close enough. These unicorns fear not maidens, but men they are greatly wary of."

Shea pondered, then drew Chalmers aside, leaving Belphebe to guard Artegall against Dolon. "Doc, can you conjure up sugar?"

"Harold, you are a continual source of astonishment to me. I really feel quite worn out, though. I'm incapable of coherent effort—"

Shea shook him by the shoulders. "Listen, Doc!" he said fiercely. "I'm pretty close to the edge of collapse myself, but if you ever want to see Florimel again, you can't let me down! This is just a little applied psychology; to wit, setting up an androphiliac fixation in the libido of one female unicorn. Now, go to it!"

Water, charcoal from the remains of one of the Da Derga's cooking fires, and a spell produced a double handful of neat patty-shaped molds of maple sugar, which Shea rather dubiously guessed would do. The unicorn sniffed suspiciously from a distance, then under Belphebe's coaxing teetered close enough to taste. It munched meditatively, wiggling its ears, then reached out its muzzle for more. Shea fed it another piece, then ostentatiously put the remainder in his pocket.

"All right," he said, "we're off. Say, Belphebe, maybe you better hitch J. Edgar Hoover's feet to the unicorn and haul him off before the Da Derga come back to see what happened." He glanced at the glowering Dolon. "Two hours truce now, and you can thank Heaven they took her bow away."

The dark was beginning to close in. As they reached the road, Dolon worked a spell and produced a horse. He mounted.

"Hey!" said Shea. "What about us?"

"I say a pox on you, 'prentice, for a rebellious rogue. Wend afoot and learn what it is to flout the great Dolon."

Shea put on a sly grin. "You don't understand, master. Don't you think it pays for the Chapter to have someone that the opposition thinks is a real man of honor? I'm just building myself up for the job. When we get ready to put something really good over on that bunch and catch a lot of them at once, instead of just these two, I'll come in handy."

Dolon considered a moment, then a smile ran round his red, full lips. "Oho! Sits the wind so? You want that red-polled baggage, eh? Well, when we capture her, you shall have her before she goes to the torture chamber—if the Chapter chooses to admit you. For I tell you fairly I doubt you are skilled enough in the more practical forms of magic."

Chalmers spoke up. "Ahem. You confessed, Dolon, that you of the Chapter occasionally...uh...work at cross-purposes."

"Aye. 'Tis the nature of things. For look you, magic is an art disorderly."

"But it isn't! We can show you how to change all that."

"Here's strange doctrine! Do you jest?"

"Not at all. Didn't you notice the Druids' methods of doing magic?"

"Those priests of the Da Derga? Magic they have, aye, but so meager a sort any lout can outdo them."

"That's not the point. It's not what they do, but how they do it. One man invokes their gods; another changes the altar from wood to stone, and so on. One man per function, and all timed to work together. That's real organization. Now, if...uh your Chapter were organized like that—"

Shea cut in: "You've been trying to break down Queen Gloriana's government and set up a council of magic to rule in its place, haven't you?" Nobody had told him that, but it seemed a reasonable guess.

"That we have; but the others worked singly, without any such leaders as myself to guide them."

"But even you, master, you're only one, and can't be everywhere at once. As it stands, your Chapter is a professional guild. It keeps you from cutting each other's throats by competition, but that's all. You won't get anywhere just bopping off an occasional knight. We can show you how to make a real organization out of it with all the parts working together as smoothly as the Faerie knights work together. The beauty of such an organization is that when it gets such a man of genius as yourself to guide it, everyone in the organization becomes a kind of extension of the leader's personality. It's just as though your Chapter were made into twenty-one Dolons. Gloriana's government could never stand against that."

"Ho-ho!" cried Dolon. "Now this proves once more that I am, as some are good enough to say, the great Dolon, and practically infallible in my judgment of men. I knew from the beginning that your minds held some noble and worthy plan for the advancement of the Chapter and the cause of magic. But I was forced to test you to bring it out. So—we are friends again, and I'll seal the bond by bringing forth your beasts and belongings."

He wheeled his own horse behind a tree. He worked a spell that sent a pillar of smoke towering through the branches to catch the last rays of the sun. From beneath it Adolphus and Gustavus trotted out to stand in the twilight beside their masters, the former with Shea's epee at the saddle. Dolon came back, grinning as though at some private joke.

"I shall present you to the Chapter as specialists in strange beasts," he remarked amiably. "That monster you rode to our rescue was as fearsome a hobgoblin as ever I saw, friend Harold. You see, I have the custom, not common among great men, of being affable to my juniors."

It was growing very dark under the trees, and the horses began to stumble on the ruinous road. Another hour of riding brought them to an opening. Midway along it and fairly close to the road, a thatched hut stood in the inadequate moonlight. One window was lighted.

"The castle of Busyrane," remarked Dolon.

"It seems somewhat...uh...exiguous," offered Chalmers timidly.

"Ho-ho! You know not our Archimage, who is a master of show and illusion, and sets such gulls to catch the unwary. Do but watch."

As Dolon spoke the moon was blotted out. Shea heard a flutter of wings. Something brushed past his face. There was a sensation of insectlike crawling on his left hand that made him snatch it from the bridle. A long, low ululating shriek rose from out of the dark. The horse quivered uncertainly beneath him. Its hoofs clacked on stone in the velvet black. Down at stirrup level a face appeared. It had huge, drooping ears and ragged teeth fixed in a permanent grin above the pendulous lower lip. There was no source of light for it to be seen by, nothing but that face floating by itself.

"The master makes you welcome and bids you dismount," mouthed the face indistinctly.

A clawlike hand reached up to help Shea from his mount. Though by now well inured to shocks, he could not help a shiver at the clammy cold touch. Dolon chuckled behind him. He shook off the horrors and followed the guidance of the corpselike fingers down a corridor of utter dark. Something rustled, and he caught the sickening odor of cockatrice. A door closed. He was standing in a big room, blinking in a flood of light, with the other two beside him.

An elderly man, wearing a palmer's robe like Chalmers', came forward to greet them. He smiled graciously. "Welcome, good Dolon! To what fortunate chance owe we your presence here before the meeting?"

"To the same chance that brings me here with these two stout fellows, whom I rescued but today from Artegall's curst clutches." This version was a trifle startling, but Shea had the sense to lay low as Dolon described his thrilling rescue of Shea and Chalmers. He went on: "Most noble Archimage, a plan has occurred to me. As you know, people are good enough to say that I have a talent for plans amounting almost to genius.

"Surely, noble Archimage, you are sib to the fact that you are but one and cannot be all places at once. As it stands, you head the Chapter well; but it is a professional guild. It prevents our cutting each other's throats by competition, but no more. What we need is an organization that will work together as the Faerie knights work together. It would be as though our mastership were composed of twenty-one Busyranes. Gloriana's government would have ill hap against it, eh?

"By the favor of fortune, I fell in with these two, desirous of admission to the Chapter. With that skill at judging character for which I am well known, I saw at once that they were experts in exactly the form of organization we need, I present you, therefore, Reed de Chalmers, magician, and Harold de Shea, apprentice, as worthy members of our society. In magic, their art is the conjuration of singular and unheard of beasts. The Blatant One himself has fled before their spells."

"Enchanted, magical sirs," said Busyrane, with a polite bow. "Your application shall receive the most earnest attention. We presume, good Dolon, you have heard the sad news?"

"That have I not."

"Poor Malvigen is slain—spitted with an arrow by that she-devil Belphebe."

"The curst vile tripping wench!" Dolon turned to Shea and Chalmers. "Magical sirs, I ask you, is this not a hard thing? Here's a man who spent a lifetime in the study and practice of magic; Malvigen. Made himself a great specialist in erotic dreams, excelling even the great Dolon in that one art. Now he's snuffed out in a second, like a wild boar, and for why? Because his attainments violate what those at the court choose to call morality."

Shea woke from a dream of being shrunk to a statue of one inch and swallowed by a snake. His clothes lay over a chair. They had evidently been given a magical laundering and mending, since they looked as good as new, in contrast to their worn and dirty state of the previous evening.

Chalmers came in. His clothes also were clean, and he looked younger than Shea remembered having seen him. He burst out: "I've found Florimel!"

"*Shhh!* For Pete's sake not so loud. Tell me about it."

"She was walking on the battlements. Really, this place is quite large when seen by daylight. Busyrane was most affable. It appears he intends to use her for the object—perfectly legitimate from his point of view—of causing dissension—"

"Okay, Doc. Okay! I get it. You're all excited. What did you really find out? Who is this Florimel, anyhow?"

"She was...uh...manufactured out of snow by a person called the Witch of Riphoea, as a duplicate or double of the genuine Florimel, who seems to have disappeared. Busyrane tells me it is at least theoretically possible to find a magical spell that will endow her with a genuine human body. He was most kind, most kind. I am afraid we may have misjudged—"

"Yeah. He promised he'd help you fix her up, I suppose."

Chalmers was suddenly dignified. "As a matter of fact, he did. But I cannot see how this affects—"

Shea jumped up. "Oh, my God! Next thing you'll be selling out to the magicians and letting Gloriana's crowd go chase themselves—as long as you can make this snow girl."

"That's not fair, Harold! After all, you were the one who insisted that we go ahead with our campaign, when I was willing to—"

"Yeah? Who had the bright idea of getting pally with the magicians in the first place? Who got up this marvelous plan—"

"Young man, let me tell you that you're grossly unreasonable as well as grossly reckless. You've placed us in one predicament after another by getting into fights for no good reason. You force my hand by making me use spells before I've tried them out. Now, when I wish to embark on a really important scientific experiment—"

"I suppose it never occurred to you that Busyrane might be trying to suck you in to work for him by means of this girl. He controls her, and—"

"*Shh!* You needn't shout!"

"I'm not shouting!" roared Shea.

A knock on the door made them both go silent. "Uh...ahem...come in!" said Chalmers.

Busyrane stood on the threshold, rubbing his hands. "Good morrow, magical sirs. We heard your conversation and bethought us there might be something our humble household might supply or our feeble powers obtain for your use."

Chalmers made a good recovery. "We were wondering— You know, the job of providing organization requires a special...uh...methodology. The science of combinational magic...uh...uh—"

Shea took over. "What we mean is, could we have the loan of some laboratory facilities?"

"Oh, certes, that lies within our gift. We have a disused chamber that would admirably serve. A few prisoners, even, on which you may experiment. We shall be happy, also, to furnish you with a cockatrice. If your honors will have the goodness to follow our poor person—"

When the head enchanter had left them, Shea and Chalmers drew deep breaths. They had watched him for the least sign of suspicion, but he had displayed none—so far.

Chalmers said: "Let me offer my apologies for...uh...my hastiness."

"That's all right, Doc. I shouldn't have flown off the handle. And I'm sorry for running you ragged by being reckless."

They shook hands, like a pair of shamefaced small boys. "What's the program now?" asked Shea.

"Well...ahem...I'd like to restore Florimel—that is, to give her a human body. Also, she might not find a person of my years peculiarly congenial. I observe Busyrane is able to assume almost any age he wishes."

"Ha—" Shea had started to laugh, but stopped as Chalmers gave him a hurt look. "After all, Harold, what's so heinous about wishing to be young?"

"It isn't that, Doc. I just remembered something you said—about amorous adventure having few attractions for a person of your age."

Chalmers smiled in mild triumph. "You forget that if I succeed in the rejuvenating process, I shall no longer be a person of my age!"

8

"Good gracious," said Chalmers. "that's the second time you've wandered off the incantation! Whatever is on your mind, Harold?" Shea stared absently at the big steel cage filling half the laboratory. Into it, with the aid of a pot containing a small fire, they were trying to conjure a dragon—one dragon. "Nothing much," he replied, "except I'm wondering about this flock of bogymen that's due to show up for the meeting tomorrow."

It was only half the truth. Shea had not given up his idea of a grand assault on the place and the capture of all the enchanters at once. The previous evening, without telling Chalmers, he had been out to look over the ground.

At the precise point where the gate began to fade from view, with rocks and trees on the other side of the building showing through it, he stopped and took careful bearings on the nearby landmarks. He chuckled internally over the thought that these invisible castles wouldn't be practical if the people of Faerie knew a little elementary surveying. Then he wedged the gate open with a small stone and slipped off among the trees.

There he cautiously whistled the tune Belphebe had taught him. No result. He went through it a second time and a third, wondering how long it would be before his absence were noticed. He was just about to give up when he saw a unicorn, apparently the same one Belphebe had ridden, peering from behind a tree. It sniffed suspiciously before coming forward to mouth one of the maple sugar lumps.

Shea wrote:

> DEAREST BELPHEBE: We are at Busyrane's castle. It lies about two hours' ride along the road from the place where we got away from the Da Derga. Looks like a hut till you turn off the road east and follow a track till you get to a big oak tree, the biggest in the neighborhood, in line with a hill that has a round top. Then you can see the castle. Could you arrange to be in the neighborhood in about forty-eight hours? I'll call the unicorn at that time and if you're riding it, will see you. Be careful about the magicians, will you?
> H. S.

He impaled the note on the unicorn's horn and shooed the animal away. *Now,* he thought, *if I make a break from the castle, I'll have a guide. If I don't, at least I'll see her again.*

That was last night. During the morning, he was more and more nervous and preoccupied, and now for the second time he had wandered from the incantation he and Chalmers were trying to work. "Nothing much," he had answered Chalmers' inquiry. Chalmers glanced at him shrewdly and hummed:

> *Heighdy! Heighdy!*
> *Misery me, lackadaydee!*
> *He sipped no sup, and he craved no crumb,*
> *As he sighed for the love of a layde!*

Shea looked at his partner sharply, but Chalmers' expression was bland. *How much did he suspect?*

But Chalmers was wrapped up in the task. "Now," he said, "let's try again.

> *By Fafnir and Python, Midgardsormr and Yang—*

the incantation rolled out. The smoke from the fire in the cage thickened, and the amateur enchanters went on, ready to yell the counterspell Chalmers had worked out if the thing got out of hand.

It was a variant on the original dragon spell, with wording and preparations slightly changed. There was a shrill metallic hiss and a minor convulsion in the smoke. The incantation stopped. The incantators stood gauping.

They had produced a dragon all right. One dragon, not a hundred. But this dragon was ten inches long, with bat wings and a prominent sting on the end of its tail. It breathed fire.

The bars of the cage had been made strong enough to hold a dragon of conventional size. But this little horror fluttered up to them, squeezed through, and flew straight at the experimenters.

"Yeow!" yelled Shea, as a blast of flame from its jaws singed the hair off the back of his hand. *"Awk!"* shrieked Chalmers as the sting got him in the ankle. They tumbled over each other and dashed around the laboratory, Shea brandishing his epee and Chalmers swinging a pestle. The dragonlet dodged past them and flew through the door into the corridor. There was a rustle and a heavy clank.

Shea went down the corridor. He came back with his face a trifle white.

"The cockatrice looked at it," he said, and held out a perfect stone dragon, ten inches long.

"Put it down," said Chalmers gloomily. He hobbled around, looking for something to put on his stung ankle. "Damnation, Harold, if there were only some way to control these things quantitatively—"

"I thought that was it," replied Shea. "What went wrong to give us that animated blowtorch?"

"I don't know. The only...uh...certitude is that we got our decimal point off again. We got point oh oh oh one dragon instead of a hundred dragons. I confess, the solution eludes me. The calculus of classes contains no aspect of quantitative accuracy—"

The rest of the day gave them a sea horse three feet long and, after some effort, a cask to put it in; six stuffed owls with blue glass eyes; and finally a large and amiable tomcat with nine tails. The last experiment found a moon looking in the castle window, so they gave up and went to bed. Chalmers murmured sadly that if he tried to give Florimel a human body in the present state of his knowledge, he'd probably make her into a set of lovely but embarrassing Siamese triplets.

There were noises during the night. Neither slept well till toward morning. When they rose, someone was tapping at their door.

It proved to be a long-eared, potbellied imp, who handed them a sheet of parchment, grinned, and sped off down the corridor. Shea and Chalmers read:

Ye Enchaunters' Chapter
Will meete in Council this daye
In ye greate Hall of Castle Busyrane

Archimage	Maistre Magitian Busyrane
Viceregente	M. M. Dolon
Archibiste	M. M. Courromont
Keeper of ye Moneys	M. M. Voulandoure
Ye Fyrst Daye	
Addresse of ye Archimage	M. M. Busyrane
Reading of ye minutes	M. M. Courromont
Report on ye treasurie	M. M. Voulandoure

Here will neue members be Thought on

Now cometh ye professional meeting

I.   M. M. Dolon—"Ye Powers magickal of six selected Water Fay-Human Hybrids."
II. M. M. Sournoy—"A neue use for ye Bloud of unbaptized infants."
III. M. M. Nuisane—"Of ye Comparative efficacie of ye Essence of ye Spotted Frogge & ye Common Green Frogge in sleeping Enchauntments."

These all with Diverse experiments and shews by ye Maistres aforesaid.

Day ye Second
Ye Maistres will meet in Executive Council in ye P. M.

Banquet	at Vespers
Maistre of ye Toasts	M. M. Nuisane

Ye Black Masse will be Celebrated after, followed by a Graund Ball, with various Comely Witches, Sprites, and Succubi.

"Sounds like a big occasion," observed Shea. "Let's go down to the great hall and see whom can we find."

They found their way to a huge room whose stained-glass windows bore pictures of mystical signs grouped round centerpieces of knights in magical torment. Already five people were gathered at one end, talking earnestly. Shea recognized Busyrane, Dolon, and Duessa. He caught a fragment of a story Dolon was telling:—"and I say he was no more than a bungling poursuivant, journeyman though he ranked. Imagine summoning up a devil, but leaving one corner of the pentagon open! He deserved no better than he got—ho-ho!—which was to have his head torn off by the demon's red-hot pincers! Ha, here come my pair! Busyrane, do 'em the honors!"

The Archimage bowed, first to Duessa and then to the new arrivals. "We are highly favored," he said, "to present Master Reed de Chalmers, who has applied for elevation to the honorable state of mastership in our Chapter. He is most expert, in the production of singular monsters, also a man full of ideas for the benefit of our order. Also his apprentice, Harold de Shea."

Was there a slight change in the voice on that last sentence? Shea could not be sure, and Duessa was curtsying, pronouncing in a fine contralto: "Enchanted, good magical sirs." With that red hair she was certainly a beauty when she wanted to be gracious. If only—

Plop! A bare-necked vulture flopped through the window and lit beside them, then changed into a hook-nosed man in a long monk's outfit. "The good Fripon!" exclaimed Dolon. "How wags the world with you?"

"By your leave, not well," croaked the good Fripon, sadly. "I had all but trapped that wretch Belphebe when what does she do but get a counter-spell from Cambina, then shoot an arrow through one of the best sprites I ever had. Curse her! She's killing off the Losels, too."

"I live for the day when I can tear her toenails out," said Duessa venomously. Shea's scalp tingled. A dust whirlwind that puffed in the window set everyone coughing, and dissolved into a short, fat man, who mopped his brow.

"Whew!" he said. "Fatiguing! Still it's better than walking for a man of my figure. Hope you have an ample lunch, Busyrane. Always thinking of my belly, that's me, Voulandoure, at your service. Ah, fair Duessa! And the good Fripon! Still cheating the gravedigger, my gloomy friend?" He poked Fripon's ribs.

Now magicians began to pour into the hall, by window and door, so many of them Shea could not keep up with their names. The trumpet for the midday meal found him vainly trying to catch up—and also separated him from Chalmers, who was taken in tow to sit at the masters' table.

Shea found himself next to a fuzzy-haired youth who said shyly: "Pray, generous sir, may I see your enchanted blade?"

"Huh?" said Shea. "But it—" before it occurred to him that no useful purpose would be served by disillusioning these people about the epee. He produced it and handed it over. The fuzzy young man waved it over the table, making noises of approval.

"I feel no sudden access of strength," he remarked. "The spell must be very subtle. Or perhaps it is one you use on yourself—no, that could not be, for Cambina's magic prevented the use of such spells at the tournament. Hey,

Grimbald!" He reached across and touched the blue-jowled man on Shea's other side. "He beat two of the most renowned knights of Faerie with this toothpick!"

"Aye," replied the other, looking up from his plate, "including one of ours." He addressed Shea directly. "Knew you not that Blandamour and Paridell, though they wear the Faerie livery, are in the service of this Chapter? Nay, you're not a member—how could you? But 'ware both in the future."

That explained a lot, thought Shea: the actions of the two knights, for one thing; and for another, why the magicians were so polite to him, though his rating was no more than that of an apprentice. There would be something practically supernatural about modern fencing technique to these people.

Busyrane had arranged his hair so that the light falling through the stained-glass window touched it to a halo. He might have been some kindly saint as he began:

"Magical sirs and ladies: Many are the pleasures that have fallen to our lot, but none equal to that of beholding you here assembled beneath our humble roof to carry on the good name and high purpose of magic. Ah, how much better and brighter a world it were if all in it could but know you all—could but see you all. My friends—"

The afternoon was warm, the lunch had been ample, and Shea had a feeling of having heard something like this before. His eyelids began to weigh on him. The smooth voice rolled on:

"—in the days of King Huon of glorious and blessed memory, my friends, when we lived a more abundant life—"

Shea felt himself itching, now here, now there, now all over. He made one more effort to keep awake, then lapsed into an unashamed doze.

He was aroused by a mild patter of applause. Busyrane's place was taken by the keeper of ye archives, Courromont, a thin-lipped, bloodless-looking man, who hardly moved his mouth as he read:

"At the council of the Enchanters' Chapter on August 1st following the address of our beloved archimage six members were advanced in grade from apprentice to journeyman and one journeyman member to wit the esteemed Sournoy was advanced to the full rank of master magician it was furthermore decided to raise the annual dues from seven and a half to ten elfars papers were read at the professional session by Master Magicians Malvigen and Denfero with various works of magical prowess in illustration it was furthermore resolved in the executive session to empower a special committee for drastic action against certain representatives of the Old Order whose activities have become threatening to wit the knight Sir Cambell and Belphebe of the Woods and the Princess Britomart the knights of the Chapter Blandamour and Paridell were accordingly—"

Shea came wide awake, but there were no details. Busyrane merely asked if it were moved and seconded that the minutes be accepted. They were.

Voulandoure's fat face shone greasily in the heat as he droned off figures and urged members to pay their dues on time. What could those plans for drastic action have been? Presumably the late Malvigen had tried one of them when he got Belphebe's arrow through him, but what else?

His attention was snapped back by Busyrane's use of his name: "—proposed that the magicians Reed de Chalmers and Harold de Shea be admitted with the ranks of master magician and apprentice. If these gentlemen will kindly leave the room—"

Outside, Shea said softly: "Did you hear what they said about Belphebe?"

"Dear me, yes. Duessa seems quite determined on that point. She used a most vulgar term in speaking of her—one normally employed in the...uh...propagation of dogs. When—"

"What are they going to *do*? Specifically?" Shea's voice was urgent.

"I—" The door opened and a voice called: "Master Reed de Chalmers."

Shea was left to fidget for five minutes before being summoned. Busyrane grasped him by the hand at the door and led him to the front of the hall. "We present to you the apprentice Harold de Shea as a member of this Chapter," he said. "A very worthy magical person, adept in the production of strange monsters, adroit in enchantments connected with the profession of arms. Apprentice Harold de Shea"—he turned toward the new member—"as members of a high intellectual calling we despise the silly ceremonies of admission such as the court uses for its orders of knighthood. Therefore, we will merely bid you welcome; but doubtless the other apprentices will have something to say to you tomorrow night after the Black Mass."

Voulandoure came over and squeezed Shea's hand in his own thick, moist ones. "My 'gratulations, also, magical sirs!" He lowered his voice. "May I point out the initiation fee—"

"Ahem," said Chalmers, who had joined the group. "How much?"

"Fifty elfars for yourself, Master Magician Reed, and twenty-five for 'Prentice Harold."

Chalmers looked slightly stricken. He fished out the money bag. His face showed some relief, but not much, when its contents proved adequate. "I should think," he remarked, "that with so many fine magicians about, you'd have no difficulty in conjuring up...uh...all necessary funds."

A shadow crossed the face of ye keeper of ye moneys. "Alas, magical sir, our great problem! 'Tis a department involving the use of the philosophers' stone and the blood of infants, this much we know. But our research in the question has been interrupted by the activities of that curst court and the Companions, and I fear me we shall never succeed till we rid ourselves of them."

"Aye," said Dolon. "The one who came nearest the solution was the enchantress Acrasia. She did make a conjured gold that was all but permanent; met every test, and would only turn to ashes when one pronounced a Pater Noster. But where's Acrasia now? Eh? Dead, down and drownded by one of Gloriana's Companions, a murrain on them all!"

"Good Master Dolon!" It was Busyrane. "The professional meeting is called, and I doubt not the other masters are as eager as we ourselves to hear your paper."

Shea found the fuzzy-haired youth at his elbow. "D'you play at checks? We 'prentices are left much to our own devisings when the masters gabble."

"Checks?"

"Aye, you know, king, queen, knight, fool, pawn, check and you're mate. I'm hand in glove with one of Busyrane's imps, who'll furnish us a mug or two of musty ale to pass the time while we play."

It sounded an attractive program. But Shea remembered that chess game afterward. The fuzz-haired apprentice was not naturally a good player. Shea beat him in the first two games easily, winning the small bets the youth insisted on "to make the sport more interesting." Then the musty ale or the youth's magic—too late Shea remembered what profession he was an apprentice in—rose up and bit him. The fuzzy one's pieces turned up in the most unexpected places, executing the most astonishing gambits and combinations. With every new defeat Shea grew more annoyed. Whether through annoyance or the musty ale, he began offering to double the bets for the next one.

When the doors at the end of the hall were flung open and the master magicians emerged, the fuzzy youth was remarking gaily: "That makes eighty-six elfars, sixteen you stand in my debt. Ha-ha, that reminds me. Did I ever tell you about the journeyman Sligon, who owed my master, Voulandoure, sixty elfars over a box of dice? He refused to pay—said he couldn't—even when Voulandoure sent him a plague of boils. Well, wasn't it funny, when Sligon was playing with his own cat one day, that he should turn into a fish? I say a good magician should never lack for money, when there are people who can be kidnapped and ransomed. Don't you agree?"

"That's right," said Shea with a heartiness which he hoped didn't sound too hollow. He got up to join Chalmers.

The elder psychologist was looking pleased with himself. "A trifle harrowing that session, but gratifyingly informative," he said as they went toward their rooms. "I really feel I've learned something about quantitative control. In fact, I'm confident that in a few months' research I can learn enough not only to transform Florimel and to rejuvenate myself, but also to... uh...revolutionize the entire practice of magic in Faerie, to make its benefits available to all."

"Yes, but"—Shea looked worried—"did you find out what they intend to do about Belphebe?"

"I gather that that is a matter for the uh...executive session of tomorrow. But as I understand the outlines of the plan, it is not to direct the enchantments against her in person. She's protected against them. They intend rather to place spells on the two or three places where she sleeps, with the design of causing her to fall into so deep a slumber that she can be captured."

They paused on Chalmers' threshold. He added: "However, I wouldn't worry about the young woman's...uh...safety, Harold. As I understand it she is to be brought here, and I am sure that as a member of the Chapter I can persuade them not to harm her. In fact—"

"For the love of Mike, Doc, are you throwing in with these guys, or just plain daffy? Didn't you hear Duessa talking about pulling Belphebe's toenails out, come the Revolution, and Dolon mentioning the torture chamber? Wake up! You're being an old fool!"

"Harold, I must request you not to use such intemperate language. After all, I'm somewhat your senior, and I require the uninterrupted use of all facilities as well as your own cordial cooperation to put this matter on a scientific basis. In a few months I shall be in a position to effect an industrial revolution in magic—"

"Theory! Months! I might have known that's what you'd be after! Can't you realize somebody's in danger?"

"I shall certainly give my most earnest attention to persuading the other members of the Chapter that this young woman to whom you are so attached is innocuous, and—"

"Oh, for Pete's sake! Forget it! Good night." Shea stalked out, more angry with Chalmers than he had ever been before. He did not hear the velvety click of the Judas window in Chalmers' room. Nor could he overhear the two men in the secret passage that led to that window.

Busyrane's voice was bland. "We were good enough to warn you that the young man was a suspicious character and mingled somehow in the affairs of the court."

"Can it be that my judgment, usually so keen, was altogether thrown off?" asked Dolon.

"Oh, you were right about the older. He's a proper magician and devoted to the Chapter. But the younger—he'll bear more than watching. A friend of Belphebe, forsooth!"

9

Shea lay in bed, staring at the black ceiling. No use trying to get the Doc to do anything. His heart was in the right place. But between his devotion to Florimel and his devotion to theory he could not be convinced that these enchanters, who talked so glibly of intellectual achievements, were bloody-minded racketeers who intended to put Belphebe, Britomart, and a lot of others to a slow and intricate death.

Shea shuddered as he thought of it. Whatever was done to save them, he would have to do, quickly. Yes, and to keep Chalmers from turning the products of his really fine scientific mind over to these rascals.

The castle was silent. He slipped out of bed, dressed, and buckled the faithful epee over his shoulder. It would not be much use against enchantments. But as long as the enchanters themselves believed it had magical power, it would help.

The door swung open noiselessly. There was no light in the corridor. The stone floor was cold under Shea's feet. His soft leather boots made soundless progress. If he kept one hand along the wall, he thought he could find the way to the great hall, and so out. Step—step—the hand that had been following the wall touched nothingness. An appalling odor of cockatrice assailed his nostrils. Evidently the door of somebody's laboratory. He went down to hands and knees and slithered past an inch at a time, hoping the creature would not wake up.

So. Here was the head of the stair. He took one step down, two—and felt something soft touch his ankles. Another step and the something soft was clear to his waist, catching at him. It felt ropy and vaguely slimy, a whole tangle of slime—cobwebs! For a moment Harold Shea felt unreasoning panic, as it seemed that going ahead and turning back would be equally fatal. Then he realized that this would be some of Busyrane's magic, part of the ordinary castle safeguards, and of no special significance.

Yet what would cut through or destroy cobwebs? Fire. He had no fire. But in his previous adventure in Scandinavian myth, Surt's giants had made use of flaming swords, and he had the epee. With an incantation to make use of the law of similarity it might become a flaming sword. On that narrow, stone-walled spiral staircase it was altogether unlikely that anyone would be able to see the light.

With the ghostly fingers of the cobwebs clutching at his legs, Shea stood on the stair and thought as he never had before of a spell:

Sword, sword, sword that is now my salvation,
Make me a light to cut through these cobwebs;
Be like Surt's sword to cut through this maze.

He could feel the hilt growing warm.

Help my escape to reach consummation;
In the name of Durandal, help me to be free.

It was not outrageously good poetry, but the hilt was so hot that he snatched it out. A smoky red flame ran down the blade and dropped from the point, revealing the whole stairwell from wall to wall and as high as Shea stood, filled with a solid mass of the hideous gray material. A man could smother in it easier than not. Busyrane left nothing to chance.

Shea slashed at the stuff with the flaming epee. It shriveled left and right before him, back against the wall with hissing, foul-smelling flames running along the strands. He advanced slowly, cutting one step at a time. As he reached the bottom and the last cobwebs, the fire in the blade went out. He was in the great hall; but a few steps carried him through it, across the forecourt and to the gate.

A moon looked down out of a cloudless sky. Shea cursed it softly to himself, wondering whether he ought to take a chance on crossing the open stretch between gate and the shelter of the trees before it set. He decided to try it.

Bending low, he scuttled rapidly across the space, his cloak, flapping like a vampire's wings. He made it without stumbling and looked back. The castle had disappeared. There was nothing visible but stony ground with the hut in the middle.

Once among the trees, he began pacing the circuit of the clearing, whistling very softly to himself the unicorn tune and pausing to listen. A quarter of the way round he was halted by a tense whisper, "Stand, sir!"

"Belphebe!"

"Aye." She stepped from her place of concealment, arrow drawn to the head. "In good sooth you look like Harold de Shea. But show me how you hold that narrow sword."

Shea drew the still-warm epee and demonstrated.

"Certes, then you are indeed he. I feared lest the enchanters had sent a phantom forth to beguile me. Right glad I am to see you, Squire Harold."

Shea said: "Say, I'm glad to see you, too. I knew I could depend—"

"Save your fair speeches for another hour. Here is danger. What is toward?"

Shea explained. Belphebe said: "For myself I fear not, though I thank you for the warning. Yet it's somewhat otherwise with Britomart, who has not the protection of the woods so close as I. And sure it were shame to miss the chance of catching the entire Chapter at once. Let me think. I left Artegall at a woodcutter's cot on the far flank of Loselwood. His man Talus had gone to fetch Cambina, that she might heal his bruises and calm his mind."

"So Cambina's a psychologist too! Why does he need his mind calmed?"

"Why, sir, he's the chief justiciar of all Faerie. Without a calm mind, how shall he hold the balance even? Let us go thither and lay this matter before him. Certes, we two cannot lay so many rogues by the heels alone."

Two hours of walking brought Shea to the yawning stage. The moon had set. Under the black trees, even the sure-footed Belphebe found the going hard. She was ready to listen to suggestions for a nap.

"Sleep is still far from me now," she said. "If you wish, I will keep watch for the first hour—which should be till the stars of the Bear sink to the top of that tree." She pointed. Shea, too drowsy to notice, composed himself to rest.

The next thing he knew, he was being shaken awake in a brightening world.

"Hey, young lady," he said through his first yawn, "I thought you were going to wake me up after the first hour?"

"And so thought I. But you were so in comfort that I wanted the heart to rouse you. I need but little sleep."

"Naughty. What about my masculine pride?"

She made a face at him. "I forgot that. Men are such foolish carls about it. But come." She danced a step or two. "Tirra-lirra, a brave day! Let's forth and seek our breakfast."

As they walked along, Belphebe peering toward thickets for an edible target, and Shea a bit woozy from lack of sleep, he asked: "D'you suppose Cambina will have calmed Artegall down so he'll listen to my explanations before he starts carving?"

"A thing to think on! Will you hide whilst I speak him fair?"

"Guess I'll take a chance on his temper." Shea wasn't going to have his dream-girl suspect him of timidity at this stage. He was sure he could outrun the bulky justiciar if necessary.

"Marry, I would not have you answer otherwise!" She smiled at him, and he felt rewarded. She went on, scrutinizing him: "Many knights, squires, and yeomen have I kenned, Master Harold, but never a wight like you. You speak fair, yet half the time with words I wot not of. You promised to explain the meanings of those wherewith you put the Blatant Beast to rout."

Shea replied: "Curiosity killed a cat."

"*Miauw!* Yet of this cat's allotted nine, I have several left to draw upon."

"I really can't, Belphebe. Magical reasons."

"Oh. Well then, tell me the meaning of the strange thing you called the Lady Cambina even now."

"Psychologist?"

"Aye."

Shea gave an account in words of one syllable of the science of psychology, and of his own experiences in its practice. Under the girl's admiring curiosity he expanded. Before he knew it he was practically telling her the story of his life. As soon as he realized this, he cut his autobiography off short, not wanting to leave her with nothing to be curious about.

Belphebe said: "A strange tale, Squire. Gin you speak truth, this homeland of yours were worth the seeing." She sighed a little. "The wilds of Faerie I know like my own palm. And since I will not tarry at Gloriana's tedious court, there's nothing left for me but to hunt the Losels and such vile—*Sst!*" She broke off, moved slowly a couple of steps, and loosed an arrow. It knocked over a rabbit.

While they dressed and cooked their breakfast. Shea thought. He finally ventured: "Look here, kid, some day Doc and I will be going back, I suppose. Why don't you plan to come with us?"

Belphebe raised her eyebrows. " 'Tis a thought audacious. But stay—could I live among the woods-paths as I do here?"

"Unh." Shea imagined the horrible complications that would ensue if Belphebe tried to lead her present life in Ohio's close-fenced farmland. "I'm afraid that wouldn't be practical. But there's plenty else to do."

"What then? How should I live in one of your great towns?"

That problem had not occurred to Shea. He revised his estimate of Belphebe. The girl might look like something out of a medieval romance, but she had a core of hard common sense. The only job he could think of for her was giving bow-and-arrow lessons, and he hardly supposed the demand for professional archers to be large.

He said vaguely: "Oh, we'll figure something out. Doc and I would see to it that you were—uh—uh..."

"Harold!" she said sharply. "What are you proposing? Think not that because I lead a free roving life, I—"

"No, no, I didn't mean—uh..."

"What then?"

He thought again. One obvious solution was staring him in the face; yet to bring it up so early might spoil everything. Still, nothing ventured...

He drew a deep breath and plunged: "You could marry me."

Belphebe's mouth fell open. It was some seconds before she answered: "You jest, good Squire!"

"Not at all. People do it in my country, you know, just like here."

"But—knew you not that I am affianced to Squire Timias?"

It was Shea's turn to stare blankly.

Belphebe said: "Nay, good friend, take it not so to heart. I had thought it known to the world, else I should have told you. The fault was mine."

"No...I mean...it wasn't...let's skip it."

"Skip it?" said Belphebe wonderingly. Shea bent over his rabbit-haunch, muttering something about the meat's being good.

Belphebe said: "Be not angry, Harold. Not willingly would I hurt you, for I like you well. And had I know you sooner...But my word is given."

"I suppose so," said Shea somberly. "What sort of man is your friend Timias?" He wondered whether the question had a useful purpose, or whether he was showing a slight touch of masochism in keeping the painful subject alive.

Belphebe's face softened. "A most sweet boy; shrinking and sensitive, not like these brawling knightly ruffians."

"What are his positive qualities?" asked Shea.

"Why—ah—he can sing a madrigal better than most."

"Is that all?" said Shea with a touch of sarcasm.

Belphebe bridled. "I know not what you mean. 'Tis even the core of the matter that he's no bold confident venturer like yourself."

"Doesn't sound to me like much of a reason for marrying anybody. I came across a lot of cases like that in my psych work; usually the woman lived to regret it."

Belphebe jumped up angrily. "So, Squire, you inquire of my privy affairs that you may sting me with your adder's tongue? Fie on you! It regards not you whom I marry, or why."

Shea grinned offensively. "I was just making general remarks. If you want to take them personally, that's your lookout. I still say a woman is taking a lousy chance to marry a human rabbit in the hope of making a lion out of him."

"A murrain on your general remarks!" cried Belphebe passionately. "An you would company me, I'll thank you to keep your long tongue in its proper groove! Better rabbit than fox with pretense of marriage—"

"What do you mean, pretense?" barked Shea. "I meant that when I said it! Though now I see that maybe it wasn't such a good idea—"

"Oh, you do? You change your mind quickly! I'll warrant me you'd have done so in any case!"

Shea got himself under control, and said: "Let's not go any farther with this, Belphebe. I'm sorry I made those cracks about your boyfriend. I won't mention him again. Let's be friends."

Belphebe's anger wilted. "And right sorry am I that I threw your proposal in your face, Squire Harold; 'twas a sad discourtesy." Shea was surprised to see a trace of moisture in her eye. She blinked rapidly and smiled. "So, we are friends, and our breakfast done. Let us be on."

The new sun was a patch of flecks of orange fire through the foliage. They found a sluggish little stream and had to squeeze through the thickets on its banks.

They reached a stretch of drier ground where the glades expanded to continuous meadow and the forest shrank to clumps of trees. They left one of these clumps and were swishing through the long grass, when a leathery rustle made them look up.

Overhead swooped a nightmarish reptile the size of an observation plane. It had two legs and a pair of huge batwings. On its back rode Busyrane, all clad in armor but his face, which was smiling benignly. "Well met, dear friends!" he called down. "What a pleasing thought! Both at once!

Twunk! went Belphebe's bow. The arrow soared through one wing membrane. The beast hissed a little and banked for a turn.

"Into the woods!" cried Belphebe, and set the example. "The wyvern cannot fly among the trees."

"What did you call it? Looks like some kind of a long-tailed pterodactyl to me." Shea craned his neck as the sinister shadow wove to and fro above the leaves.

Belphebe led the way to the opposite side of the grove. When Busyrane circled above the segment away from them, they dashed across the open space and into the next clump. A shrill hiss behind and above warned them that they had been spotted.

They worked their way through this grove. From under the trees they could see Busyrane silhouetted against the sky, while he couldn't see them.

"Now!" said Belphebe, and ran like an antelope through the long grass. Shea pounded after. This was a longer run than the first, a hundred yards or more. Halfway across he heard the hiss of cloven air behind and drove himself for all his strained lungs were worth. The shadow of the monster unblurred in front of him. It was too far, too far—and then he was under the friendly trees. He caught a glimpse of the reptile, horribly close, pulling up in a stall to avoid the branches.

Shea leaned against a trunk, puffing. "How much more of this is there?"

Belphebe's face had a frown. "Woe's me; I fear this forest thins ere it thickens. But let's see."

They worked round the edges of the grove, but it was small, and the distance to all others, but the one they had come from, prohibitively great.

"Looks like we have to go back," said Shea.

"Aye. I like not that. Assuredly he will not have pursued us alone."

"True for you. I think I see something there." He pointed to a group of distant figures, pink in the rising sun.

Belphebe gave a little squeak of dismay. "Alack, now we are undone, for they are a numerous company. If we stay, they surround us. If we flee, Busyrane follows on that grim mount—What are you doing?"

Shea had gotten out his knife and was whittling the base of a tall sapling. He replied: "You'll see. This worked once and ought to again. You're good at tree climbing; see if you can find a bird's nest. I need a fistful of feathers."

She went, puzzled but obedient. When she returned with the feathers, Shea was rigging up a contraption of sapling trunk and twigs, tied together with ivy vine. He hoped it wasn't poison ivy. It bore some resemblance to an enormous broom. As Shea lashed a couple of crosspieces to the stick he explained: "The other one I made a single-seater. This'll have to carry tandem. Let's see the feathers, kid."

He tossed one aloft, repeating the dimly remembered spell he had used once before, and then shoved it in among the twigs.

"Now," he said, "I'm the pilot and you're the gunner. Get astride here. Think you can handle your bow while riding this thing?"

"What will it do?" she asked, looking at Shea with new respect.

"We're going up to tackle Busyrane in his own element. Say, look at that mob! We better get going!" As the pursuers came nearer, thrashing the brushes of the nearby groves in their hunt, Shea could see that they were a fine collection of monsters: men with animal heads, horrors with three or four arms, bodies and faces rearing from the legless bottoms of snakes.

They straddled the broom. Shea chanted:

> *By oak, ash, and yew,*
> *The high air through,*
> *To slay this vile caitiff,*
> *Fly swiftly and true!*

The broom started with a rush, up a long slant. As it shot out of the grove and over the heads of the nearest of the pursuit, they broke into a chorus of shouts, barks, roars, meows, screams, hisses, bellows, chirps, squawks, snarls, brays, growls and whinnies. The effect was astounding.

But Shea's mind was occupied. He was pleased to observe that this homemade broom seemed fairly steady though slower than the one he had hexed in the land of Scandinavian myth. He remembered vaguely that in aerial dogfighting the first step is to gain an advantage in altitude.

Up they went in a spiral. Busyrane came into view on his wyvern, beating toward them. The enchanter had his sword out, but as the wyvern climbed after them Shea was relieved to see that he was gaining.

A couple of hundred feet above the enemy he swung the broom around. Over his shoulder he said: "Get ready; we're going to dive on them." Then he noticed that Belphebe was gripping the stick with both hands, her knuckles white.

"Ever been off the ground before?" he asked.

"N-nay. Oh, Squire Harold, this is a new and very fearsome thing. When I look down—" She shuddered and blinked.

"Don't let a little acrophobia throw you. Look at your target, not the ground."

"I essay."

"Good girl!" Shea nosed the broom down. The wyvern glared up and opened its fanged jaws. He aimed straight for the red-lined maw. At the last minute he swerved aside; heard the jaws *clomp* vainly and the bowstring snap.

"Missed," said Belphebe. She was looking positively green under her freckles. Shea, no roller-coaster addict, guessed how she felt.

"Steady," he said, nosing up and then dodging as the wyvern flapped toward them with surprising speed. "We'll try a little shallower dive."

Shea came down again. The wyvern turned, too. Shea didn't bank far enough, and he was almost swept into the jaws by the centrifugal force of his own turn. They went *clomp* a yard from the tail of the bottom. "Whew," said Shea on the climb. "Hit anything?"

"Busyrane, but it hurt him not. He bears armor of proof and belike some magic garment as well."

"Try to wing the wyvern, then." They shot past the beast, well beyond reach of the scaly neck. *Twunk!* An arrow fixed itself among the plates behind the head. But the wyvern, appearing unhurt, put on another burst of speed and Shea barely climbed over its rush, with Busyrane yelling beneath him.

Belphebe had her acrophobia under control now. She leaned over and let go three more arrows in rapid succession. One bounced off the reptile's back plates. One went through a wing membrane. The third stuck in its tail. None of them bothered it.

"I know," Shea. "We aren't penetrating its armor at this range. Hold on; I'm going to try something."

They climbed. When they had good altitude, Shea dove past the wyvern. It snapped at them, missed, and dove in pursuit.

The wind whistled in Shea's ears and blurred his vision. Forest and glade opened out below; little dots expanded to the pursuers on foot. Shea glanced back; the wyvern hung in space behind, its wings half furled. He leveled out, then jerked the broom's nose up sharply. The universe did a colossal somersault and they straightened away behind the wyvern. In the seconds the loop had taken, the beast had lost sight of them. Shea nosed down and they glided in under the right wing, so close they could feel the air go *fuff* with the wing beat.

Shea got one glimpse of Busyrane's astonished face before the wing hid it. The scaly skin pulsed over the immense flying muscles for one beat. "Now!" he barked.

Twunk! Twunk! Belphebe had drawn the bow hard home, and the arrows tore into the beast's brisket.

There was a whistling scream, then catastrophe. The wide wing whammed down on the aviators, almost knocking Shea from his seat. They were no longer flying, but tumbling over and over, downward. The top of a tree slashed at Shea's face. Dazedly, he heard the wyvern crash and tried to right the broom. It nosed up into a loop and hung. A cry from behind him, receding toward the earth, froze him. He saw Belphebe tumble into the grass, twenty feet down, and a wave of the monster men close over her.

Shea manhandled his broomstick around, fervently wishing he had a lighter one—a pursuit job. By the time he got it aimed at the place where he had last seen Belphebe, there was no sign of her or of Busyrane either. The wyvern sprawled bloatedly in the grass with hundreds of the enchanter's allies swarming round it.

Shea drew his epee and dove at the thick of them. They screeched at him, some of them producing clumsy breast bows. He swooped toward a monster with a crocodile head as the strings began snapping. The arrows went far behind, but just as Shea stiffened his arm for the gliding thrust, Crocodilehead thinned to a puff of mist. The epee met no resistance. As Shea held his glide, parallel with the ground, he found the crowding monsters disappearing before him. He pulled up, looking back. They were materializing behind. More arrows buzzed past.

He circled, cutting another swath through them. No sign of Belphebe.

At the third charge an arrow caught in his cloak. The flint head of another drove through his boot and a quarter inch into his calf. The goblins were learning anti-aircraft fire. But of Belphebe there was still no sign, and now the ghost men were streaming toward him out of the woods on all sides. In every direction they were hopping, yelling, drawing their crude bows.

He climbed out of bowshot and circled, looking. No luck. It would have to be some other way. He felt slightly sick.

He went up higher, till the vast green expanse of Loselwood spread out before him. The sun was well up. Under it he fancied he could see the region where he had tangled with the Da Derga. Beyond should be the edge of the forest, where he and Chalmers had met their first Losels.

10

An hour of cruising showed him a clearing with a little garden, a thatched cottage, and a circular palisade of pointed stakes around the whole. He helixed down slowly.

A man came out of the wood and entered the palisade through a gate. Shea caught a glimpse of red face and black beard as his own shadow, whisking across the grass, brought the man's eyes upward. The man dashed into the cottage as if all the fiends of Hell were after him. In a moment two armored men came out. The shield of one bore the striking black and silver gyronny of Sir Cambell.

By oak, ash and yew;
My broomstick true,
Like a dead leaf descending,
So softly fall you!

That was not quite the right way to put it, as Shea immediately learned. The broom settled slowly, but remorselessly literal, carried the imitation of a dead leaf to the point of a dizzying whirl. Cottage, forest, and waiting knights came to him in a spinning blur.

Shea felt ground under his feet. He staggered dizzily.

Artegall roared: "By'r Lady, 'tis the enchanter's varlet!" His sword came out, *Wheep!*

Shea said: "You're just the man I'm looking for—"

"That I warrant!" His laugh was a nasty bark. "But you'll accomplish no more magician's tricks on me. I have a protection, which is more than you have against this!" He shook the sword and swung it back.

"*Wait* a minute!" cried Shea. "I can explain, honest—"

"Explain to the devils of Hell, where you soon will be!"

At that moment Britomart and Cambina came out of the cabin. Shea wondered frantically whether to run toward them, try to start the broom, or— What was that? A set of little patterns was faintly visible on Artegall's breastplate as he turned in the morning sun. They were the type of pattern that would be left by soldering on brass oak leaves and then prying them off.

"Hey!" he said. "You're the guy who showed up in the oak leaves at Satyrane's tournament and won the second prize but didn't stop to collect it!"

"Huh? How knew you—What mean you, rogue?"

"Just what I say. You fought for the challengers, and Britomart knocked you off your pony, didn't she?"

" 'Tis to be said...ah—" Artegall turned his scowl on Britomart. She glared back.

"Come, good friends," said Cambina, "no variance. I proclaim it was Sir Artegall, for I penetrated his disguise. Come, Artegall, confess; you cannot hide the sun at the bottom of a bucket."

"I suppose I must," growled the knight. "I did but wish to make proof whether I were as strong in the lists as I seemed, or whether certain of the knights would rather fall off their horses than oppose the queen's justicier." He turned to Britomart. "You have a rude way toward an affianced husband, my lady!"

Shea caught Britomart's eye and winked violently. She turned on Artegall a look that would have melted granite. "Ah, my dear lord, had I but known! Yet surely you shall feel no shame at that one overthrow, for 'twas the combination of that enchanted ebony spear I bear and your own horse's stumbling, neither alone sufficient." She reached for his mailed arm. "When we are wed I shall leave these broils and tournaments to you."

Cambell and Cambina looked at Britomart, then at each other. The look implied they had never seen her act *that* way before. Shea repressed a grin. The brawny blonde learned fast.

Artegall smiled shamefacedly. "Why, dearest dame, that were a great sacrifice indeed. I knew not you cared so." His voice hardened. "But we have here a most villainous young rascal."

"No rascal," said Britomart, "but a true and loyal squire, whom I have sworn to my service and that of the queen."

"Then what of his soaring through the sky like a bug or witch? Nay, he's of the tribe of enchanters—"

"Not so," interrupted Cambina. "His magic is white, even as my own; and my art tells me that this Harold de Shea will speak the truth if you'll let him."

Artegall scowled, but asked: "Then what's the truth he would speak?"

Shea told his story quickly before a new argument could start. "That is good truth, I guarantee," said Cambina, when he had finished, "and Belphebe is in deadly danger."

"Then why stand we here at words?" snapped Artegall. "Ho, woodcutter! We start at once. Food and horses, as soon as they may be had, for all of us."

Shea disapproved of this cavalier treatment, but didn't feel called upon to comment. He said: "Going to collect an army?"

"Nay, not I. Time presses us too close. Here we must count on our own good arms and Cambina's magic. Art afraid?"

"Try me."

"There's a stout younker." The frown in Artegall's brows cleared a bit. "I will be just and admit I held you wrong."

The moon in this world, Shea observed, set only twelve or thirteen minutes later each night, instead of the fifty minutes later of his own earth. He and his four companions were crouched at the edge of the opening that held Busyrane's unseen castle. They did not attempt it till the moon had disappeared.

As they crossed the open space Shea whispered: "I'm afraid I can't find the gate. Too dark to see my landmarks."

"Small loss," answered Cambina. Shea saw her dimly, doing things with her wand. Out of nothing grew a faint phosphorescence that resolved itself into a row of bars.

Cambina pointed the wand at it. The instrument elongated, flexing itself like some tame worm. The tip groped with the lock, inserting itself gently. There was a faint click.

The wand withdrew, then poked its end through the bars. Under the night song of the insects there came a faint grate as the bolt slid back. The gate was open.

As they tiptoed through, the infinitesimal jingle of the knight's armor sounded to Shea's ears like an earthquake in a kitchenware factory. Cambina pointed. Over their heads on the wall appeared a sentry, visible only as a cloak and hood, glowing with a phosphorescence almost too faint to be visible. The hood swung its black cavity toward them. Cambina pointed her wand, and the sentry froze in that position.

Light and music streamed from the windows of the great hall. Shea, leading because of his knowledge of the place and the fact that his tread was most nearly soundless, was heading for the door, when he tripped over a huge, hairy leg.

With simultaneous grunts a pair of Losels who had been stretched out on the steps rolled to their feet. While the one nearest was fumbling in the dark for his club, Shea drove the epee through the creature's throat. Behind him he heard the other's club swish up

But the club failed to come down. He looked around and saw the Losel, club aloft, frozen to a statue like the sentry. The other Losel was expiring with quiet bubbling noises.

Cambina did things with her wand, and the door of the building swung open. There was light and noise within, but no one to see them. Across the corridor in which they stood was the entrance to the great hall, the door slightly ajar. Within, the revelers were too occupied with their grand ball to be watching the door.

Shea beckoned the four heads close to his and breathed: "This corridor runs around to the serving entrance."

"Are there other doors beside those two?" asked Artegall, and when Shea shook his head went on: "Then do you, Squire, with Cambell and Cambina, take that entrance. Here Britomart and I will take our stand; for this is the place where they will naturally come and we are, I think, the best men-at-arms."

Heads nodded. Shea and the other two stole down the corridor. Just before they reached the service entrance, an imp crossed the corridor from the kitchen with a tray in his hands.

He saw them. Cambell bounded forward and cut the imp in two. The bottom half of the imp ran back into the kitchen. There was an instant uproar.

The three ran a few steps to the service entrance and flung open the door.

Shea got one brief static picture of a roomful of magicians and red-lipped women looking at him. Some had their mouths open. Busyrane sat at one end of the horseshoe facing him, and he thought he recognized Chalmers. Before he could be certain, the photograph came to frenzied life.

He turned to face the noise behind. Out of the kitchen boiled a mass of imps and hobgoblins, bearing spits, knives, rolling pins. Shea neatly spitted the first on his epee, dodging the counter. The imp leaped backward off the blade and came on again. Behind him Shea heard the roar of the Chapter, Cambell's deep war cry, and the whack of swords against his shield.

"I can...handle these," panted Cambina. Her wand darted to and fro, freezing imp after imp. The rest started to run.

Shea turned back toward the hall, just in time to thrust through the throat a magician trying to roll under Cambell's legs with a knife, while others engaged the knight's attention.

The noise was ear-splitting. Cambell filled the door, and at the far end Britomart was doing equally well. Artegall had leaped into the hall and was swinging his great sword with both hands. His temper might be bad, but he was certainly a good man to have around in a roughhouse.

The lights dimmed to negligible red sparks. Cambina cried a spell and waved her wand; the magicians glowed with blue phosphorescence in the dark. The scene became that of a photographic negative—a wild one, with some of the enchanters turning themselves into winged things to flee, others hurling themselves upon the fighters, striking sparks.

A whole press at once bore down on Cambell. Shea saw a glowing head fly from its shoulders, and himself thrust past the knight's shield arm against something that gave before his blade. Then he was out in the room. A green mist whirled about him, plucking. A pink flash and it was gone.

Right in front of him a magician became a monstrous crab. Shea dodged it, clashed weapons with a still-human enchanter, thrust him through, and then went down as the falling man grabbed him by both ankles. He was stepped on four times before he kicked himself free. Colors, sparks, flashes of light danced about the room.

Just ahead a whole crowd were boiling around Artegall. Shea took one step and found himself confronting Busyrane in person. Busyrane's eyes were twice their normal size with slit pupils, like a cat's. For all his venerable appearance the enchanter was swinging a huge sword as though it were a foot-rule.

Shea gave back, almost slipping on a spot of blood. Busyrane came leaping nimbly after, slashing. The big sword, half seen, whirled in a continuous snaky blur. Shea parried, parried, backed, parried, and parried. The wall was against him.

There was no time even for ripostes against this demoniac attack. Shea took the last refuge of an outmatched fencer; leaped into a corps-a-corps and grabbed Busyrane around the waist with his free arm.

The magician seemed made of rubber and piano wire. One hand clawed at Shea's face. Shea ducked and buried his face in Busyrane's cloak, trying to trip him. The magician fumbled for a dagger. Shea reflected that the weapon was probably poisoned.

But just at this moment Busyrane was jerked backward, dragging Shea to his knees after him. Shea threw himself back and up. Then he saw what was the matter with Busyrane. Around the archimage's neck was clasped a pair of large, knobby hands. Just that and nothing more. Around the room, above, flitted a dozen more pairs of those disembodied hands, swooping at the throats of the enchanters.

Shea lunged. But Busyrane was made of stern stuff. He got the hands loose, his own sword up, and came back with a low cut. Shea lunged again. The magician, groggy from that strangling grip, had strength enough left to beat off Shea's remises and one-twos. Shea tried a coupé and one-two and felt his point go home. He held his lunge, stabbing and stabbing.

Down went Busyrane. Shea looked around. The windows of the hall were jammed with the bats and owls and things into which the magicians had changed themselves. They were beaten. The knobby hands clustered around them, tearing off wings and wringing necks with fine impartiality.

The lights flared up again. It was all over. Dead and dying monsters about the great hall changed back into men. Cambell, Artegall, and Britomart picked themselves up from the floor, slowly and with effort. Cambina drooped against the service door, almost fainting.

Artegall's deep voice boomed: "Ha! Lives one yet?" Shea turned to see him kick over a table and swing back the big blood-dripping sword. He gave a leap and clutched the arm in time.

"Thank you, Harold," said Chalmers from the foot where the table had been. Florimel was beside him. He was squeezing the neck of a bottle in both hands. The large joints of those hands were familiar. Shea realized that the disembodied pairs that had wrought such havoc among the enchanters were outsize copies of his partner's.

"Nice work, Doc," remarked Shea. To Artegall he said: "Don't. He's on our team."

Chalmers gave a hand to Florimel. "You observe," he remarked. "the improvement in my technique, although, goodness gracious! I didn't expect the hands to be quite as efficacious as that!" He looked round the room, where nearly half the corpses showed marks of strangulation.

Cambell carried his wife to a seat and supported her. He said: " 'Twill pass. She is much fordone with the labor of defeating those enchanters' spells, and 'tis well she did so or we were all dead men."

Artegall growled: "Master Harold has slain this Busyrane, a good end for as bad a man as drew breath; and Master Reed has slain more than any two of us with his own magic."

"Said I not they were true and gallant gentlemen?" said Britomart.

"True, my sweet." He wiped the sword on the skirt of an enchanter's robe. "Kneel, sirs!"

Shea and Chalmers went to their knees, but Cambell plucked at their sleeves. "Nay, on one knee only."

Artegall tapped each on the shoulder. "I dub you knights. Be brave, honest, and true in the name of our gracious majesty. Rise, Sir Harold; rise, Sir Reed."

Shea's irrepressible grin broke out as he stood up. "How does it feel to be named official racket buster, Doc?"

"Quite...uh...normal, I assure you. The really important fact about this evening's work is that I've discovered the secret of quantitative control. Frege's definition of number solves the problem with relation to the calculus of classes."

" 'The number of things in a given class is the class of all classes that is similar to the given class'?"

"Precisely. By treating numbers as classes—that is, the number two as the class of all pairs, the number three as the class of all triples, we can—"

"Say!" cried Shea. "Where's Belphebe?"

"I don't recall having seen the young woman. As I was saying, once the problem of introducing a quantitative element—"

"But I've got to find Belphebe! Busyrane caught her this morning. He must have brought her here."

Nobody else had seen her. Florimel offered: "There be gruesome great dungeons below. Mayhap—"

"How do you get to them?"

Chalmers said: "Before you go searching, Harold, I have a spell against magicians that you really must learn."

"To hell with that! She may be down there now!"

"I know. But Duessa and Dolon certainly escaped this...uh...holocaust, and there may be others."

"Be warned," rumbled Artegall. "The rash falcon strikes no game, Sir Harold. We shall need all and more than all the protection we can get to prowl those passages."

Cambell spoke up: "Cambina, I greatly fear, can do no more for the present, gentle sirs."

"Okay, okay," groaned Shea. "Why didn't you use this spell before, Doc?"

"Why," said Chalmers, innocently, "it would have blown me back into my own universe! And I have too much to live for here." He exchanged beams with Florimel. "You see, Harold, the casting of a spell produces on both the caster and the...uh...castee an effect analogous to that of an electrostatic charge. Ordinarily this has no particular effect and the charge dissipates in time. But when a person or thing has passed from one space-time vector to another, he or it has broken a path in extradimensional space-time, creating a permanent...uh...line of weakness. Thereafter the path is easier for him—or it—to follow. If I accumulated too much magicostatic charge at one time, it would, since this charge is unbalanced by the fact that I am at one end of this space-time path...uh...it would by reaction propel—"

"Oh, for God's sake! Let's have the spell now and the lecture later."

"Very well." Chalmers showed Shea the spell, relatively simple in wording but calling for complex movements of the left hand. "Remember, you've been doing spells, so you probably have a considerable charge at present."

They left Florimel and Cambina with Cambell and divided into two parties. Artegall went with Shea.

Smooth stone changed to rough ashlar as they went down. Their torches smoked, throwing long shadows.

The passage turned and twisted until Shea had no idea where he was. Now and then they stopped to listen—to their own breathing. Once they thought they heard something, and cautiously crept to peer around a corner.

The sound was made by water dripping down a wall. They went on. Shea could not help glancing over his shoulder now and then. Artegall, his iron shoes echoing, paused to say: "I like this not. For half an hour we have followed this passage into nothing."

A side passage sprang away. Shea proposed: "Suppose you go a hundred steps ahead, and I'll go the same distance this way. Then we can both come back and report."

Artegall growled an assent and set off. Shea, gripping his epee, plunged into the side passage.

At a hundred paces the passage was the same, receding into blackness ahead of him.

He returned to the T. It seemed to him that he reached it in less than half the time it had taken him to leave it. There was no sign of Artegall, just black emptiness enclosed in rough stone.

"Artegall!" he called.

There was no answer.

He yelled: "Sir Artegall!" The tunnels hummed with the echo, then were silent.

Shea found himself sweating. He poked at the stone before him. It seemed solid enough. He was sure, now, that this T had appeared in the passage after he passed it, about halfway to where he had gone.

He set off to the right. If Artegall had gone this way, he should catch up with him. An impulse made him stop to look back. The leg of the T had already disappeared.

He ran back. There was nothing but solid stone on both sides.

His skin crawled as if a thousand spiders were scuttling over it. He ran till he began to puff. The passage bent slightly, one way, then another. There was no end to it.

When he rounded a corner and came on a human being, his nerves seemed to explode all at once. The person shrieked. Shea recognized Belphebe. "Harold!" she cried.

"Darling!" Shea spread his arms—torch, epee, and all. She threw herself into them.

But almost immediately she pulled loose. "Marry, I'm but a weak woman and forgot my pledged word! Nay, dear Harold, dispute me not. What's done is done." She backed away determinedly.

Shea sagged. He felt very tired. "Well," he said with a forced smile, "the main thing's getting out of this damned maze. How did you get down here?"

"I sprained my ankle in my fall this morning. And Busyrane's minions—"

"Hah, hah, hah!" Dolon, large as life, stepped through the side of the wall. "The two mice who would kill cats!"

Shea crouched for a fleche. But Dolon made a pass toward him. Something wrapped around his legs, like an invisible octopus. He slashed with his epee, but met no resistance.

"Nay, there shall be a new Chapter," continued Dolon, "with my own peerless presence as archimage. First, I shall prove my powers on your bodies—a work worthy of my genius, doubt it not!"

Shea strained at the invisible bonds. They crept up his body. A tentacle brushed his sword arm.

He snatched his arm out of the way, reversed his grip on the hilt, and threw the weapon point-first at Dolon, his whole strength in the movement. But the epee slowed up in midair and dropped with a clang to the floor.

His hands were still free. If Belphebe was set on marrying this guy Timias, what did it matter if he got squirted back by the rocket effect of a magicostatic charge?

He dropped the torch and raced through the spell. Dolon, just opening his mouth for another pontifical pronouncement, abruptly looked horrified. He shrieked, a high womanish scream, and dissolved in a mass of tossing yellow flame. Shea caught Belphebe's wrist with his right hand to snatch her back from the blaze...

Pfmp!

Walter Bayard and Gertrude Mugler jumped a foot. One minute they had been alone in Harold Shea's room, the former reading Harold Shea's notes and the latter watching him do it.

Then, with a gust of air, Shea was before them in a battered Robin Hood outfit, and beside him was a red-haired girl with freckles, wearing an equally incongruous costume.

"Wh-where's Doc? asked Bayard.

"Stayed behind. He liked it there."

"And who..."

Shea grinned. "My dream-girl. Belphebe, Dr. Bayard. And Miss Mugler. Oh, damn!" He had happened to glance at his hands, which showed a lot of little blisters. "I'm going to be sick for a few days, I guess."

Gertrude showed signs of finding her voice. She opened her mouth.

Shea forestalled her with: "No, Gert, I won't need a nurse. Just a quart of calamine lotion. You see, Belphebe and I are getting married the first chance we get."

Gertrude's face ran through a spectrum of expressions, ending with belligerent hostility. She said to Belphebe: "But—you—"

Belphebe said with a touch of blithe defiance: "He speak no more than truth. Find you aught amiss with that?" When Gertrude did not answer, she turned to Shea. "What said you about sickness, my love and leman?"

Shea drew a long breath of relief. "Nothing serious, darling. You see, it was poison ivy I tied the broom with."

Belphebe added: "Sweet Harold, now that I am utterly yours, will you do me no more than one service?"

"Anything," said Shea fondly.

"I lack still the explanation of those strange words in the poem wherewith you bested the Blatant Beast!"

The Castle of Iron
by L. Sprague de Camp & Fletcher Pratt
Unknown, April 1941, revised, Gnome Press, 1950

"Listen, chum," said the one who breathed through his mouth, "You don't hafta kid us. We're the law, see? We'll pertect you both all right, but we can't do nothing unless we got facts to go on. You sure they haven't sent you no ransom note?"

Harold Shea ran a hand desperately through his hair. "I assure you, officer, there isn't the least possibility of a ransom note. Since it's a matter of paraphysics, she isn't even in this world."

The red-faced one said: "Now we're getting somewhere. Where'd you put her?"

"I didn't put her anywhere. Didn't have anything to do with it."

"You say she's dead but you don't know who done it, is that right?"

"No, I didn't say anything about her being dead. Matter of fact, she's probably much alive and having a fine time. She just isn't in this space-time continuum."

"That's just dandy," said the mouth-breather. "I think you better come down to the station-house with us. The lieutenant wants to see you."

"Do you mean I'm under arrest?" asked Shea.

The one with the red face looked at his partner, who nodded. "Just holding you for investigation, that's all."

"You're about as logical as the Da Derga! After all, it's my wife that's missing, and I feel worse about it than you could. Will you talk to a colleague of mine before you take me down there?"

The one who breathed through his mouth looked back at his companion. "I guess that's right, at that. We might get something."

Shea stood up and at once was patted from breast to hip with a flowing motion. "Nothing," said the red-faced one disappointedly. "Who's this friend of yours, and where do we find him?"

"I'll get him," said Shea.

"You'll get a poke in the puss. You just sit quiet and Pete will get him for you." The one with the red face motioned Shea back to his chair and, unlimbering an unpleasant-looking automatic pistol from his hip, sat down himself.

"Oh, all right. Ask for Dr. Walter Bayard in the next office."

"Go ahead, Pete," said the red-faced one. The door closed. Shea viewed his visitor with wary distaste. A mild schizoid of the suspicious variety; an analysis might turn up something interesting. However, Shea had too many worries of his own to be much interested in uncovering a policeman's suppressed desire to do ballet dancing.

The policeman regarded Shea stolidly for a while, then broke the silence. "Nice trophies you got there." He nodded towards a pair of Belphebe's arrows that hung on the wall. "Where'd you get 'em?"

"They're my wife's; she brought them from the land of Faerie. Matter of fact that's where she probably is."

"Okay; skip it." The cop shrugged. "I'd think you brain experts would start on yourselves..." His mouth gave a quirk at the strange disinclination of the prisoner to discuss things on a rational basis.

There were steps in the hall; the door opened to admit the one who breathed through his mouth, followed by big, blond, slow Walter Bayard and (of all the people Shea did not want to see) the junior psychologist of the Garaden Institute, Vaclav Polacek, otherwise known as "Votsy" or "the Rubber Czech."

"Walter!" cried Shea. "For God's sake will you—"

"Shut up, Shea," said the red-faced one. "We'll do the talking." He swung ponderously toward Bayard. "Do you know this man's wife?"

"Belphebe of Faerie? Certainly."

"Know where she is?"

Bayard considered gravely. "Of my own knowledge, no. I assure you, however—"

Votsy's eye brightened and he grabbed the arm of the one who breathed through his mouth. "Say! I know who could tell you—Doc Chalmers!"

The policemen exchanged glances again. "Who's he?"

Bayard cast a vexed glance at the junior. "As a matter of fact, Dr. Chalmers left only day before yesterday on a rather extended sabbatical, so I'm afraid he cannot be of much help. May I ask the nature of the difficulty?"

The red-faced one, quick on the trigger, said: "Day before yesterday, eh? That makes two of 'em. Know where he's gone?"

"Uh—uh—"

"Couldn't have gone off with this Mrs. Shea, could he?"

In spite of the situation there rose a unanimous laugh from Shea, Bayard, and Polacek. "All right," said the red-faced one, "she didn't. Now I'll ask you another one. Do you know anything about a picnic day before yesterday to Seneca Grove?"

"If you're asking whether I was there, no. I know there was a picnic."

The one who breathed through his mouth said: "I think he's covering up too, Jake. He talks like Snide Andy."

The red-faced one said: "Leave me handle this. Dr. Bayard, you're a physicologist just like Dr. Shea, here. Now how would you explain it in your own language that at this picnic Dr. Shea and his wife goes off in the woods, but only one of 'em comes back, and that one ain't this wife of his, and besides he goes around saying 'She's gone!' "

"I can explain it perfectly well," said Bayard, "though I don't know whether you will understand my explanation."

"Okay, suppose you come along too and tell it to the lieutenant. I'm getting a bellyfull of this runaround. Bring him along, Pete."

Pete, the mouth-breather, reached for Bayard's elbow. The effect, however, was like touching the button that set off a nuclear reaction. As far as Pete, Bayard, Polacek, and Shea were concerned, the lights in the room went into a whirl of motion that became a gray-gleaming circle. They heard Jake's voice cry thinly: "No you don't!" with the accent at the end rising to a squeal, and felt rather than saw the orange, dahlia-shaped flame of the unpleasant automatic, but the bullet never touched any of them, for—

Pmf!

The floor was cold beneath their feet.

Shea braced himself and looked around. Marble all right: there seemed to be miles of it in every direction stretching out in a tesselated pattern of black and white to where pillars leaped from it on every side, slender and graceful, supporting a series of horseshoe-shaped Moorish arches, and thence reaching back invisibly into the distance. The pillars were of some translucent substance that might be alabaster or even ice. *Oriental*, Shea thought.

"Listen," said Pete, "if you try to get away with this you'll go up for it all. This ain't like New York; they got a Lindbergh law in this state."

He had dropped Bayard's arm and was dragging out the twin of the red-faced cop's pistol. Shea said: "Don't bother shooting; it won't go off."

Bayard looked vexed. "Look here, Harold, have you been working some of your damned symbolic logic formulas on us?"

"Holy Saint Wenceslaus!" said Votsy, pointing. "Look there!"

From among the pillars that receded into the gloom a procession advanced. It was headed by four eunuchs—they must be that, loathsomely fat, grinning, wearing turbans on their heads and blue silk bloomers on their legs, each bearing a long curved sword. Behind came a file of Negroes, naked to the waist, with earrings, carrying a pile of cushions on their heads.

"You're under arrest!" said Pete, pointing the gun at Shea. He turned toward Polacek. "You want to preserve the law, don't you? Help me get him out of here."

The eunuchs went down on their knees and bumped their heads upon the pavement as the Negroes, in perfect step, broke left and right to dump piles of cushions behind the four. Pete turned his head uncertainly, then turned back quickly as Shea sat. The reflex tightened Pete's finger on the gun, which gave a loud click.

"I told you it wouldn't go off," said Shea. "Make yourself at home." He was the only one who had done so thus far; Polacek was turning his head round and round until it looked as though it might come off; Bayard was staring at Shea with an expression of furious bewilderment, and the policeman was clicking his pistol and working the slide in a futile manner between clicks. Behind the file of Negroes another procession of butter-faced men emerged from the shadows of the colonnades, bearing an assortment of zithers, brass gongs, and eccentric-looking stringed instruments, to group themselves at one side.

"Nothing you can do about it. Honest," said Shea; then, addressing himself to Bayard particularly: "You know about the theory of this, Walter. Sit down."

Bayard sank slowly into the pile of cushions. Polacek, bug-eyed, and Pete the cop, distrustfully, imitated him. One of the eunuchs pranced before the musicians, clapping his hands. Instantly they struck up an ear-wracking combination of shrieks, growls, groans, and howls, with a bearded vocalist, who seemed to have wildcats tearing at his entrails, raising his voice above all. Simultaneously, a door seemed to have opened somewhere among the darknesses behind the colonnades. A breeze fluttered the musicians' garments; underneath their squallings came the sound of distant, rushing waters.

"Cheer up," said Shea. "Here comes Room Service."

A dark-skinned dwarf, with a big aigrette held to his turban by an emerald clip, scuttled toward them, his arms filled with cushions. He flung them on the floor at the feet of the four, salaamed, and was gone. The caterwaulings of the music changed sharply, all the instruments together emitting seven high-pitched notes. Among the pillars, in the direction where the dwarf had disappeared, a flicker of motion appeared, grew, and developed into seven girls.

At least they appeared to be girls. They wore Oriental costumes, whose only resemblance to those pictured on calendars, however, lay in cut and color. Their long, loose pajamas were of the heaviest wool; so were the veils that covered all but seven pairs of black eyes and mops of black hair, while the bodices concealed everything above the waist. The howling of the musicians waxed as the girls cut a series of capers that could only by the remotest courtesy be called a dance.

"The vaudeville's corny," said Polacek, "but I'll take the one on the end."

"I'd hate to see him loose in a harem," said Bayard.

"I wouldn't," replied Polacek. "I wonder if she speaks English."

"You probably aren't speaking English yourself," said Shea. "Relax." Under those costumes it was hard to tell, but he was fairly certain that none of these was Belphebe.

The policeman, sitting bolt upright on a cushion, had stripped his gun in the space between his knees. Moreover he had gathered up the bullets that it had already disgorged, and with an expression of honest bewilderment was examining the firing-pin dents in their primers. Now he looked up.

"I don't know how you guys worked this," he said, "but I'm telling you to get us out of here or you're gonna do more time than Roosevelt was president."

"Wish I could," said Shea, "but Dr. Bayard will tell you it wasn't our doing that got you here."

"Then what *did* do it? Did you conk me on the head so now I'm dreaming? Or are we all dead? This sure don't look like the heaven they told me about at the First Presbyterian Church Sunday school."

"Not exactly," said Shea, "but you're getting warm. You know how sometimes when you're dreaming you wonder whether you're dreaming or not?"

"Yeah."

"And how sometimes when something unusual happens to you when you're awake, you again wonder if you're awake? Well, we've discovered that the universe is something like that. There are a whole lot of different worlds, occupying the same space, and by mental operations you can change yourself from one to the other."

Pete shook his head as if to clear flies from it. "You mean you can go to Mars or somepin by just thinking about it?"

"Not quite. This isn't Mars; it's a world in a whole other universe, with assumptions different from ours. What we do is fix our minds on those assumptions."

"Assump— Oh hell, if you say so I'll take your word. I'd think you was giving me a line, except..."

The seven had pranced off among the pillars. From the opposite direction another set of dancers emerged. They wore ankle-length trousers and loose embroidered coats with what might have been pairs of coffee cups beneath. "Hi, Toots!" said Polacek tentatively. Scrambling to his feet he took two steps and grabbed for the nearest, who avoided him lightly without missing a step of her dance.

"Sit down, you damn fool!" barked Shea; the dancers swung past and began to retreat.

"How long d'you think this will keep up?" inquired Bayard.

Shea shrugged. "No idea. Honest."

As though in answer, the orchestra changed beat and tune, with a violent banging from the strings and drums. From behind the disappearing dancers another pair of eunuchs stepped forward, bowed to the four, then faced each other and bowed again. Between them emerged four girls, each with a small brass tray holding a fancy jar. Bayard gasped; Polacek whistled; the policeman ejaculated: "Mother of God!" The costumes of all were ample in cut but so thin they might better have not been there at all. The wearers were definitely mammals.

The girls sidled delicately toward their customers, bowed together with the precision of Rockettes, and flopped among the cushions at the feet of the four.

"You can't bribe me," growled Pete the cop. "This only gets you smart guys another charge. Indecent theatrical performance."

Keeping time to the music, each of the girls whipped the lid from her jar, stuck her finger into it, withdrew it covered with something yellow and gooey, and thrust it into her customer's face. Shea opened his mouth and got a fingerful of honey. He heard Bayard gag and cry "No!" and turned in time to see him try to avoid the finger. Pete the cop was dabbing a honey-smeared face with his handkerchief, while his houri seemed determined to apply the stuff internally or externally.

"Better take it," advised Shea. "They're here to give it to us."

"You can't bribe me!" repeated Pete; and Walter said: "But I don't like sweets! I'd rather have beer and pretzels."

Out of the corner of his eye, Shea could see Polacek with one arm around his houri's neck, while with the other hand he conveyed finger-doses of honey to her mouth in exchange for those he received. He caught on fast.

Shea accepted another installment himself. "O moon of my delight," implored the policeman's girl, "is thy breast narrowed? Know that thou hast so infused my heart with love that I will rather drown in the ocean of my own tears than see my lord dismayed. What shall his unworthy handmaiden do?"

"Ask her for something to drink," said Bayard, tentatively touching his tongue to the finger that was being offered him, and shuddering over the taste.

"Is this truly my lord's desire? To hear is to obey." She sat up and clapped her hands three times, then snuggled down against the shrinking policeman's legs. He seemed past speech. The leader of the orchestra dropped his instrument and also clapped, and from among the pillars the dwarf who had brought the cushions came skipping forward again, this time with a big tray on which shone four elaborate silver flagons. Bayard raised himself to peer into the one set before him, then groaned.

"Milk! It needed just that to top off this mess. Who the hell wants to go to Heaven? Good Lord!"

Shea, glancing across the head of his own houri, saw that if the liquid in the flagon was indeed milk, it was milk of a most peculiar kind, with small congealed lumps floating in it. Before he could experiment, Polacek shouted: "Holy smoke, you guys try this stuff! Best cocktail I ever tasted!"

The resemblance to a cocktail might be incidental, but the flavor was delicious and the potency unlimited. As Shea took a long draft he could feel a wave of warmth running down his gullet. He handed the flagon to his girl

"What do you call this drink, little one?'"

She kissed the edge of the flagon where his lips had touched it and glanced at him archly. "O beloved youth, this is none other than the veritable Milk of Paradise."

Bayard had heard. "Paradise?" he cried. "Harold! Votsy! I'll bet you anything I know where we've landed. Don't you remember—

*—For he on honey-dew hath fed
And drunk the milk of Paradise?*

"What you giving us?" demanded Pete the cop.
"This is Xanadu, Coleridge's Xanadu," explained Bayard.

*In Xanadu did Kubla Khan
A stately pleasure-dome decree,
Where Alph, the sacred river, ran—*

"Alph! Alph" The girls scrambled to their feet and bowed in the direction of the sound of running water.

"There you are," said Bayard. "Alph, supposedly based upon the legends about the river Alpheios in Greece—"

"That's it, all right," said Shea. "Listen, officer, I'm not responsible for this, and I don't know how we got here, but he's right. Wait a minute, though, Walter. This is a jam. Remember, the poem was unfinished; as far as I know we've landed in an incomplete space-time continuum, one that's fixed in a certain set of actions, like a phonograph needle stuck in one groove. This show is apt to keep right on going."

Bayard put both hands to his head, the policeman gibbered thickly, but Polacek waved an empty flagon. "Suits me," he cried happily, reaching for his girl again. "We'll do all right, won't we, babe?"

Just then the orchestra struck a strident note. The girl at whom Polacek had snatched dodged his arm, whipped up her tray with a smooth motion, and ran. Another group of seven dancing girls emerged from the pillars. One of them, apparently a soloist, carried a pair of short curved swords, which she began to brandish.

"But look here, Harold," said Bayard, "can't you do something about this? You've been telling us how good you were at magic in cosmoi where it works. Can't you get us off this goddam vaudeville circuit?"

"Yeh," said Pete the cop. "I'll tell you, Shea, I'll make a deal with you. Know a feller in the D. A.'s office, and I'll get him to go eesh-easy with you on these here charges. Maybe, maybe, forget the indeshent performance one." The Milk of Paradise seemed to have warmed him a little.

"I can try," said Shea. "I don't know how it'll work with all this racket."

The cop heaved himself up unsteadily. "I can fix tha'," he said. In two bounds he was upon one of the astonished eunuchs, wrestling with him for his scimitar. The musicians stopped with a squeal and a murmur of voices; then one struck a gong, three times, ringingly. From among the pillars a whole parade of grim-looking janizaries advanced with long nasty spears in their hands, just as Shea wrested the scimitar from Pete. Bowing before the eunuch, Shea presented him his weapon, saying: "The humblest of your servants abases himself." Then he turned on Pete, whom Bayard was, with a little difficulty, restraining.

"You—utter—damned—jackass!" he said. "I don't care if you're the number one cop in Ohio; you can't get away with that here. How'd you like to see your head parade around on the point of one of those pikes?"

Pete shook his head as if to clear it. "How—how could I see it if—"

"Or spend the rest of your life in a specially refrigerated cell?" Shea addressed Bayard: "Remember the 'Beware, beware!' and 'caves of ice' part? This paradise has got thorns in it; you take it the way they dish it out to you, or you'll be sorry."

He led the way slowly back to the cushions. The janizaries had disappeared, and another file of dancers was coming out from among the pillars, this group specializing in bellybuttons. Pete the cop flung himself heavily into the cushions, and Walter Bayard sat down morosely.

"All right, you guys," said Shea, "try not to interrupt me while I give a whirl at a sorites. If there is something, c, such that the proposition *phi* concerning x is true when x is c but not otherwise, and c has the property *phi*, the term satisfying the proposition *phi* concerning—" His voice trailed off, and he sat with lips moving. Polacek watched him closely. Pete, head buried in his arms, murmured: "And me a married man!"

However, Shea's sorites were never completed. Through the domed building, far among the arches, rang the thunder of a cosmic voice—the kind of voice God might have used in telling the worshippers of the Golden Calf where to head in. It said: "Oh, goodness gracious, I do believe I've made a mistake!"

The voice was that of Dr. Reed Chalmers.

Shea and Polacek leaped to their feet. The musicians stopped; the dancers paused. Then musicians, dancing girls, and pillared hall began to go round, faster and faster, until they dissolved into a rioting whirl of color. The color faded to foggy gray. The gray threw up whorls that condensed into other colors, and faded into the outlines of another room, a smaller room, bare and utilitarian.

Shea and Polacek were facing a table. Behind it sat a short man and a pale, lovely, dark-haired girl. The man was Dr. Reed Chalmers. There were touches of black in the unruly gray hair that flowed from beneath the edges of a gaudy turban, and some of the lines were missing from his face.

He said: "I am glad to see you, Harold. I hoped—Oh, for goodness' sake, did I get Vaclav too?"

2

"Yeah, you got me," said Polacek. "Right away from a swell party. Walter, too."

Shea looked around. "But where is Walter? He was on those cushions—holy dewberries, Doc! He must still be back there in Xanadu with that cop, watching cootch dancers and eating honeydew. And he hates both of them!"

"Xanadu? Dear me, most unfortunate, most distressing." Chalmers fingered the papers before him. "I desired merely to establish contact with you, Harold, and I assure you the association of the others was quite accidental. I really don't know—"

Shea smiled crookedly. "I really don't know myself whether I ought to thank you or bawl you out, Doc. What have you done with Belphebe? You snatched her, too, didn't you? At least I hope so. She just disappeared when we were out on a picnic together, and they were going to arrest me for murdering her or kidnapping her or something."

"Yes—uh—there are certain difficulties." Chalmers' fingers moved nervously. "I am afraid there was rather a—uh—grave error on my part. I find the attitude of the police shocking. Though I do not think you need have worried about the legal complications. It would be well-nigh impossible to establish a *corpus delicti* under the circumstances."

"That's what you don't know, Doc. Gertrude Mugler was on the picnic, and she was the one who hollered copper when we went off on a walk together and I came back without her, nearly out of my mind because I didn't know whether some magician had hauled her back to Faerie. That woman could establish a *corpus delicti* or a society for boiling men in oil, and she would, too."

The pale girl made a small sound.

"Sorry," said Shea. "Lady Florimel, I present Vaclav Polacek, known in our country as the Rubber Czech."

"Hail, fair squire," said the girl. "The titles of your land are passing strange; yet not, methinks, stranger than that garb you bear."

Shea became conscious of a neat pin-stripe suit. "I might say the same thing about Sir Reed's headgear. What are you doing in that rig, what did you get me here for, and where are we?"

Chalmers said: "You display an unscientific tendency to confuse thought by the simultaneous consideration of different categories of information. Pray allow me to organize my thoughts and data... Ahem. I presume it was you who employed the spell against magicians on Dolon, and in so doing projected yourself to our—er—point of departure? I confess I do not understand how you also projected the young lady..."

"I had hold of her hand. We're married."

"My sincerest congratulations. I trust the union will prove happy and—er—fruitful. Your departure, you will remember, was attended by the destruction of the Chapter of Enchanters, and as a result I found myself faced by a problem rather beyond my powers. Namely, the transformation into a real person of a human simulacrum made of snow." He nodded in the direction of Florimel, who gazed at him adoringly. "I therefore—"

"Doctor, you got a chair?" asked Polacek.

"Vaclav, your interruptions are even more disturbing than Harold's. Kindly seat yourself on the floor and permit me to continue. Where was I? Ah, upon examination of available data, I was gratified to discover that there existed in Faerie the mental pattern of a universe whose space-time vector arrangement made it possible of attainment from that place by the familiar methods of symbolic logic. To wit, that of Ariosto's *Orlando Furioso.*"

"Why should that be easy to reach?" inquired Shea.

"Ahem. I was about to explain. Lodovico Ariosto was an Italian poet, who wrote the *Orlando Furioso* in what we should call the early sixteenth century. This work was considered the main source from which Spenser, a highly imitative writer, secured the ideas whence he produced *The Faerie Queene.* Since each of these universes contains the same basic mental pattern, it is easy to perceive how transference from one to the other would be a relatively light task, and I felt confident that I would find here a number of experienced practitioners of magic. Vaclav, I perceive you are not following me."

"No," said Polacek from the floor, "and I don't believe Miss—Lady Florimel is either."

"It's not necessary that she should. For your benefit, however, I will explain that this similarity of basic mental pattern establishes, as it were, certain connective roads between the two universes, over which passage in our vehicle of symbolic logic can be achieved with a reasonable certainty of reaching the desired destination."

Polacek felt in his pockets. "Anybody got a cigarette? I believe you if you say so, Doctor, but I still don't get why you had to send for Harold, and why we had to land in that cabaret."

Chalmers fussed again with the papers, uneasily. "The process was attended by—uh—certain inconveniences. I can only describe them by taking things in order, if you will permit me to do so. To localize the matter, we are in the castle of the leading magician of the *Furioso,* Atlantès de Carena, in the Pyrenees, near the Franco-Spanish border. For your benefit, Vaclav, I should explain that these places are by no means the same as we should understand by the terms employed at—uh—let us say, the Garaden Institute. "

"All right, but why jerk me back here?" asked Shea. "You might at least have asked me first."

"Surely, Harold, you realize that symbolic logic is not a thing that can be handled like a telephone. As a matter of fact, the inconveniences to which I referred had become so grave that there appeared to be no other course open to me. I may be mistaken. Working with Atlantès has been most interesting, most interesting. I have been granted the opportunity of correcting many of the principles of magic in view of the somewhat different laws that control it here.

"However, I feel that I owe this young lady here a certain duty." He indicated Florimel, and blushed as Polacek and Shea both snickered.

"Ah—Atlantès has been most cooperative, but I hope I am less easily impressed by an enchanter's affability than formerly. Not only has he been unable to accomplish anything for Florimel, but these people are also Muslims with somewhat—peculiar standards of morality. I have been led to the idea, amounting almost to an absolute conviction, that it would be necessary for me to provide additional protection for Florimel. As matters stand, or stood before I took the perhaps unwarranted liberty of—er—transporting you here, I was the only barrier between her and our, I fear, by no means well-disposed host."

"I don't get all of it," said Shea. "Why couldn't you just take her somewhere else?"

"But where, my dear Harold? That is the very nub of the difficulty. To return to our own universe would be to lose the young lady, since she is of magical origin, and there's no provision for magic in the mental pattern. It must be regarded as impossible, at least until she has attained complete humanity. It would be possible, of course, to attain the world of Dante, but I am not sure that the atmosphere of the *Inferno* would be conducive to the health of a person made of snow. Moreover, Atlantès is an extremely competent magician, quite capable of either following her to another place or preventing her going."

"A most persistent, arrant lecher," said Florimel.

Chalmers patted her hand and beamed. "I feel I owe an apology to you, and to Vaclav. However, one of the functions of friendship is to permit occasional impositions in times of emergency. And I trust you will look upon me as a friend."

Polacek waved a hand. Shea said: "It's all right, Doc, and I'll be glad to help, especially since you brought Belphebe along, even if it did get me in trouble with the cops. Where is she, by the way?"

Chalmers became more embarrassed than ever. "That is—uh—the difficulty over which I owe you my sincerest apologies. It was undoubtedly due to an error of selectivity. Er, I had not intended to transport her from our universe at all. If you are familiar with the *Furioso,* Harold, you will remember that among Spenser's imitations from it was a character called Belphegor, the cognate of Belphebe... When the young lady arrived, there was a certain amount of—uh—confusion of identity, as it were, with the result, the unfortunate result, that she had no memory of another name or a previous existence. At the present moment I really cannot say where she is, except that she is undoubtedly in this universe."

"Do you mean to tell me that my own wife doesn't even know me?" yelped Shea.

"I fear not. I cannot express—"

"Don't try." Shea looked around the room gloomily. "I've got to find her. She may be in trouble."

"I don't think you need be apprehensive, Harold. The young lady is quite competent."

"Aye, marry, that she is," said Florimel. "She dealt Sir Roger such a buffet as will make his head spin for long when he would have kept her from going without the castle but the now. Be comforted, Sir Harold."

"Who is this Sir Roger, anyway?" Shea glowered.

"I think I had better introduce you to my—uh—your associates," said Chalmers, and stepped around the desk to open the door behind Shea and Polacek. The air held an unmistakable faint odor of olive oil, and as they stepped back across the threshold, their feet gave back a metallic ring from the floor.

"Ah, yes," said Chalmers. "Perhaps I omitted to mention the fact that this castle is constructed of iron. That also is attended by certain—uh—inconveniences. Will you come this way, gentlemen?"

Another passage branched from that into which they had committed themselves, and led down a ramp towards a pair of double doors, with an oil lamp hanging from chains and throwing but little light. As they approached the doors, Shea heard the wailing sound of an instrument theoretically musical, like those in Xanadu. Polacek's eye brightened as he ran his tongue between his lips. "Babes?" he asked.

Without answering, Chalmers waved his hand at the doors, which swung open smoothly; They were looking at the backs of a pair of Arab-dressed musicians squatting on the floor, one blowing into a tootle-pipe, the other slowly tapping with his fingertips a drum about four inches in diameter. Beyond, a slinky dark girl in gauzy drapes revolved, in the paces of a slow dance. Beyond her again a dozen or more men were visible in the dim light of more oil lamps, dressed in bright Oriental costumes that seemed to have been specially spotted with grease for the occasion. Sprawled upon cushions, they gazed at the dancer with unsmiling, languid interest exchanging a word from time to time, and looking toward the farther end of the room, as though to take their cue from the man who sat there. He was bigger than the biggest of them, with the figure of a wrestler. His young face bore strong lines, but just now it showed a sulky, petulant expression. A dapper little graybeard, like a brown mouse, was whispering something into his ear to the accompaniment of fierce gestures.

He glanced up at the sound of the visitors' feet on the floor and trotted toward them. He bowed low before Chalmers. "The peace of God be with you." He bowed again. "Who be these lords?" He bowed a third time.

Chalmers returned one of the bows. "Let no less peace be with you, most magical lord of Carena. These are—uh—lords of my own country, Sir Harold de Shea and the esquire Vaclav Polacek."

"O, day of good luck!" exclaimed Atlantès de Carena, bobbing up and down like a ship in a storm. "O day of Allah's grace that has brought two mighty lords of the Franks for these poor eyes to feast upon!" Bow. "Doubtless it is by some error that you have come to so poor a hovel, but in that error I am honored." Bow. "Ho! Let the best rooms be swept out and new ceremonial garments be prepared for Sir Harold de Shea and the squire Vaclav, for these be veritably the bringers of benisons." Bow.

Shea and Polacek kept up with the first two or three bows, but gave it up as the pace threatened to make them dizzy. Apparently satisfied that he had achieved something, the little brown man took each by the hand and led them around the circle where introductions and bows were repeated as though each man they encountered could not have heard what was said to the rest. There were Lord Mosco, the Amir Thrasy, Sir Audibrad—this last one in medieval European doublet and hose, without turban—and two or three more. In the intervals Polacek kept twisting his head to watch the dancer, until, at or about the third introduction, Atlantès noticed.

"You desire this handmaid, noble lord?" he said. "By Allah, she is worth not less than a hundred pieces of gold, but you shall have her to your concubine, provided only that our Roger, for whom all things are done, puts not his claim upon her. And you will find her a pearl unpierced, a filly unridden, a gem—"

Polacek's face was reddening. "Tell him *no!*" whispered Shea fiercely. "We can't afford to get mixed up in anything."

"But—"

"Tell him no."

Atlantès' eyes were fixed on them, and there seemed to be an expression of amusement behind the wispy beard. "Listen," said Polacek, "I'll talk to you about it later. Since I am just new here, I'd like to see some more of your castle before—enjoying your—uh—hospitality. And—uh—thanks anyway, your lordship."

"Hearing is obedience." His lordship led the way to the cushion that supported the sulky youth. "And here is the light of the world, the arm of Islam, the perfect paladin and cavalier of Carena, Roger."

The perfect paladin gave a bored grunt. "More Franks?" he said to Atlantès. "Are they of better omen than that red-haired wench whom the Frankish enchanter lately brought?" Shea stiffened and his heart gave a thump. However, the light of the world was addressing him. "Are ye the new tumbling jugglers my uncle promised? Though my heart is straitened, yet may it find ease in witnessing your tricks."

Shea looked at him coldly down his long nose. "Listen, funny-face, I've been made a knight by a better man than you are, and I don't like the way you talk about the 'red-haired wench'. If you'll come outside, I'll show you a few tricks."

Roger, surprisingly, broke into a smile of pure amiability. "By the beard of the Prophet (whom God sustain)," he said, "I had not thought to find a Frank so generous. For months have I slain no man, and my muscles rot from lack of practice. Let us then to the hand-play!"

"Lords! Light of my eyes! Coolth of my heart!" Atlantès bubbled. "You have no need of another death and know well that a doom lies on it that there be none in this castle, and more, these be my noble lords and guests, fellow-magicians, for whose life I would give my own. Come, sirs, let me show you to your quarters, which, though they be but pallets in a corner, are yet as good as Carena can offer. 'Take what I have,' said the Hajji, 'though it be but half a barley-cake.' "

He clucked on ahead of them like a motherly hen. The "pallets in a corner" turned out to be rooms the size of auditoriums, elaborately hung with silks and furnished with inlaid wood. The rivet heads protruding from the iron plates of the walls and ceiling, however, reminded Shea of the interior of a warship.

Atlantès was soothing. "Coffee shall be brought you, and new garments. But in the name of Allah, magical sirs, let the voice of friendship avert the hand of disputation, and be not angry with the kinsman of your friend. Ah, lovely youth!" he brushed a hand past his eyes, and Shea was surprised to see a drop of genuine moisture glistening on it. "The glory of Cordoba. I sometimes wonder that the perfumed Hamman bath does not freeze in despair of emulating such beauty. Would you credit it that such a one could think more on blood than on the breasts of a maiden?"

He bowed half a dozen times in rapid succession and disappeared.

3

"For the love of Mike, Harold!" said Polacek, eyeing the voluminous robes with distaste. "Are we supposed to wear these nightshirts?"

"Why not? When in Rome, eat spaghetti. Besides, if you want to give any of the damsels around here the eye, you'll have to be in fashion."

"I suppose... That little wizard's a smart guy. Say, what's this, a scarf?"

Shea picked up a long red strip of textile. "I think it's your turban," he said. "You have to wind it around your head, something like this."

"Sure I get it," replied Polacek. He whipped his own turban around with nonchalant speed. Naturally it came apart in festoons around his neck, and another try yielded no better result. Shea's own more useful procedure stayed on but settled itself firmly in concealment of one ear, and with a tail that tickled his chin. Polacek laughed and made a face. "Guess we'll have to call for a tailor or wait till they dish out some real hats."

Shea frowned. "Look here, Votsy, take it easy, will you? You'll simply have to be less cocky around a place like this if you don't want to get all our throats cut."

Polacek jagged up an eyebrow. "Hairbreadth Harry telling me not to be so cocky? Getting married has made a different man out of you, all right. Speaking of which, what are the rules around this joint? I'd like to take Atlantès up on his offer and pitch a little woo at that dancer. She's built like—"

The door was flung open with a clang by a man whose hairy, pendulous-eared head bore a startling identity to that of a Newfoundland dog. Without giving time for stares, he barked: "Lord Roger!" and stood aside to let the perfect paladin and cavalier stride in. Shea noticed he moved surprisingly light for so big a man. He would be a dangerous antagonist.

"Oh, hello," he greeted the visitor coolly.

Polacek added: "Say, I'm a stranger here myself, but do you always walk in doors without knocking?"

"The lord is lord of his own saloons," said Roger, as though his name were Hohenzollern. He turned toward Shea. "It has reached me, oh man; that you are of knightly order, and I may without shame or hindrance take on myself the shedding of your blood. Yet since I am a warrior experienced, a person of prowess, it would be no more than just did I not offer to handicap myself, as by bearing no armor while you go armored in this combat when the wizards have lifted the death-doom from the castle."

If he had had the epee which served him so well in Faerie, Shea would have returned the offer. Instead, he bowed: "Thanks. Nice of you. Tell me—do I understand that Atlantès is your uncle?"

"There is no other way to it." Roger tapped delicate fingers over a yawn. "Though he is rather like a grandmother, an old nanny with one eye, who holds all here from high sports or unmannerly diversions. Yet even this may be overcome if there be one with a will to warlike valor, who yet knows something of the placing and lifting of spells."

Shea was conscious of being keenly watched from behind the mask of boredom, and began to understand the purpose of the big man's visit, but it would not do to commit oneself too soon. He said: "Uh-huh. Say, tell me what's going on, will you? Sir Reed says Atlantès is worried about something. Are you expecting an attack by the Christian knights?"

"Ha! Christian knights I fear not, though it be all twelve paladins together." He flexed his muscles. "But of ifrits and enchantments know I nothing, and there is little joy here for any since the Duke Astolph stole Atlantès' hippogriff."

Shea stood still, his eyes boring into Roger. "By the way, what was it that you were saying about a red-headed girl?"

Roger failed to notice the elaborate casualness of the question. "There is no glory but in Allah: it was but a few days since, during the time when Lord Dardinell was with us, when Atlantès and the other wizard, your friend, colluded to effect some great spell, with burnings and groans of evil spirits. There was nothing for it but that they must fetch from some far place this wench of ill-omen; well shaped, but unwomanly in garb, a huntress; and having red hair, which of all things more surely fortells some disaster, of which I fear the loss of the hippogriff is but the beginning. Have you met this unlucky one before?"

"My wife," said Shea.

"In the name of Allah! Are there no damsels of good augury in your land, that you must company with such a one? Doubtless she brought you a great dowry."

Without arguing the point Shea rushed on: "Has anything been heard of her since she left the castle?"

"It has reached me that one of the hunters saw her afoot in the mountains with Duke Astolph, a conjunction which brings a dread like midnight on the heart of my uncle, though what it may mean he knows not."

"Who's Duke Astolph, by the way?"

"Allah forgive your ignorance! He is one of the twelve whom the Christians (may they be accursed!) call paladins; yet a doughty fighter, to whom I look for the best of sport when I may measure blows with him, though he comes from an island far in the north, where it is so chill that men's faces turn blue, even though they be Franks."

Polacek asked: "Say, Roger, if you dislike Christians so much, how come you're wearing a Christian name?"

The perfect paladin went into such a grimace that for a moment Shea thought he was going to hit Votsy, but then Roger seemed to restrain himself with an effort. "Not for your question, which is the rudeness of a dog which lacks stripes," he said, "but to the good will of this knight who has offered me the sacrifice of his blood, will I answer. Learn; oh unguided one, that we of Carena are of too noble spirit to engage ourselves in the quarrels of princes, but seek honor under whatever banners may offer it, so that if the battle be hot, it matters not whose name it be fought in." Roger gave a snort, and looked at Polacek with unexpected keenness. "What said you but now of the slave-girl who danced for our entertainment?"

"Well," said Polacek, "Atlantès had—uh—made me an offer—very generous of him, I thought, and I was just saying that maybe for politeness I ought to take him up—"

"Enough, base-born," said Roger. "Learn that this castle and all in it were builded to my pleasure, and if it be my pleasure to take the damsel to concubine, there is no help for it but I must do so." He growled "Peace of God," and strolled out. The dog-headed man pulled the door to behind him.

Shea looked at the door. "You see, Votsy? Monkeying with guys like that is like telling Al Capone you don't like the color of his tie. Now let's get into those clothes and go see Doc. I noticed he solved the turban trouble and maybe he can help us."

He led the way down to Chalmers' apartment. The doctor was puttering away, chanting cheerfully:

> *We've a first-class assortment of magic;*
> *And for raising a posthumous shade*
> *With effects that are comic or tragic,*
> *There's no cheaper house in the trade.*
> *Love philter—we've quan—*

"What can I do for you, Harold?"

"These confounded cummerbunds." Shea watched as the doctor took Polacek's and adjusted it with quick, expert fingers, then began winding his own. "Look here, Roger says Belphebe's somewhere in the mountains around here. You're got to get me out of this place to look for her."

Chalmers frowned. "I fail to see the necessity for any immediate departure," he said. "The young woman impressed me as being admirably fitted to—uh—take care of herself. A perfect case of conjoined biological and psychological adaptation. And it would be most inopportune for you to leave at the present moment. We must look for the—uh—better manner of serving our united interests, and I am at present confronted with a serious problem—"

"Oh, Votsy can stay here and take care of her," said Shea.

"Vaclav is a bright young man, but I am afraid he is inclined toward irresponsibility," said Chalmers firmly, ignoring Polacek's squawk of protest. "Also, he has a—uh—deplorable weakness for the fair sex, not to mention that he lacks training in the most elementary details of magic. You, therefore, are the only person upon whom I can rely at present."

Shea grinned ruefully. "Okay," he said. "You knew you could get me with that argument. But you'll have to help me find Belphebe as soon as things are cleared up here."

"I shall be glad to help as far as I can, Harold, as soon as we have reasonable assurance of success in humanizing Florimel."

Shea turned his head to conceal the sparkle in his eye. Knowing how mulish Chalmers could get, he didn't attempt to argue. But he was a trained psychologist too, and he suspected it would transpire that he could best assist the transformation of Florimel at a distance from Castle Carena.

Polacek said: "Listen, you two. I might as well be some use around here. Why not show me how this magic works?"

"I had planned a series of talks on the subject," said Chalmers. "We will begin with the basic concepts, such as the distinction between sympathetic magic and sorcery..."

"How about teaching me a couple of good stiff spells right now? Something I can use? You can get around to the heavy theory later, and I'll understand it better if I know the practical application."

"That would be unsound pedagogy," said Chalmers. "You should be aware that I am not one of those so-called progressivists who believes that the pupil absorbs best material presented in an unsystematic and confusing manner."

"But—but—I got a reason—"

"Yeah?" said Shea. "What's going on in that object you use for a brain, Votsy?"

"That's my business."

"No tell, no spell."

"Vaclav!" said Chalmers, in a monitory tone.

Polacek struggled with conflicting impulses for a few seconds. "It's that little dame," said he. "The dancer. Of course, ordinarily I wouldn't care—" (here Shea laughed raucously) "—not having really met her, but I won't stand for that big oaf telling me what to do. I thought if you gave me a couple of spells I could put on him—"

"No!" cried Shea and Chalmers together. The doctor said: "We are, I think, involved in—uh—sufficient difficulties already without further complicating our situation. I really do not know, for instance, how to avoid Atlantès' importunities with regard to the death-doom on the castle."

"The big guy mentioned something about that," said Polacek. "What is it?"

"It appears that at some time a spell was put upon this structure, I would conjecture when it was erected. The general effect is that if a killing should be performed within it, the building will collapse, though I will not weary you with the details, which are fantastically complicated. While I would normally be most willing to assist Atlantès, it now occurs to me that should this doom be lifted, our friend Roger will no longer be restrained from cutting you or Harold into fragments by way of sword-practice."

Shea muttered: "I'm not afraid of that stupid ox. I'll bet that all he knows is saber-practice, if he knows that much."

"Perhaps not. Nevertheless, I should provide myself with a weapon. It would be most regrettable if our friendly association came to a sanguinary end. Moreover, permit me to remind you that as a married man you have incurred certain—uh—responsibilities."

Shea subsided, feeling guilty over having forgotten for some minutes that he was a married man.

"I still think you ought to teach me a couple of spells," said Polacek. "I won't turn Roger into a mud turtle or anything like that, I promise, but I ought to have enough to protect myself."

"The amount of knowledge you could acquire so hastily would be of little value for self-protection," said Chalmers firmly. "The course will be imparted as I have outlined."

Polacek jumped up. "You two give me a pain. I'm going to see Atlantès. Maybe he knows a trick or two." He stormed out, banging the door metallically.

Shea looked at Chalmers with concern on his long face. "Say, Doc, maybe I better go sit on his head, don't you think? He almost got into a jam with Roger already."

Chalmers shook his head. "I doubt whether Atlantès will impart enough magical information to enable our hasty young friend to—uh—jeopardize our safety, or for that matter, whether Vaclav can cause any particular damage in that quarter. In fact, it might be just as well if our host were allowed to gather the somewhat unfavorable impression of your characters that he is bound to form from contact with our associate. Now if you will—uh—lend a hand with this athanor, I shall finish compounding this mixture and we can retire for the night."

The last words set up a train of thought in Shea's mind that caused him to look more sharply at Chalmers. "Been rejuvenating yourself, haven't you?" he asked.

Chalmers flushed. "It seemed expedient, in view of the demands of my—uh—more active recent life. I was, as you perceive, conservative in my application of the formula, not wishing to become an adolescent by inadvertent overdosage."

Shea grinned nastily as he bore a hand with the athanor. "The more fool you, Doc. Don't you know what the statistics show about adolescents?"

4

Harold Shea dreamed he was drowning in an ocean of olive oil, too thick for swimming. Every time he reached the edge of an overhanging cliff and tried to pull himself out, a gigantic Roger with a cruel smile on his petulant face pushed him down with the butt of a lance.

He woke to see Vaclav Polacek on the edge of the other bed, holding a handkerchief to his nose. The whole place reeked with the stench of rancid oil. Shea reeled to the window, which was closed with some alabaster material. As he fumbled it open, a blast of chill but fresh air struck his face. He gulped. Beyond the castle battlements he could see the snowy crags or a range of mountains, pink in the early sun.

"What the hell?" said Shea, thoughts of some weird attempt at poisoning floating through his mind. Staying as near as he could to the open shutter, he struggled into the loose garments provided him, and, without waiting to jockey the turban into position, made his way into the hall. There the odor was overpowering. As he turned the corner he bumped head-on into the Amir Thrasy, who was toddling along with a cut open orange held under his nose.

"What the hell makes this stink, my noble friend?" asked Shea.

"Truly, sir, you're right that comes from nowhere but the ultimate pits of the damned. But as the reason, it has been whispered to me that Atlantès (may flies nest in his ears!) has forgotten to renew his spell."

"What spell?"

"Verily, none other than that by which the smell of this oil is restrained within bonds, as the Jann are bound by the seal of Solomon. It is certain that there is no spell against rusting and, unless this castle be kept well oiled, there would be no help for it that it must be overthrown. Yet is the spell for the sweetness of oil more fugitive than a leaf in tempest, and must have renewal from time to time, as..."

He stopped as Atlantès himself came bustling around a corner of the corridor. "In the name of Allah, on whom be praise!" he greeted them. "Most noble lords, forbear your anger from your unworthy servant." He was bowing up and down like a metronome. "Give me but the kerchief of your pardon that my dread may be appeased and my heart eased!" More bows. "I pray you, enlighten me with your graciousness so far as to break fast with me. See, even now the air grows purer than a spring of fresh water! And your squire as well, glorious sir. Is the youth well?"

Shea's appetite, whatever it might normally have been, had vanished under the shock of the olive oil stench. Nevertheless he called to Polacek, and the Amir Thrasy fortunately saved him the necessity of a reply.

"In sooth," said he, "our pains are borne lightly for the sake of the pleasures to come, as we bore with joy the smell of the corpses the day Lord Roger slew the two thousand serfs at the gate of Pampelona, forgetting in his warlike fury to leave any alive for the withdrawal of the bodies."

Their host conducted them to a breakfast consisting mainly of stewed lamb with a sour, whitish liquid which Shea took to be milk, rather noticeably unpasteurized. Roger, reclining on cushions across the floor from the young psychologist, gobbled horribly. There was no sign of Dr. Chalmers. When the mirror of chivalry had finished his meal by sucking leftovers from between his teeth, he stood up and said meaningfully to Shea: "Will it please your honor to slash at the pells, since under my uncle's ordnance we may not slash at each other?"

"What's pells?" demanded Polacek.

Ignoring this question in a marked manner, Shea said: "Delighted. But somebody will have to lend me a sword. I came away so quickly I left mine home."

The pells of Castle Carena were a row of battered-looking wooden posts in the courtyard. Beyond them, a couple of men in castle guards' livery were shooting at targets with short, double-curved bows. Oddly enough, they had the heads of baboons.

As Shea and Roger came out, Lord Mosco, a Saracen so pudgy that he waddled, was facing the nearest pell with a scimitar in one hand and a round shield on his other arm. He gave a blood-curdling whoop, leaped at the post light as a cat for all his bulk, and swung. Chips flew. Mosco went into a dance around the unoffending wood, slashing forehand with a drawing cut, and yelling at the top of his voice: "Allah-il-Allah! Mahound! Mahound!" He stopped suddenly and walked back to where the others stood in a little group. "My Lord Margéan, will you give me the balm of your word upon my performance?"

Margéan, in a kind of shapeless cap instead of a turban, and whose nose had once been well broken, said judicially: "I rate it but indifferent good. Twice you exposed your left side during the recovery and the war cry did not ring. The foe is always the worse for a lusty shout in his ears."

Mosco sighed. "Blessed be the name of God," he said resignedly. "I fear I am a lost man unless protected by His angels or the arm of our champion. My lords, shall we not grace our eyes with the sight of these Frankish warriors?" There was a murmur of assent. "Now there is nothing for it but you must smite at these pells, squire."

"Better say you have a sprained wrist," muttered Shea.

But Polacek had his own ideas. "I'll get along. I've been watching him, haven't I? Where do I get one of these toad-choppers?"

The Amir Thrasy handed over his own somewhat battered and nicked scimitar. Polacek marched up to the pell, yelled: "Rah, rah, rah, Harvard!" and swung up in an underhand slash. However, he had misjudged the height of the pell, missed it completely, swung himself clear round the circle, tripped over his own feet, and had to clutch the post to keep from falling.

"That's my special attack," he explained with a shame-faced grin. "I make believe I'm gonna chop him, but instead I jump into a clinch and wrassle him down where I can really get at him."

Nobody seemed to feel the episode at all funny. Margéan's face expressed disdain, while the others looked away, all but Roger, who glanced at Shea to indicate that he was next. Shea hefted Thrasy's weapon; aside from the nicks in the blade, it was altogether wrongly balanced for his type of work. "Has anybody got a straight sword I could borrow?" he asked.

Lord Margéan, who seemed to be some kind of coach, clapped his hands and called; a castle servant with the blubbering muzzle of a camel appeared with the desired weapon. Shea hefted it. The blade was straight enough, but the sword was as purely designed for cutting as the scimitars; no point whatever, the end rounded off, and the hilt made for a small-handed man. The balance was better, though, and if the weapon was too heavy for a proper parry, it might do for a little lunging practice. Shea addressed himself to the post without shouting, did a simple disengage lunge, a disengage lunge with an advance, a lunge-and-remise. In five minutes he had worked up a healthy sweat, and was pleased to hear a murmur from the spectators, partly puzzlement and partly appreciation.

Margéan said: "Marry, sir knight, here's strange bladeplay; yet methinks that with a Frankish sword you would even skewer one or two of your foes." And they began to argue about the merits of Shea's system: "Look you, lords, with a proper point like a spear you could even drive through the fine mail of Damascus..." "Nay, I like not these new-fangled tricks..." "But see the reach it gives you..." "Howsobeit, men will slash when excited..." "Oho!" (to Sir Audibrad, who was awkwardly trying to imitate Shea's lunge) "it is plainly to be seen that the noble Sir Harold's tricks are not to be picked up in an evening over the coffee cups..."

Only Roger looked contemptuous. Without preliminary words he strode up to the nearest pell, filled the castle-yard with a yell, and swung an enormous scimitar. *Chunk!* went the blade into the wood, and then quickly *chunk-chunk-chunk-chunk!* With the last blow, the upper half of the pell flew off, turning end over end. He swung round and grinned rather nastily at Shea.

Shea gulped. "Nice work, O Pearl of the Age."

Roger thrust his scimitar back into its scabbard and handed it to one of the servitors. "O Frank, this is but the tenth or the hundredth part of what would be seen if I stood in battle before a worthy antagonist. Not that you, son of an unfortunate, would be such; for you do but dance and foint like one of my uncle's entertainers."

While Shea and Polacek were giving themselves sketchy baths by standing in their washbowls and emptying the ewers over each other's heads, the latter asked: "What's the program for the rest of the day?"

"For most of them it'll be loafing all afternoon, I expect, and then Atlantès' floor show in the evening."

"I should think those guys would get too bored to live!"

"Roger does. He wants to bash somebody, and I don't quite figure why

Atlantès won't let him loose to do it. There's something funny going on besides just the business of the old guy making passes at Florimel. Wish I'd read the *Furioso;* I'd know better what we were up against. We have a date with Doc now, you know; some of that new theoretical stuff he's been working up. Ready?"

"Okay, let's go."

When they reached Chalmers' apartment there was more than a suspicion of the olive oil smell that had awakened them. Chalmers was frowning. "I am inclined to believe that the failure to renew the spell on the oil was not altogether an accident," he replied to Shea's question. "You will note that the odor persists here to a certain extent. Atlantès is extremely astute, and I have no doubt that he has become fully aware of Florimel's—uh—sensitivity. It really made the young lady quite ill."

Shea said: "Wonder why? Maybe the guy's a sadist. According to all the correlations, abnormal sex patterns should be common in this Moslem society where they keep all respectable women locked up. Besides, his personality reminds me of that sadist we used as a case study —you know the one I mean—that real estate fellow the SPCA got after."

"You mean Van Gilder?" Chalmers shook his head. "In the first place those correlations you speak of are mostly guesswork. Besides, it would be unprecedented for any genuine sadist to seek his satisfactions by indirect methods."

"You mean," said Polacek, "that a real sadist has gotta turn the thumbscrews himself?"

Chalmers nodded. "Or at least be present directing the operation. No, there are various explanations for elaborate bits of malevolent plotting of this type, but—uh—sadism is the last one to look for. An ulterior motive is inherently more probable."

"Such as?" said Shea.

"Such as—ah—if Atlantès hoped to force me to use a counter-spell, which he would then watch and adapt to lifting the death-doom which he says overhangs this castle. Harold, please for that reason do not commit yourself to indulging Roger's penchant for mortal combat. One never knows when this conflict will materialize."

"I'm not afraid of him," said Shea, but without lightness.

"Looks to me like an awful lot of guys around here are anxious to get somebody bumped off," said Polacek. "Why don't you do something about it?"

"It is merely a matter of conducting oneself with ordinary prudence," said Chalmers firmly. "In an unexpressed contention of the type wherein we are engaged with the—uh—gentlemen, the winner will undoubtedly be the party who longest restrains himself from ill-judged or impulsive action. Now, gentlemen, shall we begin?"

Half an hour later: "...the elementary principles of similarity and contagion," he was saying, "we shall proceed to the more practical applications of magic. First, the composition of spells. The normal spell consists of two components, which may be termed the verbal and the somatic. In the verbal section the consideration is whether the spell is to be based upon command of the materials at hand, or upon the invocation of a higher authority."

"That's a little different from the way you had it worked out before," said Shea.

"This is a somewhat different space-time continuum. I am trying to relate matters to our current problems, so pray do not interrupt. Now—uh—prosody is of the utmost importance if the first is the case. The verse should conform to the poetic conventions of the environment, to which the materials in question have become responsive. For instance in—uh—Asgard the verse, for maximum effectiveness, should be alliterative, whereas in Faerie it should be metrical and rhyming. In the world of Japanese mythology, on the other hand, the verse should comprise a fixed number of syllables in a certain—"

"But wouldn't any verse we made for the purpose naturally have the proper form?" asked Shea.

"It is possible. What I was about to say was that a certain—uh—minimum skill in versification is inseparable from the optimum results. That is why you, Harold, who have what might be called the literary or inspirational type of mind, often attain quite extraordinary effects—"

"Listen," said Polacek, "one of the troubles with this joint is that they're prohibitionists. You mean to say that if I made some passes and sang out:

Beer, beer, beautiful beer,
Fill me right up with it,
Clear up to here!

"I'd get a couple of seidels?"

"Vaclav!" said Chalmers sharply. "Pray give your attention to the matter in hand. If you were to perform so rash an act, you would almost certainly find yourself filled with the beverage in question, but I doubt whether your organs would retain it. The utmost precision of expression is necessary. Kindly observe that the doggerel you quoted demanded that you be filled with the liquid instead of having it to drink. Now, where was I? Ah—magic will thus, I fear, always remain to large extent an art, just as in my opinion psychiatry will as well. However, there is also the somatic element of the spell, subject to more precise regulation. There is some point in connection with this element that eludes me, and on which I shall be glad to have any light that observation of Atlantès by either of you gentlemen can throw. I refer to the very adroit manner in which he is able to employ spells as an instrumentality for teleportation of human beings or even those only quasi-human—"

Shea's mind wandered as Chalmers droned along. They had worked out most of this stuff in Faerie, with Belphebe—Belphebe! She must be the same as the Belphegor the doctor had mentioned. With the springy step and the freckles under her tan. The question of getting her back concerned the somatic element, of finding out how Atlantès...

An eruption from Polacek jerked Shea out of his daydream. The Rubber Czech was on his feet, exclaiming: "Sure, I get it, Doc. Let's take time out to do some lab work. Watch that cushion while I turn it into—"

"No!" shouted Shea and Chalmers together.

"Aw, listen; can't you ever believe a guy can learn anything?"

"I remember," said Shea, "when you blew up the lab and almost killed yourself in sophomore chem, trying to make cacodyl. You stick around for some more lectures before you try enchanting even a mouse."

"Yeah, I know, but you can check me on each step, and I'm—"

The argument was squelched by the arrival of Florimel with: "I am somewhat more myself, my lord." But so, it turned out, was the lecture on magic. Shea wandered off to orient himself, while Chalmers undertook the difficult task of restraining Polacek.

5

It was clear and bright upon the battlements, and the air had the fine tang of a mountain climate. Around a corner where a turret gave both shelter from the breeze and exposure to the sun, Shea came upon Atlantès, busy with a scroll among long cushions. The little enchanter scrambled to his feet.

"O knight of the age, you are welcome. Will the friend of my friend have sherbets?"

"No thanks, noble host. I was just looking around, trying to find where things were in this place. You certainly have a fine layout."

"Alas, my lord, that it is no better. All things shall be done for him who eases the heart and broadens the bosom of Lord Roger."

"I wasn't aware that I'd done anything remarkable in that line. Will you have something special for him tonight?"

Atlantès snapped his fingers and shrugged. "Truly, I have nothing to set before you but seven virgins of Sericane, with faces like moons. All can play at the lute and sing, or hold converse in the law of the Prophet equal to Kasis, and the dealer who sold them to me declares they are sisters of a single birth, which is a very strange thing. Yet you, O auspicious one, will have seen wonders that are to this as the sun to the crescent moon."

He had tipped his head to one side and was watching out of the corner of one eye. *What was he fishing for this time?* Shea said: "I, O doubly auspicious one, have never seen anything like it. But tell me—" he let his voice fall "—

your nephew, Lord Roger, will he like it as well as I? He seems restless."

The little man lifted his face toward the clear blue sky. "I testify that there is no god but God and I testify that Mohammed is the Messenger of God! Of a truth Roger is no less than restless, and longs for battle as a strong horse for the race course."

"Why not let him go fight one, then?"

Atlantès tapped himself once or twice on the sternum in a manner which Shea supposed was to entitle him to credit for having beaten his breast. "To you I will tell no less than the truth. Know, then, that there is a prophecy of which I have learned by my arts, that unless the wonder of the age and the son of my brother goes forth directly to battle and by the light of the full moon, he will be lost to Islam if he departs ten miles from Carena. Yet at present there is no war, nor is the moon full, and I must answer before Allah the just, the omnipotent, if he be condemned to Jehannum."

"Yeah, I see. You're in a tough spot all right."

The magician clawed at Shea's arm. "Yet it is well said: 'There is no door but a key may unlock it.' Verily, I have not seen my brother's son so content with his lot for many months as when he looked upon your exercises this morning. Doubtless you have a spell to preserve you from death by arms?"

It occurred to Shea that he had never in his life been more politely invited to let himself be killed. But he said: "What keeps Lord Roger here? If he's so keen on getting out and breaking somebody's head, why doesn't he just walk through the door?"

"In truth, that is a question asked with the answer already known, for it is not hidden from me that you are aware of the pentacles of opposition."

"I get it. This is a kind of gilded hoosegow. You don't think you can keep Sir Reed and me in that way, do you?"

This time Atlantès went through the formula of wringing his hands. "May dogs eat my flesh if I ever held such a thought! Nay, auspicious sir, should you wish to hunt in those mountains, where often I myself have had good sport when the sap of youth was in me, it would give pleasure to your slave to provide a hunter for company. And should you wish to sport with the light of Islam, the pentacles can be let down."

He certainly was persistent. "No thanks, not right now," said Shea.

The graybeard nudged him and chuckled lecherously. "Think well on it, my lord. It has reached my ears that there be maidens among the villages more dainty than gazelles, and not all hunting is done with the bow."

"No thanks, O fount of wisdom," said Shea again, wondering how much of his statement of the prophecy was true. "Right now I'm much more interested in Florimel's and Doc's—that is, Sir Reed's—project for her. Business before pleasure, you know. How are you coming along on that, by the way?"

Atlantès went through his breast-beating routine again. "There is no god but God! It has not been revealed to me how this knot may be unloosed, though I have summoned up legions of the Jann."

"Maybe I could help a little," said Shea. "I know a fair amount of magic, and once in a while I can do things that even Sir Reed doesn't pull off."

"In sooth, it were a greater wonder than burning water were matters otherwise, O master of magic. With joy and goodwill will I summon you when the hour comes that you can aid me. Yet for the present there is no aid that can be given so great as that of the contentment of my brother's son."

Again! Would this little schemer ever let up trying to get Shea shortened by a head? Shea chose to ignore the last part of the remark. "Along what lines are you working? We might check results against each other."

"If it could be so, it were the delight of my heart and the expansion of my bosom. But it is unlawful for one of our religion to initiate other than true Muslims in the magical rites; were I to do so, you would instantly be torn in pieces by an ifrit stronger than a lion and with tusks three feet in length." The little man seemed to have had enough. He started for the stairs, the motion of his feet beneath the long robe making him look oddly like a centipede.

At the head of the stairs he turned to bow another farewell. Then a thought seemed to occur to him, for he held up a hand. "O auspicious sir," he called, "take warning. These peaks be ominous; very pillars of mischance. Let the hand of friendship avert the stroke of calamity, and in the name of Allah, I pray you, do not let down the pentacles nor go forth without help from me and mine."

The afternoon light was already beginning to throw panels of shadow among the higher summits. Shea walked on around the battlements, thinking of where Belphebe might be in this world and longing for her high spirits. Damn Doc Chalmers anyway for getting them into this jam! It was a jam, too. That farewell of Atlantès, though couched in a tone of appeal, came as close to a veiled threat as he had ever heard. Suppose he did lower the pentacles and walk out, what would the old goat do? Hardly let loose the wonder of the age on him. That would run against the prophecy—if there was a prophecy. Shea thought about the question as he picked his way past a clanging iron shot tower, and reached the conclusion that the prophecy was probably quite real. Atlantès was clever enough to run a double bluff by mixing a piece of important truth with evasions and half-truths in order to steer an opponent away from the former.

The only thing he could count on, however, was that the magician was putting the heat on his guests in the matter of finding a cure for Roger's boredom. Shea considered the question for a moment. The big lug appeared to care for nothing but fighting; couldn't there be some way of meeting the wish vicariously? Back in Ohio, when children became problems along this line, the matter could be taken care of with books of adventure. That clearly wouldn't do here; or—and Shea mentally kicked himself for not thinking of it sooner—toy soldiers.

Certainly there ought to be somebody around Castle Carena with skill enough to carve passable small figures of fighting men, and he and Chalmers between them should be able to animate them magically enough to enable them to serve as miniature armies. The thought of the perfect paladin ordering battalions of six inch wooden knights about the courtyard struck him as so delightful that he slapped the edge of the battlement and laughed. At that moment someone plucked his sleeve.

It was one of the castle servants, this time with the head of a bird—a very large bird, with a great round head and a long bill like one of Tenniel's borogoves.

"What's the trouble?" asked Shea.

Although the creature seemed to understand, its only answer was to open the beak for a kind of whistling bark. It pulled at his arm insistently until he followed, looking over its shoulder from time to time and whistling encouragingly as it led him down the stairs, along one of the metal corridors, and left him face to face with Polacek.

"Hi, Harold," said the latter cheerfully, with the air of an inventor about to give birth to the atom-powered space ship. "Say, you guys need me around places like this. I got hold of one of those hobgoblins that will find all the stuff we want. The only trouble is I can't find her!"

"What stuff? Whom?"

"The little dark one that did the dance last night. All I got is her name: Sumurrud, or something like that. And what kind of stuff do you think? Tonsil-oil, of course."

"You get around fast, don't you? Lead on to the liquor, but you're out of luck on the girlfriend. If Roger hasn't got her in his room giving her the works just to spite you, Atlantès has probably sent her back where she came from by magic."

"For the love of St. Wenceslaus! I never thought of that." The Rubber Czech's face looked annoyed. "I'll cook up a spell on that guy that will make him—"

"No!"

"All right, how about this? Suppose I go to Atlantès right off the arm, and ask him can he send that little number back to Ohio. With a build like hers—"

"No! We're in enough trouble now. You don't even know her, Votsy."

"But—"

Shea sighed. "For an educated man you've got the most proletarian sexual behavior pattern—"

" 'Smatter with you; all worn out already?" said Polacek nastily, leading the way down a circular staircase in one of the castle towers. As this point in the argument was reached, so was a scullery, where the goblin, a purple-skinned object with an oversized head and spindly little legs, was at his job of dishwashing. In one corner lay a large gaunt hound with a dish between his forepaws. The goblin held up a dirty plate, repeated a formula, and whistled. Instantly the dog reacted by licking the dish before him. As he did so the detritus disappeared from the plate held by the goblin.

"Guk!" said Polacek. "How do you like your dinner?"

Shea grinned. "Don't be squeamish. The stuff gets from the outside of the plate to the inside of the dog without touching a thing." The goblin waddled over to them with a crablike gait. "Got it, Odoro?" asked Polacek with a wink. "He wants some too."

"Can get," said Odoro. "You got money, uh? Me want."

They went to Chalmers' laboratory for the money. At their knock there was a rustling from within, and when they entered, Florimel was some distance from Chalmers with her dress slightly rumpled and both of them looking hangdog. The doctor tendered some odd-looking square coins without comment.

As they made their way back to their own room, Shea laughed. "To see those two, you'd think it was a crime to hold a girl on your lap here."

"He's probably never done it before," remarked Polacek. "Well, he can have that human snowball if he wants her; I'll take that little Sumurrud. Did you know she was giving me the eye?"

The goblin joined them almost at once, producing from under one arm a small leather bottle wrapped in a ragged piece of discarded turban. Polacek gave him some of the odd-looking coins, each of which the being tested with fanglike teeth. As he turned to go, Shea said: "Just a minute Odoro." He had taken hold of the bottle. "Your master is pretty tough about liquor, isn't he?"

"Oh yes, awful! Law of Prophet." Odoro touched a hand to his forehead.

"What would happen if he found out you had a supply and were selling it to people?"

The goblin shuddered. "Anathema, second class. Red hot pincers inside." His grin vanished. "You no tell, no?"

"We'll see."

Odoro paled to lavender and made a shifting motion from one foot to the other that turned into a series of hops. "Oh, you no do! I do you boon! So do no nightly!" he squealed. "Here, you no want wine, you give me back!" He danced up to Shea, reaching. Shea held the bottle high over his head and did a snap-pass to Polacek, who caught it like a down-field end.

"Easy, easy," said Shea. "Remember I'm a magician too, and I can turn you into a red ant if I want to. This is evidence. All I want is a little information, and if you give it to us you needn't worry about our telling anything."

"No got information," said Odoro sullenly. His eyes ran round and round the room from a swiveling head.

"No? Votsy, you go find Atlantès and tell him we've got a bootlegger here, while I keep an eye on—Oh, you don't want him to go? Maybe you do know a thing or two? I thought likely. Now then, is there a prophecy about Roger?"

"Yes—yes. Nasty prophecy. If he go out before full moon he join infidels, fight true believers. *Il hamdu l'Allah!*"

"Now, isn't that nice! All right, why doesn't Atlantès let Roger out just a little way? He's a wizard and would know how to keep him from going too far."

"Afraid Duke Astolph. He magician too; stole hippogriff."

"That clears up one point anyway. But look here, if Roger's so anxious to get out, why doesn't he just make it hot for Atlantès? Cut off his head or something?"

"Not know. Swear beard of Prophet, no know. Think Atlantès do something with—you know—mind—" Odoro pointed to his head "—drive Roger like horse. But Roger not got much mind, so hard to—uh—drive."

Shea laughed. "That's about what I thought. Give him another nickel, Votsy. You see, Odoro, you stick with us and you'll be all right. Now, what's Atlantès up to with Florimel?"

"Prophecy. Find in magic book."

"I daresay. What prophecy?"

"He lose Roger by woman knight, come on hippogriff."

Belphebe was out there somewhere in the hills, and so was the hippogriff. "But what does Florimel have to do with that?"

"Not know. Think maybe he change her shape with woman knight, burn her up, poof!"

"A fine kettle of fish. What kind of spell will he use?"

"Not know."

"You know about magic, don't you?"

"Not know that. Atlantès, he very good magician."

"Okay. Votsy, suppose you ask the very good magician to come—"

"Not know! Not know! Me ignorant!" wailed Odoro, beginning to hop again.

"Maybe he really doesn't know," suggested Polacek.

"Maybe. And maybe he gets a break for that crack about Roger. Run along, Odoro. You say nothing and we'll say nothing."

"Whew!" whistled Polacek when the door had closed behind the purple shape. "You certainly have got a nerve, Harold. With your luck and my brains—we get a drink."

Shea rummaged a couple of pewter cups from a low cabinet in the corner, uncorked the bottle, sniffed, and poured some of its contents into each cup. The wine was sweet and dark, nearly black, with something the flavor of port, though he judged the proof would be lower.

Shea sipped his, remarking with the air of an experienced conspirator: "You don't want to ask questions among the hired help without getting a hold on them somehow first. They may lie to you, or they may be souped up to report anything you ask to the boss. I think we've got this bozo playing on our team for the time being—but I don't like what he said about the deal Atlantès is cooking up."

"He means Belphebe, doesn't he?" said Polacek, holding out his cup for another drink.

"I'm afraid so. No, Votsy, we've got to hang onto some of this to keep Odoro in line. Besides, Atlantès would smell it on your breath a block away and know something wasn't kosher. We have to watch our step."

6

It was plain that Roger was not enjoying the party, although the seven virgins of Sericane were giving him most of their attention. Harold Shea didn't know that he altogether blamed the big bruiser. It was good second-rate cabaret stuff, which might have been fairly enjoyable had there been a comfortable place to sit, something to smoke, and something to drink. Reed Chalmers had excused himself early and gone off to enjoy the company of Florimel.

The dance went on. In the middle of a figure Roger suddenly stood up. "In the name of Allah! Oh, uncle, this is not less than the vilest of your entertainments. My liver is constricted, and I would broaden it by hunting bears among the mountains."

Atlantès broke off his conversation with one of the lords and began fluttering his hands, not aimlessly, but in the pasted of a magical formula. However, it had no visible effect upon Roger, who trod firmly towards the door.

From besides Shea, Polacek said: "Say, I got an idea!" And wriggled to his feet and followed. Nobody but the seven girls seemed to mind the departure very much, even Atlantès going on with his whispered conversation. As the number drew to a close Shea felt uneasy; Polacek had too great a capacity for trouble to be left wondering around the castle for very long with an idea in his head. He too got up and strolled out into the corridor.

No sign of Roger or his friend. Shea ambled along the hall and around a bend without seeing anything significant. He was about to go back when his eyes lighted upon the side passage with a door at its end and where a smoky light showed the interlocked pentacles that protect magicians who deal with devils. Atlantès' own laboratory!

In a moment the direction of his attention changed. The wizard was certainly well occupied, and if he did come looking for anybody, it would be Roger. Shea stepped up to the marked door. No handle; and it and it did not move when he pushed it. Barred with a spell beyond doubt; but by this time, he knew enough magic to deal with the situation. Reaching to his turban, he plucked from the brush that adorned its front a couple of stiff bristles, detached a thread from the hem of his aba, and tied the bristles together in the form of a cross. Holding this up to the door he whispered:

> *Pentacles far and pentacles near,*
> *I forthwith command you disappear!*
> *Shemhamphorash!*

He paused, hoping there was no basilisk on guard.

There was not. The room was long and lower than it seemed from the outside. A row of alembics and other magical apparatus lay ranged on a long table at one side, faintly reflecting the blue-white phosphorescent light thrown from the eyes of an owl and a crocodile which stood on a pair of shelves. The animals were quite imobile; evidently Atlantès' private system of lighting, though not one that would ever be popular with interior decorators. Along the shelf beneath them was a row of books, terminating in little compartments, each of which had a title on its attached tag.

The books had characters on their backs which Shea tried in vain to puzzle out until he realized that in this space-time continuum he would be unable to read English or any other language in which books were printed without special instruction. With the tags on the scrolls he fared better:

Ye Principalls of Magick with ye Conjuration of Daemons Superadded; Poisons Naturall; The Lawful Names of Allah; One Thousand Useful Curses; The Carpets of the Lesser Jann; Al Qa'sib's Manner of Magickal Transformations; ...

Ah! This one might have what he was looking for. Shea pulled out the scroll and glanced at it in the eyelight of the animals. It seemed to be almost as strong on general theory as Chalmers himself, but little or nothing of the practical details. A glance showed him that, as might be expected, the scroll had neither table of contents nor index, and its style was so rambling that getting anything out of it would need a week's work.

Shea slipped the scroll back into its pigeonhole and turn to the rest of the room. If the enchanter were really trying to exchange Florimel's body for that of the menacing "woman knight," there ought to be traces of his labors about. However, the apparatus held no traces of filters, and the big scarred oak table beyond their bench laid bare. Atlantès was a neat sorcerer. Where would he keep his notebooks? Beyond the table was a stool and beyond that a low cabinet built into the wall. Like the outer door it had no handle, and as Shea bent closer he could see that its front was inscribed with pentacles. But at a touch it swung open, and Shea realized that his counter-spell must have let down barriers all over the castle. The thought that if there were any ifrits or a demons abroad tonight, they could get in and have themselves a hell of a fine time made him giggle under his breath.

The cabinet was deep, its shelves set back in, and in front of them a long straight sword hung in its scabbard from a hook. Probably an enchanted weapon, but the counter-spell would have taken care of that. Shea was about to reach past it toward the contents of the shelves when his ear caught the faint sound of a voice ordering the outer door to open.

In a flash Shea had snatched loose the sword and was on hands and knees behind the big table, which luckily had a decoration of carved wood reaching nearly to the floor.

The door opened. Shea could not see through the screening, but the light from the corridor momentarily threw the shadow of a baboon's head across the wall on the side away from the door. The newcomer was one of Atlantès servants, and a specially unappetizing member of the gang.

It stood in the doorway a moment, hesitant, as Shea himself had done. Then with the door swinging behind it, it stepped confidently toward the bookshelves. But then it fell quiet—too quiet. Shea heard it sniff, sniff again, like the puffing of a toy engine. Of course it would possess a keener sense of smell than a man. The servant worked its way over to the table that held the alembics, tracing Shea's movement, just audible as its feet pressed the carpet. Shea could imagine the snouted head turning this way and that... He gathered his muscles and shifted weight to bring his left hand free for the scabbarded weapon, planning in his mind how to snatch it out with the least lost motion.

The baboon-head reached the outer edge of the table, sniff, puff, sniff, puff, as loud as a locomotive in the oppressive silence.

Hell suddenly broke loose in the castle. A chorus of shouts and bangings echoed through the halls. The baboon-head paused for a moment, then ran to the door on almost soundless feet and out. Shea forced himself to count seven, then scrambled up and followed. The servitor had rounded the corner and the sound of its running still echoed metallically.

Shea turned towards the entertainment hall in the direction of the noise, pausing only in the side passage long enough to catch the sword on the belt beneath his flowing aba. It made him feel better.

As he approached the entertainment hall, he realized that the noise was coming from beyond. He ran past to a big winding staircase, and from where it spread to a landing he could see Atlantès and his guests coming up with swords, maces, and even musical instruments, chasing a wolf the size of a heifer. It came straight towards Shea, but with its tail between its legs and looking utterly miserable.

Shea tried to dodge, then remembered the sword, but before he could dig it out of its hiding place the creature was upon him. However, instead of leaping for his throat, the wolf threw itself on the landing and rolled over, scrubbing its back along the iron floor. It waved its paws in the air, letting out an un-wolflike "Wah-wah! Wah-wah!" Then it rolled back again, and, keeping its belly in the floor, licked at Shea's shoes.

"Hey, wait a minute," said Shea to the crowding pursuers, who were trying to take swipes at the beast. "This is a rummy kind of wolf. It wants to be a pet. Atlantès, would you mind taking a look at it?"

The sorcerer dropped one of the singers' lutes and came forward. "Verily this is a most unfortunate rare creature, a wonder of wonders. Now shall you grant me room, Sir Harold." He squatted down and peered closely into the animal's eyes; it moaned. "There is no god but Allah! This is surely a werewolf. Oh, my lords, an evil hour has brought such a shape to Carena!" He reached to the neck of his robe and made a little tear in it. "Now I must seek by my arts to find how such a creature has passed our defenses. There is no doubt but that this is the work of the Christian enchanter, the paladin Malagigi, son of a hog and a she-dog, though I had heard of him imprisoned in Albracca." He looked round the circle. "My lords, we must seek a silver weapon for one of you to slay this brute, for being myself an enchanter I cannot."

Apparently silver weapons were in short supply. "Oh greatest of enchanters," advised Margéan, "shall we not affix silver monies to a wooden club and beat it to death?"

The wolf howled piteously. Chalmers, who had popped out of his own room at the sound of the commotion, had arrived in time to hear the last remarks. Now he put in a word: "Ahem—wouldn't it be the part of—uh—wisdom to attempt disenchanting the animal first? If I am correct in my understanding, it would then lose any previous invulnerability."

Atlantès bowed. "O fortunate hour that has brought your father's son among us, Sir Reed! This is nothing less than the truth. Yet I am but a stick set in the sand beside you in such matters. As your head lives, you shall now do this for us."

"Uh—if we had some holy water, it would be a—uh—comparatively uncomplicated matter, but I will try." Chalmers turned his back, put one hand to his chin, and meditated. "I'm not sure the versification will prove adequate, but we shall see:

> *Wolf, Wolf, Wolf of the windy mountain,*
> *Wolf of fear;*
> *I conjure you by the bitter fountain;*
> *Disappear!*

His fingers moved rapidly. The wolf shuddered and turned into Vaclav Polacek rolling on the floor, clothes and all.

"Holy Saint Wenceslaus!" he cried, getting up. "Might as well shoot a man as scare him to death. Why didn't you lay off when I told you who I was?"

"You didn't tell us," said Shea.

"I did so. I kept saying, 'For the love of Mike, Harold, it's me, Votsy,' as clear as anything."

"Maybe it would've sounded like that to another wolf, but it didn't get to us," replied Shea. "How did you get into the mess anyway? Did you run into this Malagigi that Atlantès is talking about?" There was a murmur of agreement through the group, as Atlantès' eyes darted back and forth.

"Well," said Polacek. He cleared his throat once or twice before he could get going. "It's like this, see? Roger isn't such a bad guy when you get to know him. He wanted to go hunting or something, and we were talking about it, but he said as how there was some kind of spell so he couldn't get out the door, and I said I've been studying some magic, and so we went down there together, and he had the right dope; the door wouldn't open. Well, you see, I remember those somatic passes Doc was talking about and made a few of them, and boy, the door flew open, just like that!" He paused. Shea started a little, and hoped that Atlantès hadn't noticed.

"Go on, Vaclav," said Chalmers severely.

"Well, then I figured I knew enough about magic to maybe—uh—get that babe back—you know, the one you were going to introduce me to." He appealed to Atlantès. "So I worked a little spell, just like you said, but it turned me into a wolf instead. I'm sorry I made so much trouble."

"Must be your Slavonic ancestry," said Shea. "The Czechs are full of werewolf stories, and—"

He had not noticed the gathering clouds on Atlantès forehead. Now the storm burst. "Son of a dog!" he shouted at Polacek. "Where is the pride of chivalry, the noblest of his race, who is worth ten thousand such as you?"

"Why, he went out to do a little hunting, like I said," said Polacek. "He said he'd be back before morning with something good."

This time Atlantès really did beat his chest. "Ah, woe to me! The doom has stricken!" Then he swung around to the three Americans. "But as for you, Nazarene dogs, who have plotted against me by the hand of your servant while partaking of my bread and salt, you deserve nothing more than to be flayed alive and to have your bodies buried in a pit with the excrement of hogs!"

"Hey!" said Shea, reaching forward to take Atlantès by the arm. "Those are fighting words where we come from. If you want to get tough about it—"

"Harold!" Said Chalmers. "Let me handle this. We don't want—"

"We don't want anything to do with this thrip except to hand him a sock in the puss. D'you know what he's up to?"

Chalmers said: "Never mind, Harold. You have already informed me sufficiently. I'll defend—uh—myself and the young lady to any extent necessary."

Atlantès' fury had burned down to a glower. "O, ill-omened sorcerers! Know that this castle was wholly established by the arts of which I am master, and within its walls I have such power that I could turn you to a beetlegrubs in less time than the snapping of the fingers. Yet in the name of Allah, the omnipotent, the merciful, will I spare your lives to the undoing of the harm you've done, for it is written that once in his lifetime may the just man prefer mercy to justice without endangering his hope of paradise."

He extended both arms, closed his eyes and cried in a high voice: *"Beshem hormots vahariman tesovev ha-esh, asher anena esh, et metzudat habistell!"*

There was a whoosh and a buzz, like an electric fan in the adjoining room. Atlantès' permanent smile came back; so did his bow. "Behold, fellow practitioners of the noblest of the arts, if you will look beyond the walls of this castle, you will see it circled by an outer barbican of flame, sufficient to roast a sheep in less than a minute. For the hardest of men to try to pass it the punishment would be no less than death. Yet if the Lady Florimel attempt it, who is a woman and yet no woman, she would leave no more memory than steam from the coffee cup. My gracious mercy extends so far that the fire shall instantly be removed when by your arts you bring Lord Roger back; I will add to that bags of jewels so great that three men can hardly carry them. The peace of the one true God be with you in your meditations."

He bowed again and turned his back. The lords looked solemnly at the three (except Audibrad, whose sympathies, judging from the fact that he was trying not to smirk, were evidently in the other direction) and Chalmers began to dither. "I—uh—am unsure whether I am sufficiently advanced in the science of apportation, which I had presumed something of a specialty—"

"S-st!" said Shea. "If magic doesn't work, I'll take a running jump through and go hunt Roger myself. I don't mind having my eyebrows singed a little."

Atlantès, who seemed to have sharper ears than a cat, turned back. "Learn, rash youth," he said, "that the very marrow of your bones would be incinerated; and yet, of a truth, you say a thing I had not thought on; for it will be far easier to remove the Pearl of the Orient from thence to hither if he be found by human eyes than only by arts magical; and it will greatly please my brother's son to cut your throat from ear to ear beyond these walls. Go then; I undertake to pass you unharmed through the flame."

"I'd like to go, too," said Polacek. His expression showed that he did not look forward to a pleasant time at the castle after his venture into wolfishness.

"Go, then, and Allah give you neither peace nor long life unless you bring my nephew home again." He turned away again, this time for keeps.

Shea found Chalmers looking at him keenly. The doctor said: "I wonder, Harold, if helping me and Florimel was your most important motive in offering to find Roger?"

Shea grinned. "It's the only one you know about officially, Doc."

7

The whole castle turned out to see Shea and Polacek off on their Roger-hunt the following morning. During the evening, Chalmers had tried to establish thought-contact with the peerless chevalier as a preliminary to getting him back by magical means, but he had been forced to give up with the remark that Roger had about as few thoughts as the human brain could hold. In any case, there seemed to be interference, either from Atlantès himself or from the curtain of flame he had thrown around the castle, so the job clearly devolved upon Chalmers' two juniors.

He did not believe that the threat of Atlantès' plan to exchange the shapes of Florimel and the prophesied woman knight represented an immediate danger. Perhaps later; "But let us take first things first, Harold," he said cheerfully. "I think I can profitably employ my time in study and in attempting to establish communication with this Christian sorcerer Malagigi. It was—uh—remiss of me not to have thought of him before coming to Carena. I presume it would be superfluous to express a wish for your good fortune?"

Beyond the gate and a drawbridge over a dry ditch, the flames rose in a wavering wall, obscuring the nearby peaks. Shea could feel their heat on his face as he stood at the break of the drawbridge while Atlantès dipped a finger in a small bottle of oil and drew an isosceles triangle on his forehead and then a right triangle over the first, muttering a small spell as he did so. He repeated the process with Polacek and with the chief huntsman of the castle, a broad-shouldered swarthy man named Echegaray. Atlantès was all smiles as though they had no hard words the previous evening, although Shea overheard the other lords making up a small pool as to who would find Roger and when.

Echegaray strode beside them towards the flame, a crossbow over his shoulder. When he came to the magic barrier, however, he stopped and looked inquiringly at Shea. The flames streaked soundlessly far over their heads; the light was so intense that it hurt their eyes and looked altogether real and terrifying, though the grass from which the flames sprang seemed unharmed. Shea felt like stopping too, but with Echegaray watching and the eyes of the whole castle boring into the back—he threw out his chest and marched straight through. Two steps did it, and the fire only tingled.

For a moment his companions did not appear. Then there was a half-choked yell and Echegaray came through, dragging Polacek with him. The hunter looked at Shea, spat, and jerked his thumb at Polacek, who was swelling with indignation that had not yet quite reached the stage of words. "Tried to change his mind," said the hunter. "This way."

The road was no more than a track down the mountain whose peak the castle occupied, a track so steep moreover, that one had to walk with care, watching the skirts of one's jelab. They were already below the timberline and had to duck under the branches of tall trees along their way. A cool mountain breeze hissed through the pines and ruffled the brushes on Shea's and Polacek's turbans.

Shea unhooked the sword he'd taken from Atlantès' cabinet, drew it out, and looked it over before fastening it to his outside. Like the one he had used in the courtyard, the sword had a rounded point and a thick, heavy blade—useless for thrusting and awkward on the parry, altogether better suited to a slashing fanatic on horseback into a methodical epee fencer.

"Think we're going to run into anything?" asked Polacek, with wide eyes. "I ought to have something like that if we are." He turned to Echegaray and pointed to the huge broad knife in the latter's belt. "Hey, how about letting me have that thing for a while? If we have any trouble it would be better to have all of us armed."

"No. Mine," said the hunter shortly, and took up the way again. Three hours brought them to the foot of the main peak. There the path began climbing and dipping across a series of spurs reaching down from another crest which thrust in from their right. The forest grew thicker here. Echegaray led them into the throat of a valley, where a stream dropped past in a series of waterfalls and the ten a.m. sun failed to reach the bottom. The gorge widened to a valley which held a patch of swamp, where they had to squish almost ankle deep along the edge of a pond. Shea jumped and Polacek stopped at a glimpse of white skin and gauzy wings as the water-fays, or whatever they were, ducked out of sight. Echegaray pushed ahead without looking back, and they had to follow.

Beyond, the valley narrowed again. The mountain wall closed in so sharply on their side of the stream that they had to cross on a bridge which was formed of a single log. Echegaray simply walked across as if the log had been level land. Shea followed with difficulty, waving his arms for balance, and just barely making it with a leap at the end. Polacek struck his thumbs into his sash and tried to imitate the hunter's jaunty step, but failed to watch his footing and fell in.

"Time to eat," said the hunter as Polacek climbed out of the shallow water, rubbing his shin and cursing with a verve to curl the leaves.

Echegaray abruptly perched himself on the edge of the bridge-log, unslung his pack and brought out a piece of bread and a slab of dried meat, each of which he expertly divided into three portions with a slash of his knife, then waved a hand at the stream. "Water," he said.

As they munched and flexed tired muscles, Polacek said: "Say, Harold, how do you know where we're going and whether we'll find Roger there—not that I want to?"

"I don't," said Shea. He turned to the hunter. "How are you sure we'll find

Roger in this direction?"

"Best place," said Echegaray with mouth full.

"Yes, but where are we?" He produced a piece of parchment on which Atlantès had drawn a sketch-map when the journey was decided upon. "We've twisted around so many times in this valley that I'm not quite sure which direction the castle lies in."

"Magic?" Asked Echegaray, pointing to the map.

"No. Just a map."

"What?"

"A map. You know, a picture of the country with the roads and castles and things."

"Magic," said Echegaray flatly.

"Okay, it's magic, if you like it that way. Now, if you'll show us just where we are on the map—"

"We aren't," said Echegaray.

"What do you mean, we aren't? We can't have walked far enough to get off the map."

"Never on map. We're on log." He patted it to make sure.

Shea sighed. "All I want is for you to show me a spot on the map, corresponding to the place where we are now."

Echegaray shook his head. "Don't understand magic."

"Oh, to hell with magic. Look at this thing. Here's Castle Carena."

"No. Castle's a long way from here. We walk fast."

"No, no! This place on the map means Castle Carena. Now we want to know where we are on the map."

Echegaray pushed back his leather cap and scratched his short black hair. Then his brows cleared. "Want us on map?"

"Yes. You're getting the idea."

The hunter took the map from Shea's hand, turned it around a couple times, laid it on the ground, smoothed it out, and stood up—

"Hey!" yelped Shea. He caught at Echegaray's shoulders and pushed him back just as the hunter's boot was coming down on the parchment. "What's the idea of stepping on my map?"

Echegaray sat down, a resigned expression on his face. "Said you wanted us on map. Magic carpet, no?"

"No. I didn't mean you were to be put on the map physically." How the devil, wondered Shea, could you explain the principles of semantics to a one groove mind like this?

"Why'n't you say so? First you want us on map. Then you don't. Can't make up your mind. Never saw such people."

Shea folded the map and put it back in his sash. "Let's forget it. What makes you think you're going to find Roger in this direction?"

"Best place."

"One-two-three-four-five-six-seven. Why is this the best place? What would he be doing in this direction rather than any other?"

"Crossroads. Knights always fight at crossroads." The hunter broke off a twig and whittled it to a toothpick. He used it with relish, pausing now and then to belch.

"Ready?" he asked presently. Shea and Polacek nodded. Echegaray adjusted his pack, picked up his crossbow, and swung ahead.

The stream hung with them past another waterfall, where an animal of some sort went crashing through the thicket and Echegaray with an instinctive motion whipped up his crossbow. Shea could not help thinking how Belphebe—if it were she—would be enjoying this country. Beyond, the path carried them across to another high spur and through a screen of trees down to a three-pronged fork, the tracks in both directions broader and scarred by hoof marks. Echegaray strode to the junction and looked along first one leg of the fork and then the other, his forehead contorted by thought.

"What's the matter?" said Shea. "I don't see our friend Roger here. It is that it?"

The hunter gave him a look that showed disesteem for those who waste words pointing out the obvious, and pointed in the direction that must be south by the sun's position. "Crossroads; village. Four miles." Then he pointed north. "Crossroads. Village. Twelve miles. Which?" He looked at Shea for orders.

"Say," said Polacek. "Why don't we split up and play the field? One of us would have more chance of talking that big lug into coming back than both together, and besides, I know enough magic now to take care of myself—"

"No," said Shea, firmly. "You just try one more spell and I'll have your neck and ears." He turned to Echegaray. "Which way is Lord Roger most likely to go?"

The hunter shrugged. "Both. You tell."

Shea thought: after all, why not let Polacek and Echegaray take one road while he took the other? Votsy couldn't get into too much trouble with this simple-minded but knowledgeable retainer holding his hand; and as for himself, he would just as soon not have the Bouncing Czech around if he should chance to meet Belphebe. The way to the north wound among trees.

"Look here," he said, "maybe that's a good idea of yours after all, Votsy. Suppose you and Echegaray take that road to the south and let me strike off on the other one. That way we'll be all right. Watch out for Belphebe, will you? She's supposed to be wandering around here somewhere, and I shouldn't want anyone taking pot-shots at her."

"Me neither," said Polacek. "Boy, I could use one of those cocktails she used to mix, right now! She's better than you since you taught her."

They shook hands, and Shea said: "Got any money? Good. Might be an idea to buy yourself some kind of weapon in the village if you can. Probably a mace; anybody can swing a club without practice. Start back in about four days, whether you find him or not."

"Don't worry about me," said Polacek. "I figure I know how to get along with these types. Look how I contacted that purple guy with the booze in the castle, when all you did was sit around on your duff."

Shea turned up the road, looking back once to wave as the other two disappeared down a slope behind trees. He wondered how long Polacek's short legs would stand the pace. It was in such a wood that he had first seen the girl, light-footed, with a feather in her hat, who announced her presence with an arrow that slew the Losel. Belphebe. His feet picked the way along without any conscious help from his mind, except that he was aware of going forward. And they'd been getting so beautifully adjusted, too... No, not quite such a wood either. This one was more open; the trees were smaller, and there was less brush. One could see—

One could see something moving among the trunks to the right, too large and too steady of progress to be an animal. Shea snapped to attention, whipped out the sword, and slipped into the cover of a tree. Then something answered his movement with a call of "Olé!" and stepped into plain view. Echegaray.

"What in the blue-belted blazes have you done with Polacek?" demanded Shea, gripping his sword firmly as the hunter trotted up.

"Left him. Talks too much. Go with you."

"Don't you know he's not fit to be allowed out without keeper? Suppose you get right back there and keep an eye on him!"

For answer, the hunter shrugged and gazed at the top of a tall tree with an elaborate lack of interest in anything else. Shea felt his temper rise, but there didn't seem to be much he could do about it, short of turning back along the road to overtake Polacek or going for Echegaray with the sword. He stuck his nose in the air and started along the path the way he had been going. Echegaray followed.

The trees began to crowd in from both sides, and from the bottom of a draw the way commenced to climb steeply. Shea found himself puffing, although he noted that the hunter in less hampering clothes was coming along like a machine. At the crest, the spur they had been climbing broadened out into a little plateau with colonnades of trees. Shea leaned against a big trunk, breathing deeply; Echegaray posted himself against another, the toothpick twirling in a corner of his mouth.

Twunk! Twunk! The tree jarred with the blows. Shea jumped—or tried to and found he couldn't. A long white-shafted arrow had pinned his sleeve to the tree, and another was affixed just beside his right leg. He caught a glimpse of Echegaray's astonished brown face as the hunter flung himself flat, then began to snake forward to the shelter of a fallen trunk, the crossbow dragging.

He whipped a curved iron rod out of his boot and slipped one end of it over a stud in the side of the bow. A bolt dropped in; Echegaray's arm brought the piece of metal back and the bow was cocked.

There were no more arrows and the forest was silent. Echegaray's right hand scrubbed loose a pebble, which he tossed with a little noise into a brush at the far end of the log, at the same time peering cautiously around the near end.

"Drop!" he told Shea in a stage-whisper.

"Can't," said Shea. Thinking what a beautiful target he made for the unseen archer, he was trying to get the arrows out with his left hand. However, the position was awkward, and the deeply embedded shaft was made of some springy wood that would not break under his fingers' best efforts. His clothes were of a heavy, tweedy wool that would neither tear nor slide up the arrow. He gave a heave, then began trying to work his arm loose from the garment itself. Out of the corner of his eye he saw Echegaray watching the woods with bright-eyed attention, then bring the crossbow up slowly...

Snap! The bolt flashed away among the trees with it a bee-like hum. Someone laughed and Echegaray snatched up his cocking-lever.

Before he could finish reloading a voice roared: "Yield thee, sirrah! Halloo, halloo, and a mort!" Out of nowhere an oversized man had appeared over the hunter, waving a two-handed, cross-hilted sword. He was ruddy-faced, with features so strikingly regular that they might have been copied from those of an imaginary Apollo. Around his neck was a scarf with diagonal stripes of red, blue, and brown, the ends of which were tucked into a leather jacket. A light steel cap allowed curling blonde hair to escape around its edges, and a huge curled horn was strapped to his back.

Echegaray rolled over twice, whipping out his knife and coming up to one knee, but the point of the big sword was right in his face and he thought better of it. He sullenly dropped his weapon and spread his hands.

Down among the trees whither the crossbow bolt had flown, a hat with a feather came into view. The hat was bobbing on the end of the stick held by a girl in a knee-length tunic, a girl with freckles and reddish-gold hair cut in a long bob. She trotted toward them as though she were going to break into a dance step at any moment, and the other hand held a long bow with an arrow already nocked.

"Belphebe!" cried Harold Shea, his heart giving a great leap.

The girl, who had been looking at Echegaray, turned towards Shea with her eyebrows up. "What said you, Saracen? I hight Belphegor."

Shea looked blank. "Don't you remember? Harold Shea. Just an old husband of yours. The picnic."

She laughed. "Nor husband nor loveling have I, and had I such, 'twould be no son of black Mahound."

"You don't know anyone named Belphebe?"

There was a flicker between her brows. Shea remembered with a sinking heart what Chalmers had told him about his wife's loss of memory. She turned to the big man: "Nay, my lord Astolph, methinks this rogue doth seek to cozen us."

"Rather. This other chappie is Atlantès' hunter again, right?"

"Aye. Small tiding shall we have from him, even though he be ware of all. Recall you not, when erst we caught him? Your bolts, Master Echegaray!" She held out a hand, and the hunter, muttering something about "damned women...spinning-wheels" thrust forward a fistful of bolts.

"So? Have we them all?" The girl pulled the bandolier toward her and snatched out another bolt. "A clever rogue, is it not?"

Echegaray shrugged. "Worth trying," he said, resignedly.

"Very well, my man, you may go," said the man who had been addressed as Astolph. "And I'll trouble you to keep on your own side of the line hereafter." Echegaray picked up his crossbow and silently disappeared among the trees.

The big man turned to Shea: "Now let's have a word with you, my fine Saracen fowl!" He stepped to the tree and wrenched out the arrows with a strength that made the task look easy. "I don't believe I've seen you before. Do you claim you know Belphegor?"

"Look here," said Shea. "I'm neither a Saracen or a fowl, and I either married this girl or someone enough like her to be her twin sister. And she doesn't remember me."

"Daresay. It's a woman's privilege to forget, you know. They call it changing their minds, haw haw. But that's neither here nor there. We simply can't have you boffers from Carena running around and treating people the way Atlantès did this young lady. So you'd better stand and deliver an account of yourself if you want to keep that jolly head of yours."

Shea and flared up. "Stand and deliver! Listen here, Dick Turpin, suppose *you* give *me*—"

"Dick Turpin? Wasn't he the highwayman chap from old England? Haw, haw, well said, oh. But I say, how would you know about him?"

"How would you?"

"We're asking the questions here, young fella. Belphegor, keep that arrow on him to—by Jove, don't tell me you're a wizard from my own universe, the one that's built around the British Isles?"

"I don't know how much of a wizard I'd rate, but I am from there, all right. Only from the state of Ohio."

"American, as I live! Extrawdinr'y people, Americans—give me a million dollars, or I'll cut your rug for a loop of houses, what? Isn't Ohio where the cinema colony is? Hollywood? No, that's in your province of Florida. Are you a gangster? I would say so, or you'd not be hand-in-glove with those paynims at Carena."

"I'm not a gangster, and I keep telling you I'm not a Saracen. In fact, if you'll step into the woods with me I'll prove it. These are the only clothes they gave me to put on," and Shea launched into a thumbnail sketch of his apportation.

"I say," said Astolph, "this chap Chalmers, your colleague, must be quite an adept. Don't know that I could do as well, though Malagigi could. Unfortunately they've laid him by the heels. Do you know my old friend Merlin?"

"You mean the famous one, the Welsh wizard? Is he still around?"

"Certainly. I meet him at the Sphinx club in London. Do you know him?"

"I'm afraid I never met him personally."

Astolph's handsome face went a trifle grim. "That's unfortunate. Really, you know, with a war toward, we can't have strange wizards running around the borders of the Emperor Charles' dominions. Someone must vouch for you."

"There is Doc Chalmers."

"Another American. Doubtless another gangster."

"Echegaray."

"Atlantès' man. Come, you don't expect me to accept that, do you? Anything he said in your favor would be a guarantee of bad faith, assuming you could get him to say anything."

"Well, there's Lord Roger. He won't say anything in my favor."

"A fool."

"I have a friend around here somewhere, who came with me—"

"Still another gangster! Really, old man, you're only making things worse. I can't let you go under the circumstances, and I can hardly use you as a prisoner for exchange, since there's no war as yet. So there's only one thing to do..."

Shea, perspiring at this reasoning, cried: "Belphebe!"

There was a frown of puzzlement on the girl's face, but she shook her head. "He has the proper figure of a man, but—my lord, I know him not."

"I have the high justice," said Astolph, as though that settled everything. "Kneel down."

"Damned if I do," said Shea, tugging at his sword and reckless of Belphebe's nocked shaft.

"Righto," said Astolph, making a restraining motion at the girl. "But half a tick. Are you base-born? Most Americans are."

"I'm not a Duke or anything, but I've been made a knight, if that will do. By Sir Artegall of Faerie."

"Splendid. Ordeal of battle, and sound law, too. Only right to let a chap go out on his feet. Too bad you can't be shriven."

Shea got the sword out and shucked off his Muslim coats. As soon as he came within reach, Astolph took a stance, swung the big blade up, and struck down over hand with a wood-choppers swing. Clang! Clang! Clang! Shea parried with the awkward blade, though the force of Astolph's stroke almost drove it from his hand. He took a backhand cut with it, which Astolph parried easily, then came back forehand, but his opponent jumped away with a lightness surprising in so big a man. His return was so rapid that he forced Shea to give ground.

The Duke was good but not too good. After the third exchange Shea felt he could parry anything the big blade sent at him. However, the next clash brought a trickle of worry. Astolph's reach and length of blade were keeping him too far away for this clumsy weapon to be used as it was supposed to be used. If he could parry, he could not cut home, and in time, the big man would wear him down.

Another whirl and he almost lost his sword. The handle was slippery in his grasp. He began to grow angry at the unfairness of this big lug, and with difficulty remembered that an angry fencer is a losing one.

Astolph drove him back again, almost into a tree, and lowered his blade for a second to get a better purchase. The site of the exposed chest brought Shea's fencing reflexes to the surface. His right arm shot out, with the whole weight of the his body behind it in a long lunge. The rounded point of the sword hit jacket and chest with a thump. Astolph, a little off-balance and not expecting such a push, sat down.

"Yield thee yourself!" shouted Shea, standing over him and sighting on the Englishman's neck.

The duke's left arm came around like a jibing main boom and swept Shea's ankles from under him. Down went Shea. He was struggling in the bone crushing wrestler's grip when he heard the girl cry: "Hold, enough! By the power of woods and water which is my domain, I bid you cease!"

Shea felt Astolph relax unwillingly and climbed to his own feet. A rill of blood trickled from the Duke's nose where Shea had butted him, while Shea's turban was in his eyes, one of which was swelling, and the other end of the headdress was draped around him like one of Laocoön's serpents.

"I say, my dear," said Astolph, "you can't do this, you know. Ordeal of battle goes to a finish, and anything left of the loser has to be burned. I shall complain to the Emperor." He bent over, reaching for the big sword.

"Halt, sir! Would you try my bodkin?" She had drawn the tough shaft to the head, and it pointed steadily at the big man's midriff. "I care not for the Emperor Charles or the Lord of Circassia in this domain. But I say this is a true man that has fought well, and that spared you when he might have slain, and be he Saracen or no, there shall henceforth be peace between you."

Astolph grinned and held out his hand to take Shea is in a hearty grip. "Needs must take the fortune of war. Jolly good thing you didn't make that hit with a pointed blade or I should have been properly skewered. I daresay you can show me a trick or two. Care to join forces?"

"I'm not sure," said Shea. "What kind of campaign do you have on?" He thought: *If I can only get her to Chalmers, he can bring back her memory. In the meantime, not all of Atlantès ifrits will pry me away from her.*

"This bloody—excuse me, old girl—this castle of Carena. Atlantès has Lord Roger in there, and there is a prophecy that our side can't win the war unless we convert him."

Shea snickered. "From what I've seen of that guy, I'd say you'd have a rough time converting him to anything he didn't want to do. He hasn't got enough mind to convert with."

Astolph waved a hand. "That's all right. He saw Bradamant, the lady warrior, you know, at the Fountain of Love, and fell in love with her when he drank from it, so he can't do anything but what she wishes, at least until the spell is taken off. Atlantès was going to fly him to the Fountain of Forgetfulness, but I've bagged the mount."

A wave of relief swept over Shea. "You mean Bradamant is the lady warrior who was supposed to steal Roger from the Saracens? I was afraid—" and he gave a quick resume of Chalmer's position with Florimel at Castle Carena, and why he had come hunting the big beef.

When he had finished, Belphebe, said: "My lord duke, said I not it was a proper man? Sir, I thank you for your gentleness towards me; you may make me your devoirs." She whipped a knife like a steel sliver from her own belt and, taking down her cap, daintily split the feather in it along the middle, and handed Shea one half. "My favor."

Feeling awkward and a trifle confused, he tried to fix it in his breast. Silly, starting one of those formalized medieval courtships with its gambits and counters at this stage in their relationship...

Said Astolph: "So Roger's on the scram, as you fellas say? Very interesting; should have told me sooner. Stupid ass, Roger, though an awfully good fighter." He paused. "Do you know, this won't quite do, my friend. You and I are rivals in a sense. We both want Shaykh Roger, and for that matter so does the Lady Bradamant, though I really can't understand why. But I'll make you an armistice, matter to be decided by dicing, or whatever you say, but no magic. Are you genuinely a wizard, by the way?"

Shea looked down. "Not a very good one, I'm afraid."

"Come, young fella; no false modesty. Just cast me a little spell and demonstrate, so that we can have confidence in each other. Nothing like confidence, you know."

"Or leather either," said Shea. "It lasts." Belphegor-Belphebe was looking at him expectantly, and for his life he could not recall the passes of the somatic element that seemed so important in the magic of this space-time continuum. Wait a minute, though—there was the little spell Chalmers had used the other day to demonstrate that very point. The passes were simple and made a plant grow before the eyes; in Doc's case, a snapdragon. Grass would do to start with; it ought to make some kind of important looking plant. Shea plucked a handful, laid it on the ground and knelt over it, closing his eyes in the effort of memory as he whispered:

> *Though sore be my sowing,*
> *And more than ye know,*
> *And the end of my growing*
> *Is only to grow;*
> *Yet I cease not of growing*
> *for lightnings above me*
> *or death-worms below.*

When he looked around again there was no sign of a plant. Nor any of the grass. He wondered what he had done wrong this time. Astolph was looking straight at him. "By Jove! That's a neat bit, Sir Harold. Quite as good as Malagigi could have done. Apologies, old man."

"What is?" asked Shea. His voice sounded strangely muffled as though he were speaking through a blanket. Which, as he learned by putting his hand to his face, was just what he was doing. His beard, sprouting at about an inch a second, had already spread down his chest and across his shoulders, the ends twisting and curling like the tips of thin and inquisitive worms. The beard passed his belt-line and engulfed his arms.

Frantically he tried to think of a counter-spell, and felt as though he were in Hell when the only thing he could remember was Chalmers' all-too-effective spell for raising dragons. Live dragons growing out of one's face, ugh! Or would it be snakes? The beard had passed his knees, his ankles, its questing points had reached the ground. Belphegor stared at him open-mouthed.

"Oh, bravo!" said Astolph.

The stuff was piling up on the ground in a little haycock. If it would only lay off a minute; give him a respite to think! He wondered desperately how long it would keep going if he failed to find the counter-spell. There was the mill that had ground the ocean full of salt. That might be legend, but in a universe where magic worked there was apparently nothing to stop such a process until coils of hair filled the forest and rose like a tide round the magic flames that now encircled the Castle of Carena. He stepped back, almost tripping over a root. If that pulsating hair got him down—But wait, maybe he could get Astolph to stop it. If the Duke claimed Merlin as an acquaintance, he ought to know something of magic.

"Had enough?" he called over the growing mattress of wool to Astolph, whose head was now just visible.

"Thanks, yes."

"All right, fair's fair. Let's see you take the spell off."

"Righto." Astolph shifted his big sword to his left hand and swung it through the air, making a few expert passes with his right and mumbling a spell. The young mountain of first-rate upholstering-material vanished, and Shea tenderly felt his smooth cheeks. "You must meet Merlin some day," said the Duke. "Nobody likes a good joke like old Merlin. But I say, shall we get on with the business? Do you know, I believe the whole problem would become rather simple if we could get your friend out of Carena..."

"I'm not sure he wants to get out," said Shea. "There's the question of Florimel."

"No trouble at all, old man. With a pair like you and your principal, we ought to be able to rescue Malagigi from Albracca, and it would be jolly odd if he couldn't do something for the lady. But I really don't see—" he went off into frowning concentration.

"What?" asked Shea.

"That wall of flame. Deuced awkward. That is, I know well enough how to deal with it only we can't apply the solution."

"Sir Harold has been made immune to it," said Belphegor.

"Ah, but the problem is not smuggling him in, but getting this Lady—ah—Florimel out. It's this way, you see—" the big man turned to Shea with a wide gesture. "The Lady Bradamant owns a magical ring, very superior production, which protects one from any sort of enchantments, and also makes one invisible if taken into the mouth. It would be just the thing for your Florimel. Bradamant intended to use it to break into Carena for Roger, but she loaned it to Roland for no reason, and the silly beggar accidentally drank at the Fountain of Forgetfulness and lost his wits. Completely blotto. Can't remember where he put the ring or that there is a ring; can't even remember his name."

"I think I see," said Shea. "If we can get Roland to remember where the ring is, then one of us can extract Florimel from Carena and start all over again. But who's Roland? Is he important?"

"Really, old man! One of the twelve. The paladins. The companions of Emperor Charles. Best man of the lot in a fight."

"Oh," said Shea. The thought had occurred to him that this was not a problem of magic at all. Roland sounded like a fairly simple case of amnesia, and there was no reason why the techniques of the Garaden Institute should not work quite as well among these mountains as in Ohio. "I think I know a spell that will restore Roland's wits," he said. *And if Roland's,* he thought, *why not Belphebe's?* He must watch for a chance to try.

"Really? That would be wonderful. What do you say we go about it? Buttercup must be about somewhere." He put his forefingers in his mouth and whistled piercingly. Something moved in the forest and a hippogriff trotted into view, wings folded neatly back against its flanks. The wings were mainly white with pulsations of rainbow hues flickering through them. The animal pricked up its ears as it came and poked at Astolph with its beak. He scratched among the roots of its feathers. "It answers me better than it ever did Atlantès," he said. "Those confounded Saracens don't know how to treat animals."

"What does it eat?" asked Shea practically. "I don't see how that eagle's head goes with a horse's digestive apparatus."

"Blooms from some of those African plants, I believe. Buttercup's not a heavy eater. Very well, everybody, all aboard! Bit crowded, what? What's that remark you Americans make when punching cattle? Brutal business that, by the bye; I never could see why you don't just herd the poor things instead of punching them. Oh, yes, yippee. *Yippee!*"

8

The hippogriff trotted swayingly up a rise. Shea imagined that it would not be very fast on the ground, thanks to the interference between the magnified claws on the forefeet and the hooves behind. As they reached the granite hogback of the crest, the claws clung securely enough to the rock, but the hooves skidded alarmingly. Shea clutched Belphebe-Belphegor around the midriff, and she clutched Astolph, who did not seem at all perturbed. The hippogriff spread its wings, blundered along the ridge, flapping furiously, slipped again, teetered over a fifty-foot drop, leaped into the air, swept down and then up in a smooth curve that just missed the treetops.

"Whew!" said Shea, the wind of the heights on his face and a jellylike feeling in his center. "Sir Astolph, I think your Buttercup should use a rocket-assisted take-off."

"Wouldn't do, old man," said Astolph, over his shoulder. "Laws of nature diff...frame of reference..." His words whirred away down the wind of their passage as Shea reflected that according to the theory of dynamics, this beast wouldn't even be able to get off the ground. The contact with Belphebe sent tingles up his arms; he wanted to get her away for a good long talk. She seemed unaware of the emotion she was provoking.

The hippogriff apparently disliked the weight of its triple load and at every landing it sighted below, tried to spiral in for a landing. Astolph had to bark to keep it on course. After the third of these aborted efforts, Shea saw a cleared area of some extent; the details grew slowly to those of a small village with thatched roofs, surrounded by a patchwork of planted fields, plowed ground and weedy meadow. The hippogriff, its horse end sweating, swooped eagerly down, skimmed the ground, pulled into a stall, and made a four-point landing that jarred Shea's teeth.

He climbed down and reached up a hand to help Belphebe, but she vaulted down without seeing him and he felt foolish. With the half-unconscious effort one makes to cover embarrassments, he swung toward the cottages, and as he did so, a chorus of screams burst from them. Men and women boiled out one after another, running for their lives. They were either deeply or suspiciously sunburned, and most wore nothing but long, dirty, ragged shirts. At the speed of their passage, they took no notice of hippogriff or riders.

After the spreading rout came two men. The shorter of the pair, a good-looking, youngish fellow with strong hands, seemed to be trying to pacify the other. The second individual wore the medieval-type garments with the hosen and the turned-up shoes Shea had seen in Faerie, but with the laces of his jacket dangling. His face was unbarbered and his eyes roved. The fists waved in jerky motions; the voice growled.

"Upon my soul!" said Astolph. "Look here, you chaps, cheerio, and all that."

The shorter man gave a glance, waved a momentary hand, clamped a wristlock on the other and led him over to the newcomers. Shea perceived that the wild man would be handsome in a Latin sort of way if cleaned up.

"Greetings, most noble Astolph," said the short man, with as near an approach to a bow as he could manage with his grip on the other "and to you, fair Belphegor, hail. The wrath is on our great companion once more; he had slain half the village, had I not let him. Yet in true gentilesse, the fault be not wholly his own."

"Indeed? Tell us about it, old man," said Astolph.

"Would you believe it, fair lady, and you, gentles? A hart of eight brought I home, as pricksome a bit of venison as ever a man saw before vespers. A meal for the Emperor's own majesty, one might think; make it a pie, or what will you? Nay, these base varlets must even serve it up boiled, as though 'twere salt stockfish in Lent. I gagged, but our friend Roland put down the first two bites fairly enough. At the third, meseems he must have recovered a whit of the laws of cookery, for he gave a great howl like a lion and set upon the knaves, beating in their heads with his fists. But alas, to what purpose? Not even a crack will let savor into such skulls."

He looked round the group and his eye came to rest on Shea. "A paynim, ha! I thank you, Lord Astolph; a cut from his haunch will recompense me my venison." He gave a barking laugh to demonstrate that this was meant for humor. Shea smiled dutifully.

"Ah—er—" said Astolph. "Lord Reinald of Montalban, may I present to you Sir Harold de Shea? A johnny from England—that is, from one of our subject allies." He swung to Shea. "I'd be glad to present you to Count Roland d'Anglante, except that as you see, the poor lad wouldn't recognize you." The

Count, who was apparently the wild man, was alternately sucking one finger and tapping the end of it in the palm of the hand on which Lord Reinald retained his grip. It seemed to provide him with deep satisfaction. "Sir Harold is also looking for Roger of Carena. Small world, isn't it?"

"The chase is like to be longer than that for Angelica," said Reinald, reaching his free hand inside his jacket and producing something which Shea did not quite make out to kiss before he went on. "We have it on the word of the kerns that Sir Roger passed through at spark of dawn, moving as though Saint Beelzebub were on his slot."

"Really, old man!" cried Astolph. "I must be losing my grip; to hear that he slipped past my watch is more startling than your canonization of Beelzebub."

Reinald shrugged and resisted a sudden jerk by his companion. "Let buy a candle for Lucifer, then. The thing's established—would you doubt my word?"

"No, but—look, here, old man, it's rather important for the Emperor. Whyn't you stop him?"

"Can a man live forever like a priest? Roland slept; I tied him to a rafter and sought a damsel who had made certain signs by the fountain."

"How perfectly rotten of you!" cried Astolph. "What the devil did you funk the job for?"

Reinald grimaced. "Angelica lost, and fair Belphegor drives me to a distance with arrows sharper than Saint Cupid's own. What's left of life?"

There seemed not much more to say. They walked back toward the village, Astolph fingering his chin. He looked up to remark: "Do you know, I believe Sir Roger will head west, then double back to join Agramant's army. Sort of thing he would consider the height of cleverness." He turned to Shea. "Your gangster friend with the odd name won't find him. That direction would be the double bluff."

He paused and, pulling the hippogriff's head down to his lips, said something in his ear that sounded like a series of low-toned whistles. The animal cocked an intelligent eye at him and stood still.

Among the huts a table stood under a tree, and on it lay two large wooden plates with boiled meat which gave off a powerful odor of garlic and was framed in congealing grease. There were no other plates in sight, nor anything to drink.

While the others waited patiently, Reinald went from door to door, shouting in each without result, then returned, shaking his head gloomily. "The rats have fled the larder," he said. "Beyond the mind of reasonable man to riddle out. Sir Harold, how wags it in your country? Would not men without number be glad and overglad to have lords of Charles' own court to hold them from harm?"

Shea raised his eyebrows. "It couldn't be that they're afraid of your friend's tempers?"

"Think you so, indeed?" Reinald's eye brightened and he nodded his head as though something new and important had come into his life. "They be base-born enough. Three or four has he slain, but no more; and even those without pretension to gentle blood. It might be, though; fear of death is ever dreadful to those who know it not for a mocker. A mystery."

The five made room on a couple of rough-hewn benches and divided the meat with knives supplied by Reinald and Astolph, washing it down with water from the village well, drunk from the bucket. Shea hoped that the fauna of this continuum did not include typhoid germs, the back of his mind assuring him comfortably that the deadliest disease present would probably be African fever induced by night air. All the same when he noticed a crawfish clinging to the moss inside the bucket, he and the crawfish pointedly ignored each other.

Reinald gnashed his teeth across a bone and addressed Astolph: "Start we tonight or attend the Lady Bradamant, the mirror of true valor?"

Said Astolph: "I don't really believe we gain anything by a night march, do you? After all, it will be hard going with Count Roland in such a state, and we shan't really lose anything, since I doubt if Roger is up to a night march. Up with the birds, then...but wait a tick. Our young friend here is a jolly good qualified magician, and says he knows a spell to bring Roland's wits back."

Reinald crossed himself. "Holy Saint Virgil, protect us! Those wits lost to black Mahound!"

"Would simplify—"

Count Roland, who had been slobbering over his meat, suddenly turned round to look at Shea and said in a loud, clear voice: "You Saracen! I slay you!" and leaped from his place, trotting around the table with dirty hands outstretched.

"Get him—" yelled Astolph, as the others scrambled to their feet, but the latter was upon Shea before he could more than get on his feet. He did the only thing he could think of at the moment to save his neck without bringing the others down upon him; viz, ducked, knocked the clutching right hand up with his own left and dug his own right with all his strength into the Count's belly. It was like punching a truck tire, but Roland staggered two steps, almost upset the table, sat down with a fishlike expression spreading across his face, as he recovered his breath, began to cry.

Shea, shaking his hand to get the tingle out of his knuckles, almost laughed at the sight of Reinald's open mouth. "By my halidome!" said the paladin. "A rude stroke was that."

"Oh, yes," said Astolph. "Quite good at the thrust, this young fella; nearly gutted me like a bird a bit back. If you ever fight him, Lord Reinald, guard against that straight lunge. Now look here, I think we can reach an agreement. Sir Harold, I take it, only wants Roger to exchange him for a brace of friends, now in durance in Castle Carena, where that blighter Atlantès is holding them in chancery. If he can restore Roland's wits for us, I say that with three paladins, we ought to be able to set him on the right track."

Reinald blinked once or twice in a way Shea found not altogether pleasing. "The Lady Bradamant would stand our certain aid, I doubt not," he said. "Is aught of philosophical apparatus required for your enchantment, Sir Harold?"

"No-o-o. Not that I know of; unless you have a nightlight."

"That wot I not of; but since there be no bar and our composition waits but on your action, speed on. It is good law that the vavassour render his service before he have his sustention."

Shea looked at Belphegor (whom he insisted upon calling Belphebe in his mind), but she was looking in the other direction, after a single glance. He was not at all sure that he understood what Reinald was saying and he would much rather have a tête-à-tête with his wife, but as near as he could make out, the two paladins were making a deal with him to get Doc and Florimel out of Castle Carena if he got Count Roland out of what seemed to be a case of simple throwback amnesia. He sighed and addressed himself to the task by turning toward the still softly sniffling paladin:

"There, there, that didn't really hurt much, did it? But when little boys are bad, they have to learn..." Belphegor's mouth fell open a little as he droned on, but the wild man looked at Shea interestedly, then suddenly seized him around the neck and implanted a greasy kiss on his cheek.

Reinald laughed openly; Astolph seemed to have some difficulty in controlling his breath for a moment and announced that he was for bed. Shea turned toward the pale blue eyes now fixed on his in adoration.

"Want a story?" he asked. "If you'll come along I'll tell you one about three—dragons." The pattern seemed simple; age was suppressed beyond about a three-year-old level. He said rapidly over his shoulder to the others: "This is going to take some time, if the spell will work at all. You-all will have to get away from here and wait a while. I could use insulin shock, but that piece of philosophical apparatus isn't around, so I'll probably have to work half the night by my own method."

They went, willingly enough and yawning under the declining light. Roland listened with interest to the story of the three bears, translated into dragons, and demanded more. "No," said Shea. "You tell me a story instead, 'cause it's way past my bedtime. Then I'll tell you one."

Roland laughed delightedly. "They're all silly go-to-bed-earlies. What 'tory you want?"

"Well, tell me who you are."

"I'm me."

"Sure. You live in a cave, don't you?" Bits of the *Orlando Furioso* were floating through Shea's head; or was it the *Chanson de Roland*? He wished he could get them straight, but seemed to be doing all right so far, since his patient remained attentive. "And your mother's name is Madame Bertha. But what does she call you?"

"Gay-gay. That means 'snookums,' an' it's white and red."

Shea grunted internally. This mass of muscle, hair and dirt was about as far from a snookums as he could conceive. But at least the white and red was a tiny advance; those were Roland's colors. That was in the book. "What else do they call you?"

"Ruffy."

Not much there. "What's your father like?"

A pout. "Don't know. Gone to fight Saxons."

"Didn't he come back?"

The heavy face became woebegone. "Don't know."

"Yes, you do. No tell, no story."

Roland began to sniffle a little and Shea did not altogether blame him. It must have been pretty rough to move out of a castle into a cave where you didn't get enough to eat. But he was inexorable; Roland finally stopped sniffling and remarked: "Mama said he gained glory, and the syndics said we mustn't live there any more, and I was cold and had a fight and saw a fat man sitting in an inn and somebody blew a music and I don't like it here and I'm hungry."

The ice was beginning to crack. Shea felt a jump of joy in his heart and looked around for Belphegor, but she had vanished. With elaborately affected scorn, he said: "I know a better story than that."

"You do not, either! The fat man was a crowned king, and he was my mama's brother..."

A solemn moon came up and winked through the leaves, then settled slowly toward disappearance-point again as Shea desperately flogged his own memory and the paladin's on the details of the vanished career. Once he thought he was going to lose his man, when Roland mentioned the name of Angelica, put down his head and wept for quite five minutes; once he thought all would come clear at once, when Shea threw in the name of the giant Ferragus, and the paladin seized a bone from the table, leaping up and shouting "Montjoie!" But that one only collapsed, into babbling. It must have been well past midnight, a poor hour for this country, when Roland once more got to his feet, and pressed the heels of both palms to his eyes.

"Sir," he said, "I know not your name aright nor true condition, and I am hindered from giving you the kiss of peace, since I perceive my own condition is less than that which knight and gentleman should hold. You have my favor; are you a necromancer?"

"I suppose I know something about magic," said Shea, suddenly feeling modest.

"I trust your penance will be small. There be others of our brotherhood about, an I mistake not?"

He looked toward where the moon was losing its struggle. "Let us seek them; I see it all, we must seek mount and away for time will press. Is the Lady Bradamant among them?"

9

The Lady Bradamant was not in the headman's house where Duke Astolph and Reinald were laid out with straw in their ears, the latter on his back and snoring like a Diesel engine. What was more important for Shea, neither was the Lady Belphegor. He felt defeated, but Count Roland was quite evidently not of the same mind.

"Ho!" cried that worthy paladin, in a voice that would have made the windowpanes shake if there had been any windowpanes. "Will you lie slugabed when there are deeds to do? Rouse out, I say!"

In the dimness of the hut, Shea saw Astolph roll over, swinging his arms. Reinald's snores checked for one moment, then began again in a higher key.

"Ha, rouse!" Roland shouted again, and somewhat unexpectedly, deposited a resounding kick on the recumbent form as Astolph came up, all standing. Reinald whipped up, light as a cat, one hand to his belt, and Shea caught a gleam of steel, but Roland laughed and extended both arms: "Nay, nay, my noble lord and brave friend, will you slit my weazand while still the paynim danger lies on France?"

Reinald relaxed with a growl. Astolph threw a branch on the dying fire, and as it blazed up, looked keenly into Roland's face. "I believe he's all right again," he remarked.

"Aye, my own man; grace to this young knight." Roland swung toward Shea. "Sir Harold, were I not sworn to poverty, the treasures of Babylon would be too small for your reward. Yet know that you have all my heart and true support in whatsoever shall not run counter to my knightly vow of fealty to the Emperor Charles. I have the ring. And now gentles, we must out and away." He cocked his head on one side. "Hark, I hear the shrill trumpet!"

"Then the trumpeter will have outwatched the bear," said Reinald, dryly. "Look you, good Roland, this quest of Roger gains naught by a night-march while we have Astolph, who can ride after him by day on the wings of the wind. Take then your rest; with the dawn we'll woo fortune."

"He's quite right, you know," said the Duke through a yawn. "Besides, I daresay you could do with a bath and some weapons before undertaking anything serious, and tonight there's precious little chance of your getting—"

He stopped, looking over Shea's shoulder, and the latter turned with a jump of the heart to see standing in the low doorway—Belphegor, arrow on string and the firelight throwing lovely shadows on her face.

She came a couple of paces into the room. "I heard the bruit, my lords, and thought—"

Said Reinald: "That there was something toward which might permit that after all you should take comfort in my arms?"

"Nay, my lord, I sleep lonely this night—and every other, where you're involved." She returned her arrow to its quiver and relaxed the string.

"Hey!" said Shea. "I want to see you." If that antiquated technique could work such wonders on Roland, there was better than a good chance that—

The girl inclined her head gravely. "Sir knight, you have made me your service. You may see me to my rest."

"Where is it?" he asked, as they reached the door.

"I have made my bed in the branches of an oak that overlooks these cots," she said. "My lonely bed."

Shea smiled a narrow little smile. "Mean to say you positively, positively don't remember being my wife?" and thinking that at best he'd probably have to break her of claustrophobia all over again. Being married to a girl who wouldn't sleep in a bed, he had found, was an experience that did not grow on one with repetition.

She drew away from him a little. "Now, sirrah, seek you to cozen me again? Certes, you'd be a more adroit seducer than yonder lord of Montalban, but I'll not be seduced."

Shea grinned. "I should hope not by that big lug, anyway. But say, don't you remember things?"

"Nay—that Water of Forgetfulness whereof he drank have I never seen. I am free of the forests...and yet, and yet—there is a passage. I know not how I came to Castle Carena, save that I stood within beside a gray-haired wizard whom they called Sir Reed and his fair bride—ah, faugh!" She made a gesture of disgust.

"What's the matter with Sir Reed?"

"Not he, but that great loutish booby of a Roger. It had been insupportable but for the visit of Lord Dardinell and his squire Medoro."

"Huh?" said Shea in alarm. "What about this Medoro?"

"A most sweet lad. He took my part when all the others would have trapped me like a hare. Could I but count that he'd be more true to me than to a religion that bids him keep four wives—"

"My God, you can't do that!" cried Shea. "That's bigamy! Maybe I'd better—"

"Sir, you lose my favor when you still hold to the old tune like a musician who has only one note."

"Oh, all right, all right. Honest, darling, I'm only trying—well, skip it. How did you get out?"

"How—? Oh, one of the men there leaned on a staff, so I borrowed it from him, clouted a couple of pates, and it was ho!—and away."

"Didn't they chase you?"

"Marry, that they did, but I am somewhat light-foot." (Shea could believe that. Looking at her hungrily as she paused under the big oak, he could remember her in a red bathing suit, easily outdistancing himself and a squad of friends along the beach of Lake Erie.)

"Okay. Now to go back a little. You don't remember meeting Reed Chalmers and me in Faerie by shooting a Losel that was after us? And you don't remember joining us in the campaign against the Enchanters' Chapter? Or that fight in the air with Busyrane on his dragon?"

"No. Should I? These names have a barbarous, outlandish sound to me."

"You certainly should remember, and you should remember some other things, too," he said, grimly. "I think I can—"

"Put a spell upon me to work me to your will? Nay, I will assuredly contempt you from my grace, though I bade you accompany me that I might do you service."

"I'm sorry. Honest." (Shea wondered whether he ought to get down on one knee and kiss her hand, but decided he'd be damned first.)

She reached out one hand and touched his arm. "So. Well, the service is yours in any case—not for the pretty apology, but because we of the woods love not injustice."

"What injustice?"

"Think you you have a true composition with these lords? Then think again. Duke Astolph may be moderate well affected toward you, but not Lord Reinald, who holds it lawful to deceive and despoil all Saracens, among which he'd place yourself and all your friends."

Shea grinned. "I imagined they might be trying to clear out. But I'll be watching."

"Small service will that be. Astolph is to cast a spell of deep sleep on you tonight and they depart at dawn. He offered to take me and make me his leman, but I'd have none of him."

"The—excuse me for what I'm thinking. I thought Astolph was on the square."

"Oh, aye; a good wight, surely. But wrapped in law, like all the English, and when Lord Reinald spoke of his liege duty to the Emperor, and how with Roger beyond the castle, the victory of Christendom would be delayed by contention with you for his body—why then, Duke Astolph let himself be overborne."

Shea mused. "Will Roland let them get away with it? He seemed grateful enough when I saw him, and he certainly owed me a favor."

Belphegor laughed tinklingly. "I give him not a fig's weight—oh, a most accomplished gentle knight that will swoon devotion like a rose, but will set duty to the Emperor and his war above all else, even more than Duke Astolph.

Has he found the Lady Bradamant's ring?"

"He said so."

"Then even more. For look you, this Castle Carena is a haunt of paynim sorcery and nest of vipers, which being entered by the power of the ring, Roland would destroy and hold it for the day's best deed."

It was probably true. Shea remembered that the Count had made a reservation in favor of the Emperor in his promise of gratitude. "I guess I'm stuck with finding Roger on my own, then," he said, a little sadly. "What are you going to do?"

"I? In sooth, live my free life of the woods and fountains, sobeit Medoro... Since Roger's free of the castle, I hold myself free of my promise to help Duke Astolph hale him forth."

"Why not help me find Roger then?"

"Wherefore should I?"

Shea felt his throat dry up. "Oh, to help beat injustice, or just for the fun of the adventure...or something." He finished lamely, then went on again. "After all, you did promise to help Astolph."

"Ah, sir, but a debt lay there. It was Astolph and none other who turned the pursuit from Castle Carena when they would have taken me with horse and hound."

"What! You didn't tell me that." Shea felt a homicidal impulse toward Sir Reed Chalmers, who hadn't told him, either. Sir Reed, evidently felt that he'd put his foot into it about as far as he cared to.

"Aye; slew one of the Saracens and scattered the rest. But come, sir, you impose sleepless hours upon me to no purpose. You must find me an acuter reason, if I am to join your search for this Roger."

"Well—he'll head for the Saracen camp to get into the war, won't he. You might find—Medoro—there."

"Oh, fie, Sir Harold! Would you have me pursue a man like that great, buxom warrior-wench, the Lady Bradamant? You think but ill of those to whom you pay your devoirs... Not that you are wrong as to the fact; poet though he be, Medoro will hardly neglect the summons of the trumpet at such an hour. Nay, your reason is against companioning with you for a search in that quarter. Now I must have a new one, doubly strong."

So, the dope's a poet, is he? thought Shea. "I don't know any more reasons," he said stoutly. "Except that just I want you to come along because I love you."

Belphegor-Belphebe caught her breath for one second, then extended her hand. "So you have found the key at last, and are my true knight. It is covenanted. I give you rendezvous at this spot, so soon as the paladins be again in slumber. Now go, ere stark suspicion o'er-spread their minds."

"What shall we do? Steal their horses?"

"Nay, the hippogriff? And Roland's steed is the great Bayard, who'd rouse his master on the instant."

"Oh, damn. I know a man named Bayard, but he'll never wake anybody up. What else—?"

"Go, sir, I said. Nay, no embraces."

"Goodnight," said Shea, and made for the hut, feeling a tremulous half-hope such as he had not known since they were both prisoners of the Da Derga in Faerie.

He found the three squatting around the small fire on a hearth in the center of the floor. A hole in the ceiling above let out about a third of the smoke.

Astolph stretched, yawned, and with the air of a man preparing for a long sleep, began carefully unwinding his red-blue-brown scarf. Catching Shea's eye fixed on him, he remarked "School" briefly, then: "One can't exactly wear a tie in this country, you know. I had the colors made into a scarf instead."

"What school is it for?"

"Winchester," said the Duke, with just the right note of pride. "Oldest of 'em all, you know. Merlin's on the board of trustees. Wonderful thing, the public school system, though I don't know what will become of it with all this Socialism."

"I went to a public school in Cleveland myself."

"I daresay." Astolph regarded him with an air redolent of mistrust, and Shea perceived he had not taken the right way to influencing people. Before he could smooth matters out, Reinald lifted his head from where he was already down in the straw again: "Peace, you twain! A pox on your babble that keeps honest men from their rest."

"Righto. But first I fancy I'd better make certain Sir Harold here doesn't wipe us in the eye. Oh, you're a man of honor and a jolly good fellow, but this is merely a sensible precaution." Astolph had reached his feet as lightly as a cat while speaking and picked up the big sword, which he now pointed at Shea. "Lie quietly, old thing and take your medicine."

You lie on a blanket of cloud, soft and white,
And you sleep, sleep, sleep through the murmuring night,
Your limbs are so heavy, your eyelids must close,
You're torpid, you're drowsy; you loll, drift, and doze—

Shea, fully aware that this was a sleeping-spell, fought to keep his mind alert while casting about for a counter-spell. There was the one with the paper, no, that was a weakness spell...no...his thoughts were losing coherency.

Come, ye spirits who generate pandiculation
And your brothers who revel in wide oscitation—

The spell corresponded to something like hypnotism, and it was hard to keep his eyes from the tips of Astolph's fingers, moving in the passes. It was almost not worth the trouble of trying to beat it. After all...

Come Morpheus hither, and Somnus and Coma—

There was a story where you mustn't sleep. *King of the Golden River?* No... Kim—and the boy there had used the multiplication table. The memory jerked him to effort. Three times three is nine...if he could only keep on...this part was too easy...six times seven is forty-two, six times eight... The spell droned on, apparently without end...eleven times thirteen is one hundred forty-three...

I by this authority conjure you, sleep!

It was over. Shea lay with his eyes closed, but his brain wide open, working on seven times fourteen. Reinald's voice came drowsily, as though the paladin were talking through fur: "Will he sleep till the morrow?"

"Through several morrows, I should say," said Astolph. "I gave him a jolly good dose."

"Almost put me to sleep myself," said Reinald. He rolled over once, and in less than a minute was back in the low-register snore that had preceded Roland's kick.

Shea waited, wishing his nose would stop itching, or that Astolph would quiet down next to him, so he could scratch without being caught at it. His eyebrow began to itch, too, then the rest of his face in patches, so agonizingly that he wriggled it, trying to throw off the feeling. Astolph turned over and Shea froze into immobility, wondering whether a snore would be convincing, decided against it and discovered that the itch had shifted to a point inside his left ear. The Duke made another turn, loosed a sigh of comfort and seemed to drift off. But it was a good ten minutes—every one of which Shea counted—before he dared to let his eyelids flicker open.

There was a small red glow at the center of the room and an oblong of gray that was the door. Beyond, he judged it would be near the hour of false dawn; the moon had long since disappeared. The three figures in the draw made darker blacks in the blackness of the hut, but lay perfectly still. Under the beat of Reinald's snores the rhythmic breathing of the other two was audible. Asleep all right, but he could not afford to take chances, therefore gave it another good ten minutes before stirring an experimental arm. The dark gray patch of the door turned abruptly bright blue, then dark gray again. Far away, thunder purred softly.

Shea thought a few unpleasant things about his luck and the weather. If the storm came this way, it would rain through that hole in the roof, certainly rousing Astolph and probably Roland. If he were to make a getaway, it would have to be right now.

He moved his hands slowly in the straw beside him, gathering up his turban, which had been serving as a pillow, and his sword. At the next rumble, he rolled to his feet, took two cautious steps and lifted his flowing outer garments from the peg where they had hung. The next two steps took him out.

A flash showed a huge pile of thunderheads nearby and the sound came long-continued, rolling closer. A little puff of wind whirled down the village street. The hippogriff was huddled where Astolph had left it, squatted head down and eyes closed. It trembled unhappily in the lightning flashes, its feathers stirring in the vagrant dashes of wind. When Shea touched it, the beast, bound by the Duke's magic, did not lift its head. To loose the spell on it would take fooling around, time, and maybe more skill than he had. The first drop struck his hand.

A brilliant flash and an avalanche of thunder. Shea, thinking he had heard a shout from the direction of the headman's house, whipped the jelab around him and ran just as the rain came pattering down, heading without equivocation along the street and toward Belphebe's tree. As he reached the edge of the forest shade, she stepped out before him, as wide-awake as an owl, unperturbed by the rushing rain.

"Did they—" she said; a crash of thunder drowned the rest.

"I think the storm woke them up," said Shea, shedding his outer cloak and hanging it around her. "How are we going to get out of here?"

"You an enchanter and know not this?" She laughed gaily, turned and whistled a low, lilting tune in a minor key, less than a third audible under the pattering leaves and whipping branches.

Shea strained his eyes toward the village and in the repeated lightning-glare, was sure he saw figures moving. "Hurry," he said. Then he heard a trampling behind and a voice shouted "Whee-he-he-he! Who calls?" Almost instantly it was answered by another and higher one: "Who calls?"

"Bel—Belphegor of the woods—a daughter of—" her voice seemed to check oddly.

"In whose name call you us?" bellowed the first voice.

"In the name of Sylvanus, Ceres, and the Fountain of Grace."

"What desire you?"

"To be carried faster and farther than man can run or beast gallop."

The trampling sounds closed in. Shea smelled damp horse, and the next flash showed that the voices belonged to centaurs, led by one with a grizzled beard. He said: "Belphegor of the mountains, we know you by all names, but who is this? Is it our mission to carry him as well?"

"Aye."

"Is he an initiate in the mysteries of wood, wold and fountain?"

"Nay, not, that I wot on. But that am I, and he a friend in need."

"Whee-he-he-he! We are forbid by an oath more dreadful than death to take none but those who have reached the degree of the three great mysteries."

"Hey!" shouted Shea. Another flash had shown him the three paladins, leading their mounts more accurately in his direction than one would have believed possible. "What's this? Those lugs'll be here in a couple of minutes."

"There be rituals and vows through which all must pass who seek to live by the forest ways, Sir Harold," said Belphegor. "A thing of many days."

"Okay, skip it. I'll shin up a tree and hide."

"Nay, not from Duke Astolph's magic. One blast of that great horn, and you'd come tumbling like a ripened nut. Will you stand, then? My bow is useless in this wet, but we have made compact, you and I, and will guard your bare side with my hunting knife."

"It won't work, kid," said Shea, "even though it is damn white of you." The pursuers were a bare two hundred yards away. Astolph had the big sword out, and the lightning-flash was reflected from it. Then inspiration reached him. "Wait a minute, I used to be a boy scout, and I had to pass an examination and take vows for that. Would that get me by?"

"What says he?" asked the bearded centaur. "I know not the chapter, yet—" Shea snapped out a brief account of the organization and the merit badge he had won in woodcraft, looking over his shoulder. Two or three centaur heads came together, and the bearded one returned. "It is believed, that we can lawfully take you, man, though this is the first we hear of such wonders, and your craft be that of the small things. Mount!"

Before he had finished the sentence, Belphegor had vaulted lightly onto his back. Shea scrambled somewhat less gracefully onto the back of the other centaur, finding it wet and slippery.

"Ayoi! Ready, brother?" asked Shea's mount, pawing with its front feet.

"Ready. Whee-hee-hee!"

"Whee-he-he-he!" The centaur began to bounce, and as Shea, unused to this kind of ride, wiggled on its back, turned around: "Put your arms around me and hold on," it said.

Shea nearly released his grip in surprise as the first long bound was taken and a shout came from behind. It was a female centaur.

He looked over his shoulder. The last flash showed the pursuing paladins before they were hidden among the trees. The hippogriff, its feathers bedraggled, looked more melancholy than ever, and its expression would remain with him all his days.

10

The centaurs halted upon a smooth knoll. Behind them rose the slopes of the western Pyrenees, and before them the country rolled and flattened away into the high plateau of Spain. The sun was just pinking the crests.

"Here we rest," said Belphegor's centaur. "We cannot take you further, for lo! the Amir's camp is in sight, and our forests lie behind."

Shea slid off—legs stiff, eyes red, behind feeling as though it had been paddled, and teeth as furry as chows. Belphegor came down lightly on the balls of her feet, increasing Shea's already vast admiration for his wife. They thanked the centaurs, who waved farewell and galloped off as though their all-night run had been merely a warm-up, sending their "Whee-he-he-he!" after the travelers.

Shea turned in the other direction and shaded his eyes. Through the early morning haze he could just see a village with white walls and flat roofs three or four miles off. And away beyond it, a patch of little tan humps would be the tents of Agramant, Commander of the Faithful.

Shea gave Belphegor a long, searching look, noting how fresh she seemed after an all-night ride.

"Is it the chivalry of your land to stare?" she asked coolly.

"Sorry. I was just wondering what made you sort of—hold up and change your mind about your name. Last night, when the centaurs asked you."

A tiny frown appeared between her brows. "In sooth, I know not. 'Twas as though a veil were drawn, and I swam between worlds with my tongue framing words spoken by another."

"I can clear that up so it won't happen again."

"Nay, no more of your spells, Sir Magician. I lay it upon you as a condition of this adventure we undertake, that you attempt no enchantments on me for whatever purpose." She looked at him earnestly, but her regard faded into a small yawn.

"Oh—all right," said Shea ruefully. "Wouldn't take much of an enchantment to put you to sleep though, now would it?"

"Marry, that shaft is not far from the clout. Could I but find a grove!" She looked around. "But this country is bare as a priest's poll."

"Shucks, why don't you try sleeping in a bed again?"

"Again? I have never—"

Shea suppressed a grin. "Sure, sure, I know. But lots of people do without dying of it, you know, and it even gets to be fun after a while." He looked towards the village. "There ought to be an inn in that town, and we'll have to go there anyway if we're going to stand any chance of finding Roger."

Amiably doubtful, she fell in beside him as he led the way down the slope to where a track took them toward the village. The matter still hung in abeyance when they reached the place, which did have an inn. This was a small house that differed from the private dwellings only by having a dry bush affixed over the door.

Shea banged with the hilt of his sword. Above, the shutters of a window swung outward. A villainous-looking head peered out to look in astonishment at the unshaven man in Saracen costume and the red-golden-haired girl with a longbow. Presently the proprietor appeared at the door, scratching himself under a leather jerkin whose laces were not yet tied. The request for breakfast and lodging seemed to depress him.

"O lord of the age," he said, "know that neither in this village nor for miles around is there so much food as would satisfy a sparrow, save in the camp of the Amir Agramant, on whose sword be blessings."

"Heigh-ho," said Belphegor, "then sleep we supless and dine our souls on dreams." She yawned again.

The innkeeper looked more lugubrious. "On my head and eyes, Allah preserve me from your displeasure, lady; but there is lacking in my poor house a place where such a moon of delight as yourself may companion with her lord. For behold, I have neither secluded alcoves nor a bath for the performance of the Wuzu ablution."

The girl's foot began to tap dangerously. However, Shea averted the storm by saying: "Don't let it worry you. We really want to sleep; and besides we're Christians, so the bath doesn't matter."

The landlord looked at him with an expression of cunning. "O man, if ye indeed be Christians, then there is nothing for it but you must pay ten dirhams before entering, for such is the regulation of the prince of the place, who is none other than that light of Islam, the Lord Dardinell."

Shea hearing the girl catch her breath slightly, remembered that Dardinell was the name of the man who had brought the poetic Medoro to her attention. It also occurred to him that the innkeeper was probably lying, or cheating him, or both. To these peasant-village characters, a member of an outgroup was fair game... Shea, becoming annoyed, reached into the twist of the cloth belt where he had put the remainder of the coins Chalmers had given him. He pulled out a handful—a small handful.

"Listen, pickle-puss," he said menacingly, "I haven't got time to argue with you, and the lady is tired. You take these and give us a place to sleep, or you can take a piece of this." He indicated the sword.

"Hearing and obedience," mumbled the innkeeper, dropping back a couple of steps. "Enter, then, in the name of Allah the Omnipotent."

The entry was dark and somewhat smelly, with a set of stone steps going up to the right. The innkeeper clapped his hands twice. A door opened at the rear, and a very black Negro, so small as to be a dwarf, and naked to the waist, scuttled in. He grinned from ear to ear, and the speed with which he came suggested that he had overheard some of the conversation. The innkeeper did not seem to like his cheerfulness, for he fetched the dwarf a crack on the ear that sent him spinning against the wall, and said: "O miserable buffoon, cease from mockery! You shall conduct these guests to the upper room and provide them with coffee of the night, as is the custom, for they have been long abroad and desire to sleep the day."

The dwarf got up, rubbing ear and cheek with one hand, and wordlessly motioned Belphegor and Shea up the stairs. The room at the top ran the whole width of the inn. It held ten beds like very low couches, only a few inches off the floor and covered with thin and moth-eaten Oriental rugs.

Belphebe looked at them with distaste. "Sir Harold, I know not how men can bear such shabby habitation, when they may live among clean trees."

She began to pace the floor, looking out of one window after another.

"It could be better," Shea admitted. "But anyway, we won't get rained on. Come on, kid, try it for once."

He yawned. The dwarf came trotting upstairs with a brass tray holding two little cups from which floated the appetizing smell of coffee. He set it on one of the beds, then bowed low. More out of the habit of tipping then anything else, Shea fumbled one of the odd-shaped coins and held it out. The little black man half-reached toward it, looking at Shea's face as though he suspected him of playing a joke in questionable taste.

"Go on, take it," said Shea. "It's for you. Honest."

With a snatch it was in the dwarf's hands, and he rolled over and over, holding the precious thing before his eyes and gurgling with delight. Shea picked up the coffee and took a long pull, then almost gagged. It was so cloyingly sweet as to be almost syrup. He asked Belphegor: "Is all the coffee like that around here?"

" 'Tis coffee. What else would you have?" she said, sipping her own.

"Why, you know how I like..." He checked himself; no use starting the same old argument with a real amnesiac, and it would only antagonize her. He amended: "I'd have a lot else. Hey, George!"

The dwarf, having ceased his antics, came trotting over to duck his head three times. Shea asked: "Have you got any of this stuff without sugar in it?"

The servitor seemed to be overtaken by some inner ill, for he put both hands to his belly and rocked from side to side, pointed to the cups and put both hands beneath one ear, then closed his eyes, jumped up, ran to the window and went through the motion of leaping out, then pointed to Shea.

"What's the matter?" asked Shea. "Can't you say anything?"

For answer the little man only opened his mouth and pointed again. He had no tongue.

"That's too bad, George." Shea turned to the girl. "What's he trying to put over?"

She gave a tired little laugh. "Meseems he would convey that this be a brew so potent another cup would make one leap from a height. Marry, the one will not affect me so." She set down her cup, raised a small hand over another yawn, picked out one of the less dirty beds, and stretched out on it.

"Me, either," said Shea. It was too much trouble to argue. He stretched out on another; it might be straw under the disintegrating rugs, but his weary muscles found it softer than down. "Sweet dreams, kid." At least the fact that there was a multitude of beds precluded any silly arguments about laying his sword down the middle, as in the medieval romances. Though if a man were too feeble to climb over...

Just as he was whirling down into the pool of sleep it occurred to him that maybe the dwarf was trying to let them know that the coffee was doped, but he forgot before he could do anything about it...

Somebody was shaking him, and the side of his face stung with the memory of a slap. That goddam innkeeper! "Lay off!" he growled, his head fuzzy, and wriggled from the grasp. Slap!

This was too much. Shea rolled to his feet and started to swing; or tried to, for his arms were instantly pinioned from behind. Clearing eyes showed that he was in the center of a circle of armed Saracens. In another and larger group, some of whom turned as he came erect, he caught the sheen of Belphegor's bright hair, now mussed. Two of them were holding her. One had a black eye; the other had lost his turban, and his face bore an interesting criss-cross pattern of scratches.

"O my lord," said the innkeeper's voice from well in the rear, "did I not warn you that these were indeed Franks, and violent?"

"Verily, you are a mountain of wisdom," said a commanding voice. "What shall be your reward for having at once provided a pearl beyond price for my couch and an arm of the best for my battle?"

"Lord, I ask no more than the sunlight of your favor, and the payment of my proper reckoning. This unlucky Frank keeps the gains he has doubtless made from the robbery of true believers in his belt."

The owner of the commanding voice turned: a tall man with an unpleasant, dish-shaped face. "Seek if this be so," he ordered one of the men holding Shea. The latter, seeing that it would do no good to struggle, refrained from doing so.

"Verily, Lord Dardinell," said the one who was robbing him, "he has fourteen dirhams and a half."

"Give them to the innkeeper," said Lord Dardinell, and, turning back to that worthy, added: "You shall surely wait upon me in my tent after the hour of the second prayer tomorrow, when I shall have made proof of this Frankish damsel. If she prove a filly, as you have declared, your reward shall be ten times this amount; but if not, then only the double."

"Hey!" shouted Shea. "You can't do that. She's my wife!"

One of Shea's holders hit him across the face as Dardinell, expression going glum, turned to the girl. "Is this indeed the truth?" he demanded.

Before she could answer, another voice, somewhat high-pitched, spoke up: "O Lord Dardinell, it cannot be. When lately we saw this damsel at Castle Carena, she was surely neither wife nor widow, but a free maid of the forest, the inspiration of poetry."

Dish-face ran a tongue around red lips. "There is but one resource," he said, "and that is to smite the head of this dog of a Frank from his body, so that if wived, the damsel shall be widowed."

"Yet it is written," said the other voice, which Shea noticed belonged to an olive-skinned young man with delicate features, "that one shall not deal unjustly even with unbelievers, lest it be held against you at the last day. It is also lawful that even if the damsel be widowed this very day, the three-day ceremony of purification is necessary before one shall go in unto her. Therefore I say, my lord, that we should hold them both in a secure place until a learned Kazi can find the line of truth among these thickets. Moreover, O Prince of warriors, was it not your own word but now that here was a good arm to the service of the Prophet, on whose name be peace? Yet of what avail the arm without a head to guide it?"

Lord Dardinell put a hand to his chin and bowed the spiked helmet surmounted by a crescent. "O Medoro," he said finally, with somewhat ill grace, "you argue more finely than a doctor of law, and in a manner to make one believe that your own eyes are set on the damsel. Yet I can find small flaw in your doctrine." Shea, who had been holding his breath, let it out in a long *whoosh*, and the other Saracens murmured approval.

Dardinell stepped over to Shea and felt his biceps. "How came you hither, Frank?" he asked.

Shea said: "I had a little run-in, you might say, with some of the Emperor's paladins." That ought to put him in the best light, and had the advantage of being true.

Dardinell nodded. "Are you a fighter of proved worth?"

"I've been in a few scraps. If you'd like a little demonstration, just turn me loose from this gent holding my right arm..."

"That will not be needed. Will you faithfully serve the Amir Agramant in this war?"

Why not? Shea felt he owed nothing to the paladins, while consenting would at least keep him alive long enough to figure out something. "Okay. Bring on your dotted line. I mean, I'll swear to uphold your just and merciful Amir and all that, et cetera, so help me Allah."

Dardinell nodded again, but added severely: "It is not to be thought that even if the Kazi decides that your marriage to this damsel be lawful, you shall retain ownership in her, for it is my wish that you pronounce upon her the formula of divorcement. Yet if you bear yourself well, I will give you sixteen others from the spoils, with faces like full moons. How are you named?"

"Sir Harold Shea."

"Sir Harr al-Shaykh. Hear a wonder: he bears both Nazarene and Muslim titles! How became you a chieftain?"

"I inherited it," said Shea ambiguously. "You know, border family," he added, remembering the Carenas. He felt easier as the grip on his arms relaxed. No, he decided looking around, there was no chance of getting the jump on the situation and releasing Belphegor. Too many of these guys had sharp-looking scimitars in their hands.

Lord Dardinell appeared to have lost interest in him. "Let the maiden be bound, but lightly, with silken cloths," he ordered. "O Medoro, you shall take this new warrior into your troop and see him armed; and your courage shall be responsible for his."

As the girl was led past, she looked toward Medoro instead of him, and Shea's heart ached. At the street a number of horses were tied, one of which was held for him to mount. It was a damn shame that there was no chance of going back for one crack at that innkeeper, but that would have to wait until more important things were cleaned up.

Shea winced as he climbed into the saddles, for his crotch muscles were as hard as cables after the long centaur ride. But they soon loosened under the rugged massage of the high saddle, and Shea was able to go along with only nominal discomfort.

As the cavalcade set off through a hot sun that had already passed noon, it occurred to Shea that it would take something more than magic to make his wife try sleeping in a bed again after this.

11

Tents were pitched in all directions with a maddening disregard of order. Over the whole brooded a smell suggesting that the sanitary arrangements were primitive. Muslims of every size and complexion wandered among the tents, though there was little about them to suggest that this was an army. In fact, it looked more like an imitation Oriental bazaar at a big fair. Little groups argued and haggled over bargains or just argued; men lay asleep, ignoring the flies that crawled over them; from somewhere came the banging that might mean a smith. As the cavalcade picked its way among the tents, the arguers stopped arguing and some of the sleepers sat up to watch.

They made audible and highly personal comments on Belphegor. Shea felt his own face burning and began to invent a long series of ingenious tortures for them. However, she held her head high, paying no attention as she was carried past sidesaddle on a led horse. She had not so much as spoken to Shea since their capture. He did not blame her, remembering how much his fault it had been for not being careful about that scoundrelly innkeeper and for failing to interpret the dwarf's warning aright. It was certainly a poor payoff for the way she had got him out of a jam to dump her into one like this. Still, the question was...

Medoro touched his arm: "We ride this way," and led off to the left, followed by three or four of the group. Presently they arrived before a large striped tent, before which stood a pole from which hung what looked like the tail of a horse. Medoro dismounted and flung open the flap. "Will you enter, O Harr?"

Inside it was at least cooler than on the road. Medoro motioned toward a pile of carpets near the cloth partition that divided this outer room from another, and sat down cross-legged on another pile adjoining. As far as Shea, no expert on Oriental ruggery, could judge, they were very expensive specimens. The young man clapped his hands, and then said to the scraggly-bearded servitor who appeared from within: "Bring bread and salt. Also sherbets."

"To hear is to obey," said the man, and ducked out. Medoro stared moodily at the carpet in front of him for a minute, then said: "Will you have a barber? For I perceive that you follow the Frankish custom of shaving the face, even as I myself, and are long from the pleasure of this cleanliness."

"It might be a good idea," said Shea, feeling his rasplike chin. "Say, tell me, what are they going to do with her?"

"It is written that the tree of friendship may grow only beside the fountain of security," said Medoro, and lapsed into silence again until the servitor returned, followed by two more. The first carried a ewer of water and an empty basin. As Medoro extended his hands over the latter, the servitor poured water on them and then produced a towel. Then he performed the same service for Shea, who was glad to get off a little of the grime.

The second man had a tray on which stood something that looked like a flannel waffle, with a little dish of salt. Medoro broke off a piece of the waffle, sprinkled a pinch of salt on it, and thrust it toward Shea's face. The latter reached for it, but Medoro skillfully avoided his fingers and poked the morsel closer. Shea inferred that he was supposed to open his mouth; when he did so Medoro popped the object in and waited expectantly. It tasted fierce. As something more seemed to be expected, Shea in his turn broke off a piece of the flannel waffle, salted it, and returned the favor. The servitor disappeared. Medoro picked up his bowl of sherbet and sighed heartily.

"In the name of Allah, the Almighty, the Gracious," he said, "we have partaken of bread and salt together and have no harm towards each other. I have written a poem on that theme; would it broaden your bosom to hear it?"

The poem was long and, as far as Shea was concerned, did not make much sense. Medoro accompanied himself on a goose-necked lute he picked up from behind the rugs, caterwauling his refrain in a series of minors. Shea sat, sipping his sherbet (which turned out to be merely fresh orange juice) and waiting. In the midst of one of the refrains there came a squalling of many voices outside. Medoro flung down his lute, seized up one of the smaller rugs, and rushed outside for the afternoon prayer.

When he returned he flopped down on the rugs again. "O Harr, verily you shaykhs of the Franks know no more of the spirit of life in Allah, whose Prophet is the True and Indubitable, than a pig knows of the nuts whereon it feeds. Yet you shall now tell me nothing less than the truth: are you indeed an approved warrior?"

Shea thought that one over for a moment. "How the hell do I know?" he said finally. "I've done a little fighting when I had to, but I've never been in a regular formal battle, if that's what you mean."

"Aye. On bread and salt I cannot conceal it; I am myself as a stick in the sand. None dare love me but for my verses alone; yet I am of great family, and nothing less than the tradition of might will serve."

He picked up the lute again and struck a few melancholy chords. "May I be forgiven," he said languidly, "and let it not be borne overlong against me on the Day of Days. The Lord Dardinell said nothing less than that you were to be armed. Are you one of those Franks who will strike with the lance?" He brightened momentarily. "I have composed a poem on the subject of blood. Would your soul be soothed to hear it?"

"In a while, maybe," said Shea. "Don't you think we ought to get this arming business over with first, chum? Lord Dardinell will be coming around on a tour of inspection, and I don't think it would look good."

"Ah, Allah, deliver me from this life whose weight is irksome to me!" said Medoro, and without appearing to exert himself threw the lute across the tent, so that Shea heard it crack against some solid obstruction on the far side. Medoro, after a moment of silence, clapped his hands and ordered the thin-bearded servitor: "Summon my armorer."

The armorer was a squat, brawny man with black hair clipped close and black eyes. Shea judged he might be a Basque like Echegaray, but he spoke in the manner of the Muslims: "Will the wonder of the centuries deign to stand? Ha, hum; I have a suit of mail that may fit the Light of the East, but how will you be weaponed: A target, ha, hum. No doubt your magnificence will wish a scimitar also?"

"If you have a small straight sword with a point, it will do me swell," said Shea. Medoro appeared to have gone to sleep, with his mouth in a determined pout.

"O Shaykh Harr," said the armorer, "there may be such a weapon among the booty of Canfrano, but it is not to be hidden that these Frankish blades fail to hold the edge."

"Let's see one anyway. If it won't do, I'll take the longest and straightest scimitar you can find. With a point, too."

"May Allah strike me dead if you be not one of those who use the thrusting stroke! My father, who was smith before the Prince of Hind, has spoken of such in that land, but never have mine eyes been delighted by beholding such a one."

Medoro opened his eyes, clapped his hands, and told his valet: "Another lute, and tell the cook to set forth meats for the evening meal of my guest."

"Aren't you going to eat too?" asked Shea.

"My breast is straitened. I will dine on the food of thought." He took the new lute, struck it a couple of times, and gave vent to a long, howling note like that of a pin scratched across a windowpane.

The smith was still fussing and bowing. "It is revealed to me, O lord of the age," he said, "that there will be need for mail of unusual strength both on the shoulder and the upper arm—"

Medoro set down the lute. "Begone!" he shouted. "Master of noise, whose mother was mistress to a pig! Make your vile armor if you must, and send it here, but in silence."

As the smith scuttled out and the servitor began placing dishes before Shea, the young man relapsed into his playing and singing. It was not the ideal accompaniment to a meal. Shea managed as best he could the sticky mess before him without a fork; it was heavily spiced, but he was too ravenous to let that bother him. Coffee was brought, of the same appalling sweetness as that at the inn. Medoro laid aside his music to accept a cup. As he lifted it delicately to his lips, Shea said:

"What's eating you so, anyway? You act as though you'd lost your last friend."

"Nay," said Medoro, "I have found one, but—" he put down the cup, picked up the lute again, and sang:

> *Ah, bittered is the heart*
> *Which with all love must part;*
> *The sun declines, and as it sinks*
> *The tears from out my eyeballs start.*

Although Shea was not overwhelmed by the pathos of the poetry, Medoro laid down the lute and began to sob.

"Pull yourself together, pal," said Shea. "Is it about our friend Belphebe—Belphegor, I mean?"

" 'Tis true. Spake you sooth when you said she was your wife? Or was that a ruse to balk my lord Dardinell?"

"Well," said Shea, "that's a long and complicated story..."

"Nay, fear not to open your soul to your comrade of bread and salt. True friendship is above the base weakness of jealousy, as says the philosopher Iflatun."

Shea calculated his reply with the care of a sharpshooter. "I've known the girl for some time. But as for the rest of it, her status now is exactly what it was when you met her at Castle Carena. Doesn't that make you feel better?" When Medoro only sighed gustily, Shea added: "I should think we could hire a lawyer or something—"

"Verily, Shaykh Harr," interrupted Medoro, "your understanding is darkened. Know that the Kazi will surely decide that it is lawful for the Lord Dardinell to go in unto the damsel; for if you pronounce not the formula of divorce, he will cause her to do so himself. Ah, what have I done that a mere woman should bring this sorrow upon me? It was clear that with hair of gold-red she would be of ill-omen. Woe's me! I have but delayed the inevitable hour for the three days of purification."

Shea said: "Anyway, I can tell you that anybody who tried to make proof of our girlfriend without her consent has got his work cut out for him."

But Medoro's tears were flowing again. Shea sat back, thinking furiously. This twerp was about as much use as a third leg, though Shea tried to be fair, balancing his natural jealousy of Medoro's libido towards Belphegor against the fact that the youth had, in a manner of speaking, saved Shea's life at the inn. However, Medoro knew the rules, and there was one resource which he had not yet exploited: his own knowledge of magic.

"Where have they got her?" he asked.

"Nowhere but in the harem-tent of Lord Dardinell."

Said Shea: "Do you know whether Roger—you know, the one from Carena—has joined the army?"

The Saracen's woebegone expression changed to one of fine contempt. "It has reached me that the misbegotten son of a whore is indeed among us."

"You don't like him, then?"

"By Allah, if a cup of water would save him from Hell, I would give him fire to drink. At Castle Carena but lately, when I was reciting my stanzas in lament of Farragus, which is the best and longest poem I have composed, he snatched the lute from my hands."

For the first time Shea felt a certain sympathy with Atlantès' bull-like nephew. However, he said: "Okay, then, I need Roger in my business. Specifically, I want to kidnap him and get him back to Carena. You help me do it, and I think I can show you how to get Belphegor out of hock."

The handsome face distorted into lines of fear. "O Harr, Roger is so potent that no ten could stand against him. In Allah alone is protection, but we two would be to him as mice before an eagle."

"Take it or leave it," said Shea coolly. What he really wanted was to get Belphegor out of there and never mind the small change, but the chances of restoring his wife's Belphebe memory were not too good unless he could get her to Chalmers, with the latter's superior knowledge both of psychiatry and of magic. If Medoro just wouldn't play, however, he could back down at the last moment.

Someone howled at the door of the tent. The servant scampered through, and returned presently with a package that proved to contain the arms. Shea examined them while Medoro remained sunk in gloomy thought. The sword, while still a curved saber with most of the weight toward the point, was straighter than most, and the smith had ground a fine needle point to it. There was also a spiked steel cap with a little skirt of chain mail to protect the neck, a dagger, a small round shield of brass hammered thin, and a mail shirt.

Shea laid them down and turned to Medoro. "Well?"

The young Saracen looked at him craftily. "O Lord Harr, how lies it in your power to perform things for which half this army were not enough?"

"You just leave that to me." Shea grinned. "I'll give you a hint, though; I know something about magic."

Medoro touched both sets of finger tips to his temples, and said: "There is no God but God, and it is written that none shall die before the appointed hour. Speak, and I will obey as though I were your Mameluke."

"Will Roger come here if you ask for him?"

"Nay, he would rather whip my slave from his door."

"Then we'll have to go to him. Do you know where he hangs out?"

"It is even so."

"Okay. But we won't do it just yet. I'm merely laying out the program. How much authority do you have around here?"

"O Shaykh, under Lord Dardinell I am captain of fourscore men."

Shea thought it would go hard with a Saracen army if it had to rely on captains like this languishing lady-killer to lead it, but just now he was too busy to pursue that question. "Can you bring them here, three or four at a time?"

"Hearing and obedience," said Medoro, who salaamed and began to get up.

Shea, who did not altogether like the scared look that persisted in Medoro's eyes, said: "Hold it; let's have just one to start with. We can try out the magic on him to make sure it works."

Medoro reseated himself and clapped his hands. "Bid Tarico al-Marik enter and stay not, on the value of his head," he told the servant. Picking up the lute, he began to strum chords, the jewels in his bracelets flashing in the light of the Greek lamp that had been brought in with dinner.

"Lend me one of those bracelets, will you?" asked Shea. When the guardsman came in, Shea had Medoro order him to sit down and relax, then placed the lamp before the soldier. As the young Saracen continued to pick the lute, Shea dangled the bracelet before the soldier's eyes, twirling it this way and that, meanwhile repeating in a low voice as much as he could remember of the sleeping-spell Astolph had used on him.

Either as magic or as hypnotism the method was a little unorthodox; it seemed to work nevertheless. The man's eyes went blank, and he would have tumbled over if he had not been leaning against the wall of the tent.

Presently Shea said: "Can you hear me?"

"Aye."

"You will obey my commands."

"As the commands of a father."

"The Amir wants to surprise the camp. Discipline needs tightening up. Do you understand?"

"It is as my lord says."

"As soon as the evening prayer is over, you will draw your sword and run through the camp, cutting tent-ropes."

"To hear is to obey."

"You will cut all the tent-ropes you can, no matter what anyone says to you."

"To hear is to obey," repeated the soldier.

"You will forget all about this order till the time for action comes."

"To hear is to obey."

"And you will forget who gave you this order."

"To hear is to obey."

"Wake up!"

The man blinked and came out of it, wiggling as though his foot had gone to sleep. As he stood up, Shea asked: "What were your orders?"

"To watch well the door of Lord Dardinell's tent tonight. But as my head lives, Lord Medoro has given me none others."

"He forgot. You were to send in four more men. Isn't that right, Medoro?"

"It is as has been spoken," said Medoro languidly. The man shifted his feet. "There was—"

"Nothing else," said Shea firmly. He looked at Medoro, who laid down his lute and stared back.

"Verily, Shaykh Harr," said the latter, "this is as though the prophets were again on earth. Will he assuredly cut the tent-ropes as you commanded?"

"If he doesn't, I'll put a spell on him to make him eat his own head," said Shea, who had decided that he could count on all the cooperation the twerp was capable of giving. "Listen, when those others come in, keep it up with that oriental swing, will you? I think it has something to do with putting them under."

12

When the last of the fourscore guards had been given his orders, Shea felt tired. Medoro, placing a delicately-formed hand over his mouth, said: "Surely we have now done so much that the darkness of Eblis must fall on the camp, and we can easily seize the damsel and make off with her. I am wearied, though somewhat comforted by the excellence of your plan. Let us sleep and await the deliverance of Allah."

"Nothing doing," said Shea. "In my country we have a proverb about Allah's helping those who help themselves, and there's one thing we've got to help ourselves to right now. That's Roger. Remember, you promised." He stood up, put on the steel cap, buckled on the sword and stuck the sheath of the dagger through the sword-belt. The mail shirt, he decided, would have to stay behind, since for the kind of work he envisaged it was important to keep down weight. Medoro sulkily imitated him.

Outside the shadows were already stretching across the valley below the slope that held the encampment. Although Shea did not know when the hour of evening prayer was, he guessed it would be soon. That meant they must hurry if they wanted to catch Roger as part of the combined operation. Once the bruiser got loose with an uproar going on there would be no finding him.

But Medoro only sauntered along, possessed of a perfect demon of slowness. Every now and then he stopped to give or acknowledge a greeting, and those to whom he spoke seemed all to want to start an interminable discussion of nothing.

Shea thought these must be the most garrulous people on earth. "Listen," he said finally, "if you don't come along, I'll put a spell on you that will make you challenge Roger to a duel."

Shea had heard of people's teeth chattering, and not from cold, but this was the first time he had actually heard it. Medoro mended his pace.

Roger, it appeared, lived in a tent of Spartan simplicity as to outline, but as big as Medoro's. Two fierce-looking bearded men were pacing back and forth in front of it with naked scimitars.

"We want to see Roger of Carena," said Shea to the nearest. The other paused and joined his companion, who was examining the callers.

The first guard said: "There are many tents in the camp. Let the lords seek another, since all are friends under Allah." He held his sword about waist high, just in case.

Shea glanced over his shoulder to see the sun sinking fast. "But we've got to see him before the evening prayer," he insisted, shaking off the fingers Medoro was plucking at his sleeve with. "He's a friend of ours. We knew him in Carena."

"O lord, the Prince Roger's withers will be wrung. Yet it is written that it is better that one man should have an unhappiness, which endures only the appointed hour of God, than that two should lose their lives. Learn that if Lord Roger should be roused before the hour of evening prayer, we two should lose nothing less than our heads, for so he has sworn it by the hair of his beard."

"He hasn't got one," said Shea. Medoro, however, plucked insistently and whispered: "Now there is no help for it but we must leave this project for the other, since we are evidently not to be admitted by these two good men. Would you try steel against them and so provoke the shame of Islam?"

"No, but there's something else I'd try," said Shea, whipping round on his heel. Medoro followed him dubiously until they reached the side of the tent next door. With his dagger Shea cut eight long slivers of wood from one of the tent pegs. Two of these he stuck under the brim of his helmet, so that they projected like horns, and two more he inserted under his upper lip, hanging down like tusks. Then he decorated Medoro's wondering face likewise with the remaining four.

That ought to do for what Doc Chalmers called the "somatic" part of the spell. As for the verbal part, how could he do better than Shakespeare, slightly modified for the occasion? Shea turned round and round on his heel, moving his hands in Chalmers' passes and chanting in a low voice:

> *Black spirits and white, red spirits and gray,*
> *Mingle, mingle, mingle, you that mingle may;*
> *Fair is foul and foul is fair;*
> *Change, O change the form we bear!*

"Okay," he said to Medoro, "come along."

They swung round the corner of the tent. The guard who had been talking to them was just facing their way. He took one look at them, gasped: "The Jann!", dropped his sword, and ran for his life. The other guard looked also, turned a curious mottled color, screamed: "The Jann!" Falling on the ground he tried to bury his face in the grass.

Shea lifted the flap and led the way boldly in. There was no light in the outer compartment, and it was already dim with exterior twilight, but there was no mistaking the mountain of flesh piled among the rugs. Shea started toward it, but in the darkness tripped over some small object. He pitched forward and, unable to stop himself, struck the mass of Roger in the midriff in the position of a man kneading a vast vat of dough.

Roger awoke at once, rolling to his feet with incredible speed. "La-Allah-il-Allah!" he cried, snatching a huge scimitar from the wall of the tent. "Ha, Jann! I have not fought Jann!" The sword curved back for a blow as Medoro cowered away.

"Wait!" yelled Shea.

The scimitar checked. "Hold it a minute, will you?" said Shea. "We're really friends. I'll show you." He stepped over to Medoro, pronouncing the counter-spell and pulling at the chin-length tusks into which the slivers beneath Medoro's lips had turned.

Nothing happened. The tusks did not give. Between them Medoro still wore his foolish, frightened grin, and above, a pair of bull-like horns continued to project from neat holes in the young man's helmet.

Shea repeated the counter-spell again, louder, feeling of his own face and head, and discovering that he was likewise festooned with horns and tusks. Again, however, nothing happened.

Far away somewhere a voice rose in a banshee howl. That would be an imam whose alarm clock, or whatever he used for the purpose, was a little fast, calling the faithful to prayer. The others would soon follow.

Shea faced Roger and said: "Listen, let's talk this over. We're Jann, all right, sent here by the big boss to fight with the best mortal fighter in the world. But we have some pretty terrible powers, you know, and we want to arrange things so you don't have to put on a scrap at odds of more than two to one."

It sounded phony as hell in Shea's own ears, but Roger let the scimitar droop and grinned beefily. "By Allah the Omnipotent! The hour of good fortune has come upon me. Surely there would be no greater pleasure than to be with two of the jann in battle bound."

Roger flung himself among the rugs, half-turning his back toward Shea, who motioned frantically to Medoro to sit beside the colossus. Shea hoped Medoro would keep doing what he did best, namely talking. The twerp was probably too scared to do anything else, for he flopped beside Roger, saying: "Among our people we have a poem of the combats of the jann. Would your lordship care to hear it? If you have a lute—"

"O Jinn I would hear it not much more than a poem about dogs pissing in the street. Learn that at Castle Carena I acquired the taste for the despisal of poetry, since the worst of all poets came among us to visit: Medoro by name."

Shea caught the glance of appeal and indignation which Medoro flashed over his shoulder through his jinn makeup, but continued to stroll about the tent, out of the conversation. A large dagger with an ornate gold-hilted handle hung on the wall; he hefted it by the scabbard blade and looked at the back of Roger's head.

"Know, O Lord Roger," said the poet rapidly, "that by poetry and song alone is the world advanced. For it is the rule of the Prophet, on whose name be blessings..."

A steel spike stuck up through the center of Roger's turban, meaning that he had on some kind of helmet beneath the cloth. If Shea hit him while he wore that, the dagger-hilt would merely go bong, and Roger would turn and grapple.

Medoro was talking a perfect flood of words that made little sense.

Shea reached down, gripped the spike firmly, and switched it forward, tumbling helmet and turban both over the big man's face.

"Ho!" cried Roger's muffled voice as he reached upward.

Thump! The dagger-hilt hit his shaven poll in the medular region. Shea was left with the helmet-and-turban combination in his left hand as the ox rolled over and down. From outside came the united squalling of the call to prayer.

A thread of spittle ran down Medoro's chin beside the left tusk, and his hands fluttered wildly. "There—there is no gug-grace or goodness but in Allah," he babbled. "What thought is now to be taken for preservation?"

"Suppose you just leave that to me while you get busy and find some extra turbans. I haven't steered you wrong yet, have, I?"

Medoro, familiar with camp life, quickly found the turbans in the inner compartment, and they tied Roger firmly, winding him round and round with them and knotting them until he looked like a cocoon. He seemed to be breathing all right; Shea hoped his skull was not fractured. Time was getting shorter and shorter, with the show outside about to begin.

Medoro said: "O Lord Harr, surely we shall never be able to move him hence, and what of the fearsome appearance you have put upon us?"

"Shut up," said Shea. "I'm thinking."

"If we had but the magic carpet of Baghdad—"

Shea snapped his fingers. "Right on the button! I knew I'd forgotten something. Here, find stuff that'll make a small fire with a lot of smoke. Is there a feather anywhere around here? Don't argue with me, damn it. This is important if you want to see Belphegor again."

When Medoro returned from the inner compartment of the tent with a few twigs and the aigrette of an ornamental turban, he found Shea already busily at work. The journeyman magician had caught a couple of the big blue flies that buzzed about in vast numbers, and looped a silken thread from Roger's wrappings about them, attaching one end of it to the fringe of Roger's main carpet. The flies tried to take off as he released them.

"Put those twigs in a little pile here and light them," Shea directed, rolling back the carpet to leave a bare space on the ground.

While Medoro made the light with flint and steel and a tinderbox, Shea pulled the aigrette apart and began weaving it into the carpet, knotting it into the fringe. Outside something seemed to be going on. As the flame caught, shouts and the sound of running became audible.

The twigs, aromatics, filled the tent with a pungent smoke as Shea recited the spell he had been composing:

> *Be light*—cough!—*carpet, as the leaves you bear;*
> *Be light as the clouds that fly with thee.*
> *Soar through the skies and let us now but share*
> *The impulse of the strength. Let us be free*
> *From*—cough! cough! cough! *If even*
> *The Roc and all the Jann could fly like we*
> *Then were they*—cough! *right aerial indeed.*
> *To you the spirits of the sky are given*
> *That they may help us in our sorest need.*
> Cough-cough-cough!

The smoke died. The carpet was beginning to wiggle, parts of it rising from the ground and settling down again with a slight *whump*, while the tumult outside increased. The jinn that was Medoro rubbed smarting eyes.

"O Shaykh Harr," he said, "this is not the worst of poetry, though it must be admitted that you failed to accompany it with the lute. Moreover there was a foot missing from the fifth line, and the end is somewhat weak."

"Never mind the higher criticism, but help me get this elephant onto the carpet, will you?" said Shea.

They rolled Roger over and wrapped him in one of the sitting carpets before depositing him on the—Shea hoped—flying one. His eyes had come open and regarded them balefully. Where the gag allowed, the muscles of his face moved in something like prayer.

Shea flung back the tent door and looked out. There was certainly something happening in the gathering dusk; people running in all directions with manifold shoutings. As Shea watched, a big square tent with a pennon on top, farther along the hillside, corkscrewed down into collapse.

"Sit down and hold on," Shea told Medoro. He himself climbed on the carpet, which seemed to be showing signs of restlessness even under Roger's weight. Reaching to his full height, Shea swung his sword at the roof, which split to show an indigo sky from which one solemn star winked back at him. He squatted and declaimed:

> *By warp and by woof,*
> *High over the roof—*

Chop! went a sword into one of the tent-ropes outside. *Chop!* went another. "Stand, in the name of Allah!" shouted a voice.

Shea finished:

> *Fly swiftly and surely*
> *To serve our behoof!*

The tent collapsed, and the carpet swooshed up and out through the gap, its fringes flapping.

13

A bareheaded man and one of Shea's ropecutters were arguing so violently that neither noticed the carpet as it soared over their heads. Agramant's camp was in pandemonium beneath; everywhere tents were wobbling and collapsing. Some were as large as circus-tents, and great was the fall thereof. Lumpy objects moved under the enshrouding canvas, and here and there men fought. Out on one of the spurs of the hillside a tent had gone down into a fire which blazed brightly in the gathering gloom, while people ran around it, trying to beat out the flames or douse them with futile small buckets of water.

The carpet heaved and bucked, swirling this way and that. A little experiment showed Shea that he could direct its movements by pulling left, right, up, or down at the fringe of its leading edge. However, further experiment added the information that it was so very sensitive on the controls that he must be careful lest he throw them into a loop. Roger almost rolled off as the vehicle took a vicious down-curve. Medoro, though he had not eaten, seemed to be having trouble keeping whatever was in his stomach.

"Where is it?" shouted Shea.

Medoro pointed to one of the largest tents of all, well up on the slope, with a swarm of pennons floating from its multiple peaks. Dardinell's pavilion. Shea jerked at the fringe, and the carpet did a sweeping bank towards it.

The pavilion was a young city in itself. Besides the main tent, a score of lesser, outlying structures were connected to it by canopies. Among them the powerful figure of Dardinell himself could be seen among a group of officers on horseback who were trying to bring order into those on foot.

"Where's the harem?" demanded Shea. Medoro put one hand to his tusks to hold back a gulp, and with the other pointed toward an elongated tent that sprang from one side of the main structure.

As the carpet swooped, the, sound of Shea's voice brought a face in their direction. There was a yell, the whole group flowered with faces, and a flung javelin went past. Before more could follow they were over the tangle of lordly tents and out of range. They sailed in toward the roof of the harem tent. As they did so, Shea, controlling the carpet with his left hand and some difficulty, whipped out his sword and made a twenty-foot gash in the fabric.

He then took the carpet around in a curve and back to the hole he had made. "Duck!" he said to Medoro. Aiming carefully, he drove for the hole, which had been widened by the tension of the ropes. One of Shea's horns caught the edge for a moment, then ripped through. They were inside.

They were in a room full of women, so little below that Shea could have joined hands with them by leaning over the edge. The women, however, did not seem in a mood to join hands; instead, they ran in all directions, screaming: "The Jann! The Jann!" Shea encouraged them by leaning over and gibbering a little.

The carpet moved smoothly to the nearest partitions and then stopped, its leading edge curling where it met the cloth, and its side edges flapping like some lowly marine organism. Shea reached out and slit the camel's hair across. The next room was a kitchen, empty save for the furniture of the trade. The next compartment held nothing but a pair of eunuchs throwing dice. These screamed in high voices, and one of them tried to crawl away under the outer edge of the tent, as Shea slit his way through the next wall.

"Damn maze," said Shea. The outer tumult of the camp had been dampened to a whisper by the many thicknesses of cloth. Two more partitions, both yielding empty rooms, and the coolness of the evening was once more on their faces. Shea could see a couple of soldiers afoot and a horseman running past, silhouetted against a fire further down the hill. He hastily maneuvered the carpet around another curve and cut his way into the wall of the tent again. It was only the kitchen once more, and the whole structure of the tent seemed to be growing ricketty from the repeated slashings.

Nevertheless Shea warped his craft up to the kitchen's one unslit wall. A gash—and they had found their goal.

The room Lord Dardinell used for his more personal pleasures was full of precious things. Over against the wall, under a hanging out of which eddied a slow smoke of incense, priceless cushions had been piled on priceless carpets to make one of the most elaborate beds Shea had ever seen. In the midst of these cushions a bound figure writhed.

Shea tried to bring the carpet to a halt by pulling up on his leading edge, but that only took him to the ceiling; by pulling down, but that only brought him to the floor. He considered trying to snatch the girl on the way past as a bronco-buster picks a handkerchief from the ground, but rejected the idea as too risky. One hand would be needed for the carpet, and Medoro was no help at all.

He came around the room in another curve and recited:

> *By warp and by woof,*
> *In the midst of the roof,*
> *To save the fair lady*
> *Stand still and aloof.*

The carpet halted. It was a long way to the ground, and this would be no time to sprain an ankle. However, Shea, swung over the side, let himself down to his full length by gripping the yielding fringe, and dropped. He landed in the midst of the cushions on all fours, and got to his knees.

The figure on the bed rolled over and glared at him with furious eyes from under a disordered mop of graying hair, grunting through its gag.

"Eeek!" shrieked Medoro from above. " 'Tis the Amir himself! We are surely at the last hour. There is no God but God."

And in fact it was indeed the Amir Agramant, Commander of the Faithful, Protector of the Poor, just and merciful Lord of Hispania, trussed, bound, and gagged with his own turban.

"By the mass! More magic!" said Belphegor's voice. Shea turned and saw her poised to spring at him, dagger in hand.

"Stop!" he said. "I'm Harold. Don't you know me?"

"A horned demon the lord of Shea? Nay but—and yet the voice—"

"Come on, you know me. This is just a gag; a magical gag. The other spook, up there on the rug, is your boyfriend Medoro. Now do you get it? We're here to save you."

"Nay, 'tis assuredly some trick. Come not nigh, or man or monster, your weasand will be slit."

"Medoro," called Shea. "She won't believe we're us. Make a poem for her, will you, chum?"

To judge by Medoro's expression, his muse was not in the best of fettle, but he valiantly cleared his throat and began in a whining voice:

> We are not lost to prudence, but indeed
> Stand here bewildered. What shall be our rede?
> Since none will aid us from this tent to flee,
> By spells of great Lord Harr must we be free;
> But ah! my heart is lost and passion spent;
> To none but Allah can we trust in need.

"Nay, I begin to trow," said Belphegor, her mouth losing its hard line. "This is Medoro's veritable voice which comes from the shaping. But what is now your counsel, friends?"

"We're going out of here on that flying carpet, the way we came in," said Shea.

The girl stood on tiptoe and reached. "But how to attain it?"

"More turbans needed," said Shea, practically. "Where would they be?"

Belphegor leaped across the tent. "This chest—" and flung it open. Sure enough, it was filled with fine silk turban-cloths, neatly folded. He linked three of them together with solid square-knots and tossed one end up to Medoro, who caught it on the second try, and braced himself while Belphegor swarmed up it, light as a squirrel. Then Shea took a firm grip on the lowest knot and began to climb, but he had barely cleared the ground when the turban-rope went slack and he came down on his behind, the rope on his head.

"Hey!" cried Shea, stepping on the Amir and he stumbled to his feet. He saw Medoro, his jinn-eyes shifting as he crouched at the edge of the carpet and muttered. The edge of the carpet fluttered and it shifted position a little.

Shea would have said something else and more vigorous, but before he could get the words out, Belphegor leaned over the edge, with: "Throw up your end!" She caught it neatly, took a turn round her waist and called: "Mount, Sir Harold!"

Shea hesitated, afraid of pulling the girl off, for though he did not doubt her strength, she weighed a hundred and sixty. But just at this moment a troop of eunuchs flung aside the curtain and came waddling into the room, pointing, yelling and waving scimitars at least a foot wide. He swarmed up the turban-rope clumsily but effectively as a thrown dagger tumbled past him.

"Get over and let a man run this thing!" he said to Medoro. He spoke to the carpet and they slid through the gap in the tent-wall, out into the rapidly descending twilight. The fire at one side of the camp was still burning; figures appeared to be dancing before it.

Shea jockeyed the carpet up to what he judged was an altitude safe from arrow-shot and turned to Medoro. "Well, what's the alibi? You better make it damn good."

"I—I—but friend Harr, let the shield of our bread and salt turn aside the sword of your anger. Truly is it said by Al Qa'sun that he who sees into the hearts of many can seldom see into his own. Ah, most miserable of men!" He bent his head and the jeweled bracelets flashed as he beat his breast. "Your servant had no other thought but that when the end of the bond was lost, so much was lost that I should regret it to the end of days. But there is no might save in Allah, who has preserved you to be the delight of our eyes."

"You damn twerp," said Shea, through his teeth. "So you thought you'd sneak off and leave me and then make a poem about it. That's the idea, isn't it?"

"Nay, I am but a reed in the wind of your displeasure, and my breast is straitened, my brother," said Medoro, and reaching to the hem of his robe at the chest, gave it a little rip. (Shea noticed that it appeared to have been resewn several times; it was evidently a habit with the young man.) "Now there is no help for it but I must die." Two big tears rolled down his cheeks and stood gleaming on the tusks.

Belphegor put her arm around his shoulders. "Ah, unhappy wight, grieve not! Sir Harold, I charge you straitly that you shall not overbear him, for he is a troubadour, and I hold it somewhat less than knightly to treat him as less than one who has sustained you throughout this deed."

"Okay, okay," said Shea. "He's a hero and a pet. I just don't know why we bothered rescuing you at all. You were doing all right when we came in."

It was Belphegor's turn to be hurt, as Shea observed with a touch of vindictive relish. "Fie, for shame!" she said. "If you'll magic me with your enchantments into the most ungrateful of wenches, I'll have my favor back."

Her nostrils moved and Shea, feeling suddenly wretched, turned to the business of navigation. It had been a splendid exploit, and they should all have been elated. Instead of which...

After a moment he got a grip on himself, realizing that he was being pretty immature in getting sore at Medoro, who was merely one of those schizoid types who can no more help disintegrating under stress than he, Shea, could help pulling himself together under similar circumstances. Aloud he said: "All right, folks, I think we've done enough quarrelling for one night." (He realized that he had done most of the quarrelling, but he was also captain, and an apologetic attitude would undermine the position.) "Are we for Castle Carena?"

"My bow," said Belphegor. "I am undone without it. Perchance 'twill be at the inn where we were taken. Will you do me the grace to see, Sir Harold?" The voice was still chilly.

"Good idea," said Shea, trimming the carpet a trifle in the direction of the town. "I'd like to take a poke at that innkeeper myself, and now I have the equipment." He stroked his tusks appreciatively.

Behind him he felt the girl shift herself gingerly on the yielding surface to a sitting position on the rolled-up rug that was Roger. A sound somewhere between a groan and a growl emerged; Belphegor leaped to her feet, making the carpet tip perilously. "What's here! Do carpets speak as well as move in your enchantments?"

Shea grinned over his shoulder. "That's your old boy friend, Roger of Carena. We're taking him back to uncle."

"Verily?" She pulled back an edge of the rug and stared in the fading light, then gave a peal of silvery laughter. "Nay, this joys me much, and for this joy you are restored to favor as my true knight, Sir Harold. But I'd have one of the great bear's ears as a trophy." She whipped out her small hunting knife and the carpet heaved as Roger strove to wriggle in his bonds. Medoro's jinn-face took on a greenish cast. Shea said: "Cut it out, will you, girl friend? We're getting there."

The town was below them, lemon-colored gleams picking out the windows of the inn. Shea circled the carpet round the structure and carefully maneuvered it up to one of the windows that lighted the upstairs dormitory, peering in. There seemed to be no sleepers, only a feeble oil-lamp on a low table.

"I don't see it," he said. "Where did you leave it?"

"I deemed I had laid it upon the bed next to my own, with my quiver," she said.

"Not there now. Medoro, you and I will have to do a little searching. Beautiful, you stay here and see that the carpet doesn't drift away from the window, because we may come back running and dive through. You can move it by pulling gently on the fringe here, but don't do it if you don't have to. If Roger makes a fuss, you can have *both* his ears."

Medoro said: "Oh, my lord and brother, is it not more meet that I should wait, both as one who can defend this carpet from attack, and because I know not one bow from another?"

"No!" said Shea. "Come along."

He let himself carefully through the window, reaching up a hand to help

Medoro. They scoured the dormitory from end to end, peering under carpets and in corners, but not a trace of archery-tackle.

"Inshallah!" said Medoro. "It was ordained from the beginning of the world that we should not..."

He broke off at the sound of approaching horses, and then of voices downstairs. Shea tiptoed to the head of the stairs. A voice was just saying: "Uncle, are there within your caravanserai certain fugitives from the justice of the Commander of the Faithful?"

"My head be your sacrifice!" came the voice of the innkeeper. "Were there such, I had long since delivered them to the servants of the Prince, straitly bound. But are there not other inns than mine?"

The owner of the other voice replied: "By Allah, our breasts are narrowed, and an enchantment lies upon this expedition for the abatement of the Nazarenes! For behold, Lord Dardinell must bring home to the camp a damsel with hair of ill-omen, a very Frank, who indeed aroused the jealousy of the sons of Satan the stoned. For with the setting of the sun what should befall but there came unto the camp an army of furious Jann, each taller than a tree and pinioned with four wings of brass, who spurned over our tents as though they had been toys. By the grace of Allah, few were slain, though many ran in panic, and we have come to recall those who fled, lest they be taken later and fire be applied to their feet so they may flee no more."

The innkeeper apparently turned around to show them into the lower rooms, for his voice became inaudible and there was a sound of feet. But a moment later he picked up again "...the apartments for sleeping, which be untenanted."

Medoro jerked at Shea's arm and cast an imploring glance toward the window. Shea got out his sword and putting his lips close to his fellow jinn's ear, murmured: "Draw, and we'll scare the living bejesus out of them after that story he told. When I jump and yell, you do the same." He waved the weapon; Medoro produced and waved his own though with somewhat uncertain gestures. The footsteps started up the stair; Shea leaped with a whoop, in time to see three soldiers, with the innkeeper behind them.

He must have looked a hundred feet tall, coming down from above, and behind him Medoro emitted a shrill yell that was even more blood-curdling than his own. An answering scream came from the men below, mingled with a clatter of dropped weapons and the sound of heavy bodies hurling themselves any old way toward escape. For a few seconds the bottom of the stair was a confused mass of trunks and limbs; then the soldiers fought their way loose and raced out the door.

The last one to get to his feet was the innkeeper, who as low man had been trampled by all three others. He was a little too slow on the getaway as hoof beats diminished into the distance. Shea noted that he had both hands up for the formal tearing of his garments and his mouth open for a scream, but that both his motor nerves and his vocal seemed paralyzed.

He was not quite up to cutting the fellow down in cold blood, so he gave him a stiff left to the nose. The innkeeper dropped like an English heavyweight and rolled over, burying his face in his arms and awaiting the end.

"Look for that bow while I play footsie with this guy," said Shea, digging his toe into the innkeeper's ribs.

Medoro sidled past, his eyes rolling as though he expected Shea to begin carving steaks off the unfortunate man at any moment, but the latter contented himself with goosing the fellow tentatively with the point of the sword, until the young Saracen returned, waving the bow and saying: "By the omnipotence of Allah, it is indeed found!"

"Uncle, or whatever your name is," said Shea, "if you want to stay alive a little longer, lie where you are till you count slowly up to one hundred. Then you may get up and tell anybody you like about how the Jann spared your life. Okay, Medoro."

As the carpet resumed its slightly undulating flight, Medoro inched forward and patted one of Shea's feet. "Know, O auspicious Lord Harr," he said, "that this is a deed worthy to be written in the most divine verse on tablets of silver with letters of gold. It is given to poets, in the name of the Prophet, on whose name be blessings, to know all that passes in the minds of men, and had I but a lute, I would compose verses—"

"Too bad you haven't got the lute," said Shea. "But right now I'm more interested in figuring out the shortest way to the Castle of Carena."

Belphegor pointed. "Sir Harold, it lies almost under the star of the Lion, thitherward. Behold that triad of bright stars; the lowest lies under the pole. And for your help in aiding Medoro to find my weapon, much thanks. It was knightly done to accompany him."

Shea, looking down at the broken ground where the shadows were now deep, guessed that they were making twenty to thirty miles an hour. As the rolling highlands gave way to swollen, solid peaks of mountain, he had to put his vehicle into a climb to avoid the crests. All three began to shiver in their light clothes, and Medoro's teeth rattled. Shea envied Roger the rug.

That gave him an idea. They must be far enough from Agramant's camp so that over those stony mountains it would take days for the Amir's men to catch up. Why not rest comfortably through the remainder of the night? He put the carpet into a glide toward a low rounded peak and set it down, murmuring (under his breath so that Medoro would not hear) a spell to keep it there.

The Roger-rug grunted again as the rear end of the carpet touched a stone. It occurred to Shea that there was no particular reason why the big man should be comfortable while Belphebe-Belphegor was cold that night, so the prisoner was unrolled from his rug; and then it occurred to him that it would be interesting to hear what Roger had to say, so he removed the gag.

The perfect chevalier had plenty to say, beginning by calling them offspring of Marids and one-eyed sows, then running up and down the chain of their ancestry and remarking that his uncle would have them pickled in brass bottles under the seal of Solomon. With academic interest Shea noted that the invective had a certain weakness toward the end. The slow brain of the big lummox had evidently not quite been able to resolve the contradiction of Jann who spoke with the voices of Shea and Medoro.

The poet plucked at Shea's sleeve. "O brother," he said, "shall we not rather release him for the night; for it is contrary to the law of the Prophet that a man shall not be allowed to take his relievements. As is said by Abu Nowas—"

"As is said by myself, nothing doing," replied Shea. "I don't want to sit up guarding this big lug all night, and if Bradamant gets hold of him, he'll forget all about the law of the Prophet, anyway."

He was astounded to hear the big lug groan, and see a glistening tear on his eyelids in the star-shine; and even more astounded when Roger shut up completely.

Belphegor and Medoro moved a little apart and sat on a rock, talking softly and looking at the bright, near stars. Shea saw his arm go round the girl's waist and guessed he didn't dare try anything at this stage, and under the circumstances, there didn't seem to be much point in building a campfire. He pulled a twig from the top of a scrubby bush and bit down on it, trying to pretend that it was a pipe and recalling the ad for some brand of tobacco— "A gentleman's solace."

Solace! That was what he needed. What was the use, anyway, of this running across a parade of universes not even real and having nothing to show for it? What he ought to do was go back to Garaden, finish getting his doctor's degree, become a big-shot psychiatrist, consulted by alcoholics and the affluent screwy and make money. With money you could have everything—even affection. He recalled a statistic that Garaden had itself gathered, to the effect that something over sixty per cent of women could be happy and affectionate with any really good provider.

It wasn't really as simple as that, though. That red-haired spearshaft of a girl over there was his wife, none genuine without this signature, and just any girl who wanted a good provider wouldn't take her place. Anyway, he had a responsibility. He had married her and promised to keep her safe—particularly from such things as the Medoro menace. He had seen the thing so often in case-histories: women of her forceful type, thoroughly competent as long as sex was left out, falling for good-looking weaklings whom they felt the impulse to mother, and unhappy because of it. They usually ended up by despising the men in question.

Well, what? He couldn't very well murder Medoro, that was not in the limits of his own *ethos*, and it would probably have the contrary effect on the girl than the one he wanted. It would fix the love-image in her memory forever as something desirable and lost. Moreover, he had no desire to bump off Medoro. The guy was perfectly frank about his own weakness as a fighter or man of action of any kind, no sham about him. He was only miscast as a Saracen warrior, like one of the Marx brothers trying to play Hamlet. With the right kind of stage-manager...

The whole problem was one to pass on to Chalmers, that very well-integrated personality, who didn't mind tearing other people's lives apart to mend the details of his own.

Meanwhile, it would be a good idea to get some sleep. Medoro was supposed to watch Roger during the early part of the night. He hoped the idiot would not do anything stupid, like turning the perfect cavalier loose, but consoled himself with the thought that if Medoro did that, Roger would probably fall on the poet first and make enough racket to wake the other two up.

A wolf howled in the distance. Everybody moved, rustlingly at the sound. Another howl answered it. The howlers set up a duet, the howls became shorter and closer together, then they ceased. About that time Medoro began to croon in a minor key, presumably a poem of his own.

Lucky stiff, thought Shea, meaning the wolf.

14

"Now where the hell are we?" demanded Harold Shea.

Below the edge of the carpet nothing was visible but rocky peaks, pine-clad slopes and steep gorges, with now and then a metallic flash of water in them. "We've been flying for hours, and all we get is more of the same. I think we ought to stop at a gas station and ask."

A little frown came between Belphegor-Belphebe's lined brows. "As oft erst, Sir Harold, I wot not—right well—what you would say."

"It's like this; we seem to be a long time getting nowhere, and I could do with something to eat."

She looked at him, then glanced quickly sidewise and down. "I marvel that you are so eager to end this, our adventure; yet since you will have it so, there lies a road now below us which, an I mistake not, will lead us to Carena."

"You have the damndest eyes, kid. Where?"

She pointed. It was a mountain track like two or three they had glimpsed already, snaking down one side of a gorge, across a stream by stepping-stones, and up the opposite slope.

Shea banked and spiraled down toward the track. Belphegor indicated four dots ahead on the road which, as they approached, resolved into a man leading three laden asses. Shea slid in toward him, and just above head level, called: "Hi, there!"

The man looked up, his whole face seemed to dissolve, he gave a squawk of terror and began to run, the asses rocking behind him. The carpet zipped past a hairpin turn and came round in a long curve as Shea brought it back, crying to the girl: "You talk to him!"

"Nay, hold rather," she said. "He is so sore affrighted with your grim aspect that an you clip him close, he'll but leap a cliff and take the known death rather than the terror unknown."

"Allah upon you if you do!" said Medoro. "This is most excellent sport to see a merchant so buffooned."

"No, she's right," said Shea, slanting the carpet upward and away. "But it leaves us with a problem. How are we going to get close enough to anybody to ask questions, looking the way we do?"

"What need of question?" asked Belphegor. "I have given you the direction general; you have but to wait for night, then put this strange steed of yours aloft and to its pace, seeking for that ring of flame around the castle."

Shea glanced down to be sure he was following the road. "It isn't just finding the place," he said. "We've got to consider tactics, too. Duke Astolph is somewhere around with that damn hippogriff, and this thing's slow freight by comparison. I don't want to be enchanted down in flames, especially with you aboard, kid."

"Grammercy for your thought of me, fair sir," said the girl: "but I charge you that while we keep this quest, you shall no longer treat me as a woman *par amours,* but as a full companion."

The words were sharp enough, but did he imagine it, or had she said them in a tone anything but sharp?

There was not time to make a decision, for peering over the carpet's leading edge, Shea caught sight of a little fan of detritus at the side of a mountain which might be a mine entrance. "I'm going to land there," he told the others. "Belphebe—that is, Belphegor, suppose you go first and smooth out anyone inside."

The carpet slanted smoothly down to a landing in front of the mineshaft, which did not appear to be a mineshaft after all when one got close to it. As Shea stood up to stretch cramped muscles a man appeared at the low entrance. He was old, he was whiskery, and a dirty brown robe was gathered around his waist by a piece of cord.

For a moment he looked at the visitors with widening eyes, then took a step backward, and planting his feet firmly, lifted his right hand with two fingers upraised: "In the name of St. Anthony and the Virgin Mary," he said in a high voice, "depart, cursèd enchantments!"

Shea felt the muscles of his face relax into different patterns and reached a hand up to find that his tusks were gone. He looked at Medoro; the poet had lost his, too.

"Nothing to worry about, Father," he said to the old man. "We're really not enchantments ourselves, just had some put on us, and we're looking for directions."

The old man beamed. "Surely, surely, my son. There be many great and good men of your race, some of whom draw nigh unto God, though in strange wise. And all respect the hermit who has nought but his poverty. Whither wish you to go?"

"Castle Carena," said Shea, the thought flashing through his mind that even if this were the holiest hermit in Spain, his protestation of poverty was laid on with a trowel.

"By the road before you, my children. Over the next pass lies the valley of Pau; beyond it, the village of the same name, wherein stands the church of St. Mary of Egypt, whose vicar is an Austin friar. Beyond that again, a fork in the route—"

"Uh-huh," said Shea. He turned to Belphegor. "That must be the valley where my partner went hunting for Roger just before I met you and Duke Astolph." He turned back to the hermit. "Have you seen any Christian knights going in that direction?"

The old man's face took on a troubled expression. "Nay, children," he said. "I know naught of warlike men or their contentions. These be vanities, even as gold."

Medoro plucked Shea's sleeve. "Of a truth," he said, "there is no truth in this man, and he has evidently seen more than he has told. Let us question him more nearly." He fondled the hilt of his dagger.

Out of the corner of his eye Shea saw Belphegor's fine features take on a look of distaste. He said: "Nothing doing. You don't know Christian hermits, Medoro. Roughing them up only makes them more obstinate, and besides, it wouldn't look good. Anyway, now we're rid of those Jann disguises, we can find out what we want to know anywhere. So long."

He flipped a hand at the hermit, who lifted his two fingers again and said: "The blessing of God on you, my son."

The three took their places on the carpet and Shea recited:

> *By warp and by woof,*
> *High over the roof*
> *Of mountain and tower*
> *You shall fly in this hour.*

Nothing happened.

Shea repeated the verse, and then tried several variations in wording. Still no result. The hermit smiled benignly.

The girl said: "Methinks I can unriddle this, Sir Harold. This religious has not only blessed us, but pronounced an exorcism against enchantments, so that whatever virtue the carpet possessed by your magic is departed, nor may return in his presence. 'Tis not the first such wonder of holy men, nor the last, belike."

"Are you a holy man?" asked Shea.

The hermit folded his arms complacently. "In my humble way, my son, I strive to lead the sinless life."

"Oh, Lord!" said Shea. "Now I suppose we'll have to walk."

Said the hermit: "It were better for your soul to mortify the flesh by walking a thousand miles with bleeding feet than to travel at ease for one."

"No doubt," said Shea, "but right now there are a couple of things more important to me than my soul, and one of them is getting a good friend of mine out of a jam." He was talking over his shoulder as he unbound Roger's legs and made a loop in the knotted turbans to serve as a halter.

Something made a gruesome noise in the cave. Shea cocked his head. "You got an ass, Father?"

The old man's complacency gave way to a look of apprehension. "You would not rob me of my stay and sole companion, my son?"

"No. I told you we were on the square. I just wondered if you'd be interested in selling him."

With surprising alacrity the hermit disappeared into the shaft, to return presently with the ass; a big, tough-looking animal that would help them a good deal in the marching that evidently lay ahead. Shea asked how much; the hermit replied that the service of God could hardly be accomplished on less than five bezants, a figure at which Belphegor made a little round O of her mouth.

Shea felt at his belt, then remembered that the innkeeper had picked him clean and he had forgotten to repossess the money. "Damn," he said. "You got any money, Medoro?"

The Moor spread his hands. "Oh, my lord and brother, had I but a piece of copper, it were at your service. But it was ordained that my monies should be left in my casket, which is in the camp of the Commander of the Faithful, the blessed."

"Hm," said Shea. "Okay, then, let's have one of those bangles," indicating Medoro's jeweled bracelets.

Medoro looked sour. "It is not to be concealed, O friend Harr, that such a jewel is worth a dozen such vile, scrawny beasts as that which stands before us. Has not your Nazarene imam pronounced that gold is vanity to him?"

"That's his risk," said Shea, folding the carpet into a saddle-pad and slinging it on the back of the animal.

"It will be devoted to the increase of business," said the hermit, unbinding the rope around his waist and helpfully installing it as a cinch. Shea turned to Roger, who had not said a word: "Okay, big boy, you get the ride."

The direct address seemed to touch off a spring within whatever nest of complexes served the big man for a brain. "Vile cozener!" he shouted. "May Allah descend on me if I separate your bones not one from another. Yet since you do me at least the honor to give me the better place, I will accord it in my mercy that you die before these others, Alhamodillah!"

"Nice of you," said Shea, firmly, tying Roger's feet together under the animal's belly. "But that's not quite the idea. It's just that you're less likely to get loose and massacre us while you're in this position."

They set out. The track had never been intended for wheeled traffic. It was so narrow that no more than two could go abreast, a distinctly less comfortable method of travel than the flying carpet. Shea took the lead, one hand on the ass' rope. It was an hour later when he held up a hand to halt the others. "People ahead," he said.

Belphegor came up to join him, bow bent and arrow nocked. The people turned out to be three asses, biting the tops off weeds at the cliff-side and a stout, weather-beaten man, sitting in the shade and resting. The man scrambled up at their approach, hand to knife, then relaxed as Shea said: "Good morning, mister. How's business?"

"Peace and good luck to you, friend," said the man. "Business have I none at the moment, but count that at sundown I shall have much; for look you, I am bound for Pau, where they are holding an auto-da-fé on a paynim sorcerer the day beyond tomorrow. Now that is thirsty work; and I have the wine to slake it." He gestured toward the asses, and Shea perceived that they were laden with skin bags that gurgled liquidly.

Shea thought of Votsy and Dr. Chalmers and didn't quite like the sound of that "paynim sorcerer." But before he could question further, Belphegor burst out:

"No more on this. Behold, Medoro, why I still love the free wildwood, when men will still do such things to one another. Have you other tidings, sirrah?"

"Why, not such as you would name tidings, now that you ask," said the man, unabashed. "A small thing only, that will serve as a tale when tales are told. If I were a timorous man, the tale would doubtless be longer and have an unhappy ending, but—"

Belphegor's foot tapped.

"To make a long matter short, as I was taking the short route over the mountain from Doredano, I was set upon by flying demons with horns and great tusks—doubtless a sending of that same sorcerer who will be so finely cooked tomorrow. Had I not fought my way through the press with this single blade, you would not see me here and I should have lost my profit. Ware them on the way. To what lord do you take your prisoner?"

"We're taking him to a lady," said Shea, firmly. "He has four black children and won't pay alimony. But she'll probably need a bodyguard who isn't afraid of anything, and we'll tell her you applied for the job. So long."

Heedless of Roger's howls of anger, he set out again.

It took them all day to reach the pass. The rests at Medoro's request became more and more frequent, and he finally developed a blister, which had to be examined by Belphegor, to Shea's intense disgust. She pronounced the infection so bad that he would have to ride, and this time there was nearly a quarrel, Shea insisted on the danger from the big man's strength and skill with weapons, the girl equally insistent that Medoro was a third of their fighting strength and they would be in poor shape against any attack if he were eliminated.

She won, of course. Medoro mounted the ass, while Roger's feet were unbound and Shea made a slip-noose of turban for his neck, so that any sudden jerk would cut off the big man's wind. They declared a kind of tacit truce; Shea began to talk to him, and for a time wished he hadn't, since the only thing Roger wanted to discuss was broken heads and spilled guts. In desperation he turned to the subject of Bradamant, which had previously produced so strange an effect on the big bruiser. The effect was all that could be asked. Roger looked at the ground and tittered.

"What's she like?" asked Shea. "I've never seen her."

Roger appeared to be undergoing an internal revolution. Finally, with a masterful effort, he produced: "There is no blessedness but in Allah and his Prophet. Her arms are like ash-trees and her buttocks like full moons. Should chance bring union between us, I will contest with you in arms in celebration. But it is to be remarked that your death will not make me master of your Frankish slave girl with the ill-omened hair; for I would prefer consort with the uttermost daughters of Eblis."

The tables were neatly turned, decided Shea, and let well enough alone till they had crossed the pass and a mile or two down found a camping spot beside a stream. It was not yet twilight, but Belphegor declared that there would be little chance of game later, so she and Medoro went off hunting, while Shea built a fire.

Half an hour later they came back laughing, with four rabbits. She displayed her well-remembered skill at skinning and cooking them; Shea thought he had never tasted anything better, nor for that matter seen anything more pleasant than the spectacle of Medoro inserting morsel after morsel of meat into Roger's mouth, which the latter gulped with a rapidity that suggested he was trying to snap the fingers off.

After the meal, all felt better; Roger almost genial in spite of the fact that he had to be led behind a bush, and Medoro positively brilliant. He improvised comic rhymes; he effectively parodied Dardinell's parade-ground manner; he did a superb imitation of Atlantès working a complicated spell, including his dismay when the spell produced the wrong results. It came close enough so Shea laughed loud and carefree—whereupon Medoro suddenly went serious.

"Lord Harr," he said, "now that your breast is broadened, I would seek unto your advice, as that of an uncle or a learned man in the law. According to the most excellent book of the Prophet of God, on whose name be grace, which is the Book of the Cow, it is lawful for a Muslim to take unto wife what woman he desires. Yet it is written also that one wife is insufficient, whereas two quarrel with each other, and if there be three, the two will combine against the third, so that there is no safety but in a fourth. Yet this woman whom I would wed will have me as single wife only."

Shea smiled wryly. A delicious question to ask him! *However,* he thought, *let's roll with the punch.* He said: "It's a tough case. If you marry her that way, you violate your religion, and if she marries you any other way, she violates whatever religion she has, if any. I suggest you both become Zoroastrans. That can't be far from either one."

Belphegor said: "Who be these Zo-ro-astrans?" She stumbled over the word.

"Oh, they seem to have a pretty sound theology, for my money. They hold the existence of equal and opposed powers of good and evil, Ormazd and Ahriman. Gets around the difficulty of the doctors of theology. If God is omnipotent, how come there's evil?"

Said the girl: " 'Tis not far—" and stopped at the gasp of horror from Medoro.

His mouth was flapping open and shut, rather like that of a carp in a pool. When he found words, it was to say: "The Ghebers! To be a fire-worshipping alchemist! Why, they are filthy cannibals, who dance naked and eat the limbs of human beings. Why, I'd not union with the Queen of the Diamond Isles, had she all wisdom and the bed-arts of the Ethiopians, were she a Gheber! Nay, were she the most beauteous of mortal women to outward seeming, I would know her for the foulest of harlots by such token, who dined only on broiled rats' bones and hired Negro slaves to do her service."

Belphegor drew in a long breath. "My Lord Medoro," she said, "that is somewhat ungentle of you. I would pray you to think more deeply on't while we make our couches." She was on her feet, all one graceful movement. "I'm for a tree."

Next morning they breakfasted on the proceeds of the girl's hunting, Medoro slightly querulous over the lack of salt and Roger grumbling that there was no Imam to call the proper hour of prayer. Shea said: "The way I figure it out, I doubt whether we can make the castle today, unless we get some animals to carry us in Pau."

Medoro looked at the girl. "By Allah, if we reach that castle never, it were soon enough for me, unless there be a good Kazi with witnesses there to marry us at once."

Shea opened his mouth, but the girl beat him to it. "Nay, fair Medoro," she said, "let us think not so fast on marriage. For behold, I am as bound by my plighted word as ever knight was, to stand by Sir Harold till this quest be fully accomplished. Whatever faith holds, one must keep faith."

The dampening of Medoro's spirits was only temporary. By the time they were ready to start, he was gay and cheerful again. When Shea led Roger to the ass with the intention of repeating the previous day's arrangement, the poet darted ahead and mounted it at once.

"Hey!" said Shea. "You had your turn yesterday. Now look here—"

Medoro looked down from his seat. "Now Allah burn my liver if I ride not this ass today," he said. "O, son of shame—"

Smack! It was a long reach but Shea landed right on the side of the jaw and Medoro landed with a plunk on the ground. He heaved himself up on one elbow as Shea looked at his own tingling knuckles, wondering what had made his own temper depart to the region where the woodbine twineth.

When he raised his eyes Belphegor was between them, hand on her little belt-knife. "De Shea," she said, in a grating voice, "this passes bearing; a most vile peasantish discourtesy. You are no more my knight, nor I your lady, till you make full apology, nor will I hold communion with you else."

Medoro rode the ass. Shea, trudging along in the dirt and stones, with his hand on Roger's halter, wondered whether the light of his life were exactly bright.

Proceeding grumpily under the pillar of disagreement that kept them all silent, they were still well short of Pau when afternoon drew in and Belphegor announced shortly that if they were to sup, she would have to hunt. This time Medoro did not accompany her, but as he got down from the ass, he suddenly shaded his eyes against the sun and pointed:

"Inshallah!" he said. "Lord Harr, look on a marvel. That tree is surely of peach, such as they have in the land of Circassia, and as the Prophet is the Witness, we shall have fruit to our repast." He skipped off with no sign of blister or limp and in a few moments was back with his arms full of ripe peaches.

It was at that moment that inspiration descended on Harold Shea. "Sit down and take care of Roger while I prepare them for eating," he said. Medoro wrinkled his eyes round a glance that might have been one of suspicion. "Listen, take it easy," said Shea. "I'm sorry I got sore at you this morning."

The poet's face broke out in a beatific smile. "Of a truth, Lord Harr, it is said that the Franks are in fury uncontrollable; but if one bear with them, in friendship generous." He took the slip-knot turban and led Roger to one side.

Shea took off his helmet, stuck it in the ground on its spike; it made a magnificent punchbowl. Four of the peaches went into it. Shea scratched the letters C, H and O with his knife-point on the remaining peaches and arranged them as Doc Chalmers had done which he so unexpectedly produced the Scotch whiskey in Faerie. Accident that time, Shea told himself, but this time whatever happened would be on purpose. He leaned over the helmet and with one eye cocked in the direction where Medoro was rather languidly holding to Roger's noose as the latter recounted one of his tales of assault and battery, repeated softly what he could remember of Doc's spell:

> *So frequently as I with present time*
> *The earlier image of our joy compare,*
> *So frequently I find our less than prime,*
> *And little joy than that we once did share:*
> *Thus do I ask those things that once we had*
> *To make an evening run its magic course,*
> *And banish from this company the sad*
> *Thoughts that in prohibition have their source:*
> *Changes, peaches! From the better to the worse.*

For a moment he had the dreadful fear that this would give him a mess of rotten peaches, but when he opened his eyes, the helmet was brimmed to overflowing with a golden liquid in which peach-pits and deflated peachskins floated. Shea fished one of the latter out and tasted the surplus. It was peach brandy all right, of a magnificent flavor, and now that he caught it at the back of his palate, a potency rarely equaled in his own cosmos—about 120 proof, he would judge.

"Hey!" he called. "Bring him over here, Medoro. I've made some peach sherbet for you."

The poet got to his feet, jerking the prisoner along. He leaned over the helmet and sniffed. "By Allah, it has a noble perfume, Lord Harr. You are the best of the shah-bands; but it should be cooled with snow for fair sherbet."

"I'll trot right over to one of the mountains and get some," said Shea.

Medoro knelt and thrusting his face down to the edge of the helmet, took a long pull. "Allah!" he said. "Of a truth, snow is sorely needed, for this sherbet burns like fire. If this be poison—" he glared at Shea.

"Then I'll be poisoned, too," and Shea took a drink for himself. It certainly did warm the gullet going down.

"Give me some of this sherbet, I pray, in the name of Allah," begged Roger. Shea cautiously disengaged the spike of the helmet from the ground and held it for him, as he took a sip, then a drink.

When he lifted his face from the cup, Medoro said: "O lord and brother blest and to profit increased, I would have more of your Frankish sherbet; for the eve is chill, and it does provide a warmth interior."

The helmet went round, and then again, Shea not stinting when it came his turn. Belphegor's anger with him began to fade a little into the background. She'd get over it as soon as she realized her real identity, and he could think of a dozen, twenty, thirty schemes to produce that desirable result, only requiring slight details to be filled in. He could take care of that any time; in the meanwhile, Medoro was one of the most fascinating conversationalists he had ever met, and even Roger was not so bad a guy when you got to know him. The Saracen paladin was telling a tale of his adventures in Cathay, which Medoro was weaving into a ballad of immensely complicated rhythm-scheme, but he kept missing the rhyme at the third line of each stanza, and Shea was correcting him when Belphegor suddenly stood in the center of the little group, a brace of black-plumed birds in her hand.

Medoro looked up, and his mouth fell open. "Now may ifrits remove me to the outermost depths of the sea an I futter not this damsel," he shouted, and lurched half way to his feet, then sat down. His brows contorted with effort; he tried to get up again and made it. Belphegor dropped the birds.

"I love you for your exceeding loveliness and surpassing beauty," said Medoro, "and you shall grant me the desire of the body, as All bin-Hayat says:

> *Men craving pardon will uplift their hands;*
> *Women pray pardon with their legs on high:*
> *Out on it for a pious, prayerful work!*
> *The lord shall raise it in the depths to lie.*

He giggled at the girl's horror-filled face, hiccupped, spread his arms and ran at her.

Smack! Medoro sat down abruptly. Shea cried triumphantly: "A most vile peasantish discourtesy!"

The young Moor heaved himself up again, his handsome features contorted. "By Allah!" he said. "You foulest of tribades and filthiest of harlots, that would reject the love of one of the house of Hassan for base-born Negroes! Farewell! I seek the camp where there are boys a thousand times lovelier and more faithful." Before any of them could guess his intention, he took three staggering steps to the ass, was on its back and belaboring it to a gallop in the direction whence they had come with his scabbarded scimitar.

Belphegor stood at gaze a second, then snatched up her bow and sent an arrow after him—too late.

"Shurr Harol'," said Roger with owlish gravity, "ish even as I have shaid. Thish red Frankish hair ish ill-omened. You had better be drowned in the shee if you sell not that slave."

Shea ignored him to take the helmet over to Belphegor. "Here, take a drink of this," he said.

She gave him a long, slow glance and accepted the offer with slightly trembling hands. The shaking quieted. "My thanks and good grace to you, Sir Harold," she said, "for I perceive that it is to you I owe this. It is like—like—" She seemed to flounder for a lost memory.

Shea said: "In Latin they would say *In vino veritas.*"

"Oh, aye. Taunt me not; I should have seen him with clear eyes when he would have left you in the tent or put the hermit to the torture. A niggling and wittold does not make himself a true man with a lute and fair words."

She sat down and pressed the palms of both hands to her eyes. Shea sat beside her and put an arm round her shoulders, but she shook him off. From the back-ground Roger croaked: "Flee away from thish ill-omened wench."

Shea could not be sure whether she was crying or not, and his heart turned flip-flops as he tried to think of something to do. He wished he had not drunk so much of the peach brandy; there seemed to be a haze between him and what he was trying to think.

The hands came down and Belphegor turned a woe-begone face toward him. "Nay, the fault's my own," she said, in a flat voice, "and you have been my true knight that would have saved me from a villain. Heigh-ho!" She sighed and stood up. "It falls dusk and we must sup soon if we're to take the road of our quest tomorrow. Nay, no hand-kissing; I'll not have these empty courtesies."

15

They came down a hill toward Pau through the morning light. "I suppose we could get some horses there," remarked Shea, gazing at the range of thatched roofs. "Has nobody any money? I'm broke, and we haven't got Medoro with his gold bracelets."

Belphegor laughed. "Not a groat, I. To those of the woodland seed 'tis the forbidden thing."

Shea looked at Roger. "O man," said the paladin, "know that the hardest of riding is better than the easiest footgoing, as says al-Qa'saf. But as for money, what need? You have a sword to take or magics to make as does my uncle Atlantès when he would have money."

Shea gazed at Roger in astonishment. It was about the first time he had ever heard the big man express an idea, and for a wonder, it seemed a fairly good one. The only trouble was that he had a little less than no idea what type of spell would produce money. The passes, yes—one could manage those—but the psychosomatic element?

Well, one could only try. A hundred yards or so back, a bank had caved in on a deposit of fine golden sand. He scooped up a double handful of this, laid it on a handkerchief and tied the corners together. Then he laid the improvised pouch on the ground and traced out a pair of interlacing pentacles, like those on the doors of Atlantès' room in Castle Carena. Belphegor was watching him, and it disturbed him slightly.

"Take this guy a little way off and cover him, will you?" he asked. "Don't let him watch."

The spell—ah, yes, of course, good old Kipling. He chanted:

> *Iron's for the soldier, silver for the maid,*
> *Copper's for the craftsman, working at his trade.*
> *Sand is but silly stuff, sifting to a fall;*
> *But gold, red gold! is the master of them all.*

The handkerchief sagged and looked lumpy. Shea picked it up and heard a gratifying clink within. "All right," he called. "I guess we're set now."

The approaches to Pau seemed curiously deserted, the brown and green fields vacant of working men, no women and children at the doorways. Shea puzzled over it until he recalled what the wine-merchant had said about the auto-da-fé, and felt a sudden need for haste. But just at that moment a clanging sound came to his ears, and across the street he perceived a village smith, hammering away at an open-air anvil.

Shea led his prisoner over, and greetings were exchanged. "Where is everybody today?" he asked.

The smith jerked a thumb. "Down the road. Saint's shrine," he said shortly. "Auto-da-fé for the monster. Can't waste time myself." He hefted his hammer, in evident desire for them to be gone so he could carry on with his job. Shea thought these Basques a singularly uncommunicative lot. Nevertheless, he tried again:

"Monster? What monster?"

"Devil. Looks like a wolf. Caught in a wolf net."

That would be Votsy, all right. The need for hurry was becoming acute, but horses would help. "We'd like to buy horses." He jingled the handkerchief of money.

The lines round the smith's eyes wrinkled craftily. "Have some," he said. "Come, see."

"I don't think I need to. You see, we're rather in a hurry with this prisoner, and We can get any money we spend back from the baron where we're taking him."

Suspicion mingled with the craft. The smith was clearly not used to dealing with customers who bought without asking the price. "Ten bezants," he said, flatly.

"Okay," said Shea. "Lead them out." He opened up his handkerchief-purse and produced a handful of bright gold pieces. As they touched the anvil, however, they instantly changed to little pinches of sand. The smith looked at them and then at Shea. "What's this?" he demanded.

Shea could feel a flush creeping up his face. "Ha, ha, just a joke," he said hollowly, and reaching into the pile, selected another handful to hand them to the smith. But suspicion had now completely gained the upper hand in the man. He rang each piece on the anvil, or tried to, for as soon as metal touched metal, these too dissolved into little cones of sand.

"Scoundrel! Cheat! Magician!" bellowed the man, gripping his hammer in both hands. "Out! Out! Ha, priest!"

Fortunately, he did not offer to pursue as the three beat a hasty retreat. Too late, on the road again, Shea remembered that Kipling's original poem had made iron, not gold, the master of them all, so that of course the spell had gone sour. It did not help matters any that even with the halter around his neck Roger was snickering.

Shea turned toward the girl. "Look," he said. "This hasn't anything to do with the job we're working on—" he glanced at Roger "—but I think a friend of mine is in trouble. Would it put you out too much to speed up the works?"

For answer she actually smiled at him. "Lead on," she said, and taking one of the arrows from her quiver, prepared to urge Roger to speed; but then: "Hold. Here's one that weeps and may not, for chivalry, be neglected."

Shea turned. With her back toward him and feet in the ditch that bordered the road, there was indeed one that wept. Her back hair was neatly ordered and her figure was young, which lent a certain predisposition toward relieving her distress. As the three halted beside her, she turned a face definitely pretty, though tear-streaked and somewhat dirty, toward them. "They—they—they seek to slay my sweetheart," she got out, before dissolving in another torrent of sobbing.

Belphegor said: "Sir Harold, whatever else you be charged with, here is a quest that turns all quests aside; a woman unjustly in trouble, to wit."

"I don't know about the unjustice," said Shea. "But let's see." He addressed the weeping girl. "Who's they? You mean the people who are holding the auto-da-fé on the monster?"

"Aye. No more monster than me. Am I a monster?" She spread her arms and Shea noticed that her dress was low cut in front.

"Marry, tears mend no torn bodices," said Belphegor, just a trifle acidly.

"The—the priest t-t-took him down to the Saint's cross for burning. Save him!"

Shea hesitated, then looked at Belphegor. The girl was frowning, but she said strictly: "Sir Harold, meseems that her plaint would be of that friend you bespeak."

"I'm afraid so," he said. "You take—no, you'll need both hands for the bow, and I only need one for the sword. Giddy-ap, Roger." He unsheathed the blade; the girl who had been doing the weeping tagged along behind.

The road turned a shoulder and slanted up a hillside from which figures were visible, moving against the skyline. One or two people turned round, but nobody seemed in the least curious about the spectacle of a Saracen and a red headed bow-girl leading a monstrous warrior by a noose. As he topped the rise and pressed forward, Shea saw why. The road here ran along the outer edge of a wide terrace on the side of the mountain. On the innermost edge of the terrace, against the cliff, something had been carved which looked rather like a phallic symbol with a halo round its head. In front of this singular erection a huge pyre of wood was erected, and around it a hundred or so peasants were crowding.

The wood was burning vigorously, and in its center, bound to a stake by neck and all four legs, was a huge gray wolf. The logs on which it sat were already a bed of hot coals, the flames around it were consuming its bonds, but except for the fact that the wolf had its tongue out and was panting, it seemed utterly unconcerned with the proceedings.

Shea suddenly recalled the spell under which Atlantès had let Polacek and himself out of the castle's flaming border, and wanted to laugh. Instead he said: "Hello, folks."

Talk died in a circle like ripples spreading from a thrown stone in a pool. A man in a patched black robe, who had been throwing sticks toward the center of the fire, turned and came toward him, blinking with nearsightedness.

"What goes on, Father?" asked Shea.

The priest produced a cross and began to mumble. "Oh, that's all right," said Shea. "I'm not a Saracen, and anyway I'm a friend of the hermit of the mountain." He indicated his prisoner. "See? We've captured Roger of Carena."

The priest studied the prisoner's face, pressing his own close. Roger hawked and spat, but only succeeded in adding another spot on the patched gown. The priest came toddling back toward Shea. "Worshipful sir," he said, "I perceive you are a very mighty man, and I trow, a good Christian. Sir, in your might, perchance you can aid us. Here have we a very demon from the uttermost depths of hell, in monster form, but his master Beelzebub, who is the Lord of Fire, will not permit him to burn."

Shea said: "I'm not sure he's as bad as you think. Had it occurred to you that he might be just a good man under an enchantment?" He stepped forward and raising his voice, addressed the wolf: "Are you Vaclav Polacek?"

The wolf barked twice and nodded vigorously, then raising one paw to emphasize the point, tore away the burned rope that held it. There was a universal "Ooooh" and backward movement in the crowd.

"I thought Doc Chalmers told you to lay off that stuff," said Shea, disgustedly. "Can you get loose?"

"Oow! Ououw! Ouououw!" said the wolf.

"Well, lay off it for a minute, for the love of Mike, till I get you off the hook." He turned toward the priest. "It's like I said. He's a Christian squire under an enchantment. I am Sir Harold de Shea." He did his best to strike an attitude. The priest looked at him with nearsighted skepticism.

"Votsy!" said Shea. "This guy don't believe you're the goods. If those ropes are burned through enough, come over here and lick one of his feet."

"Wrrrower!" howled the wolf, and leaped against his ropes. They gave; there was a universal scream of terror from the assembled peasants and they scattered as the animal came leaping through the flames, throwing burning coals in all directions. The priest stood his ground, but his face was set in tight lines and he was vigorously fingering his rosary as the wolf that was Votsy sat down and licked at his feet. After a moment or two the priest put one hand down and gingerly patted his head, but removed the hand instantly as up the valley, in the direction they were going, a bugle sounded "Rump-te-umpte-um-tum." At least it sounded like a bugle. All the notes were flat.

Everybody gazed. Up the rise came a column of horsemen, headed by three who bore slender spears with dirty pennons of colored wool too heavy for the slow motion of their progress to lift and make clear. Behind them came the bugler, and behind them again, three knights in full plate armor with their helmets banging at their knees. Shea recognized Count Roland d'Anglante and Reinald of Montalban; the third had slightly more delicate features and a surcoat over his mail divided red and white across the middle, with a huge gold buckle occupying the center. They were followed by a score or more of mounted men-at-arms in iron hats with brims and mail-shirts of overlapping metal scales. His eyes were torn from the sight by an inarticulate burp from Roger, who suddenly seemed to have difficulty with his breathing, though the halter had not been pulled tight.

There was no point in trying to conceal anything, Shea stepped boldly to the center of the road and, holding his hand up like a traffic cop, said: "Hey!"

The bugle gave a toot, and the riders pulled up. Reinald cried: " 'Tis the turban-knight! How hight he—Sir Harold de—du Chaille? No matter. Hail, fair Belphegor!"

"Regard!" said the knight in the surcoat, in a high voice. "Roger of Carena, and in bonds. This may not be borne!" The knight vaulted down and Shea realized that "he" was a handsome, brown haired woman of show girl size. She whipped a dagger from her belt. Roger was apparently trying to use one of his feet to dig a hole to fall into, his gaze fixed on the ground. Shea thrust himself between the two. "Listen," he said, "this guy's my prisoner."

Count Roland looked down from his horse benignly. "My lady and fair cousin Bradamant, peace; for this is good law. This young sir is a dubbed knight, Sir Harold de Shea, to wit, and if he holds Lord Roger bound it is by right of fair conquest."

"Then I challenge him!" said Bradamant, picking at her belt for a pair of gloves. "For this is my very soul and love and I will assay all desperately upon the body of any who holds him. Lord Reinald, be my aid."

"Cut them down!" said Reinald harshly.

Roland leaped down from his own horse, clanging like an earthquake in a kitchen. "Then must I even stand his, to make the balance fair; for this is a very gentle knight that has done me much service. Ho, Durandal!" He lifted up a great cross-hilted sword, and Belphegor drew back a couple of steps, snatching an arrow from her quiver and bending her bow—not at Bradamant but at Roger. Shea admired his wife's presence of mind, even if the mind was not entirely her own. Reinald looked black, but Bradamant checked her rush; and gave a little laugh.

"Nay, gentles," she said, "let us not fall on contention when Saracen banners be over the next crest, but dissolve this in amical agreement. Sir Harold, my hand." She put the dagger back and extended it.

Shea reached out and took it. "Okay, lady," he said. "My story is that I need this guy in my business. A friend of mine is in Castle Carena and can't get out, because Atlantès has built a wall of fire around it, and unless I deliver Roger there it's no dice."

"Ah, but—" said the lady warrior "—this is my more than friend and most dear love." She waved a hand at Roger, who said "Allah!" under his breath. "Surely, it is less than knightly to keep us one from the other."

"Yet even more so," said Belphegor, putting her arrow back and stepping forward in evident enjoyment of the prospect of a legal argument, "—were he to fail his duty to his vavassour and liege lord who is held prisoner."

"Ah, but the greater wipes out the less," said Bradamant. "In making deliverance of Lord Roger to this Saracen, Sir Harold would fail in duty to the Emperor Charles, who is liege lord to us all."

"Not to me," said Shea.

The three knights gasped, and Roland's face went a trifle grim. "Sir knight," he said, "a truce to profitless discourse. You know me for your friend; you will hear my judgment in this cause?"

Shea looked at the surrounding men-at-arms. Might as well put a good face on it, especially as Roland didn't seem to be a bad guy. "Sure," he said, "anything you say is all right with me."

"And you, my lady Bradamant?"

"That will I."

"Then hark." Roland unslung his big sword from his belt and kissed the hilt. "This is my judgment, given in honor, as the holy St. Michael stands my aid: that Sir Harold de Shea release the Lord Roger to the Lady Bradamant. But since she has the ring that daunts all enchantments, she shall forthwith take oath to rescue Sir Harold's lord from durance in Castle Carena. This deed I lay on her; and none other shall be accomplished till it be done."

Belphegor clapped her hands. "Oh, well thought on!" she said. Bradamant's face also expressed pleasure. She stepped to her horse, produced a sword almost as large as Roland's and held it out to him. He lifted the hilt up before her; she kissed it and extended one hand: "I swear it," she said, and turned to Shea. "Now handsell me your prisoner."

"What do I do?" he asked.

"Place his hand in mine."

"I can't. He's tied up."

"Loose him, want-wit!" She stamped her foot.

Shea was not sure this was a good idea, but nobody else seemed to have any objections, so he stepped around behind the big man, and untied some of the knots, then as Roger gave an explosive sigh of relief, took one of his hands and laid it in Bradamant's.

"Do you assign me all rights of war and ransom in this man?" she asked.

"Sure."

"Then I receive him." She dropped Roger's hand, and with a roundhouse swing, hit him a terrific slap on the side of his face. "Come, varlet!" Roger slowly lifted a numbed arm, and then, instead of hitting her back, surprisingly began to titter. "You accompany us to Carena."

Roger's face straightened out. "O my lady, I pray you, take me not back thither, where mine uncle will coop me up like a chicken."

"Tish! have I not the ring, which is proof against all that he can do? Sir Harold, will you ride with us?"

"Sure," said Shea. He looked around.

The wolf that was Vaclav Polacek was nowhere to be seen.

16

Shea thought rapidly. Bradamant could probably be trusted to keep her word, and even if she couldn't, there was no particular immediate danger to Doc and Florimel. But the danger to Vaclav was both immediate and particular. If they captured him again, someone was almost certain to think of strangling or using a silver weapon instead of the fire that failed. Very likely they would get him, too. He turned to the others:

"I think you could operate better at Castle Carena without us," he said. "There's a friend of mine in trouble, and I'm afraid I've got to do something about it. Bel—Belphegor, it's the sweetheart of that girl. Will you come along?"

She put two fingers to her lips. " 'Tis not in our compact. But—aye, that will I. Whither go we?"

"My guess would be that he'd be looking for that girl. Maybe we ought to go back to about where we found her."

"Think you he would return by the village where so late they'd have burned him?"

"You have something there, kid. Votsy is as nutty as a fruit-cake, but I think he'd be bright enough to cut around the back way."

"Come, then," said the girl. "I know some little of woodland trails." She turned to the paladins. "Gentles, I salute you farewell till a happier meeting."

The armored men raised their hands, the bugle blew again and the group broke up. A horse had been brought for Roger; Shea noticed that as he and Bradamant rode off in the direction of Castle Carena they were holding hands and not giving any particular attention to their route. In their condition, he wondered how good they would be at the business of getting Doc out of Castle Carena.

Behind the shrine the ground dipped sharply, then rose up a bank set with low bushes to the veritable forest beyond. Belphegor's eyes swept it from side to side: "Thither lies his slot," she said, pointing.

Shea could see nothing that looked like a trail, but when he plunged across the declivity at the girl's heels and up the other side, there was a broken branch on one of the bushes, and beyond, where she waved a hand, the mark of a wolf's pad, deeply impressed on the soft ground.

"Hey," he said, "wouldn't we save time by short-cutting along the road?"

She turned a laughing face. "Nay, who'd go road-wise when they could walk the free way of the forest? And more—it is the nature of the wolfish kind to be somewhat scatterwit in purpose. Trust me, we shall come on him the sooner by following direct. See, there turned he to the left."

She went more rapidly than Shea would have believed possible. The sun slanted down through the leaves in speckled patterns and occasionally a bird chirped or dipped and swooped away before him. His Saracen costume was not exactly what he would have chosen for the occasion, but he found himself suddenly happy.

Belphegor hummed a little air to herself as she examined some markings at the side of another little clump of bushes. "Here he turned aside to strike at some small game," she announced. "A rabbit, belike. And here he lay to rest after the pursuit. We gain; press on."

She was tireless; it was he who had to ask for the first halt, and later, for another. Toward what he judged to be noon they made the third pause by the side of a little stream from which they drank and shared half one of the birds left from the previous night's supper. The girl frowned suddenly.

"Sir Harold," she said, "it is passing strange, but meseems there is in this something familiar and not unsweet, as though all this were a twice-told tale. Yet sure am I that we have never wandered the wildwood together before."

"Oh, yes we—" began Shea and then stopped. No use giving her a jar that might set up a resistance to her redeveloping memory. "Do you think we'll find him?" he said instead, changing the subject rapidly.

"Oh, aye, and that soon. Come, let us be afoot again."

She was on her feet in a single graceful motion and they were off. The wolf had certainly done a good deal of circling, either because he couldn't make up his own mind, or perhaps because he had lost his way. Twice more they found places where he had rested, and then, as they passed another brook, the girl pointed suddenly. Shea saw a footprint into which the water was just oozing. He stopped, filling his lungs, and shouting: "Vaclav!"

There was a sound in the underbrush, and the wolf came trotting from behind a tree with his tongue out, shaking his head and bouncing in delight.

Shea said: "What was the matter? Get lost?"

"Arf!" said the wolf.

"Okay, now you're found. Listen here, you prize idiot. You've nearly gummed the works for all of us. Now you stick by us and don't get out of sight. I can handle some magic all right, but I don't understand the higher sorcery well enough to disenchant you, so we'll have to wait till we find Doc. As it is it's damned lucky Atlantès fireproofed you before you turned into a werewolf again."

The wolf put its tail between its legs and emitted a moan of contrition. Shea turned his back and said to Belphegor: "Can you get us on the road to Castle Carena again?"

"Assuredly. It lies that way." She pointed. "But do you find the woods that are my joy so comfortless?"

"It's not that, kid. We got business. Afterward, we can come back here, if you like, and—oh, what the hell, let's go."

The approach of dusk found them still among trees. While Shea made a fire the wolf, under strict instructions, went to help Belphegor with her hunting, flushing game for her arrow and retrieving it afterward. She came back with five rabbits, two quail and a larger bird of some kind, remarking: "If we keep this adventure, I must even find some means of gaining new arrows. Two were lost on that bout, and though I have some skill as a fletcher, both tools, and seasoned wood are wanting."

The evening's bag looked like a lot for three people, but the wolf ate everything they left and looked hungrily for more. Shea was glad that they didn't have much farther to go at this rate. It would wear both of them out to feed the confounded animal.

The sun was already high in the morning when they came out on the track, a few hundred yards short of the fork where he had separated from Polacek on the outward journey. Now they were on the last lap. The wolf, which had been alternately trotting on ahead and dropping back as though it found their pace unbearably slow, suddenly came tearing up, whining and emitting little sharp howls.

"What's the matter, old man?" asked Shea.

The wolf bounded, stifflegged, nuzzling Shea's legs and running a few steps back in the direction of Pau.

"Wants us to go back and find that girl, I guess," said Shea. The wolf howled some more; then nipped Shea by the bagginess of his trousers and tried to lead him in the desired direction.

"Listen, I'm not—" began Shea, and then saw what the wolf had been trying to tell him. A column of dust was rising along the track, with heads moving beneath it. Belphegor shaded her eyes, then gave a little squeal. "The Saracens! By the foul fiend, how slipped they past Count Roland? And see— Medoro among them."

"He must have gone over the pass and picked up a party looking for us— or else that damned smith put him on our track," said Shea.

The heads jerked forward in more rapid movement. "They have spied us!" cried Belphegor. "Up yon hill-shoulder! They cannot reach us mounted there, and mayhap we shall gain the shelter of the trees."

The horsemen were coming on fast, about twenty of them. High pitched yells announced that they had seen their quarry.

Shea and his companion reached the round of the shoulder and pelted through a clump of scrubby oaks. Beyond, a slope of crumbled shale towered over them. They sank in the loose stuff halfway to their knees, every effort to go higher loosening a minor landslide that carried them staggering back. It was like a treadmill.

Below, a couple of horsemen were picking their way through the rocks at the base of the shoulder; others were spreading left and right. An arrow zipped into shale above Shea's head. He wished he knew some kind of magic that would work quick.

"No use," he said bitterly. "We'll have to stand and try to fight it out." He gripped the girl's hand and ran the few steps back down toward the trees.

The Saracens were skirmishing around the base of the shoulder, stopping now and then to yell. A few of them had double-curved bows and were letting off arrows.

Belphegor crouched behind a rock and let off one of her own shafts at a dodging shape. The shot missed, splintering on a stone behind. The next hit a horse, which reared and threw its rider. Belphegor dodged as half a dozen arrows clattered around her in return.

Medoro was on a fine white horse, well out of range. His voice floated up thinly. "Cease from shooting lest you do her a harm! She shall be taken alive, but I will give five thousand dirhams for the head of the man!"

A man threw up one arm and rolled out of his saddle, an arrow right through his body and tipped with a spurt of blood. The rest drew back, dismounted, and leaving one or two to hold horses, ran at the base of the shoulder with swords and spears.

Out from behind a rock slipped a big gray hairy shape which lit on the back of a Saracen with a long bound. Good old Vaclav! The man went down, screaming, in a voice that was suddenly choked, and Belphegor's bowstring snapped like a harp.

Thump! Down went one of the attackers, clutching his stomach and chewing at the grass. An arrow glanced up and away from the helmet of another. *Thump!* The leader of the rush was down, with an arrow right through the eye.

"Allahu Akhbar!" screamed Medoro from below. "Ten thousand dirhams!"

A Saracen stopped with an arrow through his forearm. The others set up a discordant yell and came rushing and stumbling up from all sides, clambering over those who had taken the girl's arrows. The wolf got the hindmost by the leg, wolf and man rolling down the hill, the latter squealing with terror as his weapon failed to bite. Belphegor nailed the man with the helmet neatly through the throat.

"My last shaft, Harold," she cried.

Smart girl, he thought, *to plant it where it did the most good,* and drove his arm forward in a long lunge. The scimitar-like blade was unhandy, but it went right through the open mouth of the man before him. Shea parried a cut with his dagger and swung, but the man had a helmet, which took the blow with a clang, and Shea's blade snapped off at the hilt. However, the blow had force enough to knock the man over backward, and he carried the legs from under a couple of others.

Someone hurled a barb-headed javelin just as Shea recovered from the stroke. The weapon missed and hung quivering in a tree. Shea and Belphegor grabbed for it together. He reached it first, jerked it loose, snapped it over his knee, and gripped the pointed end like a rapier. "Get into a tree," he called to the girl. The Saracens were closing in fast; Shea had just time to turn around, feint at the nearest, dodge his swinging cut, and lunge. The point got him right below the chin.

The next man gave ground, so that Shea's lunge fell short. He leaped back, barely parrying a cut from the side with his inadequate blade. They were ringing him, he couldn't face three ways at once, and was too busy parrying even for a quick thrust. A blow on the side of the head made his senses spin; only his helmet kept the edge out.

Then a sound drowned the shouts of the Saracens; a blast on a horn, deep, full and resonant. It sounded like the horn of Heimdall that had made the glaciers shake; but this one had a wild discordant edge that made Shea's skin crawl and his teeth ache. A dreadful feeling of fear and horror seized him; he wanted to burst into tears, to get down on his knees. The horn sounded again, and all at once the Saracens were bounding down the shoulder, their shouts changed to cries of panic. Shea almost ran after them.

A shadow floated across the shoulder and he looked up to see Duke Astolph soaring past through the air on his hippogriff. He was outlined against the sky as he raised the horn to his lips once more and blew the Saracens along the valley.

But not all of them. Shea looked down in time to see a short, bearded character—who must have been deaf, for he showed no sign of being affected by the horn—on one knee, not twenty yards away, drawing a curved bow. As the man released, Shea ducked almost instinctively and the arrow went over his head.

A cry made him turn round. Belphegor had reached for a dropped scimitar, and now she was sinking to her knees, the arrow sticking in her side.

Shea hurled himself at the Muslim archer, who dropped his bow and whipped out a short yataghan. For three seconds their weapons flickered like sunbeams. Shea parried and drove the javelin-point into the fellow's forearm, where it stuck between the bones.

The man dropped his weapon and pulled back, tearing the javelin from Shea's grasp.

Shea snatched up the yataghan. His antagonist fell on his knees and lifted the one good arm. "In the name of Allah! Would you strike a man unarmed?"

"Damn right I would," snarled Shea and did so. The head came off, bounced, bounced again and rolled down the hill.

Shea went back to where Belphegor lay among the rocks, her face pale and her eyes half closed. He took her in his arms.

"Harold," she said.

"Yes, dearest."

"All is crystal clear. I am Belphebe of the woods, daughter of Chrysogone, and you are my dearest dear."

Shock was often a good cure in amnesia cases. But what the hell good did it do either of them now? He gulped.

"I would have borne your sons," she said faintly. " 'Twas a brave match and a joyous."

"It's not as bad as that."

"Aye, I fear me. I go to Ceres and Sylvanus. Kiss me before I go."

He kissed her. The lips smiled wanly and he placed his hand over her heart. It was beating, but slowly and weakly.

She sighed a little. "A brave match..."

"What ho!" said a familiar deep voice. Astolph stood over them, the horn in one hand, the hippogriff's bridle in the other. "Oh, I say, is the young lady hurt? That's a bit of too bad. Let me have a look at her."

He glanced at the projecting arrow. "Let's see the pulse. Ha, still going, but not for long. Internal bleeding, that's the devil. Quick, young fellow, get me some twigs and grass and start a fire. I believe I can handle this, but we'll have to work fast."

Shea scrambled around, cursing the slow inefficiency of flint and steel, but getting the fire going. Astolph had drawn an enormous pentacle around them with a stick and had whipped together a tiny simulacrum of an arrow out of a twig, with a bunch of grass representing the feathers. He tossed this in the fire, muttering a spell. The smoke billowed around chokingly, much more than so small a fire had any right to make. Belphebe was invisible.

Shea jumped violently as he observed, beyond the border of the pentacle, a pair of eyes hanging unsupported in the air on a level with his own. Just eyes, with black pupils. Then there were more pairs, sometimes at angles or moving a bit, as though their invisible owners were walking about.

"Stay where you are," said Astolph between spells. His arms were outspread and Shea could see him waving them through the smoke as he chanted in several languages at once.

Something deep inside Shea's head kept saying: *Come on out; come out, come out; it's wonderful; we'll make you a great man; come out; just step this way; this will be the greatest thing you've ever known; come with us...*and something stirred his muscles in a movement toward the eyes. He had taken a full staggering step toward the eyes before he got a grip on himself, and sweat stood on his forehead with the effort of trying to keep from another step.

Suddenly the fire went out, the smoke died as though it had been sucked into the ground and the eyes disappeared. Astolph stood by the ashes, big beads of perspiration on his handsome face. The lines around his mouth were drawn. "Bit of warm work that," he said. "Lucky you didn't put your head outside the pentacle."

Belphebe sat up and smiled. The arrow was gone and there was no trace of where it had pierced the tunic save a big bloodstain down the side.

"I'd jolly well like to fix that for you," said Astolph, "but I'm not exactly a magic laundryman, you know."

"My lord, you have done enough and more than enough," said the girl, getting a little unsteadily to her feet. "I—"

"Bye the bye," interrupted Astolph, "you could do with a bit of leaching yourself, Sir Harold."

Shea realized that he had been wounded. There was blood on his face from the blow the helmet had stopped, a cut on one arm and another on the thigh. All responded readily enough to Astolph's magic, by no means so drastic this time. As the Duke finished his passes, Belphebe reached for Shea's hand: "So now we are whole and united. Will you forgive the seeming churlishness of one who knew not her own mind?"

"Listen, kid, do I have to answer that?" said Shea, and took her in his arms. Astolph looked down the slope.

17

After a few minutes Astolph said: "If you two don't mind, you know, I'd like a word of explanation. I thought it a bit odd when you toddled off together, but—"

Belphebe swung round, with her gay laugh. "Duke Astolph, wit you well that this is my very true and beloved husband; yet save for the wound of which you leached me in such marvelous wise, I had not known it, for I was magicked here in a strange manner by Sir Reed."

"Really? Glad to hear it. Wonderful thing, marriage—increases the population. You might have done worse; he's been a stout fellow." He began counting "—six, seven, eight. You'll want your arrows back, won't you, old girl? Those Saracens have certainly had it. Shouldn't care to take that many on at once myself. Must be something to that swordplay of yours."

"Oh, we had them at a disadvantage," said Shea. "And while you're about accepting our thanks for saving our lives, will you tell us how you happened along so opportunely?"

"Simple matter, really," said Astolph. "I was out scouting. Agramant's on the move, and I daresay we shall have a battle. Too bad we haven't Roger on our side; bad man in a brawl, only Roland can stand up to him. I hear he reached the Mussulman camp."

Shea grinned. "He got out of it, too. I ought to know. I brought him. The last I saw of him, he and Bradamant were on their way to get my friend Sir Reed out of hock."

Astolph's eyebrows wiggled. "Indeed! Jolly good of you, and tit for tat, what? I daresay the Emperor will give you a title. Hello, what's this?"

This was Vaclav Polacek, in the form of a werewolf, who had disentangled himself from one of the bodies on the slope and was coming slowly up the hill. "A werewolf, as I live! Extraordinary! Doesn't belong in this time-stream at all."

Shea explained, and with a few expert passes, Astolph changed the wolf back into Vaclav Polacek. The Rubber Czech felt his throat. "That last guy nearly strangled me," he complained, "but I got him. And I'm still sore all over from the pounding those peasants gave me with their clubs. Boy, when they let me have it I sure was glad I was the kind of wolf it takes silver to kill."

"But how'd you get into that shape?" asked Astolph. "I know enough magic to be sure lycanthropy isn't exactly a habit with you."

Polacek smiled with embarrassment. "I—uh—I got fed up with walking and I tried to turn myself into an eagle so I could look for Roger better, but I came out a werewolf instead. I guess I made a mistake."

"Rather," said Astolph. "Now look here, young man. I shouldn't try that again, if I were you. It's quite on the cards that you'd make the transformation permanent, and you'd find it deuced embarrassing."

Polacek said: "It nearly was this time. I kept getting the most awful craving for human flesh. Belphebe was in a tree and I couldn't reach her, but you'll never know how close you came to being eaten last night."

Shea gulped. Astolph laughed and said: "I really must buzz off, you chaps. Now that we're well rid of that scouting party, the Emperor will very likely want to use this valley for his main advance. Cheerio! Come, Buttercup." He was off.

"If we're going to run into any more armies, I want some equipment," said Shea. "Come on, Votsy, let's see what we can pick up."

They made their way slowly down the slope, trying various weapons while Belphebe retrieved her arrows and tried, but rejected, some of those the Moors had used in their short bows. At the foot of the slope, the girl put her hand to her mouth.

"My love and lord," she said. "I am much foredone with weariness, and I doubt not it is the same with you. Shall we not rest a space?"

"Yes, let's, but not here, where there are so many stiffs lying around," said Shea.

They moved along the valley, slowly picking their way across stones, till they reached a spot where a grassy slope slanted down past trees from the left, and stretched out. Polacek said: "The only thing I could want now would be a three-decker sandwich on rye and a cup of coffee. How about it, Harold, could you conjure one up?"

"Might, but it probably wouldn't have any nourishment in it," said Shea with a yawn. "I don't know all about this magic business yet. I wish I knew what made that spell about the Jann go wrong..." His voice trailed off. Belphebe's head was nestled in the hollow of his arm.

He thought he had only closed his eyes a minute, but when he opened them Polacek was snoring and the sun was already dropping toward the mountain rim.

"Hey," he said, "wake up, everybody. Company's coming."

It was indeed the sound of hoofbeats that had roused him. Up the valley four riders were visible. As they drew nearer, he recognized Bradamant, Roger, Chalmers and Florimel, the last riding side-saddle. They pulled up before the three at the roadside; there was a general shaking of hands and making of salutations.

Shea said: "I wasn't sure you could make it without help. How did you manage it?"

Said Bradamant: "Sir knight, if knight you be, know that the power of this ring against all enchantments whatsoever is very great. Therefore holding the ring in my mouth and Lord Roger by the hand, it was a light matter to cross so feeble a wizardry as the wall of flame, and thus to draw your companions forth with me. Do I stand acquit of my oath to you?"

"Yep," said Shea. "We're square."

"Then I'm for the north and the Emperor's army with this, my prisoner and new aid."

She motioned at Roger, who tittered again, and wriggled in his saddle so much that he almost fell off.

"Okay," said Shea. "Thanks and so long." He reached up to shake her hand but before the contact was made, there was a flash of light that seemed to split the evening sky and a violent explosion which sent a tall tree by the roadside spraying round the travelers in a fine rain of burned chips.

They turned with a simultaneous gasp to see Atlantès of Carena standing on the stump, outlined in shimmering light and with a wand in his hand.

"Link hands everybody!" said Chalmers, quickly. "He can't hurt us under the protection of Bradamant's ring."

"Vile traitors!" squealed the little magician. "Know that you had already been a thousand times worse than dead but that there stood among you the peerless paladin, the pearl of the age, my nephew. But now that I am near enough to direct my vengeance, you shall no longer escape." He pointed the wand at Chalmers and began muttering a spell. Blue lights flashed around the tip, but nothing happened.

"Better try the other barrel," said Shea. "That one missed fire."

Atlantès stamped and grimaced. "Allah upon me that I should forget the ring of enchantment!" He clapped a hand to his head. "Yet it is said: no victory without some pain of defeat." He began to trace patterns in the air. "Stir you from this spot and you shall receive the reward of your betrayals."

"Hold my hand carefully, Harold," said Chalmers, squatting and reaching with his other hand to trace a circle on the ground round the party. He added other geometrical elements to make a full grown pentacle, reciting his own spells as he did so.

"There," he said, letting go Shea's hand. "We're safe from him for the time being, though we seem to be besieged. Dear me!"

Atlantès had pointed his wand again, the group felt something rush past them in the air, and a rock on the other side of the road split in a blaze of light. Belphebe placed an arrow on her string.

"I do not believe that will be of any service, young lady," said Chalmers. "I am afraid, Harold, that this gentleman is a much better magician than I, and the most that can be accomplished at present is to accord a certain amount of protection—"

"Maybe I could do something," said Polacek.

"No!" said Chalmers and Shea together. Then the former went on. "However, Harold, you do possess a rather extraordinary skill with the poetic elements in magic. If we were to work together, we might be able to accomplish something."

"I dunno, Doc," said Shea. "We can try, but my spells haven't been going too well in this cosmos." He described what had happened with the growing of the hair on his face and the jinn disguises. Beyond the pentacle the sun was behind the peaks. In the long shadows Atlantès was incanting busily and under his wand a swarm of misshapen hobgoblins began to appear among the rocks. Apparently he meant to make a real siege of it.

"Goodness gracious, I am somewhat at a loss," said Chalmers. "You're certain you made the passes correctly, Harold? Hmmm—what was your poetic element?"

Shea described how he had used elements from Shakespeare and Swinburne.

"Oh, I am relieved. The explanation is quite simple. Like all semi-Mohammedan universes, this one is extremely poetic, and since you employed highly inspired poetry, the effect was somewhat beyond your original calculations. This also suggests a means of relief from our present situation. Do you happen to recall any lines from the major poets having to do with motion or progress?"

"How would Shelley do?" asked Shea.

"Quite well, I believe. Are you ready? Very well, suit the rhythm of your recitation to my movements." He began to make the passes with his hands as Shea recited:

> *My coursers are fed on the lightning,*
> *They drink at the whirlwind's stream,*
> *And when the red morning is brightening*
> *They have strength for the swiftness I deem:*
> *Then ascend with me, children of ocean!*

The result was somewhat unexpected. The four horses on which the party from Carena had come bounded straight into the air as though on springs and before anyone could stop them, leaped at Atlantès' collection of monsters, who scattered in all directions, but not rapidly enough to keep themselves from squashing under the flying hooves like so many tomatoes. Roger whooped with laughter; Chalmers looked a trifle dismayed. "I confess—" he began, and then stopped, looking up.

Against the fading evening sky Duke Astolph on his hippogriff was soaring in to a four-point landing.

He addressed Shea: "Did you summon me, old man? I hope it's important; that children of ocean spell is deuced wracking, but being English I couldn't well resist. Oh, I see; a spot of trouble with our old friend Atlantès."

The proprietor of Carena sneered unpleasantly from outside the pentacle. "O noble and puissant lords, now there is no help for it but that you release to me my beloved nephew, the pearl of Islam. For know that I am of greater power than all magicians of the Franks, save Malagigi alone, and he lies still in durance."

Astolph cocked his head on one side. "Indeed," he said. "Do you want to be released, Roger?"

The pearl of Islam seemed to be having difficulty with his breathing. He looked at the ground, then at Bradamant, then quickly away. "By Allah, nay," he finally managed to get out.

Astolph turned to the enchanter. "Tell you what I'll do, old thing; I'll make you a sporting proposition. I believe Sir Harold's friend here wants his lady to receive human form. I'll take you on in a contest to see who can do it, winner take all, including Roger."

"By Allah, 'tis some Frankish trick," said Atlantès.

"Suit yourself, old man. I can transport them all away from you on Buttercup, you know." He scratched the hippogriff behind the ears.

The magician lifted his hands to heaven. "I am afflicted by the sons of Satan," he wailed. "Nevertheless I will even accept this offer."

Both he and Astolph began making rapid passes. The Duke suddenly vanished, and a mist condensed out of the air around the pentacles, growing and growing until the spectators could no longer see one another. The air was filled with rustlings.

Then the mist thinned and vanished. Florimel had vanished from her own pentacle and stood in that of Atlantès. The latter said: "Behold—" and stopped as Astolph reappeared with a man as tall as himself; a man with a long white beard, neatly combed, and a mane of white hair. He was dressed with formidable correctness in cutaway, pin-striped trousers and spats, with a top hat at a rakish angle on his head and a pink carnation in his buttonhole.

"Permit me, said Astolph, "to present the Honorable Ambrose Sylvester Merlin, C.M.G., C.S.I., D.M.D., F.C.C., F.R.G.S., F.R.S., F.S.A., and two or three et ceteras."

Merlin said in a deep bell-like voice: "That girl's a sham of some sort. Just a trick, and I'll fetch the right one back." He whipped a wand out of an interior pocket, traced his own pentacle and began incanting. Again the mists thickened, this time shot with little lights.

Five minutes later they cleared and there were two Florimels, identical in dress, pose and appearance.

Merlin calmly slipped his wand in his pocket and stepped to the nearest girl. "This one's the real one, mine. Are you not, my dear?" He lifted his plug hat courteously.

"Aye, good sir." She gave a little squeal of pleasure. "And I do feel that blood, not snow flows in my veins."

Merlin held out a finger. A yellow flame appeared at the tip, bright in the dusk. He held up Florimel's arm and ran the flame along it. "Observe. No more reaction than any normal person." He blew the flame out. "Must be off, Astolph. That numismatic exhibition at the Phidias Club."

"Many thanks, old man," said Astolph. Merlin vanished.

"Spawn of the accursed!" shouted Atlantès. "Here stands the veritable Florimel."

Shea noted that Chalmers was making passes. The other Florimel, the one in Atlantès' pentacle, blinked once or twice as though just awakened, and turned into the peasant girl Shea had seen weeping at the roadside near Pau. Polacek gave a gurk. "Hey, Cassie!" he called.

The girl gave one glance, and leaped for him, crying: "Oh, my wolfie!"

"I should say that settled the matter," said Astolph. "Come along, Roger."

"Nay!" said Atlantès. "May my hair turn to scorpions if I permit this!"

"Ah, but you can hardly prevent it, you know," said the Duke imperturbably. "Your spells won't hold these people any more. Laws of magic, you know; you made an agreement, and spells to keep from fulfilling it will fail."

"By the seven imps of Satan, Sir Duke, there was no agreement that I should not have your head," said Atlantès and raising his wand, began to incant again. So did Astolph.

Shea touched Chalmers on the shoulder. "Let's get out of here," he said. "I think there's going to be fireworks."

The three psychologists and their ladies turned their backs on the disputants and through the lulling dark started toward Pau. They had not gone fifty paces when there was a crack like a cannon-shot and the landscape flashed with electric blue. One of the magicians had thrown a thunderbolt at the other.

"Hurry!" said Chalmers. They ran. Crack followed crack, merging into a frightful thunder. The earth began to quiver beneath them. A boulder came loose from the hillside and lolloped down past.

As they ran they glanced back over their shoulders. The side of the hill was hidden by a huge, boiling thundercloud, lit from beneath with flashes, and a forest fire was already spreading from its base. A piece of the mountainside came loose and slid. Through the repeated thunderclaps they heard the piercing sound of Astolph's horn.

"My word," said Chalmers, slowing down. "I—ah—perceive...that some further steps in rejuvenation will be necessary before I can indulge in much more athletics. I should mention, Harold, the reason why Atlantès was so very anxious to detain us. Apparently he has not yet learned the secret of interuniversal apportation, however adept he may be in other respects."

"I bet he never does learn it now," said Shea, a little grimly, looking back to where the battle between the two magicians had now settled down to a mere tornado.

"It would be just as well," said Chalmers.

"Say, you two," remarked Polacek, "while you're speaking about that, what about Walter?"

"Holy smoke!" said Shea. "He's been back there in Xanadu eating honey for a week and he doesn't like it."

A grin spread slowly over the face of the Rubber Czech. "That isn't all," he remarked. "Remember how long we were in Xanadu? It was hours, though it couldn't have taken Doc more than a few minutes to find out that he'd made a mistake."

"Goodness gracious!" said Chalmers. "Then Walter has been there a month or more. I must certainly address myself to the problem."

"What I want to know," said Shea, "is how we're going to get that cop back to Ohio. But I'm not going to lose any sleep over it."

He squeezed Belphebe's hand.

The Wall of Serpents
by L. Sprague de Camp & Fletcher Pratt
Fantasy Fiction, June 1953

The mail was neatly stacked on the table in the front hall. Belphebe said, "Mrs. Dambrot is having cocktails on the fifteenth. That's Thursday, isn't it? And here's a note from the maid, poor wretch. The Morrisons are having a lawn party Sunday and want us to come. This one's really for you; it's from that McCarthy wittold who was in your class last semester, and he wants to know when he can call on us and talk about psionics."

"Oh, that," said Harold Shea. He pushed back his black hair and stroked his long nose.

"And will we subscribe five dollars to the Guild for..."

"Hell!" said Shea.

She cocked her head to one side, eyeing him from under arched brows. He thought how pretty she was and how remarkably she had adapted herself to his own space-time continuum since he had brought her from the universe of the *Faerie Queen,* and later rescued her from that of the *Orlando Furioso,* whither his collaborator Chalmers had accidentally snatched her while angling for Shea to help him out of a private predicament.

"My most sweet lord," she said, "I do protest you want in courtesy. When you cozened me to wed with you, 'twas with fair promise that my life would be a very paradise."

He slipped an arm around her and kissed her before she could dodge. "Life anywhere with you would be a paradise. But lawn parties! And the home for homeless poodles, five dollars!"

Belphebe laughed. "The Morrisons are gentle folk. There will be lemonade and little sandwiches. And we shall probably play charades, 'stead of being pursued by barbarous Moors."

Shea seized her by both shoulders and looked intently at the expression of wide-eyed innocence she had assumed. "If I didn't know you better, kid, I'd say you were trying to persuade me to get out of it somehow, but getting me to make the proposition. Just like a woman."

"My most dear lord! I am but a dutiful wife, that loves but to do her husband's will."

"When it's the same as your own, you mean. All right. Ohio bores you. But you don't want to go back to Castle Carena and that gang of tinplated thugs, do you? We never did find out who won the magical duel, Atlantès or Astolph."

"Not I. But come, sir, let us reason together on this." She led the way into the living room and sat down. "In serious sooth, though we are but newly returned and though this Ohio be a land of smiling peace and good order, I think we too lightly promised each other to wander no more."

"You mean," said Shea, "that you can take only so much peace and good order? I can't say I blame you. Doc Chalmers used to tell me I should have taken to politics or become a soldier of fortune instead of a psychologist, and damned if..."

"It is not solely that whereon I think," she said. "Have you any word further on your friends who were lately with us?"

"I haven't checked today, but none of them had come back yesterday."

She looked worried. In the course of their incursion into the continuum of Ariosto's *Orlando* epics, they had left no less than four colleagues and innocent bystanders scattered about sundry universes. "That were a week complete since our return."

"Yes," said Shea. "I don't know that I blame Doc Chalmers and Vaclav Polacek for staying in the world of the *Orlando Furioso*—they were having a good time there. But Walter Bayard and Pete the cop were stuck in Coleridge's Xanadu the last I know, and I don't think they were having a very good time. Doc was supposed to send them back here, and he either couldn't make it or forgot."

Belphebe said: "And there are those who would take it amiss if they did not come? Even as you have told me that the police sought you out when I was missing in the land of Castle Carena?"

"I'll say so. Especially since one of them is a cop. In this land of peace and good order it's a lot more dangerous to monkey with a policeman than with a professor."

She looked down and moved one hand on the edge of the couch. "I feared as much...Harold."

"What's the matter, kid?"

"There is a kind of knowledge we woodlings have that those in the cities do not know. When I went abroad today, I was followed both here and there without once being able to see by whom or for what purpose."

Shea leaped up. "Why, the dirty skunks! I'll..."

"No, Harold. Be not so fiery-fierce. Could you not go to them and tell them the simple truth?"

"They wouldn't believe it any more than they did the last time. And if they did, it might start a mass migration to other space-time continua. No, thanks. Even Doc Chalmers hasn't worked out all the rules of transfer yet, and it all might turn out to be as dangerous as selling atomic bombs in department stores."

Belphebe cupped her chin in one hand. "Aye. I do recall how we were ejected from my own dear land of Faerie, never to return, in spite of your symbolic logic that changes all impressions the senses do receive. Yet I like the present prospect but little." She referred to Shea's final desperate spell in his conflict with the wizard Dolon. Dolon had been destroyed, but Shea had worked up so much magical potential that he had been thrown back into his own universe, dragging Belphebe with him.

Belphebe's brows went up. "Never before have I known you so lacking in resource. Or is it that you do not wish to go? Hark!—is there not some frame of thought, some world to which we could remove and find a magic strong enough to overcome this of Xanadu? Thus we might outflank our trouble rather than essaying to beat it down by assault direct."

Shea noticed that she was assuming the question of whether she should accompany him to be settled, but he had now been married long enough to know better than to make an issue of it.

"It's an idea, anyway. Hmm, maybe Arthurian Britain. No—all the magicians there are bad eggs except Bleys and Merlin. Bleys is pretty feeble, and Merlin we couldn't be sure of finding, since he spends a lot of time in our own continuum." (Merlin had put in an appearance in the final scene of their Orlandian adventure.) "The *Iliad* and *Odyssey* haven't any professionals except Circe, and she was a pretty tough baby, not likely to help either of us. There aren't any magicians to speak of in *Siegfried* or *Beowulf*... Wait a minute, I think I've got it. *The Kalevala!*"

"What might that be?"

"The Finnish epic. Practically all the big shots in it are magicians and poets, too. Vainamoinen could be a big help—'Vainamoinen, old and steadfast...' A guy with a heart the size of a balloon. But we'll need some equipment if we go there. I'll need a sword, and you had better take a knife and a good bow. The party might get rough."

Belphebe glowed. "That lovely bow of the alloy of magnesium, with the sight, that lately I used in the contest for the championship of Ohio?"

"N-no, I think not. It probably wouldn't work in the Finnish frame of reference. Might turn brittle and snap or something. Better use the old wooden one. And wooden arrows, too. None of these machine-age steel things you're so crazy about."

She asked, "If this Finland be where I think, will it not be uncomfortable cold?"

"You bet. None of that perpetual summer you had in Faerie. I've got enough backwoods clothes to do me, and I'll make out a list for you. This sounds like a breeches-and-boots expedition."

"What kind of country would it be?"

"Near as I can make out, it's one vast subarctic swamp. A flat land covered by dense forest, with little lakes everywhere."

"Then," she said, "boots of rubber would serve us well."

Shea shook his head. "Nothing doing. For the same reason that you shouldn't take that trick magnesium bow. No rubber in this mental pattern. I made that mistake among the Norse gods and nearly got my ears beaten off for it."

"But..."

"Listen, take my word for it. Leather boots, laced and well greased. Wool shirts, leather jackets, gloves...you'd better get a pair of those mittens that leave one finger free. After we get there, we can get some native clothes. Here's the list—oh, yes, woolen underwear. And drive slow, see?"

He looked at her as sternly as he could manage; Belphebe had a tendency to drive the Shea Chevrolet as though she were piloting a jet fighter.

"Oh, I'll be a very model of prudence." She shifted from foot to foot.

"And while you're gone," he continued, "I'll get out the symbol-cards and grease up our syllogismobile."

When Belphebe returned two hours later, Harold Shea was squatting cross-legged on his living-room floor with the cards laid out in front of him. They looked something like the Zener ESP cards, except that the symbols were the little horseshoes and *cruces ansata* of symbolic logic. He had ordered these cards on the Garaden Institute's money when he brought Belphebe from Faerie into his own continuum, and they were ready on his return from the *Orlando Furioso*. They ought to make the task of leaping from one universe to another considerably easier than by drawing the symbols on blank cards or sheets of paper. Beside him lay a copy of the *Kalevala*, to which he referred from time to time as he tried to sort out the logical premises of the continuum for proper arrangement of the cards.

" 'Lo, sweetheart," he said abstractedly, as she came in with the big bundle. "I think I've got this thing selective enough to drop us right into Vainamoinen's front yard."

"Harold!"

"Huh?"

"The slot-hounds are surely on the trail. Two men in a police car sought to follow me on my way home."

"Oh-oh. What happened?"

"I spun sprackly wise about a few corners and so eluded them for the time, but..."

"Oh, boy. They'll have your license number and be here any time."

"A pox and a murrain on them! What is there more to assemble? I'll have all ready in half an hour's space."

"Not half an hour. Now. Stay there! No, don't try to put on those new clothes now. Hug the bundle and it'll come along with us. Get your bow and stuff."

He jumped up and ran up the stairs. Presently his voice came, muffled from the depths of a closet. "Belphebe!"

"Yes?"

"Where the hell are those thick wool socks of mine?"

"In the big carton. You haven't used them since last winter."

"Okay... And that yellow scarf? Never mind, I found it..."

Minutes later, he reappeared in the living room with his arms full of clothing and equipment. To Belphebe he said, "Got your bow? Good. And plenty of arr—"

The front doorbell rang.

Belphebe took a quick look out the window. " 'Tis they! There squats their car! What's to do?"

"Beat it for the Kalevala, quick. Sit on the rug beside me and hold my hand with one hand and your duffel with the other."

The bell rang again. Shea, throwing himself into the lotus posture of Yoga, concentrated on the cards in front of him.

"If A is not not-B, and B is not not-A..." The room went out of focus.

There was nothing in front of him save the cards, arranged in a square of five cards on a side. Twenty-five cards.

"...and if C be the Land of Heroes, the Kalevala..."

On went the spell. The cards dissolved into a million little spots of light, whirling in a rigadoon of their own mysterious meaning. Shea tightened his grip on Belphebe's hand and his bundle of gear.

There was a sensation of being borne, feather-light, along the avenues of a gale. Colors. Sounds that could not quite be heard. A feeling of falling. Shea remembered how he had been scared witless the first time this happened to him—and how at the end of it he had landed in Norse myth at the Ragnarök instead of the Irish myth he had desired...

The whirling lights sorted themselves out into a fixed pattern, solidified, materialized. He was sitting in long, worn grass, with Belphebe and a couple of piles of clothes beside him.

2

The grasses, nodding to a gentle breeze, closed in the view around them. Overhead a blanket of close-packed low clouds marched across Shea's vision, shutting off the sky. The air was mildly cool and moist. At least they had not arrived in the midst of one of those terrifying Finnish winters.

Shea gathered his long legs under him and rose with a grunt, pulling Belphebe up after him. Now he could see that they stood in a wide meadow. To their right, the meadow ran out into the edge of a forest of mixed birch and fir. To their left...

"Hey, kid! Look at those," said Shea.

"Those" were a group of animals grazing around a big old oak that stood alone in the meadow. Shea made out three horses, rather small and shaggy, and another animal, belonging to the deer family. With antlers. Either a caribou or a very large reindeer.

"We shall not lack for meat," said Belphebe. "Certainly this is a noble stag, and too proud to fear."

The four animals, after a ruminant look at the space-time continuum travelers, had returned to their grazing.

"It must be a reindeer," said Shea. "They use them for draft animals around here."

"Like the gift-giving sprite called Santa Claus in your legends of Ohio?"

"Yeah. Let's get our junk over to that fence and put on our woods clothes. Damn, I forgot toothbrushes. And extra underwear..."

He thought of other items he'd forgotten in their haste to get away, such as grease for their boots. However, there were two of them, and they had his well-tempered epee and her longbow, not to mention his command of magic. By the use of these in such an environment, it should be possible to get whatever else was really necessary.

The fence was one of the wood-rail, Abraham Lincoln type. As they neared it, picking up their feet to force them through the long grass, the forest opened out a bit, and Shea glimpsed a group of low, long log houses, half hidden among the trees. A thin blue plume of smoke issued from a hole in the roof of one. There was a faint sound of voices.

"People," said Shea.

"Grant they may be friendly," said Belphebe, glancing toward the building as she inserted herself into an angle of fence and began to pull her dress over her head.

"Don't worry, kid," said Shea. "Vainamoinen's the best egg in this whole space-time continuum."

He began to change to his woods clothes.

"Oh, Harold," said Belphebe. "We brought with us no scrip or other carrier wherein to transport our possessions, and I am loath to leave this good dress. It was the first you bought me, when we were in New York."

"Fold it up, and I'll make a bag out of my shirt. Hello, company's coming!"

They hurriedly completed their change and were lacing their boots, when the man who had appeared from the direction of the houses reached the gate in the fence and came toward them.

He was a short man, of about Harold Shea's own age (in other words, on the naive side of thirty), with a snub nose, wide Mongoloid cheek bones, and a short, straggly black beard. His thumbs were thrust into a broad embroidered leather belt that gathered in a linen blouseshirt which fell over a pair of baggy, woolen pants, which in turn were tucked into boots with hair on the outside. A cap of some high-grade fur sat precariously on one side of his head. He swaggered notably.

Shea buckled on the scabbarded epee and said: "Good day, sir!" confident that his transition to this continuum had automatically changed his language to the local one.

The man cocked his head on one side and combed his beard with his fingers, surveying them from head to foot. Finally he spoke.

> *Oh, ye funny-looking strangers,*
> *It is plain for all to witness,*
> *Ye are from a foreign country!*
> *Tell me of yourselves, O strangers;*
> *Whence ye come from, what your station,*
> *Who your forebears, what the purpose*
> *Brings you to the land of heroes?*

Oh, no you don't, thought Shea. *I've read the* Kalevala, *and I know that when you get the ancestry of a man you can clap all sorts of spells on him.* Aloud he said courteously, "I'm Harold Shea, and this is my wife, Belphebe. We come from Ohio."

"Harolsjei? Pelviipi? Ouhaio?" said the man.

> *Truth to tell, I do not know them.*
> *From a distant land ye must be,*
> *Farther than the realm of Hiisi,*
> *Than the dreaded deeps of Mana.*
> *Though ye come a long way hither,*
> *Never shall ye lack for welcome,*
> *So that beautiful Pelviipi*
> *Ever smooths the path before you*
> *By her smile so warmly radiant,*
> *Warmly radiant as the sunbeam.*

"Thanks," said Shea dryly. "And if it's all the same to you, I'd just as soon you spoke prose. My wife was bitten by a poet once, and it gave her an allergy that makes her uncomfortable when she hears more of it."

The man glanced at Shea suspiciously and at Belphebe appreciatively. "Hear me now, O Harolainen..." he began, but Belphebe, playing up nobly, made a face and a slight retching sound, so he checked, and lowering his voice, said, "Is it not that in far Ouhaio you control your women?"

"No, they control us," said Shea rapidly.

Belphebe frowned; the stranger smiled ingratiatingly. "In our noble land of heroes early do we learn the manner of teaching women their places. Now will I make you the fairest of offers—we shall for one wife exchange the other, and fair Pelviipi shall be returned to you, made most obedient, and with a knowledge of poetry gained from the greatest singer in all Kalevala, all the land of heroes."

"Huh?" said Shea. "No, I don't think I'd care to go into a deal like that..." and as he caught the stocky man's frown "...at least until I know more about your country. Is Vainamoinen up there at the houses?"

The stranger had been leading them toward the gap in the fence. He said sullenly, "Not there now nor ever will be."

"Oh," said Shea, thinking that he must somehow have made a positional error. "Then whom does this establishment belong to?"

The man stopped, drew himself up, and with as much hauteur as a shorter man can give himself before a taller, said,

> *Stranger, it is clear as water*
> *You are new to Kalevala.*
> *No one from the land of heroes*
> *Could mistake great Kaulkomieli,*
> *Oft as Saarelainen mentioned.*
> *Surely have the fame and glory*
> *Of the lively Lemminkainen*
> *Wafted to your distant country!*

"Oh-oh," said Shea. "Pleased to meet you, Lemminkainen. Ye-es, your fame has come to Ohio."

He shot a nervous glance at Belphebe. Not having read the *Kalevala*, she was in no position to appreciate exactly how serious the positional error was. Instead of reliable old Vainamoinen, they had made contact with the most unreliable character in the whole continuum: Lemminkainen, the reckless wizard and arrant lecher.

But trying to pull out now would only make things worse. Shea went on, "You have no idea what a pleasure it is to meet a real hero."

"You have met the greatest," said Lemminkainen, modestly. "Doubtless you have come to seek aid against a fire bird or sea dragon that is laying waste your country.

"Not exactly," said Shea, as they reached the gate. "You see, it's like this: We have a couple of friends who got stranded in another world, and the magic of our own world isn't strong enough to bring them back. So we thought we'd come to a country where they had real magicians and find somebody with skill enough to manage the job."

Lemminkainen's broad face assumed an expression of immense craftiness. "What price shall be offered for this service thaumaturgic?"

Damn it, thought Shea, *can't the man speak plain language?* Aloud he said, "What might you want, for instance?"

The stocky man shrugged. "I, the mighty Lemminkainen, have few needs of anybody. Flocks and herds in plenty have I, fields of rye and barley, girls to kiss and serfs to serve me."

Shea exchanged a glance with Belphebe. As he stood there, debating whether to mention his own technique in magic, Lemminkainen went on, "Perhaps, if the beautiful Pelviipi..."

"Not on your life!" said Shea quickly.

Lemminkainen shrugged again and grinned. "As you wish, O Harolainen. I have no desire to haggle—and in any case, I have my own wrongs to right. Curses on the Mistress of Pohjola, who refused to let me wed her daughter, and not only that, did not even invite me to her wedding with Ilmarinen the smith. I will slay these wretched people of the land of fog and darkness!"

He suddenly snatched off his cap, flung it on the ground and danced up and down in a paroxysm of rage. Shea tried to recall his *Kalevala*. There was something about a journey of revenge like that in it, and it had not turned out too well for Lemminkainen, as he recalled.

"Wait a minute," he said, "maybe we can make a deal at that. This Pohjola is a pretty tough nut. If you take the two of us along, we might be of a good deal of help in cracking it."

Lemminkainen stopped his capering. "Shall a hero of my stature fear the land of frost and midnight?" he asked. "Tall you are, but lack the mighty thews of Kalevala's heroes. You might help if the battle were with children."

"Now look here," said Shea, "I may not be built like a truck-horse, but I can do one or two things. With this." He whipped out the epee.

At Shea's draw, Lemminkainen's hand flashed to the hilt of his own broadsword, but he refrained from producing it when it was evident that Shea had no immediate intention of attacking him. He looked at the epee. "Certainly that is the oddest swordblade ever seen in Kalevala," he said. "Do you use it as a toothpick or with thread to patch your breeches?"

Shea grinned in his turn. "Feel that point."

"It is sharp, but my wife Kylliki does my darning."

"Still, it wouldn't do you any good if it poked into you, would it? All right, then. Want to see how I use it?"

Lemminkainen's short, broad blade came out.

"No, Harold," said Belphebe, putting down her own bundle and beginning to string her bow.

"It's all right, kid. I've dealt with these cut men before. Remember the hillside near Castle Carena? Besides, this is just practice."

"Do you wish to try at flatsides?"

"Exactly. Ready?"

Clang-dzing-zip! went the blades. Lemminkainen, pressing forward, was as good a swordsman with the edge as Shea had ever encountered. He swung forehand, backhand and overhand with bewildering speed, not seeming even to breathe hard. His theory seemed to be to get in close and hit as hard and as often as possible, and to hell with the consequences.

Shea, backing slowly, parried the vicious swings slantwise, wondering what would happen if one of them caught his thin blade at a square enough angle to snap it off. A crack like that could maim or kill a man, even though only the flat of the blade was used. Once Shea tried a riposte; Lemminkainen leaped backward with catlike agility.

Round and round went Shea, giving ground steadily, trying to save his own breath. Once his foot was not quite firm; a swing almost got him and he had to stagger back three steps, with Belphebe's "Oh!" in his ears. But at last the whirlwind attack slackened. The epee slid out and scratched along Lemminkainen's forearm.

"You can tickle with that piece of straw," admitted the hero. He swung again, not so accurately this time. Shea turned the blade aside and the epee darted forward to scratch Lemminkainen's shoulder.

"See," said Shea. Lemminkainen growled, but a quick attack brought the point squarely against his midriff before he could even begin an attempt at a parry.

"Now what would happen if I pushed?" said Shea.

"Boastful stranger, that was but a chance occurrence."

"Oh, yeah? Well, let's try it again, then."

Dzing-zip-tick-clang went the blades. This time Lemminkainen, though not in the least winded, was frowning and overanxious. There were only a couple of exchanges before he was off balance and once more Shea put his point against the broad chest before him. He said, "That, my friend, was no accident. Not twice in a row."

Lemminkainen sheathed his blade and waved a contemptuous hand. "Against an unarmored foe your tricks might gain you a few minutes more of life. But the men of black Pohjola go to war in mail. Do you think that little skewer will do them damage?"

"I don't know what kind of armor they have, but it had better be tight at the joints if they're going to keep this point out."

"I will take you to Pohjola—but enough has not been shown me that I should put the service of my magic to your need. You may be my servant."

Shea shot a glance at Belphebe, who spoke up. "Sir Lemminkainen, the men of your land are marvelous boasters, it appears, though falling somewhat short of the fulfillment of their claims. Yet if losing a contest makes one a servant, you shall be mine, for it would greatly astonish me could you or any of yours surpass me in archery."

Shea suppressed a grin. Belphebe might not have any formal training in psychology, but she knew how to deal with braggarts. The trick was to out-brag them on some point where you knew you could deliver the goods.

Lemminkainen squinted at Belphebe and said, "Harolsjei, I withdraw my offer. In this wife of yours I see she a vixen who needs nothing but chastisement. Wait for my returning."

They were close to the buildings now. Shea noticed for the first time a row of ill-clad serfs who had been watching the contest with their mouths gaping open. "My bow!" shouted Lemminkainen as they fell back before him.

Presently he was back with a crossbow under his arm and a fistful of bolts stuck in his belt. Shea noticed that the instrument had a bow of steel, with a strip of copper for backing and silver inlay. Quite a handsome piece of artillery, in fact.

"Harold," said Belphebe, softly, "not so certain am I that I can in truth best this knave. A strong crossbow of steel in practiced hands can prove most deadly sure."

"Do your best, kid, you'll slaughter him," said Shea, feeling a good deal less confident than he sounded.

Lemminkainen said, "Will you have a fixed mark, red-haired baggage, or shall I set a serf to run that we may have the better sport?"

"A fixed mark will do," said Belphebe. She looked as though the only moving target she wanted was Lemminkainen.

The hero waved a hand. "See that knot in yonder fencepost, distant from us forty paces?"

"I see it. 'Twill do as well as another."

Lemminkainen grinned, cocked his bow and let drive. The steel-tipped bolt struck the fencepost with a loud crack, three or four inches below the knot.

Belphebe nocked an arrow, drew the string back to her ear, sighted a second and let go. The shaft grazed the edge of the fencepost and whistled off into the long grass.

Lemminkainen's grin widened. "Another, would you?" This time he did even better; his bolt struck the post squarely, about an inch above the knothole. But Belphebe's shot stood quivering about the same distance below.

Lemminkainen shot another bolt, then shouted: "I will not be outdone on this turn." He seemed to be right; his quarrel was squarely in the knot.

A little frown appeared between Belphebe's eyes. She drew, held her draw for a couple of seconds, then lowered the bow and brought it up again to the release point in a single motion. The arrow struck the knot, right beside the bolt.

Shea said, "Seems to me you're both about as good as you can get...Hey, why not try that?"

He pointed to where a big crow had flung itself on flapping wings out across the meadow, emitting a harsh haw!

Lemminkainen whipped up his crossbow and shot.

The bolt whizzed upward, seeming to go right through the bird. A couple of black feathers drifted down, but after staggering in its flight the crow kept on.

As the crow steadied, one of Belphebe's arrows sang upward and struck it with a meaty thump. It started to tumble; three more arrows streaked toward it in rapid succession. One missed, but two hit, so that the bird plummeted to earth with three arrows criss-crossing in its carcass.

Lemminkainen started open-mouthed. There were murmurs from the serfs around the buildings. Belphebe said calmly, "Now, sirrah, I should like my arrows back."

Lemminkainen swung an arm to indicate that the serfs should take up the task. Then he brightened, and tapped his own chest. "I, the lively Lemminkainen, am still the greater hero," he said, "because I have excelled in two contests and each of you only in one. But it is not to be denied that you are very good persons of your hands, and in exchange for your help I will chant for you the magic runes you wish."

3

Two women appeared at the door of the main house as they approached in a little procession, with serfs now carrying the bundles. One of the women was old and wrinkled, the other young and rather buxom. It occurred to Shea that with a little makeup and a Mainbocher dress, she would be a very nice dish indeed. Lemminkainen seemed to be a good picker.

He said, "Get you to the kitchen, women. We will have food, quickly, for it never shall be said that the great Kaukomieli is less than the most generous of hosts."

As the pair started to turn away, Belphebe stepped forward and extended her hand to the older one. "Gracious dame," she said, "forgive Sir Lemminkainen's seeming want of courtesy in not making us known to each other. He has no doubt been too much concerned with high matters. I am Belphebe of Faerie, wife to Sir Harold Shea here."

The old woman grabbed Belphebe's hand. Her eyes filled with tears, and she murmured something unintelligible; then she turned and toddled rapidly into the depths of the house. The nice dish curtsied. "I am known as Kylliki, the maid of Saari, wife of Lemminkainen," she said, "and she there is his mother. You are welcome."

Lemminkainen regarded her sourly. "Women always must be gabbling," he said. "Come, guests from Ouhaiola, let yourselves sit down and tell me of this conjuring you wish. I need the names and stations of the persons you wish brought here; who were their forebears, where they now may be, all that is known to them. Moreover, though your skill in magic may be small as compared with that of so accomplished a wizard as myself, it were well if you added your spells to mine; for it is by no means to be concealed that this is a very difficult task, to draw men from one world to another."

Shea frowned. "I can tell you a good deal about one of them. Dr. Walter Simms Bayard, Ph.D. in psychology from Columbia University, class of—umm—nineteen-forty. He's from—mmm—born in Atlantic City, New Jersey, I believe. Father was—Oswald Bayard, a businessman. Had a department store in Atlantic City. Died a couple of years ago."

Lemminkainen said, "Strange and hard are the names you pronounce, O Harol! And the mother of this Payart? I must have the smallest details of his pedigree and background."

Shea gave what little he knew about Bayard's mother, who lived in New York with another son of the family, and whom he, Shea, had met briefly.

Lemminkainen closed his eyes in an effort of memory then asked, "And the other whom you would draw to the land of heroes?"

Shea scratched his head. "That's a tough one. All I know about him is that he's a detective of our police force, that his name is Pete and that he breathes through his mouth. Must have adenoids or something. A suspicious character and not too bright."

Lemminkainen shook his head. "Though it is well known that I am one of the greatest of all magicians, I can have no power over one so meagerly depicted as this."

Belphebe spoke up. "Why don't you try getting Walter here first by himself? Perchance in Xanadu, where he is now, he will have learned enough of this Pete to enable Lemminkainen to conjure him up."

"Okay, kid, I think you've got it. Go ahead with Bayard, Lemminkainen, and we'll worry about Pete afterward."

Just at this moment the women came back from the kitchen with another wearing the crude clothes and deferential air of a serf, all three carrying big wooden plates. Each plate bore a huge hunk of rye-bread, a couple of pork chops and a wedge of cheese the size of Shea's fist. Another serf followed with huge mugs of beer.

Lemminkainen said, "Eat as you will. This little snack should edge your appetite for supper."

Shea's eyes bugged. He said to Belphebe: "I wonder what these people would call a real meal."

Lemminkainen said, "We must eat whole mounds of victuals to enhance our souls for such a journey."

The old woman, his mother, gave a little cry. "Do not go, my son. You are not proof against death."

Lemminkainen spoke around a huge mouthful of food. "No, it is now a thing decided. Little though a hero of my prowess needs the help of others, it is still true as the proverb has it, that bare is the back with no brother behind it, and these strangers of Ouhaiola may help me much."

"But you promised me you would not go," said Kylliki.

"That was before I met these strangers with the strange sword and the strange bow."

The old woman began to cry, wiping her eyes with the hem of her dress. "You are not wanted there. They will set traps of magic all across your way as soon as they know you are coming, and neither the strangers nor your own strength can keep you from death."

Lemminkainen laughed, spraying the table with fragments of cheese. "Fear is for the women only—and not all of those," he said, and gave Belphebe an admiring glance. Shea began to wonder whether he had not been a little hasty in persuading this buck to accept their services. "Now, go fetch me my finest shirt, for I will no longer delay in starting to show those snakes of Pohjola how we keep feast in the land of heroes."

He stood up and walked around the table toward Kylliki with one hand drawn back. Shea wondered if the hero was going to hit her and wondered what he himself would do if Lemminkainen did, but the nice little dish saved him the trouble of doing anything by getting up hastily and scuttling out of the room. Lemminkainen came back, sat down, took a long drink of beer and wiped his mouth on the back of his hand.

"Let us to our spells, O Harol," he said amiably. "I must think a moment that the verses run smoothly."

"So must I," said Shea, producing pencil and a piece of paper from his pocket, and beginning to set up a sorites. He would have to allow for the fact that the poetic element in this Finnish magic was very strong indeed, and probably interminably long. Belphebe slid down toward the end of the bench where Lemminkainen's mother was sitting and began talking to her in a low tone. She seemed to be getting results, too, because the old lady was looking noticeably less woebegone.

After a few minutes Kylliki came back with a clean white shirt, and another of some kind of leather with fishscale metal plates sewed onto it in an overlapping pattern, which she laid on the bench beside Lemminkainen. The hero rewarded her by pulling her down beside him.

"Now you shall hear one of my greatest spells," he said, "for I have composed well and truly. Are you ready, Harol?"

"About as ready as I will be," said Shea. Lemminkainen leaned back, closed his eyes, and began to sing in a high tenor voice.

> *O, thou distant Valter Payart,*
> *Caught in Xanadu's enchantments,*
> *I am sure I know thy father,*
> *Since thy father's name was Osvalt...*

There didn't seem to be much of a tune, or rather each line had a tune of its own.

> *Osvalt of Atlantic City,*
> *And thy mother's name was Linda,*
> *Of the New York City Jacksons,*
> *See I know of all thy people...*

He droned on and on, while Shea tried to concentrate on the sorites. With the back of his mind he was forced to concede that the big lug was probably a pretty good magician. His memory was prodigious, for he hadn't left out a single item of the Bayard biography and connections, though he had heard them only once.

Lemminkainen's verses came faster and faster, until with his voice climbing the scale, he ended,

> *Come thou now, O Valter Payart,*
> *From the pleasure-dome of Kubla,*
> *To the land of Kalevala.*
> *Thou canst not resist my singing,*
> *Canst not delay your coming;*
> *Thou art standing here before us!*

Lemminkainen's voice rose to a scream on the last words; he stood up and swept both hands around his head in a series of magical passes.

Foomp!

There was a rush of displaced air, which rattled the wooden plates around the room, and there was Dr. Walter Simms Bayard of the Garaden Institute, Ph.D in psychology.

Not, however, standing before them. He was sitting cross-legged on the floor, and lying on her back across his lap, clinched in a passionate kiss with him, was one of the houris of Xanadu, wearing about as much as a burlesque queen at the climax of her performance.

Bayard removed his mouth from that of the girl to look around him with amazed eyes.

Lemminkainen said, "Now is it to be seen that I am truly the greatest of wizards. For not only have I conjured this man from another world, but his handmaiden also. O Valtarpayart, fitting it is that you should give her to me in reward for my services."

As Bayard released her and both of them began to scramble up, Belphebe plucked at Shea's arm.

"Look at Kylliki," she said in a low voice. "She looks as though she wanted to scratch somebody's eyes out."

"She'll get over it," said Shea. "Besides, if I know Walter, he isn't going to fall for Lemminkainen's bright ideas any more than I did."

"That's what I mean. Harold." Her voice became still lower. "Isn't it true that in this continuum if you know everything about a person, you can always put some kind of spell on them?"

"Gee, you're right, kid. I never thought about it. We'll have to keep an eye on Walter."

4

Bayard's face slowly turned the color of a well-ripened strawberry. "Look here, Harold," he said, "these tricks of yours..."

"I know," said Shea, "you were just getting acclimated." Belphebe giggled and Lemminkainen guffawed. "Skip it—we haven't got time for temperament. This is Lemminkainen. He's a hero with a capital H."

"How do you do," said Bayard, a trifle loftily, and held out his hand. The hefty man, grinning all over his face at the complimentary description, did not appear to notice it, but ducked a kind of bow from where he sat on the bench. It occurred to Shea that the custom of handshaking probably hadn't been introduced in this continuum.

The thought apparently did not occur to Bayard. He frowned darkly, placed a protecting arm around his houri's shoulders, and said, "This is Miss Dunyazad—Mrs. Shea, Mr. Harold Shea. Now, Harold, if you'll tell me how to get out of this Norse madhouse, I'll get about it. I don't blame you for bringing me here, of course, but I haven't your taste for adventure."

"It isn't Norse, it's Finnish," said Shea. He grinned. "And I don't think you're going to get out right away. I don't think it would look good if you turned up at the Garaden Institute with your Miss Dunyazad and without Pete the cop. At least Belphebe and I found it that way. By the way, I hope he didn't get himself impaled or anything?"

Bayard looked a little mollified as the houri snuggled closer to him. "Oh, he's making the best of a bad business, trying to beat off the Rockette chorus. He's really a very proper Presbyterian, a deacon of the church. The last thing I heard him doing was trying to teach one of the girls the doctrine of original sin. By the way, is there anything solid to eat around here? I'm fed up to the ears with that sticky mess they gave us in Xanadu."

Lemminkainen had been engaged in a huge yawn that showed his tonsils and a great deal else. Now he brought his mouth closed with a snap. "True it is, O noble guestlings, that in the fatigue of my mighty magic, I forget the first duty of a host. Kylliki! Mother! Fetch supper." He counted guests on his fingers. "A couple of dozen ducks will do. Valtarpayart, I see your handmaiden is dressed for the bath. Does she wish one prepared?"

"No," said Bayard, "but I think she could use the loan of some clothes if you have a few to spare. Couldn't you, my dear?"

Dunyazad nodded dumbly and, as Lemminkainen shouted for clothes, Bayard led her over to a bench and sat down. Shea noticed it was as far as possible from Lemminkainen.

Bayard said, "I don't wish to cavil, Harold, but I really don't see why it was necessary to involve me in this escapade of yours."

Shea explained the magical reasons for the flank attack on Xanadu. "But we still haven't got Pete the cop, and if we ever want to get back to Ohio, we'd better. How much do you know about him? Irish, isn't he?"

"I should say not! I talked with him enough to find out that in spite of being a Presbyterian, his real name is Brodsky, and he's about as Irish as Jawarharlal Nehru. He only wishes he were Irish, tells Irish jokes and sings Irish songs. With that polyp or something he has in his nose; the result is below Metropolitan Opera standards."

Kylliki came through the door, bringing with her an odor of cooking duck and a long, loose dress which she threw at rather than handed to Dunyazad. Lemminkainen's eyes followed the houri admiringly as she struggled into it. Then he yawned again and said, "Scanty is the tale you give me of this Piit whom you are seeking."

"Well," said Bayard, "let's see. He was promoted to second grade detective for the work he did on the Dupont case. I've heard that a dozen times. He works out of the Madison Street station. His mother is named Maria, and his father was named Pete, too, and was a bricklayer, and wanted him to tend bar when he grew up. He himself had the idea of being a pro football player. Will that do?"

Lemminkainen shook his head gloomily. "Only such a master of magic as I would dare attempt the passing-spell with materials so scanty. And even I must meditate on it until morning, for I am foredone with labors mighty."

"Why not now?" Bayard appealed to Shea. "I'd like to see how this is done. I may be able to use it."

Shea shook his head. "Won't do, honest, Walter. You don't know the first thing about magic yet. It has rational rules, but they follow a different kind of logic than anything you've had any experience with. And I wouldn't advise you to stay around while Lemminkainen is fishing for Pete, either. You've worked up quite a bit of magical potential by being pulled here from Xanadu. So if Lemminkainen does fetch Pete, and you're right here handy, you're a little bit apt to pop right back into Xanadu along the lines of weakness created by the spell while he's coming here. Remember the trouble we had, dear?"

"Marry, that do I," said Belphebe. "But let us not dwell upon it, for here's our sup."

This time there were seven servants in the procession. Each bore a wooden tray upon which a mountain of bread was surrounded by three whole roast ducks except the one who served Lemminkainen. He had six.

When he had finished the last of them, with one of the ducks Shea was unable to eat, he stretched, yawned again, and said, "Harol, friend and helper of the lively Lemminkainen, you shall have tonight the lock bed. Will you lead Pelviipi to it? As for these guests, the latecomers, they shall have my best of bearskins to compose them by the hearth-fire. Come, Kylliki, lead me bedward, for I cannot walk unaided."

Shea thought the spell must have taken a lot out of the big oaf at that as he watched him stagger toward his sleeping quarters, but had to admit that Lemminkainen was cheerfully keeping to his side of their bargain, even if he did talk in that phony poetry.

One of the servants with a rush torch showed him and Belphebe down to the end of the hall where the lock bed was. It was bigger than a Pullman section, but not very much, and both of them had to roll up clothes for pillows...

"What the hell's that?" said Shea, sitting upright and cocking an ear toward the foot of the bed.

Belphebe giggled where she lay. "That, my most puissant and delectable lord, would seem to be the hero and his spouse engaged in a sport we wot of—to wit, a quarrel within the household. Hark! She has just called him frog spawn."

Shea gazed at the partition which separated them from the room to which Lemminkainen had retired. "Well, I hope they get over it soon," he said. "With your woods-trained ears, you can make out what they're saying and enjoy the show, but all it sounds like to me is a racket."

They did get through with it fairly soon, at that. But now the reindeer skins that served as blankets were too hot when they were on and he was too cold with them off. Besides, the straw mattress resembled a relief map of the Himalayas, and he never could get used to sleeping in a place where there weren't any windows, even if cracks in the outer wall did admit enough air.

Something scratched at the door of the lock bed. Shea listened for a minute, then turned over.

The something scratched again, this time in what was clearly a signal, for the scratching came one—two—three.

Shea jacknifed to a sitting posture in the Pullman berth and slid the door of the lock bed open a crack. Down the hall, the fire on the hearth was at the ember stage, throwing a red light over the two mounds beside it that must be Bayard and his Dunyazad. It gave just illumination enough for Shea to make out the figure of the nice little dish, Kylliki, bending over at the entrance to the lock bed. One finger went to her lips and then beckoned.

Shea experienced a dreadful if momentary sinking of the heart at the thought he might have a female wolf on his hands, but Kylliki settled the question for him by sliding the door of the lock bed farther open and reaching past him to touch Belphebe into wakefulness, then sat down on the edge of the lock bed. When the couple had taken their places beside her, she leaned close and said in a stage whisper, "There is treason afoot."

"Oh—oh," said Shea. "What kind?"

"My husband, the hero Kaukomieli. Who can resist him?"

"I dunno, but we can give it the old college try. What's he up to?"

"I learned but now his purpose. 'Tis to evade the making of the spell for bringing from hence to hither your other friend. Such wizardries leave him always weak and foredone, as you saw but this evening."

"Why, the..." began Shea, reaching for his epee, but Belphebe said, "Hold, Harold, there must be more in this than meets the eye, and meseems it's more a matter for craft than violence." She turned to Kylliki. "Why do you give us this tale? It cannot be a matter of concern for you whether this Pete be summoned or no."

In the darkness they could plainly hear the girl grind her teeth. "Because of the other wing to his bird of thought," she flared. "Instead of going to Pohjola, he'd be off to the lakes with that immodest she-devil who wears no clothes."

"Dunyazad. What do you want us to do about it?"

"Be off," said Kylliki. "Take him to Pohjola with the dawn. It is the lesser peril."

Shea thought of Lemminkainen's barrel-like chest and huge arms. "I don't see how we're going to make him do anything he doesn't want to," he said.

Kylliki laid a hand on his arm. "You do not know my lord. This night he lies weaker than a newborn reindeer calf with the back-whip of his spell-making. I have a rope. Bind him while the weakness is on him, and steal him away."

Belphebe said, "I think she has the key that will unlock our troubles, Harold. If we bind Lemminkainen tonight, then we can keep him tied up until he makes the spell that will bring Pete. And then he will be too weary to think on revenges."

"Good for you, kid," said Shea, heaving himself to his feet and reaching for his pants. "All right, let's go. But I think we'll need Walter to help."

Getting Walter was not so easy as it looked. He was sleeping the sleep of the just after his prolonged vacation in Xanadu, and shaking him only produced a series of contented grunts. Dunyazad's head came out of the bearskins though, to look at the three standing over her with mild, cow-like eyes, not saying a word, even when Kylliki hissed at her like a cat. Shea decided that Dunyazad belonged to the beautiful-but-dumb type.

After an interminable time, Bayard pulled himself together and accompanied Shea into Lemminkainen's room, where a rush-light held by Kylliki showed the hero sprawled cornerwise across the bed with all his clothes on, fully dressed and snoring like a sawmill. He didn't even move when Shea cautiously lifted a leg to put a coil of rawhide rope around it, and only changed the rhythm of his snores as they rolled him back and forth, wrapping him like a cocoon in the tough rawhide.

Kylliki said, "His mother will think little good of this, the old harridan! She cares for nothing save that he stays by her hand. I could tear her hair out."

"Why don't you?" suggested Shea, with a yawn. "Well, come on, kid, let's try to get a little shut-eye. When that big lug comes to, it will be like trying to sleep in the same house as a steam calliope."

He was amply borne out after what seemed little more than ten minutes of slumber, and jerked out of bed to follow Bayard into the other room, from which a series of truly majestic howls were emerging.

Lemminkainen was rolling around the floor of the room, shrieking curses and trying to writhe loose, while Kylliki, with no attempt at all to disguise the sneer on her pretty face, was cursing just as fast at him. Suddenly, the hero relaxed, screwed up his face, and in his singing voice began to chant:

> *Think you that I'll heed your wishes,*
> *Now you've flouted and provoked me,*
> *By your stratagems and insults?*
> *I will live to see you, strangers,*
> *All except the fair Tunjasat,*
> *Hurled into the depths of Mana,*
> *Down to Hiisi's kingdom tumbling!*
> *Think you that this rope can hold me,*
> *Me, the wizard Kaukolainen?*

Just observe how from my members
Are the cords impotent falling!

Shea stared; it was true. The cords around his feet were working loose. He tried to think of a counter-spell. Bayard said, "Hey, cut that out!" He seemed to be addressing a point a foot or two beyond Lemminkainen.

"Cut what out?" asked Shea.

"Untying him."

"But if his magic..."

"Magic my foot! I'm talking about the old lady."

"What old lady?" said Shea.

"I guess she's Lemminkainen's mother. Are you blind?"

"Apparently I am. You mean she's there, invisible, untying him?"

"Certainly, but she's not in the least invisible."

The coils of rope had worked themselves loose from feet, ankles and knees. The triumphantly grinning Lemminkainen gave a massive wriggle and came to his feet.

"Well, for Lord's sake, stop her!" said Shea.

"Huh? Oh, yes, I suppose so." Bayard stepped over to where Lemminkainen was standing and grabbed at the air. There was a scream; a couple of feet away from the hero, Lemminkainen's mother materialized with her hair over her eyes, glaring as Bayard held both her hands. Kylliki glared right back at her.

"Now, now," said Shea. "We're not going to hurt your son, lady. Only make sure that he carries out his part of the bargain."

"An evil bargain. You will take him to his death," croaked the old woman.

"And you would make him a woman-bound weakling instead of a hero," snapped Kylliki.

"That's right," said Shea. "Must say I'm disappointed in you, Kauko."

A portentous frown had replaced Lemminkainen's smile. "How mean you?" he demanded.

"Here I thought you were the greatest hero of Kalevala, and you get cold feet over the Pohjola project."

Lemminkainen gave an inarticulate bellow, then subsided to a mere roar. "Me, afraid? By Jumala, loose me from these bonds and I'll make you a head shorter to show you how afraid I am!"

"Nothing doing, Toots. You fetch Pete from Xanadu, and then we'll discuss any changes of plan."

The hero put on his crafty expression. "If your friend the spry detective is brought here from Xanadu, will you, Payart, give me the fair Tunjasat?"

"I really don't think..." began Bayard, but Shea cut him off with, "Nothing doing. That wasn't in the original contract. You go right ahead, or the whole deal's off."

"Well, then. But from these bonds you must release me, else my magic spells will falter."

Shea swung to Kylliki. "Can I trust him?" he asked.

Her head came up. "Fool! My husband is no promise-breaker... But—he may put a spell on Payart to make him yield up the maiden."

Shea stepped across to Lemminkainen and began to untie knots. "That's right, Walter. And besides, there's the danger that you might get blown back into Xanadu by the spell. You better get out of here, as far away from the building as you can. I don't know what the local range of magic is, but it can't be very high."

Bayard made for the door. As the last loop fell from his arms, Lemminkainen stretched them over his head, sat down and corrugated his forehead in thought. At last he said, "Are you ready, Harold? Good—let us begin."

He tilted back his head and sang.

*Oh, I know thee, Peter Protsky,
And from Xanadu I call thee...*

He droned on. Shea quietly worked away on the sorites. Up and up went the voice of Lemminkainen, and just as it almost reached screaming pitch, in through the door came Dunyazad, her lovely, vacant face inquiring.

"Have you seen my lord?" she asked.

"...thou art with us!" finished Lemminkainen, on a high C.

There was a rush of air; for a moment only a cloud of burning sparks hung where the houri had been, and then they went out, leaving the space occupied by a solid-looking man in a rumpled brown American business suit.

5

"What the hell is this?" Pete said, and then his eye fell on Harold Shea. "Shea! You're under arrest! Kidnapping and resisting an officer!"

Shea said, "I thought we'd been all through that."

"Oh, you did, did you? And you thought you could stash me away in that screwball fairyland while you went on and rolled your hoop? Well, you've got staging an indecent theatrical performance on top of the other charges now. How do you like that? You better come along with me."

"Come along where?" said Shea.

"Huh?" Pete Brodsky looked around the room and at the slumping Lemminkainen. "Bejabbers, where is this dump?"

"In Kalevala."

The Wall of Serpents

"And where would that be? Canada?"

Shea explained. "And here's the wife I'm supposed to have kidnapped or murdered. Darling, this is Detective Brodsky. Pete, this is Belphebe. Does she look dead?"

"Are you really the dame that disappeared at that picnic, back in Ohio?" asked Brodsky.

"Marry, that I am," said Belphebe, "and through no fault of my husband's, either."

"And in the second place," said Shea, "you're out of your bailiwick. You haven't any authority here."

"You con-merchants always try to play it smart, don't you? The law of close pursuit takes care of that. Constructively, I've been in close pursuit of you ever since you pulled that fast one on me back in Ohio. Where's the nearest American consul?"

"Better ask Lemminkainen. He's the local boss."

"The big guy? Can he speak English?"

Shea smiled. "You got along all right in Xanadu, didn't you? You're speaking Finnish without knowing it."

"Okay. Say, mister..."

Lemminkainen had been sitting slumped over. Now he lifted his head. "Get you hence and let me sorrow," he said. "Ah, that by my own efforts I should be deprived of the embraces of the beautiful Tunjasat!" He glared at Shea. "Man of ill-omen," he said, "if I but had my strength, there would be an accounting."

Kylliki said, "Much strength will come to him who eats good food."

Lemminkainen appeared to brighten at the thought. "Then why do you waste time in foolish chatter when food is lacking?" he said practically, and Kylliki scuttled out, followed by his mother.

Shea went off to hunt up Bayard and explain what had happened to Dunyazad. The psychologist did not seem unbearably grieved. "An excellent exercise for the libido," he said, "but I fear that in time she would have become importunate. Persons of her order of intelligence frequently consider that beauty entitles them to great consideration without effort." He accompanied Shea back into the house for breakfast.

Lemminkainen took his in his bedroom while the other three ate with Pete Brodsky, who did prodigious execution to a breakfast of roast meat, cheese and beer, belching appreciatively afterward.

"Maybe I got you Joes kinda wrong," he said, as he wiped his mouth with a dirty handkerchief. "You may be all right guys at that—sorta elect, if you get me. Gimme the pitch, will you?"

Shea told him as well as possible what had happened in the continuum of Ariosto's *Orlando Furioso* and why Vaclav Polacek and Dr. Reed Chalmers were still there. "But," he continued virtuously, "we couldn't very well leave you and Walter Bayard in Xanadu, could we?"

"I get it," said Brodsky. "You figured you had to spring us out of that reefer-dream or else pull a bit yourself. Okay, so you're a square. What's the next lay?"

Shea told him about the Pohjola project. Brodsky looked glum. "So we gotta go up there and crack this box with a lot of them doorshakers on the lay? Me, I don't like it. Why can't we just take it on the lam for Ohio? I'll kill the rap for you."

Shea shook his head. "Not me. Especially after the fuss I made about Lemminkainen running out on his end of the bargain. Listen, you're in a place where magic works, and it's funny stuff. When you get something by promising something else, and then try not to deliver, you're apt to find yourself without the thing you wanted."

"You mean if we went lamester, this Bayard and me would land back in that de luxe hop-pen?"

"Something like that."

Brodsky shook his head. "You're shot with horseshoes that you got a Joe with you that believes in predestination. Okay, when do we take it?"

"Probably tomorrow. Lemminkainen knocked himself out bringing you from Xanadu and won't be fit till then."

"I got it," said Brodsky. "What we got for today? Just bending the ears?"

Shea turned around and looked out the window. "I guess so," he said. "It seems to have started raining."

It was a long day. Kylliki and Lemminkainen's mother trotted in and out, carrying trays of food to the recumbent hero, and occasionally dropping one off at the table in the hall, where Brodsky and Walter Bayard had started an endless discourse on predestination, original sin, and Cartesianism. After a while, Shea and Belphebe wandered off into a corner and let them talk, since neither Kylliki nor the mother seemed very sociable. It had already grown toward evening and the lowering skies were definitely darker, though none of the rush-lights had been kindled, when Bayard and Brodsky approached the couple.

"Say, listen," said the detective. "Me and this Bayard, we been thinking, and we worked up a hot lineup. You know this magic stuff. How about you putting one of these spells on Lemon Meringue there, and make him drop his score on this Pohjola joint—just skip it? Then he just springs us back where we belong, see?"

Shea was doubtful. "I don't know. There's likely to be a kick-back. He's a pretty hot wizard, and playing on his home grounds, where he knows all the rules and I don't. Besides, I warned you about what happens when you try to get out of a magical bargain."

"But look here," said Bayard, "we aren't proposing anything unethical, even in the terms of magic. All we're suggesting is a spell that will make him see things our way. He'll have the credit of having performed a great action in rescuing us, which these heroes of romance prize more highly than anything else, as I gather it. As a more material reward, you can leave him some of your artifacts. That sword of yours, or Belphebe's bow, for instance."

Shea turned to his wife. "What do you say, kid?"

"I like it none too well, but I can see no true argument contrarious. Do as you will, Harold."

"Well, I suppose doing almost anything's better than doing nothing." He stood up. "Okay, I'll try."

He managed to waylay Lemminkainen's mother to ask her something about the hero's background, bearing in mind that one of the requirements of Kalevala magic was a fairly intimate acquaintance with the person or thing you were going to put a spell on. It was like putting soap in a geyser; the old dame prattled away at a furious pace, and Shea soon discovered that his own memory was by no means the equal of Lemminkainen's, so that he had to re-open the floodgates a couple of times by asking her to repeat.

The process lasted through another of the gigantic Kalevalan meals; when it was over, Shea retired to the corner of the fireplace with a big mug of beer and tried to work out a chant in iambic tetrameters along the line Lemminkainen had used. The form wasn't very familiar to him and he kept forgetting lines, so he got a charred stick and tried scratching some of the keywords on the floor. While he was about it, the others drifted off to bed. Bayard was already snoring from his pile of bear skins when Shea, satisfied at last, took one of the rush-lights, made his way to the door of the hero's bedroom, and in a low voice, chanted his composition.

As he finished, something seemed to flash before his eyes and he felt a little dizzy. It might be the beer, but he rather thought the spell had worked, and he staggered weakly across to the lock bed, almost missing the bracket when he put the rush-light in it.

Belphebe sat up, with the skin-blankets gathered close around her chin; her expression was far from welcoming.

" 'Lo, sweetheart," said Shea. He hiccupped slightly, sat down on the bed and started to take off his boots. Belphebe said, "Begone, sir. I'm an honest wife."

"Huh?" said Shea. "Who ever said you were anything else? And why the fire alarm?"

He reached out an arm for her. Belphebe wriggled toward the back of the bed, her voice suddenly going high. "Harold! Walter! Help—I am beset!"

Shea looked at her in bewilderment. Why was she dodging him? He hadn't done anything. And why was she calling for "Harold" when he was right there?

Before he could think up anything intelligent to say, Bayard's voice said from behind him, "He's at it again—grab him and tie him up till Harold can do something about it."

"Is everybody crazy?" demanded Shea, and felt Brodsky grab his arm. He pulled loose and threw a punch at the detective, which the latter dodged with a slight movement of his head. Then the light went out.

Shea awakened with a splitting headache and a dark brown taste in his mouth. There had been too much beer; and on top of that he was hog-tied even more efficiently than he had bound Lemminkainen the previous night. It was just about dawn; somewhere outside he could hear a clink of metal as a serf went about the early business of the house. The two piles of bearskins near him on the floor would be Bayard and Brodsky.

"Hey, you guys!" he called. "What happened?"

One set of snores bit off, a head lifted and Brodsky's voice said, "Listen, glom. We dropped you dead bang. Now dummy up before I let you have it again."

Shea fumed inwardly. From the feeling at the side of his cranium Brodsky had let him have it all right, and with a peculiarly solid blackjack. The prospect of another treatment had no appeal. But he could not understand why everybody was behaving that way—unless perhaps Lemminkainen had put some kind of spell on him while he was trying to work on the hero. That must be it, Shea decided, and lay uncomfortably, trying to work out a counterspell in Kalevalan terms. While he was doing that, he must have drifted off into a doze again. He wakened to a roar of laughter.

It was fully light. The entire household was standing around him, including Belphebe with a worried expression, and the laughter came from Lemminkainen, who was doubled up, choking with mirth. Bayard merely looked surprised.

The master of the house finally got his breath long enough to say: "Fetch me a pail of water, Kylliki—ho, ho, ho!—and we'll give his proper semblance to this son of Ouhaiola."

Kylliki brought the pail. Lemminkainen crooned a spell over it, then dashed it into Shea's face.

"Harold!" cried Belphebe. She threw herself down on Shea and covered his wet and sputtering face with kisses. "You left me burning anxious when you came not to me last night. I had thought you taken in some trap."

"Help me off with this rope," said Shea. "What do you mean I didn't come to you? How do you think I got in this jam?"

"Nay, I see it now," said the girl. "You put on the appearance of Lemminkainen. Was it to test me?"

"Yeah," said Brodsky. "Sorry I sapped you, Shea, but how the hell was we to know?"

Shea stretched cramped arms and scratched a stubbly chin. He had put a line about "As if we were twins identic" into his spell the previous night, and it appeared now that this had been a mistake. "I was trying a little spell," he said, "and I guess it must have backfired."

"You were twin to Lemminkainen," said the hero. "Learn, strange man from Ouhaiola, that the laws of magic tell us when a spell is falsely woven, all things wear another semblance. Nevermore seek to equal the master of magic until you know more of the art." He turned. "Mother! Kylliki! We must fall to eating, for we have a journey before us."

Belphebe said to Shea, "Harold, it is well to be warned. This saying that if a spell isn't accurate it will give another look to things is well to remember."

"Yeah, the laws of magic are different here. But I wish we'd known that last night."

They took their places at the table. Lemminkainen was in the best of humors, crowing over Shea's discomfiture and boasting of what he would do to the Pohjolans when he got to them. He seemed to have forgotten about Dunyazad or any other squab.

His mother looked more and more melancholy. At last she said, "If you will not hear me for your own sake, at least listen for mine. Will you leave your mother alone and unprotected?"

"Little protection is needed," said the hero. "But such as you need. I give you. This Payart, this Piit shall stay with you. Not that the two together would be of one third as much use as such a hero as myself."

"Harold..." began Bayard, and Brodsky said, "Hey, ain't we going with?"

Lemminkainen shook his head firmly. "Never shall I consent. This is hero's work. Harolsjei has shown he can be a fighting man of sorts, and this shield maiden is not the worst archer in the world, though far from so good as I am—but you, frogs of Ouhaio, what can you do?"

"Listen, lug," said Brodsky, getting to his feet. "Come on outside, and I'll show you. I don't care if you're as big as Finn McCool."

Bayard put out a restraining hand. "Just a minute, Pete," he said. "I rather think he's right, at that. The kind of activity in which we are skilled is of little value in this continuum, and we might be more useful preserving the base, as it were." He glanced at Kylliki. "Besides, it occurs to me that perhaps you could improve the hour. I doubt if any of these people have heard of predestination and original sin."

"Say, you're a good head," said Brodsky, sitting down again. "Maybe if we make that grift good, I could get a couple of converts."

Lemminkainen was already on his feet, leading his way to the door. He took down a long rawhide lariat from a peg and headed out toward the meadow, where the same quartet of animals were gazing. They started walking away; the hero swung the rope and cast it over the nearest antler of an enormous reindeer. Then, chanting something about "Elk of Hiisi," he climbed down the rope and made a loop around the animal's neck with the other end. The reindeer bucked; Lemminkainen gave one jerk and it went down on its knees.

Pete Brodsky's eyes opened wide. "Lord!" he said softly. "Maybe I copped the right dope not trying to go on the muscle with that ghee."

Lemminkainen started back across the meadow, leading the reindeer as though it were a puppy. Suddenly he stopped and stiffened. Shea followed his glance and saw that a man, too well dressed for a serf, was standing at the door of the main house, talking to Kylliki. As they came closer, it was apparent that the man was about Lemminkainen's own height, but stouter, with a great gray Santa Claus beard. He turned a beaming smile on the hero; they fell into each other's arms and administered powerful slaps on their respective backs, then held each other at arm's length. The stranger declaimed,

Hail, the lively Lemminkainen!
Is it true thou plan'st to visit
In the fogbound land of Turja,
And with help of foreign swordsmen
Teach old Ilpotar a lesson?

They fell into each other's arms and slapped again. "Will you go with me to Pohjola?" bawled Lemminkainen.

"Nay, I still seek a new wife!" shouted the gray-beard, and both of them laughed as though this were a peculiarly brilliant jest.

Brodsky and Bayard pressed close to Shea and muttered questions. Shea said, "The old guy must be Vainamoinen, the great minstrel and magician. Damn, if I'd known where to find him, I wouldn't have made that deal..."

"What old guy?" asked Bayard.

"The one talking to Lemminkainen and whacking him on the back. The one with the beard."

"I don't see any such person," said Bayard. "He's hardly more than an adolescent, with only the beginnings of whiskers."

"What!"

"Not over twenty."

Shea exclaimed, "Then this must be another magical illusion, and he must be after something. Watch him!"

The pseudo-Vainamoinen seemed to be trying to question Lemminkainen, but every now and then one of them would get off five or six lines of poetry, they would fall into each other's arms and begin back-slapping again. Suddenly, at the beginning of one of these declamations, Brodsky leaped, catching the stranger's wrist just as it came sweeping down. The detective twisted deftly, pulled the wrist across his own shoulders and stooped forward. The man's feet flew up, he came down on his head in the long grass with a wicked-looking knife in his hand. Brodsky deliberately kicked him in the ribs. The knife dropped.

The man sat up, a hand pressed to his side and the Santa Claus face twisted with pain. Lemminkainen looked bewildered. Shea said, "Walter says this man is not what he seems. Maybe you better make him use his right face."

Lemminkainen crooned a spell and spat on the man's head. A sallow young face glowered up sullenly. The hero said, "So, my cousins of Pohjola send me greeting for my journey! Bow your head, spy of Pohjola." He drew his broadsword and felt the edge.

"Hey!" said Brodsky, "you can't just bump the ghee off like that."

"Wherefore not?" said Lemminkainen.

"He ain't gone up or got his bit or nothing. Where's the law?"

Lemminkainen shook his head in honest puzzlement. "Piit, you are surely the strangest of men, whose words are without meaning. Spy, will you bow your head, or shall I have the serfs deal with you in their manner?"

Shea said to Pete, "They don't have judges or trials around here. I told you this guy was the big boss and made his own law."

Pete shook his head. "Some connection man," he said as Lemminkainen's sword whistled through the air. The man's head thumped on the grass in a little fountain of blood.

"Serfs, bury this carrion!" Lemminkainen shouted, then turned toward the visitors from Ohio. Shea noticed that the expression of shrewdness had come back into his eyes.

"You have the gratitude of a hero," he said to Brodsky. "Never have I seen a wrestle-hold like that."

"Jujitsu," said Pete. "Any shamus is hep to it."

"On our trip to far Pohjola you shall go with us and show it." His eyes swept the group. "Which of you is so skilled in magic as to have penetrated the false shaping that deceived even me, the master of spells?"

"Why, I guess that was me," said Bayard. "Only I'm not skilled in magic at all. Not the way Harold is."

Shea said, "Walter, that must be just the reason. That's why Doc Chalmers couldn't get you out of Xanadu, too. And remember how you saw Lemminkainen's mother untying him when none of the rest of us could? You must be too rational or something, so that spells working a change of appearance make no impression on you." He turned to Lemminkainen. "This guy would be more help on the trip than all the rest of us put together."

The hero appeared to be making a convulsive and prodigious effort to think. Finally, he said, "For your eyes, O Valtarpayart, so be it, since it is not to be concealed that many and strange are the enchantments that beset the road to this land of fog and darkness."

6

Under Lemminkainen's direction, the serfs dragged out the largest of four sleds that stood in a shed stacked high with harness and similar gear.

"What do you know!" said Pete Brodsky. "Is the big shot going to take a sleigh ride?"

"We all are," said Shea. "It's the only way they have of traveling here."

The detective shook his head. "If I tell them that back at the precinct, they'll think I'm on the snow myself. Why don't they get wised up and use a heap? Say, Shea, maybe we could dope one out for them! It wouldn't have to be no gold-plated boiler, just something that would buzz. These jakes always go for the big sounding show."

"It wouldn't work here, even if we could build it," said Shea. "Any more than your gun. You want to remember that nothing that hasn't been invented yet will."

He turned to watch the serfs carrying out armfuls of deerskin blankets and vast sacks of food, which they lashed in position with rawhide ropes. Two of them trundled out a keg of beer and added it to the heap. It looked as though the Elk of Hiisi would have his work cut out for him; but, gazing at the gigantic beast, Shea decided that it looked capable of meeting the demand. Lemminkainen bawled orders about the stowing of the gear and warmer clothes for Bayard and Brodsky, whose twentieth-century garments he regarded with unconcealed contempt.

Presently the tasks were done. All the serfs came out of the building and formed in a line, with Lemminkainen's two women in the middle. He kissed them smackingly, shouted the others into the sled, and jumped in himself. It immediately became crowded. As he cracked his whip and the giant reindeer strained forward, the whole line of serfs and women lifted their heads back and burst into a high-pitched doleful chanting. Most of them seemed to have forgotten the words of what they were supposed to be singing, and those who remembered were off key.

"Marry!" said Belphebe. "Glad am I, Harold, that these farewells do not come often."

"So am I," said Shea behind his hand, "but it gets Lemminkainen. The mug's eyes actually have tears in them!"

"I wish my schnozz was okay again," said Brodsky. "I used to could make them fill a bucket with eye-juice when I gave them 'Mother Machree.' "

"Then I'm rather glad you got the polyp or whatever it is that prevents you doing it now," said Bayard, and grabbed the side of the sled, as the Elk of Hiisi went into a swinging trot and the sled bounced and skidded along the muddy track northward.

"Now, listen..." began Brodsky, but just at this moment a flying clod of mud from the animal's hooves took him squarely in the face. "Jesus!" he shouted, then with a glance at Belphebe, "Write it on the ice, will you, lady? That was such a nut-buster I forgot for a minute that we gotta take what's laid out for us in the Lord's book, even if he throws the whole package at us."

Lemminkainen turned his head. "Strange the language of Ouhaio," he said, "but if I hit rightly your saying, O Piit, it is that none may escape the course laid down for him."

"You got it," said Brodsky.

"Then," said the hero, "if one but knew the incantations, one might call forth the spirits of the future to tell what will come of any doing."

"No, wait..." began Brodsky, but Shea said, "They can in some continua."

Bayard said, "It might be worth trying in this one, Harold. If the thought pattern is right, as you put it, the ability to see consequences might keep us out of a lot of trouble. Don't you think that with your magic..."

They hit a stone just then, and Shea collapsed into the lap of Belphebe, the only member of the party who had been able to find a place to sit in the jouncing sled. It was not that the road was worse than before, but the strain of hanging on and being bumped made it too difficult to talk. The trunks of birch and fir fled past them, close by on both sides, like the palings of a fence, the branches closing off all but fugitive glimpses of the sky overhead. The road zigzagged slightly—not, so far as Shea could determine, for topographic reasons, since the country was flat as an ironing board—because it had never been surveyed. Now and then the forest would clear a little on one side and a farmhouse or a small lake would appear among the trees. Once they met another sled, horse-drawn, and everybody had to dismount and manhandle the vehicles past each other.

At last, as they reached one of the lakes, Lemminkainen reined in his singular draft-animal, said, "Pause we here a while for eating," jumped out and began to rummage among the food bags.

When he had consumed one of the usual gargantuan snacks, belched and wiped his mouth with the back of his hand, he announced, "Valtarpayart and Piit, I have allowed you to accompany me on this journey, but learn that for all your arts, you will be worse than useless unless you learn how to fight. I have brought swords for you, and as we take our ease, you shall learn to use them under the greatest master in all Kalevala."

He dragged a pair of clumsy, two-edged blades out of the baggage and handed one to each, then sat down on a root, evidently prepared to enjoy himself. "Cut at him, O Valtarpayart!" he said. "Try to take his head off."

"Hey!" said Shea, with a glance at the woebegone faces of his companions. "This won't do. They don't know anything about this business and they're likely to cut each other up. Honest."

Lemminkainen leaned back. "Or they learn the swordsman's business, or they go with me no further."

"But you said they could come. That isn't fair."

"It is not in our agreement," said the hero firmly. "They came only by my permission, and that has run out. Either they practice with the swords or turn homeward."

He looked as though he meant it, too, and Shea was forced to admit that legally he was right. But Belphebe said, "In Faerie, when we would teach young springalds the use of blades without danger to themselves, we use swords of wooden branch."

After some persuasion, Lemminkainen agreed to accept this as a substitute. The pair were presently whaling away at each other under his scornful correction with single-sticks made from saplings, and lengths of cloth wound round their hands for protection. Bayard was taller and had the better reach; but Brodsky's jujitsu training had made him so quick that several times he rapped his opponent smartly, and at last brought home a backhand blow on the arm that made Bayard drop his stick.

"An arm was lost that time," said Lemminkainen. "Ah, well—I suppose not everyone can be such a swordsman and hero as Kaukomieli."

He turned away to harness up the reindeer again. Belphebe laid a hand on Shea's arm to keep him from reminding the hero of their own little bout.

The afternoon was a repetition of the morning's journey through country that did not change, and whose appearance was becoming as monotonous as the bumping that accompanied their progress. Shea was not surprised when even Lemminkainen wanted to camp early. With Bayard and Brodsky he set about building a triangular lean-to of branches, while Belphebe and the hero wandered off into the woods in search of fresh game for their evening meal.

While they were picking the bones of some birds that resembled a chicken in size and a grouse in flavor, Lemminkainen explained that he had to make this journey to Pohjola because he had learned by magic that they were holding a great wedding feast there and he had not been invited.

"Crashing the party, eh?" said Brodsky. "I don't get it. Why don't you just give those muzzlers the air?"

"It would decrease my reputation," said Lemminkainen. "And besides, there will be a great making of magic. I should undoubtedly lose some of my magical powers if I allowed them to do this unquestioned."

Belphebe said, "We have bargained to accompany you, Sir Lemminkainen, and I do not seek to withdraw. But if there are so many present as will be at a great feast, I do not see how even with we four, you are much better than you would be alone."

Lemminkainen gave a roar of laughter. "O you maiden, O Pelviipi, you are surely not quick-witted. For all magics there must be a beginning. From you and your bowstring I could raise a hundred archers; from the active Harolainen set in line a thousand swordsmen—but not until you yourselves were present."

"He's right, kid," said Shea. "That's good sympathetic magic. I remember Doc Chalmers giving me a lecture on it once. What have you got there?"

Lemminkainen had picked up several of the long wing and tail feathers from the outsize grouse and was carefully smoothing them out. His face took on the expression of exaggerated foxiness it had worn once or twice before.

"In Pohjola they now surely know that the greatest of heroes and magicians approaches," he said. "It is well to be prepared for all encounters with something that can be used." He tucked the feathers in one of his capacious pockets, glanced at the fire, which was beginning to show brightly in the gathering dusk, and lumbered off to bed.

Bayard said, "It strikes me, Harold, that the magic in this continuum is quantitatively greater and qualitatively more potent than any you have reported before. And if Lemminkainen can turn you into a thousand swordsmen, can't the other people do something like that? I should say it's rather dangerous."

"I was just thinking of that," said Shea, and went to bed himself.

The next day was a repetition of the first, except that Brodsky and Bayard were so stiff they could barely drag themselves from their deerskin blankets to go through the sword-exercises on which Lemminkainen insisted before breakfast. There was not much conversation in the sled, but when they assembled around the fire in the evening, Lemminkainen entertained them with a narrative of his exploits until Shea and Belphebe wandered off out of earshot.

It was followed by more of the same. On the fifth day, the singlestick practice at noon had progressed so far that Lemminkainen himself took a hand and promptly knocked Brodsky out. It appeared to improve relations all around; the detective took it in good part, and the hero was in the best of humor that evening.

But soon after the start the next morning, he began weaving his head from side to side with a peering expression and sniffing. "What's the trouble?" asked Shea.

"I smell magic—the strong magic of Pohjola. Look sharp, Valtarpayart."

They did not have to look very sharp. A glow soon became visible through the trees, which presently opened out to reveal a singular spectacle. Stretching down from the right and losing itself round a turn in the distance, came a depression like a dry river bed. But instead of water this depression was filled with a fiery red shimmer, and the stones and sand of the bottom were glowing like red-hot metal. On the far side of this phenomenon rose a sharp peak of rock, where sat an eagle as big as a beach cottage.

As Shea shielded his face against the scorch, the eagle rotated its head and gazed speculatively at the party.

There was no necessity to rein in the Elk of Hiisi. Lemminkainen turned to Bayard. "What do you see, eyes of Ouhaiola?"

"A red-hot pavement that looks like the floor of Hell, and an eagle several times the size of a natural one. There's a kind of shimmer—no, they're both there, all right."

The giant bird slowly stretched one wing. "Oh-oh," said Shea. "You were right, Walter. This is..."

Belphebe leaped from the sled, tested the wind with an uplifted finger and began to string her bow; Brodsky looked round and round, pugnacious but helpless.

Lemminkainen said, "Save your arrows, dainty Pelviipi. I myself, the mighty wizard, know a trick worth two of this one."

The monster eagle leaped into the air. Shea said, "I hope you know what you're doing, Kauko," and whipped out his epee, feeling how inadequate it was. It was no longer than one of the bird's talons and nowhere near so thick.

The eagle soared, spiraled upward, and then began to come down on them in a prodigious power dive as Bayard gasped. But Lemminkainen left his own weapon hanging where it was, contenting himself with tossing into the air the feathers of the big grouse, chanting a little staccato ditty whose words Shea could not catch.

The feathers turned themselves into a flock of grouse, which shot off slantwise with a motorcycle whirr. The eagle, almost directly over them—Shea could see the little movements of its wing-tips and tail-feathers as it balanced itself on the air—gave a piercing shriek, flapped its wings, and shot off after the grouse. Soon it was out of sight beyond the treetops westward.

"Now it is to be seen that I am not less than the greatest of magicians," said Lemminkainen, sticking out his chest. "But this spelling is wearisome work, and there lies before us this river of fire. Harol, you are a wizard. Do you make a spell against it while I restore myself with food."

Shea stood gazing at the redness and pondered. The glowing flicker had a hypnotic effect, like a dying wood fire. A good downpour ought to do the trick; he began recalling a rain spell he and Chalmers had been working up, in the hope of putting down the flaming barrier around Castle Carena during their adventures in the world of the *Orlando Furioso*.

He muttered his spell and made the passes. Nothing happened.

"Well?" said Lemminkainen, with his mouth full of bread and cheese. "When does the spell begin?"

"I tried," said Shea, puzzled, "but..."

"Fool of Ouhaiola! Must I teach you your business? How do you expert a spell to work when you do not sing it?"

That's right, thought Shea. He had forgotten that in this Kalevalan magic, song was an indispensable feature. With his own ability at versification, the passes Lemminkainen did not know how to make, and singing, this spell ought to be a humdinger. He lifted his arms for the passes again and sang at the top of his voice.

The spell was a humdinger. As he finished it, something black seemed to loom overhead, and the landscape was instantly blotted out by a shower of soot lumps as heavy and tenacious as snowflakes. Shea hastily cancelled the spell.

"Truly, a wonderful wizard!" cried Lemminkainen, coughing and trying to slap the clinging stuff from his clothes. "Now that he has shown us how to make soot of the river of fire, perhaps he will tell us how to bring fog to Pohjola!"

"Nay," said Belphebe, "you shall not be so graceless to my lord. I declare him an approved sorcerer—but not if he must sing, for he cannot carry one note beyond the next." She reached out one hand comfortingly.

Brodsky said, "If I could flag down a right croaker to fix my schnozz, maybe we could work something together."

"I must even do it myself then," said Lemminkainen. He tossed soot-contaminated beer from his mug, drew a fresh fill from the keg, took a prodigious swig, leaned back, meditated a moment, and sang:

> *Ice of Sariola's mountains,*
> *Ice of ten years' snow compacted,*
> *Forged into Turja's glaciers,*
> *Glaciers ever downward flowing,*
> *In the sea with thunder breaking...*

For a while it was not clear what he was driving at. Then a shimmering something appeared in the air over the fiery trench, and gradually hardened with a sparkle of color. A bridge of ice!

But just as Lemminkainen reached the climax of his song which should have materialized the ice and welded it into a solid structure, there was a slip. Down into the trench roared the bridge of ice in fragments, to shatter and hiss and fill the landscape with vapor.

Lemminkainen looked sour and started again. Everyone else held his breath, watching. This time the bridge melted and vanished even before it was complete.

With a yell of rage, Lemminkainen hurled his cap on the ground and danced on it. Bayard laughed.

"You mock me!" screamed the wizard. "Outland filth!" He snatched up his beer mug from where he had put it and flung the contents in Bayard's face.

There was less than an inch of beer remaining, but even so it was enough to produce a lively display of suds.

"No!" cried Shea, reaching for his epee as Belphebe grabbed her bow.

But instead of leaping up in anger, instead of even wiping the beer from his face, Bayard was staring fixedly at the trench of fire, blinking and knitting his eyebrows. At last he said, "It's an illusion after all! There isn't anything there but a row of little peat fires made to look big and only burning in spots. But I don't see how I came to miss it before."

Shea said, "Must be the alcohol in the beer. The illusion was so strong that you couldn't see through it until you got the stuff in your eyes. That happened to me once in the continuum of the Norse gods."

"The spells of Pohjola grow stronger as we approach their stronghold," said Lemminkainen, his anger forgotten. "But what counsel shall we take now? For I am too undone with spell working to undertake the labor of breaking so powerful a magic."

"We could wait till tomorrow when you'd have your punch back," suggested Shea.

Lemminkainen shook his head. "They of Pohjola will surely know what has happened here, and if we are checked by one magic, another and stronger will grow behind, so that at each step the way becomes more impassable. But if now we break through, then their magic becomes weaker."

"Look here," said Bayard. "I think I can resolve this. If you'll give me some beer for eyewash, I can lead the way through. There's plenty of space, even for the sled."

The Elk of Hiisi snorted and balked, but Lemminkainen was firm with him as Bayard walked ahead, dipping his handkerchief in a mug of beer and applying it to his eyes. Shea found that although he was uncomfortably warm, he was not being cooked as he expected; nor did the sled show any signs of taking fire.

On the far side, they went up a little slope and halted. Bayard started back toward the sled and then halted, pointing at a tall dead pine. "That's a man!" he cried.

Lemminkainen leaped clumsily from the sled, tugging at his sword, Shea and Brodsky right behind him. As they approached the pine, its branches seemed to collapse with a gentle swoosh; then they were looking at a stocky man of about Lemminkainen's own proportions, his face wearing an expression of sullen bitterness.

"I had thought there must be someone near us for illusion-making," roared Lemminkainen, happily. "Bow your head, magician of Pohjola."

The man looked around quickly and desperately. "I am Vuohinen the champion, and I challenge," he said.

"What does he mean?" asked Shea.

"A true champion may always challenge, even in another's house," said Lmminkainen. "Whoever wins may take off the head of the other or make him his serf. Which of us do you challenge?"

Vuohinen the champion looked from one to the other and pointed to Bayard. "This one. What is his art?"

"No," said Lemminkainen, "for his art is the seeing eye that penetrates all magics, and if you challenge him, you have already lost, since he penetrated your disguise. You may have Harol here, with the point-sword—or the shieldmaiden Pelviipi with the bow, or Piit in wrestle, or myself with the broadsword." He grinned.

Vuohinen looked from one to the other. "Of the point-sword I know nothing," he said, "and while there is doubtless no bowman in the world half as good as myself, I have other uses for women than slaying them. I choose Piit in open wrestle."

"And not the lively Kaukomieli!" said Lemminkainen with a laugh. "You think you have chosen safely. But you shall see what unusual arts lie among the outland friends of Kalevala. Will you wrestle with him, Piit?"

"Okay," said Brodsky, and began shucking his shirt. Vuohinen already had his off.

They circled, swinging their arms like a pair of indifferently educated apes. Shea noticed that Vuohinen's arms reminded him of the tires of a semi-trailer truck, and the detective looked puny beside him. Then Vuohinen jumped and grabbed. Brodsky caught him by the shoulders and threw himself backward, placing the sole of his foot against Vuohinen's midriff and shoving upward as he fell, so that his antagonist flew over him and landed heavily on his back.

Lemminkainen gave a bellow of laughter. "I will make a song about this!" he shouted.

Vuohinen got up somewhat slowly and scowling. This time he came in more cautiously, then when at arm's length from Brodsky, suddenly threw himself at the detective, the fingers of his left hand spread straight for the other's eyes. Shea, heard Belphebe gasp, but even as she gasped, Brodsky jerked his head back and, with a quickness wonderful to behold, seized the thumb of the clawing hand in one of his, the little finger in the other and, bracing himself, twisted powerfully.

There was a crack; Vuohinen pinwheeled through the air and came down on his side, then sat up, his face contorted with pain, feeling with the other hand of a wrist and fingers that hung limp.

"There was a creep in Chi tried to pull that rat caper on me once," said Brodsky pleasantly. "Want any more, or have you got the chill?"

"It was a trick," Vuohinen bleated. "With a sword..."

Lemminkainen stepped forward cheerfully. "Do you wish his head as trophy or himself to serve you daily?"

"Aw," said Brodsky, "I suppose he ain't much use as a patsy with that busted duke, but let's let him score for the break. The pastor would put the run on me if I hit him with the lily." He walked over to Vuohinen and kicked him deliberately. "That's for the rat caper. Get up!"

Vuohinen made the sled more crowded than ever and, as Brodsky had said, was of no great value as a servant, but he did make lighter the job of collecting firewood in the evening. Moreover, Brodsky's victory had improved relations with Lemminkainen. He still insisted that Bayard practice daily with the detective—they were at the point where they used real swords now—but now the hero himself practiced jujitsu falls and holds and tumbles almost daily. He was an apt pupil, too.

Around the travelers the air was colder; plumes of vapor appeared at their nostrils and those of the reindeer. The sun never seemed to break through the overcast any more. The trees became sparser and stunted, growing scattered among little grassy hillocks. Sometimes Belphebe brought home no game at all in the evening. More often than not, it would be two or three rabbits, which sent Lemminkainen back to the stored provisions after he had eaten his share.

Still the sled bumped and slid along the muddy track northward, until one afternoon, as they came over a little hill from behind a group of trees, Lemminkainen cried, "Great Jumala! Look at that!"

Before them, stretching out of sight in both directions a prodigious fence ran across the valley. A row of palings, less than a foot apart and reaching almost to the low cloud canopy; but it was the sight of the horizontal members that really made Shea's scalp prickle. For the palings were bound together by an immense mass of snakes, wound together in and out, though whether they got that way because they wanted to or because someone had tied them in that grotesque fashion, it was impossible to tell.

As the sled slid up, the reindeer shying and trembling, the snakes turned their heads toward the party and began hissing like a thousand teakettles.

"It must be an illusion," said Bayard, "though at present I can't see anything but that mass of serpents. Give me some beer." Lemminkainen drew some of the fluid from the cask. Vuohinen's face held a sneer of triumph. The reason was apparent as soon as Bayard dabbed the liquid in his eyes, stared at the remarkable fence again, and shook his head.

"They still look like serpents to me," he said. "I know it can't be true, but there they are."

Shea said, "Couldn't we just assume they're fakes and cut our way through?"

Lemminkainen shook his head. "Learn, O Harol of Ouhaio, that within this field of magic everything has all the powers of its seeming unless its true name be known."

"I see. And we're now right into Pohjola, where their magic is really strong. You couldn't try a spell yourself to take this one off, whatever it is?"

"Not unless I know the real name beneath this false seeming," said the hero.

"Maybe we can play it straight," said Shea, and turning to Belphebe, "How about trying a shot with your bow at one of those beasties? The way I understand it, if you killed one, it would have to return to its proper form."

"Not so, O Harolainen," said Lemminkainen. "It would be a dead serpent merely until we learned its true form. And there are thousands."

They gazed at the spectacle for a moment or two. It was fairly revolting, but the snakes made no movement to leave their position.

Suddenly Pete Brodsky said, "Hey! I got a idea."

"What is it?" asked Shea.

Brodsky jerked a thumb toward Vuohinen. "This gummy belongs to me, don't he?"

"Under the laws of this country, I believe that's right," said Shea, and "He is your serf," said Lemminkainen.

"And he's on this magic lay in this joint?"

Shea said, "Why, so he is, now that you mention it. He must have been the one who worked the river of fire and the eagle."

Brodsky reached a hand out and grabbed Vuohinen by the collar. "All right, punk! What's the right name for them potato-water dreams out there?"

"Awk!" said Vuohinen. "Never will I be a traitor..."

"Bag your head on that stuff. Come across with the right dope, or I'll have shorty here let you have it." He pointed significantly to the sword that hung at Lemminkainen's side.

"Awk!" said Vuohinen again, as the hand twisted in his collar. "They are—made from lingonberries."

Walter Bayard said, "Why, so they are!" He walked across to the hissing, snarling barrier, reached out his hand, twisted the head off one of the serpents, and ate it.

Lemminkainen laughed. "Now there will be a removing of spells, and then we shall have lingonberry dessert to our meal. I thank you, friend Piit."

7

The lingonberry wall came down to a tangled mat of vegetation under Lemminkainen's ministrations and they camped just beyond. The hero was in hilarious humor, making a series of jokes which nobody but Brodsky found diverting, and shouting with laughter over his own sallies, until Shea said,

"For the love of Mike, Kauko, what's got into you tonight? You sound as though you had just won the first prize."

"And have I not, Harol? For I know well that we are through the last barrier that Louhi can throw against us, and tomorrow we shall arrive at Pohjola's hall—perhaps to fight."

Shea said, "I can see that would be just about the best thing that ever happened."

He himself didn't feel the same way, not even in the morning when they began to sight tilled fields with a few domestic animals. Presently there was a stead of considerable size visible among the tops of the low trees. Lemminkainen clucked at the Elk of Hiisi, and the giant reindeer pulled up beside a slow stream that wound across the featureless landscape.

The hero dug into the duffel at the rear of the sled for his shirt of scale-mail and put it on. "For you, my friends," he said, "I have brought armor second in quality only to my own."

He dragged out four sleeveless hip length jackets of a double thickness of leather, tanned so stiff that Shea found it was all he could do to get into the thing. It was just as heavy as a well-made steel cuirass would have been, far more clumsy and less effective, but he supposed the metallurgy of Kalevala would not be up to such an article. Belphebe wriggled out of hers almost as soon as she was in it. "Marry," she said, "you may keep your beetle's bodice, Sir Lemminkainen. I shall need free arms if I'm to go to war."

Lemminkainen produced for each of them a skull cap of the same thick leather, with a strip of iron around the rim and a pair of semicircular strips that sprang from it to meet at the top of the wearer's head. These fitted better, though Brodsky's gave him the odd effect of wearing a rimless derby hat.

They climbed back into the sled. The Elk of Hiisi splashed across the little stream toward a group of buildings. Brodsky pointed, "These Hoosiers sure play it for the works. Look at them sconces!"

Shea saw that a nearby hillock was decorated with a row of stakes—about fifty, he judged—each stake surmounted by a severed human head. The heads were in various stages of decrepitude; only one stake, at the end of the line, lacked its gruesome ornament. A score of ravens flew croaking up from the heads as they approached, and Bayard remarked, "I'm glad there's only one vacancy."

Vuohinen said sourly, "You will soon learn how little the stakes of Pohjola are exhausted."

Lemminkainen pivoted round, hit him a solid back-hand blow on the ear, and said, "Now my friends, you shall see that the handsome Kaukomieli is not less skillful with magic than he is with the sword."

He brought the reindeer to a halt, leaped to the ground and, pulling a number of twigs from the stunted trees, began arranging them in rows, crooning to himself. Presently there were enough twigs to satisfy him; he stepped back, and his voice rose higher as he made a series of passes with his hands. Shea could see that they were sound magic, of a type he had seen in other space-time continua, but the hero moved too rapidly for him to follow the precise pattern. Then there was a little rush of air and, where the first twig had been, Shea was looking at a replica of himself, complete with epee, leather jacket, and ironbound cap.

Another, and another, and another Shea flashed into being, a whole row of Harold Sheas, who at once began to crowd round the sled.

Belphebe gave a little squeal. "Am I wed to all of these?" she cried. But, as she did so, the quota of Sheas was apparently filled up, and Belphebes began to leap from the ground where Lemminkainen had arranged his twigs. They mingled with the simulacra of Shea as the magician's voice went up one more tone, and copies of Brodsky joined the growing crowd, shaking hands and clapping one another on the back.

Lemminkainen's song came to an end; the sled was surrounded by at least a hundred replicas of the three. In it remained one Lemminkainen, one sour-looking Vuohinen, and a single Bayard. Bayard said, "A brilliant piece of work, Lemminkainen, but could these reproductions actually cut somebody up, or are they phantoms? They look all right to me, but I haven't tried it with beer in my eye."

"Seek to wrestle with one of these Plits, and you shall see," said Lemminkainen. "They will have all the strength of life unless someone finds which is the real one and which the shadow and make a counter-spell, using the true name of the one."

"Wait a minute," said Bayard. "Haven't we got someone here who can identify all these people for the Pohjolans?" He pointed at Vuohinen.

"By the mill!" said Lemminkainen. "It is clear that I am wise as well as brave, for no one else would have thought to bring on this journey a person so capable of seeing through millstones as yourself. Piit, Harol, Pelviipi, you must mingle with your other selves and let some of those other selves come upon the sled, lest these people of Turja find the true ones."

Shea stared a second, then said to Belphebe: "He's right, kid. See you later." He squeezed her hand and jumped over the side into the mob. Walter came with him. "I don't want to lose sight of the real one myself," he said.

Behind them, three or four Brodskys tried to climb into the sled at once. The one who made it first promptly kicked Vuohinen. "Get wise, punk," he said. "Pull any fast ones on me, and I'll let you have it,"

Shea observed that, while the various Brodskys had formed a compact group to march behind the sled, chattering with each other, most of the reproductions of himself and Belphebe had paired off. One of the unengaged ones sidled up to him and pressed his hand. It couldn't be the real one, and yet her touch was as cool and her step as light as though it were. It occurred to him that unless someone pronounced the counter-spell fairly soon, some neat marital problems would arise in a continuum that contained about thirty-five Sheas and as many Belphebes, all presumably supplied with the due quota of emotions.

Bayard said, "There's one point, Harold. It seems to me that it should be possible to tell within easily determinable limits how our presence here will affect the outcome of the epic. We have all the elements. We know what happened in the original story, and we have fairly accurate information about ourselves. It seems to me that an equation could be set up..."

"Yeah, for one of those electronic thinking machines," said Shea. "Only we don't happen to have one, and if we did, it wouldn't work."

"There was a witch once in Faerie," said the Belphebe by his side, "that warned people from danger after she had looked in a pool by magic and seen to where a course would lead."

"That's what I mean," said Bayard. "Apparently you can do things by magic in this continuum that a calculating machine couldn't think of equalling. Now if before we start something—say going into that hall there—we found out it was going to turn out badly, then we could change it to the right kind of future by taking another action."

"That's a bum steer," said one of the Brodskys, who had fallen into step with them. "Get smart, will you? Everything that's gonna happen has been put on the line by God ever since the clock began to tick. It says so in the Bible."

"Listen, my predestinarian friend," said Bayard, "I shall be glad to prove the contrary..."

"Not with magic," said Shea. "You're the only one it doesn't affect now, and if you got to working spells, you might lose your immunity. Hey, they've spotted us."

A man was running, shouting, toward one of the buildings from which came sounds of revelry. The door of this building opened as the sled came to a stop, and several broad, black-bearded faces appeared in the opening. Shea saw one of the other Sheas put an arm around a Belphebe and felt a quite illogical pang of jealousy over the thought that this might be the real one.

Lemminkainen jumped out of the sled, followed by Shea, a Belphebe and a Brodsky, who clamped a wrist lock on Vuohinen. Men began to file out of the hall stand opposite the company of visitors, who drew up a rough line. They looked much like other Kalevalans though perhaps even shorter and with more Mongoloid faces. They were armed and looked thoroughly unpleasant. Shea felt a prickling at the back of his neck an loosened his epee in its scabbard.

But Lemminkainen looked unimpressed. "Hail, my cousins of Pohjola!"

he said. "Do you wish to keep me standing here outside the hall of feasting?"

Nobody answered him; instead, more of them came frowning out. Lemminkainen turned.

"Fair Pelviipi," he said, "show them your art, that they may learn how silly it is to oppose the friends of the heroic Kaukomieli."

As though actuated by a single brain, thirty-five Belphebes, placed one foot each against the ends of the bows and snapped the strings into place. Like so many Rockettes, they each placed an arrow in the string, too one pace back, and looked around for a target. One the ravens from the palisade of heads chose that moment to come flapping over, with a loud "Kr-awk."

Thirty-five bowstrings twanged; the raven came tumbling downward, looking like a pincushion, transfix by all the arrows that could find room in its carcass "Nice work, kid," said Shea, before he realized he was talking to a simulacrum.

It impressed the Pohjolans, too. There was a quick, low-toned gabbling among them, and a couple disappeared inside. In a moment they were back and the company began to disappear through the door. Lemminkainen said, "Follow me!" and stamped up behind them. Shea hurried, not wishing to be left outside, and reached the door simultaneously with the Shea who had been in the sled.

"Sorry," said the other Shea, "but I came here to go to this party with my wife."

"She's my wife, too," said Shea, grabbing a Belphebe at random and leading her through the door behind the other couple. Thank Heaven, there were enough of them to go round.

Inside, several rushlights flickered. A fire blazed on the central hearth, to some extent counteracting the inadequate illumination characteristic of Kalevalan houses. The whole long hall was crowded with benches and tables, at which sat scores of men and quite a few women. All heads were turned toward the newcomers.

Shea's eyes followed Lemminkainen's toward the center of the hall, where a table with some space about it was apparently the place of honor. At it sat the tallest Kalevalan Shea had ever seen; this was undoubtedly the bridegroom. There was a sharp-featured, snag-toothed, muscular-looking woman—Louhi, the Mistress of Pohjola, no doubt. The stout man with his eyes drooping sleepily and a mug of drink before him must be the Master of Pohjola. The girl with the fancy beaded headdress was probably the bride, Louhi's daughter.

The duplicate Shea touched him on the arm. "Even nicer dish than Kylliki, isn't she?" he whispered. It was odd to have one's own thoughts come back at one out of one's own mouth.

Lemminkainen strode to the nearest bench, reached out and pitched the last man on it to the floor. Then he slammed his muddy boot down on the bench and shouted:

> *Greetings to you on my coming,*
> *Greetings also to the greeter!*
> *Hearken, Pohjola's great Master,*
> *Have ye here within this dwelling,*
> *Beer to offer to the hero?*

Louhi dug her elbow into her husband's ribs. He forced his eyes open, gave a grunt and replied, "If you care to stand quietly over there in the corner, between the kettles, where the hoes are hanging, we will not prevent you."

Lemminkainen laughed, but it was an angry laugh. "Seems to me that I'm unwelcome," he chanted:

> *As no ale is offered to me,*
> *To the guest who has just entered.*

"No guest you," cried Louhi, "but a troublemaking boy, not fit to sit among your elders. Well, if you seek trouble, by Ukko, you shall find it!"

"Yes?" said Lemminkainen, sitting down heavily on the bench.

> *Pohjola's illustrious Mistress,*
> *Long-toothed Mistress of Pimentola,*
> *Thou hast held the wedding badly,*
> *And in doggish fashion held it...*

He chanted on, comparing Louhi to various species of unpleasant fauna and extending the compliments to most of her guests. There seemed to be a routine about this sort of thing, Shea decided; the others merely sat, waiting till Lemminkainen had finished.

Behind him he heard the duplicate Shea say to Bayard, "All right, I admit it might work, and it's within the laws of magic. But if anybody's going to try it, you better let me. You just haven't had enough experience with it, Walter."

He whirled. "What might work?"

His twin said, "Walter's been watching Lemminkainen, and thinks he's worked out a magical method for determining the future results of a given series of events."

"I just want to show up this predestination business for..." began Bayard.

"Sssh," said the duplicate Shea. "They've finished saying hello. Here comes the floor show."

The Master of Pohjola had at last opened his eyes fully and was chanting a spell. In the space between the table of honor and the hearth, there appeared a pool of water. The Master cried:

> *Here's a river thou mayst drink of,*
> *Here's a pool that thou mayst splash in!*

"Ha, ha!" bellowed Lemminkainen.

> *I'm no calf by women driven,*
> *Nor a bull with tail behind me,*
> *That I drink of river water,*
> *Or of filthy ponds the water.*

His tone went lower, and without apparent effort he sang up an enormous ox, under whose hooves the floor creaked alarmingly. The ox, after a vague look around the company, began schlooping up the water by the bucketful.

Shea said to his Belphebe, "Probably brought up in somebody's parlor, so he doesn't think a thing about it."

The Master of Pohjola was already at work on a new spell. Its result was a great gray wolf, which took one look at the ox and bounded toward it. The ox gave a bawl of terror, whirled, and thundered toward the door, while the Pohjolans fell over one another to get out of the way. It plunged through, taking part of the doorframe with it, and vanished, with the wolf right behind.

Louhi sneered. "You are vanquished in the contest of magic, O Kaukomieli! Now begone, or ever worse come upon you."

"No man who deserves the name would let himself be driven from any place where he chose to stay," said Lemminkainen, "least of all a hero like myself. I challenge."

The Master stood up. He moved lightly for so beefy an individual. "Let us then measure our swords together to see which is the better."

Lemminkainen grinned and drew his broadsword. "Little of my sword is left me, for on bones it has been shattered. But come, let us measure them."

The Master crossed over to the wall and took his sword from a peg. The Belphebe next to Shea said, "Shall I notch a shaft?"

"I don't think so," he replied. "It's not likely to turn into a general riot unless somebody breaks the rules. They're too nervous about those bows."

The contenders were measuring their swords in the cleared space. From where he stood, it seemed to Shea that the Master's was a trifle longer. The guests crowded forward to watch, while those behind yelled to them to sit down. At last the Master ordered them back to their seats.

"And you newcomers, too!" he shouted. "Back against the wall!"

That seemed to remind Lemminkainen of something. He said, "Before that we work out our challenge, I will challenge any present—to the point-sword against my companion Harol, or to the wrestle with my companion Piit. It will be rare sport to watch, after I have disposed of you."

The duplicate Shea said, "Isn't he generous?" But one of the Belphebes put her hand on his arm and he felt better.

"You will be watching no more sports," said the Master. "Are you ready?"

"I am ready," said Lemminkainen.

The Master leaped forward, swinging his sword up for a tremendous overhand cut, as if he were serving a tennis ball. The blow was never completed, however, for the sword blade struck a rafter overhead with a loud chunk. Lemminkainen made a pass at his opponent, who leaped backward with wonderful agility.

Lemminkainen roared with laughter, saying, "What has the rafter done to you, that you should punish it? But that is always the way with little men when confronted by a true hero. Come, there's too little room in here. And do you not think that your blood would look prettier on the grass outside?"

He turned and shouldered his way toward the door. As Shea followed him, Lemminkainen leaned close and, with his foxy expression, whispered, "I think that some of them are false seemings. Let you friend Payart watch sharply."

Before Shea could reply, the others were coming. Outside, the phantom company sat or stood on the grass, talking. Shea wondered whether, when the spell came off, he would find himself remembering what the others had said. He wished he had Doc Chalmers around; there were times when this magic business got pretty complicated for an incomplete enchanter.

The Master and Lemminkainen halted in the yard, between the main house and the hillock with its head-decorated row of stakes. A couple of serfs brought a big cowhide, which they laid on the grass to provide securer footing. Lemminkainen took his stance at one edge of it, stamping his feet to test the give of the hide. He jerked his thumb toward the heads, saying, "When we finish, that last stake will no longer feel ashamed of its nakedness. Are you ready?"

"I am ready," said the Master of Pohjola.

Shea glanced at his companions. The version of Belphebe nearest him was watching with an intent, studious expression that showed duels were nothing particularly new to her. One of the Brodskys said, "Shea, this may be for the monkeys, but these birds are no flukers. If we could make TV with this show, there'd be enough scratch in it to…"

"Sh!" said Bayard. "I'm concentrating."

Clang! went the blades, the Master of Pohjola forcing the attack. His longer blade flashed overhand, forehand, backhand. "Wonderful wrists," said one of the phantom Sheas. Lemminkainen, not giving an inch, was parrying every swing. There was little footwork in this style of swordplay. They faced each other squarely, hewing as if trying to fell trees, pausing occasionally for a rest, then slashing away again.

Once the Master's blade came down on Lemminkainen's shoulder, but at a slight angle, so that the scale mail slipped the blow aside. Then Lemminkainen got in a cut at the Master's neck that the latter did not quite parry in time. Blood trickled from a small cut.

"Ho, ho!" cried Lemminkainen. "Hearken, Master of Pohjola, true it is, your neck so wretched is as red as dawn of morning!"

The Master, stepping back half a pace, rolled his eyes downward for a fraction of a second as though to assess the damage. Instantly Lemminkainen, advancing so fast that Shea could not quite see how he did it, struck again. The blade went right through the Master's neck. The head, turning over in the air, fell in a graceful parabola, and the body, half-twisting as the legs buckled under it, fell spouting upon the cowhide. There was a gasping groan from the crowd. Louhi shrieked.

Lemminkainen, grinning until it seemed as though his mouth must meet behind, like Humpty-Dumpty's, cried: "So much for the heroes of Pohjola!"

He stepped forward, wiped his blade with care on the trousers of the corpse, and sheathed it. Then he picked up the head and strutted to the empty stake.

"Now, wicked wretches, fetch me beer!" he bellowed.

Shea turned to say something to the nearest Belphebe. It was not until that moment that he remembered Bayard had said, "I'm concentrating." He turned around and looked. Sure enough, there was Bayard, his back to the arresting spectacle of␣emminkainen's victory march, crouched on the ground over a little pile of grasses. He seemed to be muttering to himself; a tiny curl of smoke came from the pile.

"Walter, no!" shouted Shea, and dived for him. Too late.

There was a little flash of fire, a sound of displaced air, and in an instant all the duplicate Sheas, Belphebes and Brodskys had vanished. As Shea and Bayard rolled over together, they heard Lemminkainen's shout, "Fool! Bungler! Traitor! Your spell has cancelled mine. The agreement is ended!"

Shea pulled himself to his knees in time to see the hero walking, not running, toward the sled with his sword out. Nobody seemed anxious to be the first to stop him.

Down toward the edge of what had been the Pohjolan cheering section around the combatants, there was a half-muffled cry, and out of a struggling group projected a leg, dainty even in the shapeless garment.

"Belphebe!" shouted Shea, getting to his feet and tugging at his sword with the same motion. Before he could get the epee out of its scabbard, he too went down under a swarm of bodies. He had just time to notice that they didn't bathe often enough and that Brodsky had laid out one of the assailants with a neat crack of his blackjack, and then he was hopelessly pinioned, being marched along beside Bayard.

"Put them in the strong-house!" said the Mistress of Pohjola. Her face did not look as though she intended it to be a place of entertainment.

As the captives were frog-marched along, Shea saw the Elk of Hiisi retreating into the distance, with the sled bouncing along behind him.

8

The four were tumbled unceremoniously over each other on to a stone floor. Shea heard a massive door slam, and the clash as several large bolts were driven home behind them. He got up and pulled Belphebe to her feet.

"Are you hurt, kid?" he asked.

"Nay, not I." She rubbed one wrist where someone's grip had come down hard. "But there are places I would rather be."

"It's a real jook-joint, all right," said Brodsky. "You got me on how we're going to push a can from this one."

He was looking around the place in the dim illumination furnished by the single, eight-inch window, which was heavily barred. The strong-house itself was composed of massive tree-trunks, and its roof seemed abnormally thick.

"Alackaday," said Belphebe. "What happened to those shapings of ourselves that so confounded these gentry but lately?"

"Walter took care of that," said Shea. "I admit I'm just as glad to have only one wife, but he was a little precipitate. What in hell were you up to, Walter?"

Bayard said, "I was merely trying in a small way to carry out the plan I mentioned of divining the future. It worked, too."

"What do you mean, it worked?" said Shea.

"I was trying to find out who would win the duel. There were little fiery letters on the ground that said 'Lem' as clearly as could be."

"A big help," said Shea, "especially as he took off the other guy's head about that time, anyway."

Bayard said, "The principle is established. And how was I to know it would counteract Lemminkainen's spell? Nobody warned me of any such outcome. What is the logical nexus between the two, by the way?"

Shea shrugged. "I haven't the least idea. Maybe we can work it out some time when we have the leisure. But in the meanwhile, we need to figure out some plan for getting out of here. These people don't fool around at any time, and that old witch has just lost her husband."

He went to the little window and looked out. Or tried to, for he found his vision blocked by a familiar-looking bewhiskered countenance: Vuohinen, who spat through the bars at him.

Shea dodged, wiped his shoulder with the cuff of the other hand, and turned to Brodsky. "Pete, he's your serf. Maybe you can order him..."

"Ha!" roared Vuohinen. "This one to order me? I am free of all serfdom now, and have been charged to see that you outlandish tricksters do not escape before the Mistress of Pohjola undertakes your punishment."

"What do you mean?"

"All details I do not know, but be assured it will be a memorable occasion. She is like to have you flayed and rolled in salt, to be followed by slow burning."

Shea fell back and looked around. Whoever had planned this box had built for keeps. The massive simplicity of the structure would defy any amount of tinkering. For instance, there was no opening whatever on the inside of the door through which one could get at the outside.

"I know your names!" shouted Vuohinen from the window. "Your wizardries will have no power on me."

He was probably right, at that. But an idea occurred to Shea. He returned to the window. "Look here," he said. "I'm a champion and I challenge you."

Vuohinen shook his head. "I am no longer a champion myself since losing the wrestle to this Piit, and cannot take your challenge until he has been beheaded."

"Wait a minute," said Bayard, "If..."

"Ya!" said Vuohinen. "I see your plot. Be known that I shall take care that your head comes off first, and his the last of all." He turned his back and walked away from the window.

Shea turned to Brodsky. "Pete, you should know a lot about busting out of places like this. What do the chances look like to you?"

Brodsky, who had been moving slowly around the cell, poking and testing, shook his head. "This is a real tough can. It would be a soup job, and even then there'd be the strong-arm squad out there to play."

Bayard said: "Couldn't we lure Vuohinen up to the bars and then grab him and choke him?"

"No good," said Brodsky. "What do you get except a good feeling in your biscuit? He ain't got no keys."

Belphebe said, "Yet while you are an approved sorcerer, Harold, it seems to me that we are not utterly without resource." She took her turn at stepping to the window. "Ohe, Vuohinen," she called.

"What now, female toad?"

"I understand how you are angry with us. We were lacking in sympathy, in not thinking of the damage to your hand. But we will make amends. If you will tell us somewhat of yourself, my lord, who knows no little magic, will make it good for you."

Shea squeezed her hand. "Nice try, kid," he said under his breath. But Vuohinen saw the point, too.

"And put myself in his power? Ya, the hand will heal itself quickly enough when I see your heads on stakes."

Shea took over with, "You're a pretty tough guy, aren't you?"

"That I am."

"Yes, sir," said Shea. "Some of them are good where I come from, but for plain toughness, I'm afraid we're not in your class. Must be the diet or something. How did you get that way, anyway?"

"Ya," said Vuohinen, "you seek by flattery to disarm me, so that you may persuade me to let you go. I am not so simple."

Bayard said, "He seems to be up on psychology, too, doesn't he?"

Shea sighed. "Psychology worked in the world of Norse myth when I got thrown in the jug."

"The trouble seems to be," said Bayard, "that this animal is a Finn. In our own world the Finns are about the stubbornest race on earth, like the Dutch and maybe the Basques. There's something in the culture pattern. I don't think you're going to get anywhere with him... I wonder how much time we have left?"

Belphebe said, "Harold, my love, I think the answer stares us in the face, but we have so looked at small details as to miss the great. Why cannot we leave this whole world of Kalevala by the same door we entered in: item, your symbolic magic?"

Shea slapped his thigh. "Just the thing! Wait a minute, though...Any kind of magic in this continuum takes a lot of music, and I guess my voice just isn't equal to it. That's why I've had trouble so far."

"Alas, I fear I can do but little more for you," said Belphebe. "Not that I croak like you, my love, but my voice is so slender. I could attune a harp if we had such a thing. Timias, my fiancé in Faerie, taught me the art."

Bayard shook his head. Brodsky said, "Not that I want to noise off, but if my schnozz was on the up-and-up..."

Shea said, "Wait a minute here. I think I see a way. Have you ever had that polyp taken out, Pete?"

"Naw."

"Why not?"

"I been busy... And besides, I don't want no croaker putting me through the mill."

His voice was defensive, but Shea rushed on. "Well, why don't we begin by curing your polyp by magic? That ought not to take much of a spell, and if your voice were working right, we could tackle something harder."

"Say, maybe you got a right steer there. But how are you going to wrap it up without music?"

"I think that Belphebe's voice with the help of a harp ought to be enough for the smaller spell. Then she could accompany you, and I'll work out the big one. Wait, I'll try."

He stepped to the window again. "Oh, Vuohinen!"

"Well, what now?"

"Do you know what a kantele is?"

"What child does not?"

"Good. Could you get us one to lighten our last hours?"

"Why should I lighten your last hours, filth?" He turned away again.

Shea sighed again. "No cooperation—that's the trouble with this damned continuum," he said.

Bayard asked, "What's a kantele?"

"The primitive harp. Vainamoinen invented it at some point in the runes, by making it out of a fish's jawbone, but I wasn't sure he'd done it yet, so I asked this guy if he knew what it was."

"If we had a fish's jawbone..."

"We could make one ourselves. Yes, I know. But our chances of getting a fish's jawbone out of that big lump of insensitivity are about as good as those of biting our way through those logs."

"I can fix that," said Brodsky, suddenly.

"Oh, yeah?" said Shea, and "Can you, indeed?" said Bayard, both together.

"Oh, yeah," said Brodsky firmly, and strode to the window again. "Hey, lug!" he called. "So you're going to clip our pumpkins tomorrow. Okay. But where's the kiss-off banquet?"

"What use is food to you, who will so soon be beyond the need of it?"

"That's right, play it dumb, lug. Listen, we're from Ohio, see? In our country, when a ghee doesn't get what he wants for his last meal, his ghost comes back on the roach that turned him down, and pretty soon the muzzier is playing with the squirrels."

"It is a lie," said Vuohinen, but he turned his head from side to side to look at the others, and Shea felt his heart leap. He nodded solemnly in support of the detective.

"That's right," said Bayard.

"Boy!" said Brodsky gleefully. "Am I going to get a bang out of watching you cut off your own toes?"

"Maybe we could make him take off his nose and ears, too, while we're about it," said Shea.

"That's the dope," Brodsky continued. "None of them fried pigs' ears, either. It's gotta be fish, or else."

The head disappeared. Shea turned to Brodsky. "You're a better psychologist than I am. How did you know that would fetch him?"

"Ah, I never saw the gorilla yet that didn't fall for the yudd racket," said

Brodsky, modestly. "They're so afraid of going wack, they'd rather turn themselves in."

He seemed to have struck oil. Outside there was the sound of feet and a murmur of voices. Then there was a wait, the bolts were drawn back, and the door opened to show Vuohinen, surrounded by a phalanx of the black-bearded Pohjolan warriors. He bore a big wooden platter.

"I told the Mistress of your outlandish custom," he said, "and though she says her magic is strong enough for any protection, she will grant you so much."

He slammed down the platter and stamped out. Shea bent to examine the platter. There was no doubt that it was fish, and more than a little on the high side, some large member of the salmon tribe. He said, "Well, here's our harp. Walter, help me get the jawbones out of this critter's head."

"What with? They took all our knives and things."

"With your fingernails. We can't be squeamish. Ssh, let me think. I'll have to work out the verse for Belphebe."

"Now," said Shea, "can you break off a few hairs, sweetheart?"

Belphebe complied. Shea undertook to tie the strands of hair, one at a time, to the jawbone, so that they spanned its gap like the strings of a harp. In the dim light, it took some doing.

She touched the strings and bent her head close. "It's awfully small and weak," she said. "I don't know."

"I thought of that," said Shea. "Listen carefully, kid, and memorize after me, because you'll have to do it all yourself. Keep your voice way down, as though you were crooning, to match the harp. I'll make the passes, just to be on the safe side, though they may not be necessary."

Belphebe seated herself on the floor, with the harp on her uplifted knees, cocked her ear down toward it, and began:

> *Oh, you harp of fish's jawbone,*
> *Hail, you kantele of magic...*

while Shea ran rapidly through some of the passes he had used in Faerie. She was from there, and it would probably help. Belphebe ended:

> *...be you forthwith ten times greater.*

And fell over on her back as a five-foot harp of fish's jawbone pushed her off balance. Shea helped her up, and she began testing the strings. "It needs tuning."

"All right, you tune it, while I work out a verse for that polyp. Pete, what's the name of your wife, and what church do you go to?"

In a few moments they were ready. Pete placed himself before the couple, Belphebe twanged the strings of her harp, and in her light, clear soprano sang the spell for the removal of the polyp.

Brodsky cried, "Ouch! Damn near took my sconce off." He felt his nose and a smile spread across his face in the semi-darkness. (Outside the summer day was just ending.) "Say, Shea..."

Whatever he was going to say was never said. The window turned dark, and all four looked up to see Vuohinen's face peering in, bearded and furious.

"Where did you get that?" he shouted. "Magic! Magic! I know your names! I will..." The face abruptly disappeared.

"Sing!" cried Shea to Brodsky. "Sing anything you can think of! Quick! I'll take care of the sorites. Belphebe, you accompany him, and Walter hold one of his hands. Now if the class A..."

Pete Brodsky tilted his head back, and in a tenor that would have done credit to John McCormack, burst into:

My wi-ild I-rish rose,
The swe-etest flower that grows...

Outside, beneath the piercing tenor and the twanging of the harp, there was a sound of distant shouting and running feet.

You may look everywhere...

The walls of the cabin seemed to turn round and round as though they were on a pivot and only the four in the center fixed in position. And as Pete's voice rose higher and higher, the solid walls turned gray and dissolved, and with them the whole world of the *Kalevala*.

The Green Magician
by L. Sprague de Camp & Fletcher Pratt
Beyond Fiction, Vol 2, #3, 1954

In that suspended moment when the gray mists began to whirl around them, Harold Shea realized that, although the pattern was perfectly clear, the details often didn't work out right.

It was all very well to realize that, as Doc Chalmers once said, "The world we live in is composed of impressions received through the senses, and if the senses can be attuned to receive a different series of impressions, we should infallibly find ourselves living in another of the infinite number of possible worlds." It was a scientific and personal triumph to have proved that, by the use of the sorites of symbolic logic, the gap to one of those possible worlds could be bridged.

The trouble was what happened after you got there. It amounted to living by one's wits; for, once the jump across space-time had been made, and you were in the new environment, the conditions of the surroundings had to be accepted completely. It was no good trying to fire a revolver or scratch a match or light a flashlight in the world of Norse myth; these things did not form part of the surrounding mental pattern, and remained obstinately inert masses of useless material. On the other hand, magic...

The mist thickened and whirled. Shea felt the pull of Belphebe's hand, clutching his desperately as though something were trying to pull her in the other direction.

Another jerk at Shea's hand reminded him that they might not even wind up in the same place, given that their various mental backgrounds would spread the influence of the generalized spells across different space-time patterns. "Hold on!" he cried, and clutched Belphebe's hand tighter still.

Shea felt earth under his feet and something hitting him on the head. He realized that he was standing in pouring rain, coming down vertically and with such intensity that he could not see more than a few yards in any direction. His first glance was toward Belphebe; she swung herself into his arms and they kissed damply.

"At least," she said, disengaging herself a little, "you are with me, my most dear lord, and so there's nought to fear."

They looked around, water running off their noses and chins. Shea's heavy woolen shirt was already so soaked that it stuck to his skin, and Belphebe's neat hair was taking on a drowned-rat appearance. She pointed and cried, "There's one!"

Shea peered toward a lumpish dark mass that had a shape vaguely resembling Pete Brodsky.

"Shea?" came a call, and without waiting for a reply the lump started toward them. As it did so, the downpour lessened and the light brightened.

"Curse it, Shea!" said Brodsky, as he approached. "What kind of a box is this? If I couldn't work my own racket better, I'd turn myself in for mopery. Where the hell are we?"

"Ohio, I hope," said Shea. "And look, shamus, we're better off than we were, ain't we? I'm sorry about this rain, but I didn't order it."

"All I got to say is you better be right," said Brodsky gloomily. "You can get it all for putting the snatch on an officer, and I ain't sure I can square the rap even now. Where's the other guy?"

Shea looked around. "Walter may be here, but it looks as though he didn't come through to the same place. And if you ask me, the question is not where we are but when we are. It wouldn't do us much good to be back in Ohio in 700 A.D., which is about the time we left. If this rain would only let up..."

With surprising abruptness the rain did, walking away in a wall of small but intense downpours. Spots and bars of sky appeared among the clouds wafted along by a brisk steady current of air that penetrated Shea's wet shirt chillingly, and the sun shot an occasional beam through the clouds to touch up the landscape.

It was a good landscape. Shea and his companions were standing in deep grass, on one of the higher spots of an extent of rolling ground. This stretch in turn appeared to be the top of a plateau, falling away to the right. Mossy boulders shouldered up through the grass, which here and there gave way to patches of purple-flowered heather, while daisies nodded in the steady breeze. Here and there was a single tree, but down in the valley beyond their plateau the low land was covered with what appeared at this distance to be birch and oak. In the distance, as they turned to contemplate the scene, rose the heads of far blue mountains.

The cloud-cover thinned rapidly and broke some more. The air had cleared enough so they could now see two other little storms sweeping across the middle distance, trailing their veils of rain. As the patches of sunlight whisked past, the landscape blazed with a singularly vivid green, quite unlike that of Ohio.

Brodsky was the first to speak. "If this is Ohio, I'm a peterman," he said. "Listen, Shea, do I got to tell you again you ain't got much time? If those yaps from the D.A.'s office get started on this, you might just as well hit yourself on the head and save them the trouble. He's coming up for election this fall and needs a nice fat case. And there's the F.B.I. Rover boys—they just love snatch cases, and you can't put no fix in with them that will stick. So you better get me back before people start asking questions."

Shea said, rather desperately, "Pete, I'm doing all I can. Honest. I haven't the least idea where we are, or in what period. Until I do, I don't dare try sending us anywhere else. We've already picked up a rather high charge of magical static coming here, and any spell I used without knowing what kind of magic they use around here is apt to make us simply disappear or end up in Hell—you know, real red hell with flames all around, like in a fundamentalist church."

"Okay," said Brodsky. "You got the office. Me, I don't think you got more than a week to get us back at the outside."

Belphebe pointed, "Marry, are those not sheep?"

Shea shaded his eyes. "Right you are, darling," he said. The objects looked like a collection of lice on a piece of green baize, but he trusted his wife's phenomenal eyesight.

"Sheep," said Brodsky. One could almost hear the gears grind in his brain as he looked around. "Sheep." A beatific expression spread over his face. "Shea, you must of done it! Three, two, and out we're in Ireland—and if it is, you can hit me on the head if I ever want to go back."

Shea followed his eyes. "It does rather look like it," he said. "But when..."

Something went past with a rush of displaced air. It struck a nearby boulder with a terrific crash and burst into fragments that whizzed about like pieces of an artillery shell.

"Duck!" shouted Shea, throwing himself flat and dragging Belphebe down with him.

Brodsky went into a crouch, lips drawn tight over his teeth, looking around with quick, jerky motions for the source of the missile. Nothing more happened. After a minute, Shea and Belphebe got up and went over to examine a twenty-pound hunk of sandy conglomerate.

Shea said, "Somebody is chucking hundred-pound boulders around. This may be Ireland, but I hope it isn't the time of Finn McCool or Strongbow."

"Cripes," said Brodsky, "and me without my heater. And you a shiv man with no shiv."

It occurred to Shea that at whatever period they had hit this place, he was in a singularly weaponless state. He climbed on the boulder against which the missile had destroyed itself and looked in all directions. There was no sign of life except the distant, tiny sheep—not even a shepherd or a sheepdog.

He slid down and sat on a ledge of the boulder and considered, the stone feeling hard against his wet back. "Sweetheart," he said, addressing Belphebe, "it seems to me that whenever we are, the first thing we have to do is find people and get oriented. You're the guide. Which direction's the most likely?"

The girl shrugged. "My woodcraft is nought without trees," she said, "but if you put it so, I'd seek a valley, for people ever live by watercourses."

"Good idea," said Shea. "Let's..."

Whizz!

Another boulder flew through the air, but not in their direction. It stuck the turf a hundred yards away, bounced clumsily, and rolled out of sight over the hill. Still—no one was visible.

Brodsky emitted a growl, but Belphebe laughed. "We are encouraged to begone," she said. "Come, my lord, let us do no less."

At that moment another sound made itself audible. It was that of a team of horses and a vehicle whose wheels were in violent need of lubrication. With a drumming of hooves, a jingle of harness, and a squealing of wheels, a chariot rattled up the slope and into view. It was drawn by two huge horses, one gray and one black. The chariot itself was built more on the lines of a sulky than those of the open-backed Graeco-Roman chariot, with a seat big enough for two or three persons across the back, and the sides cut low in front to allow for entrance. The vehicle was ornamented with nail-heads and other trim in gold, and a pair of scythe-blades jutted from the hubs.

The driver was a tall, thin, freckled man, with red hair trailing from under his golden fillet down over his shoulders. He wore a green kilt and over that a deerskin cloak with arm-holes at elbow length.

The chariot sped straight toward Shea and his companions, who dodged away from the scythes round the edge of the boulder. At the last minute the charioteer reined to a walk and shouted, "Be off with you if you would keep the heads on your shoulders!"

"Why?" asked Shea.

"Because himself has a rage on. It is tearing up trees and casting boulders he is, and a bad hour it will be for anyone who meets him the day."

"Who is himself?" said Shea, almost at the same time as Brodsky said, "Who the hell are you?"

The charioteer pulled up with an expression of astonishment on his face. "I am Laeg mac Riangabra, and who would himself be but Ulster's hound, the glory of Ireland, Cuchulainn the mighty? He is after killing his only son and has worked himself into a rage. *Ara!* It is ruining the countryside he is, and the sight of you Fomorians would make him the wilder."

The charioteer cracked his whip, and the horses raced off over the hill, the flying clods dappling the sky. In the direction from which he had come, a good-sized sapling with dangling roots rose against the horizon and fell back.

"Come on!" said Shea, grabbing Belphebe's hand and starting down the slope after the chariot.

"Hey!" said Brodsky, tagging after them. "Come on back and pal up with this ghee. He's the number one hero of Ireland."

Another rock bounced on the sward and from the distance a kind of howling was audible.

"I've heard of him," said Shea, "and if you want to, we can drop in on him later, but I think that right now is a poor time for calls. He isn't in a pally mood."

Belphebe said, "You name him hero, and yet you say he has slain his own son. How can this be?"

Brodsky said, "It was a bum rap. This Cuchulainn got his girl-friend Aoife pregnant way back when and then gave her the air, see? So she's sore at him, see? So when the kid grows up, she sends him to Cuchulainn under a geas..."

"A moment," said Belphebe. "What would this geas be?"

"A taboo," said Shea.

Brodsky said, "It's a hell of a lot more than that. You got one these geasa on you and you can't do the thing it's against even if it was to save you from the hot seat. So like I was saying this young ghee, his name is Conla, but he has this geas on him not to tell his name or that of his father to anyone. So when Aoife sends him to Cuchulainn, the big shot challenges the kid and then knocks him off. It ain't good."

"A tale to mourn, indeed," said Belphebe. "How are you so wise in these matters, Master Pete? Are you of this race?"

"I only wisht I was," said Brodsky fervently. "It would do me a lot of good on the force. But I ain't, so I dope it this way, see? I'll study this Irish stuff till I know more about it than nobody. And then I got innarested, see?"

They were well down the slope now, the grass dragging at their feet, approaching the impassive sheep.

Belphebe said, "I trust we shall come soon to where there are people. My bones protest I have not dined."

"Listen," said Brodsky, "This is Ireland, the best country in the world. If you want to feed your face, just knock off one of them sheep. It's on the house. They run the pitch that way."

"We have neither knife nor fire," said Belphebe.

"I think we can make out on the fire deal with the metal we have on us and a piece of flint," said Shea. "And if we have a sheep killed and a fire going, I'll bet it won't be long before somebody shows up with a knife to share our supper. Anyway, it's worth a try."

He walked over to a big tree and picked up a length of dead branch that lay near the base. By standing on it and heaving, he broke it somewhat raggedly in half, handing one end to Brodsky. The resulting cudgels did not look especially efficient, but they could be made to do.

"Now," said Shea, "if we hide behind that boulder, Belphebe can circle around and drive the flock toward us."

"Would you be stealing our sheep now, darlings?" said a deep male voice.

Shea looked around. Out of nowhere, a group of men had appeared, standing on the slope above them. There were five of them, in kilts or trews, with mantles of deerskin or wolfhide fastened around their necks. One of them carried a brassbound club, one a clumsy-looking sword, and the other three, spears.

Before Shea could say anything, the one with the club said, "The heads of the men will look fine in the hall, now. But I will have the woman first."

"Run!" cried Shea, and took his own advice. The five ran after them.

Belphebe, being unencumbered, soon took the lead. Shea clung to his club, hating to have nothing to hit back with if he were run down. A glance backward showed that Brodsky had either dropped his or thrown it at the pursuers without effect.

"Shea!" yelled the detective. "Go on—they got me!"

They had not, as a matter of fact, but it was clear they soon would. Shea paused, turned, snatched up a stone about the size of a baseball, and threw it past Brodsky's head at the pursuers. The spearman-target ducked, and they came on, spreading out in a crescent to surround their prey.

"I—can't—run no more," panted Brodsky. "Go on."

"Like hell," said Shea. "We can't go back without you. Let's both take the guy with the club."

The stones arched through the air simultaneously. The clubman ducked, but not far enough; one missile caught his leather cap and sent him sprawling to the grass.

The others whooped and closed in with the evident intention of skewering and carving, when a terrific racket made everyone pause on tiptoe. Down the slope came the chariot that had passed Shea and his group before. The tall, red-haired charioteer was standing in the front, yelling something like "Ulluullu" while balancing in the back was a smaller, rather dark man.

The chariot bounded and slewed toward them. Before Shea could take in the whole action, one of the hub-head scythes caught a spearman, shearing off both legs neatly, just below the knee. The man fell, shrieking, and at the same instant the small man drew back his arm and threw a javelin right through the body of another.

"It is himself!" cried one of them, and the survivors turned to run.

The small dark fellow spoke to the charioteer, who pulled up his horses. Cuchulainn leaped down from the vehicle, took a sling from his belt and whirled it around his head. The stone struck one of the men in the back of the neck, and down he went. As the man fell, Cuchulainn wound up a second time. Shea thought this one would miss for sure, as the man was now a hundred yards away and going farther fast. But the missile hit him in the head, and he pitched on his face.

"Get out the head bag and fetch me the trophies, dear," said Cuchulainn.

2

Laeg rummaged in the rear of the chariot and produced a large bag and a heavy sword, with which he went calmly to work. Belphebe had turned back, as the rescuer came toward the three. Shea saw a smallish man with curly black hair, not older than himself; heavy black eyebrows and only a faint fuzz on his cheeks compare with the heavy beards of the defunct five. He was not only an extremely handsome man; there was also a powerful play of musculature under his loose outer garment. The hero's face bore an expression of settled and brooding melancholy, and he was dressed in a long-sleeved white cloak embroidered with gold thread, over a red tunic.

"Thanks a lot," said Shea. "You just saved our lives, in case you wondered. How did you happen along?"

" 'Twas Laeg came to me with a tale of three strangers, who might be Fomorians by the look to them, and they were like to be set on by the Lagenians. Now I will be fighting any man in Ireland that gives me the time, but unless you are a hero it is not good to fight at five to two, and it is time that these pigs of Lagenians learned their manners. So now it is time for you to be telling me who you are and where you come from and whither bound. If you are indeed Fomorians, the better for you—King Conchobar is friends with them this year, or I might be making you by the head shorter."

Shea searched his mind for details of the culture-pattern of the men of Cuchulainn's Ireland. A slip at the beginning might result in their heads being added to the collection bumping each other in Laeg's bag like so many cantaloupes. Brodsky beat him to the punch.

"Jeepers!" he said, in a tone which carried its own message. "Imagine holding heavy with a zinger like you! I'm Pete Brodsky—give a toss to my friends here, Harold Shea and his wife Belphebe." He stuck out his hand.

"We do not come from Fomoria, but from America, an island beyond their land," said Shea.

Cuchulainn acknowledged the introduction to Shea with a stately nod of courtesy. His eyes swept over Brodsky, and he ignored the outburst hand. He addressed Shea. "Why do you travel in company with such a mountain of ugliness, dear?"

Out of the corner of his eye, Shea could see the cop's wattles swell dangerously. He said hastily; "He may be no beauty, but he's useful. He's our slave and bodyguard, a good fighting man. Shut up, Pete!"

Brodsky had sense enough to do so. Cuchulainn accepted the explanation with the same sad courtesy and gestured toward the chariot. "You will be mounting up in the back of my car, and I will drive you to my camp, where there will be an eating before you set out on your journey again."

He climbed to the front of the chariot himself, while the three wanderers clambered wordlessly to the back seat and held on. Laeg, having disposed of the head bag, touched the horses with a golden goad. Off they went. Shea found the ride a monstrously rough one, for the vehicle had no springs and the road was distinguished by its absence, but Cuchulainn lounged in the seat, apparently at ease.

Presently there loomed ahead a small patch of woods at the bottom of a valley. Smoke rose from a fire. The sun had decided to resolve the question of what time of day it was by setting, so that the hollow lay in shadow. A score or more of men, rough and wild-looking, got to their feet and cheered as the chariot swept into the camp. At the center of it a huge iron pot bubbled over the fire, and in the background a shelter of poles, slabs of bark and branches had been erected. Laeg pulled up the chariot and lifted the head bag with its lumpish trophies, and there was more cheering.

Cuchulainn sprang down lightly, acknowledged the greeting with a casual wave, then swung to Shea. "Mac Shea, I am thinking that you are of quality, and as you are not altogether the ugliest couple in the world, you will be eating with me." He waved an arm. "Bring the food, darlings."

Cuchulainn's henchmen busied themselves, with a vast amount of shouting, and running about in patterns that would have made good cat's cradles. One picked up a stool and carried it across the clearing; a second immediately picked it up again and took it back to where it had been.

"Do you think they'll ever get around to feeding us?" said Belphebe in a low tone. But Cuchulainn merely looked on with a slight smile, seeming to regard the performance as somehow a compliment to himself.

After an interminable amount of coming and going, the stool was finally established in front of the lean-to. Cuchulainn sat down on it and with a wave of his hand, indicated that the Sheas were to sit on the ground in front of him. The charioteer Laeg joined them on the ground, which was still decidedly damp after the rain.

But, as their clothes had not dried, it didn't seem to matter.

A man brought a large wooden platter on which were heaped the champion's victuals, consisting of a huge cut of boiled pork, a mass of bread, and a whole salmon. Cuchulainn laid it on his knees and set to work on it with fingers and his dagger, saying with a ghost of a smile, "Now according to the custom of Ireland, Mac Shea, you may challenge the champion for his portion. A man of your inches should be a blithe swordsman, and I have never fought with an American."

"Thanks," said Shea, "but I don't think I could eat that much, anyway, and there's a—what do you call it?—a geas against my fighting anyone who has done something for me, so I couldn't after the way you saved us." He addressed himself to the slab of bread on which had been placed a pork chop and a piece of salmon, then glanced at Belphebe and added, "Would it be too much trouble to ask for the loan of a pair of knives? We left in rather a hurry and without our tools."

A shadow flitted across the face of Cuchulainn. "It is not well for a man of his hands to be without his weapons. Are you sure, now, that they were not taken away from you?"

Belphebe said, "We came here on a magical spell, and as you doubtless know, there are some that cannot be spelled in the presence of cold iron."

"And what could be truer?" agreed Cuchulainn. He clapped his hands and called, "Bring two knives, darlings. The iron knives, not the bronze." He chewed, looking at Belphebe. "And where would you be journeying to, darlings?"

Shea said, "Back to America, I suppose. We sort of—dropped in to see the greatest hero in Ireland." Cuchulainn appeared to take the compliment as a matter of course. "You come at a poor time. The expedition is over, and now I am going home to sit quietly with my wife Emer, so there will be no fighting."

Laeg looked up with his mouth full and said, "You will be quiet if Meddling Maev and Ailill will let you, Cucuc. Some devilment they will be getting up, or it is not the son of Riangabra I am."

"When my times comes to be killed by the Connachta, then I will be killed by the men of Connacht," said Cuchulainn, composedly. He was still looking at Belphebe.

Belphebe asked, "Who stands at the head of the magical art here?"

Cuchulainn said, "It is true that you said you have a taste for magic. None is greater, nor will be, than Ulster's Cathbadh, adviser to King Conchobar. And now you will come with me to Muirthemne in the morning, rest and fit yourselves, and we will go to Emain Macha to see him together."

He laid aside his platter and took another look at Belphebe. The little man was as good with a trencher as he was with a sling; there was practically nothing left, and he had had twice as much as Shea.

"That's extremely kind of you," said Shea. "Very kind indeed." It was so very kind that he felt a twinge of suspicion.

"It is not," said Cuchulainn. "For those with the gift of beauty, it is no more than their due that they should receive all courtesy."

He was still looking at Belphebe, who glanced up at the darkening sky. "My lord," she said, "I am somewhat foredone. Would it not be well to seek our rest?"

Shea said, "It's an idea. Where do we sleep?"

Cuchulainn waved a hand toward the grove. "Where you will, darlings. No one will disturb you in the camp of Cuchulainn." He clapped his hands. "Gather moss for the bed of my friends."

When they were alone, Belphebe said in a low voice: "I like not the manner of his approach, though he has done us great good. Cannot you use your art to transport us back to Ohio?"

Shea said, "I'll take a chance on trying to work out the sorites in the morning. Remember, it won't do us any good to get back alone. We've got to take Pete, or we'll be up on a charge of kidnapping or murdering him, and I don't want to go prowling through this place at night looking for him. Besides, we need light to make the passes."

Early as they rose, the camp was already astir about them and a fire lighted. As Shea and Belphebe wandered through the camp, looking for Brodsky, they noted it was strangely silent, the elaborate confusion of the previous evening being carried on in whispers or dumb show. Shea grabbed the arm of a bewhiskered desperado hurrying past with a bag of something to inquire the reason.

The man bent close and said in a fierce whisper, "Sure, 'tis that himself is in his sad mood, and keeping to his booth. If you would lose your head, it would be just as well to make a noise."

"There's Pete," said Belphebe.

The detective waved a hand and came toward them from under the trees. He had somehow acquired one of the deerskin cloaks, which was held under his chin with a brass brooch, and he looked unexpectedly cheerful.

"What's the office?" he asked in the same stage whisper the others were using, as he approached them.

"Come with us," said Shea. "We're going to try to get back to Ohio. Where'd you get the new clothes?"

"Aw, one of these muzzlers thought he could wrestle, so I slipped him a little jujitsu and won it. Listen, Shea, I changed my mind. I ain't going back. This is the real McCoy."

"But we want to go back," said Belphebe, "and you told us just yesterday that if we showed up without you, our fate would be less than pleasant."

"Listen, give it a rest. I'm on the legit here, and with that magical stuff of yours, you could be, too. At least I want to stay for the big blow."

"Come this way," said Shea, leading away from the center of the camp to where there was less danger of their voices causing trouble. "What do you mean by the big blow?"

"From what I got," said Pete, "I figured out when we landed. This Maev and Ailill are rustling out the mob and heeling them up to give Cuchulainn a bang on the head. They got all the cousins of people he's bumped off in on the caper, and they're going to put a geas on him that will make him go up against them all at once, and then boom. I want to stay for the payoff."

"Look here," said Shea, "you said only yesterday that we had to get you back within a week. Remember? It was something about your probably being seen going into our house and not coming out."

"Sure, sure. And if we go back, I'll alibi you. But what for? I'm teaching these guys to wrestle, and what with your magic, maybe you could even take the geas off the big shot and he wouldn't get shoved over."

"Perhaps I could at that," said Shea. "It seems to amount to a kind of psychological compulsion by magical means, and between psychology and magic, I ought to make it. But no—it's too risky. I daren't take the chance with him making eyes at Belphebe."

They had emerged from the clump of trees and were at the edge of the slope, with the early sun just touching the tops of the branches above them. Shea went on, "I'm sorry, Pete, but Belphebe and I don't want to spend the rest of our lives here, and if we're going, we've got to go now. As you said. Now, you two hold hands. Give me your other hand, Belphebe."

Brodsky obeyed with a somewhat sullen expression. Shea closed his eyes, and began: "If either A or (B or C) is true, and C or D is false..." motioning with his free hand to the end of the sorites.

He opened his eyes again. They were still at the edge of a clump of trees, on a hill in Ireland, watching the smoke from the fire as it rose above the trees to catch the sunshine.

Belphebe asked, "What's amiss?"

"I don't know," said Shea desperately. "If I only had something to write with, so I could check over the steps... No, wait a minute. Making this work depends on a radical alteration of sense impressions in accordance with the rules of symbolic logic and magic. Now we know that magic works here, so that can't be the trouble. But for symbolic logic to be effective, you have to submit to its effects—that is, be willing. Pete, you're the villain of the piece. You don't want to go back."

"Don't put the squeeze on me," said Brodsky. "I'll play ball."

"All right. Now I want you to remember that you're going back to Ohio, and that you have a good job there and like it. Besides, you were sent out to find us, and you did. Okay?"

They joined hands again and Shea, constricting his brow with effort, ran through the sorites again, this time altering one or two of the terms to give greater energy. As he reached the end, time seemed to stand still for a second; then crash! and a flash of vivid blue lightning struck the tree nearest them, splitting it from top to bottom.

Belphebe gave a little squeal, and a chorus of excited voices rose from the camp.

Shea gazed at the fragments of the splintered tree and said soberly, "I think that shot was meant for us, and that that just about tears it, darling. Pete, you get your wish. We're going to have to stay here at least until I know more about the laws controlling magic in this continuum."

Two or three of Cuchulainn's men burst excitedly through the trees and came toward them, spears ready. "Is it all right that you are?" one of them called.

"Just practicing a little magic," said Shea, easily. "Come on, let's go back and join the others."

In the clearing voices were no longer quenched, and the confusion had become worse than ever. Cuchulainn stood watching the loading of the chariot, with a lofty and detached air. As the three travelers approached he said, "Now it is to you I am grateful, Mac Shea, with your magical spell for reminding me that things are better done at home than abroad. It is leaving at once we are."

"Hey!" said Brodsky. "I ain't had no breakfast."

The hero regarded him with distaste. "You will be telling me that I should postpone the journey for the condition of a slave's belly?" he said, and turning to Shea and Belphebe, "We can eat as we go."

The ride was smoother than the one of the previous day only because the horses went at a walk so as not to outdistance the column of retainers on foot. Conversation over the squeaking of the wheels began by being sparse and rather boring, with Cuchulainn keeping his chin well down on his chest. But he apparently liked Belphebe's comments on the beauty of the landscape.

As it came on to noon he began to chatter, addressing her with an exclusiveness that Shea found disturbing, though he had to admit that the little man talked well, and always with the most perfect courtesy.

The country around them got lower and flatter and flatter and lower, until from the tops of the few rises Shea glimpsed a sharp line of gray-blue across the horizon; the sea. A shower came down and temporarily soaked the column, but nobody paid it much attention, and in the clear sunlit air that followed everyone was soon dry. Cultivation became more common, though there was still less of it than pasturage. Occasionally a lumpish-looking serf, clad in a length of ragged sacking-like cloth wrapped around his middle and a thick veneer of dirt, left off his labors to stare at the band and wave a languid greeting.

As last, over the manes of the horses, Shea saw that they were approaching a stronghold. This consisted of a stockade of logs with a huge double gate.

Belphebe surveyed it critically and whispered behind her hand to Shea, "It could be taken with fire-arrows."

"I don't think they have many archers or very good ones," he whispered back. "Maybe you can show them something."

The gate was pushed open creakingly by more bearded warriors, who shouted: "Good-day to you, Cucuc! Good luck to Ulster's hound!"

The gate was wide enough to admit the chariot, scythe-blades and all. As the vehicle rumbled through the opening, Shea glimpsed houses of various shapes and sizes, some of them evidently stables and barns. The biggest of all was the hall in the middle, whose heavily thatched roof came down almost to the ground at the sides.

Laeg pulled up. Cuchulainn jumped down, waved his hand, and cried, "Muirthemne welcomes you, Americans!" All the others applauded as though he had said something particularly brilliant.

He turned to speak to a fat man, rather better dressed than the rest, when another man came out of the main hall and walked rapidly toward them. The newcomer was a thin man of medium height, elderly but vigorous, slightly bent and carrying a stick, on which he leaned now and again. He had a long white beard, and a purple robe covered him from neck to ankle.

"The best of the day to you, Cathbadh," said Cuchulainn. "This is surely a happy hour that brings you here, but where is my darling Emer?"

"Emer has gone to Emain Macha," said Cathbadh. "Conchobar summoned her..."

"Ara!" shouted Cuchulainn. "Is it a serf that I am, that the King can send for my wife every time he takes it into the head of him? He is..."

"It is not that at all, at all," said Cathbadh. "He summons you, too, and for that he sent me instead of Levarcham, for he knows you might not heed her word if you took it into that willful head of yours to disobey, whereas it is myself can put a geas on you to go."

"And why does himself want us at Emain Macha?"

"Would I be knowing all the secrets in the heart of a King?"

Shea asked, "Are you the court druid?'

Cathbadh became aware of him for the first time, and Cuchulainn made introductions. Shea explained, "It seems to me that the King might want you at the court for your own protection, so the druids can keep Maev's sorcerers from putting a spell on you. That's what she's going to do."

"How do you know of this?" asked Cathbadh.

"Through Pete here. He sometimes knows about things that are going to happen before they actually take place. In our country we call it second sight."

Cuchulainn wrinkled his nose. "That ugly slave?"

"Yeh, me," said Brodsky, who had approached the group. "And you better watch your step, handsome, because somebody's going to hang you up to dry unless you do something about it."

"If it is destined none can alter it," said Cuchulainn. "Fergus! Have the bath water heated." He turned to Shea. "Once you are properly washed and garbed you will look well enough for the board in my beautiful house. I will lend you some proper garments, for I cannot bear the sight of those Formorian-like rags."

3

Along the side of the main hall was an alcove made of screens of wattle, set at an angle that provided privacy for those within. In the alcove stood Cuchulainn's bathtub, a large and elaborate affair of bronze. A procession of the women of the manor were now coming in from the well with jugs of water, which they emptied into the tub. Meanwhile the men were poking up the fire at the end of the hall and adding a number of stones of about five to ten pounds' weight.

Brodsky sidled up to Shea, as they stood in the half-light, orienting themselves. "Listen, I don't want to blow the whistle on a bump rap, but you better watch it. The racket they have here, this guy can make a pass at Belphebe in his own house, and it's legit. You ain't got no beef coming."

"I was afraid of that," said Shea, unhappily. "Look there."

"There" was a row of wooden spikes projecting from one of the horizontal strings along the wall, and most of these spikes were occupied by human heads. As they watched Laeg brought in the head bag and added the latest trophies to the collection, pressing them down firmly. Some of those already in place were quite fresh, while others had been there so long that there was little left of them but a skull with a little hair adhering to the scalp.

"Jeepers!" said Brodsky, "and if you start beefing, he'll put you there, too. Give me time—I'll try to think of some way to rumble his line."

"Make way!" shouted a huge bewhiskered retainer. The three dodged as the man ran past them, carrying a large stone, smoking from the fire, in a pair of tongs. The man dashed into the alcove. There was a splash and a loud hiss. Another retainer followed with a second stone while the first was on his return trip. In a few minutes all the stones had been transferred to the bathtub. Shea looked around the screen and saw that the water was steaming gently.

Cuchulainn sauntered past into the bathroom and tested the water with an inquisitive finger. "That will do, dears."

The retainers picked the stones out of the water with their tongs and piled them in the corner, then went around from behind the screen. Cuchulainn reached up to pull off his tunic, then saw Shea.

"I am going to undress for the bath," he said. "Surely, you would not be wanting to remain here, now."

Shea turned back into the main room just in time to see Brodsky smack one fist into the other palm. "Got it!"

"Got what?" said Shea.

"How to needle this hot tomato." He looked around, then pulled Shea and Belphebe closer. "Listen, the big shot putting the scram on you now just reminded me. The minute he makes a serious pass at you, Belle, you gotta go into a strip-tease act. In public, where everybody can get a gander at it."

Belphebe gasped. Shea asked. "Are you out of your head? That sounds to me like trying to put a fire out with gasoline."

"I tell you he can't take it!" Brodsky's voice was low but urgent. "They can't none of them. One time when this guy was going to put the slug on everyone at the court, the King sent out a bunch of babes with bare knockers, and they nearly had to pick him up in a basket."

"I like this not," said Belphebe, but Shea said, "A nudity taboo! That could be part of a culture pattern, all right. Do they all have it?"

"Yeh, and but good," said Brodsky. "They even croak of it. What gave me the tip was him putting the chill on you before he started to undress—he was doing you a favor."

Cuchulainn stepped out of the alcove, buckling a belt around a fresh tunic, emerald-green with embroidery of golden thread. He scrubbed his long hair with a towel and ran a comb through it, while Laeg took his place behind the screen.

Belphebe said, "Is there to be but one water for all?"

Cuchulainn said, "There is plenty of soapwort. Cleanliness is good for beauty." He glanced at Brodsky. "The slave can bathe in the trough outside."

"Listen..." began Brodsky, but Shea put a hand on his arm, and to cover up, asked, "Do your druids use spells of transportation—from one place to another?"

"There is little a good druid cannot do—but I would advise you not to use the spells of Cathbadh unless you are a hero as well as a maker of magic, for they are very mighty."

He turned to watch the preparations for dinner with a somber satisfaction. Laeg presently appeared, his toilet made, and from another direction one of the women brought garments which she took into the bathroom for Shea and Belphebe. Shea started to follow his wife, but remembered what Brodsky had said about the taboo, and decided not to take a chance on shocking his hosts. She came out soon enough in a floor-length gown that clung to her all over, and he noted with displeasure that it was the same green and embroidered pattern as Cuchulainn's tunic.

After Shea had dealt with water almost cold and a towel already damp, his own costume turned out to be a saffron tunic and tight knitted scarlet trews which he imagined as looking quite effective.

Belphebe was watching the women around the fire. Over in the shadows under the eaves sat Pete Brodsky, cleaning his fingernails with a bronze knife, a chunky, middle-aged man—a good hand in a fight, with his knowledge of jujitsu and his quick reflexes, and not a bad companion. Things would be a lot easier, though, if he hadn't fouled up the spell by wanting to stay where he was. Or had that been responsible?

Old Cathbadh came stumping up with his stick. "Mac Shea," he said, "the

Little Hound is after telling me that you also are a druid, who came here by magical arts from a distant place, and can summon lightning from the skies."

"It's true enough," said Shea. "Doubtless you know those spells."

"Doubtless I do," said Cathbadh, looking sly. "We must hold converse on matters of our craft. We will be teaching each other some new spells, I am thinking."

Shea frowned. The only spell he was really interested in was one that would take Belphebe and himself—and Pete—back to Garaden, Ohio, and Cathbadh probably didn't know that one. It would be a question of getting at the basic assumptions, and more or less working out his own method of putting them to use.

Aloud he said, "I think we can be quite useful to each other. In America, where I come from, we have worked out some of the general principles of magic, so that it is only necessary to learn the procedures in various places."

Cathbadh shook his head. "You do be telling me—and it is the word of a druid, so I must believe you—but 'tis hard to credit that a druid could travel among the Scythians of Greece or the Scots of Egypt, with all the strange gods they do be having, and still be protected by his spells as well as at home."

Shea got a picture of violently confused geography. But then, he reflected, the correspondence between this world and his own would only be rough, anyway. There might be Scots in Egypt here.

Just then Cuchulainn came out of his private room and sat down without ceremony at the head of the table. The others gathered round. Laeg took the place at one side of the hero and Cathbadh at the other. Shea and Belphebe were nodded to the next places, opposite each other. A good-looking serf woman with hair bound back from her forehead filled a large golden goblet at Cuchulainn's place with wine from a golden ewer, then smaller silver cups at the places of Laeg and Cathbadh, and copper mugs for Shea and Belphebe. Down the table the rest of the company had leather jacks and barley beer.

Cuchulainn said to Cathbadh, "Will you make the sacrifice, dear?"

The druid stood up, spilled a few drops on the floor and chanted to the gods Bile, Danu, and Ler. Shea decided that it was only imagination that he was hearing the sound of beating wings, and only the approach of the meal that gave him a powerful sense of internal comfort, but there was no doubt that Cathbadh knew his stuff.

He knew it, too. "Was that not fine, now?" he said, as he sat down next to Shea. "Can you show me anything in your outland magic ever so good?"

Shea thought. It wouldn't do any harm to give the old codger a small piece of sympathetic magic, and might help his own reputation. He said, "Move your wine-cup over next to mine, and then watch it carefully."

There would have to be a spell to link the two if he were going to make Cathbadh's wine disappear as he drank his own, and the only one he could think of at the moment was the "Double, double" from "Macbeth." He murmured that under his breath, making the hand passes he had learned in Faerie. Then he said, "Now, watch," picked up his mug and set it to his lips.

Whoosh!

Out of Cathbadh's cup a geyser of wine leaped as though driven by a pressure hose, nearly reaching the ceiling before it broke up to descend in a rain of glittering drops, while the guests at the head of the table leaped to their feet to draw back from the phenomenon. Cathbadh was a fast worker; he lifted his stick and struck the hurrying stream of liquid, crying something unintelligible in a high voice. Abruptly the gusher was quenched and there was only the table, swimming with wine, and the serf women rushing to mop up the mess.

Cuchulainn said, "This is a very beautiful piece of magic, Mac Shea, and it is a pleasure to have so notable a druid among us. But you would not be making fun of us, would you?" He looked dangerous.

"Not me," said Shea. "I only..."

Whatever he intended to say was cut off by a sudden burst of unearthly howling from somewhere outside.

Shea glanced around rather wildly, feeling that things were getting out of hand. Cuchulainn said, "You need not be minding that at all, now. It will only be Uath, and because the moon has reached her term."

"I don't understand," said Shea.

"The women of Ulster were not good enough for Uath, so he must be going to Connacht and courting the daughter of Ollgaeth the druid. This Ollgaeth is no very polite man; he said no Ultonian should have his daughter, and when Uath persisted, he put a geas on Uath that when the moon fills he must howl the night out, and a geas on his own daughter that she cannot abide the sound of howling. I am thinking that Ollgaeth's head is due for a place of honor." He looked significantly at his collection.

Shea said, "But I still don't understand. If you can put a geas on someone, can't it be taken off again?"

Cuchulainn looked mournful, Cathbadh embarrassed, and Laeg laughed. "Now you will be making Cathbadh sad, and our dear Cucuc is too polite to tell you, but the fact is no other than that Ollgaeth is so good a druid that no one can lift the spells he lays, nor lay one he cannot lift."

Outside, Uath's mournful howl rose again. Cuchulainn said to Belphebe, "Does he trouble you, dear? I can have him removed, or the upper part of him."

As the meal progressed, Shea noticed that Cuchulainn was putting away an astonishing quantity of the wine, talking almost exclusively with Belphebe, although the drink did not seem to have much effect on the hero but to intensify his somber courtesy. But, when the table was cleared, he lifted his goblet to drain it, looked at Belphebe from across the table, and nodded significantly.

Shea got up and ran around the table to place a hand on her shoulder. Out of the corner of his eye, he saw Pete Brodsky getting up, too. Cuchulainn's face bore the faintest of smiles. "It is sorry to discommode you I am," he said, "but this is by the rules and not even a challenging matter. So now, Belphebe, darling, you will just come to my room."

He got up and started toward Belphebe, who got up, too, backing away. Shea tried to keep between them and racked his brain hopelessly for some kind of spell that might stop this business. Everyone else was standing up and pushing to watch the little drama.

Cuchulainn said, "Now you would not be getting in my way, would you, Mac Shea, darling?" His voice was gentle, but there was something incredibly ferocious in the way he uttered the words, and Shea suddenly realized he was facing a man who had a sword. Outside, Uath howled mournfully.

Beside him, Belphebe herself suddenly leaped for one of the weapons hanging on the wall and tugged, but in vain. It had been so securely fastened with staples that it would have taken a pry bar to get it loose. Cuchulainn laughed.

Behind and to the left of Shea, Brodsky's voice rose, "Belle, you stiff, do like I told you!"

She turned back as Cuchulainn drew nearer and with set face crossed her arms and whipped the green gown off over her head. She stood in her underwear.

There was a simultaneous gasp and groan of horror from the audience. Cuchulainn stopped, his mouth coming open.

"Go on!" yelled Brodsky in the background. "Give it the business!"

Belphebe reached behind her to unhook her brassiere. Cuchulainn staggered as though he had been struck. He threw one arm across his eyes, reached the table and brought his face down on it, pounding the wood with the other fist.

"Ara!" he shouted. "Take her away! Is it killing me you will be and in my own hall, and me your host that has saved your life?"

"Will you let her alone?" asked Shea.

"I will that for the night."

"Mac Shea, take his offer," advised Laeg from the head of the table. He looked rather greenish himself. "If his rage comes on him, none of us will be safe."

"Okay. Honest," said Shea and held Belphebe's dress for her.

There was a universal sigh of relief from the background. Cuchulainn staggered to his feet. "It is not feeling well that I am, darlings," he said and, picking up the golden ewer of wine, made for his room.

4

There was a good deal of excited gabble among the retainers as Belphebe walked back to her place without looking to right or left, but they made room for Shea and Brodsky to join her. The druid looked shrewdly at the closed door and said, "If the Little Hound drinks too much by himself, he may be brooding on the wrong you are after doing him, and a sad day that would be. If he comes out with the hero-light playing round his head, run for your lives."

Belphebe said, "But where would we go."

"Back to your own place. Where else?"

Shea frowned. "I'm not sure..." he began, when Brodsky cut in suddenly, "Say," he said, "your boss ain't really got no right to get bugged up. We had to play it that way?"

Cathbadh swung to him. "And why, serf?"

"Don't call me serf. She's got a fierce geas on her. Any guy that touches her gets a bellyache and dies of it. Her husband only stands it because he's a magician. It's lucky we put the brakes on before the boss got her in that room, or he'd be ready for the lilies right now."

Cathbadh's eyebrows shot up like a seagull taking off. "Himself should know of this," he said. "There would be less blood shed in Ireland if more people opened their mouths to explain things before they put their feet in them."

He got up, went to the bedroom door and knocked. There was a growl from within, Cathbadh entered, and a few minutes later came out with Cuchulainn. The latter's step was visibly unsteady, and his melancholy seemed to have deepened. He walked to the head of the table and sat down in the chair again.

"Sure, and this is the saddest tale in the world I'm hearing about your wife having such a bad geas on her. The evening is spoilt and all. I hope the black fit does not come on me, for then it will be blood and death I need to restore me."

There were a couple of gasps audible and Laeg looked alarmed, but Cathbadh said hastily, "The evening is not so spoilt as you think, Cucuc. This Mac Shea is evidently a very notable druid and spell maker, but I think I am a better. Did you notice how quickly I put down his wine fountain? Would it not lift your heart, now, to see the two of us engage in a contest of magic?"

Cuchulainn clapped his hands. "Never was truer word spoken. You will just do that, darlings."

Shea said, "I'm afraid I can't guarantee..." but Belphebe plucked his sleeve and with her head close to his, whispered, "Do it. There is a danger here."

"It isn't working right," Shea whispered back.

Outside rose the mournful sound of Uath's howling. "Can you not use your psychology on him out there?" the girl asked. "It will be magic to them."

"A real psychoanalysis would take days," said Shea. "Wait a minute, though—we seem to be in a world where the hysteric type is the norm. That means a high suggestibility, and we might get something out of post-hypnotic suggestion."

Cuchulainn from the head of the table said, "It is not all night we have to wait."

Shea turned round and said aloud, "How would it be if I took the geas off that character out there training to be a bar-room tenor? I understand that's something Cathbadh hasn't been able to do."

Cathbadh said, "If you can do this, it will be a thing worth seeing, but I will not acknowledge you can do it until I have seen it."

"All right," said Shea. "Bring him in."

"Laeg, dear, go get us Uath," said Cuchulainn. He took a drink, looked at Belphebe and his expression became morose again.

Shea said, "Let's see. I want a small bright object. May I borrow one of your rings, Cuchulainn? That one with the big stone would do nicely."

Cuchulainn slid the ring down the table as Laeg returned, firmly gripping the arm of a stocky young man, who seemed to be opposing some resistance to the process. Just as they got in the door Uath flung back his head and emitted a blood-curdling howl. Laeg dragged him forward, howling away.

Shea turned to the others. "Now if this magic is going to work, I'll need a little room. Don't come too near us while I'm spinning the spell, or you'll be apt to get caught in it, too." He arranged a pair of seats well back from the table and attached a thread to the ring.

Laeg pushed Uath into one of the seats. "That's a bad geas you have there, Uath," said Shea, "and I want you to cooperate with me in getting rid of it. You'll do everything I tell you, won't you?"

The man nodded. Shea lifted the ring, said, "Watch this," and began twirling the thread back and forth between thumb and forefinger, so that the ring rotated first one way and then the other, sending out a flickering gleam of reflection from the rushlights. Meanwhile Shea talked to Uath in a low voice, saying "sleep" now and then in the process. Behind him he could hear an occasionally caught breath and could almost feel the atmosphere of suspense.

Uath went rigid.

Shea asked in a low voice, "Can you hear me, Uath?"

"That I can."

"You will do what I say."

"That I will."

"When you wake up, you won't suffer from this howling geas any more."

"That I will not."

"To prove that you mean it, the first thing you do on waking will be to clap Laeg on the shoulder."

"That I will."

Shea repeated his directions several times, varying the words, and making Uath repeat them after him. There was no use taking a chance on slipups. At last he brought him out of the hypnotic trance with a snap of the fingers and a sharp "Wake up!"

Uath stared about him with an air of bewilderment. Then he got up, walked over to the table and clapped Laeg on the shoulder. There was an appreciative murmur from the audience.

Shea asked, "How do you feel, Uath?"

"It is just fine that I am feeling. I do not want to be howling at the moon at all now, and I'm thinking the geas is gone for good. I thank your honor." He came down the table, seized Shea's hand and kissed it and joined the other retainers at the lower part of the table.

Cathbadh said, "That is a very good magic, indeed, and not the least of it was the small geas you put on him to lay his hand on Laeg's shoulder at the same time. And true it is that I have been unable to lift this geas. But as one man can run faster, so can another one climb faster, and I will demonstrate by taking the geas off your wife, which you have evidently not been able to deal with."

"I'm not sure..." began Shea, doubtfully.

"Let not yourself be worried," said Cuchulainn. "It will not harm her at all, and in the future she can be more courteous in the high houses she visits."

The druid rose and pointed a long, bony finger at Belphebe. He chanted some sort of rhythmic affair which began in a gibberish of unknown language, but became more and more intelligible, ending with: "...and by oak, ash and yew, by the beauty of Aengus and the strength of Ler and by authority as high druid of Ulster, let this geas be lifted from you, Belphebe! Let it pass! Out with it! It is erased, cancelled and no more to be heard of!" He tossed up his arms and then sat down. "How do you feel, darling?"

"In good sooth, not much different than before," said Belphebe. "Should I?"

Cuchulainn said, "But how can we know now that the spell has worked? Aha! I have it! Come with me." He rose and came round the table, and in response to Shea's exclamation of fury and Belphebe's of dismay, added, "Only as far as the door. Have I not given you my word?"

He bent over Belphebe, put one arm around her and reached for her hand, then reeled back, clutching his stomach with both hands and gasping for breath. Cathbadh and Laeg were on their feet. So was Shea.

Cuchulainn staggered against Laeg's arm, wiped a sleeve across his eyes and said, "Now the American is the winner, since your removal spell has failed, and it was like to be the death of me that the touch of her was. Do you be trying it yourself, Cathbadh, dear."

The druid reached out and laid a cautious finger on Belphebe's arm. Nothing happened.

Laeg said, "Did not the serf say that a magician was proof against this geas?"

Cathbadh said, "You may have the right of it there, although, but I am thinking myself there is another reason. Cucuc wished to take her to his bed, while I was not thinking of that at all, at all."

Cuchulainn sat down again and addressed Shea. "A good thing it is, indeed, that I was protected from the work of this geas. Has it not proved obstinate even to the druids of your own country?"

"Very," said Shea. "I wish I could find someone who could deal with it." He had been more surprised than Cuchulainn by the latter's attack of cramps, but in the interval he had figured it out. Belphebe hadn't had any geas on her in the first place. Therefore, when Cathbadh threw at her a spell designed to lift a geas, it took the opposite effect of laying on her a very good geas, indeed. That was elementary magicology, and under the conditions he was rather grateful to Cathbadh.

Cathbadh said, "In America there may be none to deal with such a matter, but in Ireland there is a man both bold and clever enough to lift the spell."

"Who's he?" asked Shea.

"That will be Ollgaeth of Cruachan, at the court of Ailill and Maev, who put the geas on Uath."

Brodsky, from beside Shea spoke up. "He's the guy that's going to put one on Cuchulainn before the big mob takes him."

"Wurra!" said Cathbadh to Shea. "Your slave must have a second mind to go with his second sight. The last time he spoke, it would only be a spell that Ollgaeth would be putting on the Little Hound."

"Listen, punk," said Brodsky in a tone of exasperation, "get the stones out of your head. This is the pitch: this Maev and Ailill are mobbing up everybody that owes Cuchulainn here a score, and when they get them all together, they're going to put a geas on him that will make him fight them all at once, and it's too bad."

Cathbadh combed his beard with his fingers. "If this be true..." he began.

"It's the McCoy. Think I'm on the con?"

"I was going to say that if it be true, it is high tidings from a low source. Nor do I see precisely how it may be dealt with. If it were a matter of spells only..."

Cuchulainn said with mournful and slightly alcoholic gravity, "I would fight them all without the geas, but if I am fated to fall, then that is an end of me."

Cathbadh turned to Shea. "You see the trouble we have with himself. Does your second sight reach farther, slave?"

Brodsky said, "Okay, lug, you asked for it. After Cuchulainn gets rubbed out, there'll be a war and practically everybody in the act gets knocked off, including you and Ailill and Maev. How do you like it?"

"As little as I like the look of your face," said Cathbadh. He addressed Shea. "Can this foretelling be trusted?"

"I've never known him to be wrong."

Cathbadh glanced from one to the other till one could almost hear his brains rumbling. Then he said, "I am thinking, Mac Shea, that you will be having business at Ailill's court."

"What gives you such an idea?"

"You will be wanting to see Ollgaeth in this matter of your wife's geas, of course. A wife with a geas like that is like one with a bad eye, and you can never be happy until it is removed entirely. You will take your man with you, and he will tell his tale and let Maev know that we know of her schemings, and they will be no more use than trying to feed a boar on bracelets."

Brodsky snapped his fingers and said, "Take him up," in a heavy whisper, but Shea said, "Look here, I'm not at all sure that I want to go to Ailill's court. Why should I? And if this Maev is as determined as she seems to be, I don't think you'll stop her by telling her you know what she's up to."

"On the first point," said the druid, "there is the matter that Cucuc saved your life and all, and you would be grateful to him, not to mention the geas. And for the second, it is not so much Maev that I would be letting know we see through her planning as Ollgaeth. For he will know as well as yourself, that if we learn of the geas before he lays it, all the druids at Conchobar's court will chant against him, and he will have no more chance of making it bite than a dog does of eating an apple."

"Mmm," said Shea. "Your point about gratitude is a good one, even if I can't quite see the validity of the other. What we want mostly is to get to our own home, though." He stifled a yawn. "We can take a night to sleep on it and decide in the morning. Where do we sleep?"

"Finn will show you to a chamber," said Cuchulainn. "Myself and Cathbadh will be staying up the while to discuss on this matter of Maev." He smiled his charming and melancholy smile.

Finn guided the couple to a guest-room at the back of the building, handed Shea a rush-light and closed the door, as Belphebe put up her arms to be kissed.

The next second Shea was doubled up and knocked flat to the floor by a super-edition of the cramps.

Belphebe bent over him. "Are you hurt, Harold?" she asked.

He pulled himself to a sitting posture with his back against the wall. "Not—seriously," he gasped. "It's that geas. It doesn't take any time out for husbands."

The girl considered. "Could you not relieve me of it as you did the one who howled?"

Shea said, "I can try, but I can pretty well tell in advance that it won't work. Your personality is too tightly integrated—just the opposite of these hysterics around here. That is, I wouldn't stand a chance of hypnotizing you."

"You might do it by magic."

Shea scrambled the rest of the way to his feet. "Not till I know more. Haven't you noticed I've been getting an overcharge—first that stroke of lightning and then the wine fountain? There's something in this continuum that seems to reverse my kind of magic."

She laughed a little. "If that's the law, why there's an end. You have but to summon Pete and make a magic that would call for us to stay here, then hey, presto! we are returned."

"I don't dare take the chance, darling. It might work and it might not—and even if it did, you'd be apt to wind up in Ohio with that geas still on you, and we really would be in trouble. We do take our characteristics along with us when we make the jump. And anyway, I don't know how to get back to Ohio yet."

"What's to be done, then?" the girl said. "For surely you have a plan, as always."

"I think the only thing we can do is take up Cathbadh's scheme and go see this Ollgaeth. At least, he ought to be able to get rid of that geas."

All the same, Shea had to sleep on the floor.

5

Harold Shea, Belphebe, and Pete Brodsky rode steadily at a walk across the central plain of Ireland, the Sheas on horses, Brodsky on a mule which he sat with some discomfort, leading a second mule carrying the provisions and equipment that Cuchulainn had pressed on them. Their accouterments included serviceable broadswords at the hips of Shea and Brodsky and a neat dagger at Belphebe's belt. Her request for a bow had brought forth only miserable sticks that pulled no farther than the breast and were quite useless beyond a range of fifty yards, and these she had refused.

All the first day they climbed slowly into the uplands of Monaghan. They followed the winding course of the Erne for some miles and splashed across it at a ford, then struck the boglands of western Cavan. Sometimes there was a road of sorts, sometimes they plodded across grassy moors, following the vague and verbose directions of peasants. As they skirted patches of forest, deer started and ran before them, and once a tongue-lolling wolf trotted parallel to their track for a while before abandoning the game.

By nightfall they had covered at least half their journey. Brodsky, who had begun by feeling sorry for himself, began to recover somewhat under the ministrations of Belphebe's excellent camp cookery, and announced that he had seen quite enough of ancient Ireland and was ready to go back.

"I don't get it," he said. "Why don't you just mooch off the way you came here?"

"Because I'm unskilled labor now," explained Shea. "You saw Cathbadh make that spell—he started chanting in the archaic language and brought it down to date. I get the picture, but I'd have to learn the archaic. Unless I can get someone else to send us back. And I'm worried about that. As you said, we've got to work fast. What are you going to tell them if they've started looking for you when we get back?"

"Ah, nuts," said Brodsky. "I'll level with them. The force is so loused up with harps that are always cutting up touches about how hot Ireland is that they'll give it a play whether they believe me or not."

Belphebe said in a small voice, "But I would be at home."

"I know, kid," said Shea. "So would I. If I only knew how."

Morning showed mountains on the right, with a round peak in the midst of them. The journey went more slowly than on the previous day, principally because all three had not developed riding calluses. They pulled up that evening at the hut of a peasant rather more prosperous than the rest, and Brodsky more than paid for their food and lodging with tales out of Celtic lore. The pseudo-Irishman certainly had his uses.

The next day woke in rain, and though the peasant assured them that Rath Cruachan was no more than a couple hours' ride distant, the group became involved in fog and drizzle, so that it was not till afternoon that they skirted Loch Key and came to Magh Ai, the Plain of Livers. The cloaks with which Cuchulainn had furnished them were of fine wool, but all three were soaked and silent by time a group of houses came into sight through air slightly clearing.

There were about as many of the buildings as would constitute an incorporated village in their own universe, surrounded by the usual stockade and wide gate—unmistakably Cruachan of the Poets, the capital of Connacht.

As they approached along an avenue of trees and shrubbery, a boy of about thirteen, in shawl and kilt and carrying a miniature spear, popped out of the bushes and cried: "Stand there! Who is it you are and where are you going?"

It might be important not to smile at this diminutive warrior. Shea identified himself gravely and asked in turn, "And who are you, sir?"

"I am Goistan mac Idha, of the boy troop of Cruachan, and it is better not to interfere with me."

Shea said, "We have come from a far country to see your King and Queen and the druid Ollgaeth."

He turned and waved his spear toward where a building like that at Muirthemne, but more ornate, loomed over the stockade, then marched ahead of them down the road.

At the gate of the stockade was a pair of hairy soldiers, but their spears were leaning against the posts and they were too engrossed in a game of knucklebones even to look up as the party rode through. The clearing weather seemed to have brought activity to the town. A number of people were moving about, most of whom paused to stare at Brodsky, who had flatly refused to discard the pants of his brown business suit and was evidently not dressed for the occasion.

The big house was built of heavy oak beams and had wooden shingles instead of the usual thatch. Shea stared with interest at windows with real glass in them, even though the panes were little diamond-shaped pieces half the size of a hand and far too irregular to see through.

There was a doorkeeper with a beard badly in need of trimming and lopsided to the right. Shea got off his horse and advanced to him, saying, "I am Mac Shea, a traveler from beyond the island of the Fomorians, with my wife and bodyguard. May we have an audience with their majesties, and their great druid, Ollgaeth?"

The doorkeeper inspected the party with care and then grinned. "I am thinking," he said, "that your honor will please the Queen with your looks, and your lady will please himself, so you had best go along in. But this ugly lump of a bodyguard will please neither, and as they are very sensitive and this is judgment day, he will no doubt be made a head shorter for the coming, so he had best stay with your mounts."

Shea glanced round in time to see Brodsky replace his expression of fury with the carefully cultivated blank that policemen use, and helped Belphebe off her horse.

Inside, the main hall stretched away with the usual swords and spears in the usual places on the wall, and a rack of heads, not as large as Cuchulainn's. In the middle of the hall, surrounded at a respectful distance by retainers and armed soldiers, stood an oaken dais, ornamented with strips of bronze and silver. It held two big carven armchairs, in which lounged, rather than sat, the famous sovereigns of Connacht.

Maev might have been in her early forties, still strikingly beautiful, with a long, pale, unlined face, pale blue eyes and yellow hair, hanging in long braids. For a blonde without the aid of cosmetics, she had remarkably red lips.

King Ailill was a less impressive figure than his consort, some inches shorter, fat and paunchy, with small close-set eyes constantly moving and a straggly pepper-and-salt beard. He seemed unable to keep his fingers still. *An ulcer type*, thought Shea, *he would be a chain smoker if tobacco existed in this part of the space-time continuum.*

A young man in a blue kilt, wearing a silver-hilted short sword over a tunic embroidered with gold thread, seemed to be acting as usher to make sure that nobody got to the royal couple out of turn. He spotted the newcomers at once, and worked his way toward them.

"Will you be seeking an audience, or have you come merely to look at the greatest King in Ireland?" he asked. His eyes ran appreciatively over Belphebe's contours.

Shea identified himself, adding, "We have come to pay our respects to the King and Queen...ah..."

"Maine mac Aililla, Maine mo Epert," said the young man.

This would be one of the numerous sons of Ailill and Maev, who had all been given the same name. But he stood in their path without moving.

"Can we speak to them?" Shea said.

Maine mo Epert put back his head and looked down an aristocratic nose. "Since you are foreigners, you are evidently not knowing that it is the custom in Connacht to have a present for the man who brings you before a King. But I will be forgiving your ignorance." He smiled a charming smile.

Shea glanced at Belphebe and she looked back in dismay. Their total possessions consisted of what they stood in. "But we have to see them," he said. "It may be as important to them as to us."

Maine mo Epert smiled again.

Shea said, "How about a nice broadsword?" and pushed forward his hilt.

"I have a better one," said Maine mo Epert, exasperatingly, and pushed forward his. "If it were a jewel, now..."

"How about seeing Ollgaeth the druid?"

"It is a rule that he will see none but those the Queen sends him."

Shea felt like whipping out the broadsword and taking a crack at him, but that would probably not be considered polite. Suddenly Belphebe beside him said: "Jewels have we none, sirrah, but from your glances, there is something you would prize more. I am sure that in accordance with your custom, my husband would be glad to lend me to you for the night."

Shea gasped, and then remembered. That geas she had acquired could be handy as well as troublesome. But it had better not be taken off till morning.

Maine mo Epert's smile turned into a grin that made Shea want more than ever to swat him, but he clapped his hands and began to push people aside. Shea had just time to whisper, "Nice work, kid," when the usher pushed a couple of people from the end of a bench and sat them down in the front row, facing the royal pair. At the moment a couple of spearmen were holding a serf and giving evidence that he had stolen a pork chop.

Maev looked at Ailill, who said, "Ahem—since the lout was starving, perhaps we ought to exercise mercy and let him off with the loss of a hand."

"Do not be a fool," said Maev, "when it is not necessary at all. What! A man in Connacht of the heroes who is so weak-witted that he must starve? Hang him or burn him, would be my decision if I were king."

"Very well, darling," said Ailill. "Let the man be hung."

Two little groups stepped forward next, glaring at each other. Maine mo Epert began to introduce them, but before he got halfway through, Maev said, "I know of this case and it promises to be a long one. Before we hear it I would willingly learn something of the business of the handsome pair of strangers you have brought in."

Maine mo Epert said, "This is a pair from the distant island called America. The Mac Shea and his wife, Belphebe. They wish to pay their respects."

"Let him speak," said Maev.

Shea wondered whether he ought to make an obeisance, but as no one else seemed to be doing it, he merely stepped forward and said, "Queen, you have become so famous that even in America we have heard of you, and we could not restrain the desire to see you. Also, I would like to see your famous druid, Ollgaeth, since my wife is suffering from a most unpleasant geas, and I am told he is an expert at removing them. Also, I have a message for you and the King, but that had better be private."

Maev rested her chin on her hand and surveyed him. "Handsome man," she said, "it is easy to see that you are not much used to deceiving your people. Your embroidery is in the style of Ulster, and now you will be telling me at once what this message is and from whom it comes there."

"It doesn't come from there," said Shea. "It's true I have been in Ulster, in fact at Cuchulainn's house of Muirthemne. And the message is that your plan against him will bring disaster."

King Ailill's fingers stopped their restless twitching and his mouth came open, while Maev's eyebrows formed a straight line. She said in a high voice, "And who told you of the plans of the King of Connacht?"

Look out, said Shea to himself, *this is thin ice.* Aloud he said, "Why, it's just that in my own country, I'm something of a magician, and I learned of it through spells."

The tension appeared to relax. "Magic," said Maev. "Handsome man, you have said a true word that this message should be private. We will hear more on it later. You will be at our table tonight, and there you will meet Ollgaeth. For the now, our son, Maine Mingor, will show you to a place."

She waved her hand, and Maine Mingor, a somewhat younger edition of Maine mo Epert, stepped out of the group and beckoned them to follow him. At the door Belphebe giggled and said, "Handsome man."

Shea said, "Listen..."

"That I did," said Belphebe, "and heard her say that the message should be private. You're going to need a geas as much as I do tonight."

The rain had stopped, and the setting sun was shooting beams of gold and crimson through the low clouds. The horses had been tied to rings in the wall of the building, and Pete was waiting, with an expression of boredom. As Shea turned to follow Maine Mingor, he bumped into a tall, dark man, who was apparently waiting around for just that purpose.

"Is it a friend of Cuchulainn of Muirthemne you are now?" asked this individual, ominously.

"I've met him, but we're not intimates," said Shea. "Have you any special reason for asking?"

"I have that. He killed my father in his own house, he did. And I am thinking it is time he had one friend the less." His hand went to his hilt.

Maine Mingor said, "You will be leaving off with that, Lughaid. These people are messengers and under the protection of the Queen, my mother, so that if you touch them it will be both gods and men you must deal with."

"We will talk of this later, Mac Shea dear," said Lughaid, and turned back to the palace.

Belphebe said, "I like that not."

Shea said, "Darling, I still know how to fence, and they don't."

6

Dinner followed a pattern only slightly different from that at Muirthemne, with Maev and Ailill sitting on a dais facing each other across a small table. Shea and Belphebe were not given places so lofty as they had been at Cuchulainn's board, but this was partly compensated for by the presence of Ollgaeth the druid just across the board.

Only partly, however; it became quite clear that Ollgaeth—a big, stoutish man with a mass of white hair and beard—was one of those people who pretend to ask questions only in order to trigger themselves off on remarks of their own. He inquired about Shea's previous magical experience, and let him just barely touch on the illusions he had encountered in the Finnish Kalevala before taking off.

"Ah, now you would be thinking that was a great rare thing to see, would you not?" he said, and gulped at barley beer. "Now let me tell you, handsome man, that of all the places in the world, Connacht produces the greatest illusions and the most beautiful. I remember, I do, the time when I was making a spell for Laerdach, for a better yield from his dun cow, and while I was in the middle of it, who should come past but his daughter, and she so beautiful that I stopped my chanting to look at her. Would you believe it now? The milk began to flow in a stream that would have drowned a man on horseback, and I had barely time to reverse the spell before it changed from illusion to reality and ravaged half a county."

Shea said, "Oh, I see. The chanting..."

Ollgaeth hurried on, "And there is a hill behind the rath of Maeve this very moment. It looks no different from any other, but it is a hill of great magic, being one of the hills of the Sidhe and a gateway to their kingdom."

"Who..." began Shea, but the druid only raised his voice a trifle: "Mostly now, they would be keeping the gateways closed. But on a night like tonight, a good druid, or even an ordinary one, might open the way."

"Why tonight?" asked Belphebe from beside Shea.

"What other night would it be but the Lughnasadh? Was it not for that you would be coming here? No, I forget. Forgive an old man." He smote his brow to emphasize the extent of his fault. "Maine mo Epert was after telling me that it was myself you came to see, and you could have done no better. Come midnight when the moon is high, and I will be showing you the powers of Ollgaeth the druid."

Shea said, "As a matter of fact..." but Ollgaeth rushed past him with: "I call to mind there was a man—what was his name?—had a geas on him that he would be seeing everything double. Now that was an illusion, and it was me he came to in his trouble. I..."

Shea was spared the revelation of what Ollgaeth had done in the case of the double vision by King Ailill's rapping on his table with the hilt of his knife and saying in his high voice, "We will now be hearing from Ferchertne the bard, since this is the day of Lugh, and a festival."

Serfs were whisking away the last of the food and benches were being moved to enlarge the space around Ferchertne. This was a youngish man with long hair and a lugubrious expression; he sat down on a stool with his harp, plucked a few melancholy twangs from the strings, and in a bumpish baritone launched into the epic of the "Fate of the Children of Tuirenn."

It wasn't very interesting, and the voice was definitely bad. Shea glanced around and saw Brodsky fidgeting every time the harpist missed a quantity or struck a false note. Everyone else seemed to be affected almost to the point of tears, however, even Ollgaeth. Finally Ferchertne's voice went up in an atrocious discord, and there was a violent snort.

The harp gave a twang and halted abruptly. Shea followed every eye in the room to the detective, who stared back belligerently.

"You would not be liking the music now, dear?" asked Maev, in a glacial voice.

"No, I wouldn't," said Brodsky. "If I couldn't do better than that, I'd turn myself in."

"Better than that you shall do," said Maev. "Come forward, ugly man. Eiradh, you are to stand by this man with your sword, and if I signal you that he is less than the best, you are to bring me his head at once."

"Hey!" cried Shea, and Brodsky: "But I don't know the words."

Protest was useless. He was grabbed by half a dozen pairs of hands and pushed forward beside the bard's seat. Eiradh, a tall, bearded man, pulled out his sword and stood behind the pair, a smile of pleasant anticipation on his face.

Brodsky looked around and then turned to the bard. "Give a guy a break, will you?" he said, "and go back over that last part till I catch the tune."

Ferchertne strummed obediently, while Brodsky leaned close, humming until he got the rather simple air that carried the words of the ballad. Then he straightened up, gesturing with one hand toward the harpist, who struck a chord and began to sing:

Take these heads unto thy breast, O Brian...

Pete Brodsky's voice soared over his, strong and confident, with no definite syllables, but carrying the tune for Ferchertne's words as the harp itself never had. Shea, watching Queen Maev, saw her stiffen, and then, as the melancholy ballad rolled on, two big tears came out on her cheek. Ailill was crying, too, and some of the audience were openly sobbing. It was like a collective soap opera binge.

The epic came to an end, Pete holding the high note after the harp had stopped. King Ailill lifted an arm and dried his streaming eyes on his sleeve, while Maev dried hers on her handkerchief. She said, "You have done more than you promised, American serf. I have not enjoyed the 'Fate of the Children' more in my memory. Give him a new tunic and a gold ring." She stood up. "And now, handsome man, we will be hearing your message. You will attend us while the others dance."

As a pair of bagpipers stepped forward and gave a few preliminary howls on their instruments, Maev led the way through a door at the back, down the hall to a. bedroom sumptuous by the standards that obtained here. There were rushlights against the wall, and a soldier on guard at the door.

Maev said, "Indech! Poke up the fire, for it is cool the air is after the rain."

The soldier jabbed the fire with a poker, leaned his spear against the door, and went out. Maev seemed in no hurry to come to business. She moved about the room restlessly.

"This," she said, "is the skull that belonged to Feradach mac Conchobar, that I killed in payment for the taking of my dear Maine Morgor. See, I have had the eye holes gilded."

Her dress, which had been a bright red in the stronger illumination of the hall, was quite a deep crimson here, and clung closely to a figure that, while full, was unquestionably well shaped. She turned her head and one of the jewels in her coronet threw a red flash of light into Shea's eyes.

"Would you be having a drop of Spanish wine, now?"

Shea felt a little trickle of perspiration gather on his chest and run down, and wished he were back with Ollgaeth. The druid was verbose and hopelessly vain, but he had furnished the tipoff on that chanting. It was some kind of quantity control for the spells that went with it. "Thanks," he said.

Maev poured wine into a golden cup for him, more for herself, and sat down on a stool. "Draw close beside me," she said, "for it is not right that we should be too much overheard. There. Now what is this of planning and disasters?"

Shea said, "In my own country I am something of a magician, or druid as you call it. Through this I have learned that you're going to get all Cuchulainn's enemies together, then put a geas on him to make him fight them all at once."

She looked at him from narrowed eyes. "You know too much, handsome man," she said, and there was a note of menace in her voice. "And what is this of disasters?"

"Only that you better not. You will succeed against Cuchulainn, but it will end up in a war, in which you and your husband and most of your sons will be killed."

She sipped, then stood up suddenly and began to pace the floor, moving like a crimson tide. Shea thought etiquette probably required him to get up, too, and he did so.

Not looking at him, Maev said, "And you have been at Muirthemne... Which is to say you have told the Hound of what we hold in store for him... Which is to say that Cathbadh knows of it also... Ha!" She whirled with sudden panther-like grace and faced Shea. "Tell me, handsome man, is it not true that Cathbadh sent you here to turn us from our purpose? Is not that tale of wars and disasters something he made up and put into your mouth?"

Shea said, "No, it isn't. Honest. I did talk to Cathbadh, and he'd like to stop this chain reaction, but I came here for something quite different."

She stamped. "Do not be lying to me. I see it all. Cathbadh can no more protect Cuchulainn against the geas of Ollgaeth than a pig can climb trees, so he would be sending you here with your talk of magic."

This was getting dangerous. Shea said, "Cathbadh did admit that Ollgaeth was the better druid."

"I thank him for the sending." She turned and stepped across the room, opened a big jewel case, from which she took a gold bracelet. "Come hither."

Shea stepped over to her. She rolled up his sleeve and snapped the bracelet on his arm.

"Thanks," said Shea, "but I don't think I ought to accept..."

"And who are you to be saying what you will accept from Queen Maev? It is a thing decided, and I will never come to terms with Cuchulainn, no matter if it costs me my life and all. Come, now."

She filled the wine cups again, took his hand, guided him to the stools and sat down close beside him. "Since life will be so short we may as well have what we can out of it," she said, drank off the cup and leaned back against him.

The thought leaped across his mind that if he moved aside and let this imperious and rather beautiful woman slip to the floor, she would probably have his head taken off. He put his arm around her in self-defense. She caught the hand and guided it to her bosom, then reached for the other hand and led it to her belt. "The fastening is there," she said.

The door opened and Maine mo Epert came in, followed by Belphebe.

"Mother and Queen..." began the young man, and stopped.

To give Maev due credit, she got to her feet with dignity and without apparent embarrassment. "Will you be forever behaving as though you were just hatched from the shell, now?" she demanded.

"But I have a case against this woman. She made a promise to me, she did, and she has a geas on her that makes a man as ill as though bathed in venom."

"You will be having Ollgaeth take it off, then," said Maev.

"'Tis the night of Lugh. Ollgaeth is not to be found."

"Then you must even bed by yourself, then," said Maev. She looked at Belphebe and her expression was rather sour.

"I think we had better be going along, too, Harold," said Belphebe, sweetly.

7

When they were outside, Belphebe said, "Tell me not. I know. She looked so fine in that red robe that you wished to help her take it off."

Shea said, "Honest, Belphebe, I..."

"Oh, spare me your plaints. I'm not the first wife to have a husband made of glass and breakable, nor will be the last. What is that you have on your arm?"

"Listen, Belphebe, if you'll only let me tell you..."

A form stepped out of the shadows into moonlight which revealed it as Ollgaeth. "The hour is met if you would see the Hill of the Sidhe, Mac Shea," he said.

"Want to come along, kid?" said Shea. "This might be useful for both of us."

"Not I," said Belphebe. "I'm for bed—geas and all." She lifted a hand to stifle an imaginary yawn.

Shea said, "Maybe I..." and stopped. He hated to leave Belphebe alone in her present mood, no matter how really unjustified it was. But it occurred to him that if he wanted to get any cooperation out of the vain druid, he would have to play along and butter him up. And it was distinctly important to learn about the system of magic here.

"All right," he said. "See you later, dear."

He turned to follow Ollgaeth through the dark streets. The guards at the gate were awake, a tribute to Maev's management, but they passed the druid and his companion through readily enough. Ollgaeth, stumbling along the track, said, "The Sidhe, now, they have the four great treasures of Ireland—Dagda's cauldron that will never let a man go foodless, the stone of Fal that strikes every man it is aimed at, Lugh's spear and Nuada's great manslaying sword that is death to all before it but protection to the bearer."

"Indeed," said Shea. "At the table you were saying..."

"Will you never let a man finish his tale?" said Ollgaeth. "The way of it is this: The Sidhe themselves may not use the treasures—there is a geas on them that they can he handled only by a man of Milesian blood. Nor will they give them up, for fear the treasures may be used against them. And all who come into their land, they use hardly."

"I should think..." began Shea.

"I do call to mind there was a man named Goll tried it," said Ollgaeth. "But the Sidhe cut off both his ears and fed them to the pigs, and he was never the same man after. Ah, it's a queer race they are, and a good man one must be to sit at table with them."

The Hill of the Sidhe loomed in front of them.

"If you will look there carefully, handsome man," said Ollgaeth, "to the left of that little tree, you will see a darkish patch in the rocks. Let us move a little closer now." They climbed the base of the hill. "Now if you will be standing about here, watch the reflection of the moon on the spot there."

Shea looked, moving his head from side to side, and made out a kind of reflection on the surface of the rock, not so definite and clear as it might be, more like that on a pond, wavering slightly with ripples. Clearly an area of high magical tension.

Ollgaeth said, "It is not to everyone I would be showing this or even telling it, but you will be going back to your America, and it is as well for you to know that—because of the spells the Sidhe themselves place on these gates, they may be opened without the use of the ancient tongue. Watch how."

He raised his arms and began to chant:

> *The chiefs of the voyage over the sea*
> *By which the son of Mil came...*

It was not very long, ending

> *Who opens the gateway to Tir na n-Og?*
> *Who but I, Ollgaeth the druid?*

He clapped his hands together sharply. The wavering reflection faded out and Shea saw nothing but blackness, as if he were looking into a tunnel in the side of the hill.

"Approach, approach," said Ollgaeth. "It is not like that the Sidhe will be dangerous against a druid as powerful as myself."

Shea went nearer. Sure enough, he was looking down a tunnel that stretched some distance into blackness, with a faint light beyond. He put out a hand; it went into the hole where solid rock had been without resistance, except for a slight tingly feeling.

Shea asked, "How long will it stay open?"

"Long enough for whatever passes to reach the other side."

"Do you suppose I could open it, too?"

"Are you not a qualified magician, now? To be sure you could, if you will learn the spell. But you will give me something in exchange."

"Certainly," said Shea. He thought; there was the one he had used in Faerie. "How about a spell to change water into wine? I can teach it to you first thing in the morning." If he did it himself, the result would probably be rum of an uncommonly potent brew, but qualitative control was this guy's own business.

Ollgaeth's eyes almost glittered in the moonlight. "That would be a thing to see, now. Raise your arms."

He followed Ollgaeth through the spell a couple of times, then repeated it alone. The wavelike shimmering disappeared, and the tunnel came open.

"I am thinking," said Ollgaeth, as they made their way back to the town, "that it would be as well not to come here again the night. The Sidhe will be noticing their gate clap open and shut and setting a guard over it, and though they are poor in arms, it's a bad-tempered lot they are."

"I'll be careful," said Shea.

Within, he tapped at the door of the guesthouse. "Who's there?" asked Belphebe's voice.

"It's me—Harold."

The bolt slammed back, and the door opened to show her still fully dressed, a little line of worry in her forehead.

"My lord," she said, "I do pray your pardon for my angers. I do see now 'twas no more your fault than it was mine at Muirthemne. But we must be quick."

"What do you mean?"

She was collecting their small amount of gear. "Pete was here but now. We are in deadly danger, but more especially yourself. The Queen has given permission to this Lughaid who accosted you to take your head if he will."

Shea put his hand on his sword. "I'd like to see him try it."

"Foolish man! He is not coming alone, but with a band—six, half a score. Come." She pulled him toward the door.

"But where's Pete? We can't go back without him."

"Nor can we go back at all if we do not live out the night," she said, leading out into the dark, silent street. "Pete is doing what he can to gain us time—his singing's wholly caught them. Hurry!"

"I don't see what good merely running away tonight will do us," said Shea. "Wait a minute, though. I can get in touch with Ollgaeth. You're right."

There was only one guard at the gate, but he held his spear crosswise and said, "I cannot be letting you out again the night. The Queen has sent word."

Belphebe gave a little cry. Shea half turned to see sparks of light dancing, back among the houses. Torches. He swung round again, bringing his sword out with a sweep, and without warning, drove a thrust at the guard's neck. The soldier jerked up his buckler just in time to catch Shea's point in the edge of the bronze decorations. Then he lowered his spear and drew it back for a jab.

Shea recovered, knocking the spear aside, but was unable to get around the shield for a return lunge. He thrust twice, feinting with the intention of driving home into an opening, but each time a slight movement of the buckler showed it would be futile. The soldier balanced, drew back for another thrust, and then swore as Belphebe, who had slipped past him, caught the butt end of the weapon.

He shouted, "Ho! An alarm!"

They would have to work fast. Shea aimed a cut at the man's head, but he ducked, simultaneously releasing the spear into Belphebe's hands, who went tumbling backward as the man did a quick side step and whipped out his sword.

Shea made a lightning estimate; the guard's face and neck were too small a target and too well protected by the shield, and the torso was doubly protected by shield and mail. Down.

He made a quick upward sweep that brought the buckler aloft, then drove the blade into the man's thigh, just above the knee and below the edge of the kilt. He felt the blade cleave meat; the man's leg buckled, spilling him to the ground in a clang of metal with a great groaning shout.

Behind them in, the rath there were answering cries and the torchlight points turned. "Come on!" cried Belphebe, and began to run. She still clutched the big spear, but was so light on her feet that it did not appear to matter. Shea, trying to keep up with his wife, heard more shouts behind him. "The hill," he gasped, and as he ran, was suddenly glad that the Irish of this period were not much with bows.

There were only occasional trees, but the moonlight was tricky and dubious. A glance backward showed the torchbearers had reached the gate and were beginning to spread. There ought to be just barely time if he could remember the spell correctly. Whatever dangers the country of the Sidhe held, they were less than those to be encountered by staying.

He was getting short of breath, though Belphebe beside him was running as lightly as ever. The hill loomed over them, dark now by reason of the movement of the moon. "This way," gasped Shea, and led up the uneven slope. There was the black rock, still shining queerly mirrorlike. Shea lifted his arms over his head and began to chant, panting for breath:

> *The chiefs of the voyage—over the sea—*
> *By which—the sons of Mil came...*

Behind one of the pursuers set up a view-halloo. Out of the corner of his eye, Shea saw Belphebe whirl and balance the spear as though for throwing; he didn't have time to stop and tell her that such a weapon couldn't be used that way.

"Who but I, Harold mac Shea?" he finished; resoundingly. "Come on."

He dragged Belphebe toward the dimly seen black opening and then through it. As he entered the darkness he felt a tingling all over, as of a mild electric shock.

Then, abruptly, sunlight replaced moonlight. He and Belphebe were standing on the downward slope of another hill, like the one they had just entered. He had time to take in the fact that the landscape was similar to the one they had quitted, before something crashed down on the back of his head and knocked him unconscious.

8

Briun mac Smetra, King of the Sidhe of Connacht, leaned forward in his carven chair and looked at the prisoners. Harold Shea looked back at him as calmly as he could, although his hands were bound behind his back and his head was splitting. Briun was a tall, slender person with pale blond hair and blue eyes that seemed too big for his face. The rest of them were a delicate-looking people, clad with Hellenic simplicity in wraparound tunics. Their furnishings seemed a point more primitive than those in the Ireland from which they had come—the building they were in had a central hearth with a smoke hole instead of the fireplaces and chimneys he had seen there.

"It will do you no good at all to be going on like this," said the King. "So now it is nothing at all you must lose but your heads, for the blackhearted Connachta that you are."

"But we're not Connachta!" said Shea. "As I told you..."

A husky man with black hair said, "They look like Gaels, they speak like Gaels, and they are dressed like Gaels."

"And who should know better than Nera the champion, who was a Gael himself before he became one of us?" said the King.

"Now look here, King," said Shea. "We can prove we're not Gaels by teaching you things no Gael ever knew."

"Can you now?" said Briun. "And what sort of things would those be?"

Shea said, "I think I can show your druids some new things about magic."

Beside him Belphebe's clear voice seconded him. "I can show you how to make a bow that will shoot—two hundred yards."

Briun said, "Now it is to be seen that you are full of foolish lies. It is well known that we already have the best druids in the world, and no bow will shoot that far. This now is just an excuse to have us feed you for a time until it is proved you are lying, which is something we can see without any proof being needed. You are to lose your heads."

He made a gesture of dismissal and started to rise. The black-thatched Nera said, "Let me..."

"Wait a minute!" cried Shea, desperately. "This guy is a champion, isn't he? All right, how about it if I challenge him?"

The King sat down again and considered. "Since you are to lose your head anyway," he said, "we may as well have some enjoyment out of it. But you are without armor."

"Never use the stuff," said Shea. "Besides, if neither one of us has any, things will move faster." He heard Belphebe gasp beside him, but did not turn his head.

"Ha, ha," said Nera. "Let him loose and I will be making him into pieces of fringe for your robe."

Somebody released Shea and he stretched his arms and flexed his muscles to restore circulation. He was pushed rather roughly toward the door, where the Tuatha De Danaan were forming a ring, and a sword was thrust into his hand. It was one of the usual Irish blades, almost pointless and suitable mainly for cutting.

"Hey!" he said. "I want my own sword, the one I had with me."

Briun stared at him a moment out of pale, suspicious eyes. "Bring the sword," he said, and then called: "Miach!"

The broadsword that Shea had ground down to as fine a point as possible was produced. A tall old man with white hair and beard that made him look like a nineteenth-century poet stepped forward.

"You are to be telling me if there is a geas on this blade," said the King.

The druid took the blade and, holding it flat on both palms, ran his nose along it, sniffing. He looked up. "I do not find any smell of geas or magic about it," he said, then lifted his nose like a hound toward Shea. "But about this one there is certainly something that touches my profession."

"It will not save him," said Nera. "Come and be killed, Gael." He swung up his sword.

Shea just barely parried the downstroke. The man was strong as a horse, and had a good deal of skill in the use of his clumsy weapon. For several panting minutes the weapons clanged; Shea had to step back, and back again, and there were appreciative murmurs from the audience.

Finally, Nera, showing a certain shortness of breath and visibly growing restive, shouted, "You juggling Greek!" took a step backward and wound up for a two-handed overhead cut, intended to beat down his opponent's blade by sheer power. Instantly Shea executed the maneuver known as an advance-thrust—dangerous against a fencer, but hardly a barbarian like this. He hopped forward, right foot first, and shot his arm out straight. The point went right into Nera's chest.

Shea's intention was to jerk the blade loose with a twist to one side to avoid the downcoming slash. But the point stuck between his enemy's ribs, and, in the instant it failed to yield, Nera's blade, weakened and wavering, came down on Shea's left shoulder. He felt the sting of steel and in the same moment the sword came loose as Nera folded up wordlessly.

"You're hurt!" cried Belphebe. "Let me loose!"

"Just a flesh wound," said Shea. "Do I win, King Briun?"

"Loose the woman," said the fairy King, and tugged at his beard. "Indeed, and you do. A great liar you may be, but you are also a hero and champion, and it is our rule that you take his place. You will be wanting his head for the pillars of the house you will have."

"Listen, King," said Shea. "I don't want to be a champion, and I'm not a liar. I can prove it. And I've got obligations. I really come from a land as far from the land of the Gaels as it is from Tir na n-Og and, if I don't get back there soon, I'm going to be in trouble."

"Miach!" called the King. "Is it the truth he is telling?"

The druid stepped forward, said, "Fetch me a bowl of water," and when it was brought, instructed Shea to dip a finger in it. Then he made a few finger-passes, murmuring to himself, and looked up.

"It's of the opinion I am, he said, "that this Mac Shea has obligations elsewhere, and if he fails to fulfill them, a most unfavorable geas would come upon him."

"We may as well be comfortable over a mug of beer in deciding these questions," said the King. "We command you to follow us."

Belphebe had been dabbing at Shea's shoulder. Now she caught his hand and they went in together. The big sword was awkward, and they had taken his scabbard as well, but he clung to it anyway. When they were inside, and King Briun had seated himself again, he said, "This is a hard case, and requires thinking, but before we give judgment, we must know what there is to know. Now, what is this of a new magic?"

"It's called sympathetic magic," said Shea. "I can show Miach how to do it, but I don't know the old tongue, so he'll have to help me. You see—I've been trying to get back to my own place, and I can't do it because of that." He went on to explain about the court of Maev and Ailill, and the necessity of rescuing Pete and getting back with him. "Now," he said, "if someone will give me a little clay or wax, I'll show you how sympathetic magic is done."

Miach came forward and leaned over with interest, as someone brought a handful of damp clay to Shea, who placed it on a piece of wood and formed it into a rather crude and shapeless likeness of the seated King. "I'm going to do a spell to make him rise," said Shea, "and I'm afraid the effect will be too heavy if you don't chant. So when I start moving with my hands, you sing."

"It shall be done," said Miach.

A verse or two of Shelley ought to make a good rising spell. Shea went over it in his head, then bent down and took hold of the piece of wood with one hand, while he murmured the words and with the other began to make the passes. He lifted the piece of wood. Miach's chant rose.

So did a shriek from the audience. Simultaneously an intolerable weight developed on Shea's arm, a crack zigzagged across the floor, and he half-turned his head in time to see that the royal palace and all its contents were going up like an elevator, already past the lower branches of the trees, with one of the spectators clinging desperately to the doorsill by his finger-tips.

Shea stopped his passes and hastily began repeating the last line backward, lowering his piece of wood. The palace came down with a jar that sent things tumbling from the walls and piled the audience in a yelling heap. Miach looked dazed.

"I'm sorry," began Shea. "I..."

Patting his crown back into position, King Briun said, "Is it ruining us entirely you would be?"

Miach said, "O King, it is my opinion that this Mac Shea has done no more than was asked, and that this is a very beautiful and powerful magic."

"And you could remove the geas on this woman and return the pair to their own place?"

"On the wings of the wild swan."

"Then hear our judgment." King Briun stretched forth a hand. "It is the command of the gods on all of us to help others fulfill their obligations, and this we will do. Yet it is equally true that a doing should be met with a doing in return, and this we cannot escape. Now, Mac Shea has killed our champion, and does not wish to take his place. There must be a balance against this, and we set it that it shall be this wonder-working bow of his wife's, which if it is as good as his magic, will surely shoot holes through the walls of the mountains."

He paused and Shea nodded. The man could be quite reasonable after all.

"Secondly," Briun went on, "there is the matter of removing his wife's geas. Against this we will place the teaching of this new magic to our druid. Now respecting the transfer of these two to their own country, there is no counterweight, and it is our judgment that it should be paid for by having Mac Shea undertake to rid us of the sinech, since it is so troublesome a monster and he is so great a champion and magician."

"Just a minute," said Shea. "That doesn't help us find Pete or get him back, and we'll be in trouble if we don't. And we really ought to do something for Cuchulainn. Maev is going through with her plan against him."

"We would most willingly help you in this matter, but you have no other prices to pay."

Miach said, "Yet there is a way to accomplish all they ask, save the matter of the man Pete, in the finding of whom I have no power."

Briun said, "You will be telling us about it, then."

"Touching the geas," said Miach. "Since it is one that was imposed, and not a thing natural, it can be lifted at the place and in the presence of the druid who laid it, and it will be needful for me to accompany these two to the place where it was put on. Touching the sinech, it is so dreadful a monster that even Mac Shea will be hard put against it by his own strength. Therefore let us lend him the great invincible sword of Nuada, which is forbidden to us by its geas, but which he will be able to handle without trouble, at all. Then he can lend it to this hero Cuchulainn, who will make a mighty slaughter of the Connachta we detest, and as I will be with the sword and Mac Shea, I can see that it is returned."

The King leaned his chin on one hand and frowned for a minute. Then he said, "It is our command that this be done as you advise."

9

Miach was an apt pupil. At the third try he succeeded in making a man he did not like break out in a series of beautiful yellow splotches, and he was so delighted with the result that he promised Shea for the hunting of the sinech not only the sword of Nuada, but the enchanted shoes of Iubdan, that would enable him to walk on water. He explained that the reason for the overcharge in Shea's magic was that the spells were in the wrong tongue; but, as the magic wouldn't work at all without a spell of some kind and Shea didn't have time to learn another language, this was not much help.

About the sinech itself he was more encouraging. He did a series of divinations with bowls of water and blackthorn twigs. Although Shea himself did not know enough of the magic of this continuum to make out anything but a confused and cloudy movement below the clear surface of the bowl, Miach assured him that in coming to this world of legendary Ireland, he had himself acquired a geas that would not allow his release until he had accomplished something that would alter the pattern of the continuum itself.

"Now tell me, Mac Shea," he said, "was it not so in the other lands you visited? For I see by my divinations that you have visited many."

Shea, thinking of how he had helped break up the chapter of magicians in Faerie and rescued his wife from the Saracens of the *Orlando Furioso*, was forced to agree.

"It is just as I am telling you, for sure," said Miach. "And I am thinking that this geas has been with you since the day you were born without your ever knowing it. We all of us have them, we do, just as I have one that keeps me from eating pig's liver, and a good man it is that does not have trouble with his geasa."

Belphebe looked up from the arrow she was shaping. Her bow was a success, but finding seasoned material from which to build shafts was a problem. "Still, master druid," she said, "it is no less than a problem to us that we may return to our own place late, and without our friend Pete. For this would place us deeply in trouble."

"Now I would not be worrying about that at all, at all," said Miach. "For the nature of a geas is that once it is accomplished, it gives you no more trouble at all. And the time you are spending in the country of the Sidhe will be no more than a minute in the time of your own land, so that you need not be troubling until you are back among the Gaels."

"That's a break," said Shea. "Only I wish I could do something about Pete."

"Unless I can see him, my divination will not work on him at all," said Miach. "And now I am thinking it is time for you to try the shoes. King Fergus of Rury was eaten up by this same sinech because he did not know how to use them, or another pair like them."

He accompanied Shea to one of the smaller lakes, not haunted by sinechs, and the latter stepped out cautiously from the shore. The shoes sank a little, forming a meniscus around them, but they seemed to give the lake water beneath a jellylike consistency just strong enough to support him. A regular walking motion failed to yield good results. He found he had to skate along, and he knew that, if he tripped over a wave, the result would be unfortunate. The shoes would not keep the rest of him from breaking through the surface and, once submerged, would keep his head down. But he found he could work up quite good speed and practiced making hairpin turns until night put an end to the operation.

Next morning they went out in a procession to Loch Gara, the haunt of the monster, with King Briun, Belphebe, and the assorted warriors of the Tuatha De Danaan. The latter had spears, but they did not look as though they would be much help. Two or three of them fell out and sat under trees to compose poems, and the rest were a dreamy-eyed lot.

Miach murmured a druid spell, unwrapped the sword of Nuada, and handed it to Shea. It was better balanced than his own broadsword, coming down to a beautiful laurel leaf point. As Shea swung it appreciatively, the blade began to ripple with light, as though there were some source of it within the steel itself.

He looked around. "Look, King," he said, "I'm going to try to do this smart. If you'll cut down that small tree there, then hitch a rope to the top of that other tree beside it. We'll bend down the second tree..."

Under his direction the Tuatha did away with one tree and bent the other down by a rope running to the stump of the first. This rope continued on, Shea holding the rest of it in a coil. "Ready?" he called.

"We are that," said King Briun. Belphebe took up her shooting stance, with a row of arrows in the ground beside her.

Shea skated well out in the lake, paying out the rope, which dragged in the water behind him. The monster seemed in no hurry to put in an appearance.

The Green Magician 401

"Hey!" called Shea. "Where are you, sinech? Come on out, Loch Ness!"

As if in answer, the still surface of the lake broke like a shattered mirror some fifty yards away. Through the surface there appeared something black and rubbery, which vanished and appeared again, much closer. The sinech was moving toward him at a speed which did credit to its muscles.

Shea gripped the rope with both hands and shouted, "Let her go!"

The little figures on shore moved around, and there was a tremendous tug on the rope. The men had untied the tackle, so that the bent tree sprang upright. The pull on the rope sent Shea skidding shoreward as though he were water skiing behind a motorboat. An arrow went past him and then another. Shea began to slow down, then picked up again as a squad of King Briun's soldiers took hold of the rope and ran inland with it as fast as they could. His theory was that the sinech would ground, and in that condition could be dispatched by a combination of himself, the soldiers with spears, and Belphebe's arrows.

But the soldiers on the rope did not yank hard enough to take up all the slack before Shea slowed down almost to a stop. Still twenty yards from shore, he could see the sandy bottom below him, looking a mere yard down.

Behind him he heard the water boiling and swishing under the urge of the sinech's progress. Shea risked a glance over his shoulder to catch a glimpse of a creature somewhat like a mosasaur, with flippers along its sides. Just behind the pointed, lizard-like head that reared from the water, a pair of arrows projected. Another had driven into its cheek-bone, evidently aimed for the eye.

The instant of looking back brought Shea's foot into contact with a boulder that lay with perhaps an inch projecting from the surface. Over it and down he went, head first into the water of the marge. The sinech's jaws snapped like a closing bank vault door on empty air, while Shea's head drove down until his face plowed into the sand of the bottom. His eyes open under the water, he could see nothing but clouds of sand stirred up by the animal's passage. The water swished around him as the sinech came in contact with solid ground and threshed frantically in its efforts to make progress.

The shoes of Iubdan kept pulling Shea's feet up, but at last he bumped into the boulder he had stumbled over. His arms clawed its sides and his head came out of water with his legs scrambling after.

The sinech was still grounded, but not hopelessly so. It was making distinct progress toward Belphebe, who valiantly stood her ground, shooting arrow after arrow into the creature. The same glance told him that the spearmen of the Tuatha De Danaan had taken to their heels.

The monster, engrossed in Belphebe as its remaining opponent, threw back its head for a locomotive hiss. Shea, skating toward it, saw her bend suddenly and seize up one of the abandoned spears to distract it from him. Tugging out the sword of Nuada, he aimed for the sinech's neck, just behind the head, where it lay half in and half out of water, the stiff mane standing up above Shea's head. As he drove toward the creature, the near eye picked him up and the head started to swivel back.

In his rush, he drove the sword in up to the hilt, hoping for the big artery.

The sinech writhed, throwing Shea back and ejecting the sword. There was a gush of blood so dark it looked black, the animal threw back its head and emitted a kind of mournful whistling roar of agony. Shea skated forward on his magical shoes for another shot, almost stumbling over the neck, but reaching down to grasp a bunch of mane in his left hand, and climbing aboard, cutting and stabbing.

The sinech threw back its head violently, it seemed to a height of thirty feet. Shea's grip on the mane was broken, and he was thrown through the air. All he could think of was that he must hang on to the sword. He had hardly formulated this thought before his behind struck the water with a terrific splash.

When he got his head out against the resistance of the shoes at the other end of his anatomy, the sinech was creaming the water with aimless writhings, its long head low on the bank, and its eyes already glassed. The sword of Nuada had lived up to its reputation. for giving mortal wounds, all right. Shea had to develop a kind of side-winding dog paddle to carry him into shallow water past the throes of the subsiding monster.

Belphebe waded out to help Shea to his feet, regardless of the wet. She put both arms around him and gave him a quick, ardent kiss, which instantly doubled him over with cramps. Behind her the Sidhe were trickling out of the wood, headed by King Briun, looking dignified, and Miach, looking both amazed and pleased.

Shea said, "There's your job. Do you think that lets me out from under that geas you say I've got?"

Miach shook his head. "I am thinking it will not. A rare fine change you have made in the land of the Sidhe, but it is to the land of men you belong, and there you must do what is to be done. So we will just be going along to see if you can avert the fate that hangs over this Cuchulainn."

10

Shea and Belphebe were bouncing along in a chariot on the route from the section of Tir na n-Og corresponding to Connacht to the otherworld equivalent of Muirthemne in Ulster. They had agreed with Miach, who was coming in another chariot, that this would be better than to reenter as they had come and possibly have to fight their way through hostile Connacht, even though he was wearing the invincible sword of Nuada.

The country around seemed very similar to that from which they had come, though the buildings were generally poorer, and there were fewer of them. Indeed, none at all were in sight when they stopped at a furze-covered hill with a rocky outcrop near its base. Miach signaled his charioteer to draw up and said, "Here stands another of the portals. You are to draw off a little while I cast my spell, as this is not one of the holy days and a magic of great power is required."

From the chariot, Shea could see him tossing his arms aloft and catch an occasional word of the chant, which was in the old language. A blackness, which seemed to suck up all the light of the day, appeared around the outcrop, considerably larger than the tunnel Shea himself had opened. The charioteers got down to lead the horses, and they found themselves on the reverse slope, with Cuchulainn's stronghold of Muirthemne in the middle distance, smoke coming from its chimneys.

Shea said, "That's queer. I thought Cuchulainn was at Emain Macha with the King, but it looks as though he came back."

"By my thinking," said Belphebe, "he is most strangely set on having his own will and no other, so that not even the prophecy of death can drive him back."

"I wouldn't..." began Shea, but was interrupted as a horseman suddenly burst from a clump of trees to the right, and went galloping across the rolling ground toward Cuchulainn's stronghold.

Miach called from the other chariot, "That will be a warden, now. I am thinking the fine man there is expecting company and is more than a little ready to receive it."

They went down a slope into a depression where the fold of the ground and a screen of young trees on the opposite side hid the view of Muirthemne. As they climbed the slope, the charioteers reined in. Glancing ahead, Shea saw that the saplings and bushes on the crest had all been pulled down and woven into a tangle. At the same time a line of men jumped out of cover, with spears and shields ready.

One of them advanced on the travelers. "Who might you be?" he demanded truculently, "and for why are you here?"

Miach said, "I am a druid of the Sidhe, and I am traveling with my friends to Muirthemne to remove a geas that lies on one of them."

"You will not be doing that the day," said the man. "It is an order that no druids are to come nearer to Muirthemne than this line until himself has settled his differences with the Connachta."

"Woe's me!" said Miach, then turned toward Shea. "You will be seeing how your geas still rules. I am prevented from helping you at the one place where my help would be of avail."

"Be off with you, now!" the man said and waved his spear.

Behind her hand, Belphebe said to Shea, "Is this not very unlike them?"

Shea said, "By George, you're right, kid! That isn't Cuchulainn's psychology at all." He leaned toward the guard. "Hey, you, who gave the order and why? Cuchulainn?"

The man said, "I do not know by what right you are questioning me, but I will be telling you it was the Shamus."

An inspiration struck Shea. "You mean Pete, the American?"

"Who else?"

"We're the other Americans that were here before. Get him for us, will you? We can straighten this out. Tell him that Shea is here."

The man looked at him suspiciously, then at Miach even more suspiciously. He pulled a little aside and consulted with one of his companions, who stuck his spear in the ground, laid the shield beside it, and trotted off toward Muirthemne.

Shea asked, "How comes Pete to be giving orders around here?"

"Because it's the Shamus he is."

Shea said, "I recognize the title all right, but what I can't figure out is how Pete got away from Cruachan and got here to acquire it."

He was saved from further speculation by the creaking of a rapidly driven chariot, which drew up on the other side of the hedge. From it descended a Pete Brodsky metamorphosed into something like the Connecticut Yankee at King Arthur's court. His disreputable trousers projected from beneath a brilliantly red tunic embroidered in gold; he had a kind of leather fillet around his head and a considerable growth of beard; and at his belt swung not one, but two obviously home-made blackjacks.

"Jeepers!" he said, "am I glad to see you! It's all right, gang—let these guys through. They're part of my mob."

Shea made room for him to climb in their chariot, and the spearmen fell back respectfully as Pete directed the driver through the winding gaps in the entanglement. When they had cleared it Shea asked, "How did you get here, anyway?"

Pete said, "It was a pushover. They had me singing until I almost busted a gut. I tried to get this Ollgaeth to send me back to Ohio, but he nixed it and said I'd have to throw in with their mob when they came over here to rub out Cuchulainn. Well, hell, I know what's going to happen to the guys in that racket. They're going to end up with their heads looking for the rest of them, and anyway I figure that if you go anywhere after you do your fadeout, it will be here. So one day when this Ollgaeth has me in the King's ice house showing me some of the flash, I figure it's a good chance to take along some presents. I let him have one on the conk, snatched everything I could and make a getaway."

"You mean you stole Ailill's crown jewels?" asked Shea.

"Sure. I don't owe him nothing, do I? Well, when I get here, they roll out the carpet and send for Cuchulainn. Well, I give him a line about how this Maev mob is coming to hit him on the head, like I told him before, but I add that they're gonna put a geas on all his gang so they'll go to sleep and can't do any fighting. That was different, see? They all want to get into the act, but they can't figure what to do about it. I been watching this Ollgaeth, see, and the line I got is that if he can't get close enough, he can't make this geas business stick."

"That's good magicology," said Shea. "Couldn't Cathbadh send you home?"

"Home? What do you mean, home? They told me to go to it, so I stashed the combination around the place like we done in the army. Then they made me head shamus of the force. Do you think I want to go back to Ohio and pound a beat?"

"Now, look here..." began Shea, but just then the gate of Muirthemne loomed over them, with Cuchulainn and Cathbadh beside it, accompanied by a tall, beautiful woman who must be Emer.

The hero said, "It is glad to see you that I am, darlings. Your man is less beautiful than ever, but you will be handselling him to me, for I think that with his help I may escape the doom that has been predicted."

Shea climbed down and helped Belphebe out of the chariot. "Listen," he said. "Pete's already done all he can for you, and we don't dare go back to our own country without him."

Pete said, "Look, I'll write you a letter or something to put you in the clear. Leave a guy run his own racket, will you? This is my spot."

"Nothing doing," said Shea. "Go ahead, Miach."

The druid lifted his arms, mumbled one or two words, and lowered his arms again. "The geas is still upon you, Mac Shea," he said. "I cannot."

"Oh, I forgot," said Shea, and pulled the sword from his belt. "Here, Cuchulainn, this is the sword of Nuada. I borrowed it from the Sidhe for you, and it will have to go back to them after you're through with the Connachta, who ought to be here any minute. But it will protect you better than Pete could. Does that leave us square?"

"It does that," said Cuchulainn, holding the great sword up admiringly. Light rippled and flowed along the blade.

"Now, Miach," said Shea.

Miach lifted his arms. "Hey, I don't want..." began Pete, as the chant rose. *Whoosh!*

Shea, Belphebe, and Brodsky arrived with a rush of displaced air in the living room at Garaden, Ohio, and almost in a heap. Behind them, the door of Shea's study stood open. As the trio landed, a couple of heavy-set men with large feet turned startled faces, their hands full of Shea's papers.

"It's them!" said one.

The other said, "And by gawd—Pete Brodsky, the synthetic harp, in a monkey suit!" They both began to laugh.

"Hell with that, you punks," said Pete. "I've had enough Ireland to last me. From now on it's *na zdorowie Polska!* See?"

Shea paid little attention. He was too busy kissing Belphebe.

FLETCHER AND I

BY L. SPRAGUE DE CAMP
1975

My late friend and collaborator Fletcher Pratt (1897–1956) was a connoisseur of heroic fantasy before that term was ever invented. He read Norse sagas in the original and extravagantly admired E. R. Eddison's *The Worm Ouroboros*. Curiously, he despised Robert E. Howard's Conan stories—next to Tolkien's *Lord of the Rings* three-decker, the most successful books in the genre—because their occasional crudities and lapses of logic exasperated him. He had no use for heroes who merely battered their way out of traps by their bulging thews, without using their brains.

(Murray) Fletcher Pratt, the son of an upstate New York farmer, was born on the Indian reservation near Buffalo. He claimed that this gave him the right to hunt and fish in New York State without a license, but he never availed himself of the privilege.

As a youth, five foot three but wiry and muscular, Pratt undertook two careers in Buffalo. One was that of librarian; the other, that of prizefighter in the fly-weight (112-pound) class. He fought several times, lost a couple of teeth, and knocked one opponent cold. When the story appeared in the Buffalo papers, the head librarian told him that it simply would not do to have one of their employees knocking people arsy-versy. Forced to choose between the two careers, Pratt chose the library.

Soon afterward, Pratt entered Hobart College at Geneva, New York, on Lake Seneca. When the coach learned that Pratt had been in the ring, he tapped him for an assistant in his boxing class. Word got around that this funny-looking little freshman who was showing the boys in the gym how to do rights over lefts was the real thing. Hence, somewhat to his disappointment, Pratt was never hazed.

At the end of Pratt's freshman year, his father fell on hard times. Pratt had to leave college. In the early 1920's, he worked as a reporter on the Buffalo

Courier-Express and on a Staten Island paper. Later, he settled in New York with his second wife, the artist Inga Stephens Pratt.

For several years, Pratt held a succession of fringe literary jobs, such as editing a "mug book" (a biographical encyclopedia), in which people of small importance were persuaded to pay money to have their pictures and biographies included. He also worked for one of those writers' institutes that promise to turn every would-be scribbler into a Tolstoy and that keep the money coming in by fulsome flattery of the veriest bilge submitted to them. Later, as an established author, Pratt drew on these experiences in lecturing to writers' groups on literary rackets.

In the late 1920's, Pratt got a foothold as a free-lance writer. From 1929 to 1935 he sold a number of science-fiction stories to *Amazing*, *Wonder*, and other science-fiction pulps of the time. He also worked for Hugo Gernsback, then publishing *Wonder Stories*. Pratt translated European science-fiction novels from the French and the German. Gernsback had a habit of not paying his authors what he had promised, but Pratt got around him. He would translate the first installment or two of a European novel and then, when the material was already in print, say:

"I'm sorry, Mr. Gernsback, but if you don't pay me what you owe, I don't see how I can complete this translation."

He had Gernsback over a barrel. He also took off more than a year to live in Paris on the insurance money that he collected after a fire gutted the Pratts' apartment. He studied at the Sorbonne and did research for his book on codes and ciphers, *Secret and Urgent*.

Pratt learned Danish among other languages, spoke French with a terrible accent, and became friends with the curator of arms and armor at the Louvre, who once let him try on the armor of King Francois I. In his day, the king had been deemed a large, stout man. The flyweight Pratt found all the armor too small except the shoulder pieces; Francois had tremendous shoulders from working out with sword and battle-ax in the tilt yard.

Back in New York, Pratt—now a self-made scholar of respectable attainments—attacked more serious writing. After an abortive history of Alexander's successors, he hit his stride with books like *The Heroic Years*, about the war of 1812, and *Ordeal by Fire*, a popular history of the American Civil War.

The Pratt ménage in New York attracted a wide circle of friends, drawn by Pratt's lavish hospitality and extraordinary sense of fun. One room of the apartment was cluttered with cages full of squeaking marmosets, which Pratt successfully raised by feeding them on vitamin tablets and squirming yellow larvae.

As a history, military, and naval buff, Pratt devised a naval war game, to which his friends were invited once a month. In odd moments, he had whittled out scale models (55 feet = 1 inch) of the world's war-ships, using balsa wood, wires, and pins, until there were hundreds of models crowding his shelves. The game called for the players to crawl around on the floor, moving their models the distances allowed on scales marked in knots; estimating ranges in inches to the ships on which they were firing; and writing down these estimates. Then the referees chased the players off and measured the actual ranges, penalizing ships hit so many points, according to the size of the shells, and depriving them of so many knots of speed, so many guns, and so on. When a ship had lost all its points, it was taken from the floor. There were special provisions for merchant ships, shore batteries, submarines, torpedoes, and airplanes.

For several years, the war garners met in the Pratts' apartment. When this became too crowded, with fifty or more players at once, the games moved to a hall on East Fifty-ninth Street. After World War II, interest declined.

Pratt's interests also included the reading of sagas and gourmet cookery. He wrote a cookbook, *A Man and His Meals*. He taught at the Bread Loaf Writers' Conference, was a Baker Street Irregular, and served for seven years as president of the New York Authors' Club. In 1944, he founded a stag eating, drinking, and arguing society, the Trap Door Spiders, which still meets periodically in New York.

In 1939, my old friend and college roommate, John D. Clark; introduced me to Pratt. A naval buff of long standing myself, I was soon an enthusiastic war gamer and a regular attendant at the Pratts' evenings, along with such colleagues as Laurence Manning, Malcolm Jameson, Ted Sturgeon, George O. Smith, and L. Ron Hubbard, who had not yet manifested himself as the pontiff of Scientology.

I had been free-lancing for a year and a half, having been fired as an economy measure from an editorial job on a trade journal. I was also in the midst of getting married. With the appearance of John W. Campbell's fantasy magazine *Unknown*, Pratt conceived the idea of a series of novellas, in collaboration with me, about a hero who projects himself into the parallel worlds described in our world in myths and legends. We made our protagonist a brash, self-conceited young psychologist named Harold Shea.

First we sent Harold to the world of Scandinavian myth, in "The Roaring Trumpet" (*Unknown*, May 1940). Pratt furnished most of the background for this story, since at that time my knowledge of Norse myth was limited to popular digests and retellings. I had not yet read such splendid sources as the *Heimskringla* and the *Prose Edda*.

For the second episode, we transferred Harold to the world of Spenser's *Faerie Queene* in "The Mathematics of Magic" (August 1940). I was never so enthusiastic about the *Faerie Queene* as Pratt was, finding it tedious for long stretches. Years later, however, when I took to writing verse, I composed a poem, "The Dragon-Kings", using the Spenserian nine-line stanza, which is a most exacting verse form. Having sweated through three such stanzas, I was awed by the feat of Edmund Spenser, whose *Faerie Queene* comprises over four thousand.

The first two novellas were followed by *The Castle of Iron* (April 1941), which took Harold to the world of Ariosto's *Orlando Furioso*. Also in that year, Holt brought out the first two novellas as the clothbound book *The Incomplete Enchanter*, which has since been through a number of editions. While Pratt proposed the basic themes for the first two stories, those for the later ones were worked out by discussion between us.

After World War II, Pratt and I rewrote and expanded *The Castle of Iron* to full-novel length, in which form it appeared in 1950. We also wrote two more novellas of the saga, placing Harold first in the world of the Finnish *Kalevala* ("The Wall of Serpents") and then in the world of Irish myth ("The Green Magician"). After magazine publication, these two stories were combined in, a cloth-bound volume, *Wall of Serpents*. It was not possible to include them in the present volume, first because of considerations of space and second because of contractual complications.

For obvious reasons, I cannot assess the virtues and faults of these works. I will say only that they were certainly heroic fantasy, or swordplay-and-sorcery fiction, long before these terms were invented. While Robert E. Howard is justly hailed as the major American pioneer in this subgenre, neither Pratt nor I, when we started the Shea stories, had even read a Conan story or ever heard enough about Howard to recognize his name.

Our method of collaboration was to meet in Pratt's apartment and hammer out the plot by long discussions during which I took shorthand notes. Observing the utility of Pratt's knowledge of shorthand from his journalistic days, I soon taught myself Gregg and have found it valuable ever since. I took the notes home and wrote a rough draft. Pratt then wrote the final draft, which I edited. In a few cases—our later stories of Gavagan's Bar, for example—we reversed the procedure, Pratt doing the rough draft and I the second. This did not work out so well. In such collaborations, it is generally better for the junior member to do the rough draft, since the senior member, as a result of experience, is likely to have more skill at polishing and condensation.

A fan magazine once asserted that in the Harold Shea stories de Camp furnished the imaginative element and Pratt the controlling logic. Actually, it was the other way around. Pratt had a livelier and more creative imagination than I, but I had a keener sense of critical logic. In any case, I learned much of what I think I know about the writer's craft in the course of these collaborations. Pratt's influence on me in this matter was second only to Campbell's.

In 1941, L. Ron Hubbard wrote one of his several hilarious fantasy novels for *Unknown: The Case of the Friendly Corpse* (August 1941). This tale had some of Hubbard's funniest passages but let the reader down badly at the end. The hero, Jules Riley, had swapped souls with an apprentice magician on another plane, who up to then has been a student at the College of the Unholy Names. Another student tells Jules (now on this other plane) that Harold Shea appeared before him, claiming to be a magician from another world. The student challenged Harold to a sporting contest: the student would turn his wand into a super-serpent, and Harold could summon up his own monster, and they would see which creature won. But "...the snake just grew up and then grabbed him and ate him up before I could do anything about it."

Some fans were indignant at Hubbard's so brusquely bumping off a colleague's hero. Pratt and I thought of writing a story to rescue Harold from the serpent's maw and turn the tables, but after some floundering we gave up. Another writer's *mise en scène*, we found, so severely cramps the imagination that fancy plods when it should soar. In the end, we ignored Hubbard and sent Harold on to other milieux.

During 1941-42, Pratt and I wrote two fantasy novels, *The Land of Unreason* and *The Carnelian Cube*. Pearl Harbor came just as I was finishing my part of *The Carnelian Cube*. I volunteered for the Naval Reserve, was commissioned, and spent the war navigating a desk at the Philadelphia Naval Base. I did engineering on naval aircraft along with Heinlein and Asimov.

Pratt, a strong patriot and nationalist, described himself as a political conservative—although, when one discussed actual current issues with him, one found in him a surprisingly objective, pragmatic, almost liberal attitude. Kept out of the armed forces by his physical limitations and age, he wrote a war column for the New York Post. This ended when his editor forced him to guess on the outcome of the battle of the Coral Sea, and he guessed wrong. He also wrote a number of books on the war, especially the part played in it by the U. S. Navy.

Then Pratt became a naval war correspondent assigned to Latin America. An old Brazilophile who spoke fluent Portuguese, Pratt visited Brazil. He had long worn a mustache and, in the early 1930's for a while, a goatee. Now he grew a straggly full beard, graying reddish in color and of Babylonian cut. He hated razors, and the Navy forbade him to use his electric shaver on shipboard in the Caribbean. This was long before the revival of beards in the 1950's and '60's. His small size, whiskers, thick, tinted glasses, and loud shirts made an ensemble not easily forgotten.

After the war, Pratt resumed living in New York, while my family and I stayed on in the suburbs of Philadelphia. We continued our collaborations with the two later Harold Shea novellas and the Gavagan's Bar stories—a series of barroom tall tales, comparable to (though conceived independently of) Arthur C. Clarke's *Tales of the White Hart*. Pratt also wrote two first-class heroic-fantasy novels of his own: *The Well of the Unicorn* and *The Blue Star*.

When he had finished *The Blue Star*, Pratt told his friends that he planned a third fantasy novel, about a modern woman who finds herself in the body of another woman of 1,800 years ago. With the approach of the Civil War centenary, however, Pratt became so busy with better-paying nonfiction that, during his last few years, he gave up fiction altogether. He had written over fifty books, including many science-fiction stories, books on Napoleon, biographies of Edwin M. Stanton and King Valdemar IV of Denmark, and a history of the U. S. Navy.

He and I had discussed possible future works of fiction, such as another Harold Shea story laid in the world of Persian myth, or a Gavagan's Bar story about a vampire with a sweet tooth who attacked only diabetics

But they were never written. For, in 1956, when he was fifty-nine and had just begun to hit the best-seller lists, Pratt suddenly fell ill of cancer of the liver and soon died.

I have not tried to carry on any of our series alone, because I think that the combination of Pratt and de Camp produced a result visibly different from either of us alone. Besides, I have always had more ideas waiting to be actualized in writing than I could find time to get down. But some of those who have not read the tales of Harold Shea's adventures may still, I trust, get some entertainment out of them.

Sir Harold and the Gnome King
BY L. Sprague de Camp
The Enchanter Reborn, Baen Books, 1992

"Darling," said Belphebe, "will you *please* stop worrying! The doctors all confirm that it be nought but a normal, healthy pregnancy."

"I know," said Harold Shea. "But I just can't help—"

"And you really must go off on your syllogismobile to fetch back Walter. If you do it not soon, he'll lose his tenure; the committee meets next month."

"What sort of husband goes off on some goofy quest when his wife's time is getting near?"

"Oh, cease your fussing and get along with you! Marry, I shall be just as pleased if, when you return, the babe's born and I have my wonted shape. Besides, the police are prey to ever-waxing suspicions—"

"Oh, all right," grumbled Shea. "But if anything goes wrong, I'll never forgive myself..."

Thus it came to pass that Harold Shea, incomplete enchanter, sat on the floor of his study arrayed in boots and breeches for his journey through other space-time dimensions, with a feathered hat on his head and a saber by his side.

He had decided that the epee, which he had used on other journeys to mythological worlds, was too specialized a weapon. It had served him well against opponents afoot and unarmored; but even so, it was more by luck than by management that the slender blade had not been snapped in parrying the ferocious cuts of edge-men, nor bent to breaking against stout armor.

His present weapon was a nineteenth-century officer's saber, with the blade shortened by a few inches. The original thirty-six-inch blade, suitable for a horseman, was too unwieldy for combat on foot. The swordsman who swung it might swing himself right off his feet.

As a backup weapon, Shea wore a bowie knife in a sheath at his belt. Moreover, whereas he had formerly scorned protective devices, he now wore beneath his outer garments a shirt of fine mesh-mail.

The last he had seen of Walter Bayard before his recent brief visit to mythical Ireland, his fellow psychologist at the Garaden Institute, was in the hut wherein he, Bayard, Belphebe, and Detective Peter Brodsky had been imprisoned by the chiefs of the world of the Finnish *Kalevala*. Shea's spell, with help from Belphebe and the cop, transferred them all to the world of mythical Ireland, with Cuchulainn and Queen Maeve. But Bayard, if indeed he came through the dimensions, was nowhere to be seen. Shea thought that he had probably been dumped somewhere else in the same world of myth.

But should Shea go back to Cuchulainn's Eriu to look for his colleague? The search might take years, with no end in sight. Moreover, these quasi-Irishmen showed a disturbing fondness for collecting peoples heads as trophies.

There was, however, a plausible shortcut: the Land of Oz, as chronicled by L. Frank Baum and later by Ruth Plumly Thompson. In Oz, a major magical artifact was the Gnome King's Magic Belt, confiscated by Dorothy Gale of Kansas after the King had treacherously tried to imprison her. The Belt was effective as a teletransporter. If Shea could enlist the help of the Belt's present custodians, he could fetch Bayard from mythical Eriu to Oz, whence the custodians could send the two of them back to Ohio.

Shea launched into the sorites that, he hoped, would bring him to the world of Oz: "If P equals not-Q, then Q implies not-P, which is the same as saying either P and Q or neither, but not both. But the counter-implicative form of the proposition..."

On went the sorites, adjusting Shea's senses to the stimuli of the other world he sought.

At length the study around him dissolved into a whirl of spots of color. He seemed suspended in nothing, as if in free fall. Then things solidified.

Shea found himself standing on a pavement of onyx squares among several small buildings of boxy shape. Behind these structures rose towering crags, in which yawned large black openings. Paved paths led up to these apertures. Up and down the paths walked figures in ankle-length gowns, with hoods drawn over their heads.

Shea stood still, trying to orient himself. Wherever he was, he did not think that this was the land of Oz—at least, not any section of it in the books by Baum and Thompson. Of course it had been years since...

He began to sort out the pedestrians. Some were of normal human stature and aspect, in hooded gowns of various colors, running strongly to somber purple. Others, inhumanly tall and lean, wore black; these had a single horn emerging from each hood. A closer view showed that those in black walked on hooves instead of human feet.

Looking around, Shea saw, rearing against the surrounding cliffs, a single lofty spire. Overhead the sky was overcast and so dark as to imply a dawn or a sunset. Flames of cressets and torchères mitigated the gloom. The orange light flickered, making it hard to be sure of anything.

Pedestrians walked past Shea without evincing interest. The hooves of the horned ones went *clop-clop* on the sable flagstones. Some of the walkers passed in pairs, conversing in quiet tones.

A shriek from the direction of the slender tower brought Shea about. He turned in time to see a gown-clad figure falling, doubtless from high in the tower. The garment fluttered with the body's rising speed, and the arms and legs thrashed the air. The figure landed with a sound that reminded Shea of hitting a melon with a mallet.

The hooded pedestrians continued their ways without even looking around. Soon a pair of horned, black-gowned beings picked up the corpse and bore it off.

Unable longer to stand the suspense, Shea touched a passerby on the arm. "Excuse me, sir."

The passerby, in a purple gown and holding a walking stick, turned and threw back his hood. "Eh? What is it?" He was a tall, handsome, swarthy, black-haired young man.

At least, thought Shea, the sorites had worked to give him fluency in the local language, whatever that was. From its wealth of gutturals, Shea suspected Arabic. He said:

"Could you please tell me where I am?"

The tall youth stared. "Do you mean you don't know?"

"No, I don't. A magical journey just dropped me here, but I don't think it's where I wanted to go. Could you set me right?"

"All right. You are on the campus of the University of the Unholy Names, in Death Valley."

"But what world?"

"You mean you don't even know *that*? You must be a little touched here..." The youth tapped his forehead.

"Maybe so, but I really must know. Please!"

"Well," said the tall youth, "this is the world called sometimes Dej, an acronym of Dâl Ay Jim—or, as the infidels say, Delta Epsilon Gamma."

"And you, sir?"

The youth ducked a little bow. "Bilsa at-Tâlib, an undergraduate at good old UUN, at your service. And you? You must be a pretty good magician, to go flitting from world to world."

Shea smiled warily. "Oh, I know a trick or two. My name's Shea, Harold Shea."

Shea almost put out a hand before realizing where he was. Recovering, he touched his fingertips to his heart, lips, and forehead. Bilsa, he was relieved to see, did likewise.

"What about that fellow who just fell from the tower?"

"Failed his exams and was dropped." Bilsa shrugged, then continued with an eager rush of words: "Say, you see this stick? I was on my way to show it to the dean. When I throw it down, it turns into a snake, which gets bigger and bigger until I hit it with this little wand, and it shrinks back into a walking stick again. I've got a swell idea! I'll turn this stick into a snake, see, and you conjure up your own monster; and we'll see which one of 'em wins!"

The youth was evidently of the kind that, in a college chemistry laboratory, starts mixing chemicals at random to see which mixture will go *boom*. Before Shea could protest, Bilsa threw down the stick, which instantly turned into a snake of the python kind. It grew and grew, soon reaching a size beyond that of any earthly serpent. It reared up and swung its tapering head, now as big as that of a horse, toward Shea. It opened fangsome jaws and hissed like the safety valve of a steam boiler.

Shea had no monster-conjuring spell to hand and did not wish any such contest. He must, he thought, have substituted a Q for a non-Q in the sorites. Against such a foe, his sword was of little avail. Frantically he again began the series:

"If P equals not-Q, then Q implies..."

The monstrous head, now of tyrannosauric size, swooped. The jaws came down upon his head and snapped shut like the door of a bank vault, cutting off the meager light. Shea felt himself snatched off his feet as the jaws clamped on his midriff. The mail shirt kept the teeth, now spikes the size of fence palings, from piercing his body, but the pressure of the jaws blew the wind out of him. By a mighty feat of concentration, he continued the spell:

"...which sets down Harold Shea near the abode of Dorothy Gale in the Land of Oz!"

The agonizing pressure on Shea's midsection let up. Again he seemed to be suspended in nothing and surrounded by a galaxy of whirling colored dots.

Then he landed on solid earth, rolling over and over as if he had fallen at a slant from a height. The scabbarded saber banged and poked him.

He sat up, wincing at the pain of the places bruised by the pressure of the reptile's jaws. Every movement of his trunk was painful. Around him rose a forest of green-leaved cornstalks, several of which he had broken in his fall. They were just coming into ear.

Battered, bruised, and sore, Shea gathered his legs and rose. His head and the upper part of his torso were covered with gooey serpent saliva, to which the brown dirt clung in patches. He must, he thought, look like nothing on Earth. He was bareheaded; his hat must have gone down the sorcerous serpent's gullet. Had he not finished the correct sorites, he would surely have followed the hat. He was thankful that, more by luck than by management, the spell had translocated him alone and not both him and the super-snake.

He had begun to thread his way out from the cornfield when a man shouted: "Hey, you there! What are you doing in my field?"

"Trying to get out without damaging anything," said Shea, picking his way among the cornstalks.

"The blazes you ain't! You mean without doing any *more* damage. You've knocked over a dozen stalks already!"

"I'm very sorry. In going from world to world, one can't always count on a soft landing."

"Jeepers Cripus, what world do you claim to come from?"

The speaker was a man of medium size, with work-roughened hands and a sun-wrinkled neck. He wore yellow knee breeches and a yellow shirt, both faded and patched, and a broad-brimmed straw hat. He gripped a cultivator like a weapon.

"From Ohio, in the United States of America," said Shea.

"Oh, the mundane world," said the man. "Well, now, that's interesting..."

"Is Dorothy Gale's house near here?" asked Shea.

"Huh? Oh, you must mean my wife! She was Dorothy Gale before she became Mrs. Stidoth. Well, now..."

"Stidoth!" came a woman's voice.

"Yeah, honey? Hey, come on over here! We got a visitor from your world!"

A woman approached—a blonde of middle years, well-featured and a little plump.

"Says he's lookin' for Miss Dorothy Gale," said Stidoth.

"Okay, mister, you found her," said the woman. "Where in my world did you come from?"

"Ohio. Shea's the name."

"Back east, eh? Well, another real American's always welcome. We don't see 'em around all that often, since we moved out from the Emerald City. Come on in the house. You look like you could do with a bit of a cleanup."

"If you'd been half swallowed by a giant snake—well, you know what I mean. Lucky for all of us I didn't bring the super-serpent with me. A magician conjured it up and sicced it on me."

"Come along; you can wash up in the house and tell us all about it. We got running water and everything."

Cleaned up, Shea had finished the tale of his adventure, saying: "Things look different from what I expected."

"How different?" said Stidoth, who without his straw hat proved somewhat balding.

"I thought people in Oz stayed the same age forever, until some accident took them."

Stidoth explained: "That's how it was, more or less, before the big change."

"Big change?"

"Yeah. Seems there was this kid, Dranol Drabbo, who couldn't wait to grow up. The way things were, he'd have growed up, all right, in a couple of hundred years; but he was one of these here flibbertigibbets who can't wait five minutes for anything they happen to want.

"Well, now, this here Dranol Drabbo went to Wogglebug College and majored in magic. And one of his experiments canceled the spell that some queen of the fairies laid on Oz centuries ago. People say that there spell got rid of death, but it ain't really so. All it did was to slow down the normal business of aging to a crawl, like a snail walking. Aging was already a lot slower for us Ozians than for you mundanes. You seem to us like them there bugs that flit around for a day and then die."

"Must have been a tragedy for the Ozites."

Stidoth shrugged. "Got advantages and disadvantages both ways, like most things in life. As 'twas, the population was getting out of hand, with the old folks hangin' on forever.

"Anyway, I was Dot's age at the time. So when we growed up we got hitched, and here we are. I didn't much like the idea of our boys going to Wogglebug, on account of what happened with Dranol Drabbo. Besides, too much book-learning can spoil a good farmer. But they sold Dot on the idea, and—well, you a married man, Mr. Shea?"

"Yes," said Shea. "Quite happily—but I know what you mean."

Stidoth chuckled. "The older boy'll be out in a couple of months, looking for a way to earn his three squares. Claims he's invented some sort of calculating machine." Stidoth's eyes narrowed. "All right, Mr. Shea, now tell us just what you came here for, and in particular why you wanted to see Dot."

Shea told of Walter Bayard's predicament. "...so I thought that, if I could persuade whoever's in charge of the Gnome King's Belt to fetch Bayard here and then send us both back to what you call the mundane world..."

Stidoth sat in silence for several seconds, then said: "Mr. Shea, if you owned one of them there atomic bombs we hear about, would you keep it in the cellar, where some kid might set it off accidental-like?"

"Of course not!"

"Same way here. That there belt could be just as dangerous, in the hands of some amateur piddler in magic like Dranol Drabbo, as one of them bombs. So it's kept locked up in the palace in the Emerald City."

"What happened to Dranol Drabbo?"

Stidoth sniffed. "Queen Ozma's a fine woman, and don't let nobody tell you different. But when she was a girl, she was full of airy-fairy impractical ideas. One was you shouldn't hurt nobody or nothing, even to save your own life. She almost let Oz be conquered several times, because she wouldn't believe anyone was so wicked as to plot agin her. Even when she was warned, she wouldn't fight, because that meant hurting or killing people. Each time she was saved by some lucky, last-minute magical trick; but you can't count on that kind of luck forever.

"So the question was, what to do with young Dranol Drabbo? I'd have called in Nick Chopper and had him operate with his ax on Dranol's neck. But no, the Queen decided the worst punishment she'd allow was to send him to exile in Ev.

"Well, you know the gnomes live under the ground where Ev is, and it didn't take long for Dranol to get in cahoots with the Gnome King, Kaliko—the one who followed Ruggedo. They say Kaliko fired his chancellor, Shoofenwaller, and gave his job to Dranol. Don't rightly know what sort of devilment they're cooking up; but I'm sure it's something.

"Course, when Ozma growed up and married King Evardo, it steadied her down. He's got plenty of hard common sense."

Shea thought. "This king—is he of the royal family of Ev?"

"Sure; he's King of Ev. But he lives here in Oz and lets his brother Evring run the kingdom as regent. That way, Evardo gets the fun of being king without the headaches."

Shea grinned. "Reminds me of a song from a show back in my world:

Oh, philosophers may sing
Of the troubles of a king;
Yet the duties are delightful and the privileges great...

Stidoth chuckled and slapped his thigh. "Hey, that's good! Wouldn't mind seeing that there show. Anyway, Evardo also got the duty of providing the most beautiful woman in Oz with heirs to the throne. Boy, that's one job plenty of men—"

"Stidoth!" said Dorothy sternly.

"Sorry. Anyway, they've only got two kids so far. The older's a boy—young man, almost—and I hear he's away visiting kinfolks in Ev. The other's a girl, just starting school. But a royal family needs a whole raft of heirs, in case something happens to the older ones. So I guess Evardo has lots of fun trying—"

"Stidoth!"

"Anyway, reckon you'll have to get to the Emerald City and hand a petition to some flunkey at the palace."

Shea shook his head. "It just doesn't seem like Oz somehow, those young fairyland girls growing up and having children of their own."

"Well, that's what they do in your mundane world, ain't it?"

"Yes; I'm an expectant father myself. It's just—well, it somehow spoils the magic." *How logical,* Shea thought, *that Dorothy, though here ranked as a princess, should wed a man of background like her own!*

"Don't you believe it, Mr. Shea. We got plenty of magic left. It's a matter of this here now mental attitude. When you was a kid, didn't your mundane world seem like a kind of fairyland to you, full of exciting things you later found out didn't exist? But when you growed up, you had to trade in those exciting things for the exciting things of the real world, even if they wa'n't so pretty.

"As for Ozma's getting spliced, I mind me some years ago, before Dranol worked his spell, some little princeling named—let me think—Pomp-something. Anyway, he asked Ozma to marry him. Course, he got turned down flat. Lucky young fella found another princess, who took him on.

"Then there was that there Baron Mogodore, who captured the capital by surprise and said he was going to many Ozma whether she liked it or not. Since the law says a marriage has got to be with the free will of both parties to be legal, there ain't really no such thing as a 'forced marriage,' leastaways in Oz. It's just a fancy name for plain old—"

"Stidoth!"

"Oh, all right, Dot honey, if you won't call things by their right names. I'll say he was going to 'subject her to an indecent personal assault.' That fancy enough for you?"

Shea reflected that the Stidoths had a very normal marriage, solid but not without occasional rifts and irritations. He changed the subject: "If I have to go to the capital, how do I get there?"

"You can walk, but it's quite a piece. Don't have no magic carpets or broomsticks or nothing here."

Dorothy spoke: "Dear, why don't we lend him Alis? He can ride her to the city, turn her loose, and tell her to go home. She knows the way well enough."

"Reckon that's a good idea. How about it, Mr. Shea?"

"Who is Alis?"

"One of our mules. I forget; you mundanes ain't used to animals that talk and understand like people do. But it's too late to start now. You better stay overnight with us and set out at sun-up."

"You're much too kind, really—"

"Think nothin' of it, Mr. Shea! Anybody that's got legitimate business with the Queen, it's only right to give him a hand to get him there."

From what he recalled of the Oz books, Shea believed that Ozma's court did not go in for elaborate formalities, such as requiring presentees to prostrate themselves or knock their heads upon the floor. But his travels through alternative universes had given him a fair command of protocol. The flunkey announced:

"I present to Your Majesty Doctor Sir Harold Shea, a mundane with a petition."

Shea put his hand over his heart and bowed to the horizontal, flourishing an imaginary hat with a sweeping gesture. When he straightened up, he faced Queen Ozma on her throne. She must have been about Dorothy's age in terms of mundane maturity; but she was still one of the most beautiful women Shea had ever seen. A circlet of gold, to each side of which was fastened a large red blossom, confined her midnight hair. After scrutiny, Shea decided that the blossoms were artificial.

"Master Shea," said Ozma. "Your pardon, Doctor Sir Harold Shea. Do not, pray, take offense at our curiosity; but we should like to know whence you obtained those appellations of rank, 'Doctor' and 'Sir'?"

Shea smiled easily. "Your Majesty, the 'Doctor' was awarded in consequence of my studies at the Garaden Institute in the mundane world, and I was dubbed a knight by the warrior lady Britomart in the world of *The Faerie Queene*."

"Of what sort were these studies whereof you speak?"

"In the workings of the human mind, Madam."

"Perhaps we should keep you with us, to unravel the mystery of why people, living secure and comfortable lives, persist natheless in acts of mischief, dishonesty, and violence. But now tell us what you would of us, pray."

When Shea had again told the story of Walter Bayard's stranding in mythological Ireland, Ozma sat quietly for some time. Twice she leaned forward and seemed about to speak but then sank back on her throne. At last she spoke, not to Shea but to a flunkey:

"Where is our consort?"

"My last knowledge, Your Majesty, is that he was on the tennis courts."

"Kindly request him to join us in the Audience Room." She turned back to Shea. "Sir Harold, you appear to have led a lively career, leaping from world to world. Whilst we wait, will you tell us of one of your adventures?"

"Gladly, Your Majesty," said Shea. "When I sojourned in the iron castle of the enchanter Atlantès, in the world of the *Orlando Furioso*..."

Shea was telling how he and Polacek had bribed the goblin Odoro to fetch them a bottle of liquor in the nonalcoholic Muslimoid environment, when the consort entered, carrying a tennis racquet. King Evardo was a tall, lean, well-muscled man, with blond hair streaked with gray. He wore shorts and a T-shirt, and sweat beaded his features.

The flunkey made introductions, and Shea repeated his bow. To his surprise, Evardo thrust out a large hand. Shea shook it and got the impression of a crushing grip, deliberately held back from its full power.

"A pleasure, Sir Harold!" boomed the consort, wiping his face with the towel a flunkey handed him. He turned to Ozma. "What's the problem this time, darling?"

On request, Shea repeated the tale of Bayard's stranding. He ended: "...So I thought that if Your Majesties would use the Belt to fetch Bayard here and then send us both home..."

"I see," said King Evardo, looking through narrowed lids.

Ozma spoke: "It sounds like a praiseworthy enterprise—"

She broke off as Evardo raised a hand. The consort said: "My darling is sometimes a trifle impulsive, perhaps a bit over-accommodating. This is a lovable quality in a spouse but unrealistic in a ruler. Assuming that we can, with the Belt, accomplish these feats, wherein lies the benefit to the Kingdom of Oz?" After a pause, he added: "To put it in the mundane vernacular, what's in it for us?"

"I—I hadn't thought," said Shea. "What could I possibly do for Your Majesties?"

"One task stares us in the face, namely: the rescue of our son Oznev from captivity by the Gnome King."

"Huh? Do you mean old Ruggedo? I thought you had turned him into a potted cactus!"

Evardo gave a grim chuckle. "So we had; or to be exact, so our friend the elf Himself had. But Ruggedo's former chancellor, Kaliko, succeeded him. Kaliko's a less contrary, cantankerous character than old Rug, but you trust either at your own risk.

"Anyhow, we sent Oznev off to visit his cousins in Ev, during his summer vacation from Wogglebug U. Then, when we looked in Ozma's magic picture to see how he was getting on, it showed us poor Oznev chained in an underground cell. Next we got a note from Kaliko, delivered by messenger bat, saying he would trade the boy for the Belt. If we didn't agree, he would send Oznev home—but a piece at a time."

"So, what do you expect me to do?" asked Shea.

"We'll transport you to Ev by the Belt, dropping you off near the Gnome King's western palace, which is actually a glorified cave. We'll give you a chart, showing how to find the entrance to the Kingdom of Gnomicia. Once inside, you're on your own."

"If you know where Oznev is, why can't you fetch him home by the Belt?"

"Because the Gnome Kingdom is so well protected by magical barriers and counter-spells that no device like our Belt can get through into it. We can just barely bring it into focus in our magic picture. The Royal Wizard of Gnomicia, Doctor Potaroo, set them up and keeps adding new ones. Other wizards call Potaroo a fifth-rater, but there's nothing fifth-rate about his magical defenses."

Shea said: "I understand that Gnomicia is a labyrinth of caves and tunnels, in which an outsider could easily get lost."

"Right you are!" said Evardo.

"Then how do you expect me to find my way around it? Wandering through miles of tunnels wouldn't do your son a bit of good. Do you know a trustworthy guide?"

Ozma spoke: "The only person in Oz who knows the tunnels is Ruggedo—"

"What!" exploded Evardo. "We mustn't even think of turning that villainous old scundermuch loose on an innocent world!"

"Perhaps, if he promised to reform—" began Ozma.

"Darling! He's promised that before, more than once, and each time he backslid. It's out of the question, Sir Harold."

"Then," said Shea, "I'm sorry, but I really don't see how I can help you in this matter. Of course, Your Majesties and several of Her Majesty's subjects, like Princess Dorothy, have been in the caverns and come out again; but I don't suppose—"

"You don't suppose correctly," snapped Evardo. "It's true that the Queen and some of our friends have visited Gnomicia, but only briefly, seeing but a small fraction of the complex. Your chances of finding Oznev were as good if you went in cold as they would be with, say, the Scarecrow or Tik-Tok as guide..."

The argument growled on and on, Shea refusing to agree without a sure guide, living or documentary; the royal couple refusing to help recover Bayard unless Shea undertook the mission. At last Shea suggested:

"Maybe Ruggedo would be so pleased by a chance to oust Kaliko and get his throne back that he'd be glad not only to show me around but also to stay there, without further conditions. I believe he did once recover his kingdom but wasn't allowed to keep it."

Evardo sighed. "I still wouldn't trust him any farther than I could throw a chimney by the smoke. Sometimes you mundanes are too sharp for us poor, simple fairylanders. Let's drop the subject and take it up again tomorrow, when the Queen and I have discussed it. You are welcome to dine and pass the night in the palace."

The audience resumed at ten the next morning. Evardo said: "Sir Harold, the Queen and I have decided to take you up on your proposal to give Ruggedo back his gnomish form. Then we shall see if he'll fall in with our scheme. Pray come with us to the conservatory, good my sir!"

Following the royal couple and a brace of guards, Shea ducked right and left to avoid masses of greenery. The air was steamy. Evardo and Ozma stopped at a long bench on which were lined up flowerpots containing spiny and prickly plants, such as cacti, agaves, and thistles.

"Here they are," said Evardo, indicating two pots at the end, in which stood prickly-pear cacti of the genus *Opuntia*. "Are you sure you know which is which, my dear?"

"Certainly," said Ozma. "The tall one is the King of Silver Mountain, and the short is Ruggedo. He used to be fat and tubby, but all his efforts to best the Ozites wore him down."

"All right, my dear," said Evardo. "Just a minute while I fetch some more guards to grab Ruggedo in case he tries something..."

Evardo was gone for several minutes. During this time, Ozma showed Shea the rare plants in the conservatory, explaining the provenance and properties of each. Evardo returned with another pair of stalwart, sword-armed guards in palace livery. He handed Ozma a wand and a small phial, saying:

"Number three-forty; isn't that the one you wanted?"

"Yes. Everybody quiet, now."

The Queen made passes with the wand, speaking words of power in an undertone. At last she poured the contents of the phial over one of the cacti, crying: "Awaken!"

The flowerpot burst into fragments, spilling dirt across the bench and on the floor, as the cactus changed into an aged gnome, sitting on the bench amid potsherds and the dirt in which he had been planted. His first word was: "Ouch!"

Ruggedo pulled a large, jagged potsherd out from beneath him and threw it away. Then he slid down from the bench and ducked a bow to the royal couple, saying in a creaky voice:

"Well, well! Queen Ozma, or I'll be egged! But how you've grown! I should hardly know you but for that fancy fillet you always wore. What in Oz has been happening? Have centuries passed while I was under that villainous leprechaun's spell?"

"No," said Ozma. "A few years after Himself enchanted you and the King of Silver Mountain, a youth studying magic accidentally canceled the aging-stasis spell."

"So now Ozites die of old age as other folk do, without waiting for an accident to get them?" Ruggedo gave a sneering laugh.

"That is right. It makes less difference than one might think, because our natural lives are longer than those of mundanes to begin with."

"And what befell the King of Silver Mountain? Did he become a plant, too?"

Ozma pointed her wand. "Your fellow cactus."

"Well, strike my topsails! You will have to give me some time to gather my wits. And who are these other people?"

Shea remembered that Ruggedo had led a brief career as a pirate captain; the locutions of that milieu had evidently remained with him. Ozma said:

"My beloved husband, King Evardo of Ev, and Doctor Sir Harold Shea, a mundane."

Ruggedo chuckled. "Well, well, little Evardo! You've grown even more than she has!"

"And you've lost a lot of weight," said King Evardo, "since the time you turned me into a piece of bric-a-brac on a shelf in your palace." He added: "As you have already guessed, Sir Harold, you behold the former Gnome King, Ruggedo the Rough, a.k.a. Roquat the Red, a.k.a. the Metal Monarch. He used to be as round as a grapefruit."

Ruggedo sighed. "Life has been hard, especially that five-year stretch as a mute peddler. You have no idea how difficult it is to give customers a hard sell without a voice. No wonder I was starved down to a skinny old swabbie! The things that have befallen me in trying to recover my just rights!"

"You look better skinny," said Evardo. "You used to resemble a grape or an olive with toothpicks stuck to it."

Ruggedo put his fists on his hips. "Very funny, ha-ha. Now then, don't tell me you've revived me just out of the goodness of your hearts. Ozma just might, but I judge you, fellow monarch, to be a tougher character. You were as a boy. So what do you want of me?"

The gnome glared defiantly. Evardo said: "Just to act as a guide to Sir Harold into Gnomicia, that's all. And to help him to rescue our son—Ozma's and mine—from captivity by your successor Kaliko."

"So Kaliko worked a snatch on royalty?" Ruggedo snickered. "As chancellor, he was always warning *me* against overreaching; and here he's done the same fool thing himself! The last thing I said to him, when he threw me out of my kingdom the second time, was not to mess with the Ozites. I had tried every way I could think of and come a cropper each time. But some people don't learn from others' experience."

"And power corrupts," added Evardo. "Well, how about it? Will you undertake this quest?"

Ruggedo looked sly. "Yes, if you will give me back my Belt."

"Out of the question! We'll use it to send you and Sir Harold to your western entrance."

"No Belt, no guide," snapped Ruggedo, crossing his arms on his chest.

"Of course," said Ozma casually, "I can always turn you back into a cactus."

"Go ahead! At least it's painless, though life as a potted plant is pretty dull. Almost as tedious as being a walnut or a crockery jug, both of which I know from experience."

Shea spoke: "King Ruggedo, this trip would give you a chance to oust Kaliko and resume your kingship."

"Hmm. I'll think it over. If you offered the Belt along with this rescue mission, I'd say 'yes' like a shot."

"Forget the Belt!" roared Evardo. "Guide and help Sir Harold, and you shall have a chance at your former kingdom. Otherwise, not."

Ruggedo's normally gray complexion flushed an angry red. "You mean," he shouted, "that even if I do you a vital service, you still won't return my own hard-earned property?" The gnome began to hop about, and his voice rose to a scream. "You're all just a band of bandits, thieves, robbers! You pretend to be so noble and virtuous, but it's all a sham! Hypocrites! Plunderers!"

The gnome seized a small flowerpot holding a plant, raised it high, and hurled it to the floor with a mighty smash, sending dirt and potsherds flying.

"Grab him!" said Evardo to the guards. Two stalwarts seized Ruggedo's arms and held him fast despite his yells and struggles.

"Oh, my poor Ragbadian daffodil!" cried Ozma, stooping to pick up the remains of the plant.

"You two," said Evardo to the remaining guards, "find another flowerpot, put the dirt back in—as much as you can—and replant the bulb. We may save it."

Shea said: "In the mundane world, back when monarchs really ruled, anyone who spoke that way to a king or queen would soon find himself shorter by a head."

Ozma smiled. "We know old Rug." Then to the gnome: "You might as well calm down, Rug. You make much of your property rights in the Belt. But, you see, we know the story of how you obtained it in the first place."

"That was entirely different!" said Ruggedo. "You haven't heard my side of the tale—"

Evardo interrupted. "Later; some other time. We're getting off the subject. Do you accept our deal or not? Don't hope that, once in Gnomicia, you can hatch another plot against us. We shall watch you."

Ruggedo looked hurt. "What, me plot against Your Majesties? Perish the thought! I tried that several times without success and hope I have learned a few things in my centuries. Since I have this time really resolved to reform, I will agree to your terms, unfair though I deem them."

"Very well," said Evardo. "When shall we send you off? Tomorrow?"

"Just a minute, Your Majesty!" said Shea. "You haven't fetched Bayard yet."

"After you have released Prince Oznev," said Evardo. "Not before."

"But Bayard is a big, strong fellow, and very smart. I'll need his help, especially if it comes to a fight."

"No."

"Then no rescue mission. You can turn Ruggedo back into a cactus."

"Dear," said Ozma, "we had better consult on this. Will you gentlemen excuse us?"

She swept out, followed by Evardo and two guards. The other two guards remained, glowering uneasily at Ruggedo. The gnome said to Shea:

"Who is this Bayard? What's this all about? Since I've been a dumb plant for I don't know how long, you can't expect me to sound very intelligent."

Shea repeated the tale of Bayard's stranding in Eriu. Answering Ruggedo's questions, he was in the midst of a summary of twentieth-century mundane history when the royal couple returned. Evardo said:

"How is this, Sir Harold? We will get out the Belt and fetch Bayard from that barbarous world wherein he dwells. But we will not send him to Gnomicia with you. On such a mission, two is fine but three is a crowd, more likely to be discovered.

"Instead, Bayard shall remain here until you return from your quest. If you perish in the attempt or, despite valiant efforts, fail from circumstances beyond your control, we will send him—or the twain of you, as the case may be—back to your mundane world. Fair enough?"

"In other words," said Shea, "you'll hold Bayard as a hostage."

"That's a crude way of putting it; he'll be very well treated. And I would not insult a dubbed knight by implying that he might slip away and run out on his obligations."

"I'll buy it," said Shea, "provided you equip me with enough magical gadgets to enable me to succeed."

"The Queen and I shall consider the matter and outfit you in the morning."

On a small table before Ozma's throne lay two round, woolen, peakless caps. When Shea picked one up, he found it so much like the common Mediterranean beret that, when he looked inside, he expected to read *Fabrique en France* or *Producto de Espana*.

"Don't put it on yet," said Evardo, standing beside the throne. "They are the best we could find in the magical arsenal. Most of our magical devices will not work in Gnomicia because of Potaroo's counter-spells. These tarncaps will, I am sure. They are set for full charge, so they will render your clothes as well as your body invisible."

Shea: "The lesser charge, which would affect only my physical person, wouldn't be very practical, would it?"

Evardo smiled. "We wouldn't ask you to strip naked before invading the Gnome Kingdom. I can think of base uses to which persons of low morals might put a tarncap—"

"Evardo!" said Ozma sternly.

Evardo sighed. "My dear! I was only thinking of the loot an invisible thief could garner, and that therefore we must keep these headpieces under strict control. What had you in mind?"

"Never mind!"

She suppressed a grin. *Ozites*, he thought, *had some remarkably Victorian attitudes. Ozma and Dorothy Gale, close friends as girls, had evidently matured with similar ideas on the management of husbands.* He said:

"Your Majesties! We'll need three caps, one for Oznev when and if we release him and are on our way out. You said yourselves you couldn't use the Belt to snatch us away until we're free of the caves. Hadn't we better take a look in your magic picture to see what we'll need?"

"Right on both counts, Sir Harold," said Evardo. "Let's take a look, my dear."

Looking at the magic picture, Shea said: "We mundanes have a thing somewhat like this, called a television screen. But we can't always see what we wish, and much of what is shown gets pretty tedious."

Ozma, facing the picture, placed her fingers against her temples and whispered. Presently the scene in the picture, a conventional landscape with trees and a waterfall, faded. Instead, the picture darkened, showing an adolescent youth on a bench in some sort of crypt or dungeon. Stout chains joined the gyves on his wrists and ankles to massive staples set in the masonry.

"Is the cell barred?" asked Shea.

Ozma whispered some more, and the view moved back from the prisoner. There was indeed a set of bars with a door closing the front of the cell, but the door stood ajar.

"Shiver my strakes!" growled Ruggedo. "Kaliko's a careless sort of king. When I ruled, any jailer who left cell doors open would be fed to the slicing machine!"

"Next," said Shea, "assuming we gain entrance to the cell, how do we dispose of the chains and handcuffs? Picking locks is not one of my skills. Haven't you a wand or something I could zap the chains with?"

"I fear not," said Evardo. "If we had, it probably wouldn't work in Gnomicia."

"Is there a bolt cutter in Oz?"

"I know not, but I shall find out."

The next day saw Shea at the royal smithy, trying to explain to the royal smith, with the help of a diagram, the principles of a bolt cutter.

Back in the informal reception room of the palace Shea told the royal couple: "I think I got the idea over, but his first try at a bolt cutter may not work. The last I saw, he was muttering spells over a piece of bar stock. Are you going to fetch Bayard now?"

"Yes; we were waiting for you," said Ozma. She wore a wide belt that reminded Shea of the belts favored by motorcycle gangsters. She leaned forward, closed her eyes, waved a wand in an intricate pattern, and whispered. With a *floomp* of displaced air, something bulky landed with a bang on the carpet. Blinking in surprise, Shea realized that the object was a large bed of primitive construction, with a rough-hewn wooden frame and a network of rope in lieu of a mattress.

Moreover, the bed was occupied by two persons, who thrust up heads beyond the end of the blanket. One was that of a big man with a bushy brown beard; the other, that of a red-haired, pale-skinned young woman. As they sat up, the blanket fell down to reveal that both were naked, at least to the waist. The woman snatched up the edge of the blanket to cover herself, emitting a shriek:

"Fomorians! 'Tis a pair of dead corps that we are!"

The bearded man blinked, stared around, and finally said: "Hi, Harold! I thought you'd get me out sooner or later. But where did you get us out to?"

"The Land of Oz," replied Shea. "These are Queen Ozma and her consort, King Evardo of Ev. This is Ruggedo, the former Gnome King. Doctor Walter Bayard, Your Majesties. Sorry to have snatched you at an inconvenient time, Walter."

Bayard bowed as best he could sitting up in bed. "Pleased to meet Your Majesties. Excuse my not getting up, but as you see I don't have on my court dress. This—" (he indicated the red-haired girl) "—is my *caile dhonn*, otherwise Mistress Boann Ni Colum. Tell me, Harold, are the people here as fussy about exposure as those of mythical Ireland?"

"We observe the normal decencies," said Ozma.

"Then," continued Bayard imperturbably, "may we borrow some clothes? Had we but known in advance..."

Ozma gave orders to a bodyguard, who departed. Shea said: "I didn't know you with the whiskers, Walter."

"A druid without a beard is no druid at all."

"You're a druid now?"

Bayard smiled. "I got to the third degree in the order of Vates or wise men. A little modern psychology, tactfully applied, put me so far ahead of the competition that it was no contest."

The guard came back with four muscular flunkeys, who carried out the bed. Ozma explained:

"I'm putting them in the fourteenth guest room, with clothes to don. Do they wear clothes in this mythological Ireland, Sir Harold?"

"Indeed they do! In that climate, without them everyone would die of pneumonia."

Bayard appeared in green knee breeches, shirt, and vest; Mistress Boann, in a gauzy gown that Shea suspected of being one of Ozma's castoffs. Bayard bowed ceremoniously saying:

"I thank Your Majesties with profound gratitude." After a gracious royal dismissal, Bayard asked:

"Harold, where's Belphebe? I'd have expected to see her with you."

"Home having a baby," said Shea.

"Congratulations. I'm surprised she let you go, even to spring me from the land of poetical headhunters."

Shea frowned. "On the contrary, it was she who insisted I go. I think she feels somehow guilty over the fact that it's to be a girl. She comes of a culture that rates sons far and away above daughters. I explained about Y chromosomes and told her over and over the gender didn't matter, and I'd be delighted whichever it was; but she feels she's somehow failed me. So she practically bullied me into going before the kid was due. Silly, but there it is."

Later that day, King Evardo said: "Sir Harold, may I speak with you privily, whilst the Queen shows our new guests around the palace? In my cabinet, pray. This way."

"Okay, Your Majesty," said Shea. "Spill it."

Seated behind a big desk, Evardo twiddled his fingers uncertainly. "This subject is a trifle awkward, but the Queen insists. Your comrade Bayard and his—ah—Mistress Ni Colum are plainly on intimate terms. But—ah—is their union legitimate?"

"You mean, are they married?"

"Precisely, Sir Harold. You see, the Queen insists on the strictest standards, at least in the palace. Our new arrivals seem to expect assignment to the same quarters, but our rules cannot be stretched to cover—ah—irregular unions. Which is it in this case?"

Shea suppressed a snigger. "I don't know how they do it in the world of Irish myth. From what I recall of the legends—which may or may not accurately describe conditions in Eriu—they were pretty free and easy about sex, although puritanical about nudity. A chief could demand that a subject lend him his wife for a few nights."

"Galloping Growleywogs!" cried Evardo in horrified tones. "We can't have that sort of thing here!"

"Of course not," said Shea soothingly. "Eriu's a pretty barbarous world; I've been there. But my impression is that if a man and a woman set up house together, they were married by definition. You could say Walter and Boann were married by the local laws and customs of the place where they met."

Evardo frowned. "I know not how far that tale will go to convince the Queen, but I'll try. I was a little surprised when Doctor Bayard made no objection to being left here, as a kind of polite hostage, whilst you and Ruggedo set forth on your adventure."

Shea shrugged. "Walter's an easygoing fellow who takes things as they come, and he's seen enough adventure not to feel a need to seek it for its own sake. I'm sure he'd have come if he'd been asked. And he'll have certain—ah—amenities here that I shall lack."

Evardo smiled. "I take it you mean Mistress Ni Colum. I deem myself broad-minded, but pray do not speak thus lightly on such matters to the Queen. She might take offense."

"As you say, sir. I, too, have a strong-minded wife."

"How goes your bolt cutter?"

"The first one worked badly. The smith says he has trouble spacing the pivot pins correctly. He's familiar with scissors and pincers with a single pivot, but five in one tool baffle him. He's working on another model now."

"If I remember aright," said Ruggedo's creaky old voice, "the entrance ought to be just over yonder ridge."

"That's what the chart shows," said Shea.

Shea finished his lunch, while Ruggedo put away the concertina on which he had been playing a melancholy tune.

"Then let's go," said Shea, with a pack on his back and his saber at his side. "You lead, since you know the country."

The somber crags of western Ev rose all around them, occluding the cloudy sky to right and left and before and behind. Ruggedo tramped ahead, seeming to gather strength from contact with his native soil. He briskly poled along with a bill from the royal armory of Oz, well stocked by King Evardo after he became Royal Consort.

This was the weapon Ruggedo had chosen over an assortment of swords, axes, maces, pikes, halberds, crossbows, and arquebuses. (When Shea saw these primitive firearms, he regretted not having brought a pistol with him, since it might work in this milieu.) When Shea had questioned the choice of the bill, Ruggedo, drawing himself up to his full four and a half feet, challenged him to a practice bout, quarterstaff against wooden sword.

Padded and masked, the two squared off. In no time, Ruggedo poked Shea in the belly with the end of the quarterstaff. Shea demanded two out of three. On the second bout, he managed to drag out the match until Ruggedo began to pant and weaken, when Shea got him in the chest with a lunge.

Shea thought he had the third bout in the bag. But it had hardly begun when he received a crack over the head, which made him see stars despite the padding.

"You see, my boy," grinned Ruggedo, "it's not the particular kind of weapon so much as knowing how to use it."

Ruggedo's bill was a six-foot spear with a head that included, besides the foot-long steel blade, a hook on one side and a point on the other. It was shod with a pointed bronzen butt, which could be thrust with. Shea was girt with his saber. Ruggedo, marching ahead, snarled:

"Klumping Kaloogas, Sir Harold, hold that thing so it doesn't clank! The Long-Eared Hearer could hear us a mile away."

Shea grasped the scabbard in his left hand. This silenced the clank but also made his footing less certain. He stumbled over a rock and cursed beneath his breath, wishing he had something he could use as a walking stick. He could have drawn his sword, but the thought of marring the needle point and razor edge he had painstakingly given it dissuaded him.

"Clumsy clodpate!" muttered Ruggedo.

They plodded along a winding trail, which led zigzag up one side of the ridge and down the other. Something flew overhead with harsh screams. It was neither a bird, a bat, nor a pterosaur but combined a little of all three.

The distance was greater than Shea had thought. After a time they stopped for a respite.

"Sir Harold," grated Ruggedo, "isn't 'Shea' an Irish name in the mundane world?"

"I believe it is. But my people have been American so long it doesn't matter."

"Humph! That's what Himself the elf used to say. Claimed he was an American leprechaun from New Jersey. I'll never trust any being more than one-sixty-fourth Irish, after what that treacherous elf did to me. What did you do for a living in the mundane world?"

"Psychologist," panted Shea.

"What's that? And don't try to confuse me with fancy words!"

"A man who studies the workings of the human mind."

"Humph! If you be so learned and all, then tell me: Why does everybody hate me so?"

"That's a hell of a question to spring on a poor innocent foreigner!"

"Well? Do you mean that, with all your studies, you still can't answer a simple question?" Ruggedo snorted contempt.

"Well, now," drawled Shea, gathering his mental forces, "let's look into the matter. From all I've heard about you, you are two things that, together, account for the phenomenon. One: You're an unscrupulous, treacherous, selfish, greedy, lying, thieving scoundrel."

"You've been reading what those mundanes wrote!" cried Ruggedo, beginning to dance with rage. "They got half the story wrong and the rest distorted. That writer couldn't even spell 'gnome' right. A farrago of half-truths, errors, and outright lies—"

"Hold on!" said Shea, raising his voice. "You haven't heard the rest, yet. If you want my answer, then shut up until I finish!"

Ruggedo, grumbling, subsided. Shea continued: "In the mundane world, we'd call you a paranoid sociopath. At the same time you're an irascible, ornery, cantankerous, ill-mannered, bad-tempered old grouch. Now one—"

"Lies! Vile calumnies!" yelled Ruggedo.

"Do you want the rest of my answer or don't you? All right, then, hold your tongue until you hear it! I was saying that some scoundrels are successful, provided they are also polite, affable, obliging, winsome charmers. In the mundane world we had a charming scoundrel of that kind, who knew something of the world I accidentally touched down in on my way to Oz. He became enormously rich despite being an even bigger villain than you've ever been.

"On the other hand, even a cantankerous grouch can be admired if he also practices honesty, kindness, generosity, and unselfishness long and hard enough. Why, do you wish no longer to be hated?"

Ruggedo grunted a vague assent. "Suppose so."

"Then you must either stop being a treacherous etcetera scoundrel or stop being an irascible etcetera grouch. If you managed to cure both, you might become as beloved as Queen Ozma."

"Humph!" growled Ruggedo. "You give me one Hades of a choice. It's not easy to change at my age; but I'll think it over. I tried to reform before, several times; but my good resolutions never seemed to stick. Still, it would be nice, just once, to be known as a good king. Come on!"

Off went the gnome, poling himself along with his bill. They crossed the crest and picked their way down the other side of the ridge. Ruggedo halted in front of a recess in the rocks, which looked like the entrance to a tunnel blocked by a granite door.

"Sure you remember the way?" asked Shea.

"Of course, nitwit! I once got my throne back from Kaliko, and I'd have had it yet but for that sanctimonious little meddler Ozma." Ruggedo flourished his beret. "Time to put 'em on," he whispered, donning the tarncap.

At once the gnome disappeared, save that by staring hard in the gloom, Shea could just make out a pair of disembodied eyeballs hanging in space. Shea put on his own cap, saying:

"How shall we keep together?"

"I'll raise this pike high enough so the point shows," said Ruggedo. "Keep your eye on it!"

The gnome then rapped the door with his knuckles in a peculiar pattern and uttered a warbling whistle. The door groaned open.

"Come on, stupid!" whispered Ruggedo. "Hurry!"

Shea started after the gnome but, trying to keep his eyes on the barely visible spearhead, tripped and fell full-length, tearing a hole in his breeches' right knee. The scabbarded sword struck the ground with a clank.

"Awkward ass!" groaned Ruggedo. "If that doesn't alert them, an earthquake wouldn't!"

Shea felt stringy but powerful arms invisibly helping him up. In they went.

The tunnel was not so dark as Shea had feared. Along the walls, enormous faceted gems—or at least prismatic glassy objects that looked like enormous gems—were set in the rock and shed soft lights: ruby, emerald, and other hues. The footing became more even, but Shea still had to look down with every limping step to avoid another fall.

Rasping voices wafted from ahead. As the invaders approached, Shea saw a pair of gnomish sentries, each standing in a recess in the sides of the tunnel. They held halberds somewhat like Ruggedo's bill, slantwise so that their shafts intersected at about man height. The gnomes complained in growls:

"...that cursed sergeant has it in for me. Nothing I do pleases him."

"Trouble with you, Ungo, is that nothing pleases you. If you were told you had no duties at all, you'd crab about that..."

"How shall we get past?" whispered Shea.

"Crawl, idiot!" The eyeballs sank down to within two feet of the tunnel floor.

Shea got down to hands and knees, wincing at the pain in his injured knee. He would, he thought, leave a trail of blood wherever the knee touched ground.

Silently Ruggedo and Shea crept beneath the halberds and past the sentries, one of whom said: "I feel something's going on, Ungo. We both heard that clank."

"Too much imagination," rasped the other. "You'll get ulcers, worrying over every little sound."

Past the sentries, Ruggedo and Shea arose and resumed their way. For an hour they stole through tunnels, now and then choosing among alternative branches. Shea tried to remember the choices, since he depended for guidance on Ruggedo. He kept repeating to himself: right once, left twice, past three side tunnels...But soon the number of forks and branches surpassed his ability to remember which was which. A few times, groups of gnomes approached them from the tunnel ahead, and they had to slip into side passages until the parties had gone past.

They passed chambers in which gnomes were noisily at work: mending weapons, polishing gems, and other gnomish tasks. A smell of cooking came from one cavern, in which female gnomes, no prettier than the males, bustled about.

They passed a huge assembly room, lined with doors of gleaming metal and commanded by an over-hanging balcony. The hall was empty save for a few gnomes polishing panels of gold and silver in the doors.

At last they turned into a downward-sloping, foul-smelling corridor. A few steps brought them to a spacious chamber, against the far wall of which yawned a row of cells. At the entrance, a gnome sat on a high chair and smoked a long-stemmed pipe.

Ruggedo walked briskly to within reach of the seated gnome and smote him over the head with the shaft of his bill. The pipe fell clattering, and the gnome slumped and fell after it.

"Come on!" hissed Ruggedo. "There's the cell we want, Number Six! The lazy bastards have left 'em all open, to save the trouble of locking and unlocking."

On the bench at the back of the cell sat the stripling whom Shea had seen in the magic picture. As the rescuers entered the cell, Shea spoke:

"Prince Oznev, can you hear me?"

The youth sat up with a start. "Who—what—where are you?"

"In your cell, invisible. We've come to get you out. Don't shout or do anything foolish!"

Shea reached into his pack and pulled out the bolt cutter. If it had worked on small-gage bar stock in the smithy in Oz, it ought to function here. He snipped off the chains near the cuffs on Oznev's wrists and ankles.

"But who *are* you?" said the youth. "All I see is two pairs of eyes floating around."

"I'm Sir Harold Shea, and this is ex-king Ruggedo," snapped Shea, snipping the final link. "Now come along, son; no time to lose. Here, put this on your head!"

"What is it?"

"A tarncap, to make you invisible like us."

"It seems a cowardly sort of trick. A prince should face his enemies in plain sight!"

"Oh, lord!" said Shea. "Rug, we've got a terminal case of chivalrous scruples."

"Leave the brat if he won't come sensibly," growled the gnome.

"Can't." Shea stepped close to Oznev and, with a quick motion, jammed the third beret down on the head of the young prince, who disappeared. "There, Your Highness. I put it on you, so it's not your fault you're wearing it."

"I'll take it off!" muttered the invisible Oznev.

"You do, and I'll knock your royal block off!" snarled Shea. "Now come along like a good princeling!" Shea felt around and caught Oznev's wrist.

"Sir Harold!" rasped Ruggedo. "The sentry's gone!"

"Must have come to and gone to spread the alarm," said Shea. "Better run for it. Pick up your feet, Your Highness, if you don't want a tumble!"

From another cell came a rattle of chains and a cry: "Hey, get me out, too!" Similar cries and chainy sounds came from other cells.

Ignoring these appeals, the three dashed up the sloping passage and then along the labyrinth of tunnels, turning right and left at forks. The ex-king, trotting ahead, made the turns without hesitation. Shea hoped Ruggedo's memory of his kingly days did not play him false.

They passed more work rooms, all of which, earlier full of gnomes, now yawned empty.

"Where have they all gone?" Shea called, as loudly as he dared.

"Kaliko's probably making a speech," panted Ruggedo. "From what—I hear, he's gotten pompous. You know—how it is with us kings, surrounded by flunkeys—and flatterers. Flattery—rots the brain."

"Better save your breath, Rug," said Shea.

On and on they went. Shea heard a buzz ahead, indicating a crowd of gnomes. The light grew, and the fugitives came in sight of the hall of assembly.

They glanced inside, where thousands of gnomes now crowded the floor. On the balcony, picked out by spotlights, stood a beardless gnome in glittering regalia. Gnomes in gleaming armor, holding spears and swords, flanked the central figure.

"Wait!" said Ruggedo. "I want to hear him."

The robed and crowned gnome, evidently King Kaliko, had just launched into a speech. To Shea it sounded like a thousand other soporific political speeches that he had heard or read:

"...We must seize the moment... Productivity must rise... Family discipline should be tightened... We must be alert against foreign influences, especially of the subversive plots of the skulking Ruggedo... We must rid ourselves of bureaucratic waste... Beware those who plot against us... My reign has brought prosperity, despite the damage by my foolish predecessor and the grumbles of malcontents..."

Another gnome, in gnomish working clothes, pushed through the attendants on the balcony. "Your Majesty! I have news of moment!"

The newcomer looked like the jailer whom Ruggedo had stunned, although Shea did not know gnomes well enough to tell one clearly from another. Kaliko turned upon the newcomer, shouting:

"What mean you, knave, interrupting my speech?"

"But, sire, this is important! Surfacers have invaded—"

Kaliko roared: "Here, *I* decide what is important! Take him away!"

Shea glanced at Ruggedo, or at least at what he thought were Ruggedo's eyeballs. Ruggedo was muttering and, from the jiggle of the eyeballs, dancing about in a rising paroxysm of rage. Then Ruggedo's beret came off in the gnome's hand.

Before Shea could interfere, Ruggedo hurled the tarncap to the floor and dashed into the chamber. He ran a few steps along the wall, past some of the golden and silver doors, until he came to a plinth, on which stood a statue of a gnome in combat with a monster. With a muscle-cracking effort, Ruggedo tipped over the statue, which crashed to the floor. The old gnome vaulted atop the plinth, waved his bill above his head, and screamed:

"Gnomes! I am Ruggedo the Rough, your rightful king! Rally to me against that pompous fool of a usurper!"

For a few seconds, silence fell. A stout gnome dashed to the plinth and knelt, crying:

"Hail, King Ruggedo! It is I, former chancellor Shoofenwaller! Hail to our true and rightful king!"

The audience burst into a roar of talk, questions, and argument. Kaliko yelled from the balcony and Ruggedo shouted from his plinth, but their words were lost in the din. Calls to arms resounded.

More and more gnomes clustered round Ruggedo's plinth. The gnomes had at first been unarmed, but now weapons began to gleam. Steel clanged and wounded gnomes screamed.

"Come on, Oznev," said Shea, pulling the prince after him. The hall of assembly, he thought, was near enough to the western entrance to enable them to find their way out without Ruggedo.

"Wait!" said Oznev's voice. "A prince should stand by his comrades! I must help Ruggedo in his fight for the throne!"

The prince wrenched loose and pulled off his tarn-cap. As he raised his arm to throw it away as Ruggedo had done, Shea, who had half drawn his sword, whipped out the weapon and smote Oznev on the head with the pommel.

The prince collapsed. Shea sheathed his blade, snatched up the discarded tarncap, and jammed it down on Oznev's head. Then he picked up the stripling and slung him over one shoulder. This took all of Shea's strength, because Shea was of no more than average size. He could not have done it if Oznev had been as big as, say, Walter Bayard.

Inside the chamber, partisans of Kaliko and Ruggedo coalesced into discrete masses. Other gnomes passed among them, handing out weapons. A roar of combat drowned all other sounds. Shea stumbled over a gnome's head, which rolled, trickling blood, out of the hall of assembly and into the corridor.

Shea limped and staggered along the tunnel, away from the hall. His battered knee hurt like blazes.

Then a figure popped out of a side tunnel. As it neared, Shea saw, by the light of the luminous gems, a human being in gnomish costume.

"Halt!" shouted this one. "I see your eyeballs! You cannot escape!"

The man advanced, swinging a sword right and left, high and low, to keep anyone from slipping past him. He was a huge man with long arms, so that he covered the entire tunnel with his sweeps. Closer he came.

"One of Ozma's tricks!" roared the man. "Well, she can't fool Dranol Drabbo! Have at you, spook!"

Another step would bring the man within sword's length of Shea, who let the limp Prince Oznev slide to the floor. He had not completely drawn his own sword when Drabbo aimed a slash that, had it gotten home, would have sent Shea's head rolling like that of the gnome.

Shea did a quick squat. The sword whistled over his head, sending his tarncap flying.

"I knew it!" yelled Dranol Drabbo, making a running attack. Shea parried and backed, backed and parried. Dranol Drabbo was a stout fighter and a skilled cut-and-thrust swordsman, who wielded a long, heavy blade as easily as if it had been a flyswatter. In parrying one mighty downward cut, Shea's sword, on which he had lavished such care, broke off a hand's breadth from the hilt.

Dranol Drabbo threw himself forward in a lunge. His point struck Shea's chest, and the force of the blow knocked Shea off his feet. His mail shirt, however, kept the point from piercing his skin.

Shea scrambled up, reaching for his bowie knife. But Dranol Drabbo was hopping about, clawing at something invisible that clung to his back.

Shea sprang forward and whacked Dranol Drabbo's skull thrice with the flat of his oversized, machete-like knife. Dranol Drabbo sank to a sitting position, not completely unconscious.

"Good!" cried Oznev's voice as the prince untangled himself from Dranol Drabbo. "I couldn't desert you in a fight, either. Here's your cap."

"Just a second," said Shea. Reaching down Dranol Drabbo's back, he sawed through the man's belt with his knife. "Okay," he said. "Now run for it!"

Soon they reached the western entrance, with Shea limping heavily. A glance back showed Dranol Drabbo, small in the distance, staggering to his feet. When the man started in pursuit, his breeches fell down, and Drabbo went to hands and knees. His roars of frustration echoed down the tunnel.

"My head aches like fury," said Oznev. "What hit me?"

"The force of destiny," said Shea.

"Why didn't you kill him?"

"Wasn't necessary, and experience teaches that today's friend may be tomorrow's foe and vice versa. Waste not, want not."

Shea hobbled along the trail. They had not gone a hundred paces outside the caves when Shea felt the now familiar symptoms of magical teleportation—the fading of the scene, the misty whirl of colored dots...

"Well!" said Queen Ozma when she and King Evardo had embraced their son. "You, Sir Harold, appear to have had a time of it!"

"Your Majesty is a mistress of understatement," said Shea, handing over the two surviving berets. "Hi, Walter! Who won?"

"Ruggedo," said Bayard. "At least, just after the Queen actuated her Belt to fetch you, we saw Kaliko and his chancellor pop out the western entrance, in flight with a few followers."

"Demonstrating," said Shea, "that gnomes show no more wisdom in picking leaders than we mundanes."

"Oh, dear!" said Ozma. "I'm sure old Rug will start plotting to conquer us again."

"He told me," said Shea, "that this time he was really determined to reform. Whether he'll succeed, your guess is as good as mine. But permit me to suggest that Your Majesties hire someone to keep him under constant surveillance in your magical picture."

Evardo: "Sir Harold, we are greatly in your debt. We should like to honor you with a fine banquet in celebration. Oz is renowned for its parties."

Shea gave his courtliest bow. "I appreciate the courtesy, Your Majesty. But back home my wife is about to give birth. So, if you will forgive me..."

"I see," said Evardo. "In other words, you would prefer to be sent home forthwith, as soon as your hurts have been mended. It shall be as you wish. Do you also speak for Doctor Bayard and his—ah—wife?"

"No, sir. If they wish to remain, that's fine by me."

Shea lay stretched out in the bathtub. Bayard came in and sat on the toilet lid, saying: "Just been watching Ruggedo in Ozma's picture. We hear from our spies he's telling the gnomes that monarchy is obsolete. So he's proclaimed himself Lifetime President and Founding Father of the Gnomic Republic."

Shea replied: "Like one of those pipsqueak dictators we have in the Third World, eh? What are your plans?"

"The Queen will send us home after you as soon as the party is over. It promises to be a real blowout, with all the famous characters, such as Ozma's father, ex-king Pastoria, hauled in from his elegant tailoring establishment. Boann will play the harp and sing sad songs. Now give me the blow-by-blow."

Shea narrated his adventures. Bayard said: "Of course we watched you in the magic picture. But it's not wired for sound, and we couldn't watch every minute. When Kaliko's chancellor—that fellow with a name like a drain-cleaning compound—got you with his lunge, we thought you were a goner. What saved you?"

"How do you suppose I got this big purple bruise on my chest? If you look yonder, you'll see a mail shirt of alloy-steel mesh."

"You, wearing armor? You used to brag you never touched the stuff."

"Circumstances alter cases," said Shea. "Do you know a verse by Kipling, called "The Married Man" or something? It begins—I won't try to imitate the cockney dialect Kipling used—but it goes something like this:

> *The bachelor, he fights for one*
> *As joyful as can be;*
> *But the married man don't call it fun,*
> *Because* he *fights for three.*

"If you ever get married, you'll find out what Kipling meant. Speaking of which, how's it with you and Miss Ni Colum?"

Bayard pondered. "I suppose I could fare further and do worse. Guess we probably are married in the sight of Crom Crutch, or whomever these bloodthirsty quasi-Celts worship. Good thing you didn't fetch us to Oz in the midst of our quasi-nuptials; might have been downright embarrassing.

"When I explained that she might either be sent back to Eriu or go to America with me, as she liked, she threw a shoe at me and burst into tears. Thought I was trying politely to 'cast her off,' as she expressed it. So I guess Boann is Mrs. Bayard henceforth. It gets us all sooner or later, I suppose."

"Your enthusiasm overwhelms me," said Shea, rising from the water. "If you do it right—and I speak from experience—it's the very best thing around. Hand me that big towel, will you?"

Sir Harold of Zodanga
by L. Sprague de Camp
The Exotic Enchanter, Baen Books, 1995

"So, Doctor Malambroso," said Professor Doctor Sir Harold Shea to the man who faced him across his desk at the Garaden Institute, "what do you want of me?"

The man facing Shea was a tall, lean person with a close-cut graying beard. His graying hair hung to his collar. He wore a cheap suit with a loud checked pattern and an eye-blinding cravat, tied in a way suggesting that Malambroso had never learned to tie a necktie. The last time Shea had seen Malambroso, in the universe of Hindu myth, he had worn white pyjamas embroidered with gold thread. Malambroso had, Shea thought, made a not altogether successful effort to adopt local coloration on the mundane plane.

"I want the Lady Florimel back!" said Malambroso in a rasping, growling voice, as if he hated asking any favor of anybody.

"Gods, what crust!" exclaimed Shea.

Malambroso frowned. "You puzzle me, Sir Harold. Methought 'crust' meant the hard covering or integument of something softer, such as the outer surface of a loaf of bread or a pie."

"Colloquially, 'crust' is also used for..." Shea paused to think. " 'Obtuse aggressiveness' is close to the colloquial meaning. That you should ask *my* help to regain possession of the Lady Florimel, who seems quite happy to be back with her husband, my colleague Reed Chalmers!... If that be not a case of obtuse aggressiveness, I don't know what is."

"I can explain," growled Malambroso.

"Then pray do so, and I hope concisely. I need to get back to these term papers."

"The fact, Sir Harold, is that, for the first time in a long and active life, I am in love. Methought I was far beyond such petty, juvenile mortal sentiments; but in that, lo, I erred. I would never admit this, save that I know you for a man of exceptional ability, at least for a native of this stupid, brutish mundane plane."

"Thanks. But I always thought you hated everybody?"

"So I did, before the tender passion awakened a side of my nature that I did not know I possessed. Anyhow, the gist is that I must have the lady for mine own paramour. I must and shall have her!" Malambroso smote the desk with a bony fist.

"Don't be silly, Malambroso," said Shea. "For one thing, you're too old for her."

"No older than Doctor Chalmers. What reason have you to think that he can perform his connubial duties to the satisfaction of all concerned?"

"He's been giving himself magical rejuvenating treatments."

"How can he, when magic does not work in this continuum?"

"I didn't say he performed the treatments *here*, and it's none of your business anyway. What makes you think that, after he and I went to so much trouble and risk, surviving dangers both natural and supernatural, to reunite the lady with her lawful husband, that I would help you to snatch her again?"

"Because if you do not, I will turn you into an insect of an especially loathsome kind!"

"You can't. Spells don't work here."

"Think ye so?" Malambroso pointed bony fingers at Shea and muttered an incantation, ending with a shout of: "...be thou a lowly Geophilus!"

Nothing happened. Malambroso's face took on expression of petulant frustration, muttering: "The Incantation of Sorax has always worked for me before! You should be a little crawler, on a hundred-odd legs."

Shea laughed. "Told you. Wrong universe. I seem to have only the two legs I started out with. Besides, if I had a hundred-odd, I couldn't be an insect. They all have exactly six."

"Oh, curse your silly pedantry!" snarled Malambroso.

"By the way," said Shea, "how did you get here from the world of Hindu myth?"

"By the Spell of the Tipulidae, which worked perfectly well in that universe. But think not that I failed to consider means of exit from this miserable, magicless world of yours. I read your publications in the Institute library anent the manipulation of symbolic logic. 'Twas right shrewd of you to have worked out your system. The papers revealed what a formidable fellow you could be, whether as foe or ally. I shall convince you that it were better for you to be mine ally rather than mine enemy. I know of universes where you could be a great man—belike an arch-wizard or an emperor. I could furnish you with mighty assistance towards those goals, Sir Harold."

"You may skip the 'Sir,' Malambroso. American citizens are not allowed titles of nobility, so it doesn't apply in this world. Anyway, I have no desire to be an emperor or even an archimage. I am quite satisfied to be a well-established academician, a fond husband, and a doting father. I've adventured enough on other planes to do me for the rest of my life."

Malambroso argued further, but Shea remained firm in his refusal, until Malambroso said: "Is this your final word? You refuse to discuss practical arrangements between us?"

"Yes and yes. Good afternoon, Doctor Malambroso."

The wizard rose. "You shall regret your contumacy, good my sir!"

"We shall see," said Shea.

Malambroso took a topcoat from the rack, picked up a cheap suitcase, gave Shea a stiff nod, and stalked out.

Some hours later, Shea looked at his watch and saw that it was nearly time to go home. Then the intercom said: "Doctor Shea? Call your wife, right away!"

"Darling!" said Belphebe, breathlessly. "That wizard Malambroso has kidnapped Voglinda!"

"Good God!" said Shea. "Have you called the cops?"

"First thing I did. Sergeant Brodsky's here now."

"I'll come right home."

"Fine, but drive carefully!"

"Pretty little thing," said Pete Brodsky, passing back the photographs. "About three, isn't she? Now, Belle, suppose you tell Harold what you told me, about how this Doctor Malefactor got away."

"Malambroso," Belphebe corrected. "He came to call, he said, ever so politely. When we sat down in the living room, he gave me a sales pitch, trying to get me to persuade you to throw in with him in an attempt to win Florimel away from Reed for his own—'paramour,' I think he said. When I said no, he tried to sway me with tales of the wonders of other universes he could take us to and make us big shots in, where I could have all the fancy clothes and jewels any girl could want. He didn't realize that my taste runs to simple, outdoorish garb, suitable for running through the greenwood.

"When I persisted in saying no, he seemed to give up. He said he wanted another look at Voglinda, who was having her nap. He stole up to her bedroom door and slithered in as quietly as a cockroach. I was right behind him; but he shut the door in my face and shot that little bolt we put in high up. I heard him reciting a sorites and called the emergency number. I couldn't break down the door myself, but Pete drove up and gave the door a good push with his shoulder, and away went the bolt. You'll have to do some carpentry, dear, to mend it.

"Well, there was nobody in the room, and the window was latched on the inside. So here we are."

Shea said: "Did you hear enough of the sorites to tell where Malambroso was going?"

"No. Sorry."

Brodsky growled: "Trouble with chasing you dimensional guys is, you can vanish into the goddam world of some jerk's imagination. Like that phony Finland and phony Ireland we visited together.

"See, if you want a guy and know he's somewhere along a line, say a railroad or a bus route, you can start at the beginning and go on to the end. Perps don't often make it that easy for us.

"If you know he's somewhere on a map, that's harder, because you got two dimensions to cover. Then, if he can go not only north-south and east-west but also up-down, it gets pretty goddam impossible, unless you get a tip from a snitch or stoolie. And I suppose chasing a peril through your alternative universes would be using the fourth dimension or something, eh?"

"You get the general idea, Pete," said Shea. "If I can examine Malambroso's personal room, I might find us a clue. Okay?"

"Sure, I can arrange it, if you promise not to touch anything."

Shea stood in Malambroso's rented room, staring at the bookcases. At last he said to Brodsky: "I think I know where he's taken our kid."

"Where's that?"

"To Barsoom."

"Huh?"

"Barsoom, Edgar Rice Burroughs' version of Mars."

"Aw, hell; I know there ain't enough air on Mars to keep a bug alive—"

"Not the real Mars, but the one Burroughs imagined for his John Carter stories—or, to put it another way, the Mars in another universe, which somehow got into Burroughs' mind and formed the basis for his stories. In fact, I suspect Malambroso's already made at least one trial there to test out our syllogismobile. You can see the books. For Barsoom, he's got a collection somebody would give real money for: the old McClurg hardbacks, the Methuen reprints, and the paperbacks: Ballantines from the sixties, the later Ace series, the Del Reys... I take it to mean he's a Barsoomian fan. So, knowing about Barsoom already, he'd naturally take off in that direction. Looks as though the only way to catch up with him is for me to go to Barsoom."

Brodsky sighed. "Wish I could go with you. But since I got promoted, seems like I'm buried under a daily blizzard of papers."

"Harold Shea!" said Belphebe in tones of exasperation. "If you think for one minute I would let you go off by yourself after Voglinda, you're as mad as some of your faculty colleagues think you are. She's my daughter, too, you know. From what I've heard of Barsoom, gun making there isn't so far advanced that a good longbow wouldn't be useful as a backup."

Shea sighed. "Oh, all right, darling. Get your stuff together."

"What do they wear on Barsoom?"

"Mostly they go naked, except for a kind of harness of straps with pockets and pouches dangling. It doesn't conceal anything."

"You mean—you mean real naked, with everything showing?"

"That's what I understand. They don't seem to have the ancient Hebrew taboo on nudity, inherited by Christianity and Islam. Maybe you'd best stay home—"

"No, sir! If I have to show the Barsoomians my personal anatomy to get our precious back, I'll do it! And if any Barsoomian makes a pass, I'll make him eat a clothyard shaft for breakfast! But then, you couldn't wear your mail shirt under your clothes, could you?"

"Not and pass myself off as a native Barsoomian, which we may have to do. According to Burroughs," said Shea in his classroom manner, "Barsoomians are pretty puritanical in matters of sex and theft. Where they go off the reservation, from our point of view, is in their permissive attitude towards homicide. If you want to kill somebody, you just up and do it, and nobody gives a damn. At least, so Burroughs says, and I don't know how accurate he was. I wouldn't very far trust any writer who put tigers and deer in Africa."

"Then I'd better pack an extra quiver!"

Shea made a slight face, knowing that it would fall to his lot to carry the extra weight on the portages, however short, that any extensive trip entailed. But he did not dissent, since the proposal made sense. He said:

"And I'll take the old six-shooter. It's not the most up-to-date firearm—everybody goes for automatics nowadays—but it's simple and rugged and has fewer things to go wrong with it."

"Is Barsoom a universe where firearms work?"

"According to Burroughs, yes; though I doubt his story of radium rifles that shoot fifty miles with radar sights."

Harold Shea and Belphebe sat cross-legged on the rug in the center of the Shea living room. Shea, in breeches and boots, with a cowboy hat on his head, sat with a scabbard containing a shortened nineteenth-century saber on his left, a sheath holding a bowie knife in front, and on his right a holster with a big Smith & Wesson .44 revolver.

Belphebe wore green slacks, a similar jacket, and the feathered hat of her home world. Her longbow, unstrung, was slung over her back by its bowstring, passing between her full, young-mother breasts. A laden quiver was also slung to her back, its strap forming an X with the longbow string.

"Okay," said Shea, "let's go!" He grasped her near hand and began: "If P equals not-Q, then Q implies not-P..."

2

Shea had been through these transitions before and so was ready for their effects. The living room dissolved into a whirl of colored spots. Momentarily he seemed to be suspended in nothing, as in a free-fall. Then, bit by bit, the world around him solidified. But this world was nothing like the one they had left.

The scene was of nighttime out-of-doors, lit by a brighter moonlight than Shea had ever seen on Earth. The source was a big, bright moon, even larger than Earth's Luna, passing overhead. Elsewhere sparkled a myriad stars, brighter and more numerous than they would appear to the naked eye anywhere on Earth.

Beside him, Belphebe said: "That moon is traveling so fast you can see its motion against the stars. Also, it seems to be going from west to east, unlike our Earthly moon."

"Quite right, darling," said Shea. "That's Thuria, the closer of Barsoom's two moons. It corresponds to Phobos in our own universe. I don't see the other satellite, Cluros as they call it here. If this were our Mars, you could only see Phobos from near the equator, and it's only a big boulder anyway."

"Why couldn't Phobos be seen from elsewhere?"

"The bulge of the planet would hide it, just as it hides the Southern Cross from viewers in the northern parts of our world."

"How do you know what the Barsoomians call them, if you've never been here before?"

"I've read Burroughs. Besides, the advantage of the sorites is that, if you compose it right, you arrive in the other universe already knowing the local language. Otherwise we should have to spend months studying Barsoomian in order to get around, as Burroughs' John Carter did on his first arrival."

"Probably several different languages, as on Earth," said Belphebe.

"No; Burroughs says they have only one spoken language for the entire planet, though different nations have different ways of writing it. I daresay there are local dialects."

"How could that be? Since languages are always changing, what would prevent the speech of Barsoom from diverging into branches, like those of the Latin or the Slavic languages on Earth?"

Shea shrugged. "I don't know, darling. Perhaps some conqueror once brought the whole planet under his sway and ordained that his particular speech was the official one, which everyone had to use on pain of death. And it hasn't had time to split into different languages yet."

Thuria sank below the eastern horizon, whereupon a deeper darkness closed down, relieved by the pyrotechnic starlight.

"Oh, my!" said Belphebe. "Look at those stars! I've never seen them so bright on Earth—or in any other world I've visited."

"It's the thin atmosphere," said Shea, "sort of like that on top of the Rocky Mountains. But if I'm not mistaken, the sun is coming up soon."

The sky was visibly paling in a strip along the eastern horizon. Little by little, a small but very bright sun climbed into view.

"I hope it warms us up," said Belphebe. "I'm cold! And you tell me the

Barsoomians go naked!"

"I think they usually put on some sort of wrap when they have to go out at night," said Shea, pulling her close for warmth. "Nudism isn't really comfortable for us Earthlings unless the air temperature is well over twenty-five Celsius. Hey!" He pointed. "I think we've landed near Lesser Helium!"

In the slowly waxing light, a few hundred meters distant rose a massive city wall, high enough to conceal any buildings within, with one exception. This was a tall, slim tower. As the light grew stronger, it lit up another tower, even taller but much farther away.

The Sheas were sitting on a flat surface covered by a pinkish-yellow moss-like growth, stretching away to the horizon in all directions, save where it ended at the foot of the city wall.

"Hurrah for us!" said Shea, rising. "I aimed for the twin cities of Helium, and that's what we got. The one in front of us is Lesser Helium; the one off in the distance, where you see the bigger tower, is Greater Helium." He gave Belphebe a hand up.

"Where next?" she asked.

"Walk around the wall till we come to the main gate. Remember, your weight is less than half what it would be on Earth. So it's easy to trip and fall if you don't step cautiously."

They set out briskly. As soon as they became used to their own reduced weights, they bounced along fast to warm their muscles. After a trot of a quarter to half an hour, they approached a road, whereon people and animals moved. The road led to a massive fortified gate, and the crowd looked like an assemblage of locals bringing in wagonloads of farm produce. They were massed around the gate, waiting, and more constantly arrived.

As the Sheas approached, Shea made out the distinctive features of these Barsoomians. They were black-haired men with bright-red skins—redder than that of any Native American, together with facial features much like those of Earthly Europeans. They shivered under blankets wrapped cloak-wise around themselves. Shea recognized the beasts of burden harnessed to the wagons as thoats—hefty animals on eight slender legs apiece, with gaping jaws and massive tails ending in broad blades, usable as weapons.

As the Sheas came near the gate, a silvery trumpet sounded. With a screechy creaking, one valve of the gate swung outward. After a pause, the other valve did likewise. Several men, naked but for a harness of straps supporting swords and other personalia, bustled out. Their harness was all of one design, thus constituting the gate guards' uniform.

The gate guards talked among themselves and with members of the waiting crowd. Then two guards strode purposefully toward the Sheas. As they neared, the low sun flashed on large, bejeweled metal buckles and badges, where the straps of the harness crossed or joined.

"Who are you?" barked the nearer guard.

"From your garb," said the second guard, "you look like Jasoomians."

"So we are," said Shea. "In fact, we are—"

"You must come with us at once!" said the first guard, seizing Shea's arm in a firm grip, while his comrade took hold of Belphebe's arm.

"Unhand me, sir!" cried Belphebe.

"Orders are orders," said the first guard. "Come along, now!"

"What orders?" said Shea.

"To bring any Jasoomians before the Jed at once!"

"Harold!" cried Belphebe. "Will you let these knaves lay hands on me?"

"Best we go along with them, darling," said Shea, "since they're taking us where we want to go anyway."

Mors Kajak, Jed of Lesser Helium, sat behind a huge desk piled with scrolls. As Shea noted, the Barsoomians had not yet made the transition to the codex, the book of separate pages all bound together along one edge. The Jed was a big red Barsoomian of what, in an Earthman, would be called early middle age. He was stouter than most Barsoomians, with a few strands of gray in his bristling, crew-cut black hair.

Shea had read that Barsoomians kept the appearance of youth longer than Earthmen until, in the last century of their millennial lives, they rapidly aged. Like other Barsoomians, the Jed wore nothing save a harness of straps, whence dangled pouches, pockets, and a pair of swords in scabbards. At last he dropped the scroll he had studied and looked up.

"Well?"

"O Jed," said the senior guard, "we found these Jasoomians trying to sneak in the main gate. Mindful of our orders, we seized and brought them hither."

Belphebe looked ready to utter an angry outburst, when a gesture from Shea silenced her.

"You did right," said the Jed. "You may return to your duties, leaving the Jasoomians here. As you go out, tell the two door guards to step into my sanctum."

The senior gate guard saluted (a gesture that reminded Shea of the Roman salute made notorious by Mussolini and Hitler). Then he did a smart about-face and departed, followed by his comrade. The two door guards entered the room and took places at either end of the massive desk.

"Well, Jasoomians," said the Jed, "how explain you your presence on this world?"

"First, O Jed," said Shea, "permit me to protest the gate guard's referring to my wife's and my approach to the gate as 'sneaking.' We came peacefully and in plain sight." Shea then plunged into the tale of Malambroso's abduction of the infant Voglinda Shea.

The Jed judiciously put his fingertips together. "You say you are Professor Doctor Sir Harold Shea, and that the lady is your wife Belphebe?"

"It may be that what you have told me is true. Pray ignore the manner whereby you were fetched hither. We have learned to be wary of Jasoomian visitors. They are such wild exaggerators and prevaricators, like my crazy son-in-law, Lord John Carter. When he bests one man in combat, he tells everyone that he has slain three. If he defeats three, they become a score.

"Moreover, Jasoomians are forever introducing subversive ideas, trying to upset our sound, stable, time-tried Barsoomian customs to make them more like those of their native world. Why, Carter has spoken of making it illegal to slay a man in fair fight!"

"You disagree, O Jed?" said Shea.

"Of course! Did we Barsoomians not kill one another off with such zest by duels and assassinations, the planet's population would soon exceed that at which its scanty resources could support its people.

"Another Jasoomian, Ulysses Paxton, goes under the Barsoomian name of Vad Varo. He urged that each Barsoomian nation adopt a written constitution, to be confirmed by popular vote. He persuaded the Zodangans to try it, with the result that the chief of the Zodangans' assassins' guild, Ur Jan, won the Jed.

"Paxton has even preached that slavery is wrong, if you can believe that an apparently intelligent being could entertain such a nonsensical idea, and an inhumane idea to boot."

"How is it inhumane?" asked Belphebe.

"Why, what else could you do with prisoners of war except to make slaves of them or kill them? If you turn them loose, they will return to their own land and come back to fight you again. The remaining alternative is to kill the lot, and Paxton deems that even more inhumane. But it is the only practical alternative to enslaving them.

"When Paxton took up residence in Zodanga, Ur Jan would have slain him for his subversive ideas had he not fled. Any such doctrine would utterly overthrow our social system and reduce the world to seething chaos!"

Shea said: "My own home world has struggled with similar difficulties. Where is Lord Carter now?"

"He has gone off to Ptarth to visit Thuvan Dinh, the Jed, and to promote some of his revolutionary ideas. It will be interesting to see how long Thuvan Dinh puts up with Carter's transgalactic nonsense."

"O Jed," said Shea, "could you tell me more about Lord Carter's mysterious arrival on Barsoom? Likewise with Paxton. Some of our wise men have speculated that they sent their astral bodies to Barsoom, leaving their Earthly ones on their native planet. But that leaves open the question of whence came the mass of their Barsoomian bodies.

"There is also a mystery about where Lord Carter was born and when. He seems to have appeared out of nowhere and to have spent several times the normal Earthly life span, earning his living on Earth as a mercenary soldier—an occupation that no longer commands the respect it once did. Truth to tell, it has fallen into disrepute."

"We have been puzzled, too," said the Jed. "Nor have questions to Lord Carter done much to enlighten us. He is a jovial man of action, with little interest in the whys and wherefores of his becoming a Barsoomian.

"Now the consensus is that he is really a Barsoomian, taken to Jasoom as a child or youth by some occult means, like that which brought you and your lady hither. It is surmised that his fair skin marks him as a descendant of the white race, so called, which dominated parts of Barsoom back when the oceans still washed the margins of the continents, before the races that then existed merged to form the present red race.

"But enough of this pleasant chatter, Sir Harold. Not for naught do some folk of Lesser Helium call me 'Mors Chatterbox'—albeit not to my face. But the man whose duty it is to stand beside me and stop me when I talk too much is on vacation. So, Doctor Shea, what mean you to do next in pursuit of your vanished offspring?"

"My first step," said Shea, "is obviously to find out whether Malambroso has actually come to Barsoom. Is that the sort of thing your Barsoomian mastermind, Ras Thavas, would know?"

"Of course! Had you not brought up the matter, I should have suggested him myself. He has his own system of keeping track of events in Barsoomian cities, which we have found useful in warning us of aggressions and revolutions." The Jed turned to one of his guardsmen. "Dator Thin, you shall send a message to Doctor Ras Thavas, respectfully requesting his presence here forthwith."

The guardsman saluted and departed. The Jed said: "Sir Harold, plan you to go about Barsoom searching for this miscreant on your own?"

"Yes, sir, unless you could furnish me with helpers."

The Jed shook his head. "Since this is a matter among Jasoomians, it concerns not the Empire of Helium. I will not, therefore, let my people become involved therein, aside from furnishing such information as you can elicit from Ras Thavas. It strikes me, however, that clad in those hideous and overheating garments, you could not hope to do aught by stealth. You are as conspicuous as an Otzian on a snow bank."

From his reading, Shea knew that by "Otzian" the Jed meant a member of the black-skinned race of Barsoom, who dwelt in Otz Valley at the South Pole. He continued:

"You will, therefore, wish to adopt Barsoomian garb and color of skin. I am sure that Ras Thavas can show you how to do that—unless you have that curious prejudice among Jasoomians, that it is shameful or improper to expose one's sexual parts to the view of one's fellow beings. You Jasoomians must be a singularly nasty-minded lot, forever thinking of copulation."

"We can overcome such feelings," said Shea. "Agreed, darling?"

"Not being a native Jasoomian," said Belphebe, "I have never suffered from this twitch. If my husband ever had it, he is cured."

The Jed rang a little bell on his desk. A red Barsoomian, with the usual harness of straps, came through a side door to the sanctum. Mors Kajak said:

"Dattok, lead these Jasoomians to one of the hospitality suites, third class. Farewell for the nonce, O Sheas. Pray hold yourselves in readiness to return hither when Ras Thavas appears."

The Jed picked up the scroll he had been reading when the Sheas arrived. He unrolled it again and hunted about his cluttered desk for weights to hold down the corners of the strip and prevent it from rolling itself up again.

The following morning, a flunkey summoned the Sheas to the executive chamber. There Shea and Belphebe found another red Barsoomian in converse with the Jed. The new arrival seemed to be in what to a Barsoomian would be youth—say, in his second or third century—of handsome aspect, but notably lean and starved-looking.

"Here," said the Jed Mors Kajak to the new Barsoomian, "are the Jasoomians whereof I have told you: Mr. and Mrs. Harold Shea, unless you prefer all the fancy titles they claim: Sir, Professor, Doctor, and so on. Sheas, this is Doctor Ras Thavas, with whom you asked to speak."

Shea raised his right hand in the Barsoomian greeting. "Kaor, Doctor."

"Kaor," grunted the young Barsoomian. "Where do you wish us to confer, O Jed?"

"Dattok will show you the way," said the Jed.

The secretary led them through a maze o hallways to a small conference room. Seated, Shea studied Ras Thavas. He asked:

"Doctor, is it true that you had your brain transferred to the body of a younger man?"

"It is true," rasped Ras Thavas. "But let us not dwell upon the circumstance of my brain transfer, since social pressures have forced me to give up that kind of neurosurgery. Nor am I a chatterbox like Mors Kajak, to waste precious research time in idle chatter. What would you of me? Pray make it brief."

Shea poured out the tale of Voglinda's abduction by Malambroso. He ended: "And so, knowing you for a far-sighted and well-informed man, I ask if your intelligence system has apprised you of the arrival of this pair on Barsoom?"

Ras Thavas chuckled. "You are a clever fellow, Doctor Shea, knowing that flattery is the surest means of procuring favors from your fellow man. But think not that it will work on a person of my superior intellect. I easily see through such childish sleights.

"Now, let us suppose that my informants have in fact told me of the arrival on Barsoom of your Doctor Malambroso and his captive infant. If I put you on this wizard's track, I shall expect a favor from you in return."

"Such as?" said Shea.

"That depends. By diligent investigation, Doctor Shea, I have learned a few things about you, if not enough to grasp all aspects of your personality."

"You mean you have a dossier on me? Where did you get your information, since I only arrived on Barsoom for the first time yesterday?"

Ras Thavas gave a lopsided grin. "Oh, I have ways; I have ways. The inventions of your fellow Jasoomian, the wireless pioneer Gridley, have been of substantial help. But to get down to cases, Doctor, what is your occupation on your native planet?"

"I am a professor of psychology at the Garaden Institute, in Garaden, Ohio."

"Just what I needed! I understand that, starting as a brash, hot-tempered, and emotionally volatile youth, you have learned by painful experience to bridle your natural impulses to as to avoid offense and disarm hostility. Your conduct here during the last few *xats* shows all the smoothness one would expect of you."

"And what has all that to do with you, Doctor?" asked Shea.

"I shall come to that forthwith. When Vad Varo—formerly Ulysses Paxton of your world—transferred my brain from the worn-out body it then occupied to the body you now see before you, he did an excellent job. That is no cause for surprise, since he had the greatest possible teacher of neurosurgery, namely me."

Shea asked. "What happened to the original brain of the body you are now using?"

"It was incinerated. That was no great loss to civilization, since it was a brain of a relatively primitive, stupid type, who had left school for good as a child. But when these facts came out, sentimentalists raised such an ebullition that I was forced to give up my practice of brain transfer.

"In one respect, however, Vad Varo was never able to complete his task. The original body retained a battery of glands, whose functions affect even my superior brain. Therefore mundane urges and desires that I thought I had long since cast aside as mere irrational sentimentalism arise to plague me.

"In fact, I seem to be turning into the very sort of creature I most despised: an emotional, irrational sentimentalist. Why, finding myself recently in the company of two of Mors Kajak's handsome nubile daughters, I found to my horror that I developed a hearty erection. Since on Barsoom we do not conceal the parts in question by those ridiculous costumes that Jasoomians wear, and since the phenomenon in question is, on Barsoom, accounted the worst possible breach of good manners, I was forced to mutter an excuse and beat a hasty retreat.

"So then, you may ask, why do I not simply mingle with others of my class and form such attachments as my glands dictate, as other mortals do? The difficulty is that, having steered my course for centuries by the ideal of a purely rational, objective, emotionless scientist, I find that I cannot freely mingle with the rabble. To be blunt, they do not like me and, further to aggravate matters, most of them bore me.

"In forming their personal relationships, they make no allowance for my obvious mental superiority. If I join a group happily chattering away about trivial matters, they fall silent at my approach. If I seek a social engagement with one of the more promising rabblites, of either sex, the object of my wish for good fellowship makes transparent excuses: he or she is unwell, or has a previous engagement, or has just lost a close relative, or some such fribbling pretext. Nobody ever invites me to anything! Intellectually I know that lonesomeness is just one more irrational sentiment, forced upon me by the primitive glands of the stupid previous owner of this body. But that fact does not make the emotion any less painful."

Shea, grinning, said aside to Belphebe: "He reminds me of Edgar Poe."

"Who or what is Edgar Poe?" snapped Ras Thavas.

"A crow I once knew."

"What is a crow?"

"A large black Earthly bird, omnivorous and relatively intelligent. Edgar was found by a couple as a fledgling who had fallen out of its nest before it was airworthy. They took him home and fed him up, so that he grew into a big, handsome adult crow. Then the couple decided it was a shame to keep Edgar penned up indoors. They took him to a place they knew a flock of wild crows frequented and turned him loose.

"A fortnight later, one of them opened the back door. There was Edgar, taking the begging attitude, like this." Shea squatted, half spread his arms, and looked up with his mouth open. "He was bald, because all the feathers had been pecked off the crown of his head.

"What had happened was that Edgar, having lived among human beings through his formative years, thought of himself as human and tried to behave accordingly. He had never learned proper crow manners and etiquette; so the other crows of the flock he tried to join set upon him. In the end, the couple had to take him back, although they confessed that the full-grown Edgar in the house was something of a nuisance. Now, what am I supposed to do about your problem?"

"You shall take me in hand and teach me the little sleights and dodges and mannerisms of friendly social intercourse—the details your Edgar failed to learn about his fellow crows. For centuries I have avoided learning such details with the rabble, lest they waste time that were better spent on my research. In other words, you shall teach me how to get along with people, even mere rabblites."

"Jeepers!" cried Shea. "That would take a lot of doing. What makes you think an alien like me would know how to tinker with your mental works? You need a Dale Carnegie type."

"A what type? Never mind; my superior telepathic powers convey the sense of your meaning. As a professional psychologist—an occupation entirely lacking on Barsoom, save for my own limited forays into that field—you are the best-qualified person on this planet. Psychologically, we Barsoomians are very close to you Jasoomians. The difference you will in due course discover and make allowances for. Your being an alien is an advantage, since it enables you to view Barsoomian society and customs with a coldly objective eye."

Shea objected: "Meanwhile, what happens to our daughter Voglinda? I can't chase after Malambroso and at the same time give you a crash course in human relations."

"That is my condition," said Ras Thavas. "Teach me the skills I have set forth, and I will do what I can to further your search for your daughter. Otherwise I will do naught, and with your ignorance of this world you will probably encompass your own speedy destruction."

"Be reasonable! What you ask is as feasible as jumping out the window and flying by flapping my arms!"

"I am always reasonable. You have my condition."

"May I make a suggestion?" asked Belphebe.

"By all means, do," said Shea. "Whenever we get really stuck, I know I can count on you to pull a rabbit out of the hat."

"What is a rabbit?" asked Ras Thavas.

"A mere figure of speech; ignore," said Shea. "What's your suggestion, darling?"

"Why don't we bring Doctor Ras with us in searching for Voglinda? You can coach him daily in polite social intercourse and scold him when he makes a gaffe. If he be half as brilliant as he thinks he is, he would be a valuable guide in this alien world."

"Depends on where we're going." Shea turned to Ras. "So, will you now tell us where we are going."

"Do you agree to the lady's scheme?" said Ras Thavas. "I hate to lose the research time; but the cold logic of my superior mind dictates that I agree to the lady's scheme. Do you also agree?"

"Yes, I do. If you will guide and help us to our objective, I'll do my best to make you over into a suave Barsoomian-of-the-world. I can't guarantee success in changing your habits, fixed by a thousand years of conditioning; but I'll do my best. So, where are they?"

Ras Thavas replied: "One of my informants in the city of Zodanga has reported that a man of alien aspect arrived from another world with a small child a day or two ago. From such details as I could elicit by wireless, the pair agree with your descriptions of Malambroso and Voglinda."

"Where is Zodanga?"

"About three thousand haads from here, in a roughly northeasterly direction."

Belphebe asked: "What's that in Earthly measurements?"

Shea replied: "I don't remember the exact conversion factor; but it's something like two thousand miles. The haad comes close to the kilometer."

"Quite a distance," said Belphebe.

"One must get used to great distances on Barsoom. Although the planet is smaller than our Earth, the fact of having no oceans makes the land area over twice ours."

"Then how do we get there?" she asked. "Borrow one of their flying machines?"

"That would not be practicable," said Ras Thavas. "If any Heliumite were willing to lend or rent such a machine, he would certainly not do it to an alien of whom he knows naught."

"How much would one cost?" asked Shea. "New or secondhand?"

"A new flier to carry three would run about ten thousand crowns."

Shea exchanged looks with his wife. "I doubt if we brought anything like that with us. And I don't suppose they accept credit cards."

"What is a credit card?" asked Ras Thavas. "Never mind. Anyway, who should pilot the craft? The Heliums, who like to think of themselves as thoroughly up-to-date, have installed a newfangled system of licenses for piloting fliers, and rules to govern air traffic. I do not have a pilot's license, so one of you Sheas would have to obtain one. That calls for a course of instructions and passing a flight test and a written examination."

"Oh-oh!" said Shea. "Looks as if bureaucracy has caught up with Barsoom at last!"

"There are reasons," said Ras Thavas. "Lord Carter was persuaded to start a course at the local university on Earthly capitalism. His praises of the free-market system proved so popular that the Jed was prevailed upon to abolish the former restrictions on free enterprise.

"Soon, enterprising Heliumites set up factories to make fliers, cheap enough for ordinary folk to buy. Some of these machines were hastily built and killed their occupants. That was only one example of the shortcomings of capitalism, which transpired little by little. So now a powerful faction is urging more regulations, which Lord Carter furiously opposes, calling such interference in business un-American, whatever that means.

"In any case, the air over the Heliums became too crowded for safety, especially when some of the younger and more reckless males began doing acrobatic stunts with their fliers. Aerial collisions became a daily occurrence. The rain of machines and bodies on roofs and streets led the Jeddak, following Lord Carter's advice, to impose a strict system of licensing."

Belphebe asked: "Isn't there any public transport on Barsoom? Say, an airline?"

Ras Thavas chuckled. "One Heliumite last year essayed to start a regular passenger service by flier to Zodanga and Zor. But it foundered on one of the weaknesses of human nature."

"How so?" asked Shea.

"You know our Barsoomian custom, of always going armed, at least with sword and dagger if not with a pistol as well? That is how we distinguish free men from slaves by sight. Thus I, being unarmed at the moment, could be mistaken for a slave, were not my repute so high that no Heliumite, at least, would commit that error. The Jed's secretary, Dattok, is a slave. I forgo sword wearing in the Heliums because the cursed things are a nuisance, forever tripping me up or hitting me in the shins.

"Well, it did not take long for the lawless element to reason out a way to turn the airline fares to their advantage. Suppose a criminal wished to fly to, say, Horz, which is halfway round the planet. So he would buy a ticket to Zor, which was vastly cheaper. Then, when the flier had taken off, he would draw sword and pistol and command the pilot to take him to Horz. This led to aerial fights and fatal crashes.

"First, the capitalist who launched the scheme tried to disarm his passengers, demanding that all weapons—swords, daggers, pistols, and so on be handed in to the gate guards. But you must understand that, for Barsoomians, the sword has a mystical prestige. To ask a free Barsoomian to surrender his sword is like asking him to become a slave.

"Hence fights broke out, with gate guards and would-be passengers slain. Hence the passengers dropped off, and his company went bankrupt by the end of last year."

"What happens to one who goes bankrupt here?"

"He is auctioned off as a slave to his creditors. Of the money paid for him, most goes to the government's tax collectors, while the remainder is divided amongst the unsuccessful creditors. I am sure that your home world, being technologically more advanced than we are, has long since mastered such problems."

"I fear not," said Shea. "Among certain classes of Jasoomians, the pistol has acquired something of the same mystical glorification that here applies to the sword. A few centuries ago, the sword on my world had much the same status. Wearing a sword proved that one belonged to the gentleman class. Now that the sword is obsolete as a military weapon, the pistol has somewhat taken its place psychologically."

Belphebe: "That's all very well, but then how do we get to Zodanga? You don't seem to have railroads or buses."

Ras Thavas said: "I fear we must either walk or ride on the backs of thoats. Do you two ride any riding animal?"

"Yes," she replied. "We are both experienced riders of a Jasoomian beast called a 'horse.' How long would it take to get to Zodanga on thoat-back?"

"Three thousand haads..." Ras Thavas frowned in thought, twitching his fingers to do sums. "With good beasts, assuming no accidents or hostile encounters, forty to fifty days."

Shea grunted and Belphebe groaned. Shea said: "Is there no way to get us there faster?"

"Not that I know of, unless Sir Harold can work his symbolic-logic spell to move us to another part of the planet."

"I fear that won't work, either," said Shea. "An attempt would probably snap us back to the planet we started from."

"Then," said Belphebe, "we must make the best of it. It might even have advantages. Harold can work on Doctor Ras to make him into the perfect Barsoomian gentleman." Ras Thavas made a face of disgust.

"Yes," said Shea. "And, Doctor, have you been eating regularly? You look starved."

Ras Thavas waved a dismissing hand. "My body keeps signaling that it wants more to eat; but I cannot afford the time away from my research to indulge its primitive lusts. Its previous owner was an athlete, and his body doubtless wishes to continue in the gluttonous habits it formed in its previous life."

"For our scheme," said Shea, "you must be in top physical trim. So be prepared to eat what and when I tell you to."

"The body I now wear," said Ras Thavas haughtily, "was the physically finest among the hundreds of specimens that have passed through my laboratories. In fact its previous owner, if weak in intellect, had a repute as a champion wrestler or something of the sort."

"It may have been a perfect body then," said Shea, "but I can see where you've let it run down. Too much crouching over lab tables, not enough food, and not enough exercise. Daily workouts will soon fix that! Then I must by you out on some sword practice, since Barsoomians have such romantic ideas about the glory of the sword."

Ras Thavas groaned.

3

Harold Shea said: "Seems to me we've ridden far enough for one day. What do you think, darling?"

"I think you're right," said Belphebe, mentally commanding her thoat to halt. Hitching her longbow up out of the way, she slid off the animal.

Shea dismounted with a grunt. "I fear we shall have some sore muscles tomorrow."

"We haven't done enough riding lately to keep in shape," said Belphebe. "It's not as if I hadn't reminded you."

"I know," said Shea. "But there's always a meeting at the damned Institute, or a stack of papers to grade. At least, with all those legs, these critters give a smoother ride than a horse."

Ras Thavas had more difficulty in halting his thoat. The animal trotted on for several thoat-lengths before he brought it under mental control and circled back to join the others.

"Accursed beast," he growled, dismounting. "How comes it that you two aliens manage to guide your beasts as well as native Barsoomians; whereas I, despite being Barsoomian-born and having the most highly developed brain on this planet, find it difficult to do so?" It was plain to see that Ras Thavas had gained weight, compared to the starveling savant whom the Sheas had first met.

"My guess," said Belphebe, "is that you take a purely intellectual approach to your beast, whereas Harold and I make friends of ours."

"Mean you that these dumb brutes are motivated by irrational emotions, like human Barsoomians of the lowest kind?"

"That's one way of putting it," said Shea, rounding up the eight thoats— two for baggage and three as spare riding animals—and staking them out. Spreading their eight spindly legs apiece, the thoats fell to grubbing up mouthfuls of the salmon-pink moss that covered most of the Barsoomian surface.

Ras Thavas growled: "It is wrong that I, the greatest mind on Barsoom, should have to truckle to the irrational whims of these animals."

"No doubt," said Shea. "It is also wrong that I, if I fell off a pier into deep water on my native Earth, should have to give a bad imitation of an aquatic animal to escape death by drowning. But that's the choice that would face me." He turned to Belphebe. "Target practice?"

Belphebe was setting up a tripod to support an archery target. "Absolutely, love. Without practice, you soon lose any skill."

Having dug the legs of the tripod into the moss, she walked away from the tripod, counting her paces as she went, and strung her bow. She and Shea, like Ras Thavas, were entirely naked save for footgear and a few straps supporting pockets and, in Shea's case, a large purse, a longsword, a shortsword, and a pistol. Both Sheas had been stained all over with bright-red pigment to match the Barsoomians. Belphebe's red-gold hair had been dyed black, not only on her scalp but also wherever else it grew.

"Time for your workout, Doctor," said Shea to Has Thavas. "We'll start with deep-knee bends."

Ras Thavas groaned, but Shea bullied him into calisthenics. At the end

Shea, sweating freely, said: "Now for a whack with the sticks."

From the pile of gear removed from one of the baggage thoats, Shea pulled out a pair of padded jackets, of wire face masks, and of wooden singlesticks with basket guards. Soon the dry clatter of the sticks resounded. Shea said:

"You're coming along, Doctor; much better than when we left Helium—*unh!*"

Has Thavas had feinted a lunge and, when Shea parried in sixte, competently doubled and poked Shea in the solar plexus with the blunt end of the singlestick.

"Hey!" said Shea. "That was good!"

"No problem to one of my intellect," said Has Thavas. "I simply listened to your instructions and applied them intelligently."

"Okay," said Shea. "But, as I've told you over and over, you'll have to get out of the habit of telling everyone who'll listen about your superior mind."

"It is a simple statement of fact!" protested Ras Thavas.

"No doubt; but to get along with your fellow mortals, you'll find it more effective to keep quiet about your marvelous intellect. Remember poor Edgar the crow!"

Ras Thavas chewed on this unwelcome advice. At last he asked: "What should I say?"

"Pass off the victory with a light laugh and say you were merely lucky."

"Rank hypocrisy!" snorted Ras Thavas.

"True; but hypocrisy is one of the factors, like liquor and religion, that enables mortals to put up with one another, at least when they form masses larger than primitive foraging bands."

"Foraging bands? Kindly explain."

Shea gave a summary of current Earthly theory of human prehistory, from the time when Australopithecines in Africa adopted erect posture and bipedal walking down to the rise of civilization.

"That is not at all our Barsoomian view," said Ras Thavas. "Know you the story of the Tree of Life?"

"I know of it. Not having done scientific investigation here on Barsoom, I won't say anything against it. But we have had similar traditional stories on Earth—the Garden of Eden, the Red Sea crossing, and so forth—which turned out to be mere myths and legends. To get back to our last subject, if one of these thoats—" Shea gestured toward the eight animals "—took a grudge against you, do you think it would do any good to lecture it on your mental superiority?"

"I suppose not," grumbled Ras Thavas. Then he looked past Shea with a widening gaze. "Behind you, Shea!"

Shea whirled. Stealing up on the fencers were half a dozen wild calots, the Barsoomian equivalent of a pack of wolves. Each had eight lean legs, bent so that the animals slithered along with their bellies brushing the moss. Their heads, which reminded Shea of those of Earthly bulldogs, had gaping jaws full of fangs, whence the animals drooled on the moss.

Shea's instant thought was for his weapons, which lay with his harness in the direction whence the calots were coming. In fact, the leader of the pack now stood over their gear, gave it a brief sniff, and resumed its stalk, leaving the fencers to face the pack with singlesticks. Over his shoulder, Shea called: "Hey, sweetheart!"

As he did so, Ras Thavas threw his singlestick at the leading calot, turned, and ran. Instantly the calot bounded erect from its crouch and sprinted after the fugitive, detouring past Shea.

Having eight legs to Ras Thavas' two, the calot, Shea could see, would overtake the savant in seconds. The rest of the pack ran after their leader.

Shea dashed to the pile of equipment that he and Ras Thavas had dumped on the moss. As he did so, he heard the snap of Belphebe's bowstring. The leading calot doubled up with a howl. A second shaft laid it, writhing, on the pinkish-yellow moss.

Ras Thavas continued his flight. The five other calots hesitated at the sight of their leader's throes, then resumed the chase.

Shea straightened up with pistol in hand. Holding it in a two-handed grip, he fired it at the calot closest to the fleeing Ras Thavas; missed, and fired again. The animal collapsed, just after another of Belphebe's arrows struck another calot. The latter beast began to turn in circles, trying to reach the shaft in its flank with its jaws. Shea fired again, and the calot fell.

The three remaining members of the pack ran away. Breathing hard, Ras Thavas came slowly toward Shea, unfastening his padded jacket. Shea said: "Well, you're a fine one to have as an ally in a tight fix!"

"On the contrary," said Ras Thavas, "it was obvious to my superior mind that singlesticks were inadequate weapons for coping with beasts of prey. That was all we had, thanks to your stupidity in leaving our swords and things out of reach."

For a few seconds, Shea struggled with a primitive lust to beat the shit out of this mastermind. When he finally got his rage under control, he said: "On the other hand, if you hadn't panicked and run, we might well have faced them down until my wife got her bow into action. Jasoomian predators hesitate to attack any prey animal who boldly faces them; but when one runs away, they go after it instantly. From what I've seen, it's the same for Barsoom."

"I did but follow the logical course," said the scientist. "I knew that I could not outrun the calots. But if I led them close by you, they might attack you instead of me, affording me a chance to escape."

Shea snorted: "Any normal Barsoomian would call that the act of a son of a calot."

"That merely shows the primitive mental state wherein most of them dwell. Any thinking person could see that, between the two of us, my mind is infinitely the more valuable to the planet."

"And you wonder why people don't like you!" roared Shea. Ras Thavas held up a hand.

"Please, let us not continue this bootless argument further. Had we known of the incident in advance, we could doubtless have planned a more generally satisfactory course of action.

"To go to a more agreeable subject, I note that you fired three shots from your alien pistol without reloading. This must be one of those repeating Jasoomian firearms whereof Carter and Paxton have told us. Our Barsoomian smiths have tried to make them, but they always jam. Our smithery is not yet accurate enough. Of course that Earthman who wrote about life on Barsoom said many things that are simply untrue, like the number of legs on some animals, and repeating firearms that shoot a distance of eighty haads."

Shea took off his jacket. Belphebe walked past him, saying: "I missed one shot; help me to find it. I don't see anything around here that we could use to make more, such as wetlands with stands of cane or reeds. I'd have done better with that Turkish composite bow, but I was afraid I hadn't had enough practice with it."

"Next time we make arrows," said Shea, "let's paint the shafts a color that contrasts with that of the moss. It may take zodes to find this one. And then we must cut the others out of the calots you hit. I could use some pistol practice, too."

She said: "There's just not enough time to practice all the skills we might find useful. Oh, there's my shaft, half buried in the moss."

Ras Thavas said; "You will find plenty of plants of the sort you mentioned in the Great Toonolian Marsh. But count yourselves lucky if the pursuit of Malambroso lead you not thither. Do you mean to cook and eat the dead calots?"

"If you consider them edible, and our little oil stove works." As Shea puttered with culinary preparations, he asked:

"Tell me something, Doctor. Barsoom, being the fourth planet from its sun, corresponds in a general way to a planet called Mars in my universe. Yet it differs from Mars in a number of striking respects. Mars, in the words of an Earthly friend, lacks enough air to keep an insect alive.

"Now, you call your sun's third planet Jasoom, and it corresponds more or less to the Earth in my universe. My question is, how much like Earth is Jasoom? Carter and Paxton both thought they were going to our Mars and landed on Barsoom instead. On our Mars they would have died of anoxia in a matter of minutes. What is the Jasoom of your universe like?"

"I do not know," said Ras Thavas. "It appears to be inhabited by a species somewhat like yours, Doctor Shea. But our means of communication are not yet perfected enough to enable me to say more."

Shea flashed a grin at Belphebe. "We must learn not to confuse Jasoom with our own Earth. Any time we get restless, darling, we can crank up the old syllogismobile and set it for Jasoom."

She replied: "You forget, sweetheart, we're parents now. We can't any more just dash off on adventures whenever the whim takes us!"

The trio, trailed by the extra thoats, trotted through the Zodangan suburbs along a road that became smoother and better maintained with each passing haad. Ras Thavas explained:

"The reason the houses all look so new is that they are new. When the city fell to besiegers in the jedship of Than Kosis, the Heliumites and their Thark allies destroyed most of the old city. But thanks to its natural advantages, it has been rebuilt and is now almost as populous as the old Zodanga."

"What are its natural advantages?" asked Shea, staring about at the monotonous, featureless, pinkish-yellow, moss-covered Barsoomian plain. "It has none that I can see."

"Why," said Ras Thavas, "it lies at the crossing of the road from the Heliums to Ptarth and Phundahl, and the road from Zor to Duhor."

"I see," said Shea.

"That attack on Zodanga," said Ras Thavas, "was one more example of the incorrigible stupidity of most of my fellow Barsoomians. Since the last big war, guns had evolved from smoothbores to rifled muskets, far more accurate. Yet Tars Tarkas repeatedly led his Tharks in massed mounted frontal attacks on the Zodangan defenses. Naturally they took tremendous losses, whence the Thark nation has not yet recovered."

"I recall similar events on Earth," said Shea. "Battles in places called Fredericksburg and Gettysburg "

Ras Thavas sighed. "You must tell me more about your Earthly history, since your people seem capable of quite as egregious stupidities as ours. Sometimes one wonders whether it be worthwhile to try to do anything for the future of this planet at least, since anything good one accomplishes will soon be undone by the stupidity and shortsighted selfishness of individual Barsoomians."

"The same can be said of Earth," said Shea. "And if the dominant species on Jasoom is similar, I daresay it could be said of that world also."

They came to the main wall of the city, where their badges, identifying them as subjects of Jed Mors Kajak of Lesser Helium, got them past the gate guards without questioning.

"That was easier than I expected," said Shea.

"We are fortunate that Lord Carter be not off on one of his lunes, such as trying to abolish assassination," said Ras Thavas. "If he were, you can be sure that Ur Jan, the elected Jed and head of the local assassins, would subject every Heliumite to minute examination ere admitting him, if he let him in at all. Inside, he would be followed night and day by the Jed's police agents. Vad Varo thinks that Barsoom needs a system of passports like that of his native world. Belike it does, but that would make travel even more difficult than it now is."

"How long does Ur Jan's term of office run?"

"According to the newfangled constitution, it should have ended some time ago. But Ur Jan pronounced the constitution null and void and declared himself supreme and absolute ruler. Since his followers had the power, no other Zodangans dared to object."

"Sounds like one of our more backward Earthly nations," said Shea. "Time for another charm lesson. I meet you in the morning and say: 'Good morning. How do you do?' Then what do you say?"

Ras Thavas grumbled: "I say 'Good morning,' too, even though it be plainly a terrible morning. As for 'How do you do?' I am sure that you would not wish a detailed account of all my symptoms—the toothache, the constipation, the sore toe joint, and so on. So what say I?"

"You say: 'Fine, and you?'"

"Oh, very well. 'Fine. And you?' though I no more want to hear a list of his symptoms than he does mine."

"What next?"

"I forget, Tell me!"

Shea: "'How nice to see you!'"

"Rubbish! Hypocrisy! Most of the people whom I meet, I do not find at all nice. Those who do not display obvious faults of intellect or character tend to be insufferable bores."

"You must say it anyway. Go on, say it!"

Ras Thavas complied, with the expression of one who has unexpectedly bitten into something sour. "What then?"

"'How well you are looking!'"

"Even if the fellow looks as if he were about to drop dead?"

"One must exercise discretion. If he really looks all in, you say: 'Can I help you?'"

"Oh, Issus! What if I care naught what befalls the wretch?"

"Make the offer anyway. Go on, say it!"

Ras Thavas groaned but complied. A few blocks further on, Shea said: "That looks like a respectable eatery. What do you think, Doctor?"

"I am no judge of such matters," said Ras Thavas. "For centuries I have devoted my superior mind to the solution of more recondite scientific problems, paying no more heed to the demands of my animal body than I must to keep the mechanism efficiently functioning."

"No bon vivant, you," muttered Shea.

Belphebe, dismounting, said: "I'll take a quick look inside and report." When she came out, she said: "At least it looks passably clean. Come on!"

The eatery served in automat style. Machines proffered dishes to patrons, who collected them on trays as they passed. Belphebe was ahead of her two men in the line, and next before her was a burly red Barsoomian. After her came Shea and Ras Thavas. The latter murmured:

"Have a care with that hoodlum in front of us, Doctor Shea. His metal says that he is one of Ur Jan's personal guards, an old comrade from the assassins' guild."

Shea loosened his pistol in its holster. The assassin meanwhile moved so that his naked skin brushed lightly against that of Belphebe. When she turned a frowning face toward him, he muttered: "Hey, you pretty spear-shaft! How about a little quick fucky-fucky? As you can see, I have the equipment!" He glanced down to where he displayed the physical symptom of lust for all to see, since Barsoomian costume made no attempt to conceal the private parts.

Angrily, Belphebe spat: "Begone, sir! I am an honest wife!"

"Is that so?" said the assassin, loosening his longsword in its scabbard. "Is one of those two behind you, wearing Heliumite metal, your husband? Tell me which, and I'll make you an instant widow. Then I'll show you some lovemaking, the like of which you have never enjoyed!"

Shea tapped the man's shoulder, at the same time bringing up his revolver. He grated: "Sir, I am the husband in question. If you bother us, I shall shoot you dead!"

"Shea!" cried Ras Thavas. "Put that pistol away! You know not what you do! To use a gun is a capital offense, even in self-defense! I will take care of this jackanapes, and you must not interfere! Stand clear! The code does not permit you to help me." Ras Thavas drew his own sword, saying:

"Sir guardsman, anyone who confronts my friend here must answer to me. He is a foreigner who does not fully understand local customs, whereas you are a mannerless *ulsio*. Draw, scoundrel!"

The guardsman's sword came out with a *wheep*. Slaves rushed out from behind the food counters and shooed people away to clear a space. The guardsman roared:

"Lay on!"

Ras Thavas and the guardsman crossed blades. In an instant they were at it, *zip-whisht-clang!*

Shea watched uncertainly, torn between a natural urge to help Ras Thavas and the command laid upon him not to interfere. He expected the guardsman to make mincemeat of the scientist, whom he persisted in viewing as elderly despite his youthful body. But to his surprise, after a few short passages, Ras Thavas nailed his opponent with a coupe and lunge, driving his sword through the guardsman's beefy chest and out his back. The guardsman folded upon the floor.

Ras Thavas wiped his blade with a napkin that someone handed him and sheathed his sword. A couple of slaves picked up the corpse by wrists and ankles and bore it out, while another cleaned up a small puddle of blood with a mop. Another staff member chivvied people back into line at the serving tables.

Shea paid for their meals and said: "Doctor, I never expected to see you such a swashbuckler!"

"That was nothing," said Ras Thavas. "I have listened to your words and practiced with you at singlesticks, and I simply put my knowledge to use. Now, I trust, there will be no more aversions on my courage!"

Evidently, thought Shea, his remarks about the incident of the pack of wild calots had rankled. Otherwise has Thavas might not have been so ready to take up Shea's quarrel with the guardsman. Shea was tempted to twit Ras Thavas on displaying a common human weakness, despite his profession of lofty superiority to such sentiments, but thought better of it. Instead he said:

"You certainly picked up fencing skill in record time. On Earth it takes years of practice to attain that level."

Ras Thavas smiled thinly. "I would attribute that accomplishment to my superior mind, did I not know that allusions thereto displease you. Let us assume that my youthful athlete's body retains some reflexes from its former life."

"What will be done about the guardsman's death? Shall we be arrested?"

"Naught, since he met it in a fair fight. I have committed no legal offense. But if you had fired that gun, we should all have been in deep trouble."

"Kindly explain. Why is it all right to puncture a man with a sword but illegal to do the same thing to him with a bullet?"

"That requires thought to make clear. For many centuries, slaves have been forbidden, for obvious reasons, to wear weapons. So a sword has, as it were, become the symbol of a free man—what one of you aliens would call a 'gentleman.'

"At the same time, the tradition grew up that, to prove his free manhood, a man must be prepared to defend his honor with his sword. So sword fights to the death, like that between me and the late guardsman, were accepted as the normal order of things. Of course, there is an element of luck in the outcome of such a duel; but at least most Barsoomians accepted the notion that such a fight was mainly decided by the skill of the fighters.

"Then, a few centuries ago, they invented guns. This obviously enlarged the role of luck in the outcome. Hence death by shooting was no longer deemed a 'fair fight' and was considered illegal. I do not personally consider these fine distinctions logically sound. To me, courage is an irrational sentiment, even though my glands may force me betimes to attempt to display it. But that is how things now stand on Barsoom."

"Seems to me," said Shea, "that Barsoom has a strong case of class rule here: a majority of slaves, bossed around and bullied by a minority of sword-wearing free men."

"True, O Shea. But from what I hear of Jasoomian or perhaps I should say Earthly—social systems, embody a similar distinction betwixt the ruling minority and the subject majority. Laws are passed and constitutions adopted to enlarge the power of the ruled majority over their own destinies; but the ruling minority somehow keeps a grip on power, whether they pass under the name of counts, colonels, capitalists, or commissars. It must be a tendency built into the species' makeup.

"If the ruled revolt and expel or exterminate the ruling class, almost instantly the more aggressive and energetic members of the ruled class form a new ruling class, lording it over the rest. In theory, a free man is not supposed to use his sword on a slave, since that is obviously unfair But every day we hear of cases where a free Barsoomian lost his temper with a slave and sworded him to death."

"Is anything ever done to the swording bully?"

"Not unless the slave's owner takes offense at the loss of his servitor and challenges the slayer. The result the duel, of course, depends on the strength and skill the combatants—and, inevitably, on luck."

"So justice has nothing to do with it," said Shea, rising to leave the eatery. Belphebe and Ras Thavas followed him out. The scientist said:

"What is justice? An ideal, which everyone interprets to his own advantage. Methinks the hostelry we are now passing might furnish us and our beasts with suitable accommodations."

Belphebe said: "Darling, your telling me what sex puritans the Barsoomians were was a little premature."

Shea sighed. "Live and learn."

The following morning, Shea and Ras Thavas had to wait at the entrance to the hostelry for Belphebe appear from the women's half of the building. Ras Thavas pestered the clerk to draw him a map showing how to find the house where dwelt Mar Vas, his local informant.

"Turn right as you leave," said the clerk, "and at the third street on the right, turn right again. Number fourteen is the last house at the end of a long block on your left. You cannot miss it."

Shea muttered: "I've had people tell me before that I couldn't miss the place I was looking for, and gotten as thoroughly lost as ever."

Ras Thavas: "I hear that on Jasoom, the streets all have names or numbers, shown by signposts; and the houses are numbered in regular order, with number fifteen following number fourteen and so forth."

"I don't know about Jasoom," said Shea, "but that's how we do it on Earth. It makes places much easier to find."

"You would never get Barsoomians to agree. Why, if anyone could be tracked down from the name of his street and the number of his house, any assassin or enemy could find and kill him! That is the reason that the costlier houses can be raised on telescoping pillars at night."

"Since Jed Ur Jan," said Shea in a lowered voice, "is himself an old assassin, I should think he'd want to make things easier for assassins."

Ras Thavas smiled crookedly. "A Jed soon discovers that he cannot rely solely upon one small part of the populace for support, especially in a world as much given to homicide as Barsoom. A ruler can keep his subjects under control for a while by terrifying penalties. But if he makes himself disliked enough, sooner or later a subject—even a mere slave—will try to shoot or stab him."

Belphebe appeared. As she and Shea exchanged a morning embrace, Ras Thavas said: "Lady Belphebe, had I met you a thousand years ago, my life might have followed a different pattern. I have watched with admiration how you and Doctor Shea act in concert, supporting each other. Even though you squabble occasionally, you always present a united front against the outside world. And I believe the building across the street is the one whereto the clerk directed us."

The building in question was a rooming house, run by a red Barsoomian landlady with four slaves. She informed them that Mar Vas had gone out earlier and had not returned. He had left word, however, that if Doctor Ras Thavas came, he was to be shown to Mar Vas' room.

The room turned out to be used as a home laboratory, with tables here and there bearing unfamiliar pieces of equipment and a tangle of wires everywhere.

"You behold Mar Vas' experiments in wireless communication," said Ras Thavas. "Do you understand this apparatus?"

"I'm afraid not," said Shea. "On Earth they used to sell do-it-yourself kits for making such apparatus, but in my time they sold complete sets, contained in a single compact box, so big." Shea illustrated with gestures. "I never mastered that skill, unfortunately."

In answer to further questions, the landlady said: "I remember his saying something about visiting the Arms Fair."

"Where is that?" asked Shea.

"Go that way along the nearest cross street till you come to the public fountain, then turn right..."

Another hour found them before a circus-sized tent, with swarms of Barsoomians going in and out. To one side of the entrance, a stand bore a spacious sign. Shea could not read the writing; for, while Barsoom spoke essentially one language, each nation had evolved its own system of writing. He appealed to Ras Thavas for a translation. The latter studied the sign for some seconds, then spoke:

"It says; 'Down with the Restrictionists! They seek to deprive us honest men of means of defending our lives, property, and honor. They would reduce all free Barsoomians to the status of sniveling slaves! Smite the cowardly scoundrels!' "

"What's that all about?" asked Shea. "Who are the Restrictionists?"

"They are members of a movement to restrict the right of free Barsoomians to go armed. Since a sword is a symbol of being a free man, any threat to take away a man's sword incites him to furious resistance."

"How about guns?"

"Meseems they have not got around to considering guns yet, since guns are a fairly new feature of Barsoomian personal armament. The gun was invented in my own lifetime and has not yet acquired the status in Barsoomian culture that the sword has. You have already learned that, if threatened with a sword, it is deemed a dreadful crime to defend oneself with a gun, which is thought a cowardly, unmanly weapon. But, because of its ability to slay at a distance, in some places the gun is inching its way into the status that the sword has long enjoyed."

"Will the Barsoomians get around to forbidding guns in private hands?"

"They may." Ras Thavas gave a cynical smile. "But even if they manage to stop all carrying of weapons, the only result will be an increase in population, until numbers are again limited by lack of food and water."

Shea frowned at the sign. "What's that squiggle down at the bottom?"

"That, my good Doctor Shea, is the colophon of the Arms Makers Guild, who paid for the sign. I would not be so misanthropic as to accuse the Guild of erecting the sign purely from selfish motives, to stimulate the arms business." The scientist snickered. "But you may judge that matter for yourself. Here, Shea, it is up to you to pay for our admission. The entrance fee is small. I trust that you changed enough of your Jasoomian—excuse me; I meant Earthian—gold pieces into local currency?"

Shea said: "I think we shall manage. The kind of man you claim you would like to be would say: 'Oh, let me pay for all the admissions!' Then I would argue the matter, and you would gradually let yourself be talked out of paying."

"Meseems a silly business, making an offer that I do not intend to keep. What if you then said: 'Thank you, Doctor; that is generous of you!'?"

"You would pay with a good grace, not even looking sour at the prospect. That is how things are done among human beings."

Shea handed in the required number of elliptical coins. Inside, they found long aisles between rows of tables, on which arms displayed by dealers were set out in lavish quantities: swords, daggers, muskets, pistols, and less usual arms such as battle-axes, pikes, halberds, maces, and fauchards. Shea remarked:

"Doctor, one thing about Barsoom puzzles me. For folk who make such a fetish of combat with hand weapons, nobody gives a thought to armor, or even shields. On Earth, at one time the art of making armor was highly developed, so that a fighter could go into battle completely encased in steel, so cleverly made that he could move about almost as freely as he could without any armor."

"The matter has been discussed on Barsoom," said Ras Thavas. "For centuries, the general opinion among the sword-wearing class has been that wearing armor is an open admission of cowardice. Most Barsoomian warriors would rather die bravely than survive by means deemed unmanly."

"Seems a little extreme," said Shea. "We Earthians admire courage, too, but not to the point of suicide."

Ras Thavas chuckled. "I know what you mean. As the philosopher Kong Dusar said, any virtue carried to an extreme becomes a vice. But the actual reason for the Barsoomian disdain of armor—albeit Barsoomians are loath to admit it—is that before guns appeared, during the first century or two of my former life, our smiths were too unskilled to make practical suits of the sort you speak of. They would have so weighed down the warrior that he could not make full use of his limbs.

"Then came the gun, and to make armor bullet-proof it would have to be even thicker and heavier. So sword wearers, unable to obtain suits of practical armor, made a virtue of fighting naked."

Shea said: "Some Earthian peoples, like the ancient Greeks and Celts, went through similar stages. When their smiths learned how to make good, practical armor, the warriors put it on. On Earth, the gun had an effect somewhat like that on Barsoom; it caused the virtual abandonment of armor."

"Doctor Ras Thavas!" cried a voice in the crowd. It was the informant Mar Vas, whom Ras Thavas introduced to the Sheas. Shea was in the midst of asking after the whereabouts of Malambroso and Voglinda, when an infantile shriek of "Mummee! Daddee!" cut through the background noise.

Between them and the front entrance stood Doctor Malambroso, in his gold-embroidered purple robe conspicuous amid the throng of naked Barsoomians. On his head he wore an obviously Earthly Panama hat. In one hand he held the end of a leash, the other end of which was affixed to a harness securing the small body of three-year-old Voglinda Shea.

"Laws or no," snarled Shea, "I'm not taking chances with that guy." He drew his revolver.

As he did so, Malambroso's free hand came out from his robe bearing an egg-like object, which he tossed on the ground between himself and the Sheas. Shea began:

"Your spells are no damned good here! So hands—"

"No magic!" shouted Malambroso. "Just an ordinary smoke—"

The egg-like object burst with a loud pop, emitting a vast cloud of smoke, which filled the area around them. Shea plunged into the cloud, while behind him Belphebe cried: "Harold! Where are you?"

"Here!" shouted Shea, coughing. "Try to reach the front entrance!"

Shea ran full-tilt into the ticket taker's booth, upsetting the stand. He groped his way out the front entrance, cursing a bruised knee. Behind him the ticket taker, cursing even more vehemently, struggled to right his stand.

As Shea emerged from the tent, he saw Malambroso, carrying Voglinda, leap into the first of a row of taxi-carriages at the curb, each harnessed to a single thoat. Malambroso shouted orders to the driver, who vaulted into the saddle of his thoat. Off went thoat, postillion, gig, magician, Shea infant, and all.

Shea and Belphebe reached the second carriage in the row just as the first disappeared at a gallop around a corner. To the second driver, Shea shouted:

"Did you hear where that one was going?"

"To the airport, sir," said the second driver.

"Then we're going to the airport, right away! Catch up with that other rig if you can!"

He and Belphebe piled into the cab. Ras Thavas, breathing hard from his dash from the tent entrance, squeezed in between them, making three on a seat designed for two. Luckily, all three passengers were lean rather than stout.

Leisurely, the driver swung into his thoat saddle, and the carriage pulled out. They wove this way and that, rounding corners until Shea felt totally lost. He called:

"Can't you go faster?"

The driver replied: "No, sir. There are three of you, and I shall have to charge extra for the load. But I will not kill poor Blossom when she has all she can do to move the vehicle!"

Shea sat fuming until they came to a broad field on which a score of slaves were at work, filling holes and raking the ground level. Off to one side, several Barsoomian fliers were parked before a row of sheds, evidently the local version of hangars. Shea asked:

"Does one need a pilot's license or a series of examinations here?"

"Not to my knowledge," said Ras Thavas. "Zodanga is still a citadel of rugged individualism, with all its advantages and disadvantages. If one has money, one can buy or rent a flier and take off whenever one wishes."

"Then we'll get a flier. Doctor, I'll let you dicker over the fare, and I'll repay you. Do they tip here, and if so how much?"

"I can manage," said Ras Thavas, pointing. "There go your magician and his captive now!"

Across the field, a boat-shaped, wingless Barsoomian aircraft was taking off on a long slant, impelled by a single airscrew in the stern. Shea groaned, saying:

"We could never catch up with that machine on thoats. We must obtain our own flier!"

"Could we rent one?" asked Belphebe.

"I daresay." Ras Thavas addressed the driver: "Put us down at the big central building!"

The driver obeyed. He and Ras Thavas settled the fare, while Shea jogged into the building and sought out the rental desk.

The man at the desk proved a stout Zodangan with an aggressively commercial manner: "...Are you sure you do not wish to buy a ship, sir? I have several repossessed craft in excellent shape, every one a steal at its present price. One was used by a former Jed of Zodanga."

"I do not wish to buy," said Shea. "As I said, what I want is to rent a ship for three or four passengers, for a few days."

"...But sir, our easy-payment plan calls for payments hardly larger than our rental fees, and you end up owning the ship." He spread out a sheet of Barsoomian paper bearing sketches of fliers. "Now here's a fine little ship, with seats for five and a stern gun for emergencies..."

"I won't buy," said Shea with emphasis, "but I do wish to rent."

"But consider, sir! This one was owned by a former dwar of the Jed's guard..."

By shouting, Shea finally convinced the salesman that his sales pitch went to waste. At long last he signed papers making him the renter of a five-seater named the Banth. He paid most of his remaining cash as a deposit to insure the return of the craft. He also insisted upon a receipt.

"Do you know how to work everything?" asked the clerk.

Shea nodded toward Ras Thavas. "I shall rely on our friend here, since he owns the finest intellect on Barsoom."

Ras Thavas explained: "You rise by dropping ballast—those bags of sand tied along the sides. This instrument tells you your altitude."

"How do you come down again?" asked Shea.

"This lever releases some of the—" Ras Thavas used an unfamiliar word, which sounded to Shea like *refufupizaidi* "—which causes the ship to descend. Be careful not to release too much at once, or we shall crash, or at best not be able to rise again."

Shea inferred that the mysterious *refufupizaidi* was some sort of lifting agent, comparable to the hydrogen and helium gases used in Earthly balloons. Burroughs, no scientist, had called it in English the Barsoomian Ray. Ras Thavas continued:

"This is the motor control. Turn it to the right and the propeller revolves, the further the faster."

"What's the source of its power?"

Ras Thavas gave a technical explanation full of words that Shea did not know. Shea got the impression that the source was analogous to an Earthly storage battery, with a much higher capacity in proportion to its weight.

"How do I steer?" asked Shea. "I see no rudder or ailerons."

"The stern post holding the propeller swivels," explained the savant. "You turn this wheel, so. Here is the compass. You can set the machine to fly on instruments and stop at a predetermined time. This is the airspeed indicator. These gauges tell you how the charge of refufupizaidi is doing."

"Tell me," said Shea to the clerk, who stood around. "Was that little ship that just took off one rented from you? It flew that way—" he pointed "—but it's now out of sight."

"Mean you that alien in the weird costume, with a tuft of hair on his chin?"

"Yes. Did he say where he was going?"

"Yes, sir. He said he was taking his granddaughter to visit her kinfolks in Toonol."

"Where can I get a map, showing the landmarks between here and Toonol?"

"There should be one in the side pocket, sir. Here you are!"

They climbed aboard. Shea studied the map as the clerk walked off, back toward the administration building. Shea said: "Are we all ready, despite the fact that this is one of the most amateurish, ill-planned expeditions of my long experience?"

Ras Thavas: "You snap the fittings on the ends of these harness straps to these cleats."

"Like Earthly seat belts," said Shea. Belphebe had already fastened hers.

"Watch me," Shea said to Ras Thavas, "and correct me if you see me doing anything wrong. Here goes!"

He released the sand in one of the ballast bags and turned the wheel controlling the motor. The Banth rose slowly, and the airscrew began to revolve in its protective cage. When it dissolved into a blur to the sight, the Banth began to move horizontally.

4

The airscrew purred in its cage behind the passengers, whose hair fluttered in the wind. Belphebe spoke to Ras Thavas:

"What surprises me, Doctor, is the ease with which we took off. On Earth you'd need a pilot's license, like those they demand in the Heliums; and you'd have to file a flight plan with the Federal Aviation Administration, and so on. More and more paperwork."

"Things have not yet got to that stage here," said Ras Thavas. "But there have been so many accidents lately people getting lost in strange parts of the planet, pilots flying drunk, and fliers running into one another—that there is a move to impose similar rules all over Barsoom. Of course, the move meets fierce resistance from those who think it a natural right of any free Barsoomian who can get his hands on a flier to fly it whensoever and whithersoever he pleases. Besides, each city-state has its own ideas of the right rules and would resist with arms any attempt to impose upon it rules written elsewhere."

Belphebe asked Shea: "Are you doing all right, darling?"

"It's not difficult, compared to flying an Earthly airplane," said Shea. "It feels much like the blimp of which I was once allowed to take the controls for a few minutes. Presently I'll give you your turn at the controls."

Ras Thavas asked: "How goes your navigation, Doctor Shea?"

"All right so far," grunted Shea, whose attention flickered back and forth from the terrain below to the flier's compass and to the map spread out on his lap. He said:

"This Barsoomian landscape is notably shy of landmarks, compared to Earth. You have to figure out where you are by dead reckoning, or you don't figure it. Nearly as I can guess, it should take us about ten zodes to reach Ptarth, which lies almost halfway from Zodanga to Toonol. Then another day's flight should take us to Toonol.

"Doctor, would Ptarth be a safe place to land, to get a bite to eat and maybe spend the night? Or is it one of those xenophobic cities where they kill strangers on sight?"

"Safe enough for us," said Ras Thavas. "Just put the Heliumite badges back on your harness. Jed Thuvan Dinh is an old ally of the Heliums."

"Harold," said Belphebe, "I'm cold! Nudism is one thing on a beach in Florida but something else up in the Barsoomian atmosphere."

Shea rummaged through the lockers until he found a pile of blankets and handed one to each of the others. Belphebe asked:

"Is there any way to catch up with Malambroso before he reaches Toonol—if that be where he is going?"

"Since I don't know the top speed of Malambroso's flier," said Shea, "I have no way of telling. I've already turned our motor control all the way to 'fast.' "

"Then," she continued, "what is that little speck in the sky ahead? Now and then it winks at us, as if the sun reflected from metal."

Shea stared. "I can't see it, darling; but then, your eyes were always better than mine at long distances."

"Too bad we don't have some sort of telescope or field glasses," she said.

"Now that you mention it," growled Ras Thavas, "I have something that may help." From a container dangling from his harness he produced a small monocular telescope, which he pulled out to full length and put to one eye.

"It is indeed a flier," he said at last. At Shea's request he handed him the scope.

The vibration from the whirring airscrew made it hard to get a fix on the target, and the magnification was so high that the scope could cover only a narrow field. After tracking back and forth, Shea finally fixed upon the image of a flier, stern-to and looking no bigger than a gnat. Belphebe asked:

"Would Malambroso follow the same route as ours, passing near Ptarth?"

"Probably," replied Ras Thavas. "Ptarth is only a slight detour, and navigation charts assume that, on a flight from Zodanga to Toonol, all ships would fly to or near Ptarth. The same would apply to Phundahl, if the Phundahlians did not shoot down any foreign flier that enters what they consider their airspace. So we give Phundahl a wide detour."

"What would happen if we landed there?" asked Shea.

"They would ask us whither we were going, and if we said 'Phundahl' without exactly using the local pronunciation, they would cut off our heads."

"Hospitable people," said Belphebe. "What is the official pronunciation?"

"It is neither 'Fundahl' nor 'Phundahl,' but something like 'Pwhundahl.' It takes practice to say it just right."

Belphebe said: "Then let's not stop at Phundahl."

"No argument there," said Shea. "Reminds me of one of those Balkan countries, where using the wrong dialect of the national language can get your throat cut." Peering through the telescope again, he said: "Maybe it's wishful thinking, but I do believe we are gaining on them."

"Let me have a look," said Belphebe. "I can't see that they're getting any closer."

"You wouldn't," said Shea, "with a difference in our speeds of only a few haads per zode. Let's have a look at that bow gun."

"Harold! Even if we catch up with them, you wouldn't dare shoot for fear of hitting Voglinda, or causing them to crash."

"I suppose you're right," sighed Shea. "If we get close enough, perhaps we can pick off Malambroso, either me with my pistol or you with your bow."

"Assuming he doesn't snatch up our child as a shield!"

"What should I do if he does? Jump from the Banth to his flier, sword in hand?"

Ras Thavas said: "That were too risky to be practicable. You would probably fall to the ground below, and at this altitude that were fatal. If we get close enough for any such leaps, I am sure that, with our gun, we could disable their ship sufficiently to let us take it in tow."

"Unless," said Belphebe, "he's holding a knife to Voglinda's throat, threatening to kill her if we make a hostile move."

"Sentimentalists!" snorted Ras Thavas.

Shea: "I've warned you not to use that word, Doctor. If you want to make people hostile, just sneer at their profoundest feelings!"

"Sorry; I forgot," said Ras Thavas.

Belphebe said: "And suppose he throws a magical spell at us."

"Wouldn't work here," said Shea, "same as on Earth."

"How about that cloud of smoke he used to cover his flight from the Arms Fair?"

"That was just a plain, nonmagical smoke grenade, such as they make on Earth."

For hours the Banth purred along, now and then rising or falling with thermal air currents, while its three passengers argued over strategies. Malambroso's flier became larger with agonizing slowness. To Shea's naked vision it grew from a speck the size of an insect to that of a small bird.

The small, brilliant Barsoomian sun was nearing the flat horizon when Ras Thavas, telescope to eye, said: "Methinks our quarry has seen us, Doctor Shea. He is turning his flier. He has a bow gun like ours, and he cannot shoot straight aft for fear of hitting his own propellor."

"I'll take a converging course," said Shea. "When we get closer, you might fire a couple of shots to throw his aim off. Be careful to miss him!"

"I am no gunner," said Ras Thavas. "The last time I fired one of these things was centuries ago, in my other body. Methinks it better than you give me the helm whilst you do the shooting."

"Maybe so. But how do you work these guns?"

"Pull this bolt handle back, opening the chamber. Place the projectile, here, in the chamber and push it forward. Place behind it this cartridge of propellant. Close the bolt, and you are ready to fire by pulling this lanyard."

Shea followed instructions. Ras Thavas said: "Try to cripple his propellor."

As the fliers came closer, Shea saw Malambroso climb out on his foredeck and swing his bow gun around. Shea aimed low and jerked the lanyard. *Boom!*

The gun discharged a vast cloud of smoke, which for an instant hid Malambroso's flier. While Shea did not know the composition of Barsoomian gunpowder, he saw that its effects were much like those of Earthly black powder.

Boom! A similar cloud erupted from the other flier's gun. There was no sound of a projectile striking the Banth, so Shea inferred that Malambroso, too, had missed. But, he thought, Malambroso might not have missed on purpose.

Shea tried to imagine what went on in Malambroso's mind. The wizard had started out by demanding Florimel and, finding Shea uncooperative, had kidnapped the Sheas' daughter in a daft attempt to compel Shea's help in the matter. But if he slew both Sheas, then what good would his possession of Voglinda Shea do him? It would hardly advance his suit for the body and soul of Florimel, who very much had a mind of her own. Altogether, Malambroso evidently did not have a well-worked-out plan. Ras Thavas might be an exasperating egotist, but at least he was smarter than that.

"Clean out your cartridge chamber before reloading," said Ras Thavas, reaching into the flier's tool chest and handing Shea a rag. "Otherwise a spark might set off your next charge of propellant."

Shea was working away on his chamber, and the ships were circling closer, when there came another *Boom!* followed by a loud clank. The Banth shuddered.

"Propellor," said Ras Thavas.

Boom! The Banth lurched. Ran Thavas said: "Hull, methinks. He is turning away."

Shea took back to the helm, but now the Banth vibrated violently. When he turned the motor control back to "slow," the vibrations eased. The other flier diminished swiftly into the evening sky.

"Guess we stop at Ptarth willy-nilly," said Shea. He brought the propellor to a halt. "How much damage, Doctor?"

"We shall have to get it repaired," said Ras Thavas, "before proceeding. One blade is badly bent."

"How about that hit on our hull?"

"Just a sofad whilst I look."

Ras Thavas shifted the ends of his safety straps to cleats on the sides of the hull. Then he climbed over the rail and lowered himself headfirst toward the keel. When he came back up, his naturally red face was further incarnadined by a suffusion of blood. Shea could not avoid a twinge of admiration for the scientist's courage. He, Shea, could not have undertaken such a human-fly stunt so casually.

"It looks like a mere graze, a glancing blow," said Ras Thavas. "Let us hope it did no damage to the interior."

"Damn, damn," said Shea.

"Be not too disturbed, Doctor Shea," said Ras Thavas. "It was luck that enabled Malambroso to fire three shots without cleaning his chamber between shots and without blowing up his flier, himself, and your infant. Perhaps luck will be on our side next time, though I am not so childish as to think that bad luck one time assures good the next."

Below, a shadow of night swept across the flat landscape toward the sinking sun. Soon the last bit of sun winked out, and darkness sharply fell. Stars blinked in. The moon Thuria was not in sight; Cluros was visible but no brighter than Venus appears at its maximum on Earth. Belphebe said:

"I see a distant patch of light off our port bow. Would that be Ptarth?"

"Bless your eyesight, darling," said Shea. "The map shows Ptarth in that direction."

Belphebe said: "Didn't Jed Mors Kajak tell us John Carter was off visiting the Jed of Ptarth? Why shouldn't we look him up? He might be glad to see an

Earthian couple and lend his help against Malambroso. From what I've heard, he throws a lot of weight on Barsoom."

Shea thought before shaking his head. "I think not, darling. Malambroso could use the time to get far ahead of us. My guess is that the time is more precious to us right now than even the help of the great John Carter."

At the following sunrise, the Banth took off from Ptarth with Shea at the controls. He studied the map and set the course for Toonol.

"Aside from padding our hotel bill with a charge for wine we never drank," said Shea, "and overcharging us for straightening our bent propellor, the Ptarthians treated us nicely enough."

"Be fair, darling," said Belphebe. "They worked, through the night on the propellor, and you know any Earthly machine shop would charge overtime rates for that."

"True," said Shea, who then had to explain to Ras Thavas what he meant by "padding a hotel bill."

"Do you think I am giving Phundahl a wide enough miss, Doctor?"

Ras Thavas looked at the chart. "Yes, I believe you have. A fellow named Fal Sivas in Zodanga is, I hear, working on a system for mental control of a flier. It were handy to whisk us out of danger if the Phundahlians should attack us in the air.

"This Fal Sivas, I am told, thinks all too well of himself. He goes about calling himself the Master Mind of Barsoom, when it is obvious that he is no such thing. If anyone deserves that title, it is I, not he... Oop, sorry, Doctor Shea. I forgot again."

Shea grinned. "You're learning, old boy. With half a year of my training, you'd be so polite and tactful that Helium could use you as ambassador to negotiate sensitive issues."

"They tried that once," said Ras Thavas sadly. "They sent me with a delegation to Manator. But something I said so enraged the Jed there we almost had a war, although Manator is halfway round Barsoom from the Heliums."

The day passed uneventfully, save for the sight of a column of the nomadic green men of Barsoom, each with four arms and twice the stature of a red Barsoomian, crossing the yellow-pink, moss-covered plain below. One green man wheeled his oversized thoat, pulled a musket from a boot in his saddle, and fired upward at the Banth, with a cloud of smoke. A projectile whistled past.

Shea hauled the Banth into a turn and pulled the rope releasing sand from one of the bags of ballast. Below, the green warrior was reloading. Shea growled:

"I'm tempted to shoot back, to teach the bastard not to take pot shots at harmless travelers just for the hell of it. But I guess that wouldn't be smart under the circs."

Ras Thavas said: "I am happy to see that some members of your species, at least, can overcome their animal urges."

By the time the green warrior raised the gun to his shoulder again, the Banth was out of range. Shea said:

"Doctor, I don't like the way the ship behaves. We ought to have risen faster."

Ras Thavas said: "It is possible that the shot that struck our hull has caused a small leak in one of the buoyancy tanks."

"We must watch our altitude," grumbled Shea, plotting the course to Toonol again.

A glance over the side showed that they were entering a widespread marshland, stretching to the horizon. Below, small streams and lakes were interspersed with patches of solid vegetation. Shea said:

"Looks like Barsoom's last wetland." Then he had to explain the term "wetland." "Time was," he said, "when it was considered the right, natural thing for any Earther to kill any wild animal he came upon, and to drain and, ditch wetlands to turn them into farmland. But lately, people have begun to see that wetlands have their essential function, too. Get rid of them and you'll be sorry."

"I understand," said Ras Thavas. "A few Barsoomians, have tried to agitate similar proposals to conserve natural features. But so far the masses have taken the view that these are mere busybodies seeking excuses to meddle in others' affairs and to deprive them of their normal means of making their livings. One might think that the length of Barsoomian lives would lead the rabble to take a long, view, extending over centuries or millennia. But most find a year as far ahead as they can or are willing to think."

"Sounds like Earth," said Shea.

"How is your altitude holding, Doctor?" asked Ras Thavas.

"Losing, little by little. I don't like to empty our last bags of ballast, because that would leave us without vertical control."

"I can see that we are flying lower and lower," said Ras Thavas. "Perhaps we had better alight on the first good landing spot we find, rather than wait for the loss of refufupizaidi to bring us down on a spot not of our choosing."

"Sound thinking," said Shea.

"What else would you expect, from one of my superior intel—Sorry; there I go again." With a shamefaced grin, Ras Thavas got out his telescope and scanned the marsh-land below and ahead of them. "Methinks I see a patch flat enough, dry enough, and sufficiently unencumbered by plant life to serve our needs. About ten degrees to port, Doctor."

The Banth came down to a quiet landing on a patch of soil overgrown with the yellow-pink moss instead of the ubiquitous shrubs, trees, and swamp plants. Shea said:

"I don't think it's practical to try to walk to Toonol."

Belphebe said: "The understatement of the year, darling. Is there any chance you could find and repair the leak? You were always pretty fast with the wrench and the soldering iron with our car."

Scrutinizing the hull, Ras Thavas said: "I cannot see any holes in the tanks. But then, we should have to take the whole ship apart to find a mere pinhole, and all the remaining refufupizaidi would escape. Have we any lift left?"

Shea worked the controls. "I think there's a little; but not enough to raise us off the ground. So we might as well manhandle the Banth into the water. If the hull leaks, we can use those mugs we brought along for lunch to bail it out."

Belphebe: "Can this flier float?"

"It should," said Ras Thavas. "When, following discovery of the refufupizaidi, these machines were first devised, their design followed that of the smaller water craft, since remnants of Barsoom's oceans still existed. That was before my time. So fliers still look something, like boats. Propose you to attempt the rest of our journey by water?"

"We can try," said Shea. "Even if the swamp watercourses wriggle like worms on a hook, I think I can figure out a route from this map."

"What are 'worms on a hook'?" inquired Ras Thavas.

Shea explained, adding: "What worries me more right now is how we shall ever get this contraption back to Lesser Helium, to recover our deposit. It took most of our liquid funds."

"I may be able to tide you over," said Ras Thavas.

"What, you?" said Shea in mock astonishment. "You being altruistic?"

Ras Thavas looked embarrassed. "I try to benefit from your pronouncements, Doctor. Since we are all in this together, it is the logical course to follow. And I am sure that we shall be able to have the ship repaired in Toonol."

"All right," said Shea, taking a grip on the stem of the Banth. "Let's see how that fine new body Vad Varo gave you works with loads. Take the bow, and grab the end of the painter."

"Grab what? Oh, you mean the rope at the bow. I fear my Barsoomian thews are not the equivalent of yours, since my body—either this one or its predecessor lacked the advantage of growing up on a high-gravity planet. On your own world, are you classed as a man of exceptional strength?"

"Not at all," said Shea. "If anything, I rate as a rather skinny fellow."

"Fortunately for me," said Ras Thavas, "my superior brain has made it unnecessary to develop musculature above that which I inherited, and the habits that I formed in the thousand years of my former life have remained with me. At least, in the Banth, you will not be able to force calisthenics upon me!"

With final grunts, they slid the ship into the stagnant water. Shea seized the painter, and the three boarded the craft, which rocked a little. Shea coiled the painter, studied his map, and bent to turn on the motor. The airscrew revolved in its case, slowly at first, then faster until it became a blur to the sight. Shea said:

"Doctor, please get up on the forward deck to watch for snags and shallows, so you can warn me off them."

"Can't we go faster?" said Belphebe.

"I don't dare, lest we run into an obstacle. So I have set the motor control to 'medium.'"

For hours, Shea navigated the flier cautiously through the countless creeks and sloughs of the Toonolian Marsh. In the bow, Ras Thavas called back warnings of snags and shallows. Once a half-submerged log turned out to be an animal of the crocodilian kind.

"I sure don't want to run into him," said Shea. "He might take it into his little reptilian brain to come aboard."

"Harold!" cried Belphebe. "Look at that thing overhead! We're going to pass right under it." She bent her efforts to stringing her bow.

"Where?" said Shea. "Oh, that! Looks like a tough customer. How about it, Doctor?"

"If you leave it alone, it will probably extend the same courtesy to you," said the savant.

The creature in question looked something like a man-sized lizard with six legs, each leg ending in formidable hooked claws. It was perched on a branch of a large tree that grew out of the water in midchannel. Belphebe shrieked:

"Watch out, Harold!"

Shea's attention had been distracted long enough for the Banth to run head-on into the tree. Ras Thavas slid off the bow into the muddy water. The tree shuddered, and the Barsoomian swamp lizard fell from its branch to land on the engine compartment of the flier, forward of the seat in which Shea sat handling the controls. Belphebe had occupied the other seat, but she had risen to string her bow. She seized one of the safety cleats to steady herself.

In falling off the bow, Ras Thavas had quick-wittedly grabbed the painter. He had scarcely emerged from the water when he began hauling himself up on the bow again.

"Don't shoot!" cried Belphebe, who had nocked an arrow but not drawn it. "If you missed, you'd hit Ras Thavas!"

Shea, trading stares with the swamp reptile at arm's length, returned his pistol to its holster and instead drew his short sword, saying: "At such close quarters, I'd prefer this."

The reptile hissed and yawned, showing formidable fangs. Further forward, Ras Thavas called: "Let it alone, Shea! I have it under control."

Shea could not see what sort of control the savant had over the swamp reptile. But after a few more seconds, the animal turned and dove over the side. It swam away with serpentine sweeps of its tail.

"How did you do that, Doctor?" asked Shea.

"All higher forms of Barsoomian life are more or less telepathic," said Ras Thavas. "I simply exerted my superior mental powers, and chide me not for referring to those powers. Without them, you and your lady might have sustained fatal wounds. These animals are difficult to kill. Is there a towel aboard, to wipe off this muck?"

Shea hunted through the lockers until he found a piece of suitable cloth. He said:

"At least, on Earth you'd be covered with clothes, which would have to be washed before you wore them again."

"Perhaps you can explain this curious Earthian custom of covering oneself with textiles, even when the air is warm enough not to need them."

Shea sighed. "Some of the leading religions insist upon it. I suppose it goes back to primitive times, when our brutish ancestors, up to then as naked as you Barsoomians, first migrated out of Africa, a hot continent, to colder climes..."

Shea was well into a lecture on the anthropological explanation of the nudity taboo prevalent in Judaism and its two offshoot religions, Christianity and Islam, when something flew past with a loud buzz. Ras Thavas uttered a shrill scream and threw himself down on the floorboards.

The flying organism whirled about in a circle and returned. Belphebe cried out and slapped at it. "It tried to sting me!"

"Keep it away from me!" shrilled Ras Thavas, cowering in the bottom of the flier.

Shea started to reach for his revolver, then changed his mind and drew his short sword. When he got a good look at the flying organism, he saw something resembling an Earthly hornet, but several times as large, with a length the span of his hand and a wingspread the length of Shea's foot.

"There's another!" yelled Ras Thavas. "Save me, Doctor Shea!"

The first intruder hovered, rising and falling with a bouncing motion. Shea swung his short sword. His blade struck the flier with a click and sent its body whirling away in two pieces. The second pseudo-hornet instantly swooped down and stung Shea in his right buttock.

Shea jumped with an angry yell and, with a backhand slash, slew this attacker also. A third buzzed up and was likewise bisected by Shea's blade.

"We must be near a nest!" wailed Ras Thavas. "Speed up the motor! The smell of dead stiths will fetch more of them!"

Shea stuck the point of his short sword into the floor-boards, leaving it standing upright and gently rocking back and forth. He advanced the motor control, and the Banth surged forward. Another stith circled the Banth and swooped toward its passengers, but it tried to fly through the propellor and was hurled away in pieces.

"Are they all gone?" quavered Ras Thavas.

"Seem to be," grunted Shea, running a hand over his swollen fundament. "Get up, Doctor; you're not hurt. I'm the one with a sore arse, who'll have to eat standing up for a while."

"I—I am sorry that you should behold me in such contemptible shape," said Ras Thavas. "It is my only weakness."

"You mean a phobia about creeping things?"

"Yes, I am shamed to say. The mere sight of even a harmless one sends me into a panic. I trust you will not regale the other Barsoomians, as a great joke, with the tale of the downfall of the mighty Ras Thavas."

"The story is safe with me," said Shea. "In my trade as psychologist, I come upon all sorts of phobias. Some I can cure, at least in my own species. Do you know how you came to have this phobia?"

"I have a vague notion that a stith must have stung me as a child. But it would have happened a thousand years ago, and I have no clear memory of the incident. Could you cure me?"

"Doubt if I had a chance to try, Doctor. It would take many days of conditioning."

"How would you do it?"

"By gradually habituating you to the sight of such a bug, let's say starting with a picture of one, then a mounted dead one, and so on, until you could handle a live one without a shudder."

"I must by such a cure on myself," mumbled Ras Thavas. "It were painful but better than the risk of making a fool of myself in public." The savant cracked a wintry smile. "At least, you can tell the folk back on your Earth that the stith does not grow to the size of a thoat, as that writer would have his readers believe."

"They couldn't," said Shea, "because of having to have soft bodies during times of growth. That doesn't work when you wear your skeleton on the outside. There are also difficulties with increases in size in getting enough oxygen to the muscles..."

5

Vantos Vaz, the Chief Constable of Toonol, said: "Yes, yes, Doctor Shea. I understand that you are an alien on this world. But I must put you down on this form as of a place on this world, not some other. Nobody's identification is complete without it."

"All right," said Shea. "Call me Sir Harold Shea of Zodanga; that's where we were a few nights ago. I could say 'of Ptarth,' but I think Zodanga has a prettier name. Now, how about our fugitive wizard and our daughter?"

"Yes, Doctor Shea, such a person did arrive in Toonol a few days past. A tall, gray-bearded man of alien aspect, with a light-tan skin, wrapped in a robe ornamented with golden thread. He insists on retaining this robe, as if Toonol were in the polar regions. He had with him an unmistakable alien child with yellow hair, whom he kept under control by means of a harness and leash. I must get such an apparatus for my wife, to control our own hatchlings. Why do you wish to know?" Shea told of Malambroso's abduction of Voglinda.

Ras Thavas added: "I have been traveling with Doctor and Mrs. Shea and have found them persons of exceptional faithworthyness."

The Chief Constable sighed. "If the world-famous Ras Thavas says it is so, it must be so. Mean you to slay this Malambroso person? I warn you, homicides are not permitted save in accordance with the code and through the licensed guild of assassins."

"No," said Shea. "While Malambroso's demise would not cause me inconsolable grief, our main objective is to get our daughter back, unharmed. All else is secondary."

Belphebe added: "If Malambroso would just go away and leave us alone, we should be satisfied. Where is the scoundrel now?"

"According to the last report from the officer assigned to watch him," said Vantos Vaz, "he and the little have put up at the Purple Apt. Were you going thither forthwith?"

"Not quite, sir," said Shea. "First we must make arrangements for the repair of our flier. Who gives first-class service in such matters, at reasonable prices?"

Vantos Vaz suggested a repair shop, adding: "Do not be surprised if I assign a man to watch you. Since a confrontation is likely betwixt you and this off-world magician, we must make sure that any slaying is done in accordance with the law. Undermanned as we are, we find it hard to make all killers follow the code. Had you a difficult trip through the Toonolian Marsh?"

"Not too hard," replied Shea, "except that we ran out of food and starved, although we killed and tried to cook a swamp lizard. We've been eating like pigs since we arrived to make up."

"What is a pig?" asked the Chief Constable.

Ras Thavas, Shea, and Belphebe returned to Van Larik's Inn after a fatiguing morning of hunting down the machine shop recommended and then waiting while the mechanics disassembled the Banth and examined the buoyancy tanks for signs of a leak.

Shea opened the door to his room and stepped aside to let Belphebe enter. He and Ras Thavas followed her in, when a sound caused all three to whirl.

For a closet, the room had a simple conservatory consisting of a rail curving out from the wall and back to the wall again. From this rail hung a curtain. Now the curtain had been thrust back on its curtain rings, revealing Malambroso in a purple robe, Voglinda in her harness, and a naked red Barsoomian in his caparison of straps and sheaths, longsword in hand. Malambroso trained on the Sheas a large black automatic pistol of a common Earthly make.

"Well!" grated Malambroso. "It seems that I am destined to encounter Doctor Sir Harold again! Reach not for your pistol, Doctor Shea. If you do, I shall shoot you dead. Or better yet..." Malambroso trained his gun on Voglinda. "Force me not to end the life of this winsome young lady. I have become quite fond of her in the short time that we have been traveling companions. Would you believe it, last night we stopped at a place where an orchestra was playing and couples were dancing. Voglinda insisted that I take her out on the dance floor, too. Imagine me, at my age, wheeling this tot around on the floor!

"I see that you and your wife, Doctor Shea, have adopted the local costume, or lack thereof. Thank Lucifer, I at least retain a civilized sense of decency, even though my robe causes the natives to stare!"

"And who, then, is the Barsoomian?" asked Shea. "I don't believe I have had the pleasure of meeting him."

"The pleasure, I am certain, will prove ephemeral," said Malambroso. "Know that this is the honorable Spor Mopus, a leading light of the local assassins' guild. He has come with me to kill you. Lady Belphebe, think not to string your bow, or you shall suffer the same fate as Doctor Shea."

"Now why," said Shea, "should the honorable Spor Mopus wish to kill me? I am too lean to make good eating."

"He will slay you because I have hired him to do so. But he insists that the killing must be done in accordance with the highest ethical principles. He will not even let me shoot you, unless you draw a gun on me first. It must be done with honest face-to-face swordplay. If you will kindly draw your sword, he will set out upon his task."

The red Barsoomian stepped forward; bringing his sword up to guard position.

"This is childish nonsense," grumbled Ras Thavas. "So is all the elaborate politeness betwixt you twain."

"Since," said Spor Mopus, "you disdain our ancient and honorable principles, I shall tend to you after I have finished off this alien. Have at you, Doctor Shea!"

The Barsoomian threw himself into a lunge that would have spitted Shea had he not, almost unconsciously, drawn his saber and parried. In an instant the twain were at it, *tzing, zip, clang!*

Shea found Spor Mopus good but not superlative. Unless he made a stupid mistake, Shea thought, he should be able to handle this assassin. Still, there was an element of luck in these encounters, and what right had he to leave Voglinda fatherless, assuming they rescued her from Malambroso?

Back and forth they went: double, one-two, beat, and, coupé. Spor Mopus was only so-so on attack but very good on defense; Shea could not penetrate his guard. Shea began to fear that Spor Mopus would keep him in play until fatigue laid him open to attack. *Tzingg!*

Suddenly, Spor Mopus backed up and lowered his point, crying: "That is not fair! It is unethical, to bring a squad of supporters with you. Withdraw them, or I shall refuse to continue the fight!"

"What on Earth?" murmured Shea.

Spor Mopus sheathed his sword and stamped out the open door. At that instant, Belphebe's bow twanged. While Malambroso's eyes had been fixed on the combatants, she had stepped aside and quietly strung her bow. The arrow pierced Malambroso's body. Malambroso swung toward her, striving to bring the big pistol up to bear. The bow twanged again. Malambroso dropped his pistol, which struck the floor with a bright yellow flash and a deafening boom. The magician folded up, joint by joint, on the matting. Ras Thavas moved quickly to kneel over the wounded magician.

"Mummee!" screamed Voglinda, running to Belphebe.

"How did you do that?" Shea asked the scientist.

Ras Thavas looked up. "My mental superiority, that is all. I have told you that all the higher Barsoomian organisms are somewhat telepathic. I simply forced Spor Mopus and Malambroso to see, not one sword-wielding Shea, but six, all advancing upon them at once. Now, let us see about this fellow. He will soon be dead if I cannot render aid."

The innkeeper appeared at the door. "What goes on here? Did I not hear a gunshot?"

"You did," said Shea. "but it was an accidental discharge, when the magician dropped his pistol."

"Find a stretcher and a pair of slaves to carry it," snapped Ras Thavas, "and get this man to a lazaret!"

"Why try to save him?" asked Shea.

"Because I once swore an oath to John Carter himself," barked Ras Thavas, "that I would thenceforth try to help those who needed it. Besides, if he dies of the lady's arrows, you would be in trouble with the law, since he did not perish in a proper, legal sword duel.

"I know that he deserves to be let die, but my oath had no such qualifications. Ah, here come Master Van Larik with a stretcher and a pair of slaves. Be careful, boys. Slide him over; do not attempt to roll him!"

A man wearing the badges of the constabulary appeared, panting for breath. He said: "Is the fight already over? Was it conducted in proper accord with the laws on homicide? I must make out a report."

Ras Thavas assured the constable that all had been done in accordance with the code, and the cop went away satisfied.

Several days later, Shea and Belphebe, with little Voglinda in tow, visited the lazaret. They found Ras Thavas sitting by Malambroso's bed. On the other side stood a plump red Barsoomian nurse. Shea said:

"Doctor, the shop assures me that the Banth will be airworthy again tomorrow, with the buoyancy tanks full. From what I saw, I think they are right. Are you ready to go with us?"

"My patient is virtually ready for his discharge today," said Ras Thavas. "By tomorrow I am sure it will be safe for me to leave him."

"Either of those arrows ought to have killed him," said Belphebe. "Unless you Barsoomians are tougher than most civilized species."

"Either would probably have proved fatal," said Ras Thavas, "had my patient not had the luck to fall into the hands of the greatest physician and surgeon on Barsoom."

Shea cleared his throat meaningfully, at which Ras Thavas looked embarrassed. Shea said: "But I can't go off leaving him loose so long as he pursues that crackpot idea of taking my colleague Chalmers' wife away from him."

"I do not think you need worry on that score," said Ras Thavas. "How about it, Doctor Malambroso?"

"Oh," said the magician in a weak voice, "I now have completely different plans." He rolled an eye at the Barsoomian nurse, who tittered.

"Yes," he said, "I have at last discovered true love. My attachment to Lady Chalmers was just a passing fancy, an infatuation. My affianced bride, here, is Mordalia, the widow of Jan Valos, who was slain last year in one of those ridiculous duels. She has promised to accompany me whithersoever I go. If you see Lady Chalmers, present her my respects and assure her that she has naught to fear from me."

"Daddee," said Voglinda, "when are we going home?"

"As soon as I can arrange it," said Shea. "Widow Mordalia, I am happy to have met you and wish you luck." He silently added, *you'll need it!*

"May our departure be soon," said Belphebe. "My hair's beginning to show its natural color at the roots. I should soon need another dye job."

Ras Thavas said: "Are you flying back to Zodanga? If so, I am going with you."

From his bed, Malambroso said: "Could you not save some time by working your sorites here and going directly back to Earth?"

Shea grinned. "No. I must return the Banth to its owners and get our deposit back. Also, we left eight riding thoats there, which I shall want to resell. Besides, we left our Earthside clothes in Zodanga. Can you imagine the sensation if Belphebe and I, nude as we are, materialized on the grounds of the Garaden Institute? We shall have to get used to clothes again, dear."

"They'll seem unnatural for a while," said Belphebe.

"Also," said Ras Thavas, "you promised me another lesson in making friends and influencing people. I have tried out your principles and have been agreeably surprised to find that they actually work. Why, even Malambroso here—whose ethics, I fear, are not up to Barsoomian standards—seems to like me. So let us get to it forthwith!"

ARMING THE INCOMPLETE ENCHANTER
BY JERRY POURNELLE
Amra, 1965

This article is concerned with the kind of equipment Harold Shea should have carried when he went traveling in his syllogismobile. Before looking at the equipment, let's get the ground rules set. On his first adventure, Harold didn't know that firearms, matches, Boy Scout Handbooks, and other here-and-now technological devices wouldn't work, so he didn't provide himself with much of an outfit. On most of his trips after the second adventure, he wasn't able to make much preparation at all, since he was unaware of his impending departure.

We will accordingly confine this discussion to one adventure in which he not only knew where he was going, but actually arrived there, having outfitted himself in what he thought was a proper manner. This was the journey to the land of Spenser's *Faerie Queene,* which is the second episode of the book, *The Incomplete Enchanter.* We will also omit sorcery and preparations therefor; Shea and his companion never did find out how properly to prepare for that sort of thing, which is half the fun of the series; and besides, they were often called upon to defend themselves in situations where sorcery was strictly out.

Shea's preparations are, I fear, simply not in keeping with his general intelligence. Finding that the "medieval stuff"' in the costume shop was of no use whatever, what with the armor made of wool and paint, and the swords made of wood, Shea hies himself to antique shops, where he finds mostly "Civil War cavalry sabers." Shea decides to use a modern fencing epee or dueling sword, removing the button and grinding on a sharp point. I've got one myself I made some years ago, doubtless just after my first reading of *Enchanter.*

In the story, Shea makes quite a reputation for himself with this toy, skewering several good and famous knights, assorted demons and goblins, and uncounted men-at-arms. As far as I can tell from a close reading of the story, this weapon plus some rather outlandish clothing from a stage rendition of *Robin Hood* are all the gear Shea takes with him; and, I repeat, this is not in keeping with the man's general intelligence.

In fact, it is nothing short of damn foolishness; and the result would have been quite different from the way de Camp and Pratt wrote it. Our Hero would have got himself killed in the first real fight he got into, ruining the story and depriving all of us of something to talk about. Even if he would have managed to survive, he gave himself a pretty slim chance. If he couldn't find something better, he would have done well to carry one of the Civil War cavalry sabers; it wouldn't have been very good, but it was a better bet than the epee.

Let's look at the kind of opposition Our Hero was up against. I'm a little hampered by not having a copy of the *Faerie Queene* around, but I can get most of it from the *Enchanter*. The main thing is that it's set in a time of feudal chivalry, and a rather idealized chivalry at that. We have the following main features:

1. There's quite a lot of combat required. It won't be fighting in the ranks, and the opponents who count are heavy cavalry who indulge in single combat rather than charging *en masse*. The enemy is likely to be somewhat better equipped than the rider in the illustration [p. 195], but the predicament of Our Hero is obvious, and the expected outcome is that the horse will stomp his brains out.

2. Even in ground combat, one's opponent is likely to be wearing armor. The Good Guys will shed it when fighting an unarmored gentleman, but the Bad Guys are likely to be mean about the whole thing. The armor will be plate, not chain mail.

3. Missile weapons are available, but not extensively used. Arrows don't usually penetrate armor, the Welsh Longbow not having been introduced to the Yeomanry, so most people don't carry bows. I presume that archery and its associated technology is an underdeveloped art.

4. The principal weapons of the time are sword and lance, supplemented by axe, *morgenstern* and mace, quarterstaff, and even halberd. The sword is likely to be a great heavy affair without glittering net, no point, a grip long enough for it to be held with both hands but capable of being used one-handed, and a heavy pommel to balance the thing off. A very unwieldy and unhandy weapon, but well suited for combat between armored men. The hand guard is undeveloped, consisting of a simple cross-bar.

5. One's opponents aren't going to know anything about scientific fencing. Our Hero does; and his major advantage is that he knows how to lunge, while his adversary is stuck with the pass. For the benefit of those who don't know, the gent on the contents page [*Amra*, Vol. 2, No. 43] is lunging sloppily from T to O, while the unsuccessful fellow standing on the O was attempting to use the pass. Our Hero will, we trust, execute a cleaner lunge, keeping his body and legs in a line and not turning his feet.

The limiting restrictions under the ground rules imposed by the story are:

1. Neither Shea nor his companion were rich. Both were psychologists in an endowed hospital, a notoriously underpaid profession even today and more so in 1940. Still, they were not broke; and if one is about to put one's life out on the line, it's nice to have the best equipment you can afford, even if you have to eat beans for a month to get it.

2. Apparently there was a limit to the gear that could be carried along. It had to fit in a back pack or otherwise be carried on the person. We can assume that chests and chests of gear would simply not go through the transition, although you could bring along people who were not aware of what you were doing. We'll also assume that dumb animals couldn't make it: no pack or riding horses, no Alsatian dogs, etc.

3. You can take *technique*, but not *technology*. Somehow, modern fencing, although unknown in the *Faerie Queene*, will still work; guns, matches, compasses, etc. will not. I'm not sure about modern medicine, distilleries, and the like. I presume modern metals will preserve their qualities, since Shea's epee, in order to stand up to all the attacks it was subjected to, must have been damn good steel.

Therefore, it seems reasonable that armor made of Duralumin or stainless steel would work as intended, although to stay in keeping with 1940 technology, Duralumin may be out. [We seem to recall a vague reference to the rusting of stainless steel somewhere in the series, so perhaps that is out too.]

Now that we've set up the situation, we can start equipping Our Hero. Remember, he's a fair to middling modern fencer, not particularly strong, and not particularly big. He's going to be up against men who aren't big, but they're strong like Superman compared with the average modern. Those guys are used to swinging that great, heavy sword with one hand, lopping off arms and heads and like that.

We've pictured one of the less dangerous enemies [*Amra*, Vol. 2, No. 43, p 14] He's less dangerous because he's not wearing any armor except a helmet.

The first thing we have to do is dispose of that epee. I say it with some disappointment, because it makes a good story, but it won't work. It just isn't heavy enough to parry with, and Shea is going to have to rely on his parries until he can steal some armor. The likely result of epee against broadsword is this: the knight or magician steps forward, swinging his sword at Hero's arm. Hero has two choices: a stop thrust to the arm, which may work if he's fast enough; or parry. But the parry will be swept aside with consequent severe damage to the Hero's physiognomy, the epee probably broken in the process. Now it's true that even modern sabermen tend to forget there's a point on that thing, and I've won more than one bout by using epee tactics with a saber; but in each case the opponent was drawn out of line by a threatened cut, after which I managed to get the point on target. With the epee, there's no chance of threatening a cut.

No, we have to face it. You just can't make much of a parry with light weapons. I've played the game, several times, of epee versus ribbon saber, the ribbon saber being a thing like a cavalry saber rather than the thin, light affair of our modern competition saber, and I lost about as often as I won. True, my opponent with the ribbon saber knew modern fencing; but he also had a lot lighter weapon than Our Hero has to face; and even then, I didn't have enough mass in my weapon to be able to keep my point in line. Once you get out of line with an epee, you have no edge to use, so your weapon is useless. Furthermore, the method of gripping an epee, particularly a French epee, doesn't make for strong beats, strong parries, or fast recoveries from strong beats. Even the Italian, Belgian, and Spanish epees suffer from this defect. But without the capability to exert some force against the enemy's blade, you can't get him into a situation where he can conveniently be skewered. No, that epee has to go, at least as the main weapon, although it may be useful as a second weapon, and of course Shea had it free.

So far, too, we've talked about unarmored combat. That toothpick is obviously useless against a man in armor. Unfortunately, almost anything except several years of training is going to be useless under those circumstances, but we'll get back to that in a minute. There are a few items which might be worth taking along to deal with the situation.

With the epee disposed of, we have two broad categories of sword to choose from. The best known is the rapier, which is built along the lines of the weapon carried by our charmingly dressed young lady [*Amra*, Vol. 2, No. 43, p. 5]. Her sword is a bit thick at the base, which would put the center of impact well up the blade, and it lacks a proper hand guard, but it does illustrate the rapier principle, namely, that the flat is parallel to the ground. The other alternative is the saber, which has the flat vertical.

After giving the matter some thought, my vote is for saber rather than the rapier. The reasons are technical. In order to make a certain strong beat with the rapier—and I'm talking about a heavy rapier, by the way, something like the weapon the young lady [Amra, Vol. 2, No. 43, p. 5] is carrying, perhaps not so heavy—you have to rotate the hand, beat with the flat, then rotate the hand again to use the point properly. To make a good cut, you have to get your hand in an awkward position, and although we are going to use the point mostly (that part of the *Enchanter* is exactly correct), we do want to be able to cut. In particular, we want to be able to cut to the cuff and forearm against an unarmored man.

Now that indicates rotation of the hand in order to make a point attack with the saber, and this is a little slower. On the other hand, we can beat without preparation, and if we beat in quarte (high inside line), and follow through with point to elbow, we can do so with a single movement. This attack will be our most common one, varied with attack without preparation and single disengagement. If Shea must carry a rapier, he would want one somewhat lighter than that illustrated [*Amra*, Vol. 2, No. 43, p. 5], with the bell brought well down over the thumb; but I should think he would prefer the saber.

Now, of the sabers easily available to Shea, most were undoubtedly curved and therefore not suitable for the kind of fencing he would do; and furthermore they wouldn't have a real bell guard, which he'd need. The hand guard on Shea's ideal weapon need not be solid; the attacks on the hand will not be from the point, and a basket hilt would be suitable to catch cuts. It must be well made, though. Those cuts will have real force behind them.

Still, they made all kinds of swords and sabers for the Civil War (or War Between the States, if you're a diehard) [or even, War of the Slaveholders Rebellion]. Even if you couldn't find the sort of thing needed in an antique shop, and the chances of finding a good quality saber with appropriate hand guard are rather good, you could still have one made. I could have the ideal weapon forged from high quality steel for less than $200 right here in Orange County, and that's at 1965 prices. Shea should have been able to beat that by quite a bit.

I'm afraid Shea didn't use his head. He could have afforded one whale of a lot better weapon than that epee. If he had thought about it, he would have found himself something like the sword our amorous friend (p. 263) is carrying, and probably have made it a bit more probable that he would end up in such pleasant circumstances instead of in small pieces scattered about the landscape. The sword would ideally have a slight curve, be sharp along about a third of the back edge with a definite thickening along the back for added mass and impact, have a crossbar and bell guard to protect the fingers, and a leather loop for inserting the index finger into. This last gives remarkably good control. In addition, he might have had a brass strip riveted to the base of the back edge, which would be useful in hanging up the opponent's sword and thus making it easier to dispatch him.

Now, we may have spent all of his money on the sword, but supposing he has a little left to spare, what else might he carry along? After all, we've tooled him up for unarmored combat on foot; but what's he to do against a walking—or riding—tank?

Against a fully armored opponent, he can't do much. Those guys were experts, trained from an early age, and although we might at great expense outfit Shea with better armor than his enemy, he's going to be unhorsed and beaten. If he faces a mounted enemy, what he'd better do is hope his horse is faster. In the story, Shea never had to fight that way, and a good thing for him, too.

Unhorsed, but with armor, he also has troubles, but not quite as bad. Let's see what help we can give Our Hero for this situation. The first thing to do is to design some defensive equipment. It must be light enough to allow Shea to fence while wearing it. It also ought to be designed for the kind of fighting most expected: and now we come to a problem. Must we guard against arrows? It would help, of course, if Shea were immune to missile attacks; but let's just say that this isn't part of our design requirement, for the very good reason that that would get very expensive. He'll have to take his chances on missiles and concentrate on winning in combat with an armored swordsman.

We don't need to worry about point attacks. Shea's enemies are all slashers, and his stance is such that there isn't too much that can be slashed. In fact, the sword arm is Shea's most vulnerable part, followed by the head. Something like a war helmet (there weren't war surplus helmets available in 1940, but something like that would have been available), if possible with riveted or welded nose guard and shoulder plates takes care of the latter; and a leather jacket with some chain sewed into it should do nicely for the arm. Presto: at not too great cost and a lot less weight than the enemy is carrying, Shea is protected, at least temporarily. Now, how are we going to dispose of the other guy? He is more or less invulnerable to Shea's sword, and he is in a lot better physical shape than Our Hero, so he won't tire out as quickly.

In an open field, single combat, we probably have him. He's ungainly in all that equipment, and Shea can manage to get behind him and push him down, or otherwise get him prone. Then Shea can find a weak joint in the armor if Sir Muscles won't give up. In an enclosed space, though, we got troubles. Shea can parry cuts for a while, but can't hit him, and can't get around him. What to do?

It all depends on whether Shea wants to carry a rather ungainly weapon around. What we do is make him a poleaxe, a pike with axe head as well as point, with hand guards built on. Shea ought to be able to floor him with *that;* but of course it's heavy and can't be carried at all times. On the other hand, we don't expect Shea to fight armored knights on foot very often either, so it balances out. We've shown what Our Hero would look like as he prepares to face an armored man. [*Amra*, Vol. 2, No. 43, p. 71.

The equipment list goes like this:

1. A fairly straight saber-type sword, heavy enough for real parries, light enough to use for fencing, with a good hand guard and a leather finger-loop for the index finger to help control it. Second choice is a rapier-like sword with fairly heavy blade and real hand-guard.

2. A helmet, helmet liner, and suspension system; with nose-guard and shoulder plates. This thing won't protect against a real swipe from a broadsword, but it should manage to stop those cuts which get through parries or which go on to the target after Shea has put his point through the other fellow's arm.

3. A leather jacket, with chain sewed into the right arm, and—if you like—

vertical stripes of chain down the chest to protect against cuts which get through the guard. Three lengths of chain should be sufficient.

4. Optional: a poleaxe, from five to seven feet long, with both point and axe blade, and with hand guards attached. (I'm not really optimistic about surviving the armored versus unarmored combat in a confined space, even with this, but I'd rather try it than just use my sword if I can't run away. I haven't quite made up my mind about length, either; any suggestions?)

This, we assume, exhausts Shea's money. Some other time, I'll take up the question of relaxing the ground rules and allowing all kind of modern technique and gear that doesn't depend on unacceptable technology; and also, what happens if you can take your own horse and pack him up with things. For now, we'll leave Harold Shea in his apartment, under the watchful eye of the landlady, with the above equipment slung onto himself while he recites, "If P equals not-Q, Q implies not-P; which is equivalent to saying..."

Lots of luck, Harold. You'll need it.

> You know, I think Dr. P. is right. If I were writing the story today instead of thirty years ago, I'd set things up pretty much along the lines he proposes. But alas! that is not likely to happen. The lady who wrote: "Backward, turn backward, O Time, in your flight," never claimed that Time had obeyed her hest.
>
> L. S. de C.

Notes, 2006, by Jerry Pournelle

When I wrote that, it was all theory. That is, I had been a pretty good epee fencer—at the Pacific International Invitational Tournament I won against Petr Bakoney, then the world epee champion—but I had not yet participated in the Society for Creative Anachronism tournaments against medieval weapons. When I did, I found that I was about right: against unarmored man with broadsword, a good saber was quite effective.

A few SCA fighters had studied formal fencing, but most had not, and learned broadsword and shield in the old style. They weren't much able to defend themselves against a light saber with a point. Indeed, the rules were changed so that broadsword and shield were required in Crown Tournaments, and the use of the point was so circumscribed by rules supposedly adopted for safety that it was in effect forbidden.

This was just as well for the broadswordsmen.

Second, when I wrote that I wasn't really aware of the US 1913 Cavalry

Saber, designed by then Lieutenant George S. Patton. It was designed primarily for fighting with the point, but had an edge. It was sturdy and the guard was steel. In a word, it was nearly the ideal weapon for Harold Shea, and had I known of it (as Shea certainly would have had he actually done the research De Camp says he did) it is what I would have recommended; and it is I think what Shea would actually have carried.

I append below Lieutenant Patton's précis that accompanied his report on the sword in modern war. It can hardly be bettered. I did not know of it when I wrote my short essay for AMRA some forty years ago.

> By Lieutenant George S. Patton:
> In the Peninsula War, the English nearly always used the sword for cutting. The French dragoons, to the contrary, used only the point which almost always caused a fatal wound. This made the English say, "The French don't fight fair." Marshal Saxe wished to arm the French cavalry with a blade of a triangular cross section so as to make the use of the point obligatory. At Wagram, when the cavalry of the guard passed in review before a charge, Napoleon called to them, "Don't cut! The point! The point!"
>
> The point is vastly more deadly than the edge. While it might be possible to inflict a crippling blow with the edge (were the swing unrestricted by the pressing ranks of the charge or by the guard of attack) the size and power of the blow is so reduced there is grave doubt it would have sufficient power to do any damage to an opponent's body, protected by clothing and equipment. And even should the blade reach the opponent, it's power to unhorse is dubious.
>
> The cavalryman rides at a man to kill him. If he misses, he goes on to another, moving in straight lines with the intent of running his opponent through. As to the question of recovering his sword thrust into an opponent, when a man has been run through he is going to be pretty limp and will probably fall from his horse, clearing the weapon for you. It would seem, then, that the straight sword possesses all of the advantages of the curved sword for cutting, besides the proper use of the point, which the other does not, and that in using the point in the charge not a single advantage of the edge is lost, while many disadvantages are overcome. In addition, the highest possible incentive to close with the enemy is given.
>
> The Egyptian expedition under Napoleon gave fresh impetus to the saber. Many real scimitars were carried back to France at it's close. The famous sword of Marengo carried by Napoleon was of this type. Murat also carried one, probably because it gave increased possibilities for being decorated with jewels.
>
> The Cavalry Sword Model 1913 [designed by Lt. Patton] is an ideal thrusting weapon and at the same time, one which can give a cutting blow at least one third harder than our former saber.
>
> The sharpened back edge makes it much easier to withdraw from a body

than would be the case if it were single edged. The use of the point is taught exclusively. In the charge with the point, all the energy of the horse is conserved and he becomes a steel-pointed missile.

When using the point, the almost prone position of the trooper reduces the target and facilitates the speed of the horse.

Of the foregoing advantages of the point, the fact of increased reach is paramount. The point will outreach and outkill the edge in a charge; hence if we meet foes using the edge against our point, we have them. If our enemy also uses the point, we are simply fighting fire with fire and our superior swords and greater physical strength tips the scale a little our way; whereas, in such a case, had we continued to use the edge, we would have been lost. Against infantry, the point is the only thing. The bayonet has a long reach and against it the cut is of little use. Among wagons or artillery, the point alone can reach opponents behind wheels or shields.

Is it possible for the soldier in battle to always take up the extremely extended positions described in the regulations? No, not any more than it will always be possible to always get the proper sight setting for the rifle. The positions described are the best and the more rigidly and accurately they are enforced at drill, the more approximately will they be assumed in battle.

Will the edge ever be used? It will. Man is not very far removed from his cave ancestor. And as battle was a primal pastime, so modern man engaged in it more readily retrogrades to his hairy progenitor. It was for this reason-together with the added facility in withdrawing it-that the sword was made sharp. We do not teach it any more than we do biting in a fist fight. At the last extremity, both are useful and will be used. The longer we can defer, by practice, that state of hysteria in which either will be used, the more deadly we make our swordsman or boxer.

Will the point always be successful? No, but in all circumstances it gives the largest chance of success.

http://www.pattonhq.com/sword.html

REarming the Incomplete Enchanter
by Jerry Pournelle
AMRA II:58, January 1973

A long time ago when I lived in fabulous Buena Park (a peaceful place now, with no fame beyond Knott's Berry Farm and an undeserved reputation for ultra-conservative politics; but prior to 1920 they used to shoot the sheriff at least annually) my telephone rang. It used to ring quite often, what with political campaigns, siding salesmen, rug cleaning outfits, and occasionally a rush call from the Apollo program on which I worked in those dear dead days before Space took second place to the Dole; but this time the voice at the other end was the *Amra* editorial staff, who Had A Problem: they were temporarily assigned in the Buena Park environs, wanted to publish *Amra* for some nefarious reason, and had no Selectric typewriter handy.

They were also short an article. The result was that *Amra* got typed on my machine—the same one I'm using to do this article, by the way; those Selectrics are *durable*—and I wrote an article called "Arming the Incomplete Enchanter." My piece was all about what Harold Shea should have carried and didn't, when he went roaming about amongst the knights bold and ladies amorous of the *Faerie Queen,* and at its end I promised to write another carrying the tale of Shea's quartermaster corps to its logical conclusion. I promptly forgot the promise and the Amraëditorialhorde being essentially Nice Guys about not bugging people (or maybe there's a message there? No, I'm sure not) I wasn't reminded of it again until my postman brought me a Book.

Now, my postman often brings me books. Usually, though, the Post Office hasn't utterly destroyed the mailing label and container—and if it has, the book is in a similar state of decay. In this case, though, somehow at the Studio City Post Office there had arrived or appeared or materialized one each perfect copy of *The Conan Grimoire,* shorn of all wrappings. Without even looking inside to see that there was an article by me he promptly brought it to my doorstep. I'm *sure* there's a message *there.*

Naturally I read my own article first, as what writer doesn't? And being reminded of my promise, and having several publishers' deadlines to meet, bills to pay, and people screaming at me for a story or article or something that will bring in money (no, not my publishers screaming; my creditors, and the Angel of My Life and Mother of My Children—both the same creature, perhaps fortunately) I promptly sat down to fulfill my promise.

Where were we? I had last equipped Harold Shea with:

1. A fairly straight saber heavy enough for parries but light enough to fence with, with a good handguard and a leather finger-loop for the index finger inside the guard.
2. A helmet, helmet liner, and suspension system with noseguard and shoulder plates.
3. A leather jacket with chain sewed into the right arm and vertical stripes of chain down the chest to protect against cuts which get through the parries. Three lengths of chain "should be sufficient" wrote I.
4. A poleaxe some five to seven feet long with point and axeblade, with hand-guards attached.

These, I had insisted, would have been superior to that epee which was so famous, but which was likely in the actual event to have got Harold sliced into mincemeat. I note that Mr de Camp more or less agreed with my analysis and was kind enough to say so at the end of my article.

Well, I've had some Second Thoughts. Many of them come from my alter ego, a gent known as Jerome Robert, Laird o' McKenna, Knight Marshal of the Kingdom of the West, who goes about getting bashed under the auspices of the Society for Creative Anachronism, Inc, and gets to watch a number of other gents do the same. When I wrote "Arming the Incomplete Enchanter" I'd had only experience with modern fencing—i.e., I was in the same position, and suffering from the same delusions, as Harold Shea before he visited the world of the Iron Men. Since then I've had the pleasure of fighting men in armor and doing a bit of it myself, and it's illuminating. (For those who'd like some of the same information, *Tournaments Illuminated* is available from the SCA for $4/year, and well worth it; write the SCA at Box 1162, Berkeley CA 94701.)

My first conclusion is that Shea's epee wasn't as silly as I'd thought; it could be useful, but not as de Camp and Pratt intended. As I wrote in the earlier article, one swipe from a medieval broadsword would brush aside any parry you could make with an epee and probably break the toothpick in the bargain: a fact unalterably and painfully true. But Shea isn't going to parry. He isn't going to cross swords with his opponent either. I'd had a mental picture of the armored man standing in something like a modern fencing stance, but with his feet square and his body perpendicular to the line of engagement, his sword held out in front of him like Errol Flynn, making great sweeping cuts with a heavy sword that he could handle well enough but still being a bit unwieldy.

It don't Work That Way. Actually, the man in armor will stand with his left foot forward (assuming him right handed), his shield held squarely forward, and his sword upraised above his head and parallel with the ground to protect from straight-down chops. He swings the sword in a wide arc without preparatory movement—and when he does, Harold's dead.

However, if Harold's fast enough, he wins. He stands as far from his armored opponent as possible, and as soon as the "Begin" is cried he lunges, without preparation or warning, straight for the eye-slits. He'd better be accurate, because he gets one and only one chance; but a good epee man can hit a ping-pong ball bobbing about at the end of a long rubber band, so we assume Harold can do it too.

That's about the *only* thing Harold can do with that epee, though, if he's facing plate armor of good design. He has to go for a kill, and do it instantly, or else spend a lot of time retreating around the field waiting for a similar shot, and *then* do it instantly; but either way he gets one thrust only, it had better be lethal, and except for his lethal attack he can't afford to ever let his enemy get within striking distance of him. He can't be chivalrous and disable his enemy unless there is a really obvious chink in his opponent's armor, *and* a thrust to the chink will disable instantly. Otherwise he thrusts, the point goes in—and the Iron Man slices Harold's head off.

Against an armored man, though, the epee is likely to be more useful than that axe I designed. The epee will get through the armor—there *have* to be eyeslits or holes to see out of—more easily than the axe. Shea can lunge, giving him several feet more lethal radius than his enemy. His weapon is far more easily controlled than his enemy's—and the epee far more likely to succeed than the axe, because Shea doesn't expose himself until he's actually killing his enemy with the epee, while just getting into distance with the axe will probably get Harold killed. Axe and shield (or axe without shield) does not win against sword and shield with equal opponents—and Harold ain't nothing like equal in ability to the man he faces.

His fencing training will actually hamper him when he fights with medieval weapons.

Another of my conclusions that Have To Go was that Harold might be able to exploit his unarmored status, running about the field until his plated enemy tires, then approaching from behind and pushing that ton of junk down to the ground.

Uh-uh. Good plate armor doesn't tire you out that way. It doesn't hamper vision or movement very much, either. The idea of the unwieldy man unable to move is one of those myths whose origin I don't recall, but it was helped

Arming the Incomplete Enchanter 501

along by T. H. White who ought to have known better. [Shakespeare's *Henry V* helped too.] Now it is true that as gunpowder and longbow developed, plate got heavier and heavier, until we reached the period of King James VI (or I, according to the English). King James, watching one of his knights arm in the h/o/p/e/f/u/l/l/y/ wishfully firearms-proof armor of that late period, said: "I see the armor serves two purposes: it prevents anyone from harming my knights, and it prevents their harming anyone else." Harold, though, is going to fight men in really well-designed plate who wear it precisely because it is more agile than chain-mail; being suspended from many points of the anatomy rather than shoulders only (as mail is), good plate is also less tiring.

In other words, Harold better stab quick and deep; he won't get behind his enemy and push him down or do any of the other rather clever things I'd thought he could do. Actually, if I'd been thinking when I wrote that nonsense, I'd have known better—it should be obvious that the Iron Men wore armor for a reason, and they didn't dominate the peasants for centuries by making themselves ineffective. I'm reminded of the various forms of Oriental unarmed combat that are supposedly so superior to swords and like that: they were developed by subjugated peoples not allowed to have weapons; and they *stayed* subjugated by the weapons carriers.

Having saved the epee for use against single armored enemies who fight with broadsword and shield, and being glad of it because I *liked* that epee, we're faced with another problem: it won't work all that often. Those Iron Men weren't stupid, and after Harold has demonstrated that lunge—which is really his only advantage: a long, thin, pointed weapon suitable for poking through eye-slits being known as long as was armor—they're going to Take Steps. What they'll probably do is gang up on Harold and have their grooms kill him out of hand for unchivalrous combat, but assuming that one of them decides to face Harold in single combat, he'll put his shield up, crouch behind it, and overrun; literally bowl Harold over onto the ground. There are other things they could do, too.

The problem is, Harold still has no defense. He can't parry with the toothpick, he has only a limited number of places he can thrust to, and he must keep out of the swordsman's reach or die. Can we not help him?

It does no good to cover him with armor. Weight does count, and neither Harold nor any of us in the Twentieth Century can design armor more adapted for the human frame than was made in the time of the *Faerie Queen*. The Iron Men are stronger than Harold, more used to combat with their weapons, and far deadlier. Harold has only his skills as a Twentieth Century fencer, his wits, and his agility.

We *can*, however, give him some reasonable protection consistent with his advantages. A Great Kilt, for example. Now, I'm not talking about the modern, sewn, pleated kilt worn by gentlemen and paraders; I mean the old Genuine Article, about ten yards of thick woolen cloth, bunched up around the waist and over the kidneys, pleated over the legs, carried over the back in bunches and pinned over the left shoulder. I can testify that this makes pretty good armor. It probably wouldn't stand up to a really well-aimed and well-delivered blow, but it provides far more protection than you'd think; unless the Iron Man gets his weight into it and cuts just right, Harold might, given the protection of a Great Kilt, survive for a second thrust.

Of course, we don't leave him with the kilt alone. The combat helmet with liner and riveted shoulder and face guards will have to be kept; and my leather jacket with chains sewn inside is a definite must, the difference being that now I'd advocate *wire* to attach the chains, and put the chains *outside* the jacket. I'd also advocate far more than the three lengths of chain I specified in "Arming the Incomplete Enchanter."

What about fighting an unarmored man? That was Harold's first encounter in the world of the *Faerie Queen,* his opponent chivalrously shedding his iron suit to give Harold an equal chance. Well, it wouldn't go as described in the Sacred Texts. There wouldn't be any phrases, engagements, and parries. What would happen is the Iron Man would raise his sword, Harold would nimbly retreat in fencer's stance, the Iron Man would pursue—and Harold lunges to get him neatly in the wrist, forearm, or elbow, preventing that deadly chop that takes Harold's head off. The result wouldn't be much different, but the methods would. That epee would work pretty well after all.

I discovered this in practice, fighting some of the Knights of the Society. They were good with broadsword or they wouldn't be Knights; but their technique hadn't taught them anything about defending against point attack to the arm. On the other hand, they weren't stupid; and after I'd done it to one, it was difficult to do it to him again—or to someone who had seen it done. They adapted quickly, as would any man familiar with his weapons.

Thus, we are back to the requirement for a weapon with which you can parry. Harold can win an engagement or two with his epee; but after that the Iron Men will be wary of him, change their tactics, and use the weight of their swords and the strengths of their arms to dominate Harold's toothpick.

I am proud to say, then, that the basic weapon I chose for Harold in "Arming the Incomplete Enchanter" was correct: a good saber, not much curve and with a good sharp point—the point attack is still our best—but heavy enough to parry a broadsword attack, and with enough hand protection to keep Harold from getting his fingers cut off. If Harold had the strength of wrist to swing it properly, the Scottish basket-hilted broadsword—called a claymore in a lot of the literature of the time it was used, I don't care what Mr de Camp says [or the custodian of the arms museum in the Tower of London, who agrees with him], although I concede that originally "claymore" is a corruption of the Gaelic word for a two-handed broadsword—that would be the best thing he could carry. He probably couldn't afford a really good one, such as the Wilkinson I almost bought (but decided to make the house payment instead); but it would be a good investment. Armed with *that* and his ability to use the point, Harold would be a match for any unarmored man in town.

Since he won't have the strength to heft quite that much sword properly, we are back to the Civil War sabers mentioned in the Texts and rejected by Harold for unaccountable reasons; and they would have done quite nicely, again probably assuring Harold of success and survival.

In fact, I am now convinced that against unarmored men a good modern fencer would have done very well in Medieval times. Although the Society's Knights are probably not as good as the best of that era, they are good indeed, and we've been able to field-test the problem. The broadswordsman fighting the modern saberman, each using the techniques he has learned, will lose if both are unarmored. Give the broadswordsman his shield and you've got another problem. That shield is a weapon, and a good one. The Iron Man tucks himself in behind it, withholding his weapons and arms and like that out of reach of even my best lunge; and it's hard to do anything to him. Then his forward rush with shield to overrun me is damned hard to stop or retreat from. Given retreating room, and given free use of the point, the modern fencer has a good chance, though. Take the point away from him, and he's doomed, even if you give him a shield of his own. The point and the lunge are the modern's weapons, and he must be able to use them. Any attempt to fight on the Iron Man's terms gets the fencer killed rather quickly.

Where does that leave us, then? Actually, Harold is better off than I thought he might be. He carries:

1. The trusty epee, honed to needlepoint.
2. A good saber. Since both saber and epee won't weigh any more than the Iron Man's broadsword, Harold can carry both in the same scabbard, although designing a good scabbard for carrying a bell-guarded epee is far from easy, as I've learned to my sorrow.
3. Ten yards of good woolen tartan, a wide leather belt studded with metal rings, and knowledge of the arcane art of pleating this mess into a Great Kilt. He *could* (horrors) wear trousers under the kilt if he's worried about how his knobby knees look.
4. A good leather jacket sewn over with chain, the chain secured with wire.
5. A military helmet on which he has welded or riveted a nose-guard and shoulder plates; better would be that he finds out how to make chain mail and makes himself a mail hood covering head and shoulders, and puts on nasal-armored helmet over

that. (Pity that Harold couldn't have subscribed to *Tournaments Illuminated* in 1940.)

He uses the epee against unhorsed men in armor (against horsemen, he's dead anyway) and the saber against unarmored men who show some talent for fencing. He's prepared to retreat quickly—that's in character anyway—and avoid shield rushes. And although he's got some problems, he's got a better chance of living through all this than I originally thought.

Moreover, although I had promised in "Arming the Incomplete Enchanter" to look at what Harold might have taken if he'd had plenty of money, we'd stayed within the original limits of the Texts. There isn't a lot more to add to the package, even given unlimited funds and carrying capacity. He could use greaves, and they could be made reasonably cheaply from steel. Given a lot of time, he could sew iron rings flat onto his leather jacket—William the Conqueror wore that type armor in preference to anything else—starting with a knee-length leather overcoat. He could then discard the Great Kilt, but he'd want something under the jacket for padding. Quilting was used in Them There Days and would be available in 1940. A modern hunting crossbow might help keep his enemies at a distance and give him a bit of protection against cavalry. They're expensive, but anyone who can shoot a rifle can fire one pretty accurately. However, being slow on the reload, they're useable only against a single enemy (or several *very* slow ones).

With all this gear, a horse to help carry it wouldn't hurt, and a well-trained Alsatian dog might come in handy. But even with only the basics, Harold just may do all right at that. So once again we'll leave him under the curious gaze of his landlady. There sits Harold, wearing Great Kilt and greaves, two swords at his side and helmet on his head, while his landlady goes for the police. Quickly now, Harold, before the men in white coats come: "If P equals not-Q, Q implies not-P; which is equivalent to saying..."

Good luck, Harold. I think we might see you again at that.

Bibliography
of the Harold Shea Stories

Besides the stories co-authored by de Camp and Pratt and those by de Camp by himself, two volumes containing Harold Shea stories written by other authors have appeared. Both volumes were edited by de Camp and Christopher Stasheff. Additionally, two further stories touched on the Canon. Here is a list of all of the Harold Shea stories in order by their internal chronology.

The Roaring Trumpet, by L. Sprague de Camp and Fletcher Pratt, *Unknown*, May 1940. Norse myth.

The Mathematics of Magic, by L. Sprague de Camp and Fletcher Pratt, *Unknown*, October 1940. Spenser's *The Faerie Queene*.

The Castle of Iron, by L. Sprague de Camp and Fletcher Pratt, *Unknown*, April 1941, Ariosto's *Orlando Furioso*.

The Wall of Serpents, by L. Sprague de Camp and Fletcher Pratt *Fantasy Fiction*, June 1953. *The Kalevala*, Finnish myth.

"Return to Xanadu" by Lawrence Watt-Evans, *The Enchanter Completed*, ed. by Harry Turtledove, Baen Books, 2005. In an L. Sprague de Camp tribute anthology, de Camp himself visits Xanadu shortly after "The Wall of Serpents" to fix an error he'd made.

The Green Magician, by L. Sprague de Camp and Fletcher Pratt, *Beyond Fiction*, Vol 2, #3, 1954. Irish myth.

"The Case of the Friendly Corpse", by L. Ron Hubbard, *Unknown*, August 1941. (In a short segment, Harold Shea is reported killed during a magical duel at the College of Unholy Names. But see "Sir Harold and the Gnome King" for what *really* happened!)

Sir Harold and the Gnome King, by L. Sprague de Camp, *World Fantasy*

Convention Program Book in 1990 and then revised and expanded in *The Enchanter Reborn*, Baen Books, 1992. The University of the Unholy Names and Oz.

"Professor Harold and the Trustees" by Christopher Stasheff, *The Enchanter Reborn*, Baen Books, 1992. Academic politics with a quick visit back to *Orlando Furioso*.

"Sir Harold and the Monkey King" by Christopher Stasheff, *The Enchanter Reborn*, Baen Books, 1992. Chinese myth.

"Knight and the Enemy" by Holly Lisle, *The Enchanter Reborn*, Baen Books, 1992. *Don Quixote*.

"Arms and the Enchanter" by John Maddox Roberts, *The Enchanter Reborn*, Baen Books, 1992. A visit to the *Aeneid*.

"Enchanter Kiev" by Roland J. Green and Frieda A. Murray, *The Exotic Enchanter*, Baen Books, 1995. Borodin's *Prince Igor*.

"Sir Harold and the Hindu King" by Christopher Stasheff, *The Exotic Enchanter*, Baen Books, 1995. Hindu myth.

"Sir Harold of Zodanga" by L. Sprague de Camp, *The Exotic Enchanter*, Baen Books, 1995. Barsoom.

"Harold Sheakspeare" by Tom Wham, *The Exotic Enchanter*, Baen Books, 1995. *The Tempest*.

The New England Science Fiction Association and NESFA Press

Recent books from NESFA Press:

- *Years in the Making* by L. Sprague de Camp $25.00
- *Homecalling and Other Stories* by Judith Merril $29.00
- *The Masque of Mañana* by Robert Sheckley $29.00
- *Once Upon a Time (She Said)* by Jane Yolen $26.00
- *The Essential Hal Clement*, (3 volumes) .... (each) $25.00
- *The Complete William Tenn* (3 volumes) .... (each) $29.00
- *The Best of James H. Schmitz* $22.00
- *Major Ingredients* by Eric Frank Russell $29.00
- *Entities* by Eric Frank Russell $29.00
- *Transfinite: The Essential A. E. van Vogt* $29.00
- *A New Dawn: The Don A. Stuart Stories of John W. Campbell, Jr.* $26.00
- *The Compleat Boucher: The Complete SF of Anthony Boucher* $25.00
- *First Contacts: The Essential Murray Leinster* $27.00
- *His Share of Glory: The Complete Short SF of C. M. Kornbluth* $27.00
- *Ingathering: The Complete People Stories of Zenna Henderson* $25.00

Find details and many more books on our web page: www.nesfa.org/press

Books may be ordered by writing to:
NESFA Press
PO Box 809
Framingham, MA 01701

We accept checks, Visa, or MasterCard. Please add $3 postage and handling per book in the US.

The New England Science Fiction Association:

NESFA is an all-volunteer, non-profit organization of science fiction and fantasy fans. Besides publishing, our activities include running Boskone (New England's oldest SF convention) in February each year, producing a semi-monthly newsletter, holding discussion groups relating to the field, and hosting a variety of social events. If you are interested in learning more about us, we'd like to hear from you. Write to our address above!

Acknowledgments

I'd like to thank Elisabeth Carey and Rick Katze for help in scanning, Dave Grubbs, Tony Lewis, Steven Silver, Priscilla Olson, Larry Pfeffer, and Pam Fremon for proofing, and Alice Lewis for her usual lovely job of dustjacket design.

This book was typeset in Adobe Garamond using Adobe Pagemaker and printed by Sheridan Books of Ann Arbor, Michigan, on acid-free paper.

— Mark Olson
December 2006